PRAISE FOR M. L. BUCHMAN

Buchman has catapulted his way to the top tier of my favorite authors.

— FRESH FICTION

One of our favorite authors.

— RT BOOK REVIEWS

Buchman has catapulted his way to the top tier of my favorite authors.

— FRESH FICTION

A favorite author of mine. I'll read anything that carries his name, no questions asked. Meet your new favorite author!

— THE SASSY BOOKSTER, FLASH OF FIRE

M.L. Buchman is guaranteed to get me lost in a good story.

— THE READING CAFE, WAY OF THE WARRIOR: NSDQ

I love Buchman's writing. His vivid descriptions bring everything to life in an unforgettable way.

— PURE JONEL, HOT POINT

Nonstop action that will keep readers on the edge of their seats.

— TAKE OVER AT MIDNIGHT, LIBRARY JOURNAL

M L. Buchman's ability to keep the reader right in the middle of the action is amazing.

— LONG AND SHORT REVIEWS

The only thing you'll ask yourself is, "When does the next one come out?"

— WAIT UNTIL MIDNIGHT, RT REVIEWS, 4 STARS

The first...of (a) stellar, long-running (military) romantic suspense series.

— THE NIGHT IS MINE, BOOKLIST, "THE 20 BEST
ROMANTIC SUSPENSE NOVELS: MODERN
MASTERPIECES"

I knew the books would be good, but I didn't realize how good.

— NIGHT STALKERS SERIES, KIRKUS REVIEWS

Buchman mixes adrenalin-spiking battles and brusque military jargon with a sensitive approach.

— PUBLISHERS WEEKLY

13 times "Top Pick of the Month"

— NIGHT OWL REVIEWS

Tom Clancy fans open to a strong female lead will clamor for more.

— DRONE, PUBLISHERS WEEKLY

(Miranda Chase is) one of the most compelling, addicting, fascinating characters in any genre since the *Monk* television series.

— DRONE, ERNEST DEMPSEY, AUTHOR OF THE SEAN
WYATT THRILLERS

(*Drone* is) the best military thriller I've read in a very long time. Love the female characters.

— SHELDON MCARTHUR, FOUNDER OF THE MYSTERY
BOOKSTORE, LA

Superb!

— DRONE, BOOKLIST, STARRED REVIEW

A fabulous soaring thriller.

— *TAKE OVER AT MIDNIGHT*, MIDWEST BOOK REVIEW

Meticulously researched, hard-hitting, and suspenseful.

— *PURE HEAT*, PUBLISHERS WEEKLY, STARRED
REVIEW

Expert technical details abound, as do realistic military missions with superb imagery that will have readers feeling as if they are right there in the midst and on the edges of their seats.

THE COMPLETE DOG TRILOGY

A WHITE HOUSE PROTECTION FORCE ROMANCE

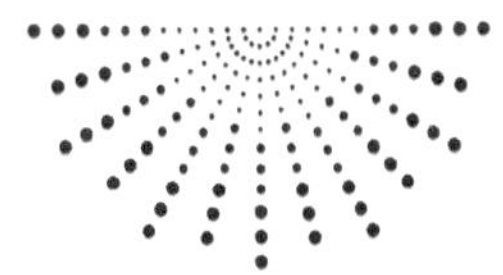

M. L. BUCHMAN

Buchman Bookworks

DON'T MISS A THING!

*Sign up for M. L. Buchman's newsletter today
and receive:
Release News
Free Short Stories
an awesome collection*

*Do it today. Do it now.
www.mlbuchman.com/newsletter*

Other works by M. L. Buchman: *(* - also in audio)*

Thrillers

Dead Chef
One Chef!
Two Chef!

Miranda Chase
*Drone**
*Thunderbolt**
*Condor**
*Ghostrider**

Romantic Suspense

Delta Force
*Target Engaged**
*Heart Strike**
*Wild Justice**
*Midnight Trust**

Firehawks
Main Flight
Pure Heat
Full Blaze
*Hot Point**
*Flash of Fire**
Wild Fire
Smokejumpers
*Wildfire at Dawn**
*Wildfire at Larch Creek**
*Wildfire on the Skagit**

The Night Stalkers
Main Flight
The Night Is Mine
I Own the Dawn
Wait Until Dark
Take Over at Midnight
Light Up the Night
Bring On the Dusk
By Break of Day

and the Navy
Christmas at Steel Beach
Christmas at Peleliu Cove
White House Holiday
*Daniel's Christmas**
*Frank's Independence Day**
*Peter's Christmas**
*Zachary's Christmas**
*Roy's Independence Day**
*Damien's Christmas**
5E
Target of the Heart
Target Lock on Love
Target of Mine
Target of One's Own

Shadow Force: Psi
*At the Slightest Sound**
*At the Quietest Word**

White House Protection Force
*Off the Leash**
*On Your Mark**
*In the Weeds**

Contemporary Romance

Eagle Cove
Return to Eagle Cove
Recipe for Eagle Cove
Longing for Eagle Cove
Keepsake for Eagle Cove

Henderson's Ranch
*Nathan's Big Sky**
*Big Sky, Loyal Heart**
*Big Sky Dog Whisperer**

Love Abroad
Heart of the Cotswolds: England
Path of Love: Cinque Terre, Italy

Other works by M. L. Buchman:

Contemporary Romance (cont)

Where Dreams
Where Dreams are Born
Where Dreams Reside
Where Dreams Are of Christmas
Where Dreams Unfold
Where Dreams Are Written

Science Fiction / Fantasy

Deities Anonymous
Cookbook from Hell: Reheated
Saviors 101

Single Titles
The Nara Reaction
Monk's Maze
the Me and Elsie Chronicles

Non-Fiction

Strategies for Success
Managing Your Inner Artist/Writer
Estate Planning for Authors
Character Voice

Short Story Series by M. L. Buchman:

Romantic Suspense

Delta Force
Delta Force

Firehawks
The Firehawks Lookouts
The Firehawks Hotshots
The Firebirds

The Night Stalkers
The Night Stalkers
The Night Stalkers 5E
The Night Stalkers CSAR
The Night Stalkers Wedding Stories

US Coast Guard
US Coast Guard

White House Protection Force
White House Protection Force

Contemporary Romance

Eagle Cove
Eagle Cove

Henderson's Ranch
Henderson's Ranch

Where Dreams
Where Dreams

Thrillers

Dead Chef
Dead Chef

Science Fiction / Fantasy

Deities Anonymous
Deities Anonymous

Other
The Future Night Stalkers
Single Titles

CONTENTS

No one knows how many terrorists and crazies they've caught near the White House...except the dogs and their US Secret Service handlers.

Come join them as they go:

Off the Leash

While they prowl the White House and have an unexpected run in with the Chocolatier.

On Your Mark

Leaving the White House fence line to risk life or death to save the Beast —the President's limo.

In the Weeds

Sniffing out the bad guys around the White House campus is one thing, doing it aboard the Marine Force One helicopter is quite another.

3 dogs.

6 hearts at risk.

A complete set of action-adventure romances...with dogs!

OFF THE LEASH

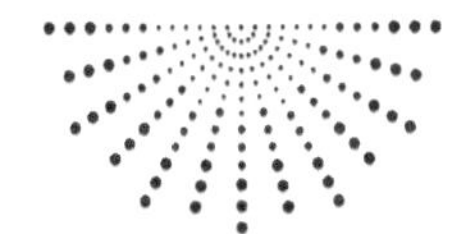

The White House Protection Force Saves the Day! *Come meet the behind-the-scenes specialists who keep our White House safe—even while they lose their hearts.*

White House Chocolatier Clive Andrews *takes pride in the subliminal messages hidden in his State Dinner showstoppers. But there's more than sensual sweets at risk when his heart begins to melt.*

Sergeant Linda Hamlin *left the Army after a decade of service. As the newest member of the U.S. Secret Service K-9 Team she expected flak. She didn't expect to be paired with a misfit mutt named Thor. Together they face down bombers, master spies, and a teenage genius.*

All of which might be manageable, if not for the handsome chocolatier who teaches her that a little indulgence can be a very good thing.

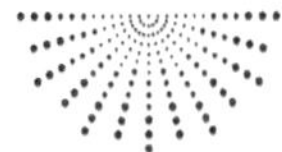

CHAPTER ONE

"**Y**ou're joking."

"Nope. That's his name. And he's yours now."

Sergeant Linda Hamlin wondered quite what it would take to wipe that smile off Lieutenant Jurgen's face. A 120mm round from an M1A1 Abrams Main Battle Tank came to mind.

The kennel master of the US Secret Service's Canine Team was clearly a misogynistic jerk from the top of his polished head to the bottoms of his equally polished boots. She wondered if the shoelaces were polished as well.

Then she looked over at the poor dog sitting hopefully on the concrete kennel floor. His stall had a dog bed three times his size and a water bowl deep enough for him to bathe in. No toys, because toys always came from the handler as a reward. He offered her a sad sigh and a liquid doggy gaze. The kennel even smelled wrong, more of sanitizer than dog. The walls seemed to echo with each bark down the long line of kennels housing the candidate hopefuls for the next addition to the Secret Service's team.

Thor—really?—was a brindle-colored mutt, part who-knew and part no-one-cared. He looked like a cross between an oversized, long-haired schnauzer and a dust mop that someone had spilled dark gray paint on. After mixing in streaks of tawny brown, they'd left one white paw just to make him all the more laughable.

And of course Lieutenant Jerk Jurgen would assign Thor to the first woman on the USSS K-9 team.

Unable to resist, she leaned over far enough to scruff the dog's ears. He was the physical opposite of the sleek and powerful Malinois MWDs—military war dogs—that she'd been handling for the 75th Rangers for the last five years. They twitched with eagerness and nerves. A good MWD was seventy pounds of pure drive—every damn second of the day. If the mild-mannered Thor weighed thirty pounds, she'd be surprised. And he looked like a little girl's best friend who should have a pink bow on his collar.

Jurgen was clearly ex-Marine and would have no respect for the Army. Of course, having been in the Army's Special Operations Forces, she knew better than to respect a Marine.

"We won't let any old swabbie bother us, will we?"

Jurgen snarled—definitely Marine Corps. Swabbie was slang for a Navy sailor and a Marine always took offense at being lumped in with them no matter how much they belonged. Of course the swabbies took offense at having the Marines lumped with *them.* Too bad there weren't any Navy around so that she could get two for the price of one. Jurgen wouldn't be her boss, so appeasing him wasn't high on her to-do list.

At least she wouldn't need any of the protective bite gear working with Thor. With his stature, he was an explosives detection dog without also being an attack one.

"Where was he trained?" She stood back up to face the beast.

"Private outfit in Montana—some place called Henderson's Ranch. Didn't make their MWD program," his scoff said exactly what he thought the likelihood of any dog outfit in Montana being worthwhile. "They wanted us to try the little runt out."

She'd never heard of a training program in Montana. MWDs all came out of Lackland Air Force Base training. The Secret Service mostly trained their own and they all came from Vohne Liche Kennels in Indiana. Unless... Special Operations Forces dogs were trained by private contractors. She'd worked beside a Delta Force dog for a single month—he'd been incredible.

"Is he trained in English or German?" Most American MWDs were trained in German so that there was no confusion in case a command word happened to be part of a spoken sentence. It also made it harder for any random person on the battlefield to shout something that would confuse the dog.

"German according to his paperwork, but he won't listen to me much in either language."

Might as well give the diminutive Thor a few basic tests. A snap of her fingers and a slap on her thigh had the dog dropping into a smart "heel" position. No need to call out *Fuss—by my foot.*

"*Pass auf!*" *Guard!* She made a pistol with her thumb and forefinger and aimed it at Jurgen as she grabbed her forearm with her other hand—the military hand sign for enemy.

The little dog snarled at Jurgen sharply enough to have him backing out of the kennel. "Goddamn it!"

"*Ruhig.*" *Quiet.* Thor maintained his fierce posture but dropped the snarl.

"*Gute Hund.*" *Good dog,* Linda countered the command.

Thor looked up at her and wagged his tail happily. She tossed him a doggie treat, which he caught midair and crunched happily.

She didn't bother looking up at Jurgen as she knelt once more to check over the little dog. His scruffy fur was so soft that it tickled. Good strength in the jaw, enough to show he'd had bite training despite his size—perfect if she ever needed to take down a three-foot-tall terrorist. Legs said he was a jumper.

"Take your time, Hamlin. I've got nothing else to do with the rest of my goddamn day except babysit you and this mutt."

"Is the course set?"

"Sure. Take him out," Jurgen's snarl sounded almost as nasty as Thor's before he stalked off.

She stood and slapped a hand on her opposite shoulder.

Thor sprang aloft as if he was attached to springs and she caught him easily. He'd cleared well over double his own height. Definitely trained…and far easier to catch than seventy pounds of hyperactive Malinois.

She plopped him back down on the ground. On lead or off? She'd give him the benefit of the doubt and try off first to see what happened.

Linda zipped up her brand-new USSS jacket against the cold and led the way out of the kennel into the hard sunlight of the January morning. Snow had brushed the higher hills around the USSS James J. Rowley Training Center—which this close to Washington, DC, wasn't saying much—but was melting quickly. Scents wouldn't carry as well on the cool air, making it more of a challenge for Thor to locate the explosives. She didn't know where they were either. The course was a test for handler as well as dog.

Jurgen would be up in the observer turret looking for any excuse to mark down his newest team. Perhaps teasing him about being just a Marine hadn't been her best tactical choice. She sighed. At least she was consistent—she'd always been good at finding ways to piss people off before she could stop herself and consider the wisdom of doing so.

This test was the culmination of a crazy three months, so she'd forgive herself this time—something she also wasn't very good at.

In October she'd been out of the Army and unsure what to do next. Tucked in the packet with her DD 214 honorable discharge form had been a flyer on career opportunities with the US Secret Service dog team: *Be all your dog can be!* No one else being released from Fort Benning that day had received any kind of a job flyer at all that she'd seen, so she kept quiet about it.

She had to pass through DC on her way back to Vermont—her parent's place. Burlington would work for, honestly, not very long at all, but she lacked anywhere else to go after a decade of service. So, she'd stopped off in DC to see what was up with that job flyer. Five interviews and three months to complete a standard six-month training course later—which was mostly a cakewalk after fighting with the US Rangers—she was on-board and this chill January day was her first chance with a dog. First chance to prove that she still had it. First chance to prove that she hadn't made a mistake in deciding that she'd seen enough bloodshed and war zones for one lifetime and leaving the Army.

The Start Here sign made it obvious where to begin, but she didn't dare hesitate to take in her surroundings past a quick glimpse. Jurgen's score would count a great deal toward where she and Thor were assigned in the future. Mostly likely on some field prep team, clearing the way for presidential visits.

As usual, hindsight informed her that harassing the lieutenant hadn't been an optimal strategy. A hindsight that had served her equally poorly with regular Army commanders before she'd finally hooked up with the Rangers—kowtowing to officers had never been one of her strengths.

Thankfully, the Special Operations Forces hadn't given a damn about anything except performance and *that* she could always deliver, since the day she'd been named the team captain for both soccer and volleyball. She was never popular, but both teams had made all-state her last two years in school.

The canine training course at James J. Rowley was a two-acre lot. A hard-packed path of tramped-down dirt led through the brown grass. It followed a predictable pattern from the gate to a junker car, over to tool shed, then a truck, and so on into a compressed version of an intersection in a small town. Beyond it ran an urban street of gray clapboard two- and three-story buildings and an eight-story office tower, all without windows. Clearly a playground for Secret Service training teams.

Her target was the town, so she blocked the city street out of her mind. Focus on the problem: two roads, twenty storefronts, six houses, vehicles, pedestrians.

It might look normal…normalish with its missing windows and no movement. It would be anything but. Stocked with fake IEDs, a bombmaker's stash, suicide cars, weapons caches, and dozens of other traps, all waiting for her and Thor to find. He had to be sensitive to hundreds of scents and it was her job to guide him so that he didn't miss the opportunity to find and evaluate each one.

There would be easy scents, from fertilizer and diesel fuel used so destructively in the 1995 Oklahoma City bombing, to almost as obvious TNT to the very difficult to detect C-4 plastic explosive.

Mannequins on the street carried grocery bags and briefcases. Some held fresh meat, a powerful smell demanding any dog's attention, but would count as a false lead if they went for it. On the job, an explosives detection dog wasn't supposed to care about anything except explosives. Other mannequins were wrapped in suicide vests loaded with Semtex or wearing knapsacks filled with package bombs made from Russian PVV-5A.

She spotted Jurgen stepping into a glassed-in observer turret atop the corner drugstore. Someone else was already there and watching.

She looked down once more at the ridiculous little dog and could only hope for the best.

"Thor?"

He looked up at her.

She pointed to the left, away from the beaten path.

"Such!" Find.

Thor sniffed left, then right. Then he headed forward quickly in the direction she pointed.

CLIVE ANDREWS SAT in the second-story window at the corner of Main and First, the only two streets in town. Downstairs was a drugstore all rigged to explode, except there were no triggers and there was barely enough explosive to blow up a candy box.

Not that he'd know, but that's what Lieutenant Jurgen had promised him.

It didn't really matter if it was rigged to blow for real, because when Miss Watson—never Ms. or Mrs.—asked for a "favor," you did it. At least he did. Actually, he had yet to meet anyone else who knew her. Not that he'd asked around. She wasn't the sort of person one talked about with strangers, or even close friends. He'd bet even if they did, it would be in whispers. That's just what she was like.

So he'd traveled across town from the White House and into

Maryland on a cold winter's morning, barely past a sunrise that did nothing to warm the day. Now he sat in an unheated glass icebox and watched a new officer run a test course he didn't begin to understand. Lieutenant Jurgen settled in beside him at a console with feeds from a dozen cameras and banks of switches.

While waiting, Clive had been fooling around with a sketch on a small pad of paper. The next State Dinner was in seven days. President Zachary Taylor had invited the leaders of Vietnam, Japan, and the Philippines to the White House for discussions about some Chinese islands. Or something like that, Clive hadn't really been paying attention to the details past the attendee list.

Instead, he was contemplating the dessert for such a dinner that would surprise, perhaps delight, as well as being an icebreaker for future discussions. Being the chocolatier for the White House was the most exciting job he'd ever had. Every challenge was fresh and new, like the first strawberry of each year.

This one would be elegant. January was a little early, it would be better if it was spring, but that wasn't crucial. A large half-egg shape of paper-thin white chocolate filled with a mousse—white chocolate? No, nor a dark chocolate. Instead, a milk chocolate mousse but rich with flavor, perhaps bourbon. Then mold the dark chocolate to top it with a filigree bird, wings spread in half flight, ready to soar upward. A crane perhaps? He made a note to check with the protocol office to make sure that he wouldn't be offending some leader without knowing it.

"Never underestimate the power of a good dessert," he mumbled one of Jacques Torres' favorite admonitions. This was going to work very nicely.

"What's that?" Jurgen grunted out without looking up.

"Just talking to myself."

Which earned him a dismissive grunt, as if he was unworthy of the agent's attention. It wouldn't surprise him. Clive was not trained like a Secret Service officer. His skills lay in his palate and his fingers for shaping the very finest chocolate work. He knew his big frame and good looks said easy-going and, while his size wasn't quite to oaf, people always assumed he was just a big and clumsy guy.

Clive often felt defensive about being a chocolatier when he was so dismissed out of hand. He had spent years learning his skills. And to be invited to join the White House kitchen…well, he couldn't think of a higher accolade. The fact that his father would agree with Jurgen didn't help matters. However, Lieutenant Jurgen didn't look like the sort of man to risk upsetting.

His own father had been a quiet, drunken merchant marine who rarely spoke when he was ashore—except for grumblings about his only child's lame excuse for a choice of profession. The one blessing of having Nic Andrews as a father was how much of Clive's life the man had spent at sea. In between, Clive and his mother had lived together in Redwood City very quietly and with some small degree of content. Their apartment had a view of the brilliant colors of the Cargill Salt Flats of San Francisco Bay. He often used their colors in his chocolates.

"They're starting." It was clear by his tone that Jurgen could break Clive over his knee like a piece of sugar work despite Clive's size and would be glad to demonstrate at the least provocation.

"Oh, thanks," seemed to be an acceptable response.

A "you're welcome" grunt sounded softly.

Miss Watson had told him to watch, so he closed his notepad and tucked it in his shirt pocket.

"Any suggestions on what I'm looking for?" Miss Watson had *not* been clear on that point. He looked down at the new officer and the small dog entering the far end of the course. He picked up a pair of binoculars from the window ledge but the dog was still small, barely reaching the officer's knees.

He scanned upward.

A woman. For some reason he hadn't expected that. Of course with the silly little dog, that somehow fit. However, officer or not, the woman offered a great deal to be looking at. Five-seven or eight. Medium chocolate brunette, about a fifty percent cocoa, with a nicely tempered shine like a fine ganache. It fell in a natural flow down to her shoulders, slightly ragged rather than in some DC socialite perfect coif. A thin face without being gaunt. Perhaps intense would be a better word.

Her jacket hid her shape, but she wore no hat or gloves despite the cold. Tan khakis hinted at nice legs. Army boots declared definitely not DC socialite.

"Well, for one thing, she's not following the damned course," Jurgen sounded puzzled.

"Is that a bad thing?" Clive could see the worn track and that they definitely weren't on it.

Jurgen made a sound that was neither yes or no.

"What's her name?"

"Linda with Thor," as if it was a single name.

Clive couldn't stop the laugh. "*That* scruffy little mutt is named Thor?"

Jurgen's grin would look appropriately nasty to be carved into the flesh of a Halloween pumpkin.

The woman had transformed once she started the course. Pretty and intent had transformed to focused to the point of lethal. She moved with all the efficiency of a fine-honed knife blade. Maybe she was Thor and the dog was Linda.

With a series of hand signs—Linda's mouth rarely moved though he did spend some time watching it—she directed the dog along a storefront. When she disappeared inside, he turned to watch the camera feeds on Jurgen's console.

"It isn't just the dog," Jurgen volunteered. "The dog has the nose, but the handler guides the dog to make sure no area is missed. Neither one can do it alone. Hundred percent a team effort."

Inside what might have been a real estate or travel agency, the dog sat abruptly and looked back at Linda. The officer stuck a red Post-it on one of the desk drawers.

"PETN. Very hard to find. Under half of the dog teams find that one," Jurgen didn't sound pleased. Maybe he was one of those people who was only happy when someone was suffering. Clive had worked for more than one chef like that.

"Linda with Thor"—or "Thor with Linda," he wasn't going to commit on that one yet despite Jurgen's evil grin—were on the move again.

Just as they stepped out of the office, Jurgen flipped a switch on his console.

Clive jumped as the blast of sirens sounded from a police car parked at the curb, even though they were muffled by distance and the observer station's windows.

It must have been painfully loud right next to the car, but Linda and Thor both merely looked at the wailing vehicle, sniffed their way around it, then continued along the street.

For an hour they left behind a trail of red Post-its and for the most part ignored sirens, gunfire, and other distractions. Once an actual explosion spattered them with dirt. For that, Linda had wrapped her arms around the dog and huddled in a bookstore doorway with her back turned toward the worst of it. Moments later they were back at their task.

Clive could look down in wonder. She'd positioned herself so that if the explosion had been lethal, rather than merely a training distraction, she'd have given her life to save her dog. Maybe the guys on the Presidential Protection Detail really would step in front of the bullet if given the chance. Would he himself step in the line of a rogue chocolate shard? Perhaps, but only because that didn't sound terribly threatening.

When they reached the end of the course, they stopped in the center of the intersection. From a small pack, she pulled out a fold-up bowl and poured some water into it for Thor before drinking herself. Then a doggie treat. Nothing for the handler.

With a tip of his head, Jurgen indicated that Clive should follow him down.

As they stepped out onto the street themselves, she was tossing a bulbous Kong toy for Thor. He'd once more turned into the dog most likely to belong at a little girl's tea party, eating all of the cookies whenever the hostess wasn't looking.

"You missed two," Jurgen snapped out his form of a polite greeting, not bothering to look at his clipboard.

Linda flinched as if she'd been slapped and her shoulders sagged.

But Clive had learned some things about Jurgen's expressions: there was a sourness there like bitter chocolate. "What's been your best score by any other team?"

"Five misses," Jurgen's scowl now included him since Clive had just spoiled his fun.

Linda still didn't look any happier. That told him a lot about her—this was one seriously driven woman. Anything less than perfect was a hundred percent failure. Which he supposed was true when your job was to make sure that no one blew up the President.

At that moment Thor stopped playing with his toy, trotted up to Jurgen's feet, circled him once, and sat abruptly with his nose aimed at one of the lieutenant's shoes.

"Damn it," he growled. "Okay, that makes one miss."

"Let me guess," Clive could get to enjoy this after all. "The observer's station also has an explosive." Then his breath caught in his throat. He wouldn't put it past Jurgen to have him sitting on an explosive the whole time he'd been in the observer's chair.

***

Jurgen's expression said it all.

"Of course," Linda couldn't believe she'd missed it. "It is always the person and place you least suspect that gets by you." *That* was certainly never going to happen again.

She was furious with herself for missing that but wasn't going to show any weakness. It was one of the great traps of serving in the military. If a woman showed the least weakness, she'd forever be tagged as unable to perform. If a guy showed ten times as much, he'd be tagged as being tired and probably told he'd done a good job. The military had taught her how to hide *anything* she was actually feeling—often until she barely felt it herself.

It was even more galling that some stranger had to be the one to point it out. He didn't sound or act like Secret Service, making it even worse.

"Usually takes a new dog-handler team weeks of hard work to get even close to that kind of performance. Fine!" Jurgen's tone said it was anything but. He yanked a sheet from his clipboard, scrawled a signature, and handed it across. "Oh eight hundred tomorrow. Report to Captain Carl Baxter at the USSS office in the West Wing of the White House. Take that damn dog with you. I've got a meeting to get to." Then he stalked off. A trumped-up meeting, because earlier he'd said he had all day.

Linda could only look down at Thor in amazement. She squatted down and gave him a big scritch. It wasn't Thor's fault that she'd screwed up and not led him into the control center to sniff around and she had to make sure that he knew that. She'd never before worked with such a well-trained dog. He flopped onto his back and presented his belly. As she rubbed it, his back leg began kicking spasmodically in joy.

"You did so good, Thor. You are such a good doggie!" She used that ridiculous high-pitched voice that so many dog trainers used. She was long past being embarrassed by it. Mostly. She couldn't care less about Jurgen, but something about the other man who'd stayed behind made her less sure.

"Maybe I should leave you two alone." He had a nice deep voice, befitting his large frame.

Linda glanced up at him. Her automatic profiling assessment kicked in: Caucasian male, closecut dark hair, dark eyes, built big like a wrestler—enough so that he'd look heavy if he wasn't six-four. Instead he looked like the guy most likely to wrap you up in a friendly bear hug, which would force her to flatten him if he tried. His standout feature was powerful hands well marked with small cuts and burns. That and an amazing smile, which lit up his whole face. He wore a fleece jacket over a maroon turtleneck and a knit scarf in a blocky pattern of brilliant colors that made his brown eyes even warmer.

"Hi," his pleasant tone not the least diminished by her own silence, which was now growing awkward.

Thor had rolled to his feet, sniffed around the man, then looked up at him wagging his short tail.

He knelt down and reached out to scratch the dog's ear.

She snapped her fingers to get Thor's attention and made the hand sign for "enemy" as a test.

He looked up at her in surprise as if she'd lost her mind.

She sighed and whispered, "*Spiel.*" *Play.* The dog could do what he wanted.

He nosed out and slipped his head under the stranger's half-extended hand. Without a moment's hesitation, the man began to rub the offered ear. Easy for the dog.

Not so easy for her. Well, she had to start somewhere and he looked kindly enough.

"Nice scarf."

He looked down at his chest. "Oh, this one. Thanks. My mom knit it for me last Christmas. It's the colors of home."

"Where did you grow up, in a kaleidoscope?"

"Almost. South of San Francisco there are these huge salt flats that turn wild colors as their salinity increases. This is the last scarf she ever knit for me. I made one of cherry blossom colors for her that same year." His smile was wistful, which was more than she'd ever feel if her mom died.

"You knit?" She couldn't imagine how with those big hands of his.

"Doesn't everyone?" But his smile said that rather than an actual expectation, it was some form of humor—not one of her strengths. It was getting strange, not knowing if he was someone to salute or not, so she held out a hand.

"Sergeant Linda Hamlin. New to the Secret Service—as of today, I suppose."

"Clive Andrews," which still didn't tell her who he was. He reached up from where he still squatted by Thor. His hand was warm—her fingers were freezing—and as powerful as it looked. His massive hand completely enveloped hers. That's when she realized that he wasn't merely big, he was immensely strong. If he was trained, she might have trouble taking him down—though she'd learned more than a few dirty tricks fending off unwanted attentions in her decade of service.

There was an easy roll to his voice that hinted at Scottish, overlaid with a soft American accent that she couldn't pin down—which must be San Francisco. It made him sound as much of a mutt as Thor.

"Not *Agent* Hamlin?"

"*Special Agent* is separate from the Uniformed Division. The canine teams are UD; we use ranks."

"Oh."

Great way to build a friendship—her first potential one outside of the military in a decade—by correcting him. It did tell her that he wasn't Secret Service or he'd have known that. Which raised the question of what he was doing on their secure base.

"And this is a White House patrol dog?" He rubbed under Thor's chin.

She looked down at Thor's shaggy appearance. Despite his exceptional performance, it was clear that she was going to be endlessly harassed about him. She sighed and changed the subject.

"And you are…?" Best way to appease a man, talk about *him*.

"The White House chocolatier." His cheery wince said that he too was expecting a certain dismissive reaction.

When she didn't take the bait, he merely acknowledged it with a shrug.

Again the silence was stretching… "Is there a reason a chocolatier is here at James J. Rowley Training Center?"

This time the shrug looked a little awkward as he rose back to standing, much to Thor's dismay.

She was an expert on reading a dog's body language. Men were a mystery to her. Well, except for a few obvious nonverbal messages that she had made it a rule to ignore. But she wasn't getting those from Clive the Chocolatier.

"Grown men actually make their living with chocolate?"

That earned her another of his dazzling smiles, "Only the lucky ones."

"Chocolate was never a big motivator for me."

He slapped a hand on his heart and staggered backward as if she'd knifed him with her Benchmade Triage foldable. "You have set me a challenge, madam. I shall expect you to visit the White House Chocolate Shop at your first convenience so that I may convince you otherwise."

"The White House has a chocolate *shop*? Like where you buy chocolate?" She was definitely back in civilian land. The places she'd been operating, a chow tent was a luxury and a mess hall mostly a distant dream.

He sighed and hung his head as if she was a hopeless case, which wouldn't surprise her for a moment. But then he smiled down at her again, as cheerful as ever. He and Thor were apparently two of a kind.

"Actually, in the world of chocolate, a chocolate shop can be either a place of sale or a kitchen. Mine is a actually a chocolate kitchen. We just call it a shop."

"Okay. Sure. Whatever. I'll look you up if I get there." A chill breeze flapped the piece of paper directing her to report at the White House tomorrow and made her shiver. "Okay, *when* I get there."

Clive cast off his fooling around. His friendliness actually made her feel warm despite the freezing temperature. She really needed to get some gloves. Did he know how powerful that smile was on his handsome features?

Her jerk-o-meter wasn't twitching either, which was unusual.

Then, of all unlikely things, he bowed deeply—once to her and once to Thor, the second bow accompanied by a brief head pat—before turning and heading for the parking lot.

A nice guy. One who remembered her dog. She didn't like being charmed by any creature with less than four legs, but he'd somehow managed it.

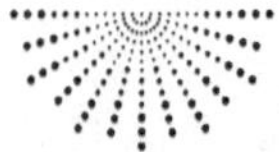

CHAPTER TWO

"*A*nd?"

Clive wondered how anyone could pack so many emotions into such an innocuous word: inquiry, curiosity, impatience, and a touch of someone busy working on a jigsaw puzzle in which he himself was but one of the smaller pieces. Not the most comfortable feeling.

That it was also Miss Watson's form of a greeting only made it all the stranger. As if they were in the middle of a conversation that he'd already missed the start of and would never catch back up with as it raced away from him.

He always felt like a cave explorer whenever he came down here.

Her office was a tiny space deep in the White House Residence's lowest subbasement. It was two stories below the kitchen and his chocolate shop, directly beneath the dishwashing room. The latter was proven by the nest of drain piping that covered the ceiling of her office. Any conversation here was punctuated by a succession of gurgles from dishwashers flushing away the remains of meals, ranging from the President's private dinners to massive state banquets.

The walls were old brick that probably dated back to the massive

Truman renovation. They were lined with packed-solid bookshelves. He'd never been able to make sense of the titles. Even an eclectic reader was unlikely to cover such a range of interests: religious texts, English law, German something or other (not one of his languages, not that he actually had any other than mostly forgotten high school French only slightly enhanced while apprenticed to the great Jacques Torres in New York), contemporary thrillers, dictionaries in a variety of languages…

As an excuse to look somewhere other than her steel blue eyes, he inspected her collection of curious artifacts—some of which he wondered how Miss Watson had gotten past White House security. Fierce knives and strange-looking rifles that were like none he'd ever seen being carried by the Secret Service or the military. Some of them looked like they'd be more appropriate in a spy movie than in real life.

High on one wall, with its own tiny spotlight as if it was a place of honor, a tattered wool scarf hung pressed in a glass frame, faded almost a uniform gray with hard usage. The sloppy knitting followed no discernable pattern. There were even holes that he could tell had been dropped stitches that had expanded with age. He'd never found the nerve to ask about it and, he thought about it a moment, today wasn't going to be the day he braved her daunting expression.

The office looked as if not even a single dust mote had been changed since his first visit here three months ago.

It had been a lovely day in October, one of the most beautiful months in DC. He'd found a note. Not a text or an e-mail, a handwritten note in a flowing black ink script. The problem was that it had been locked inside his personal recipe file box—to which he knew for a fact he had the only key.

"Come see me. Residence, Subbasement Two, Room 043." Nothing more. The paper had begun to dissolve just from the moisture on his fingers. He dropped it in the sink and it dissolved completely in the moisture accumulated there.

He'd only been called to her twice since and always left more puzzled than when he arrived. Everything about the room made the small, gray-haired woman who sat behind the battered steel desk seem all the more daunting and mysterious.

He tried not to fidget and totally failed. "Sergeant Linda Hamlin's score on the course was apparently exceptional. She—"

"I have them here," Miss Watson rested her hand on a slim file.

"Then why did you send me out to—"

"Tell me what isn't in the file."

Protesting that he didn't know what *was* included in the file didn't seem like a path that would lead anywhere good, so he abandoned it untested.

Clive wished that Miss Watson had actual guest chairs—not that the office was big enough to accommodate them. Instead, she had a single, four-legged wooden stool on which one of the legs was a half inch short. Sitting on it, he always felt out of balance…and kept checking his head to see if he should be wearing a dunce cap like the bad boy in the corner. It was also short enough that even with his stature he was barely eye-to-eye with her across the desk.

He looked at her again. Penetrating blue eyes. Silver hair back in a 1950s bun. She wore a hand-knit cable cardigan adorned only by a small bronze broach in the form of an oak leaf. She had an intricately patterned sock of gray, pale orange, and brown wool half completed on the corner of her desk. It was a Fair Isle pattern he'd learned at his mother's knee. He'd rather talk knitting than what he didn't know about Linda and Thor—but the thin needles caught the low desk light brightly, making them appear dangerous, as if they were weapons of war rather than of wool.

He'd never raised the subject of knitting with her on any of the four occasions she'd had reason to call him to her office. And he wasn't brave enough to this time either.

"Linda and Thor, a rather silly-looking little dog, moved about the course as if they were a single being connected by gesture and tone. They were more cohesive than most restaurants' menu plans, though Lieutenant Jurgen said it was their first meeting. There was a well-trodden path leading into the test area that they *didn't* follow. Linda led them onto a path of her own choosing instead."

"They see no boundaries." Miss Watson typically gave him the impression that he was only one of a myriad of more important topics she was contemplating. He now had her full attention and wished he didn't—it was rather daunting.

He tried to think of what else might not be in a performance report by Lieutenant Jurgen.

Linda's lovely face, flowing hair, and cautious eyes came to mind. Also, how hard it had been not to reach for her fine hand again as he left. He'd wanted to hold it again, however briefly, and that seemed a little creepy so he'd done his best courtly bow instead.

"During the course, there was a mock explosion that spattered them with dirt. Linda put Thor's life ahead of her own, shielding the dog with her own body. She did it so fast that I never saw it happen."

"You like her," Miss Watson made it a flat statement.

"Linda offers a lot to be admired."

Miss Watson brushed that aside with a flick of her ringless fingers. "You like her."

He grimaced. At which Miss Watson smiled like a benevolent grandmother rather than a scary old lady in the White House subbasement who was never discussed on the floors above. Did the politicians orbited through and mingled in the Residence even know she was down here?

"It is not mindreading. Your voice and expression would give you away. Your automatic use of her first name as well. Yes," Miss Watson gazed up at the waste pipes that formed her ceiling but appeared to be looking up through the two subbasements and the four stories of the Residence, right up to the Delta Force snipers permanently stationed on the roof. "Yes, I shall have to arrange to meet her."

"She promised to come by my chocolate shop."

Miss Watson tipped her head down to look at him as if she was glaring over the rims of her reading glasses, except she didn't wear any.

"Uh..."

She waited.

"Perhaps I'd best be going."

"Perhaps," her tone was drier and grittier than under-conched cocoa. "But before you depart, I would ask you to consider one question. What boundaries stop you, Mr. Andrews?" Then she picked up her knitting and he knew he was summarily dismissed.

He got out while the getting was good.

CHAPTER THREE

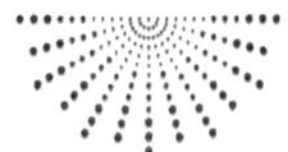

hor eyed her strangely.

"Give me a break." Linda's feet were riveted to the sidewalk. But there was no explaining to a dog that the broad green lawn and white stone building on the other side of the stout fence was anything more than a giant park specially designed for dogs to go pee in.

Even as she stood there, gawking through the black iron fence at the White House like any other tourist, a USSS dog team came working along the sidewalk. Before she could see their dog, it was easy to spot the handler: six feet of strapping immensely fit male in the black uniform and jacket of the Uniformed Division. Dark sunglasses despite the recent sunrise.

She envied the thin leather gloves protecting his hands. She'd found a battered pair of fingerless shooter's gloves in her gear, but they didn't keep her hands much warmer. Her last duties in Africa and Fort Benning, Georgia, hadn't called for anything more. DC's bitter winter was contending with fall evenings in Vermont and she'd forgotten how cold those were.

But rather than a proud German shepherd parting the crowd like a plowshare, a handsome springer spaniel nosed his way out of the crowd, swinging a little left and right to check the air swirled about by the few early morning joggers. It was still too early on a chilly morning for tourists and protestors to flock to the White House fence, but the dog team was already on duty.

The handsome dog handler stopped in front of her wearing a big smile.

"First day? I know the look. Still feels that way every time I look at the place." He turned to his dog. "*Gute Hund.*" The dog immediately relaxed its vigilance and came over to meet Thor.

"Uh, yeah. Guess so." Linda wondered if she could sound any lamer.

"Malcolm," he nodded toward the spaniel presently trading butt sniffs with Thor. "I'm Jim." Maybe he was okay despite his looks—it took a true dog handler to introduce his animal first.

"Thor. I'm Linda," and she wasn't going to get tagged with being lame. "One word about his name and you'll find yourself on your ass real fast."

Jim held up his warmly gloved hands palm out.

"Just sayin'," she put on her nicest tone.

"Hey, we floppy-eareds gotta stick together," again the unexpected genuineness of his smile. "Though Thor is kinda the extreme example I've seen."

"Floppy-eareds?"

"Friendly dogs. PSCO—Personnel Screening Canines Open Area. You'll see. The Emergency Response Team and the other behind-the-scenes dogs, they get the big muscle. We get the total sweethearts," the last he spoke in happy dog, squeaky pitch to Malcolm, who thumped his short tail against Jim's leg.

It made her like him even better—again the sign of a true dog handler. Maybe the world wasn't all made up of Jerk Jurgens. Or handsome chocolatiers.

"Well, gotta go. We got bad guys to catch. Go see the captain, he'll get you off on the right foot. See ya down the fence line. Later, Thor. *Such,*" he told Malcolm, who instantly headed forward into the thickening morning crowd along the fence line. Jim waved at her and moved off. She half wondered if he even remembered her name. Then she caught him glancing back…and she knew the timing: calculated to let him check her out, then glancing away fast when he knew he'd been caught.

Fine. Whatever.

A second UD officer separated from the crowd and followed Jim and Malcolm. He didn't have a dog; instead he had an AR-15 assault rifle slung across his chest. Teams of two.

She headed to the gate and showed her temporary ID to the guard inside the entrance's security hut. He scanned it, looking back and forth between her and the screen a couple of times before returning it. Then he waved her toward the metal scanner and she just rolled her eyes at him.

"What?"

"Collar, leash, handcuffs, sidearm, utility knife, taser, spare magazines…should I keep going?"

He leaned forward and looked down over the counter. "Oh. Didn't see your dog down there."

She held up the badge again, which said Secret Service K-9 on it rather than pulling out a baton and cracking him smartly on the head. She *was* learning patience.

"Right. Okay. But that's a temporary. Can't let you on the grounds while armed without an escort." Before she could think what to say, he was on the phone. It only took a moment. "You're expected. You can go through, but wait by the door."

She walked through the metal detector, which squealed in several nasty tones but, as no one shot her, she kept moving. She walked down a short hallway watched over by an attentive looking agent behind a tall counter made of louvered metal.

Thor swung aside and came to a halt as he sniffed at the screening.

"You're screwing up my job," the agent grumbled.

Linda tried to figure out how.

Thor was wagging his tail. The same way he had when he'd met Malcolm the springer spaniel along the fence line.

Then she felt it and looked up. Warmth! She raised her hand, the one not holding Thor's leash, closer to the source. It felt so good. A fan was blowing a slow waft of warm air down over her. It was...oh! Just enough to drive the air down and through the louvers along the counter. An EDT—Explosives Detection Team—dog would be on the other side of the louver beside the disgruntled agent.

"Tell him that Thor says hello."

"She," the agent looked down at his own dog, out of sight behind the counter, with a growl deep in his throat.

And apparently some of the White House handlers *were* closely related to Jerk Jurgens.

Linda tapped her thigh and led Thor out of the entry screening hut. Outside the air was fresh and the sun bright. She didn't mind the cold as much as she had earlier. Until she tucked her fingertips under opposite armpits and realized they were chilled to the bone.

Captain Baxter—by his shield and name badge—came up to her and held out a hand. "Sergeant Linda Hamlin. That like the Pied Piper of Hamelin or like Linda Hamilton in *Terminator?*" Naming her for the movie star was not one of her mother's kinder acts—not that her mother was known for that particular trait.

"Neither, sir." She *had* been named for Linda Hamilton, but for her role in *Beauty and the Beast* so Linda could properly deny any association with *Terminator.* An unfortunate similarity in looks that she'd never been able to live down made it even worse. She managed not to clench her jaw, but considered seeing just what attack skills *had* been taught to Thor.

The captain continued blithely on as he guided her toward the West Entrance to the White House, unaware of just how close she'd come to unleashing some wholly inappropriate response. "So, Jurgen finally found someone willing to give the little scruff ball a chance."

"Yes, sir."

"Assessment?" He asked it just a little too casually. Was he messing with her? Or did he know things she didn't and this was some sort of test?

"His acuity is exceptional. Good-natured, yet deeply trained to the handler-dog bond. Whoever trained him I suspect is highly qualified. Though I understand he's the first dog from a new kennel."

"Stan Corman. Navy SEAL, retired." The captain made a chopping motion with one hand against the biceps of his other arm. "Lost his dog and his arm at the same time. The two of them saved my life a couple years before that. Got out while I was still in one piece and came on board here. He landed at some place in nowhere Montana named Henderson's Ranch. I owe the man a chance and then some."

So, she'd done something right in accepting Thor. Wouldn't that just tick off Lieutenant Jurgen.

Through the foyer, again the badges cleared by security, and down a long hall crowded with rushing people.

Her nerves, which had bolted her to the sidewalk outside the fence line, blew up so high that she was amazed the White House roof didn't go with them. She was inside the bubble of the Commander-in-Chief. To her right were the doors to the Situation Room where any number of her last ten years' missions had been authorized. The Navy Mess.

While she gawked, the Vice President strode in chatting with the White House Chief of Staff as if it was a normal, everyday occurrence. She was *so* out of her depth. Only Thor's light pull on his leash kept her moving forward at all.

At the far end of the hall, Captain Baxter led her through a door labeled United States Secret Service. This at least felt familiar from her training. The craziness on the other side of the door? She'd be perfectly happy to never cross the fence line again. She and Thor would patrol the streets, and the people in here she'd just leave to do whatever people in here did.

The Secret Service Ready Room was packed with desks along the walls—about half of them occupied. At one end was a briefing area that could hold twenty or so agents, at the other were two glassed-in offices barely big enough to hold a desk and a chair each.

In one sat an agent with light brown, close-cropped hair. He was a few inches shorter than Clive and about half his size… Now why was she thinking about the chocolatier? She shook her head to clear it. The agent punched at a keyboard as if he was trying to kill it. The sign beside his office door didn't even bear a name, just PPD—Presidential Protection Detail.

Baxter led her into the other office marked UD—Uniformed Division.

He jabbed a finger at the lone chair as he closed the door.

She sat. Thor lay down at her feet.

Dropping into his own chair, Baxter slapped a hand on a file thick enough to be her entire personnel file and then some.

"All of this true?"

"Not having read it, sir, I wouldn't know."

"Commendations coming out of your goddamn ears, Sergeant. If *you* brought this to me, I'd have chucked it in the trash because I'd know one thing for certain—that you were a lying suck-up, forging shit to get near the President."

"Sir." Linda didn't know what else to say. She hadn't been some superstar, just a woman trying to play it dead clean in a man's world.

"Number of female dog handlers qualified to fight with the 75th Rangers: one. Number of female dog handlers in any branch of the military with not one, not two, but three medals for valor including a Bronze Star—all with the V for "in combat" on all three: one. Clearance Top Secret with SCI and SAP."

And Linda hoped that she'd never see another thing like it. Sensitive Compartmented Information and Special Access Programs information was always a nightmare.

"Seventeen of your actions over the last five years are redacted so that even I can't tell what the hell you were doing. You care to tell me?"

"No, sir." She wasn't at liberty to do so, no matter what his clearance.

"Good girl."

Okay, not girl. Not even woman. Soldier! Training in silence was all that let her keep the comment inside. Besides, only seventeen of her missions redacted? That meant that a number of her missions were so highly classified that they weren't in her file at all—at least not the version made available to the Secret Service.

"What in the name of all that's holy and the US Army are you doing in my office?"

"Reporting for duty?" What kind of a trick question was that?

Baxter stared at the closed file for a long moment before looking back at her. "Draw me a map, Hamlin. US Rangers to US Secret Service. How did you get here?"

"There was a flyer in my DD 214 discharge packet. USSS K-9 team recruiting. *Be all your dog can be.* Sounded like me."

He barked a short laugh. "I like it. But we don't do that. We don't have flyers."

"Well, someone put it there. Looked better than going back to Vermont." Throwing herself naked into the Potomac in January looked better than that.

Baxter harrumphed. Then scowled at Thor, who had lain down at her feet.

"Damned if I know what to make of it. We get good men applying for this job, a lot of them."

He didn't emphasize *men,* so she kept her thoughts to herself.

"Most of them straight out of college with some nutso ideas about glory. Takes forever to straighten them out and some we never do. That's not you."

"That's not me," Linda agreed.

"A woman with a decade of service and half of it with the 75th Rangers," he mused to himself. "I'll be damned." Without further comment, Baxter leaned over his desk and slapped a hand against the wall.

While they were waiting for whatever response, he dug a bright-brass USSS Uniformed Division badge out of his pocket and tossed it to her. She pinned it to her uniform's left lapel, taking only a moment to rub her thumb over the embossed image of the White House and the small blue plaque at the bottom with "Sergeant" etched into it.

A moment after she had it affixed, the door opened and the agent from the PPD office next door stepped in and closed the door behind him.

"This her?"

Baxter just nodded.

Her what? Linda didn't have time to be more than puzzled by the remark.

"Hello. I'm Harvey Lieber, Senior Special Agent in charge of President Zachary Thomas' protection detail."

"Linda Hamlin," she'd have stood if there was room, but there wasn't.

"Out of the friggin' blue," Baxter grumbled.

"And?"

Baxter eyed her. "Jurgen doesn't give anyone top marks. I keep him out at Rowley to scare the ego out of all the rookies, even the agents back for refresher training who are getting too cocky. He gave them to her, though. I told you about Stan Corman sending me a dog."

"That?" Lieber looked down at Thor, who began batting a front paw in his sleep as if chasing a rabbit.

Linda hoped it was a little field bunny, because he wasn't all that much bigger than a jackrabbit.

"That," Baxter agreed.

"Should do nicely."

Linda twisted around to get a better look at him, but it didn't tell her anything.

"Can you be presentable?" Agent Lieber looked down at her.

She waved a hand at herself. This was how she came. In uniform with her hair and teeth brushed.

"I mean in a high-end social crowd. Not asking if you're pretty—that's obvious and irrelevant, though not a bad thing in this situation. Asking if you know how to behave."

"My mother wishes I did." Mom had always been pushing her into the political events in Montpelier, Vermont—as if it was Albany, New York, or some other much larger and more important state's capital. Was she supposed to become a conniving politician like her mother, whose ethics had nothing to do with reality and everything to do with partisan stratagems and counterattacks? Or was she supposed to become like her father, teaching at University of Vermont, Burlington, because of all the coeds who flocked to handsome poli-sci professors whenever his wife was off to Montpelier?

"Which means you know how, you just hate it. Couldn't care. Your call, Baxter. First Family flies out in an hour, I can't deal with this right now." And just that fast he was gone.

"What the hell?"

Baxter raised his eyebrows.

"Sir."

<hr>

CLIVE WENT through his morning routine on autopilot.

The Chocolate Shop was so small that it was a good thing there was a coat closet between it and the main kitchen. The twenty-foot-square room was immaculate and, with all of the counters and equipment, left little space for anything extraneous like his coat.

The conching machine ground happily away in the corner, smoothing and heating the chocolate to uniformly distribute the cocoa butter throughout. It's background hum always made him feel as if everything was okay. The dark chocolate required three days of conching. It had taken some real magic to squeeze the machine into his tiny kitchen, but the results were absolutely worth it.

He studied several of the sketches he'd taped on the face of the spice cabinet. He peeled away the chocolate cake he'd made for Christmas and the white chocolate and strawberry streusel from New Year's Eve. He liked to think of it as clearing the decks for what came next. Many other surfaces had neat rows of images that inspired him, but the spice cabinet was only for the actual desserts he was going to make and he never repeated.

He unlocked the pantry and main chocolate storage cabinet that kept everything at fifty degrees. His supplies were all in place.

A peek inside his smaller storage cabinet, which he left at sixty degrees and never locked, said that the overnight damage hadn't been too severe. He made a point of leaving "extra" confections there, which were frequently raided when the staff had to work late. He made a mental note to keep the level of truffles a little higher and form the chocolate bars smaller. Apparently people felt too guilty taking the larger chocolate bars when raiding his kitchen. He took a few minutes with a hot knife to cut them neatly into halves and thirds. He lay a small bet with himself as to how many would survive another night.

Of course whenever Clive caught a "thief," he took deep umbrage and soundly berated the individual—it was the only time he unleashed his father's brogue. "An' what makes ye think that ye deserve such *snashters,* you blaggard?" And the like. Lasses, of course, were treated more kindly. It came out half drunken-Scot and half pirate-captain—all in good fun.

The "public" cabinet was a good testing method for new creations. He'd leave several options, and often discovered that one had been completely cleared out and another barely touched. Last night had been an even fifty-fifty, so nothing new to learn there. He found that disappointing, he'd rather thought his lavender-brushed honey truffles would be more popular than the vanilla-cream-filled extra-dark bonbon.

"Back to the drawing board, lad."

Which reminded him of yesterday's sketch. Drawn, but now he'd have to write out the process of execution.

He took his time heating milk to two hundred degrees, rinsing his favorite mug under the boiling-water tap to bring it up to temperature, and then mixing in his homemade cocoa powder. He sipped it, but it wasn't quite right. Christmas was recently gone—the holiday madness that wracked the White House kitchens every year had subsided—but it was too abrupt. He fished a whole nutmeg out of the pantry and used a rasp to grate a little over his mug. A pinch of allspice and a quick stir. He let it steep for a minute or two to blend properly, then tasted it again.

Yes, just a little nostalgia after the holidays to soften the blow of descent from the madness of the holidays into the bland, unending stretch of January. Nothing ever happened in January...except for mesmerizing dog trainers.

He sat at the marble counter with his cocoa and his notepad, finally allowing himself to flip to the sketch he'd made yesterday while out at the James J. Rowley facility. He studied it carefully. It was pretty enough—a white chocolate, half eggshell with jagged edges, filled with a bourbon mousse and crowned with fanciful dark chocolate work.

Something wasn't right there. At least not yet. Perhaps because the crane also looked like a stork and neither the President nor the Vice President had reproduced yet. That created a mixed message that he wasn't wholly comfortable with. A bluebird perhaps? Did Southeast Asians believe in the bluebird of happiness?

Something more bothered him, but he was having trouble pinning it down.

Vietnam, Japan, and the Philippines. The only thing their flags had in common was the color red. Hard to play off that.

Using Marou chocolate from Lam Dong province might please the Vietnamese delegation, but might well insult the others for perceived favoritism. While the Philippine chocolatiers were doing well, only Kablon and Malagos came close to the same standard. And Japan didn't make chocolate at all. Regrettably, to avoid offense, he'd have to go South American or African. But that still didn't solve the lack of a Japanese element.

The dessert felt almost old hat—three different grades of chocolate to make…

No. He wanted something…

The words were eluding him. He knew from experience that only when he found the right words could he then design the confection.

He studied the sketch again. It was pretty enough, but it was lacking in meaning.

He crumpled up the page and tossed it away. Yesterday it would have been good enough, but not today.

Clive doodled on the corner of the next page while he contemplated what had changed. It wasn't merely enough to achieve, he wanted to excel. Something had shifted in his understanding of what he did.

Life was like that, perceptions growing and changing in fits and starts, and he'd come to anticipate their arrival. By the time he understood that he was a chocolatier, he had already graduated from the CIA—the Culinary Institute of America—and slaved for four years under the eagle eye of two different masters, one in Chicago and another in LA before finally going to work for the great Jacques Torres in Manhattan. He sipped his hot cocoa again after raising it in a toast to the signed photograph of Torres and himself on the wall.

The invitation to the White House had shocked Clive until he had looked back at his steady climb up the ranks of the nation's dessert kitchens post-Torres: the Beverly Wilshire in LA, The Plaza in New York, The Greenbriar…

Only in retrospect did his life ever make sense.

He was less certain about what had changed last night, though something definitely had. He was no longer content with a design that just yesterday he would have happily created and he knew would have been well received.

Whatever the seed of the change, he could see more clearly now. It was not enough for his dessert to be pretty and a topic of conversation. It had to have meaning. It had to have…purpose.

There! That was the problem. He knew almost nothing about the purpose of the dinner he was designing for.

He tapped his pen on the page. Who to ask? The kitchen team wouldn't know any more than he did. Chef Klaus was not exactly an elevated thinker. An elevated chef? Absolutely. But thinking wasn't an ingredient he used very often.

Clive sipped at his cocoa for inspiration, but only found an unpleasantly lukewarm concoction that had a little too much allspice in it.

Miss Watson would know, but he couldn't imagine bothering her with anything as trivial as a chocolate design.

What was it Miss Watson had said about Linda? That she saw no boundaries.

Maybe that was it. Maybe he now saw a boundary that was behind him. One that had limited his vision. The problem was that every time he turned around, he saw Linda Hamlin's face.

It took him a moment to understand the he really *was* seeing her face.

"You came!"

LINDA COULD ONLY BLINK in surprise.

She hadn't actually come looking for Clive, but he seemed so happy about her arrival that she didn't want to gainsay him either.

Finally, in self-defense, she held aloft the map she'd been following. Rather than sending her and Thor to the fence line—the standard location for floppy-eared dogs to patrol—Captain Baxter had given her a map. Actually a book of maps—who knew the White House was such a vast complex.

"President Zachary Thomas and the First Lady are traveling—three days in Tennessee at her family's ranch," Baxter had rattled off his instructions so fast that only her military experience let her keep up with them. "Vice President Daniel Darlington is up on the Hill for the day. Go learn the White House. I want you and Thor familiar with every square inch." She was beginning to discover quite how tall an order that was.

Not wanting to bother anybody until she felt a little more sure of herself, she'd chosen to first explore everything below the Ground Floor. The West Wing was generally acknowledged to have three floors: the Ground Floor she'd entered on that included the USSS office and the Situation Room, the State Floor with the Oval and other key offices, and some more office space on the Second Floor. She'd discovered a labyrinth of two more stories below that, including several places where a Marine guard waited, so she decided to tackle those later. This included a massive new complex under the north lawn that had been built between 2010 and 2014 that she somehow doubted even her full-access pass would allow her into.

On second thought, rather than waving the book of maps aloft, with its bold "Secret" label on the cover, she tucked it in her vest pocket. She had no idea if Clive was authorized to even know that some of the areas existed.

"I'm so glad that you're here."

"You are?" She'd barely met him yesterday.

"I am," his big voice boomed about the tiny kitchen. "Welcome to my kingdom."

"Um, I don't want to appear rude, but isn't it a little small for a kingdom?" The room was perhaps twenty feet square, and that was only if it was stripped to the walls. Instead, every single nook and cranny was packed solid. White marble work surfaces, massive doors to walk-in refrigerators, and lots of fancy kitchen machinery. The center six-by-six-foot work table left barely enough room around it for two people to squeeze by each other.

On the few uncovered wall surfaces were pictures of too astonishing a variety to quite take in: peacock feathers, cobblestone streets in the rain, a postcard of modernist art. They all blurred together. Only the area around a portrait of a smiling man shaking Clive's hand seemed to rise out of the general noise.

"Nonsense!" Clive bounced to his feet. "It's a splendid kingdom! Come. I'll give you the grand tour, then I will ply you with tasty treats because you must come to my aid."

Linda tried to keep up, but three separate agendas in a single sentence seemed a bit much. "Maybe I should just…" She made the mistake of turning her head for a moment to wave down the hall that supposedly led to the Flower Shop. It was her next destination and then the three unlabeled rooms merely marked Storage beyond that. She'd found many interesting things that were marked that way on the map, none of them having to do with storing anything.

Her ill-timed distraction allowed Clive time to scoop up something from the counter and cross two of the four steps that defined the breadth of his kingdom to squat in front of Thor.

"He can't eat chocolate," she warned him off. "It's poisonous to dogs."

"I know that. How about a little bacon? I've been testing a savory treat, baked maple-glazed bacon with a chocolate drizzle that I haven't applied yet. Is this okay?" He held aloft the piece of bacon.

Thor was nearly shivering with anticipation.

"*Ja*," she whispered to the dog, who practically snatched it from Clive's fingers the moment she gave him permission. Clive clearly knew to keep his fingers out of the way when dogs and bacon were involved. Technically, it was bad form to let anyone feed a Secret Service dog other than its handler, but Clive seemed okay.

Okay?

He was on his knees by her dog, thumping him lightly on the ribs as Thor made quick work of the treat.

"Now," in a deceptively smooth and light motion for a man of his size, Clive was on his feet once more looking down at her.

At six-four he seemed too large for the kitchen, and so close that she had to crane her neck slightly to look into his eyes. He was thinking hard about something, but she had no idea what. Then he had her arm in his grip and was tugging her over the threshold that only Thor had crossed.

In moments he was describing shining machines with words she'd never have applied to them or didn't recognize at all.

A grinder was neither for coffee beans nor smoothing down the side of an M-ATV where a bullet had pierced the heavy armor.

Conching was something done for days on end though she didn't understand what or why.

The tempering vat didn't seem angry at all.

"In the past, the White House Chocolate Shop has always relied on the production of chocolate by others. Chefs took the finished product in bulk and worked it from there. Whenever I can, I step back earlier in the process. I don't have room for a cocoa nib roaster, but I have control of the rest of the line after that point. Here, I'll show you the difference."

He pulled on a latex gloves before reaching into one of the coolers. On a tiny white plate, he placed three bite-size pieces of chocolate.

"Taste these. Start with that one," he pointed.

Unable to pull back from the rushing vortex that was Clive Andrews in his element, she gave in and tasted the first one.

"Nice enough, right? Melts well. Smooth on the tongue. A little crunch when you bite it. Swallow and the flavor lingers for several moments."

She tasted all of those things, none of which she'd ever noticed before.

"Now, a sip of plain seltzer to clear the palate," he handed her a glass that he'd been pouring. "This should be lime sorbet, but I don't have any handy at the moment."

When she opened her mouth to protest that she didn't have a palate, he popped a second piece in her mouth.

"Notice the sharper snap when you bite on it. There are hints of the terroir. A suggestion of vanilla, though I haven't added any to this batch. The melt is slower, teasing at your senses as it unfolds. When you finish, it lasts, convincing you… Almost whispering in your ear," he leaned in and did just that. "More. Eat a little more."

She tried to pull back, but her body said to lean in. The two canceled each other out, but she wouldn't soon forget the way his voice lowered and teased like the chocolate did.

"More seltzer now. And now the third piece."

She didn't even make a pretense of reaching for it, instead just opening her mouth and closing her eyes as he popped it into her mouth.

"Bite it," he whispered.

She did. The snap was fresh and crisp. Behind it came a tidal wave of sensations. So smooth, it was almost like cream. Flavors wandered by, teasing, enticing, promising…and delivering. She breathed in through her nose and the flavor built and unfolded. It was just chocolate and vanilla, but it seemed to unravel and entice with so much more. She didn't know what any of them were, but they were both magnificent and subtle in the same moment.

"Now notice—"

"Hush," she reached out and clamped her hand over his mouth. "I'm having a moment here."

His smile tickled against her palm.

CLIVE HAD LONG AGO LEARNED the power of good chocolate over women. But never in his life had he so enjoyed watching one eat it.

When Linda closed her eyes, her face softened. The fiercely focused Secret Service professional revealed an unexpected gentle side—transformed from brittle, sharp-edged sugar work to smooth chocolate sculpture. No longer bundled in her jacket against the January chill, her sleek athleticism still defined her, but it was no longer all of who she was.

Then she opened her eyes. Between one eyeblink and the next, Sergeant Hamlin returned. She pulled her hand away from his mouth as if she'd been electrocuted.

"Okay. That was tasty. I'll admit that."

He couldn't help laughing. She might think she was all the tough dog handler, but now he knew better. He'd seen the woman behind the wall. And he wanted to see more.

"I have work to do. Thanks for the chocolate." And that quickly, she almost slipped out of his reach.

"Wait!"

"For what?" Linda turned to look at him from halfway out the door. The woman moved as if attached to a teleporter.

"I have a problem."

"The third item on your agenda."

"I have an agenda?"

She rolled her eyes at him, but he still didn't know what she was talking about. Under normal circumstances his next agenda might be how to get Linda Hamlin out to dinner, then into his bed, but in her Secret Service mode that wasn't going to happen.

He thought about reaching for her, but that too had shifted.

One moment she'd had her hand over his mouth—a teasingly gentle touch. So close that he could smell her. Unscented soap and shampoo left her own natural flavors to fill the air around him: the softness of honey and the warmth of fresh ground chili powder mixed with the freshness of new-fallen snow. She presented the most evocative sensations he'd ever encountered.

The next moment she was…herself. Half out the door and all about getting on with whatever business had led her past his shop.

"You said you needed my help."

"I did?" He did? "I do."

And he'd think of why in a minute, but if that was enough to hold her in place…

"Oh. Right," he moved back to the stool at the counter in front of his notepad, hoping that would draw her back into the shop.

She waited at the threshold. Well, if that was the best he was going to get, it would have to do for now.

"I need to make a special dessert. Something…relevant."

Again, the waiting silence that he was learning was Linda's answer to so many questions.

"The leaders of Vietnam, the Philippines, and Japan will be here next week. Something about some islands. Do you know why?"

"Why would I know that? This is my first day in the White House."

"Do you know what islands they'd care about?"

"For those three together? Probably the Spratlys. China has claimed them though they lie six hundred miles south of the People's Republic. They've dredged the reefs to build islands, one of which is now a heavily equipped military base offering them a significant forward projection of air and naval power. They've done all this despite United Nations' rulings that they didn't have the right to do so."

Clive could only blink in surprise. "Why would they do all that?"

"It extends their territorial control. For one thing, it places them at the center of a major oil tanker route reaching all of the way back to the Persian Gulf. They want to protect that supply chain as well as they can in future years. Possibly even preempting all three of those countries' supplies for their own benefit. Taiwan's and Korea's as well, for that matter. Without massive oil imports, there *is* no China, no matter how fast they burn coal."

She'd already completely shifted his understanding of the upcoming meal. A white chocolate egg with a bourbon mousse was completely irrelevant to the proceedings. New Birth had nothing whatsoever to do with this kind of problem. He needed to completely rethink it.

He could feel her watching him, but he didn't know what to say. How many of his desserts had he delivered with such little understanding of what was actually occurring upstairs in the State Dining Room?

Between one eyeblink and the next, his doorway was emptied.

Linda and Thor were gone as if they'd never been. He rushed to the door and caught only the briefest view of the two of them moving silently down the hallway before they turned a corner and were gone. So he hadn't imagined everything—she actually had been here.

He returned to his marble counter and looked down at his blank sketch pad trying to visualize what *did* belong there.

Except it wasn't blank.

His earlier doodle was of a small dog and just a hint of a woman's face no clearer than a ghost's.

———

"WOULD YOUR DOG LIKE A BISCUIT, my dear?"

Linda checked her map again. White House Residence, Subbasement Two, Room 043-Mechanical.

Then she looked back at the woman. She was tall, silver-haired, and had a pleasant smile. She waved a hand at a ceramic cookie jar in the shape of Snoopy's red doghouse, complete with the dog himself lying on the ridgeline as a handle. It sat on a small walnut side table.

Room 043-Mechanical had a ceiling of tangled pipes mostly lost in overhead shadows. But the room itself was warmly lit by a gas fireplace set inside a white-and-gray marble mantel at the far end. An old, disused looking desk sat close by the door, with a lone stool in front of it. Beyond that, a long room led past several bookcases to a cozy sitting area. Deep, cheerfully floral armchairs sported lace doilies over the arms.

Linda hesitated and inspected the shadows more carefully. Weapons of war were collected along the tops of some of the bookcases closer by the desk. Not just war, but clandestine war. They were the weapons that might have been used by an assassin or a spy. The Arsenal knife, with a .22 six-shot revolver built into the handgrip. A Ruta Locura single shot .22 LR rifle that could break down into a pair of carbon-fiber tubes—stock and barrel—no bigger around than her thumb and each as long as her forearm. Add a scope and it still weighed under a pound and a half. Utterly lethal and very hard to detect. It made the sniper rifle from *The Day of the Jackal* movie look clumsy.

Deeper into the room, the Tiffany lamps with their cheerfully colored shades lit framed portraits of women. Some in evening gowns, others in military uniforms.

"Yes, I'm sure Thor would enjoy a treat," Linda agreed to buy herself a moment longer to inspect the curious collection and the woman in the midst of it.

The woman made a show of lifting the lid and selecting just the right dog biscuit, then handing it off to Thor. He took it delicately from her fingers, rather than the sharp snap of Clive's bacon, before lying down to happily grind it into the room-filling, white Persian rug.

"Would his handler like some tea?"

She could only nod. Linda's head was spinning. She'd abandoned her basements-first plan after escaping Clive's chocolate shop. That had sent her tramping all through the upper floors of the Residence, feeling like a voyeuristic intruder.

Still uncomfortable approaching Clive's shop, she and Thor had investigated the East Wing from the top story First Lady's offices down to FDR's bomb shelter below the northeast lawn. A small plaque had informed her that it was rated to withstand a five-hundred-pound bomb—early WWII had been a kinder, gentler era in some strange ways.

Deep in the lowest basement of the East Wing, she'd turned away from the tunnel leading to the Treasury Building and instead followed the one that ran from the FDR shelter below the East Wing into the lowest level of the Residence, and beyond that, connected to the West Wing.

Deep under the lawn between the East Wing and the Residence, she passed The Truman Shelter. It had been built with nuclear weapons in mind and was significantly more substantial, if little more welcoming than FDR's concrete cube. It was set up as a complete safe room, but it too stood with its door open and no guard in attendance. Another part of the White House's buried history that none of the public would ever see.

Once more beneath the Residence itself, she and Thor had investigated air conditioning and heating machine spaces. She'd fed him a snack from her bag and let him rest for a while outside the elevator machine space.

She'd carefully avoided Clive's shop, though she could still feel his smile against her palm. It seemed to belong there. She wanted to go back. Taste another piece of his magnificent chocolate and perhaps see if his smile tasted as good as it felt.

Whoa! Where had *that* idea come from?

She hadn't been in a relationship since RAF Lieutenant James. Her team had been stationed with the British attack helo pilots at Kabul for six months, and she'd spent three of them happily in his arms whenever they were both on base. He'd been like the first of Clive's chocolates: not deep, but definitely nice enough while it lasted. There had never been a second-chocolate-level relationship for her. Something inside her was broken that didn't allow for any of those. Her emotions were broken, just like her mother's—a sour taste indeed.

Once more on the move, she'd rounded a corner past Electrical Switching Control in the lowest subbasement of the Residence and— stepped into a Victorian tea room complete with a silver-haired matron dispensing dog treats.

"Please, Miss Hamlin. You have walked a long way. Take a seat."

"You know who I am." A pointless statement. Somehow the woman also knew she'd walked miles today exploring the President's House. Probably knew Linda's tour was barely half done even though the day was almost over.

"I'm Miss Watson," she didn't bother wasting breath to confirm her knowledge of Linda's name. She poured tea from a white porcelain teapot covered in sweet pea flowers. On a small table between the two chairs, she placed a matching plate with unadorned shortbread biscuits.

Linda could feel Clive's pained expression two stories above. He'd have dipped, sprayed, or sprinkled them with something. Certainly he'd add elegant little designs on the tops like the ones she'd spotted on the chocolates in a small cabinet he'd shown her.

"You have an…interesting office, Miss Watson." A Victorian sitting room in the lowest subbasement of the White House made that an understatement. A pair of hinged bookcases had been swung back against the walls of the elegant room. Linda saw that if they were closed, the sitting room would disappear and only the dingy but dangerous little office would remain.

"Thank you, my dear." Miss Watson sat in a chair across from her and picked up her knitting.

Linda focused on the picture above the woman's head. It was of a dark-haired beauty in a golden, quasi-Egyptian metal bikini. "Is that…"

"Mata Hari. Margaretha Geertruida MacLeod. Falsely accused, tried, and executed by the French for being a double agent—15 October 1917." Miss Watson didn't look down at her knitting, instead watched Linda intently. "They needed a sacrifice to their flagging morale, so they shot Mata Hari for being a former wanton during a time of constricting morals as much as anything else."

Inspecting other photos that hung about the room, Linda decided that some questions were best not asked aloud. But Miss Watson began answering them anyway.

"Marthe Cnockaert, WWI—specialist in explosives." Miss Watson indicated another image with a flick of the end of her knitting needles. "Sarah Emma Edmonds was an American Civil War master of disguise: male, female, black, white. Manuela Sáenz, 1800s—a fascinating and dangerous woman who destroyed a leader in Peru and was instrumental in creating Simón Bolivar in Venezuela. Nancy Wake, WWII. One of the most highly decorated servicewomen of the war, she topped the Gestapo's most wanted lists."

Who was Miss Watson that she had a room decorated with portraits of female spies?

Linda decided that her best option was to keep quiet and sip her tea. Thor, done with his biscuit, looked at her longingly until she gathered him into her lap. He sighed happily and flopped backward with his head in the crook of one of her arms and appeared to fall instantly asleep. He acted as if they'd been together a lifetime rather than twenty-four hours.

The clicking of the knitting needles stopped abruptly and Linda became aware of Miss Watson inspecting her closely.

"What drives you, Miss Hamlin?"

"I'm not sure what you mean. Dogs, I suppose."

"That answer is too easy, Miss Hamlin. Do you not find it so?"

"I can't say that I ever thought much about it."

"Oh, that's unlikely."

Linda blinked.

"Come, my dear. You are sitting in a library built upon histories of the exploits of the world's greatest spies, male or female. Some worked for intelligence gathering, others in undercover roles to take down hated regimes. Some of them hated *our* nation, yet they too adorn these walls. Runway model Anna Chapman—2001-2010 in London and New York for the Russians," she indicated a striking redhead posed in black leather pants and a lacy bustier while holding a chromed MP-443 Grach pistol as if she knew how to wield it. "Ethel Rosenberg and Ruth Greenglass—Manhattan Project for the Soviet Union. Wild Rose Greenhow—a noted spymaster for the Confederacy versus Elizabeth Van Lew who served a similar role for the Union. A woman of such caliber as yourself has most assuredly thought long and deeply."

Miss Watson finally pointed a knitting needle at the center of Linda's own chest like an attack.

"I'm not a spy."

"If you were, you wouldn't be here—though your picture might be. But your illustrious career leaves little reason to suspect your loyalties. My question is rather what *are* you, my dear?" The pointing needle turned once more to the mundane task of turning linear yarn into a three dimensional object.

The contrast of the inquiry couched as a mild threat made Linda inspect her tea. Her cup was only half empty, but she tested herself to see if she felt woozy or drugged. The room didn't spin. She felt no more inclined to speak than normal. She closed her eyes and felt no different. She—

Miss Watson snickered quietly.

Linda opened her eyes.

The needles had again stopped clicking and Miss Watson was using an embroidered kerchief to dab at the corners of her eyes.

"What?"

"Watching your imagination is lovely, my dear," she barely managed over her quiet laughter.

"My—" Miss Watson had observed her thoughts. If not a mind reader, then she was certainly well trained in observing human expression. As well trained perhaps as Linda herself was at reading the signals of a dog's feelings. And that kind of training implied...

She scanned around the room once, twisting to make sure she didn't miss any of the pictures tucked on shelves or hanging over the mantelpiece.

"Where is your photo?"

Miss Watson's laugh brightened even more, leaving her unable to speak at all.

"Oh, that will teach an old woman," she fanned herself with her handkerchief once she had mostly recovered her composure. "After all these years, you would think that I knew better than to make assumptions. You are the first to ever unmask me." Then she unclipped a gold locket from about her neck, flicked open the cover, and gazed at it a moment before handing it across.

Linda looked down at the two tiny images within. One was of a young and beautiful woman. Though it was black-and-white, it was easy to imagine her brilliant blue eyes looking straight out of the picture from the cargo bay of a Vietnam era UH-1 Huey helo. The other was a closeup. In that one, she looked severely Russian: her blonde hair pulled sleekly back, sitting in the lap of a terribly handsome Soviet-era general with two stars on his golden shoulder boards.

"The first was shortly after my return from my third undercover mission to confirm the number of prisoners at the Hanoi Hilton and other camps, gathering intelligence used during negotiations at the Paris Peace Talks. Sergei, on the other hand," she sighed softly and a smile lit her features. "Poor Sergei had no secrets from me. Not once did he suspect any of my secrets."

Linda closed the locket and handed it back.

"You are more than you appear to be, Miss Watson."

"The best of us always are, my dear. We always are," she placed the locket once more around her neck and returned to her knitting.

CHAPTER FOUR

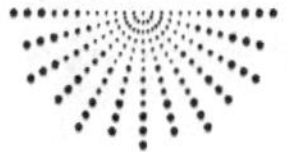

*I*t took Linda two full days to complete her White House tour and another to walk the outer grounds. Jim, Malcolm's handler, had been right. Every single moment was humbling.

Each night—while Thor snoozed on her feet in their temporary billet near the James J. Rowley Training Center—she had studied the book of maps until it was embedded clearly in her mind alongside other locations she'd had to scout over the years. It was an uncomfortable feeling to have the White House overlaid in her mind with sections of Kabul and Lashkar Gah, Afghanistan, as well as Mosul, Iraq, where the Rangers had served as "advisors" during the bloody battles clearing out ISIL.

She'd learned a lot these last few days. The Emergency Response Team dogs worked from vans parked around the perimeter of the fence line and from strategic emplacements inside the fence, allowing them to spring into action at a moment's notice. The floppy-eared sniffer dogs were afforded no such luxuries.

After the half-hour ride in on the Metro, they stopped off first at the USSS offices six blocks from the White House. There they transformed from a woman and her dog into a fully kitted out Secret Service team. Leash was traded for USSS harness that proudly announced Police K-9 on the Kevlar vest that wrapped down over the dog's vital organs (though it had taken them some time to find one small enough for Thor). For herself it included a six-pound Dragon Skin vest—the best armor in the business no matter what the Army politicians said about the twenty-two-pound "lightweight" IOTV or the thirty-plus-pound full version. Adding basic weapons to that, she was ready for duty—a day on the fences.

It was what she was coming to learn was a typical DC day in January: low thirties rising too slowly to low forties, clear blue skies with a high hint of cirrus clouds heralding incoming weather from the Atlantic.

Thor tugged ahead as they were walking to the fence line.

"Going to be on our feet all day, there's no need to hurry."

But he wasn't listening. Not at all. Instead…

Normally, he wandered about just like any other dog, checking out lampposts and fire hydrants for messages on the dog-pee telegram network. Only when she told him *seek* did he forget about that and go hunting explosive smells.

But what if he'd found one of those smells on his own?

He still moved ahead in the slight zigzag that so disconcerted oncoming pedestrians intent on their to-go coffee and reaching work on time. But she knew he was weaving to make sure that he wasn't straying from the strongest centerline of whatever scent he'd found.

Linda risked a quick glance around but spotted no other Secret Service agents on the move. This was really happening and she had no backup. What if she caught up with Thor's quarry before they reached the fence line? She rested a hand on her Taser, but using a device that delivered several thousand volts into someone wired up with explosives wasn't her first choice. The secret to dealing with a bomber was to tackle the individual, controlling both of their hands from the first instant, in case they were clutching a dead man switch or reaching for a trigger.

She felt a decade of combat training slip over her like a favorite jacket. The blast of adrenaline made her hyperaware of her surroundings. She began assessing and recording every possible relevant detail from crisscrossing pedestrians to the models of cars moving along the road. Her mind cleared of everything except the moment: possible attackers, assets, terrain, safe hides, minimum threat to innocents.

Thor picked up the pace, weaving less and less as he homed in on his quarry.

He knew nothing of the dangers involved. His sole mission was to locate the explosives and then receive a doggie treat for his vigilance.

Linda eased him back.

Thor proved just how strong his legs were in his drive to move ahead, but she kept him at bay.

They crossed 15th Avenue just north of the Treasury Building. No rental vehicles pulled to the curb where they shouldn't be. Everyone's car windows rolled up against the cold morning rather than lowered to allow firing a weapon. Once across the traffic, Thor followed the scent into the pedestrian-only area of Pennsylvania Avenue between the White House and Lafayette Square.

As pedestrians peeled off with each turning, her field of possible targets narrowed.

She was down to eleven. Two blondes with cell phones out and chatting together while barely watching where they were going (unlikely). Three couples, one holding hands and two holding coffee cups (unlikely). Three solos: black wool coat to his knees, gray suit, and brunette with a stylish jacket.

CLIVE EMERGED from the underground entrance at the Metro Center station. Though he'd ducked underground less than twenty minutes ago in Friendship Heights at the northwest corner of DC, it was always a surprise. Today, he'd descended in darkness and emerged in the light. Sunrise happened so much faster in the winter here, especially when compared to San Francisco.

Though it felt as cold as a San Francisco fog.

A pleased shiver rippled over him. It made him experience a touch of homesickness even if there was no longer any reason to return. But even that sad reminder enriched the flavor of the breaking dawn.

He disgorged onto the street with the other Washingtonians, bursting forth from the escalator like a hundred fronds of a chocolate lacework, dispersing into ever-tapering clumps but joined by others until their overlapping paths created an invisible lacework upon which the city was laid.

Interconnections.

He still hadn't resolved his dessert for the State Dinner, but he liked the word "interconnections."

He had consulted with Chef Klaus about it. As Clive had feared, no neat answers to the dessert had been forthcoming, but for his troubles, a chocolate course had been added to the front of the menu. That alone had required most of a day. He'd started with an old Jacques Torres recipe that his mentor had cooked for Julia Child's show as a young man: caramelized bananas in a milk chocolate soup with a baked meringue topping. It was good, reliable, but it was a dessert soup and Klaus wanted something for the first course. He didn't have much luck adapting it, so he finally abandoned the idea and went looking elsewhere for a first-course chocolate solution.

As the White House's head chef, Klaus was insisting on a European menu, which made the various Mexican chocolate *mole* soups unwelcome candidates. After a long afternoon of experimentation, Clive had finally recalled a white chocolate-pomegranate *baba ghanoush* that he hadn't made since school. A little testing, and now with a much more experienced palate, he had created a very pleasing dip by the end of the day. It was Middle European rather than strictly European but, with the substitution of individual miniature French baguettes rather than pita for the base, Chef Klaus had agreed that it was acceptable—high praise for him.

Another day since he'd met Linda had been filled with processing chocolate. The concher had finished a batch of Forastero nibs and had needed a thorough cleaning before he could start on the rare shipment of Criollo that had come in from Venezuela. That country was in such disarray that he rarely got his hands on any and he missed the flexibility that the rich flavor provided.

Then, he'd made a batch of chocolate-dipped lemon-coconut macaroons. The First Family was always partial to their sweets after returning from a trip and he tried to keep them pleasantly surprised.

He wasn't sure quite what had happened to the last day since meeting Linda with Thor. Perhaps daydreaming about the brunette whose dog had led her into his shop for such a brief instant. And the incredible way she had softened as he fed her chocolate. Softened… then hardened faster than an overchilled ganache. Gone so quickly that she almost hadn't been there.

It was ridiculous. He'd met her twice for less than ten minutes each time, but she left a greater impression than a Jacques Torres praline. It seemed that everywhere he looked he saw her, or at least impressions of her.

Even now, as he streamed toward the White House in the company of hundreds of others, he could spot a flounce of brunette hair just her color and in the same carelessly unfettered cut.

He hurried across 14th pushing the limits of the Don't Walk countdown. Normally he was glad to wait and simply enjoy the day, but not today.

The glimmer of shining fifty-percent-cocoa brunette was still moving quickly down the block ahead of him. It moved with a speed and determination that had his pulse and his hopes picking up a beat. It was very hard to run into a dog handler by chance while working in the White House kitchen. Even on the busy streets of a large city it was more likely.

Maybe, just maybe.

He'd long since learned to keep his stride short or he outpaced anyone with him. But to keep up with Linda—if it was her—he opened up his stride. He could cover ground quickly when needed, yet still he only gained on her slowly.

A chance gap down the half block of crowded sidewalk gave him a full view of the woman for just an instant.

It *was* her.

No one else that he'd ever met had that head-down determined walk so completely integrated into their stride. Was he shallow that he also knew her fabulous figure from behind could belong to no one else? Perhaps, but it was true. Three days ago, when she'd disappeared from his chocolate kitchen doorway and he'd hurried out into the hall to see her striding away, she had stamped an indelible impression on his memory. As fine a vision as when she'd been walking toward him. She made him smile, delectable from every angle.

She slowed abruptly, causing a snarl in the normally smooth flow that was commuter foot traffic, causing her to briefly disappear from view. When she reemerged, their separation had halved. Then he missed the crossing at the corner of 15th and the White House Gift Shop and was left at the corner while President Zachary Thomas' face stared at him from a dozen plates in the display window.

As if he needed a reminder that he was focusing on a woman rather than his job.

"Morning, Thor. Hey there, Linda. Long time no see." Malcolm and Jim from the first day's fence line. He came off the corner of Pennsylvania just as she crossed it and left the fence line to come greet her.

Relief washed through her. She was about to open her mouth to explain what was happening when Malcolm veered sharply sideways, almost jerking the leash from Jim's hand.

Jim grunted once in surprise, then his gaze shifted from his dog to Thor and then to her face. No question, just a blink of surprise. Malcolm had found a scent and the handler had understood the cue.

With quick slices of her hand, she indicated the backs of her three "most likelies."

He tried veering Malcom off to the side, but the springer spaniel wasn't having anything to do with it. All the confirmation either of them needed.

Blondes peeled off toward the White House, as did the couple with the coffee cups. One of the other couples stopped to take a picture in front of the statue of Lafayette—the French hero of the American Revolution.

That left one couple and three solos. One of the solos peeled off, the brunette, but neither dog followed.

The other two—Black Wool Coat and Gray Suit—continued as if in flight formation, continuing along Pennsylvania Avenue toward Blair House, where foreign dignitaries were frequently housed. She vaguely remembered yesterday's briefing that the Japanese Defense Minister was already in residence to help prepare the way for the upcoming State Dinner. Or perhaps arriving early to make sure that the Japanese PM could lay claim to the Blair House accommodation so close to the White House rather than being placed in the Hay Adams across Lafayette Square.

Then the two targets veered more deeply into the park.

She glanced at Jim, who offered her a small shrug as if to say, "Your find, your call."

If *only* Thor had alerted to the scent, she might have hesitated. But with both dogs catching it…

That's when she had an idea.

She pulled Thor back, much to the dog's dismay, then slipped the release on his harness. The moment before he took off, she whispered *"Fassen! Ruhig!" Attack! Silent!*

The small dog raced after the target, and in a dozen very small bounds, lunged at the back of Mr. Black Wool Coat. He grabbed a mouthful, then dug in all fours and yanked.

Because Thor hadn't made a sound, the man almost fell over backward in surprise.

His briefcase fell to the ground as he tried to turn and see what was going on.

Japanese. Five-seven. Black hair to just above the ears. Particularly prominent cheekbones. Squinting against the bright sun—now in his face—his left eye closed first. His hands were small and exposed, no gloves despite the cold weather. Perhaps to make sure he held tightly onto the briefcase—even though he hadn't.

Linda jammed Thor's harness into the front of Jim's partially open jacket—didn't he get that it was freezing out?—then trotted up, "Secret Service Police. Are you okay, sir? I've got him," She snatched up Thor before the man could kick him. She let him wrestle with the man's coattails for a moment longer before whispering, "*Gute Hund,*" just loudly enough to get Thor to settle and release. It should look as if she was the good cop, saving a passerby from a stray dog.

Meanwhile, Jim's Malcolm had stepped up to the man's briefcase and promptly sat. *Bad cop.*

Jim moved up to block the man reaching for it.

"I have diplomatic immunity. You can't touch that," Black Wool Coat protested. Gray Suit had continued on his way with hardly a sideways glance.

"May I see your card, sir?" Jim put all of his six-plus feet and workout body to good use, looming over the small Japanese man.

While he was fishing in his pocket, she set Thor down. "Get along, you," she said in English, then followed it softly with "*Such,*" in German. Thor sought. It took him three steps and he sat down in front of the briefcase beside Malcolm. Double confirmation on the explosives.

"Isn't that sweet? They're friends," she did her best to make it a coo, which sounded utterly ridiculous. Probably meant she'd gotten it right.

The Japanese man turned to look at her. Jim took the opportunity to call the bomb squad. As they were on twenty-four-hour alert and were stationed less than six blocks away, they'd be arriving very quickly.

Again the man reached for his briefcase.

Rather than telling Black Wool Coat not to touch the case, Jim called out, "*Pass auf!*" Malcolm twisted to face the man and let out a snarl befitting a much larger dog.

Thor also reacted to the command and added his higher voice to Malcolm's.

She stepped firmly between the man and the dogs.

"We seem to have a problem here, sir. Would you mind explaining it to me?"

Already she could hear the bomb squad's sirens roaring toward them along New York Avenue.

CLIVE WASN'T REALLY PAYING attention to what was going on at the other side of the morning crowd, he was just glad that he was catching up to Linda. He hurried along the path to where she'd stopped close by Andrew Jackson's statue at the center of the park. The massive edifice was topped by a bronze of the two-term President and general of the Battle of New Orleans on horseback.

At his feet, close by the wrought iron fence protecting a circular lawn, Linda and Thor stood close beside another handler-dog team, chatting with a man in a long wool coat who appeared upset.

Thor glanced in Clive's direction.

Half a heartbeat later he was staring at the yellow end of a space age gun that Linda had pointed at his chest from less than ten feet away.

"Uh…"

"Damn it, Clive! Get out of here! It's not safe." She swung the weapon down toward the ground and he recognized it as a taser. He'd seen other Secret Service agents carrying them, but never thought about it much. Now that he'd stared down the barrel of one, then into the wielder's coldest dark eyes he'd ever seen, he'd be thinking about it in his nightmares for a long time to come.

"Why isn't it safe?"

As if in answer, two vehicles jumped the curb and raced across the square in their direction. The black suburban was unmarked, but there was no mistaking the equally black truck close behind it. "FBI Bomb Technicians" was emblazoned down the side in large gold letters and it towed one of those disposal trailers that looked like a six-foot steel sphere.

Capitol Police streamed in close behind them.

Some of the early morning crowd scattered in alarm, others moved forward to gawk.

And they were all focused in their little group's direction.

"Any other questions? Now get out of here." Linda holstered her taser and turned back to the third man.

Clive hadn't noticed him before—an Asian in a long wool coat. His face looked arrogant as he held out some form of ID. Clive had seen enough of them at the White House to recognize a Diplomatic Immunity card.

When the police came up to move Clive back, he went, but he didn't leave. He joined the gawkers at the safety perimeter and didn't care if the policeman rolled his eyes at him before walking away.

Already the bomb techs were pulling on those heavily padded suits they wore making them three times their normal size.

And still Linda stood close by the fallen briefcase that commanded the dogs' attentions. She wore no bulky body armor. She looked so fragile, standing in the center of the danger.

A robot rolled out of the second truck. Bright silver with long arms holding multiple cameras aloft. A yard long and equally high—it drove forward on four rubber tires.

And still no one was moving aside.

Clive wanted to shout a warning but had no idea what it would be.

"Move it, ma'am," one of the bomb techs called out. "And get your dogs clear."

Linda kept watching the Japanese, chronicling additional facial features until she could draw him from memory, even though Jim was holding his ID and calling it in to doublecheck that it was valid.

Goro Yamashita had stopped trying to retrieve his briefcase, but he also wasn't walking away. His hands, except for retrieving his immunity card, had reached into no pockets for a hidden trigger.

There was also something odd about his attitude. Arrogant and self-righteous, yes. But not fanatical in the way she'd come to recognize as "normal" among the true jihadists of Southwest Asia. He didn't strike her as a man who would blow himself up, yet he wasn't walking away to move outside any blast zone either. Linda judged that the hazard was low.

She called Thor to heel beside her and stepped straight into the man's personal space.

Yamashita gave way, backing up. Not even a single glance at the briefcase. It made it unlikely that there was some sort of a proximity detonator on his person that would trigger the explosives if he was too far away.

He dug in his heels at ten meters. "You are not authorized to touch that case."

Jim had him covered with a sidearm that he hadn't reholstered, so she risked a glance. The robot had reached the case and extended a camera eye to inspect it closely.

"I'm sorry, sir," Linda made an effort to recover her good cop role. "But I saw no markings on your briefcase that would indicate it was a diplomatic pouch."

"That's precisely what it is!"

Now she understood some more of the elements of the Secret Service training. As a soldier, she'd have believed him. But now she knew that if it wasn't clearly labeled, it wasn't technically a diplomatic pouch—a single fact of thousands they had spent these last months pounding into her brain. Without a label, once he'd dropped it, it had become a briefcase and nothing more.

But if they opened it and discovered a pouch inside, they'd have to return it unopened no matter what the dogs said about it. They couldn't even X-ray the pouch without breaking the 1961 Vienna Convention on Diplomatic Relations.

Leaving Jim to cover the man, she trotted over to the bomb squad's truck. Two TV vans had pulled up close behind it. At least the no-fly zone over the White House was keeping the news helicopters away. She didn't like staring straight into one of the camera lenses, even if the Capitol Police were keeping them back. She turned her back on it.

Why did they even bother with television anymore anyway? She'd left for war before cell phones became the standard form of news gathering. Now there were fifty or a hundred people recording every single move she made. She could either worry about someone catching something she didn't do perfectly... Or they could all go to hell.

She opted for the second choice and erased them from her mind.

"Who's your commander?"

"Talking to him. What do we know?" He was leaning over the robot operator's shoulder and didn't bother to look up.

"Japanese male. The briefcase triggered both of our dogs."

"Please don't use the word trigger around explosives."

"Got it. Both dogs alerted. He has diplomatic immunity. We're verifying that it's genuine. He has the card."

"Diplomatic...Shit!" He looked up at her.

"He dropped the case and it has no outer markings. If you open the case and there's a diplomatic pouch inside, we're sunk. But if you X-ray it while it's still closed..."

His smile was quick. "Some light in the day. Thanks, sergeant. We're on it."

CLIVE DIDN'T like the way the man's eyes lingered on her as she and Thor trotted over to rejoin their teammates and the man in question. The fact that his own eyes had been lingering earlier was...well...

Okay, maybe he could empathize with the bomb squad officer. In the nation's capital—the city most likely to have women looking their best this side of Paris and Milan—Linda stood out as being impossibly real. Designer clothes traded in for police gear. An attitude that didn't care what others thought of her. And a lethal edge which, of all unlikely things, was attracting him a great deal. Past lovers were casual memories, two ships in the night and all that. Nothing about Linda Hamlin said that was any part of who she was.

What did she see when she looked at the world?

Danger everywhere and everything a threat until proven otherwise?

He tried to see Lafayette Square through her eyes.

The sun was well up now, the sunlight had cleared the buildings to the east enough to light the five statues at the four corners and the center of the square. The grass was green and the concrete walkways were immaculate after being cleaned by the nighttime crew. Some people stood on the park benches to get a view of the excitement over the heads of gawkers who showed no sense of self-preservation.

Of course, neither did he. Except he did. A little. Linda was out there and he couldn't leave until he knew that she'd be okay.

The robot was tipping the case upright and a man in a bomb suit was rolling out a cart. Probably the X-ray machine he'd been able to overhear Linda talking about.

Some people were looking at their watches, cursing, and pushing through the encircling crowd to hurry off to work. His time was more flexible, and even if it wasn't, at the moment he didn't care.

If Linda saw danger everywhere, she must be overwhelmed by the amount of information. How did she filter it down? He scanned the area again. Of the entire crowd, only a few people stood out. Several hecklers were shouting for an arrest. Someone else had a placard on a tall handle, protesting against police brutality. He was waving it about injudiciously enough to have cleared a space around himself of people who didn't want to be brutalized by it.

The perpetrator himself stood with his arms folded over his chest, waiting. He wasn't watching his briefcase or the bomb tech. He wasn't watching the two dogs sitting at alert by their handlers' feet. He also wasn't looking at Linda. Instead he wore a smug half smile and faced the other dog handler.

Clive scanned for anyone else who wasn't behaving as might be expected. There were too many people. Cell phones aloft, hecklers still heckling, police keeping a secure perimeter, and the bomb squad ignoring everyone while they worked through their meticulous procedures.

A third of the way around the circle, an Asian man stood at the front of the crowd. No phone aloft, no emotion on his face. His hands were unnaturally straight at his sides. As if he was standing at attention, but not in any US military form that Clive had seen around the White House.

Clive kept an eye on him as he scanned the rest of the crowd, but he didn't pick out any other anomalies.

Because he'd ended up beside the bomb squad on their initial arrival, moving away from Linda only after the police cordon had been set up, he was inside the bubble—a feeling he recognized from working at the White House.

He took a deep breath, finding a conviction somewhere inside him that was stronger than chocolate. Then he simply strode into the circle as if he belonged. It must have worked because he only saw twenty or so cell phones turning to track him, but no officers shouted at him to stop.

"Hi, Thor," he squatted down to pet the dog now sitting beside Linda. Maybe if he didn't surprise the dog, he wouldn't face the wrong end of a taser again.

Thor popped to his feet and leaned into Clive's knees hard enough that he lost his balance and fell over backward on his butt.

Linda looked down at him in surprise. "What part of get as far away as possible don't you understand?"

Thor decided it was a prime chance to sit on his chest and breathe doggie breath down into his face. He knew that his palate would be ruined for tasting chocolate at least for the morning—everything would taste like panting dog.

"Apparently this part," he looked up at Linda just in time to receive a cold, wet dog nose in one eye. "Yow! Cut that out you," he wrapped his hands around Thor and lifted him aloft so that he could at least sit up.

"What are you doing out here?"

"I saw someone who didn't fit."

"What?" Linda squatted down and took Thor from him, dropping the dog back on all fours on the concrete. Thor instantly bounded up to place his forepaws on Clive's chest. He'd have gone down again if not for Linda's support.

"I was like you."

"I like you, too, but this is a damned weird time to be telling me."

"No, I— Wait! You do?"

Linda huffed out a breath, which at least smelled of cheap coffee and a sugar donut rather than doggie biscuit. It was an improvement over Thor's, but not by much. He was definitely going to have to fix that for her. This was a woman who deserved delicate pastry and good hot cocoa.

"That isn't what I meant. I mean that I was trying to be like you. And I saw a man in the crowd who doesn't fit."

Linda didn't even look around. Instead she closed her eyes for a moment. Then she cursed vilely and looked back at him.

"Gray suit coat? Standing roughly past my right shoulder?"

"That's the one." How did she do things like that?

"Thanks, Clive. I should have seen that. I want you to leave now."

He swallowed hard. Was that all the thanks he was going to get? If he'd seen something important, it should mean more than—

"Go back the way you came. Quietly pick up a uniform cop and get behind Mr. Gray Suit, outside the crowd. I'll give you a ninety-second head start before I flush him."

Clive briefly pictured a flushing toilet and tried to imagine what that had to do with anything. Then he focused on Linda. She might not be a plumber, but she was definitely a hunter—a hunter of men. She was going to flush her quarry, as in make it run.

She rose, grabbing his hand and proving her surprising strength as she tugged him to his feet.

For just an instant they were chest to chest so that he had to look almost straight down to see her.

"And yes, I do like you. Now get out of here," she pushed him away, raising her voice for the last.

Ninety seconds later—as he rushed to be in position with two uniformed officers—Linda and Thor circled along the front of the crowd. His height allowed him to follow the progress by momentary glimpses of her beautiful hair. She was almost upon the man in the gray suit before he noticed. He faded back into the crowd quickly—straight into the officers' arms.

Clive could get to enjoy this.

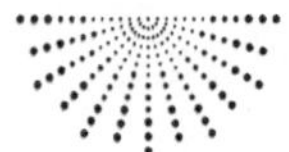

"Good work this morning."

If one more person told her that, Linda was going to... she didn't know what but she was definitely going to do it. If she ever had the energy to get out of this chair again.

She'd made the mistake of dropping into a chair in the Secret Service Ready Room on the West Wing's Ground Floor and now couldn't find the motivation to get back out of it. There were only six agents in the room at the moment, and all of them had said the same thing already, so she was safe for the moment.

She and Thor had spent the entire day, except for a far too short pee break for both her and the dog—in the room at the opposite end of the floor.

The Situation Room—a place she'd never thought she'd ever see, even with her captain's instruction to learn the entire building—had been both more and less than she'd expected. The President's Briefing Room was but one small part of the Situation Room complex. There were secure phone booths just waiting for Clark Kent to turn into Superman, and meeting rooms for smaller groups, right down to two people. The biggest room by far was given over to the operations staff who sat at a two-tiered curved desk—three in front and three behind

—each station with multiple monitors. These six watch officers were the heartbeat of the Situation Room, completely visible but never shown in the movies.

She and Thor had spent the entire day in the Briefing Room, deconstructing every moment of a situation that had lasted less than thirty minutes. The main events had lasted less than ten.

There had been a round robin of individuals. Captain Baxter. Harvey Lieber, freshly returned with the First Family, of course. A tall, slender, and somewhat terrifying woman—the White House Chief of Staff Cornelia Day—had also stepped in several times.

Secretary of State Mallinson had been of frustratingly little help. Every idea by anyone earned a ten-minute lecture on the geopolitical implications of the shifting relations among various international trade organizations.

The second man, Gray Suit, also had a Japanese diplomatic pass, but he appeared to be far less pleased about being apprehended. He was a career diplomat, stationed in DC for nearly two decades.

The bomb squad had learned nothing from the X-ray except for the block of explosive inside the briefcase. Oddly, there was no apparent trigger mechanism. There were some other materials in there—which might have been papers or might have been the outline of a diplomatic pouch.

This had earned them a thirty-minute lesson from Mallinson on the implications of violating the 1961 Vienna Convention as well as a byline history of various known times that a diplomatic pouch had been misused for the smuggling of weapons or hundreds of millions in American currency—the global bribery currency of choice.

Unable to gain sufficient resolution, the bomb squad had the robot deliver it into the bomb containment chamber that the explosives team had brought with them. The weight of the briefcase was only four kilos and the chamber was rated to a ten-kilogram explosion, so they locked it in and drove away out of her life. They'd take it to Quantico and blow it up out on the demolitions range.

A Secret Service tail confirmed that neither of the diplomatically immune terrorists—for so they were—had subsequently met with the

Japanese Prime Minister at Blair House. The minister had, predictably, denied any knowledge of the two men. Nor had they headed up Embassy Row to the Japanese Embassy. Both men had turned instead for Dulles airport where they boarded a flight...to Beijing.

That had really sent Secretary of State Mallinson off the deep end.

Were they working for China? Attempting to disrupt the upcoming meeting about China's incursions into the South China Sea?

Was it merely misdirection and the two agents would board a connecting flight to Japan? Or some other country?

While Mallinson railed, the CIA Director had contacted his Chinese counterpart. China had agreed to watch them closely to see what they did, but it was outside of US jurisdiction and no longer her problem.

Linda's best guess was that, whoever the two men worked for, their next action wouldn't vary. They would step off the plane in Beijing with different identities than they had boarded and would blend into the disembarking crowd. The US had been unable to get an agent on the plane as the flight was full.

That had brought up another puzzle. To board a full flight, they already had to have tickets. So their mission had only been delivery of the explosives. If it had been more, they would have missed their flight. It had all been pre-calculated with an impressive nicety of timing.

Linda rubbed her eyes. The only light of the entire day had been when Clive had been brought in to discuss his part of the action.

Mallinson had been called away to obstruct someone else's effort at having a coherent thought, so at least he was spared that.

Clive had been practically shaking with nerves as he'd looked about the Situation Room wide-eyed. Rather than going with the impulse to hold his hand to comfort him—especially because she had no idea where *that* came from, completely aside from it being wholly inappropriate—she'd scooped up Thor and dropped the dog in his lap.

For a moment she'd been afraid Clive would hurt Thor with how hard he hugged the dog to his broad chest, but Thor merely snuggled in and then settled on his lap while Clive was interviewed. She wasn't sure how she felt about the attachment between him and her dog. No, she wasn't in the least bit sure about that.

Thankfully, he'd left out any comments about his saying he liked Linda, changing the reason that he'd initially gone to her. "I was just being nice, wanting to check in that she was liking her new job. I hadn't seen her in three days."

Had it really been that long? She felt oddly guilty about that.

She did her best to suppress her envy that he'd been freed after only an hour. She'd spent eleven hours being grilled—or lectured.

"You look done in," a deep male voice addressed her.

"A military mission debrief is ten times easier. And thanks. Exactly what a woman always wants to hear." She rubbed her eyes one last time before forcing them open.

Clive.

"Decided to brave the West Wing a second time?" She asked him.

He shrugged. "Might not have if I knew I needed an agent escort just to see you here."

"I've got him, thanks," she waved off the agent who had accompanied him into the part of the building that his pass wouldn't admit him. A funny contrast. As a senior chef, he had one of the highest clearances available—Presidential Proximity without an agent escort. However, as a chef, he had no clearance to the political areas of the White House's operations.

"What are you doing here, Clive?"

"Checking up on you."

"I'm fine." Nothing a dozen hours of sleep wouldn't fix. Except for having the lesson driven home that terrorists weren't only on foreign soil. Nothing was going to fix that.

"You are fine," his smile said that he was talking about more than her general well-being. "But you don't look it."

"Again with the sweet talk."

"Should I whisper in your ear about chocolate ganache or hot cocoa?"

She gave a dutiful chuckle. "Might work on me at this point, who knows."

Ignoring the fact that they weren't alone, he leaned toward her until she half thought he was going to kiss her. Another image she didn't seem to mind. Instead, he placed his mouth close beside her ear and whispered with that luscious voice of his, "Shining chocolate ganache. Steaming hot cocoa. Dark cherry truffle. Butterscotch praline."

LINDA'S LAUGH WAS BRIGHT—DOUBLY so because it was so unexpected. Clive hadn't even been sure she could laugh. It filled the room and drew the attention of the other agents.

That was the moment that Clive realized what he had just done, flirted with a Secret Service agent while she was surrounded by other Secret Service agents. The heat rushed to his face, but he couldn't do anything about it. His cheeks seemed to burn.

"I—" There was no excuse for embarrassing her in her new workplace. "I'll just go now." He resisted the urge to sprint from the room but did make a point of using his long legs to advantage. Except he had no idea where he was in the rabbit warren that was the West Wing Ground Floor.

People were streaming up and down the corridors. Some pulling on coats in the hopes of escaping at the end of the day before some new crisis trapped them. Others hurried by—clearly still caught up in the frenetic business of the government. No matter what he did, he felt he was getting in deeper rather than finding his way out. His quiet, safe chocolate shop seemed to get farther away with each step.

He turned a corner and recognized the Navy Mess as much by scent as anything else. In another direction he spotted the two Marines guarding the Situation Room. He'd almost fainted in there today, would have if not for Linda's kindness. Not a chance he was going anywhere near that.

He swung the other way and plowed squarely in Linda, bowling her over. Thor stood directly behind her, taking her out at the knees, and she tumbled backward through a door and then was gone as it swung closed.

Thor looked up at him in surprise at being suddenly separated from his mistress.

Clive looked at the sign on the door and knew that his day had, impossibly, taken a turn for the worse. It read: Men's Lavatory.

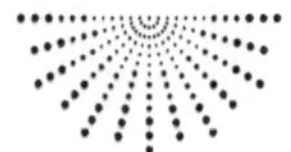

CHAPTER SIX

*L*inda wasn't quite sure how it had happened.

Clive had refused to stop apologizing until she'd agreed that he could take her out to dinner. It was one of the trigger phrases she'd learned long ago. In a guy's mind, "dinner out" meant "hopefully with meaningless sex for dessert." Her standard answer of "thanks but no way in hell" didn't appear with Clive.

Instead, she'd happily followed him to the kitchen beneath the Residence, which was apparently his idea of a dinner out.

It was late enough that the kitchen itself was quiet. A sour-faced man, introduced to her as Chef Klaus, offered her a scowl and Thor another before returning to his tiny office. An on-call chef puttered away in the pastry kitchen. The massive White House kitchen was theirs alone.

A stove with a dozen gas burners, two big grills, mixers almost as tall as she was with bowls that Thor could have slept inside. Multiple ovens with more controls than she'd ever seen before, an espresso machine that would be the envy of even a Starbucks barista, dozens of pots and pans hanging from overhead hooks, a meat slicer, knife racks... It never seemed to end—everywhere she looked there was more kitchen equipment.

But there were none of the homey touches of Clive's chocolate shop. No pictures on the walls, no sketches taped onto refrigerator doors. It felt cold despite the warmth of the room. Without thinking about it much, she'd scooted her stool closer to where Clive was cooking.

Partly to watch him. His big fingers were surprisingly nimble as he selected, sliced, and seasoned. His hands looked as if they belonged to a stone mason or a US Ranger. But after years of hard use in the field, a Ranger's hands would be hard-pressed to do any fine work—except strip and clean a weapon, of course. Clive's massive hands appeared to fly as he sprinkled a pinch of salt into a heating pot of pasta water and then began building a sauce.

She also scooted closer because it felt warmer near him. Not just the burners roaring with bright blue flames. There was something about Clive that drew her in. His willingness to walk into an explosives danger zone to warn her of something he'd seen that she should have. What man did that? Clive Andrews. And what had he said when he arrived? That he was trying to be like her...intentionally! Why anyone would do that was beyond her, but Clive had. As to his saying that he liked her—in the middle of her first-ever diplomatic crisis—well, it was beyond strange.

While the fettuccini boiled, Clive thin-sliced and sautéed chicken. At the last moment he tossed in lemon juice, shallots, and slivers of lemon complete with the peel. Thor was just going to have to wait for dinner until they got home, but it was hard to care because it smelled so heavenly.

Then Clive pulled out some hamburger. "I'm not sure what to put in this, I'm not used to cooking for a dog."

"A lump of that, raw. That's grounds to win love forever. Uh, his love." If Clive noticed her stumble, he didn't comment on it.

Instead he laughed aloud.

"Ground beef as grounds for love. Good one."

Which she hadn't actually thought of as a pun.

"That is precisely what every man needs, the love of a good dog. Doesn't he?" Clive asked Thor as he set to work. He placed a fist-sized ball of burger in a small bowl—thankfully her fist and not his, which would be nearly the size of Thor's head—and quickly beat in an egg. Then he set it upon a white plate. Somehow, with those big hands of his, he quickly shaped it into an elegant form as if it was a tiny meat Bundt cake complete with spiral flutes up the sides and a hole in the middle.

Why was she feeling a fit of pique that he was doting on her dog and not on… She needed her head fixed.

"Does he like greens?"

"I…don't know. Most dogs do." She'd given him kibble and canned dog food so far. She'd only had him five days, nowhere near enough time to learn his preferences. Not even enough time to learn her own. The scramble of these last days had relegated her meals to pizza by the slice from the corner shop near her apartment. She'd often buy an extra couple slices to have cold leftovers for breakfast.

Clive held out a small piece of spinach. Thor roused himself enough in her lap to happily chomp it down. Clive diced up enough to fill the hole he'd shaped inside the raw hamburger patty. He crumbled bacon over the top, throwing more into the sauce for their own dinner.

"That looks good enough for me to eat, forget about the dog."

"For a good tartare, I would fresh chop a much finer grade of meat and add some more spice. I make a good one, I'll do that some other time." Clive just smiled as he scooped out the finished fettuccini, let it drain for a moment, then dumped it into the sauce pan.

As if he hadn't ever so casually dropped his plans that this wouldn't be a one-time event. His confidence was amazing, which she liked, but with none of the arrogance that typically went with it.

He stirred it a few times. Then, in quick, neat motions, he mounded the fettuccini in elegant twists on a pair of white plates. Finally he grated Parmesan cheese on the top.

"I thought you were a chocolatier."

"I am."

"But you can cook as well."

"Of course."

"There's no 'of course' about it."

"Why? What's the last meal you cooked?"

Linda puzzled at that. The last time she'd cooked, something fancier than frozen pizza or a can of soup…

Clive stopped halfway through mincing some parsley. "You do cook, don't you?"

"Well, the Army sort of took care of that for the last decade. Or Mom's maid the few times I was dumb enough to go home on leave."

"Please tell me that you are joking," Clive sounded deeply offended.

"I *can* cook…" Linda gave up. "Though, honestly, nothing fancier than scrambled eggs and burnt toast."

He squinted closely at her.

"What?"

"I've spent the last five days fantasizing about a woman who can't cook? That can't be right."

"It's true. You—" His words caught up with her. "You *what?*" Her shout was loud enough for Chef Klaus to stick his head out of his office, leaning out far enough to look around the big stand mixer between them and deliver a hard stare before turning back to whatever he'd been working on.

Clive didn't appear in the least abashed. "We're in the house that George Washington built. Even if he didn't live long enough to ever take up occupancy here, it's still his house, therefore I cannot tell a lie." He dressed the plates with little spears of asparagus that she hadn't even seen him preparing, and a thick slice of crusty bread.

"But—"

"Shall we take our plates somewhere more private?" Ignoring her feeble protests, he did one of those waiter things with a plate in either hand and Thor's plate resting on his forearm. Then he led the way out the back of the kitchen and along the Basement Hall toward his chocolate shop.

Out of options, she set Thor on his own feet and followed after him.

CLIVE DIDN'T KNOW how to slow down around Linda, but it seemed to be working, so maybe he shouldn't.

He'd gotten her out of the West Wing without getting down on his knees and begging, though he'd come close while fishing her out of the men's lavatory where her boss Captain Baxter had been washing his hands. The captain had merely raised his eyebrows as he looked down at his newest officer lying prone on the tile floor.

Clive really wanted to get her back into the Chocolate Shop, where he'd made a couple of special treats for her. He'd almost screwed that up with suggesting that they go out to dinner, because that's what a man did with an attractive woman in DC, right? Dinner, drinks, a goodnight kiss that might lead somewhere or might not. He knew from past experience that leading somewhere tended to happen with him.

He'd never really given it much thought. He liked women and women liked him. Easy-peasy. It never lasted…

He glanced over at Linda as she squatted to give Thor his plate of K-9 tartare. It was easy to imagine watching her doing that, feeding her dog, day after day. He'd never really thought about having the same woman around for the long term. He knew it was in his future somewhere, but the insane hours of being a world-class chocolatier were no less hectic than being a world-class chef. He'd never found a woman willing to put up with that for long, which was fine—he was always up-front about it so it was never a big issue. But with Linda in his kitchen, the future shifted somewhere much closer.

Maybe that was why he couldn't slow down around her. All of his smooth skills around women had turned into curdles and the clumsy bloom of over-refrigerated chocolate.

And now that he had her here, in his chocolate shop, his mouth had gone dry with a sudden lack of words.

"I think he likes it," Linda patted Thor as he started eating.

"What's not to like?" He watched her and couldn't think of a thing.

He was being ridiculous, he knew, but his attraction to her pulled at him like a new confection recipe.

Then, rather than taking her seat, she stood and stared at him. "What's that look?"

"What look?" He rubbed his hand over his face and did his best to erase it.

"*That* look."

"So much for wiping it off my face. Eat," he pulled out a pair of stools from under the counter. After a moment's debate, he set them kitty-corner at his central steel worktable—placing them close but still facing each other.

"Evasion, Chef Andrews."

"Absolutely, Sergeant Hamlin."

"And you want me to let you off the hook?"

"Consider it payback for identifying that bad man for you."

She harrumphed but took her stool. "Okay, just this once." But her look said not a chance was this over. "You still owe me for dumping me into the men's room—not that I'm keeping score."

"Did you ever figure out what they were doing, or is that now some state secret you can't tell me about?" Clive went for the subject change.

"I wish it was. We don't know. And we're getting mixed signals on who they were working for. The Japanese have now disavowed both of their diplomatic passports based on today's actions."

"A little late for that, isn't it?"

"It is. Both men were gone long before it happened. Whether that is per a plan by the Japanese or an honest reaction to a betrayal is unclear. Mr. Black Wool Coat was new to the mission, but Mr. Gray Suit was a senior official who abandoned a long career the moment he stepped on that plane."

"Which explains why he was so angry when we caught him," Clive could still remember the moment. It was the only time he'd been involved in anything like that. He'd have been a basket case of nerves if it hadn't happened so fast—Linda spooking him, Mr. Gray Suit breaking through the crowd, the officers grabbing the man as Clive pointed him out, and finally his look of fury at being caught.

"Fury or dismay? It became the latter fast enough. We've seized his US assets, but those are unusually small for someone who has served in Washington for two decades, as if he knew he was at risk and had cleared out most of his holdings just in case."

"So, basically, no one is happy." Except him. The adventure had given him the narrowest sliver of insight into the richness of mysteries in Linda's world. Crisis, adrenaline, action, yet she'd remained perfectly calm and in control throughout. And having her in his shop was enough to make him happy for a long time.

"Well, Thor looks pretty happy," Linda pointed out. The dog lay on the floor licking his chops with a polished clean plate in front of him. "And me. This is fantastic."

He'd been wondering if she was eating it without even tasting. It wasn't anything much, but it had come together nicely from various kitchen leftovers. Klaus always kept a shelf of items that any chef working late could take advantage of for a quick meal. He was stretching it a little for an agent and her dog but, other than one of his patented scowls, Klaus had appeared fine with it.

"Clive?"

"Mm-hmm?" He had a mouthful of pasta at the moment.

"What you said earlier?"

"Mm-hmm?" *Uh-oh!*

"Why?"

He chewed and swallowed. No real question what she was asking, so he'd go for his honesty policy. "You're asking why I like you. Have you met many DC women?"

Her shrugs were expressive. This one reminded him that though she'd been out in Maryland for three months, her experience with DC was minimal.

"There's a sameness to them. The way I have always figured it, DC attracts two major types of women. Ambitious women deeply concerned with politics for one. The others are looking for a job that they could find anywhere else more easily but wouldn't have the prestige of being involved in the government—or the chance at a future president for a husband, because of course they can make the right man into that. Guess which type I normally meet?"

"The tall blondes."

"Well sure," he wasn't going to fall for that trap. "Who wouldn't? But I'm finding that now I've met a third type."

Linda did that narrow-eyed inspection thing of hers.

"Short brunettes who take obnoxious K-9 instructors and international terrorists all in the stride of a day's work without letting it flap them in the slightest."

"You like me because I don't fly off the handle around a man who is being an asshole?"

"It's a good hedge against the future on my part, don't you think?"

LINDA COULD ONLY BLINK. Every time she tried to corner Clive, to pigeonhole him somewhere in her mind, he didn't fit. He also didn't mind each time she caught him.

Tall blondes. It was easy to picture a tall blonde beside him. He was a tall, handsome man and would look exceptional with a beautiful woman on his arm. So why was he talking to her?

I like you.

What's not to like? he had asked of Thor's dinner—which had been sweet and thoughtful of him to make.

She turned the question around: what was there about Clive Andrews not to like?

The normal laundry list that washed men out of her life before they even got into it wasn't applying.

They weren't in the same unit.

Not even in the same branch of the service.

Her first two big issues no longer applied because she was a civilian now. They allowed fraternization within the Secret Service, provided it wasn't within a linear chain of command. But even that didn't apply to Clive.

There was a freedom to the thought that she hadn't experienced in over a decade. Every relationship in the military had a dozen ramifications: rank, reassignment, and the imminent threat of death that was definitely a factor to consider in Special Operations Forces. Yet, for the foreseeable future, she and Clive would both be stationed in DC. If things didn't work out, all she had to do was not come by his chocolate shop. The entire danger-scenario, risk-assessment part of her thoughts had been rendered meaningless by the simple act of leaving the military.

And without all of those obstacles in the way, she realized that she *did* like Clive as well. And she remembered a feeling, the memory of a smile that had continued to tickle her palm for the last few days.

"Clive?" This was a very low-risk environment. It was a freaking chocolate shop.

"Mm-hmm?" Now he was just messing with her, both of their plates were clear.

If she was going to do something, she should just do it.

She leaned forward and brushed her lips over his. He tasted of lemon and shallot. And his return kiss was warm and thoughtful, taking his time about it. He laid one of those big warm hands over hers where it rested on the cool steel table.

Clive was clearly a man who knew how to kiss a woman. She hoped that she returned even a little of the same as her bones slowly melted. With only the slightest tug on her hand, not even enough to shift it, he somehow had her body moving toward his.

The heat warmed her from the inside out and she shifted, being careful not to break the kiss. She wanted…

She *wanted.*

That alone was a miracle. A part of her she was sure was dead…*wanted!* She—who had never needed anything other than her dog and a mission—wasn't some kind of emotional zombie as she always thought. She actually groaned as Clive slid one of those wonderful hands onto her waist. If he tried to take her here and now, she wasn't going to stop him.

There was a sharp growl that she didn't think came from Clive.

Then a high "Eeep!" that she was fairly sure didn't come from her.

A growl from a dog.

Too high for Thor.

An eeep from—

She broke the taste of heaven and turned to see a young girl standing in the Chocolate Shop's doorway with her hand clamped over her mouth. At her feet, a Sheltie growled at Thor, who'd risen to his feet in surprise.

Linda snapped her fingers and signaled for Thor to sit and stay. He sat down, but strained forward to sniff at the new arrivals.

"Dilya," Clive sighed. His sigh seemed to include an entire conversation, but Linda had no way to interpret it. Her head was still trying to process the flash of heat awoken by Clive's kiss, and her higher-functioning, multitasking capabilities were not reporting for duty.

The girl wasn't as young as she first appeared—mid-teens perhaps. Very pretty. Dark skin and even darker hair that cascaded in long ruffles down to her elbows.

"Wow. He's well trained," she squatted down to Thor's level. "Okay to pet him?"

"Sure," Linda was surprised the girl thought to ask. Most didn't. "Thor, *Freund.*"

"Hi, Thor," the girl didn't even hesitate at the name, winning her several points. "Yes, I'm friendly. This is Zackie," she tugged on the Sheltie's leash, but Zackie was busy getting pets from Clive— apparently he wasn't lavishing attention on Thor just for her sake, but genuinely liked dogs. She'd been wondering.

"Zackie?" Linda asked.

"Sure. Named for the President by the First Lady back when they were still Vice President and girlfriend."

"President Zachary Thomas' dog was named Zackie by his girlfriend?"

The girl's amused giggle was answer enough. "Actually, Zackie is her dog. She only lets the President play with Zackie if he's been nice to her."

"And what does she call the President?"

"Why, Mr. President, of course." But Linda didn't quite trust the girl's blithe answer. She looked fifteen at most, yet the nuanced way she said it seemed unlikely for a girl of that age. She herself certainly hadn't understood the subtleties of grown-up relationships at that age —except that she wanted no part of anything like her parents'.

Then the girl looked up at her. She wore a hot pink sweater, black leggings, oversized boots, and a scarf knit in tiny rows of colorful splotches to match Clive's—a noisy combination that screamed youth. But her green eyes, caught by the kitchen lights, belonged to no young girl that Linda could imagine. She'd only seen such old eyes in... Syrian refugee camps. On kids who had seen things not even an adult should have to witness.

"I'm Linda," she held out a hand.

"Dilya," the girl offered in return, though it was clear she already knew Linda's name.

"You're the President's dog handler?"

"When they're traveling somewhere Zackie can't go. Or have too many meetings or stuff like that. They just got home from Tennessee, so I took her out to burn off some of her energy. She's fine on Air Force One, but riding in Marine One, even just the short hop from Andrews, always winds her up. Yes, I know," she turned to the dog and unabashedly used the high squeaky dog voice, "you just can't help yourself, can you?"

The little dog yipped happily and wiggled with delight at the attention. Under all that fur she was probably about the same size as Thor, but she seemed as young as her caretaker didn't.

"How did you get Thor to stay like that? He still hasn't moved. Can you teach me?"

"Um, sure. But Thor has had years of training."

"I've worked on Zackie ever since President and Genny Matthews left the White House and decided they no longer needed a nanny. I still get to babysit Adele whenever they're in town, once or twice a month. The First Lady and the former First Lady both work for the UNESCO World Heritage Centre, you know. So they always have all of these meetings. And President Matthews goes over to the West Wing and hangs out with the President or Vice President whenever his wife is busy. Which means I end up babysitting Zackie and a two-year-old. Terrible twos, they're really something, aren't they?"

"I wouldn't know," Linda was still puzzling at Dilya. It sounded as if she knew everything.

Clive had returned to his seat from playing with the dog.

"You've never played with babies?" Dilya looked at her in surprise. "Oh, right, you just got out of the Army. Who were you with?"

"A group called the 75th Rangers."

"Which battalion?"

"Third," Linda wondered again just who this teen was.

"Oh, I don't know any of those guys. I used to hang out with the 2nd Battalion Charlie Company when my mom was... Whoops! Sorry. We were never there. Never mind."

Linda looked over at Clive, who had the temerity to just smile at her.

"Her mom is Sergeant Kee Stevenson, formerly with the 160th Night Stalkers, now part of the FBI's Hostage Rescue Team." Then he glanced at Dilya, who was still playing with the dogs, and silently mouthed, "War orphan." Which explained a lot.

"Kee..." Linda's voice trailed off. Everyone in Special Operations knew that name—she was one of the top snipers anywhere. Which meant that her father, another former Night Stalker, was the Secretary of Defense. Okay. Dilya's knowledge and personality were making more sense in some ways, even if she was making less in others.

"You're the one who found the explosives this morning?" Dilya asked the dog.

"He was," Linda answered for him.

"Good doggie!" Dilya pet him some more.

Zackie had also apparently come to terms with the presence of another dog and closed the rest of the distance between them.

"*Spiel,*" Linda gave Thor permission to get up and play. With a single bound, the two dogs plowed Dilya over onto her back and proceeded to race loops around the small kitchen.

"Told you that Marine One wound her up," Dilya clambered to her feet and smoothed her scarf.

"That's just like Clive's," Linda couldn't help but admire it.

"She liked the one Mom made so much," Clive reached out and thoughtlessly flipped Dilya's hair into place, "that I knit one for her."

"You really can knit?"

"I CANNOT TELL A LIE," he raised a Boy Scout salute. At least not as long as she didn't ask him what he'd been thinking when he kissed her. During that he was thinking utterly ridiculous thoughts about a woman he barely knew. Things like there never being another woman for him. "Keep being nice to me, and I'll knit you a sweater someday."

"At this point I'd take a decent pair of gloves," she wiggled her fingers at him.

That would be safer. Knitting a sweater actually had a lot of potential baggage with it. He'd heard from a ton of knitters that when the knitter made a sweater for their boyfriend, the relationship had always seemed to end at the same time the massive effort of making a sweater did. Yes, mittens would be safer. He'd have to figure out Linda's hand size, maybe from the outline he could still feel from when she'd covered his mouth.

Linda Hamlin overwhelmed him in every possible way. Forthright in a city where everything was nuance and innuendo. Her emotions so clear that there was no questioning them. Okay, she couldn't cook, but the way she looked while eating his food was enough to motivate him to cook forever. And he hadn't forgotten how she looked while tasting his chocolate. And the taste of *her*... He was ruined for anyone else. It didn't matter that he barely knew her because he already knew so much about her.

"It's beautiful work," Linda was fingering Dilya's scarf once the dogs had settled down to clean themselves after the excitement—

Clive couldn't agree more. Whatever creator had carved Linda out of DNA and the ether of the unknown had forged a stunning masterpiece.

Dilya was watching him strangely.

"You came for chocolate, didn't you, you scamp?"

"Caught," Dilya admitted freely. But her look said a great deal more that he couldn't interpret. He pulled a few pieces out of the small cabinet and set them on a plate on the marble counter. The chocolate bars had indeed gone away far more quickly now that he'd made them smaller, but Dilya had never shown much interest in them.

He was about to reach for a small to-go box, but Dilya sat down on a stool beside Linda. He wanted her to himself. He wanted to kiss her again and find out if the impossible was actually real. Clive was a worldly man who definitely knew better than to be swept off his feet. But "Linda with Thor" had done just that. In a few short days, his world had completely shifted.

Shifted?

It was like the first time he had tasted couverture chocolate. His world had suddenly made sense in an instant. Years of thinking that the world was comprised of just baking chocolate and eating chocolate. On his own, he'd improved until he could create flavors and textures that won amateur awards.

Then he'd tasted couverture. The exceptional quality and increased cocoa butter content provided astonishing results in sheen, snap, mellow flavor, and a creamy mouth feel. In that instant, recipes and techniques had reconfigured in his mind until he understood just what *was* possible. Chocolate had shifted from a world he understood to one that he couldn't wait to spend the rest of his life exploring.

Linda Hamlin was exactly like that. Until now he knew women and how to please them. They were fun, like an infinite variety of chocolate chip cookies. But he now understood just how much a woman could be—the perfect, ever-unfolding truffle.

He looked at her to see how she'd been transformed by his realization—but she hadn't.

Sergeant Linda Hamlin sat beside Dilya over peppermint truffles, talking about dog training techniques. They left the candies half finished when they clambered to their feet and stood side by side in front of their dogs. That certainly put him in his place.

"The finger snap does two things," Linda was explaining. "One, it lets the dog know that whatever you do or say next is for them."

"Same as calling their name first. Simple word association for dogs," Dilya nodded hard enough to make her hair swirl about her head.

"Right. The second thing it does is actually far more important—it gets them looking at you so that they can see the next command."

"Like in a Delta Force operation, when they wave a hand at the edge of someone's vision prior to giving a silent hand signal. Got it!"

And Clive knew that meant that she did have it. He'd been on the receiving end of her brilliance enough times to know that the teen missed nothing. Though how she'd ever been witness to a Delta Force team doing anything…

Linda took it right in stride. "Exactly. The next trick is that nothing can be ambiguous. You come up with a standardized set of commands and always use precisely those words: come, come here, come along you—they're always alerting on the word *come* so don't use any other."

"Or not. Zackie isn't so hot on come. Or stay. Or…" Dilya groaned at the dog's failures.

"Or not," Linda agreed. "And why don't they come when called, especially when you *know* that they know better? Because when we shift tone, they may think that it's a different word. And each time you use it differently, it dilutes the primary. A single, consistent *come* will outperform all of the others combined. When you do use tone, keep that same balance to the word and simply increase the emotional trigger of intensity for emphasis."

"Do I have to use German? I don't think the President speaks it. Though that could be fun, actually."

"Easy, girl," Clive warned. "He is the President and it is his wife's dog."

Dilya smiled in that way that he could never interpret. He knew that most women had a smile like that—one that men were welcome to think was agreement, no matter what they were actually thinking. That's when he remembered that the First Lady *did* speak German and might enjoy teasing her husband about his inability to command her dog. As usual, Dilya was three steps ahead of everyone around her. Except maybe Linda.

Clive sat on one of their abandoned stools and tasted one of the peppermint truffles. A good balance of sweet and bright mint. The mix of textures was good, the smooth crispness of the outer chocolate and the coarser but softer mint fudge center.

The contrast.

That's what was so stunning about Linda, that contrast between who she presented to most of the world and the brief glimpses she let him see.

He fished out his notepad as they worked with the dogs.

Zackie was having trouble focusing, but Thor's steadying influence and well-honed actions were already helping.

Contrast. Contrast and... What was it he'd thought of earlier? Interconnections.

Japan, Vietnam, and the Philippines on one side. China on the other. Tension, threatening to pull everything apart. Connection, pulling it back together. More than connection—interconnection. Where their differences made a new whole.

Linda and Thor—human and dog making an exceptional explosives detection team.

The West Pacific Rim nations unifying in some fashion that was new and different.

The Vietnamese Marou and Philippine Malagos chocolates together. Not blended. No. Use the white Marou and the seventy-two percent dark Malagos. Twist them around a Japanese Pocky-style biscuit to create a chocolate candy cane look, along with a unification of the three working together in a different way. Now that was getting interesting. He had no idea how to actually do it, but that was part of the fun.

He pulled out a larger pad from under the counter and began

sketching out the likely techniques. He couldn't simply scale up the Pocky stick—the texture would be wrong. The delicacy of the biscuit was part of the Japanese finesse. And how to twist the two chocolates together without *melting* them together?

Clive was several pages in when he noticed the quiet.

The Chocolate Shop was dead silent. No, not quite, Thor's soft doggie snore sounded in the background.

Linda sat once more on her stool, her chin resting on her palm as she watched him. Dilya was nowhere to be seen.

"You're an interesting man, Clive Andrews."

"I'm hoping I'm more than that," he looked at a clock to see how much time had passed, but since he didn't know when they'd eaten or when he'd started drawing, there was no way to track how much time he'd lost. Chocolate did that to him.

"Come on," she said to him as she stood up. Nudging Thor awake so that she could retrieve her jacket that he'd been using as a doggie bed, Linda shrugged it on.

"Where are we going?"

"You're taking me home."

Clive could only nod.

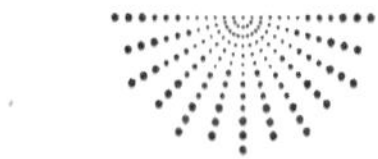

*L*inda never made decisions like this, but as Clive unlocked his front door, she swore that she wasn't going to second-guess herself. Which, of course, meant that she couldn't stop doing it.

"Would it be inappropriate for me to ask why we're here?" Clive was standing in the center of his apartment's living room.

Thor began sniffing his way around the apartment as she also checked it out.

It was a very guy space. A leather lounger, built on the same scale as Clive—big—faced a large television. Football or cooking shows? She'd bet on the latter.

Beside his chair was a large collection of books in untidy stacks. She looked closer: dessert cookbooks. The walls were mostly decorated with—she moved closer—pictures of chefs shaking hands with Clive and of knit goods. A quick scan around and she spotted a tall, glass-fronted mahogany cabinet so full of yarn that it looked like a rainbow gone mad. A massive sweater of gray wool, covered in intricately overlapping cables, had been tossed on a couch.

"You really do knit."

"You're avoiding the question."

She turned for the kitchen. Inspecting that, even if she wouldn't be able to judge most of what would be in there, would be far more comfortable than answering why she was here. There was a splendid, lived-in quality to the apartment. Her own small studio could still pass military inspection.

"Linda," he snagged her elbow as she tried to pass by.

His simplest touch brought her to a halt. It was just them now. No chef peered at them from behind a mixer. No teen was likely to drop in, seeking chocolate and dog training tips. It was just them and she didn't know what to do about it. Her plans for some sex with an interesting man whom she liked felt foolish now that she was here.

It *had* been a while. Secret Service training had kept her hopping enough that she could brush off the various passes made by the other trainees. Those had also faded away as she'd worked through the course in half the normal time—many of them hadn't liked that. And before that in the 75th Rangers she'd...

Clive kissed her.

Her whirling thoughts slammed into focus. Clive. She'd been working with Dilya and giving her the basics techniques for training Zackie when Dilya had done a teen thing that Linda remembered all too well from her own past. The girl had suddenly realized that she was learning something from an adult and that didn't fit with a teen's independent self-image. Between one eyeblink and the next, Linda had been alone with Clive, who was so immersed in his drawings and notes that someone could have indeed bombed the White House and he probably wouldn't have noticed.

Clive. His kiss deepened and she let her body mold against his as he wrapped his arms about her. Exactly as she'd guessed, it felt like being hugged by a big, warm, kindly bear. His powerful hands were gentle as they held her close.

She'd become enthralled with watching him work in his kitchen— his chocolate shop—even if it was just designing. The focus, the obvious joy he took in the process. His quick smile and bright eyes had gone quiet as he worked and she could see the man revealed. He gave a first (and second and third) impression of being light-hearted and quick-thinking, living for the banter of the moment.

But not when he was working on a chocolate recipe. To that he brought a focus she easily recognized: it was the difference of a grunt in for a tour or two and the long-term professional soldier.

And at the moment, he was bringing that same incredible intensity of concentration to melting her bones as if they were actually made of chocolate.

It was working.

Not only was he reshaping her body to his, but if he were suddenly to let go, her liquid knees would be sure to melt out from under her.

He didn't let her go, but he did ease back and break their kiss by the simple expedient of standing up straight. He had at least eight inches on her height…she'd never kissed such a tall man. Rather than uncomfortably submissive, she felt as if she was being cared for. The former she'd have to think about but the latter she had no experience with and it was confusing as hell.

"Now," he whispered as he looked down at her with those deep, warm eyes of his. "Why are you here?"

"This," she managed on an uneasy breath that didn't sound anything like her.

"Not good enough, Linda."

Not good enough? If his kiss and embrace had felt any better she'd—

Again Clive left her with no good words.

"What are you really asking, Clive?"

"We're not going to simply tumble into bed and screw each other's brains out."

"We're not?" That sounded very good at the moment.

"Linda," he practically groaned in agony.

Unable to think while looking at his eyes, she tipped her head down and placed her nose and forehead against his chest.

With his strong hands he dug into her back muscles and continued the job of melting her against him.

If they weren't here to screw… But they were. She knew enough about reading men to know that's exactly why they were here. It was why she'd said he should take her home and he hadn't argued. At least not until now when the bedroom door stood less than ten feet away. Hell of a time to stop a seduction.

Unless that's what this was. Was it?

Instead of a hot, sweaty release, what if… What if… What if she actually *wanted* to be here? To be here with Clive rather than just some guy most likely to sate her body for a night?

And it was true.

Dilya had whispered something offhand before she left the Chocolate Shop. They'd been looking down at the two dogs, and Zackie was actually sitting at alert and waiting quietly for the next command. "Such a good doggie. We can see so much more of who you are when you're being quiet, can't we?" The dog had wagged her tail in happy response, revealing that she really was a sweetheart and not just a hyperactive ball of beautiful fur.

Then Dilya had been gone, leaving Linda to watch the quietly working Clive.

And she'd seen so much more of who he was. He was a man alive with ideas. His chocolate shop had photos of them taped to every surface: a mottled orange-and-red sky, a breaking ocean wave, a red-winged blackbird's wing. He didn't merely make chocolates. Clive sought inspiration in nature. He might look like the guy most likely to play the front four on a football team, but instead she could only marvel at the delicate confections he'd created and the way he drew. Beneath that ever-so-distracting exterior, there was an intelligent, thoughtful, and skilled man.

At that moment, his probing fingers found a locked-up muscle beneath her right shoulder blade. He massaged it until it released with a suddenness that took her breath away. And when she breathed back in, with her face still planted against his chest, he filled her senses just as surely as he'd filled her thoughts.

She now knew why she was here.

"Take me to bed, Clive." She'd thought it would be the action that mattered. But it wasn't. It was the man.

It was enough.

It was too much.

Clive ached for Linda like he'd ached for no woman before.

He'd wanted her clear words that she really did want to be here. That she did want to give her body to him.

And she certainly didn't need to tell him twice.

He scooped her up in his arms, and she simply buried her face against his neck. Turning sideways, he barely managed to scoot them through the bedroom door.

Then, by the light spilling in through the doorway, he saw that the bed was unmade. His bathrobe was on the floor. The…

He hadn't known he'd be bringing home a beautiful woman or he'd have—

Linda looked up to see why he'd stopped.

"You really are a civilian. As long as those rumples are all yours, you'll get no complaints from me."

"They're all mine," his voice felt hoarse, stuck deep in his chest. "Have been for a while." Longer than usual, by far. As if he'd somehow known he was waiting for Linda Hamlin to step into his life.

She offered a thoughtful hum that might have been pleasure and might have been a cat's purr of contentment.

He was past thinking about such things. Setting her on her feet, he wasn't really sure how to begin. But Linda had taken care of that without him noticing. As he'd carried her, she'd unbuttoned his shirt.

Once again she placed her face against his chest; he now felt the tickle of her warm breath on his skin. The brush of her impossibly soft hair, even her happy sigh as she slid her arms inside his shirt until they were wrapped around him.

He wanted her to speak, though he wasn't sure why. Usually, when he bedded a woman, it was all about feeling: his hands on her skin, her reactions as he laved her body with touch and kiss as fine as decorating a chocolate. They would occasionally talk or guide and that was fine.

But with Linda, he wanted to hear her thoughts. He'd already learned that she was a woman of few words. He would have to coax her verbal responses just as he might another woman's physical ones.

"Tell me about—" his words choked off as she slipped his pants and underwear off his hips and dragged his bare body against her with fingers dug hard into his behind. She was so distracting that again he hadn't noticed her actions undressing him.

Undressing him. But she was still fully clothed. She hadn't even taken off her US Secret Service jacket, though she had unzipped it when they'd entered the apartment building.

US Secret Service. His past was filled with secretaries, aides, a lobbyist or two, and even a US Congresswoman. All professional women of the office variety. And, in hindsight, a disproportionate number of them had indeed been tall blondes exactly as Linda had teased him.

This short brunette of the military variety was something completely new.

Linda took a step back and shucked off her jacket. He almost missed the fact that if he didn't stop her, she'd strip down the rest of the way just as quickly.

He wanted her naked, but not merely stripped down.

Grabbing one of her hands before it could grab the hem of her blouse, he went to twirl her into an impromptu dance step.

Except his pants had slid from around his thighs to around his ankles and instead of stepping forward into the lead, he plunged to the carpet, nearly crushing Thor, who had come in to see what was going on. With a yip of surprise, Thor scooted back out the bedroom door.

A similar sound came from Linda because he hadn't let go of her hand as he went down. She landed hard against him, firmly planting a shoulder in his gut and knocking most of the wind out of him.

While he was busy gasping for air like a beached fish, Linda propped an elbow on his ribs and looked down at him.

"Is this how you usually run your seductions?"

"Sure," he managed on a gasp. "Dark choco-late," took two breaths.

"Smooth moves. Wrestle to carpet." He tried to reach for her, but his arms were still in his shirtsleeves and the bulk of the shirt was pinned beneath him. *Worst seduction, ever.*

Then Linda did what he'd been trying to forestall, or at least draw out. She grabbed the back collar of her blouse, yanked it off, then tossed it aside. A slightly stained gray sports bra followed moments later.

He'd been right. With Linda Hamlin, you got what you saw. No lacy lingerie purchased special for the moment. No coyness over wearing work clothes—no matter how high end—rather than date clothes.

And with absolutely spectacular results. He knew of her strength. Had witnessed it, felt it as he'd rubbed her back. But to see how so much power had been translated into the female form was astonishing. She looked only a little broader of shoulder than might be expected for her size. But with even the slightest motion, he could see the muscles rippling beneath her beautiful skin.

And what skin. It wasn't all smooth, powdered, moisturized, and who knew what else. There were scars on her arms, a big one on her shoulder that looked like…

"Dog teeth?"

She followed the line of his gaze, then shrugged. "Bite training. He caught me above the training sleeve. Seventeen stitches. I thought men only looked at one thing on naked women."

"Well, I'll admit to noting that you have exceptionally nice breasts." Again he reached for them and again he failed. He tried to raise his shoulders enough to free the trapped shirt, but she was still leaning against his chest and he couldn't get the leverage.

But Linda was about so much more than her womanly parts. Though now that she'd mentioned them, it *was* hard to look away.

That earned him a smile before she leaned down and rubbed against him chest-to-chest. He watched her eyes as she slowly gave herself over to the sensations. The tough soldier-turned-dog handler faded away and the hidden woman who intrigued him as much as the latter slowly emerged. Her eyes slid shut and her mouth opened slightly as the shift continued.

He leaned up enough to kiss her and they both groaned.

"Where?" She finally whispered.

Clive waved a hand at the nearby nightstand. She straddled his chest, still wearing her khakis as she reached over and dug out some protection. He planted a kiss on her breastbone just between her breasts and she scooped a hand to support his head and keep it there. Her breasts were soft and warm, brushing against his cheeks. He'd always been an unabashed breast man, in any size. But at her breastbone he felt as if he was somehow closer to who she was. Powerful muscle close over solid bone. The essence of this woman lay not in her splendid curves, but in her pervasive inner and outer strength.

With him sheathed and her pants shed, again in some maneuver he'd missed, she hovered over him. Her palms braced on his shoulders kept him still trapped by his shirt. Pinned by that and the most dramatic woman he'd ever been with.

LINDA FELT as if she teetered upon some brink. Men were easy. You gave them what they wanted and, if all went well, you got some of what you wanted as well.

But Clive confused her.

He kept insisting on seeing *her*, Linda, rather than merely some woman. And if she knew who that was, it would definitely help.

She knew Sergeant Hamlin. More than one unit had nicknamed her Ball-breaker because she didn't take shit from anyone. And any grunt who dared perform at one millimeter less than a hundred percent of their potential around her soon found out just how dangerous that was—though she saved literal ball-breaking just for those who didn't understand the meaning of the word *no*.

Clive had kissed right her where her dog tags had hung for a decade, as if he could somehow fill the hole that their removal had left. She didn't believe in nostalgia and had stripped them off as she'd driven out of the Fort Benning gates on that last day, but she'd missed them. Missed them horribly without realizing it until Clive planted a kiss there as if he could heal the gaping wound left by the removal of her dog tags and the end of her military career.

With a subtlety of understanding, he also didn't reach for her, merely letting his hands rest on her thighs where she knelt over him. He somehow knew that she had to find her own way through the maelstrom that being with him had stirred awake.

Men were *supposed* to be easy.

Clive Andrews *looked* easy. His sweet face and smiling eyes said that he absolutely *was* easy. But with every gesture, with every move, he proved that he was the most complex man she'd ever met.

His kindness was without question.

His humor, his ability to laugh at himself even as he tumbled to the carpet in the middle of a dance step and played the fool, was something she knew she'd be a better person if she could learn.

And the man... There wasn't a thing about him that wasn't substantial.

His impact on her thoughts was all out of proportion with any prior assignation. And to take him inside... It felt as if she was about to bare her very soul for him to see. Of course, Clive Andrews was the one proving to her that she even *had* a soul, so perhaps that wasn't a bad thing.

Easing down, she slowly took him in. One long, slow, delicious slide all the way down until she couldn't believe how extraordinarily he filled her in every way.

Definitely not a bad thing.

"It will be dawn soon," Linda mumbled from where she lay beneath the covers, her head on his chest.

"Dawn," Clive managed to acknowledge as he finger-brushed her hair so that it spread like a liquid ganache over his neck and shoulders. A featherweight as light as her kisses and the flutter of her eyelashes against his cheek when they kissed.

Dawn of a new day. New day? He had trouble even remembering the Clive of yesterday. In a single night, Linda Hamlin had transformed him. Yesterday he'd been a chocolatier who enjoyed women. Today he knew for a fact that there was no other woman for him.

He couldn't remember the last time he'd been awake a whole night and come out of it feeling more energized than when the evening had started. Yes, sex on the carpet, hard against the tile wall in the shower with the hot water sluicing over them, and finally on top of her in the bed had certainly had their impact. But it was the times between, curled up in each other's arms and talking easily, that he'd most remember.

Piece by tiny piece, like a layered chocolate truffle that continued without end, she slowly revealed herself. The triumphs and heartbreaks of working with the dogs. And with the people. He'd never given much thought to the civilians of countries caught up in war zones against their wishes. Now they seemed so real that he'd never see the war-torn, ex-military men prowling along the White House fence the same way again. They hadn't wanted war either, but everything had been stripped from them until all they had left was looking through an iron fence at the center of power. Did they find comfort there or a focus for their ire?

And he was a chocolatier. How useless was that?

Yet Linda was so compassionate that she had talked him down from that as well. "It gives me hope, knowing that normal life continues. That I can walk into the mall and hit See's Candies. It's a sign of all the things we're doing right." After that he'd made a particularly gentle love to her, for it was the best way he could think to thank her.

"I just wish I could do more," he brushed at her hair some more. Out the window, the low gray clouds reflected back the streetlights.

"You do." She pulled back the sheets enough to uncover her face so that he could trace his fingertips over her fine features. Somehow she knew that it was the same conversation they'd abandoned hours before. "Think about the dessert you just designed."

He'd told her about it earlier. Now it sounded trite. He rolled his eyes.

"No, Clive," she propped herself up to look down at him. "I'm serious. A mission isn't achieved by me and my dog leading the way, searching for IEDs. It's won by the intel analyst who found the target, the commander who planned and ordered the raid. The helo pilots. The grunts on the ground. The snipers on overwatch. The eyes in the sky of the drone operators. We each do our little piece. Even then victory isn't assured, but it's not for want of trying."

Clive blinked at the force of her tirade, but she continued.

"Your role may not seem obvious to you, but how do you know that your contribution won't be the tipping point? You don't. You just do what every good soldier does. You do the best you can; and as long as you keep doing that, no one can ask more of you. Besides, you're much farther up the chain than I am. Maybe your 'silly' dessert will help make a change so that people like me don't have to deploy in the first place."

"Have you always been such an optimist?"

"I'm not. I'm a fierce pessimist. Maybe I'll tell you about my parents someday."

Then she shuddered against him and he wasn't so sure that she was pretending. Only then did he realize that her life story to him had begun with the moment she joined the Army.

"Or maybe not," she continued softly. "But I'm also a realist who see what works."

"There must be something you're optimistic about?"

In answer she slid a hand down his chest, over his stomach, and wrapped those fine fingers around him.

"Okay," he had to agree. "I'm feeling rather optimistic about that too."

CHAPTER EIGHT

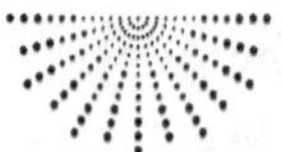

*P*erimeter patrol. It felt good to be outdoors for a change.

Even if it was snowing. She was in such a good mood that the light snowfall looked pretty. If it persisted through the day and the temperature didn't rise, she'd probably be less enamored by this afternoon. For now, it was pleasant. Each cool snowflake that landed on her face and melted seemed to freeze and wash clean an old memory leaving only the fresh and new ones behind.

Linda also appreciated having a tall fence *between* her and the White House for a change. Between her and Clive.

She'd pay for the lack of sleep later, though the Rangers had taught her to go two or three days without when needed. But she'd never felt more awake rather than less with the passage of time.

Clive had slipped past her guard. She wasn't used to guys spending the night. In all fairness, she'd been in his apartment, so it would have been up to her to leave. But she hadn't even thought about it. Two a.m. had slipped by just as pleasantly as their predawn tussle in the sheets. She was comfortable in his arms like no other's before. Which was unnerving enough to confuse the crap out of her.

Then this morning he'd given her a pair of gloves that he'd knit for his mother, but she'd died before he'd finished them.

"They were to be our cribbage gloves."

She'd inspected them carefully. Rows and rows of tiny beer glasses, some amber, some stout brown, and each with a white foam cap. "They look like drinking gloves."

"We used to go to a pub together to have a beer and play cribbage." Then he'd folded down the thumb. Sure enough, on the inside face of it was a tiny cribbage board.

Even now she felt the kiss on each palm before he'd slipped the gloves on her hands.

Clive hadn't just slipped past her guard—he'd blown by it as if it wasn't even there.

This morning, an officer named Claremont was following her along the fence line, but far enough back that she didn't have to interact with him. His job was two-fold: to act as backup if Thor found anything and to answer questions about Thor so that they could keep moving and do their job. She could hear him behind her.

"Yes, he's really a Secret Service dog."

"No, you can't pet him. Sorry."

"Yes, he may look silly, but his nose is one of the top ones in the business."

"His breed, ma'am? Pure mutt."

"Yes, he's the one who caught the bomber yesterday."

"No. He's at work right now, so he can't stop for pictures, sir."

He was repeating the last two so often that it was making Linda crazy. Thor had become an overnight celebrity. The Secret Service was generally very careful to keep quiet just how many lunatics they quietly nabbed at the fence line carrying explosives.

But the diplomat, by dropping his briefcase in the center of Lafayette Square, had turned it into a front page spectacle—below the fold, but still front page. With a big close-up of Thor. The hero dog had drawn crowds of his own to the White House fence.

Well, the public weren't the only ones who now knew who she was. The other dog handlers circling the fence offered her a nod of greeting, even the ones she'd never seen before. Outside the line, she and another floppy-eared were on opposite rotations, so they passed one another each half-rotation around the White House grounds. Even from inside the fence line, the handlers with the Malinois ERTs —Emergency Response Team dogs—nodded a greeting.

She missed the prestige of handling a Malinois war dog. They were fierce and fiercely loyal. They could also be utterly charming, but they were always impressive. Yet Thor, the least impressive dog on the entire team, had a sweetness that went all the way to his core.

And they were finding a place for themselves. She'd burned out in the Rangers. Witnessing so much death and suffering had taken its toll. But Linda had stayed an extra two-year tour just because she had no idea where she could possibly belong outside of the Army. But maybe, just maybe, she was finding it.

"You're famous," a voice whispered close beside her.

Linda prepared herself to actually deal with a tourist when she recognized the voice. "Good morning, Dilya."

The girl was dressed in a massive parka of neon blue that almost reached her knees. She wore a knit hat of blue with gold stripes with a tail so long that she had the end tied around her throat as a scarf. She existed only from her brilliant green eyes to her lower lip.

"Is that hat-scarf thing Clive's doing? *Gute Hund,*" she told Thor so that he could take a moment to greet Dilya and pee on a handy lamppost.

Dilya nodded.

"Where's Zackie?"

"I didn't want to distract Thor. Besides, I'm not supposed to take her off the grounds. It's weird how many people want to kidnap the First Dog."

It was weird, but she'd seen the statistics on threats against White House pets. More than one tour guest had tried to smuggle a First Cat out under their coats. "Good choice. We've got to get back to work, but you're welcome to walk with us. Thor, *Such.*" And once more he was back on the job, sniffing the air as he moved through the crowds gawking at the White House. Whenever someone stepped too far aside, as if perhaps shifting to avoid being smelled by Thor, she'd twitch his leash ever so slightly and he'd shift over to check them.

Dilya fell in close beside her. With a neat awareness, she stayed an extra half step to the side so that she wouldn't be in the way if Linda had to react.

"Did you get any more training done?"

"No, she's with the First Lady over in the East Wing. They're usually good together for the morning. After lunch she's off to New York."

Meeting at the UN, Linda recalled from the morning briefing. The President was scheduled to be inside all day.

"I'm usually at school in the mornings anyway."

"Why aren't you today?"

"Saturday. Duh!"

"Oh," Linda had completely lost track of the days. She simply checked the duty roster at checkout each evening to see if she was on or off the following day.

"Is that where you caught him?" They were passing Lafayette Square.

"Yes. Close by the Andrew Jackson statue in the center. Though Thor picked up his trail three blocks that way."

Dilya was looking from the statue to along G Street.

She did it enough times that Linda finally had to ask what she was thinking.

"Well…" she drew it out. "He wasn't really headed anywhere, was he. Not to Hay-Adams Hotel or he would have crossed the square on the other side of the statue. And not toward Blair House where the Japanese ambassador was meeting with their prime minister or he wouldn't have come into the square at all."

An observation that had been brought up at yesterday's debriefing, but no one knew how to interpret.

"But by walking along G Street, he was almost asking to be found. If you hadn't caught him, I wonder if he would have kept walking back and forth."

Linda froze, earning her a puzzled look from Thor. She looked up the street, imagining a map of DC in her mind. Three blocks to the Metro Center subway station. Two blocks and a block left beyond that to the Secret Service Headquarters building. It would be perhaps the *most* patrolled approach to the White House just for that reason.

Dilya continued her speculation, "I mean, if I was going to smuggle four kilos of explosives into the vicinity of the White House without a dog catching me, that isn't a route I would have followed. Combine that with a diplomatic pass and something isn't right."

"How did you know it was four kilos?" The fact of the diplomatic pass had also been kept out of the papers, yet somehow Dilya knew.

Linda didn't wait for the girl to answer. She keyed the radio mic clipped to her shoulder. "Sergeant Hamlin for Captain Baxter."

"Baxter here."

"What if the bomber *wanted* to be caught?"

There was a long silence. Then, "Get your ass in here. I'll send another team out to patrol the line."

She acknowledged and turned to thank Dilya, but she was gone. Even her neon blue parka and matching hat were nowhere to be seen.

———

It took Clive most of the day to perfect the dessert for the State Dinner. Chef Klaus liked it well enough, even if he didn't understand the higher concept. First Lady Anne Darlington-Thomas understood it the moment she saw it and was then delighted with the taste. She looked absolutely elegant and had a small entourage in tow that crowded his tiny shop badly.

"You've outdone yourself, Chef Andrews." The First Lady began handing around his Pocky-stick treats to the rest of the gathering.

"Thank you, ma'am."

An assistant stood by her side with a tablet at the ready for notetaking. The White House photographer was maneuvering for a good photo—thankfully the assistant had called ahead and he'd had time to don a fresh apron and set out his creations for the State Dinner in a neat display. Still the photograph was a challenge because the First Lady was even shorter than Linda and didn't reach his shoulder. Special Agent Detra Willand, a shapely and cheery blonde in charge of the First Lady's protection detail, smiled brightly at the contrast as she stood guard in the doorway.

Dilya slipped in quietly, leading Zackie, and took one as well.

"Yum!" Dilya broke off part of the bare biscuit and fed it to the dog. " I one heard someone say that life is uncertain…"

"*…so eat dessert first.*" Clive and the First Lady spoke in unison. Then the First Lady looked thoughtful.

"Chef Andrews, can you scale these down and serve them as a treat at the predinner reception?"

Clive considered. Yes, he could scale them down now that he had the techniques figured out. But then he'd need a suitable dessert for the dinner. Perhaps Jacques Torres' chocolate soup might have a place after all. Made of the same dark chocolate, perhaps with a passionfruit-flavored meringue. Each bowl accompanied by a single one of his scaled-up version of a twirled chocolate Pocky stick. For those who had snacked on the smaller ones at the reception, it would bring the concept full circle, emphasizing the unity of the evening.

When he laid out the idea, the First Lady had practically glowed with appreciation.

"You are thinking at a whole new level, Chef Andrews. I like that."

"I had someone offer me…" *her body and her passion* "…some clear insights."

"Oh, I do so *love* those kinds of insights." She breezed out of the kitchen with her entourage hurrying close on her heels. Dilya grinned at him, clearly not missing a thing, then took another stick of chocolate and followed the First Lady as well—Zackie's claws ticking brightly on the linoleum floor.

He could only gape after her. What was it with women? Did they simply assume that all good bounty flowed directly from them? Even if the First Lady was absolutely right in this case.

All good bounty? Who was he kidding?

He'd known Linda Hamlin for mere days and if she was willing to promise the rest of her life with him, he'd go down on bent knee right here and now in his chocolate shop. How was a sane man ever supposed to get enough of someone like her?

Well, that one he knew how to answer. The only way to get enough was to indeed commit to a lifetime together. That was the only way there would ever be enough time.

The fact that the thought was completely and certifiably insane wasn't bothering him as much as he'd expect it to. Is this what being in love was?

If love was like a chocolate, what would it be?

He wasn't sure, but he began pulling out his favorite ingredients. Rather than an ultra-high-end chocolate, he selected a Lindt couverture. It offered a taste of homey familiarity rather than a unique experience for the palate. Apricot liquor. Dried Bing cherries that he'd candy in an apricot nectar simple syrup. A sprinkle of candied ginger on a red chocolate surface. Then—

He looked at it all on the counter and knew it was wrong.

Yes, it would make a nice chocolate. But it would be about him and what he liked. He wanted it to be about Linda. Even better, he wanted it to be about them.

Once more Clive studied the ingredients on the counter. Then the ones in his pantry.

The problem was that he didn't know enough about *her*. He knew how she made him feel—like the luckiest chef on the planet. No other woman could ever offer that incredible blend of strength and surety and clarity.

But he couldn't think of how to make a chocolate out of those words.

And what words would she use?

He didn't know. Her thoughts were like the hidden center of a treat—unknown except to the baker until they were bitten into. There was no secret code worked into the finishing decoration to tell him what she had contained within.

Clive might not know her, but he couldn't deny being fascinated.

Fascinated?

Completely gone. He simply knew she was the right woman for him.

Again the thought seemed crazy, but it was as right as that first moment he'd bitten into couverture chocolate and the future had opened up for him.

Linda Hamlin was the one for him.

Now, how to go about finding more about who she actually was and convincing her that he was the one for her.

"You *what?*" Linda's body ignored her shock and kept doing what it had been doing.

She and Clive were right in the middle of another night's research into just how good it was possible to make each other feel—when he'd mumbled out those three impossible words.

"Tell me. I didn't just hear. What I just heard." It took her three gasping breaths to get the sentence out.

Clive offered one of his uncomfortable shrugs. He opened his mouth, but she cut him off.

"And don't spout anything. About George Washington. Not telling lies!" Her pulse rate was still escalating, just not for the reasons it should be.

He closed his mouth again.

"This isn't happening." She straddled over him in his big Barcalounger. It was tipped back just enough that his incredible hands had access to her chest and the wonderful things he'd proven he could do there.

"Sorry," he whispered.

Release was so close, for both of them. She'd learned to read his gasping breaths and clenching thighs to know just how close.

And then he'd said...

She couldn't even think it.

But they were so close that even the least movement...

Her body, out of her control, sank down hard one last time and the waves hammered through her, stealing the last of her breath and mind. Moments later, the pulses wracking her own body tipped Clive off the edge as well.

"So good," was all she could mumble. "So good." Sex with Clive was better than any prior experience had even hinted was possible.

He held her hips tight against his as they rode it out together. Every shudder, every breath—she could feel every nuance through his physical connection deep inside her where he was plugged directly in her nervous system.

When at last their shared body had quieted, she tipped her forehead against his. "It's okay, Clive. It's just something that guys are dumb enough to say during sex. They think that sex equals love and spout things out. Sorry I yelled, I get that."

But resting brow-to-brow, she could feel him shaking his head.

"Do *not* repeat it!"

"Okay," he whispered.

"God damn it, Clive!" Linda pushed back to glare down at him. "There's no such thing, outside of fairy tales and Hollywood movies. You do know that, right? Who the hell am I kidding? You're a guy who knits and makes chocolate for a living. You believe in the Easter Bunny, the Tooth Fairy, and true love."

"Well, I kind of outgrew the Tooth Fairy—she didn't like me much because I'm a chocolatier. I'm totally in good with the Easter Bunny, though. I'm a big fan. Huge."

"Clive," her groan felt like it was made of shards of glass. "We've known each other for maybe three days."

"Six, actually. It's past midnight."

"Clive!"

He ran his hands up her bare back and pulled her in.

She resisted. Well, she *wanted* to resist, but she knew how good it felt to lie against him. And knew just how perfectly he could hold her with those big, wonderful hands of his. Her traitorous body leaned in against him until they were chest to chest and she could rest her head on his shoulder.

"How can you believe in love?"

"How can you not?"

Linda buried her face against his neck and sure enough, his hands sliding up and down his back soothed her. But she didn't want to be soothed. She didn't want to fall into some male-engineered trap.

"No," she pushed back up. "No!" She extricated herself from Clive and his goddamn chair. Because it was tipped partway back, the angles were all wrong, but she finally managed to obtain enough leverage to stand to the side and look down at him. He was *so* beautiful. So fantastically male.

He was also a dangerous drug. She'd felt less effect from morphine ampoules delivered from field medkits when she'd been injured. The potency of Clive Andrews wasn't merely a force to be reckoned with. For a moment there, she'd almost fallen under his spell.

But no!

She *knew* better.

They always said that if you didn't know what to respond when the other person said those three awful words, then that was the answer.

But she knew exactly what to say.

"Clive. I *don't* love you." Then she couldn't stop herself. "You're a really great fuck," the best she'd ever had. "But that's all this is."

And he looked like she'd just rammed her battle knife under his ribcage.

She wanted to reach for him. Take his hand. Console him. But… she'd just forever forfeited that privilege with those four words of her own.

CLIVE COULDN'T LOOK at her, but he couldn't look away either. Naked, beautiful, her hair brushing her powerful shoulders. So strong and yet so angry.

He knew he shouldn't have said that he loved her. He knew it the instant the words had slipped out of his mouth. But they'd been so true. All of the way down to the core. It hadn't been something tossed out in the throes of passion, it had simply been clarified so perfectly in that instant. He knew its truth as surely as he knew his passion for chocolate.

And it wasn't merely how she felt, how she smelled, how she tasted. Nothing had prepared him for the way she gave with all of her being. Her open heart and the connections she built so easily with Thor and Dilya—it had taken him months to win Dilya's trust and Linda had done it in minutes. Picturing Linda with children of her own was the easiest thing in the world. Picturing her with *their* children…

It had taken his breath away and the words had spilled out.

Saying those words aloud had been a shock to him as well, but they were nothing compared to her answer: *I don't love you.* He felt as if he'd been gutted and wished he could somehow curl up and hide rather than lie bonelessly sprawled back in his chair, unable to find the leverage to climb to his feet. Spread out like a corpse whose heart had just been hacked out of his chest, inspected, and found wanting.

Linda began dressing as efficiently as she did everything else and all he could do was watch.

"You're a wonderful man, Clive."

Socks and underwear.

"The best time I've ever had." As if he was a carnival ride.

Pants and belt.

"What you don't understand is that there's no such thing as love. It's just a delusion. A mass hallucination cooked up by Hollywood and romance authors."

She bent down to tie her boots, offering him an incredible view of her naked breasts partly masked by a fall of her luxurious hair.

"No!" He protested as her words sank in. "Wait. That's wrong. Of course love exists." He finally found the chair controls and tipped it upright enough for him to really face her.

"No." Bra, blouse, fleece vest. "It's a stupid word for a cruel concept that is used only to hurt and manipulate."

Shoulder holster, sidearm, and taser.

"Linda, you can't believe—"

"I *don't* believe." USSS jacket. "I *know.*"

Her face was cold, expressionless. This wasn't the woman...or even the soldier. She'd gone somewhere far beyond either of those.

"Love is an empty word said by a husband to his wife before he goes off to screw another coed. It the word a mother uses to manipulate and guilt-trip her child: *If you loved me, you'd...* The song is right. Love isn't a weapon, it's a goddamn battlefield."

A snap of her fingers and Thor trotted to her side.

She pulled out the gloves he given her—his mother's cribbage gloves. She rubbed a thumb over them for a moment, then set them on the coffee table beside the last of the pizza he'd made for her.

"Goodbye, Clive."

"Wait! Let's talk—" But she was gone, with Thor at her heels.

The door swung softly shut.

Leaving him to sit naked and alone.

Linda didn't take the Metro.

She needed to walk it off.

Hot tracks scored her cold cheeks like the razor slice of flying shrapnel—momentary surprise, and then, after a pause just long enough to think you were lucky and had escaped this time, the slicing pain. She hadn't cried since...

She remembered the day perfectly while she strode blindly down Wisconsin Avenue. It was a good thing it was two in the morning and there was no traffic. She couldn't seem to stop herself as she strode through intersection after intersection no matter what the lights were doing.

A young girl. The day before she'd turned eleven. She could still see it with crystalline clarity in her mind's eye—sharper than the night's fluttering snow caught in successive streetlamps.

Standing outside her parents' open bedroom door. Her best friend beside her. Home from school for a play date.

Everyone always talked about how wonderful and kind her parents were. What great hosts. The joy of every party. So helpful.

But that wasn't what she and Peggy saw.

Her parents. Toe to toe in the bedroom. Screaming at each other as if they were ready to commit murder.

She recalled the images like snapshots: the rumpled bed, her father naked, a blonde college student that Father had said he was tutoring cowered in the corner trying to hide her own nakedness, her mother raging.

The words had tumbled by her, barely recognized, not understood until later: cheating fuck, icy bitch, limp-dicked loser, dried-out hag with nothing but a dusty hole where all joy died…

But worse than the words had been when they'd turned and noticed their audience.

Her father had merely sworn, "There's the other useless bitch. Why the hell did we ever have a kid?"

Her mother hadn't corrected him. Hadn't defended her. Instead she'd stridden to the door in her Armani power pantsuit and whispered harshly, "Neither of you little shits saw or heard a thing!" Then she'd slammed the door in their faces.

Peggy hadn't been there when Linda had finally recovered. Her pinkie-sworn, best-friend-forever never spoke to her again. Word got around, and not many of their classmates ever had either. Linda's eleventh birthday party, her last ever, had been attended by her golden retriever. That's what had driven her out of the social set and into sports, which had ultimately led her to the military. None of the jocks knew of the horror that was her parents. They didn't know she was now a social pariah. She never once took any of her sports friends to her house.

And that evening at dinner? Everyone just pretended that nothing had happened, including her. Her father still tutored his students at the house, often in the bedroom, sometimes more than one at a time. Her mother rarely came home from Montpelier—except when there were dinners or parties to host, of course. When Linda visited there, her mother was always with a different man—whoever's political favors she was currying at the time. Linda had spent all of her accumulated allowance to buy top-quality noise-canceling headphones—the only possession she never forgot to take from place to place.

It wasn't the night of the fight that Linda had last cried. She'd just kept her dry-eyed face buried in Beau's fur as she and her dog hid together in her bedroom closet.

When the aged golden retriever had died two months later, *that* was when it all came out. She'd cried so hard that they'd had to call the paramedics and give her a muscle relaxant before she could stop.

That had been her very last time.

Until now.

Dammit!

She wiped at her eyes with chilled fingers, all the colder as they were soaked in salt water.

A lone passerby hesitated as if he might offer to help—then hurried away fast. Smart man.

Wisconsin intersected Massachusetts. Dupont Circle sent her south along Connecticut. Until once more she stood in Lafayette Square with the White House shining like a beacon. A lone dog team patrolled along Pennsylvania. Emergency response dogs would be in their ERT vans—one of them was bound to have spotted her and was keeping an eye on her just in case.

Warning: Crazy bitch in Lafayette Square at three a.m. Alert the QRT!

In her current mood she was half tempted to do something that would get a Quick Response Team to come and put her out of her misery. How could she have done that to Clive? He *was* the best fuck of her life, but there'd been no reason to say it that way.

She brushed the thin coating of snow off a bench and sat. Thor settled at her feet. Linda cursed herself as she gathered him into her arms.

"Oh, I'm so sorry, buddy. I just made you walk five miles." She buried her face in his fur as he tried to lick the dried salt from her face. Even without his lead clipped on, he'd stuck with her.

A dog. That was all a woman could trust. Her own self and her dog.

Then she remembered the devastated look on Clive's face as she carved up his heart and fed it back to him.

She'd sworn that she'd never be cruel like her parents, but now that rule lay shattered with a direct hit. Apparently cruelty wasn't a choice, it was genetic.

Maybe not so much with trusting herself.

Thor finished cleaning her face and began on his own paws.

Okay. At least she could trust her dog.

CHAPTER NINE

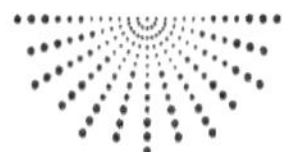

"*A* difficult night, my dear?" A homeless woman settled on the bench beside Linda.

"Could you just leave me alone?"

"Oh no. I don't think that's a good idea at all, dearie." Then the woman held out a dog biscuit.

Linda yanked Thor away before he could even sniff it. MWDs often carried ten or even twenty thousand dollar bounties on their heads in war zones—fifty times the average per capita yearly income in Afghanistan. She'd never heard of anyone poisoning a Secret Service dog, but Thor was not going to be the first.

She reached for her taser, even as it sank in that the voice was familiar. A clump of silver hair spilled out of the tattered hood of the woman's knit sweater and caught the streetlight. Bright blue eyes watched her intently.

"Miss Watson." Dressed like a bag lady, complete with a couple of badly scuffed plastic bags and wearing enough layers that she looked quite fat. Earlier she'd looked, well, it was hard to remember. Matronly? Without the voice, Linda never would have recognized her.

"You were expecting Greta Garbo?"

"Was she one of your spies?" Linda let loose her hold on Thor and Miss Watson once again offered the biscuit, which he happily took.

"She was before my time. The stories are very conflicted about her, just as everything else was."

"But…"

Miss Watson smiled. "Yes, she was deeply involved in very private ways—she did more than many in the fight against Hitler. Shall I repeat my question?"

"Please don't." She picked up some of the biscuit that Thor had broken off and dropped into her lap, holding it out for him to take once more.

"In that case, I will inquire as to the progress of your thinking about our would-be bomber."

"Is *nothing* secret in the White House?" Then Linda remembered who she was talking to and sighed. "My current, private theory is that he wasn't a bomber. The X-ray of the briefcase showed no signs of a trigger mechanism or timer. It did create the opportunity to pat down both of the diplomats and if they were hiding something like a trigger, it was well done."

"So, you have two men who carried four kilograms of explosive through an area well known to be patrolled by explosives detection dogs." Somehow Miss Watson knew about that observation as well, even if it hadn't shed any more light on the Secret Service's thinking— though Secretary of State Mallinson had poured forth a lecture that was equal parts conspiracy, xenophobia, and accusations of the Service's incompetence.

"Yes," Linda rubbed Thor's nose and received a freezing cold sneeze in her face as a reward. She sighed and wiped it away. "And yesterday I was able to trace them using the traffic and surveillance camera feeds backward from where I picked up their trail. They didn't ride the Metro, instead merely passing it. They had indeed walked directly past the Secret Service Headquarters building. We spotted them emerging from a cab. We managed to trace them backward through two more cab rides—all three were short, within the city limits. Prior to that, their trail disappears as if the film had been snipped."

"And your thoughts." Miss Watson didn't make it a question.

"My thoughts?" Linda's thoughts were that if she could undo one thing in her life—any one thing—it wouldn't be her parents, it would be hurting Clive. But if ever she'd killed off something good so thoroughly that it could never recover, that was it. "I don't have any thoughts."

Miss Watson didn't even bother to scoff as she had during their first meeting in her basement office. Instead, she held her hands out for Thor to sniff to prove they were empty of any second biscuit. He sighed and laid his head on Linda's chest to go to sleep.

"My thoughts are... Someone just wants to mess with our heads. Tomorrow, next week, at some point, they're going to actually do something and this event was merely to lay down a false trail. But whether it is to Japan, China, or freaking Tajikistan, I have no idea."

"Oh dear," Miss Watson said as daintily as a British mum about to serve tea and confronted by poorly cut cucumber sandwiches.

It was only then that Linda wondered if she'd actually been cleared to tell that information. The fact that Miss Watson somehow had an office in the subbasement of the White House—a clandestine one of long standing—said volumes about what she could do. But Linda had no spycraft of her own to estimate whether Miss Watson was good, bad, indifferent, crazy, or some sort of quadruple agent.

"I had rather feared that. However, I suspect that it will be far sooner than a week from now."

Linda swiveled to look at her more closely. "What do you know that I don't?"

Miss Watson's smile was rich with innuendo and an unlikely humor considering the situation.

"Ha. Ha. Ha. I meant about this situation."

"I know about a certain chef who has just arrived at the White House at an unprecedented hour by his standards. As to the other..." She reached out and squeezed Linda's hand with a very surprising strength, enough to dispel the frail, old woman persona. But she didn't speak.

Linda couldn't think about Clive being in the building shining right in front of her. Too close. Too real. So she set it aside.

But what did Miss Watson know? *Far sooner than a week from now.*

The pieces weren't connecting yet: a block of C-4 without being a bomb, a Japanese diplomat without being a Japanese diplomat, a flight for two to China as the first leg of a trip that would end who knew where.

Then she got it.

"It's not just *related* to the upcoming talks. It's *about* the upcoming meetings between Vietnam, Japan, and…" But even as she was saying it, she knew it was about something more.

It wouldn't be enough to merely disrupt the meetings—they'd just be held at a later date in another location.

However, if she wanted to permanently disrupt or damage the talks, or use them to showcase that no one was out of reach of whoever the true aggressor was, how would she go about it?

The meetings themselves? That wasn't very exciting. Horribly damaging, but missing that newsworthy hook. She worked with enough embedded war reporters to know they were always after the hottest hook. "What's the bin Laden-moment here?" always came out of their mouths at one time or another. Modern warfare was rarely about bin Laden-moments. It was about slow and steady attrition: one leader here, two weapon suppliers over there, a dozen fighters, an armored vehicle.

But if she was setting up a scenario specifically designed to *create* a bin Laden-media moment, she wouldn't do it during any dull meetings.

That left…the reception in the Residence and the State Dinner itself.

She swallowed hard. Both would require attacks *inside* the White House.

The State Dinner. Unless bipartisan slaughter was on the menu, it would be a hard situation to control. Would all of the potential targets even be at the same table?

That left the predinner reception on the Second Floor of the Residence.

"It's got to be—" Linda turned, but once again she and Thor were sitting alone in the center of Lafayette Square. She looked down at Thor.

"Between Miss Watson and Dilya, I really wish they'd stop doing that."

He offered a sleepy woof of commiseration.

CLIVE HAD CHASED LINDA. But by the time he'd dressed and raced out the door, she'd had too much of a head start and he didn't know where to begin looking for her.

He stood on the corner, slowly chilling down until he felt the ice form inside him as well as his freezing breath outside.

Everything had made such perfect sense just minutes before—a clarity of vision so clear that it felt prescient. He'd never believed in such things, though his mother had teased him about it often enough.

How did you know I was going to say that, Clive? Are you clairvoyant?

No. She'd simply said the same thing before when he'd done something equally stupid. He never forgot a word she said, even if he was slow to actually follow the advice. Which was too bad in retrospect—he'd eventually learned that most of Mom's advice had been good. He could use some of it now, but she'd died last spring. Her weak heart had made her so frail that the progression from cold to flu to pneumonia had been terrifyingly fast...and final. She'd died lying in a hospital bed clutching the cherry blossom scarf he'd knit for her, but she would never have a chance to wear. He'd buried it with her.

A passing thought that he wished she'd lived long enough to meet Linda just drove the knife in deeper.

And now as he stood in the freezing cold of the Washington, DC, night, he could feel the scars freshly opened.

No such thing as love.

She was wrong. He and his mother had had it—he still missed her as if she'd died yesterday. Maybe his father hadn't cared. He'd been at sea when she died and done no more than cashed the check for his share of her meager estate when he returned. He'd never even bothered to contact Clive. But that didn't negate that there was such a thing as love.

At a loss for what else to do, he'd entered the Metro and headed to work.

Now he stood in his kitchen and couldn't make sense of anything here either. The ingredients for a new dessert were still out on a prep table—the one that would be all about his heart. And his alone. He couldn't even see how the pieces fit together anymore.

He sat and put his head on the table.

What had he done wrong?

Fallen in love?

It was real. He could feel it like an agony in his chest, all curdled and sour, so he knew it was real.

But Linda didn't have a heart. He could see that now. Though he'd met few women like that, he knew men like that—his father for one.

And Clive thought he'd been so wise, so lucky. Able to recognize the woman who so rarely emerged from the soldier.

Now Clive understood that there was a reason she was a soldier.

Tonight he'd seen the other half of her. The part that made the soldier look kind and gentle. The woman who didn't merely deny love, but denied its existence. That *believed* it so deeply that she could say what she'd said.

She'd given him her body, but that was all. As if there weren't plenty of women willing to do that.

He raised his head enough to glare at the ingredients: Lindt dark couverture, apricot, ginger... His heart meant nothing to her. She'd just been using him for sex. Never in his life had he treated a woman that way. Even when it had just been purely physical, they'd both known that beforehand.

Not Linda. Her smile, her actions, her every breath had promised so much more. He'd seen the wonder on her face as she'd touched him. There was so much—

But there wasn't. Linda had made that perfectly clear.

He stood up and stowed the chocolate supplies back in his pantry. Then he began the long slow process of making the biscuit dough for the center of the dessert: reception nibbles for fifty, dessert for two hundred and forty.

CHAPTER TEN

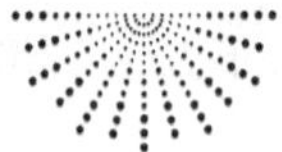

Mallinson had been in the Situation Room when she stuck her head in. He was quietly reviewing classified material for a change. They had a surprisingly pleasant discussion about her experiences overseas. He was an intelligent and insightful man, as long as she didn't mention the current situation.

So, at a loss for where else to go, Linda had once again crammed Special Agent Harvey Lieber into Captain Baxter's office, with Thor at her feet.

"What do you know that I don't?"

Lieber leaned back against a file cabinet with his arms crossed over his chest. "What are you talking about, Hamlin?"

"How did you know that the attack would be at tomorrow night's reception in the Residence?"

Both men flinched and looked at her aghast.

"You didn't know?"

They exchanged a quick glance, briefly suspicious of the other, before understanding that they were both in the dark. They *hadn't* known. But...

"Then why, the last time we met, did you ask if I could pass in a high-society environment if it wasn't to place me in that reception?"

Again that careful exchange of glances.

Linda considered the satisfaction of knocking their heads together versus her career having a future. She could feel that her nerves were frayed. She'd slept little the last two nights. The first night and a half because of Clive's splendid attentions and the last half because—she couldn't think about that.

"We have a source," Baxter began, then compressed his lips together.

"A very reliable one," Lieber acknowledged with equal reluctance.

"Let me guess, a woman in the basement."

"No." Again the dual blank look. "What woman? Which basement?"

Miss Watson. Subbasement Two, Mechanical Room 043. Librarian? Spy? Or something else entirely? Linda had no way to know Miss Watson's role, but something told her to keep that to herself. She held her silence until they got back on track.

Baxter finally rose to his feet, shoving Lieber aside, which almost pushed him into her lap because there was so little space. It was a good thing for Thor's sake that he was small enough to fit under her chair. Baxter unlocked the file cabinet, opened the top drawer, and then used a thumb print to open a safe mounted inside the drawer. He pulled out a slim folder with that same scary yellow-and-red fly sheet of an "Eyes Only" file. He handed it to her.

She opened it while the men reshuffled to their former positions.

Secure message.
From: WHPF
To: Captain Baxter
Cc: Senior Special Agent Lieber
Recommend immediate placement of Sergeant Hamlin
and dog Thor on internal White House patrol.
Level White protection.

It was dated the same day she'd passed the course at James J. Rowley Training Center.

"Who's WHPF?"

Lieber merely growled that it was Baxter's problem.

"We don't know. Something set up by the prior administration. We've learned that their advice is always good—and I mean always. But we have no idea who they are. They simply came online one day with a note from President Peter Matthews and Lieber's predecessor Frank Adams that said they had both personally certified the WHPF."

"Frank wouldn't tell me shit about who they were," and Agent Lieber's voice made it clear just how happy he *wasn't* about that. Then he held up his hands in resignation to the inevitable. "It stands for White House Protection Force and they've proven that they're good at it. Damned if I know where they get their information."

Linda could take a good guess. But maybe not. She remembered her two talks with Miss Watson. The matron was definitely in the loop, a piece of it, but last night in Lafayette Square she'd been reaching for answers as hard as Linda had. The simple memo in her hand spoke of a deep knowledge, or perhaps a broader reach than seemed likely from Mechanical Room 043.

"And Level White protection?"

Again the snarl from Lieber.

Baxter, on the other hand, actually smiled at his friend's upset expression. "It means that while you work for me, you've also been assigned undercover to the PPD."

Linda could feel the blood drain out of her face. The Presidential Protection Detail? Nobody got on that. It was the gold star times a thousand. Granted only after years of exceptional service.

"Wait! Undercover? Who else knows?"

Baxter, clearly enjoying his comrade's foul mood at having an undercover agent watching his own team, pointed a finger at the two of them. "Us and whoever the hell is behind the WHPF."

Linda couldn't speak. Couldn't think.

"We need a way to slip her in. Can't just put her there as an agent," Baxter pointed out.

Lieber looked her up and down with all the joy of inspecting a rotting piece of meat. "She and her dog as special guests for their fine work in Lafayette Square. Give Chief of Staff Cornelia Day a heads up. She'll alert the President and VP and get Hamlin on the guest list. Leak it to the press—they'll like a story about that. Do *not* reveal her true role."

"Of course not," Baxter shot back. She could hear the *Duh!* that Baxter didn't give voice to. She was starting to see the tight relationship between these two men. Their brotherly snarls back and forth would never be shown in public. But that they showed it in front of her made her wonder just *what* she'd suddenly stepped in the middle of.

Then she focused on what they'd just said. A special guest of the First Family? But she'd never met any of them.

"By the way, Hamlin," Lieber practically sneered at her. "Reception is tomorrow night. Can't wear your uniform if you're going undercover. You'd better go out and buy a dress."

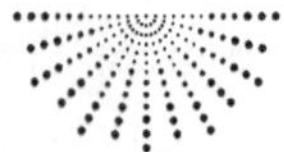

By late afternoon, Linda was out of options. She could have slipped into the subbasement to ask Miss Watson, but she didn't want to risk intruding on Clive, even if his chocolate shop was two stories above her hidden office. That was too close and she just couldn't deal with it today.

There were no female agents on shift for her to ask, not that she really could now that she was spying on them.

In desperation, she finally had the White House operator track down Dilya for her. Unable to offer any explanations, she'd simply told the girl that she needed help buying a dress.

"Five minutes at the North Portico," Dilya sounded thrilled.

"Too soon. I have to take Thor back to the kennel at the Secret Service building first. Then I can—"

"No. No. No. You've gotta bring Thor, trust me. Make sure he wears his K-9 harness and stuff."

"And I suppose I should—" but the line had gone dead. Since she didn't have another jacket, and it was still cold out, she shrugged on her USSS one. Not exactly subtle, with the six-inch letters across the back, but there wasn't anything she could do about that. She considered leaving her weapons behind, but that felt wrong as well.

Dilya was there ahead of her.

"I can't take Thor into a department store."

"Sure you can. Service dog and like that." Dilya led the way down the driveway and toward the security gate.

"Maybe I should get dark glasses and a white cane too."

"If it makes you feel better. What kind of a dress?" She waved at the guards, who grinned back at her.

Linda blinked. Her thinking hadn't gone that far. Her last dress had been when she was fourteen for her mom's swearing-in ceremony as a state representative. She often wondered why such intelligent people as Vermonters kept reelecting her mother, but such things were beyond her.

"Um, a dressy dress?"

Dilya rolled her eyes.

"A dress I can afford."

"For a hot date with Chef Andrews?"

Linda's guard was down and the gut shot punched straight in.

"No," she somehow managed. Where was a medevac bird when she needed one? "Not for that," Linda struggled to hide her feelings.

"I like Chef Andrews," Dilya sounded defensive. So much for pretending it didn't hurt.

"I like him, too. It's not like I'm cheating on him." Not like that statement would ever have meaning anyway because she'd blown that all to hell just last night.

"Then what's the dress for?" Dilya had stopped in the middle of the closed stretch of Pennsylvania Avenue as if she was considering turning around and going back into the White House.

"I have to go to the reception and dinner tomorrow night in the Residence. I have to blend in."

"Ooo! Like undercover?"

"So much for keeping *that* a secret." This kid was going to be the death of her.

"Excellent! It's so cool. An agent gone undercover at a Residence reception."

Then a brief look crossed Dilya's face. Dark. Dangerous. This pretty young teen suddenly emanated a barely-contained fury. As she heard her own words, she looked ready to take on the fight herself. She glanced up at Linda.

"Are you good at what you do?"

Linda flashed an image of how thoroughly she'd eviscerated Clive, then did her best to set that aside. *Too good.* She could only nod.

"*Really* good? Protect-the-White-House kind of good?"

Linda considered how to answer that. "I guess I'd better be."

Dilya studied her a moment longer, then nodded sharply.

"Okay then." Her expression flipped back to being the pretty teen rather than the young woman ready to go to war. No. She remembered Clive's whispered comment, 'war orphan.' Dilya was ready to go *back* to war. "I've gotta get a nice dress too."

Linda wondered at the dual personality she'd just witnessed: Dilya's public persona and the fierce child-warrior beneath.

"Don't look at me like that," Dilya's expression saddened.

"Like what?"

"Like I'm an alien. I never killed anyone. I would have, but my new mom took care of that for me so I didn't have to." And she stated it like simple fact.

"Didn't have to?"

"Two men shot my real parents point-blank because we walked into the wrong place at the wrong time. Them I could have killed." There was no hint of doubt in her voice. "It made her sad, and I get why now. Back then I was too young to understand the price. Still I would have done it—they deserved to die."

A tone that Linda instantly recognized as having come from her own mouth just this morning. *No such thing as love.* If she was so sure, then why did it hurt so much?

"Okay," Linda managed a breath, then remembering a long ago promise badly broken, she decided it was time to try trusting again. She held out a pinkie. "I hereby solemnly swear to never look at you funny again—provided you promise the same. No matter how ridiculous either of us is being. And you promise never to make fun of my dog either."

Dilya hesitated only a moment before hooking her pinky with Linda's and nodding with all the solemnity of a Supreme Court Justice.

"Maybe we should get matching dresses," Dilya firmly declared the topic closed after shaking their joined pinkies up and down three times.

"That wouldn't be very undercover, would it?" Linda did what she could to match the girl's easy tone. "Besides, I don't think we wear quite the same styles." Today Dilya was wearing distressed green jeans that clung tightly to her thin legs, massive black snow boots with all the buckles undone and tinking together with each step like muted sleigh bells, and a heavy red hoodie that asked *Is it too late to be good?* She looked like a dark-haired elf needing only a Santa hat. "You do know that Christmas was *last* month?"

"Duh!"

Right. Because it was a satiric statement about teens never getting their act together. By a teen who apparently had her act *totally* together. Linda knew that was a gift she'd never possessed herself.

"Classy but affordable," Dilya confirmed and led the way.

They walked in silence back along G Street.

"Elegant but will make men's tongues hang out," Dilya said suddenly.

"Dilya!" How old was this girl?

"What my mom—Kee, my adoptive mom, but she cried the first time I called her Mom and she never cries, so I always give that to her —would call boardroom-street-walker clothes."

"Dilya!" This fifteen-year-old was absolutely not fifteen, except perhaps in her sense of humor. Fine. "Get a grip, kid. What on earth makes you think I could pass as either one, even if I wanted to?"

Dilya stopped right in the middle of the sidewalk and they were nearly plowed under by the hurrying locals. "Hold your hair back in a ponytail and unzip your jacket to here," Dilya pointed to just between Linda's breasts.

She handed Dilya Thor's leash and did as she was ordered, while the girl inspected her critically.

Then Dilya turned to a department store window. Linda hadn't even realized there were department stores here though she'd walked this route every day—except last night of course when she'd been coming from Clive's apartment.

A mannequin in the window wore a fire-engine red sheath dress that clung so tightly that she could see the seam joints in the mannequin itself. It ended about half an inch below the mannequin's crotch. She wore matching red vinyl boots that almost reached the hem, but not quite.

"Not no, but hell no, Dilya."

"Weird," Dilya continued her inspection between Linda and the dummy.

"What?"

"You're right."

"Adults aren't supposed to ever be right?" Linda remembered that clearly from her childhood, but that was because they never were— which didn't bode well at the moment.

"Never, especially not about themselves. Mom acts like she's still working deals on the streets of East LA even when she's busy winning FBI sniper competitions. But you're right. You're super pretty, but you look too nice to be anything bad."

Oh Sweet Christ! The kid was gonna kill her. "Too nice" didn't describe anything that she was or had done since she was younger than Dilya.

"I did say *look* too nice," her smile had a distinctly diabolical twist to it, stating that she'd easily read Linda's expression.

"Dilya, if this is going to work, you're going to have to promise me two things."

"What?"

"One, stop reading my mind."

"No promises."

"Two, don't you dare abandon me in a dress store."

Dilya laughed. "Okay. That part's cool."

They worked their way down the street analyzing the window

displays together—each one a different statement: business, sexy, dressy, clubby, and something Dilya called athleisure (designed to make the rich look as if they were also sporty and might actually be willing to get their fingers dirty—if it was for the right activity and didn't muss their hair). When they reached the main entrance, Linda knew one thing for certain: she was even more out of her depth than she'd thought.

CLIVE SCRAPED his third batch of batter into the garbage just as Chef Klaus came over to him. The chocolate kitchen had warmers to melt chocolate, but for baking he had to cross over to the main kitchen.

"What was wrong with that one?"

Not trusting himself to speak in his frustration, Clive handed the chef both a large and a small Pocky stick from his latest test bake.

Klaus took his time inspecting each element. "The shape is good— even and nicely round. You have the color right." He bent each one. Both made a crisp *snap* as he did so. "Good bake."

Then he bit on the small one and grimaced. He picked up the larger one and eyed Clive.

Clive just shook his head. Yes, it was worse. The batter had been fine yesterday. He had no idea what he was doing wrong.

Chef Klaus dropped the sticks on the pile of goo in the garbage can.

"When I become stuck, what I do is go and have a walk."

Clive didn't have time to walk it off. The entire day had been wasted and he—

"Go! *Gehst du hier raus! Spazieren gehen!* Go away! Walk until whatever mess is in your head is cleared out. *Das problem, es ist nicht im* recipe. *Es ist in dem* chef." Then Klaus turned on his heel and walked away.

Clive cleared up his space and hung up his apron. The kitchen was already gearing up for tomorrow night's dinner—a half-dozen chefs scrambling through all of the prep work that could possibly be done in advance. He should be done with the sticks and moving on to the dessert soup. He should have been there hours ago.

Instead, he stepped out of the kitchen and stood in the Basement Hall that connected the kitchen, his shop, flowers, carpentry, and the one-lane bowling alley that ran outward beneath the center of the North Portico's steps.

He couldn't go outside. He might run into Linda walking the fence line with Thor. He absolutely wasn't ready to face that. He didn't know if he'd ever be ready again. His pain and disbelief had turned to the stage of anger and it didn't feel like bargaining was going to happen any time soon. The grief counselor for his mother's death had merely been irritating—anyone tried that on him right now and they might find themselves baked into a cake with four-and-twenty lethal piercings by massive pieces of sugar work.

Walk. Chef Klaus had said to walk and he didn't want to be caught in the back hall ignoring the chef's command. So he walked. When he reached a junction, he turned; when he reached stairs, he descended. When he reached others, he ascended.

All the same to him.

He wasn't going anywhere.

He and Linda weren't— They *definitely* weren't going anywhere. The woman had such a twisted up, demented view of the world that he couldn't imagine what he'd seen in her in the first place.

Sure, she was beautiful. Their bodies had a connection that he'd thought was undeniable. And she had an inner drive that was amazing to witness. So many of the women he met only had an inner drive to power. Linda's was externally focused. She caught bad guys for a living. She—

Why in all creation was he thinking of her? Done. Gone. And the anger inside him flared back to life. The only thing he could equate it to was his father. Clive had hated having a father who showed up for a week every few months and expected no more than his meals and his beer. He gave back even less before departing again—leaving his wife sadder each time. Nic Andrews had sent home his paychecks. He'd only been cruel through emotional negligence, not intention.

Okay, maybe not like Linda.

She'd slashed at him out of—

Clive stumbled to a halt and looked through the doorway in front of him. Miss Watson sat at her dingy desk, her small lamp illuminating only her knitting except for some reflection which lit up her blue eyes. She peered at him in curiosity.

She didn't speak.

At a loss for what else to do, Clive stepped in and sat down on the teetering stool and looked about the tiny, dim office.

"What's with all the books?"

"I'm a librarian."

"A basement librarian?"

She might have smiled. She might not.

"Maybe you're an alien librarian. Is there a tunnel here under the White House that leads to Area 51?"

"That's a long way off," she kept knitting without looking down. He could do that sometimes, when it was a simple pattern and thick yarn. She was doing it on a Fair Isle design, flipping the two yarn colors back and forth with perfect surety.

"Maybe you have a time-space warp under your desk." He wouldn't put it past her. It might explain a few things. "Like in *Star Trek*, you know."

"Yes, I know *Star Trek*."

Clive waited for a while, idly looking at the book titles. Then his eyes traveled up to the only other light in the room. It splashed on the faded and ill-made scarf framed high on the wall.

"It's Belgian," Miss Watson explained without prompting.

"Not a very good job of it."

"It depends on what job you are expecting it to perform."

If there was a double-meaning there somewhere, he couldn't pick it out. "What job *did* it perform? Certainly not keeping out the cold."

"Each five-stitch pairs are five train lines leading into Antwerp that were in view from a particular porch. Two purls were a passenger train, two knits a cargo train, a knit and purl equaled no train. Each group represents ten minutes, each row an hour. The scarf is a chronicle a week long."

"And the dropped stitches?" Clive stood to inspect it more closely.

"Those are the interesting ones. Those are when there was supposed to be a train, but there wasn't."

"Maybe it was running late."

"Actually, it was because the Nazis had replaced it with a war train. You are looking at a coded message of Nazi troop movements in and out of Antwerp prior to the Battle of the Scheldt to wrest it from Nazi occupation in September and October 1944."

Clive could only blink at it in surprise. "Messages in wool."

"Messages in wool," Miss Watson concurred as she continued knitting.

"Anything I should know about those socks you're working on?"

"Yes," then she smiled softly for the first time since he'd met her. It made her seem almost human. "My feet get very cold in January."

The laugh came out of him, breaking so hard in his throat that it hurt. Again and again until he wasn't sure if he was laughing or crying. He clapped a hand over his mouth to stop it before the tiny room was filled with the hysterical sound.

And he could feel the outline of Linda's fine fingers over his mouth on that first visit to his chocolate shop. Her entire face softening as his chocolate made her "have a moment."

That was the woman he had fallen for. But he couldn't reconcile her with the one who had declared there was no such thing as love. If she'd done it in anger, rage, or sorrow, he could have understood. But her voice had been so cold and emotionless that it was impossible to disbelieve her—cold, hard fact. At least for her.

"I'm so sorry, Clive."

Unable to speak, he kept his hand in place over his mouth despite the disconcerting double image of Linda's hand resting there as well.

Miss Watson had put down her knitting and leaned forward into the light so that he could see her face clearly, as if for the first time. She had been, still was, a beautiful woman and the sympathy in her eyes ran deep.

"I should have seen it when I sat with her last night in Lincoln Square. I must be getting old to have missed it. When I teased her about your early arrival at the White House, she didn't react at all. But I missed how cold she went."

He brushed at his eyes before dropping his hand. "She's good at that."

"She'll find her way through it."

He could only shake his head. "No. You didn't see her. You didn't hear what she said." And again his throat tightened too much to allow further speech.

The silence stretched as he fought against the tears—a battle he finally won sometime after Miss Watson's knitting needles began their rhythmic ticking sounds once more.

"I was in love once."

That made him blink in surprise. It was not a possibility he'd ever considered.

"He was a wondrous man and I used our love to betray him for my country. It was the hardest thing I've ever done."

Then she stopped knitting once more and looked at him with those piercing blue eyes. Any hint of softness was gone. Instead, the scary old lady was back and he didn't dare move. He even held his breath.

"It is your job not to give up on her."

"But she—" he could only wave his hand helplessly in the direction of his apartment.

"No!" Miss Watson's voice shifted from dangerous to fierce. "Had I looked deeper, maybe I could have saved him. Had I asked, perhaps he would have come with me. But now I will never know. You must not make that mistake."

"I *did* ask."

"Good! You must not stop doing that."

Clive opened his mouth and closed it again. He didn't know if he dared. Didn't know if he could take the brutal rejection again.

He looked again at the scarf. Not what it appeared to be.

The guns on the walls that barely looked like guns and probably wouldn't at all if taken apart. The crazy collection of books. Not for reading, but for some other, unknowable purpose. And the woman knitting in the Residence subbasement who was scary, kind, and deeply sad.

None of it what he would expect. None of it quite what it appeared.

He thought of the three Lindas.

The one who gave herself so completely to him...and to her dog. Who hadn't hesitated to help Dilya train Zackie. She gave so easily.

Then there was the intense soldier he'd first witnessed doing her mission at the James J. Rowley Training Center and again in Lafayette Square. Focused, competent...lethal.

And finally the one that he'd only seen once. Getting dressed in front of him as casually as if she was in a locker room. Cold, heartless, frozen to the core. That was the Linda that still made no sense to him. Unless that version wasn't what it appeared to be.

The soldier and the sharing woman were undeniable. The heartless automaton—she was the version of Linda who he couldn't reconcile.

But how to reach past that persona that he'd wager she still wore like armor at this very moment? He knew, he just *knew* that there had to be a way. He couldn't believe that he could fall in love with Linda if her inner essence wasn't the giving woman rather than the automaton.

"She's from Vermont, isn't she?"

"Yes."

He barely heard Miss Watson's reply.

"Vermont," he turned the word over in his mind. Ben and Jerry's Ice Cream. Unlikely flavor combinations. Dairy products, maple syrup, apples, honey.

"She will be attending tomorrow night's reception as a guest," Miss Watson volunteered.

"Really?" Linda at the White House reception in the President's private quarters.

What if he rethought the biscuit dough in his Pocky sticks? It could—

The concept slammed into him as hard as one of Linda's kisses.

"Excuse me."

If Miss Watson responded as he hurried out, he didn't hear it.

<hr>

"You're tricky."

Linda stared down at the pile of dresses on the bench. As Dilya's taste ran to more covered than revealing, any of them would have been fine with her. Besides, most of her issues about showing skin had died during a decade in the Army. She was fine as long as they didn't go boardroom-street-walker—or whatever athleisure was—but Dilya was clearly operating to some different standard.

"No, that bright red doesn't bring out your eyes. Makes you look kinda demonic."

Demonic fit her current mood well enough at the moment. Besides…mouse-brown, what color was there to bring out?

"OMG, that makes your hips look as wide as the Hindu Kush."

Linda had patrolled in Afghanistan's Hindu Kush Mountains and lived to tell the tale—it was the ruggedest and one of the deadliest areas in the entire war zone. She could do without the memory—as apparently Dilya also could. That got rid of the whole peplum theme, which was fine with her. The ruffled flair at the waist made her feel like a circus clown.

"Nope. Nope. Nope."

"Why not? I thought black dresses were a good thing." Linda looked at her reflection wearing the clinging jersey material. It looked good on her. She'd never worn sexy clothes before, but the startling woman in the mirror wore it well. It clung and curved in ways that… She sighed. That she'd have liked Clive to have seen back before she'd destroyed something so good. Why couldn't he have just left things the way they were?

Dilya placed her fists on her hips. "Okay, Miss Undercover Smarty

Pants. Sure, it looks majorly awesome on you. Now, where do you put your weapons?"

Linda again turned to the mirror. The cleavage was deep enough to just show where Clive's kiss had healed the wound of her missing dog tags—which now felt like a new scar all its own. But the cleavage was also just deep enough that there was no room to tuck even a Glock Slimline out of sight.

The material flowed over her hips and down to a tasteful overlap that ended mid-thigh. It left her legs bare and the male shop clerk working near the changing rooms seemed to think they were worth a second and a third look.

However, it clung enough that there wasn't anywhere to hide a knife, much less a handgun in a thigh holster or the bulk of a taser. And her draw time from under a dress would be prohibitive.

"What about a jacket of some sort? Then I could wear my usual shoulder holster."

Dilya poked around through the racks and came back with something called a bolero.

"These are so weirdly old-fashioned. I don't know why they make them anymore. It's not like you're a Spanish flamenco dancer or something."

It was the color of the Vermont leaves in autumn, all dark reds and rich golds. Frankly it looked too fancy for her, but Linda shrugged it on anyway, then gasped when she spotted the price tag dangling from the sleeve.

"Hmm," Dilya looked half-pleased, which would be a first in all this madness and which dropped the price from outrageous to incredibly painful. Not that her clothing budget was anything dramatic, but she was presently wearing more than a year's worth of it.

Linda turned to the mirror.

A sexy and sophisticated woman looked back at her. Her mother would approve, which, under the circumstances, Linda supposed was a good thing. The jacket reached down to just below her ribs, emphasizing her reflection's trim waist. It came close enough to closing in the front that she didn't feel quite so revealed, yet stood open enough that it wouldn't inhibit her drawing a weapon. The half-sleeves let the long sleeves of the black dress emphasize her arms.

She shed it, pulled on her shoulder holster, and tugged the jacket back on. A Glock 42 slimline .380 and a lightweight holster would be a better option, but even her big FN Five-seveN was acceptable. Her folding knife and two spare magazines clipped on the other side didn't show at all.

"Not too shabby."

She answered Dilya's "high" praise with an eyeroll that earned her a laugh. If it got her done and out of this store, Linda would find a way to live with the horrific price tag.

She squatted and stood. Twisted side to side testing freedom of movement. She did a quick draw of her weapon, dropping into a crouch with both arms extended and holding the firearm.

And then looked up at the startled faces of three women who had just stepped into the dressing area, their hands full of items on hangars. One of them screamed and sent clothes flying everywhere, which had the clerk rushing over.

"Sorry," Linda reholstered her weapon.

Only Thor's presence with his clearly labeled "Police K-9" harness finally calmed them down. Then they all had to pet and coo over him.

"Can we get out of here?" Linda whispered to Dilya because she didn't know how much more high, squeaky "Oh he's so cute" she could take though Thor was clearly thrilled with the attention.

"Sure. Just as soon as we get a purse you can hide the taser in, then shoes, then deal with your hair."

"You're kidding me, right?" She'd never owned a purse in her life. "No purse. I'll sign out a compact taser and mount it on the harness. I want my hands free."

Dilya's groan of exasperation said that she'd accept that—barely.

"Maybe shoes, maybe." Since all she owned were work boots and running shoes. "But nothing with heels."

Dilya's evil elf smile was back.

Crap!

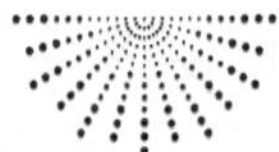

Olive was set up for the reception on the Residence's Second Floor in the family kitchen and dining room. Waiters hustled in and out bearing trays of champagne and canapes: bruschetta with smoked salmon and basil, shrimp stuffed with prosciutto and Stilton cheese, and his little chocolate bouquets.

Each bouquet was made up of five slender Pocky sticks thinner than a pencil and half as long. Three shades of chocolate: dark, milk, and white. Then to complement the white, he'd started with a white chocolate base to make two more: blueberry blue and also apple red. He'd made two separate biscuit doughs: a plain one beneath the first four, plus a maple syrup-honey-flavored core for the fifth red stick. All tied so that they stood together like a thistle bloom, using tiny golden ribbons bearing the Vermont state motto: Freedom and Unity.

Chocolate and the American flag—in the flavors and spirit of Vermont.

The guests would all interpret it one way, but he was hoping one person might interpret it another.

He'd worked straight through last night and all day to get these right. For the banquet dessert, he still had the original design: a larger Pocky of plain biscuit and the Vietnamese and Philippine chocolates to complement the soup as well as harkening back to these. But the Pocky bouquet wasn't for the diplomats. The bouquets were designed for one person alone, and never had he worked so hard or felt so inspired to achieve it.

Jacques Torres had always spoken of the dessert of the heart.

Clive had assumed he'd been talking about creating with passion and a desire to discover something new. But now he understood. This treat was so simple and delicate in one way, but in another he had never created anything so perfect. If ever there was to be a single dessert of his heart, this was the one.

He just hoped to god that it worked.

***

LINDA HAMLIN just hoped to god that she didn't faint.

Unwilling to risk the Secret Service Ready Room close beside the downstairs kitchen, she'd changed into her dress over in the West Wing. Even threats of being tasered hadn't wiped the smiles off any of the agent's faces as she'd stowed her work clothes under a desk in the ready room there.

Captain Baxter waved her into his office as he hung up his phone. He, at least, wasn't leering. Instead he looked grim.

"We just took down a car loaded with weapons. A real mash-up of conventional shit: handguns, shotguns. No sense to it. Not like someone's collection."

"Where?" Linda felt a shiver run up her spine.

"Abandoned on Embassy Row. The guys who dumped it knew where the cameras were well enough to hide their faces."

"Japan's people?"

"Or any of fifty others in that strip. Not quite in anyone's front yard. Your guess is as good as mine. Car rented by a drug runner... who then reported it carjacked."

"What makes you think it was related to us, then?"

"The drug runner was from East LA, never been here before. He received instructions, a plane ticket, and ten grand cash in an unmarked envelope. Did nothing illegal, but I'm holding him for forty-eight hours for 'protection'. He was jacked by, and I'm quoting, 'a couple of Asian dudes with some serious shit.' Chinese Type 77 handguns. He'd never seen them before, but picked them out of a book fast enough. Said having one nearly shoved up his nose had made it real memorable."

"That's a very distinctive weapon, right down to the Chinese star on the handgrip."

"That's what I was thinking. *Too* distinctive. You were right, someone is definitely messing with us tonight. We've got the grounds locked down hard, but you're inside. Keep your eyes open tonight, Hamlin."

Walking across to the Residence had been a major challenge. She'd only partially won the shoe battle with Dilya. She wasn't wearing spikes, but the black ankle boots had a wide two-inch heel that she still didn't have a feel for though she'd practiced with them in her apartment last night. She got lots of practice because it wasn't like she was having any luck sleeping.

Every time she'd lain down, her bed felt cold and empty. And while she lay there studying the ceiling, she'd only been able to remember Clive lying in that Barcalounger like the remains of some innocent, caught in the unexpected blast of an IED. She'd dozed a little. Not enough to dream, but enough for her mind to free associate in a new and hideous fashion. It was as if they had traded places and she was the one lying there with her chest cut open and someone inspecting the empty cavity where her heart should have been.

She'd even tried pulling on her dog tags as she wandered around the tiny apartment—in her new boots—because she couldn't stand being in the bed anymore. All they did was remind her of Clive's kiss that he always had made a point of planting there. She took them off and ended up watching an *I Love Lucy* marathon until it was time to go prepare for the reception.

Linda had spent the entire day at her desk studying the profiles of every guest invited to the reception until she could recite their schooling, family, and career.

And now she was here and couldn't remember how to breathe.

Zackie greeted Thor at the head of the Grand Staircase. Dilya looked elegant, if a little loud, in a bias-cut gold lamé top with a draped collar matched to black slacks. She wore a pretty scarf of green and dark blue, almost big enough to be a shawl.

"I always wear it when I want to be fancy."

"How come I'm stuck in these stupid heels and you get to wear red Converse sneakers?"

"Some of us just have better fashion sense than others." Dilya's smile flashed brilliantly before she and Zackie moved away.

Linda surveyed the layout from the staircase landing at one end of the party. The Center Hall stretched twenty feet wide and over a hundred long including the West Sitting Room through the broad archway beyond. Done in warm beiges and dark wood, it was an attractive space for a party. She almost laughed, a room that would absolutely kill her mother to know that her daughter was invited to. High time that Linda left her grudge behind.

She surveyed the crowd. A pianist played light music at a grand piano tucked close against one wall. There were eight potted palms spaced evenly down the length of the hall with a roughly equal number of Secret Service agents. Small clusters of chairs, some occupied, some not—most people stood. There should be fifty-three guests in all including the three prime ministers and their entourages, scattered in loose groups. Most held wine glasses. A few, she was pleased to see, weren't dressed any fancier than she was. Though she was definitely in the lower-tier amidst so many fine tuxedos and stunning evening gowns, but that didn't matter to her. She was a Secret Service officer here as a guest. As long as she didn't stand out, Dilya had done her job well.

Back at the store, the girl had been oddly shy about Linda's thanks, but accepted the offer of an ice cream sundae readily enough despite the January chill.

Much to her surprise, Linda had some money left over despite the hair and shoes. It was a low trick to play on an unsuspecting dog, but Dilya had leveraged Thor's fame with the store clerk and negotiated such a discount on the dress and jacket that Linda had felt it necessary to tip him generously when Dilya wasn't watching. Or when she thought Dilya hadn't been—the way she'd played with Thor afterward said that the girl had been crafty and calculated the entire deal. A child raised in a barter-based society clearly enjoyed outsmarting a retail-based one. And she'd seen it far enough ahead to tell Linda that she had to bring Thor to go dress shopping.

As she stepped into the hall, Linda almost lost her balance when her heel caught the edge of the carpet.

Thor glanced up at her.

"Watch it or I'll put you in heels and see how you do."

Thor looked unperturbed.

Linda began matching up faces and names. The First and Second Couples were easy. Former President Matthews was also in attendance—his wife's plane had been delayed and she wouldn't be here until tomorrow's meetings. She had no official capacity, but had close relations with all three guest countries through her UNESCO work.

The leaders of the three guest countries were chatting with their American counterparts. There hadn't been anything damning in any of their files.

She spotted Harvey Lieber standing in a shadow along one of the walls, but close by the President. He afforded her a brief nod before turning back to study the room. The President shifted down the hall to join another conversation and Lieber followed. A massive black man did the same for former President Matthews.

Speaker of the House. Majority and minority whips of the Senate. Secretary of Defense Archie Stevenson—a tall and spare man with light brown hair—was having a heated debate with Secretary of State Mallinson. Despite Archie's attempts to remain calm, Mallinson was waving his hands about in such a way that a nearby Secret Service agent shuffled farther along the wall to avoid being impaled.

Not a hard choice on who to root for—Secretary Stevenson was Dilya's adoptive father, which was recommendation enough for

Linda. Not wanting to enter Mallinson's sphere of intolerable officiousness, she decided to circle the other way.

Thor had already proven that he didn't need to be "on task" to find explosives—three days ago they'd just been walking to work when he'd detected the diplomat—she simply let him choose her way into the room but kept his leash short. She had tried to groom him for the event. However, his crazy tangle of fur that seemed to grow in every direction, but mostly straight out, looked much the same before and after brushing. She hoped her own hair wasn't too much the same.

Thor drifted over to Agent Lieber, sniffed, then wagged up at him in greeting.

"Go away, you." Linda couldn't tell if he was addressing Thor or herself. "Do your damn job." Okay, that one she got, and signaled Thor to keep moving. They moved slowly up the south side of the hall until they reached the grand double-arched window that seemed to be in every movie ever made about the White House. That she was suddenly standing in the real-life version of the movie set made her wish once again that she was just out walking the fence line and had never heard of Miss Watson or the White House Protection Force.

Taking a deep breath for fortitude, which didn't provide any help at all, she crossed to the north side and began working her way back along the hall.

She made it about twenty feet before she plowed squarely into Clive's back.

CLIVE HAD JUST WANTED to take a peek into the West Sitting Hall to see how his part of the appetizer was faring. None were coming back on the serving trays, which he took as a good sign, but neither was much of anything else. He wanted to know if his were being eaten first or last of the selection.

At least that's what he told himself he was doing. He'd just step out, take a quick look, and then duck back into the dining room to continue the service.

He wouldn't be searching up the hall to see if there was a flounce of shining cocoa hair anywhere among the crowd. He wasn't going to stoop that low.

Clive stepped into the hall and someone slammed into his back.

He tried to take a stumbling step forward, but a small dog—Thor—had circled around from behind him and stood with his forepaws practically on Clive's shoes, happily wagging his tail. Unable to step forward, and overbalanced from behind, he went down like a drunkard on a storm-tossed sea. No handy furniture near enough to catch himself with, he crashed down on the rug. His tall chef's hat tumbled away. Thor immediately raced over and stuck his head inside it.

Well, at least Clive knew who had hit him.

As did everyone else in the entire hall—they were all looking in his direction. As payback for bowling her into the men's lavatory in the West Wing in front of her boss, this struck him as somewhat over the top.

Thor tried to lift his head, but in the process, the chef's hat slid down to his neck. He began shaking his head trying to free himself as the crowd began laughing.

He lay there for a moment, focused on just how amazing two-inch heels made Linda's legs look. The muscles in her calves were accentuated wonderfully, especially as he knew exactly how they felt when wrapped around— The past. Again!

She helped him back to his feet with a strength that was now very familiar. Except it was attached to a woman he barely recognized. Once he was stable, she moved forward and plucked his hat off Thor's head and handed it back to him.

At the crowd's applause, Thor wagged his tail.

The only thing that Clive could think to do was bow and then retreat back into the dining room. He was not, however, so addled that he failed to drag Linda along with him.

"I'm so sorry. Are you okay?"

He looked down at her and couldn't speak.

Linda Hamlin in a dress. He'd never thought to imagine such a thing. The black dress clung to her and told him just how lucky he was…had been…to have a lover with a body like that. The jacket accentuated the color of her hair and brought out a slightest hint of deep red in the brown that he'd never noticed before. Her casually ragged cut had been transformed to accentuate all of her features and Linda was a woman with many, many fine features: bright eyes, wide mouth, pert nose…

"You changed your hair." Which was perhaps the dumbest phrase ever uttered by man.

"And I'm wearing a dress," her voice laced with deep chagrin and just a bit of the humor that he'd forgotten how much he missed.

"I noticed. My god, Linda. I can't begin to tell you…" *how much I've missed you* "…how incredible you look."

She grimaced, then scowled at somewhere near the center of his chest.

Just as she opened her mouth, the head of the PPD strode into the dining room.

"Hamlin. We aren't paying you to chat up the chefs. Now get a move on."

And without another word, he strode back out.

"What was…"

"Senior Special Agent Harvey Lieber hates me," Linda patted his arm. "But he's right. The trouble in Lafayette Square isn't over. I think it's hitting the fan tonight. Here at the reception if I'm right."

"Have you…" No, of course, she hadn't tasted one of his appetizers. She was in her focused-soldier mode. He swiveled to a passing tray and snatched a salmon bruschetta and handed it to Thor, who scarfed it down in a single bite. That delayed Linda just long enough for him to place a Pocky stick bouquet in her hand. "Try this. Please."

Then, though it nearly killed him to do so, he turned her around and pushed lightly against her shoulders to send her back into danger. Because that was a part of who she was and it wasn't up to him to keep her close and safe—no matter how much he wanted to.

Courtesy of her stupid heels, Linda practically did a Clive-style pratfall at his light push. It was either that or her weak knees. Whichever it was, she managed to keep on her feet by only the narrowest of margins. Even standing before him for just those few moments had stirred up things she didn't understand until she was nearly swept under by vertigo.

But few heads turned as she stumbled out into the long hall once more.

East. She'd been moving east along the north side of the hall when she'd run into Clive.

So she continued east and let Thor lead the way. She was a professional and could guide him, but she didn't feel up to leading at the moment. Only as she passed a small group of senators talking with Vice President Daniel Darlington did she remember to look at what Clive had given her. A tiny bouquet of multi-colored Pocky sticks in the colors of chocolate and the American flag wrapped in the golden ribbon bearing the Vermont state motto: "Freedom and Unity."

She nibbled on one while she focused on getting her mind out of the kitchen and back into the hall. The chocolate was so good, even sublime compared to the samples he'd given her a lifetime ago in his chocolate shop.

A senior aide, who she couldn't place at the moment—the head speechwriter?—stopped her to thank her and Thor for the fine work in Lafayette Square.

The blueberry one took her back to her childhood in Vermont—back before she'd understood that her family was a nightmare. There'd been a big blueberry bush in the backyard—might even still be there—and she remembered every summer, standing out in the sunshine, picking and filling her mouth as fast as she could. The little blue Pocky burst with the flavor of nostalgia so richly that she wondered if the speechwriter thought that it was his thanks that prompted her misty eyes.

She was halfway back to her original starting point when she ate the final red one. It wasn't strawberry as she'd expected. Instead it was an explosion of Macintosh apple. Vermont in the fall slammed into her senses. Then she crunched down on the biscuit center and the flavor of maple syrup washed over her like the cusp of winter-to-spring when the maple tree sap was flowing but there was still snow on the ground.

Clive had made a treat of the seasons of Vermont.

She looked around and saw that they were the first items being swept off the trays that the waiters were carrying guest-to-guest. It seemed that everyone was holding the little golden ribbons. He'd made a treat for the reception that was the clear favorite.

That wasn't right. Yes, it was a clear favorite, but how many people would understand that it was the seasons of Vermont? And Clive had said he was from San Francisco and had worked in LA, New York, Virginia… He'd never once mentioned Vermont.

She'd said nothing beyond the fact that she'd grown up there.

From that single clue, Clive had developed this magnificent treat for her alone. She had said such awful, unforgivable things to him, and he had given her back the best parts of her childhood. He'd fed a treat to the elite of Washington, DC, that was designed just for her.

"Are you okay?"

She could only shake her head and she focused on the man who had come up to her. Tall, lean, a tousle of light brown hair—Secretary of Defense Archibald Stevenson III and former major of the 160th Night Stalkers.

"You're Dilya's father."

That earned her a surprisingly cheery, lopsided smile. "You've met her?"

"She helped me buy this dress. Jacket. Shoes." Could she sound any more like a driveling idiot? "Told the salon how to do my hair." Yes, apparently she could. Because her hair was *exactly* the sort of thing that the Secretary of Defense would care about.

"Allow me to say that she did a damn nice job. And that would make you Sergeant Hamlin and Thor. I was briefed on the work you did. Thank you for that."

She considered alerting him that it wasn't over yet, but the head of the Presidential Protection Detail had deemed it need-to-know only, so she kept her mouth shut.

"What happened to your friend?" Not her smoothest subject change.

"Friend?"

"You were, uh," she'd dug the hole and couldn't figure a way out of it. Fine. Might as well dig it deeper. "What did you do with Secretary of State Mallinson's body?"

"Excuse me?" He didn't sound offended, merely surprised.

"You weren't exactly seeing eye-to-eye earlier. You're the man left standing, so I figure you won or you did him in. Should I start checking behind the potted palms?"

His smile was more of a grimace.

"He has always been stubborn man, but tonight he was being stupid to the point of irrationality. It was as if none of his thoughts were connecting. Made me positively twitchy."

"I'll definitely start checking behind the palms."

"Don't bother. He just left. Said he had a meeting to get to."

"Oh, well. It was a pleasure to meet you, sir." The prime minister of Vietnam came their way and she decided it was best if she bowed out.

She checked her watch—the pretty feminine one that Dilya had insisted that she buy to replace her favorite Luminox Blackout military one. At least she'd been able to read that one. She squinted for fashion. Never again.

Twenty-six more minutes to the reception. Then down to the East Room for the dinner. She had been so sure that whatever was planned was going to happen at this reception, but nothing looked out of place.

THEY WERE NEARING the end of service for the reception. Clive was arranging the last of his Pocky treats. Next up would be to race down the narrow spiral stairs that connected the kitchens: the Second Floor kitchen, the pantry close by the State Dining Room, the main kitchen on the Ground Floor, subbasement storage, and finally the second subbasement dishwashing room. The sous chefs should have the white chocolate-pomegranate *baba ghanoush* of the first course ready, but he wanted to check each plate himself while the diners were finding their seats.

Seeing Linda had given him such hope. Miss Watson had been right. He shouldn't give up, no matter what. One look at her and he'd known. Okay, two. The first look had been him trying to comprehend what a stunningly gorgeous woman it had been his good fortune to find. But with the second look he'd seen the pain clear in her eyes. He *knew* for an absolute fact—as surely as dark chocolate and strawberries were a perfect match—that the real woman inside Linda-the-soldier was the one with the giving heart, not the automaton.

He wanted to see her again, right now.

But, she'd said there was danger here at the reception and that meant she was working. Special Agent Harvey Lieber's furious reminder must mean that the danger was imminent and somehow Linda and Thor were the key to finding it.

Hadn't Miss Watson said something about Linda being added to the guest list?

To the *guest* list. Not the *agent* list.

That meant that she wasn't here as an agent, yet the head of the Presidential Protection Detail had made it clear that she was. And if she'd merely been a guest, she probably wouldn't have brought Thor.

Linda with Thor.

That's what was going on out there while he was in here making chocolate doodads. He looked down at the last tray of Pocky stick bouquets and felt more useless than ever before in his life. More useless than a young boy unable to attract his father's attention. More useless than holding his mother's hand as she died and unable to do anything to stop the process.

But there'd been a moment when he'd done something important. Maybe even more important than chocolate. Just a few days ago in Lafayette Square, he'd somehow managed to help Linda. A path that had led her here tonight.

Well, he couldn't help her from here in the dining room. And he'd be of even less use from the downstairs kitchen.

He returned to finishing up the last tray. This one he would carry out into the hall personally. If there was any way that he could help Linda, he wasn't going to cower in the kitchen just because it was dangerous.

OUT OF IDEAS, Linda had sought out Dilya.

She had nothing but a hunch that anything was going to happen tonight and she now doubted every assumption that had led her here.

But she'd still be happier if she could at least send Dilya out of harm's way, even if she couldn't justify clearing the room. The threat wasn't credible. A block of C-4 in a diplomatic pouch didn't mean anything. That had been outside the security bubble that enclosed the White House. It was nearly impossible to bring anything lethal through that barrier.

She found the teen near the center of the hall. It was only after she stepped into the conversation that she really focused on the man Dilya was talking to.

Former President Peter Matthews.

He was tall, handsome, and graying at the temples. He looked ten times as impressive in real life as he did on television.

Dilya still had Zackie beside her and she was arguing with the former President. "She is *not* hopeless. Her only problem is that she hasn't been trained to be more than a pet."

"And you're going to make a military dog out of Anne's Sheltie?"

"Sure," Dilya told him blithely. "And Linda promised to help me," Dilya turned to her.

She had? Well, to escape the dress store and then the shoe store and then the salon, she may have made any number of promises. "I'm glad to."

"But that dog has a brain the size of a peanut." As if to prove his point, the President tossed a stuffed shrimp on the floor in front of Zackie, who barked at it rather than eating it. "I win."

Dilya sighed. "Thor's smart though, isn't he?"

"At least around food." Linda snapped her fingers, then pointed at the shrimp. Thor—who'd been sitting patiently beside her—lunged in, snapped up the shrimp, and returned to his position to eat it happily.

"*He's* well behaved," the President bent down to pet him.

"Trained at a ranch in Montana."

"Henderson's," he acknowledged. Then he froze, half bent over, before straightening slowly.

At first she was shocked that he knew the origin of her dog. But that didn't explain why he was startled to be caught with that knowledge.

The only reason that she could think of for him to be surprised was if Henderson's Ranch was more than it seemed. What if it was…

"WHPF," Linda said to him.

"What's that?" But his poker face sucked. Even she could read it.

"White House Protection Force, sir."

Captain Baxter had said that the former President had certified the WHPF personally. Somehow, her dog and the WHPF were linked to one another.

He sighed, then shrugged his complicity.

Now it was Dilya's turn to say, "What's that? What's WHPF? And what does Major Beale's ranch have to do with it?"

"Hush, half pint," the former President looked down at her. "Keep your mouth shut on this one. Not even your parents."

Dilya nodded, but it was clear that she wasn't going anywhere.

The former President sighed again. "Always have to have your nose in it, don't you, Dilya?"

"Survival instinct," Dilya answered flatly and Linda knew that it was true, even though it made Dilya blush to be caught telling a real truth.

"I wish I could have done more," President Matthews sighed, apparently missing the depth of Dilya's statement. "Not a lot of things for an ex-President to do. I'm not exactly the kind of guy who sits around in some consulting think tank. The WHPF has a good purpose behind it. I liked it and Emily agreed to set it up for me."

Emily Beale. Major Emily Beale, formerly of the Night Stalkers. Linda had met her once, sort of. The Night Stalkers 5th Battalion D Company had transported her Ranger unit into a strike zone five years ago. There was no question that the reason they'd escaped the horrendous battle so unscathed had been largely due to the pilot of the team's DAP Hawk, one Major Emily Beale—rumored to be the best pilot they'd ever had.

Now she'd created the White House Protection Force, which had earned Baxter's and Lieber's absolute respect. And the WHPF had been the one to make sure Linda was assigned to this duty—undercover protection of the President, who was presently standing not twenty feet behind the former President.

"Be all your dog can be." The flyer in her DD 214 discharge packet had somehow come from Henderson's Ranch.

"Emily's dog trainer uses that phrase all the time," the President explained. "Ex-SEAL, quite a character."

A SEAL dog trainer at a ranch run by the Night Stalkers' best pilot who had set up the White House Protection Force and then managed to get Linda assigned right into the center of it.

No pressure.

Of course Linda was a former sergeant of the 75th Rangers. Pressure was what she ate for lunch.

She scanned the room again. These were hers to protect, but she didn't know how. The Secretary of Defense was now talking to a short, very buxom woman with a blonde streak in her Asian dark hair. The woman stood as Dilya might indeed describe a boardroom-street-walker—she looked sharp, classy, and just maybe a bit on the hustle. And quite pregnant. When she went up on tiptoes to kiss the Secretary, that confirmed her as Dilya's adoptive mother.

There was no way Linda could get them out of the room without raising the alarm. And Linda wasn't going to allow Dilya to lose another set of parents. She'd been orphaned at eleven, the same age

Linda herself might as well have been. The girl had been fortunate enough to find new parents, a gift beyond any measure.

She had to solve this.

The contrast of Dilya's mom beside Secretary Stevenson versus Secretary of State Mallinson was startling. One content to stand quietly while her husband rested a testing hand on her mounded abdomen—the other near to raving.

But Mallinson had left for a meeting.

A meeting.

Lieutenant Jurgen had used exactly that same excuse to get away from her after she'd nailed his training course—back then she had trusted the instructor to not be the agent of destruction. An oversight that still made her grind her teeth whenever she remembered it.

But no one set up a meeting during a State Dinner. And then to attend only half of the reception? What had Mallinson been trying to get away from?

The itch between her shoulder blades bloomed to life.

"Excuse me," she walked away from the former President in midsentence of teasing Dilya and strode over to Harvey Lieber, lurking in his shadow. "If he's still here, don't let Secretary of State Mallinson off the property."

"What?"

"Do it! Then have them check him for a trigger of some sort."

To his credit, whatever he thought of her, Lieber didn't hesitate to raise his wrist mic and send out the instruction.

His eyes unfocused as he listened.

"Nothing. Nothing," he echoed the reports for her. "Got him. Treasury Building tunnel—unusual exit for him. Pissed as hell. Making a lot of threats." His eyes refocused on her. "No trigger on him. Not even a cell phone. You sure about this, Hamlin?"

"Pissed or scared?"

He relayed the question and merely looked thoughtful at the reply.

"Get him back here," she looked around the room. They couldn't bring him to the Second Floor without creating a panic. She quickly reviewed the map in her head. Most of the Ground Floor would be filled with guests who even at this moment were gathering for the main party to descend the Grand Staircase and lead them to dinner. Except for...

"Take him to the Usher's Room by the North Entrance."

She didn't bother to wait. Instead, she crossed the hall—as casually as she could manage, which only got her stopped twice for congratulations and Thor petted three times—then raced down the back stairs toward the State Floor.

Clive was still somewhere in the upstairs hall. If she was wrong, or too slow, he could well be in harm's way. She moved faster, despite her unfamiliar heels.

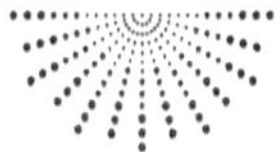

Clive made sure his chef's hat was on straight, then swept up the last finished tray of treats and carried them out into the reception himself.

Only after he stepped out did he double-check that Linda wasn't about to barrel into him or trip him up again. No sign of her and no Thor.

He turned for the main body of the room.

Everyone went out of their way to take another Pocky treat off the tray as he worked his way forward. The compliments flew thick and fast but he barely heard them, though he made sure to nod and smile as seemed appropriate.

The First Lady made a point of stopping him and complimenting him on the success. "They swept every tray clean before they touched anything else," she told him. "Of course, it *was* chocolate, so I was an easy sell and have eaten entirely too many."

He exchanged a laugh with her.

Linda, however, was anything but an easy sell—even with chocolate. Had she tried the treat? Had she understood?

He'd put everything he had into it.

And now?

He used his height to scan the crowd once more.

And now she was nowhere to be seen.

LINDA ALMOST RACED past the Office of the Chief Usher. It was on the landing between the two flights of the back stairs leading from the Second Floor of the Residence to the double-high main Entrance Hall. At the bottom of the stairs was the Usher's Room, but Thor had veered aside at this midlevel office and she saw why.

Handler Jim and his springer spaniel Malcolm were standing just inside the threshold of the Office of the Chief Usher. A number of people were packed into the small room.

"Thought it best to bring him in here," he greeted her. "Get him away from the State Floor and the main entrance. Folks are pouring in at the moment."

"Perfect," she briefly squeezed his arm in thanks as she stepped past him.

The office was on the mezzanine level—directly above the Ushers' Room and only accessible by these back stairs. At most it measured ten by fifteen feet, though it felt much smaller with Malcolm, four agents, the chief usher, and Secretary Mallinson all squeezed in around the pristine walnut desk and chairs.

Malcolm hadn't alerted to Secretary Mallinson. Neither had Thor and he still wasn't. No explosives on him. Nor had he recently handled any.

Linda's thoughts raced, just like when she and her dog were at point on a village patrol.

"I don't suppose you're willing to be helpful?"

Mallinson leaned back against the wall with his arms crossed over his chest and a worried look on his face. He glanced up at the ceiling at her question, then looked sharply away as if he'd been caught with his hand in the cookie jar.

No longer any doubt that she'd found her culprit.

But he wasn't showing any fear. Whatever he'd planted up there, he was convinced that he was safe down here.

However, his nerves were high. He checked his watch twice in under ten seconds before he caught himself.

"I don't know what you're talking about. I have a crucial meeting." He protested vehemently, but his eyes drifted to the ceiling once more.

She turned to Jim. "Is Malcolm trained in tracing lost articles?"

He shook his head, "Just explosives."

That wasn't going to help. She and Thor had checked the entire hall and found nothing.

Linda looked down at her dog. "Time to see just how good your training was, little one."

She pointed at the Secretary and said, "Thor, *verloren.*" Lost.

He sniffed the man carefully, then looked back up at her.

The Secretary stared down at him in shock. He began protesting loudly, but she ignored the distraction.

Hoping for the best, Linda pointed out the door toward the stairs leading up to the reception.

"*Such!*" Seek!

Searching among the guests, Clive had at least spotted Dilya. If anyone knew where Linda had gone, it would be the kid.

He was a little daunted by the company she was keeping, but took a deep breath and braved it anyway. In Lafayette Square, he'd stepped into danger without knowing it. That wasn't bravery. This time, he knew that whatever was going to happen, he was probably now standing near the center.

"Good Evening, Mr. President."

"Chef Andrews," President Matthews sounded delighted. "You were always one of my wife's favorites."

"And she mine as well, sir. She was kind enough to bring me

chocolate from her family's own plantation on several occasions. She has very much made me want to visit Vietnam."

"If you bring some of your finished chocolate back with you, I can't imagine you won't be welcome. This," he picked one of the last treats up from Clive's tray, "is utterly delightful."

"Thank you, sir."

Dilya, however, appeared to be too distracted to take another. That was very unusual, especially because he suspected that she was one of the chief thieves of his shop's small chocolate cabinet.

She kept watching an archway off the side of the hall. It led to one of the bedrooms, or maybe the family elevator, which he'd never used.

He was about to scan the room again when Linda and Thor appeared beneath the arch as if by magic. Or as if she'd been running, and had suddenly come to a halt and was trying to appear calm.

Then Linda softly snapped her fingers and, when Thor looked up at her, she pointed to the left.

Thor put his head down and went.

He recognized the action from the very first moment he'd seen her at the starting line of the James J. Rowley Training Center's explosives course. With gestures and small noises, she guided him forward.

Very few people were watching. Dilya. Lieber and Adams from the Secret Service agents along the wall. But no one else. Not even President Matthews, who had turned to strike up a conversation with his replacement, President Zachary Thomas—something about rival football teams.

The conversations still buzzed up and down the length of the room. The pianist still played though Clive doubted anyone was listening to him to begin with.

He and Dilya watched as Thor suddenly shifted direction, then sat abruptly at someone's feet.

"Oh shit!" Dilya whispered softly.

Clive didn't bother to correct her language. He just put an arm around her shoulder and pulled her in tight as Secretary of Defense Archibald Stevenson looked down at Thor in surprise.

"Good evening, sir," Linda managed as the shock rippled through her.

"Good evening again, Ms. Hamlin. May I ask why your dog is looking at me like that?" Both of Dilya's parents would know the meaning of the way Thor had sat so abruptly.

This couldn't be happening. She *couldn't* be the one to take away Dilya's second set of parents.

Then Thor stretched up to sniff at the Secretary's hand.

"I'm sorry to ask this, sir, but did you shake hands with Secretary of State Mallinson?"

He lifted his right hand up to near his face, inspecting it and then Thor.

Then he held it down closer to Thor—who wriggled happily in response at finding what he'd been told to find.

"I did. What is going on, Ms. Hamlin?"

"I'm sorry, but I don't have time to explain."

"Yes, I think you do," Dilya's mom stepped directly in front of her.

"No, ma'am. I really don't." Then she looked down at Thor. "*Such!*" And they stepped around the couple and continued down the room.

"Oh my god, I thought I was gonna die," Dilya bolted from Clive's grasp and raced to her parents, where she hugged them fiercely. They pulled her in close.

That was real family. That's what Clive had lost with the death of his mother. Lost and missed so much that he'd thought it was a hole that could never be filled. Until he met Linda Hamlin.

He couldn't take his eyes from the three of them holding on so tightly to everything they had, but they in turn never took their eyes off Linda and her dog as the team continued their patrol.

He and Linda and a girl of their own.

It was all he needed to be happy—a truth he no longer doubted in the slightest.

Clive could feel the seconds ticking by, so slowly that each heartbeat seemed to be a separate clap of thunder in his ears.

Linda came up to him in full soldier mode.

Thor sniffed him, then moved on. Even the dog was in soldier mode and acted as if he didn't recognize Clive.

Then, just before Thor led her away, Linda reached out to squeeze his hand.

"That chocolate was truly glorious, Clive. Thank you."

And she was gone.

But she'd left hope in her wake.

LINDA COULD FEEL the clock ticking. Inevitable. Unstoppable. How many seconds did she have? Not enough was her fear. Though at least she now knew Thor could track an odor.

But she'd taken a precious few of those seconds to try and tell Clive what he'd done to her. His chocolate treat had gifted her back so much of the past she had forgotten. She and Peggy, back when they were still friends, on the swing hanging from the old apple tree. Maple sugar eaten fresh off the snow where Old Man Kimball would drizzle it in fanciful swirls to cool. All of the tastes and flavors of her childhood, distilled down to the impossible essence of five little sticks of chocolate.

How had he reached so deep inside himself that he could do that?

He was the one who had given her that gift. And she knew he hadn't had the snack figured out yet on that awful night when she'd gone out of her way to wound him.

Instead of anger or revenge, he had reached out to her with impossible forgiveness that she didn't deserve. Forgiveness and understanding.

If he truly gave her another chance, she promised herself that she would never again cast it aside.

Of course, he wasn't the only one who had to give them another chance. She first had to make sure they all survived.

President. Vice President. Prime ministers. Some noticed Thor's inspection, but most continued their discussions, oblivious to what was going on around them.

Until Thor once again sat abruptly.

She looked up at the man's eyes.

"The one you least suspect," she whispered.

Special Agent Harvey Lieber glared back at her.

CLIVE MOVED IN FAST, using his bulk to block any escape, as well as anyone else's view.

"Not me," the agent growled.

Clive looked down and saw that Linda had a small taser pressed against the belly of the head of Presidential Protection Detail, Harvey Lieber.

"Are you sure, Linda?" Clive couldn't believe it.

"Shut up, Clive. This is out of your league."

"And yours, Hamlin," Lieber growled at her.

Clive couldn't believe it—the head of the PPD? He glanced around, but they still had no one else's attention, not even of the other agents in the hall. Only the trio of Dilya's family watched them from the far side of the hall.

"We can walk out of here quietly, Lieber. Or I can have you dragged out of here twitching like a string puppet."

"Not gonna happen, Hamlin. You and your dog screwed up. You're both gone."

Clive glanced down at Thor, who was still sitting close by Agent Lieber's feet. But he wasn't looking up at the agent the way that he'd been looking up at the Secretary's hand. Instead, he was staring down.

"Linda?"

"Clive, I said—"

"Look at Thor."

Linda and Lieber both turned to face him, then they both looked down at the dog.

Lieber took a slow, cautious step sideways, but Thor's attention didn't follow.

For the moment, Agent Lieber had been standing in the shadow of one of the potted palms.

A briefcase sat behind the pot.

"Oh shit," Linda muttered. She'd been hunting the scent of explosives before, not of Secretary Mallinson. "I knew I should have checked behind the palms."

"IT'S the same make and model," Linda was going to be sick.

"You sure?" Lieber asked.

"I spent half an hour staring at it in the middle of Lafayette Square and then another dozen looking at the photos in the debriefing. I have nightmares about this make of briefcase."

"I'll call the bomb squad. I had already alerted them and they're staging in the basement." She caught his wrist and kept him from raising his mic.

"It may not be fast enough." She tried to check her pretty ladies' watch, but there'd been no outer dial to spin and track the number of remaining minutes. And she couldn't remember now.

She squinted at it.

Five minutes to go until it was time to head downstairs?

No, three. Could the bomb squad even get here that fast?

Would it be safe to move? A motion trigger or—

"Secretary Mallinson kept checking his watch. That implies a timer, not a motion detector." Linda reached for the case and this time Lieber stopped her.

"What if it's both?"

She closed her eyes and tried to picture Mallinson's face. He'd checked his watch, not once but multiple times. He wasn't worried about her moving it. He was worried about her finding it too soon.

Brushing Lieber aside, she picked up the case.

She lived through it.

Good sign!

"This way," Clive stepped out ahead of her, and she followed closely in the wake he cut through the crowd with his empty tray leading the way.

All she could think about was that, moments ago, her hand had clutched his, perhaps for the last time. And now it was holding a briefcase that felt as if it was leaving a stain of evil that would never wash off.

By the time she noticed where he was leading her, they were past the back stairs. Past the stairs, through the dining room, and into the First Family's private kitchen.

"What?"

"Here," Clive slammed open the dumbwaiter.

No time to stop and think, she shoved it in among the dirty serving platters.

Clive slammed the door shut and hit the button for the downstairs kitchen.

Lieber called down to the bomb squad.

The three of them stood still. Unable to move away despite how stupidly close they were to the dumbwaiter filled with explosives. If the bomb went off in the shaft, it was bound to shoot a column of flame straight up at them. Still they all crowded around the glass doors and looked down.

"At the kitchen level," Lieber reported as he listened to his earpiece.

"Bomb squad has it... In a portable shock sleeve..." which would absorb at least some of the explosion. "Out of the building..."

Then a pause long enough that Linda almost screamed for them to hurry.

"Inside containment with vessel sealed..."

"Detonated! No damage. No one hurt."

And all three of them whooshed out held breaths making them laugh nervously together.

LIEBER DIDN'T SAY A WORD. He simply shook Clive's hand, a solid grip that expressed all of his relief at a close call. He held Linda's hand in both of his for a long moment as they exchanged silent nods. Then he knelt down in front of Thor and received a sharp growl for his efforts.

"*Gute Hund. Freund.*"

Thor relaxed at her command and accepted the pet, but still showed the man distrust.

Lieber rose and headed toward the hall calling instructions into his wrist mic to prepare for the processional to dinner.

Unsure what to do with his hands, Clive wiped them on his apron, then threaded his fingers together.

Linda looked up at him, inspecting him closely.

"What?"

"You're a brave man, Clive Andrews."

"You think that's brave? You should try building a three-hundred-pound chocolate White House that's going to appear on national television at Christmas. That's bravery." Then he blew out another breath at how ridiculous he sounded.

She rested her hand over his interlaced fingers. He could feel the gentle impression of each of her fingers as they held his.

"You are also the kindest man I've ever met. I can't believe that you made that chocolate treat for me after what I did to you."

"It was all for you, Linda." And if he was going to be brave… "I love you, Linda Hamlin. I know it's too soon. I know it's ridiculous. But I could never ask for more than you. I get that it may take you some time to catch up, but Miss Watson said to never stop saying it."

"Miss Watson, huh?" A ghost of a smile touched her lovely lips.

"Scary lady in the dingy basement? You know."

"Yes, I know Miss Watson. At least a little," her expression was confused for a moment, but she shrugged it away.

Clive couldn't think of what else to say.

Then the kitchen phone rang, the display showing Chef Klaus' extension. He freed one hand from Linda's grasp but made sure to keep a hold with the other so that she couldn't slip away, then pressed the speaker button.

"Andrews here."

"*Warum* are you up there? *Du musst hierher kommen.* While you are playing with your chocolates upstairs, *wir haben* bomb squads who say nothing, secret service agents who *auch nichts sagen.* All is mayhem. We start service *in neun minuten.* Get down here. *Schnell! Schnell!*" He delivered the tirade in a single breath intermixed with a thick stream of German curses, then the line went dead.

"I guess I'd better get going," Clive could stand here all night holding Linda's hand in his. He squeezed her fingers and she squeezed them back.

"I don't have the words, Clive."

He did his best not to show his disappointment.

"But," she took a deep breath and let it out slowly, "but if you can give me some time, I promise to try to find them."

Without thinking, he gathered her into his arms and held tight.

And she held him back.

For now that was enough.

The phone rang again. They both looked at the display declaring it was again from Chef Klaus.

Clive didn't bother to answer it. Instead, he kissed Linda far too briefly, then raced down the tight spiral staircase that descended close beside the dumbwaiter.

LINDA FELT a little dazed and lightheaded as she stepped out into the hall. It was completely transformed.

The crowds were all gone, as was the pianist. A waiter picked up dishes and glasses and a janitor followed closely behind cleaning every cleared surface. A large vacuum cleaner started up at the far end of the hall.

Only five people remained: Dilya with her parents, former

President Matthews, and a huge black man who must be his bodyguard.

Dilya rushed over, slamming into her arms and giving her such a hard hug that it took her breath away. Linda hugged her back and took the brief liberty of resting her cheek on the girl's hair. Her parents were so lucky. Though it wasn't all luck. They were parents who behaved the way parents were supposed to.

"It appears that you had an interesting evening," President Matthews commented drily.

Then Kee Stevenson, Dilya's mom, stepped over, planting her feet firmly on the carpet and her fists on her hips. She looked as if she could whip Linda's ass one-handed, despite being pregnant.

"Did you just nearly get our daughter killed?"

Linda could only nod. If she'd been even two minutes slower, they'd all be dead. She squeezed Dilya once more and let her go before the teen could figure out she'd actually bonded with an adult.

"Damn it!" Kee pounded a heel on the carpet. "God damn you, Archie."

Linda could only blink in surprise. She'd thought she was the one in trouble.

"You know how much I hate being out of the action. You ever try your 'wouldn't it be fun to have another kid' pitch on me again, I'm gonna bust your balls."

"Better than my arm," Secretary Stevenson, proving he was a brave man, simply stepped in and slid an arm around his wife's shoulder.

Kee slammed an elbow into his gut, but he was braced for it and merely laughed.

"That was really cool, Thor," Dilya squatted down to play with him.

"Ma'am," the massive agent came up beside them. He tapped his earpiece. "I've been asked to pass on to you that initial analysis shows that the explosive was TMETN."

"Odorless. That would explain why the dogs didn't alert to it. But the power…" The briefcase hadn't been very heavy. Linda didn't see how that little weight would do more than kill the few people closest to it.

"TMETN and sarin gas. Probably in containers shaped to look like normal objects when X-rayed. If the agents X-rayed the Secretary of State's briefcase at all," the last was delivered with a snarl that said on his watch it damn well would have been.

There was a stunned silence. Everyone on the entire Second Floor of the Residence would have been dead within ten minutes. Most within one.

"Who the—" Kee flashed from frustrated to furious.

"Mallinson," the Secretary stated. "He couldn't wait to get out of here."

"That's what you figured out," the President pointed at Linda.

"Right. His departure in the middle of the reception for a meeting was the piece that didn't fit. But I don't understand why he did it."

President Matthews laughed. It was bitter, but it was a laugh. "This one I know. The Secretary of State is fourth in line to the presidency. By the way, the first three were also in this room tonight. He was trying to stage a coup. A very bloody one."

"But the clues. Chinese, Japanese..."

"Whether they were a smokescreen or the attempt of a foreign power to gain power over our government, that will be someone else's problem to figure out. Tonight you protected the White House and this government. You are a credit to the force," the President's tone made it clear that was the end of that topic.

For a moment she wondered if he meant the Secret Service or the White House Protection Force—then understood that he meant both.

He held out his arm to her and she could only blink at him in surprise.

"We're late for dinner. And as my wife's flight from Vietnam is delayed, I believe that you are my date. I'll tell you about a rather nice ranch you and your boyfriend should visit in Montana someday."

With Thor's lead in one hand and former President Matthews' elbow in the other, she led the way down the Grand Staircase while she tried to digest the word "boyfriend."

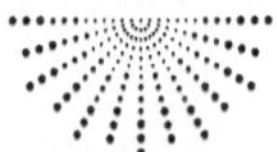

"*I* found the words," she told Thor.

He licked her face, which made her glad about her staunch refusal to wear any makeup.

"You ready?" She scrubbed her fingers into his sides and he wiggled with delight. "Of course you are," she acknowledged in her squeaky dog voice.

"He's always ready," Dilya laughed. "He's a dog. How about you?"

Linda looked over at her. This time their dresses matched, or were at least color coordinated. Dilya had insisted and Linda had known better than to argue.

"You never were fifteen, were you?"

Dilya shrugged. She could pass for twenty-five in the elegant dress of pale-lavender silk with a wide white sash emphasizing her waist. She wore her hair down—the only styling battle that Linda had won in this entire affair other than no makeup. If Dilya's hair was down, then she could leave her own down as well.

"You're still short, you know," she teased Dilya.

"So are you!" Her maid of honor stuck her tongue out at Linda.

"Taller than you," Linda returned the salute with an added raspberry.

"Not much," Dilya pointed to her own bright red boots with two-inch heels.

Linda had won the shoe battle by arguing that she wanted to dance with her new husband and didn't want to trip. Dilya had finally caved and *allowed* her to purchase white flats, but it had cost her two inches in the height battle and left her with only a narrow lead.

There was a discreet knock. Dilya answered and then let former President Matthews into the room. Linda rose to her feet.

"You look very nice in your suit, President Matthews."

"That's Secretary of State Matthews, thanks to you. It's so good to have something useful to do. I can never show you my full appreciation for coming up with the idea. And you look amazing in that dress."

"Thank you. I had the best help ever," she placed a hand on Dilya's shoulder in thanks. Then she did a slow turn for him and he made a point of applauding. She watched herself in the East Bedroom mirror, a room that the First Family had loaned her for the occasion.

The wedding would be small, but the President and First Lady had insisted on holding it in the Residence's Central Hall where she'd saved everyone's lives three months before.

Dilya had understood her well enough to choose a simple white knee-length dress, with a lace sheer and a lavender waistband to match Dilya's dress.

She'd considered a bouquet of chocolate, then thought of apple blossoms instead. How perfect a gift Clive had given her.

"You know, I tried to perform the ceremony for Emily once."

"How did that turn out?"

Secretary Matthews grimaced. "Not well. I lost a shoe in her pond."

"No ponds here, you should be safe."

"I hope so. I like these shoes. Are you ready for this? If so, we should do it before the groom melts down like one of his chocolates."

She used a bit of lace to tie the rings onto Thor's harness.

Linda bit her lower lip for a moment, then nodded. As ready as she was ever going to be to completely change her life in a single moment.

Former President Matthews had been an obvious replacement for the jailed Secretary of State Mallinson. He knew global politics from his own two terms of office; because of his wife's directorship with the UNESCO World Heritage Centre, he had continued to travel widely, and he was immensely respected around the world—by both friend and foe. The way he had lit up the moment she'd suggested the idea over Clive's luscious dessert soup, she knew it had been one of her better ones.

"Oh, wait," Linda dug into her purse—because Dilya had finally won that war—and pulled out the thin gold ribbon. It was from the one chocolate bouquet she'd gotten to eat on that night a lifetime ago. She looked at the words on it for a moment.

Freedom and Unity.

It might be the Vermont motto, but it was also a good message for herself: freedom from her past and a new unity in her future. Tied up in a gold knot.

"Could you give this to him?"

Secretary Matthews took it cautiously, then read the words and smiled. Without comment, he stepped over and gave her a hug and a kiss on the forehead. He did the same for Dilya before heading out the door to get in place so that he could officiate the wedding ceremony of Linda and Clive Andrews. It would be a relief to be rid of her family name.

Dilya followed through the door when the pianist started the Wedding March on the grand piano. The First and Second families would be rising to their feet, along with Dilya's parents. Linda had decided against inviting her own—a choice Clive had agreed to after a brief, very brief, visit to Vermont. But there absolutely was a contingent from the Secret Service K-9 teams with their dogs.

She'd found a team as fine as the 75th Rangers. They gave her a place and a purpose.

Linda might not have recognized the vivacious older woman who had offered her services as photographer if not for her gold locket and piercing blue eyes. She was tall, with long silver hair, and looked slimly elegant in a black von Furstenberg pantsuit as she wielded her cameras. If Clive had caught on that it was Miss Watson, he certainly hadn't mentioned it.

Clive.

He was the one who had given her the greatest gift of all.

His patience and love.

It had taken her two months to find the words "I love you" inside herself. The moment she'd found them and managed to speak them (which had been a whole separate challenge), they'd both wept.

Then and there—while the tears still streamed down her face for only the second time since her childhood had ended—he had gone down on bent knee to propose.

Clive had given her a promise she'd never imagined possible.

He'd promised a future and a family.

She only had to find two more words to make it all come true. She'd already written "I do" on a piece of paper clutched in her fist just in case she couldn't say them aloud.

But she knew she would, and stepped out the door in confidence. She would walk down the aisle herself with Thor to escort her.

She'd be able to say them because, just like his chocolate, Clive's promises would turn out to be ever so perfectly delightful.

DILYA'S BONUS SCENE

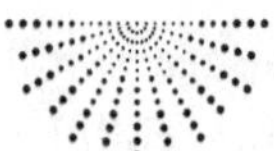

-WHITE HOUSE PROTECTION FORCE #1-

These scenes take place during the events of Off the Leash, *but they are Dilya's view of what actually was taking place, versus what the grownups thought was going on.*

Originally these were an exclusive treat for newsletter subscribers, now included here for the first time.

---

*D*ilya couldn't believe it when the Sergeant Linda Hamlin called her on the phone. She should just play the "sullen teen" card and make her go away.

Sergeant Linda had been nice about helping her train Zackie in the Chocolate Shop that day—not treating her like a little girl at all. But then yesterday she hadn't even acknowledged that Dilya was the one who figured out the bad guys were *trying* to get caught when they carried the explosives into Lafayette Square. She'd just called her boss on the radio and started talking as if it was her idea. Dilya had raced away to hide the anger that lurked so close that she sometimes feared she couldn't hide it.

Fifteen years old meant she didn't fit in anywhere. She was an adult, but no one thought to treat her that way.

Fine! She didn't need to make friends with Sergeant Linda, even if she had a nice dog.

"Please. Please. Please," Sergeant Linda begged on the phone. She sounded really frustrated. "I need help buying a dress. I don't have any friends in DC and I don't know who else to ask."

Dilya stared at the phone in surprise. Sergeant Linda Hamlin was a Secret Service officer. She was all grown up, had a job, had been kissing Chef Andrews…but she didn't have a friend?

Dilya certainly knew what that was like. At Forward Operating Base Bati she'd always been everyone's favorite sidekick, but they'd all been Night Stalkers and Rangers and Delta Force people—even the youngest had been twice her age. Not a real friend anywhere.

Here at the White House, she'd been friends with President Peter Matthews, but he had gone away and his wife and their baby had gone with him. Every time they visited, she briefly felt as if it could all be okay again, but it never was. She only knew the new President a little bit. The First Lady was cool, though, and she paid money into Dilya's college fund to train and take care of their dog after school and on weekends. She'd told them that she knew how to do it, then had barely slept for a week because she was online studying until she actually could do it.

The kids at school all treated her strangely because she practically lived at the White House and her parents were the Secretary of Defense and a sniper for the FBI. The other kids didn't know that her *real* parents had been gunned down because they'd crossed the wrong ridge of the Hindu Kush Mountains at the wrong time. That was *all* they'd done wrong. The kids at school didn't get that every time her *new* parents stepped out the door she wondered if they'd still be alive that night to come back through it. There were days she wanted to dump her classmates alone in the Hindu Kush and see how *they* survived. Now *that* was a funny image.

"No friends" she so *totally* understood. And Sergeant Linda wasn't treating her like a little kid at all—she was asking for help with dress shopping. That's something grownups didn't ask kids to do. That's something *friends* did. Together! Maybe Dilya had been wrong yesterday about Sergeant Linda not giving her credit for thinking up that the bad guys had played a trick on the Secret Service.

"I'm desperate, Dilya. You've got to save me."

"Five minutes at the North Portico," her initial hesitation disappeared in an excited heartbeat. A friend!

"Too soon. I have to take Thor back to the kennel at the Secret Service building first. Then I can—"

"No. No. No. You've gotta bring Thor, trust me. Make sure he wears his K-9 harness and stuff like that." Hadn't Sergeant Linda learned anything in all that time she'd spent in other countries? Thor was essential to getting a great discount on a new dress.

Dilya hung up before Sergeant Linda could change her mind, barely remembering to grab her parka on the way.

"I can't take Thor into a department store," was Sergeant Linda's greeting.

"Sure you can. Service dog and like that." She still didn't get it. But that was okay because Dilya did. She led the way down to the security gate before Sergeant Linda could turn back.

"Maybe I should get dark glasses and a white cane too," she followed after only a little hesitation.

"If it makes you feel better," though Dilya didn't understand why it would.

She filed the words away to look up later. There was no way to know what would save her life some day.

"What kind of a dress?" She waved at the guards who grinned back at her. Being nice would pay off eventually when she really needed it.

"Um, a dressy dress?"

Dilya rolled her eyes. Clothes were one of the best things about not being a war refugee anymore. Bright colors, fun shapes. It was *awesomeness!*

"A dress I can afford." *Duh!* That's why they needed Thor. Didn't she get that her dog was famous?

"For a hot date with Chef Andrews?" Dilya couldn't think why else Sergeant Linda would suddenly need a dress.

Then Dilya realized she was walking along the sidewalk alone. She turned around and saw Sergeant Linda frozen in place. She looked like she'd just taken a .50 cal BMG round to the chest and her body just didn't know it was dead yet. She hurried back to check, but Dilya hadn't heard any supersonic crack of a sniper round coming in. There was no splatter of blood on the sidewalk behind her. Thor remained at her side and was looking up at her waiting for a command.

"No. Not for that," Linda's voice was barely a whisper. Did Chef Andrews know she liked him and still he'd turned her down? They'd been kissing, hadn't they? That was another problem with being fifteen—boys were *so* stupid and they treated her all weird because she worked at the White House. She was *never* going to find a boy she wanted to kiss.

"I like Chef Andrews," Dilya said carefully. But if he'd hurt her new friend, Dilya was done with him *and* his chocolates.

She had to turn away for a moment and run her fingers over the multi-colored scarf that Chef Andrews had made for her. When she'd found out that he too had lost his mother and that scarf was the last thing she'd made him, Dilya had envied that. The men who killed her real mom had let Dilya live, but chased her away. She never had a chance to say goodbye much less take anything other than a memory with her. She'd never told Chef Andrews that, but he'd made her a copy of his scarf which had been really nice of him.

Could she be loyal to two friends? Well, Chef Andrews wasn't really a friend, though he was always nice to her even if she was "just a kid." And she still wasn't sure what Sergeant Linda was.

"I like him too," Sergeant Linda protested. "It's not like I'm cheating on him."

"Then what's the dress for?"

"I have to go to the reception and dinner tomorrow night in the Residence. I have to blend in."

"Ooo! Like undercover?" Dilya pumped some extra energy into it.

It was cool and it was clear that Sergeant Linda needed a boost of enthusiasm for some reason.

"So much for keeping *that* a secret."

"Excellent! It's so cool. An agent going undercover at a Residence reception." Actually it was cool. She was going to find out everything and go in there as Sergeant Linda's undercover backup. So undercover that even Sergeant Linda wouldn't know. *Secret agent Dilya Stevens at your service!*

Then she could—

Stupid! Stupid! Stupid! If Sergeant Linda was going undercover to a White House reception, that meant something bad was going to happen. Someone was trying to hurt the people who mattered to her. Well, that wasn't going to happen either. The Delta and Rangers back at Bati may have thought they were humoring a little girl, but she'd listened. And she'd learned. She knew how to use their tactics.

"Are you good at what you do?"

Linda nodded.

"*Really* good? Protect-the-White House kind of good?"

Linda tipped her head to the side for a moment. "I guess I'd better be."

"Okay then." Dilya studied her a moment longer, then nodded sharply. The mere force of the nod reminded her of that long-ago day when Kee wasn't her new mom yet, but had killed the men who had murdered her real mom.

Dilya knew that she shouldn't be showing her anger, her thirst for vengeance now, just as she hadn't shown it to Kee then. With a shake of her hair, she flipped back into "happy teen" mode.

But Sergeant Linda had seen the other Dilya, the angry one who lurked and waited. Dilya cast her mind about, looking for a kid's kind of remark before the sergeant could ask her any adult questions, then saw Sergeant Linda's face.

"Don't look at me like that," Dilya's whispered. Sergeant Linda was now looking at her like… She didn't know what, but she didn't like it.

"Like what?"

"Like I'm an…alien. I never killed anyone. I would have, but my new mom took care of that for me so I didn't have to." And again she was telling Sergeant Linda things she hadn't even told Kee.

"Didn't have to?"

Dilya sighed. She was in it this far… "Two men shot my real parents point blank because we walked into the wrong valley at the wrong time. Them I could have killed. It made Kee sad to kill them and I get why now. Back then I was too young to understand the price. Still I would have done it—they deserved to die." And she'd do it again herself next time because the war had taught her that remorse didn't keep you safe.

"Okay," Sergeant Linda nodded once, then again. Then she stood up straight and nodded to Thor as if he'd said something.

She held out a pinkie. "I hereby solemnly swear to never look at you funny again—provided you promise the same. No matter how ridiculous either of us is being. And you promise never to make fun of my dog either."

Dilya had heard about pinkie swears, but she'd never actually done one. She experimented at her side until her pinkie was the same shape as Sergeant Linda's before raising it.

Linda—if someone pinkie swore, that meant they were a friend, right? So she'd think of her as just Linda. Linda hooked their pinkies together and solemnly shook them up and down together three times.

Dilya couldn't believe what was happening. A real *friend?* "We should get dresses that match." Like they were twin sisters or something.

"That wouldn't be very undercover, would it?" But her new friend Linda smiled at her as they headed into the store together to buy secret agent dresses for their mission. She didn't look at Dilya funny, even once, the whole time.

***

Dilya had brought Zackie to the reception on the Second Floor of the Residence as part of her disguise. She didn't expect the Sheltie to be of any help, but it felt as if she also was supporting her new friends, Linda and Thor.

The whole event had turned out to be less exciting than she'd hoped. Mostly it was just politicians standing around and doing their politician thing. Her new parents were there. Archie was fighting with Secretary of State Mallinson, just the way he handled any fight—very quietly. Dilya tried never to test his patience, but Kee certainly did and yet Dilya had never seen Archie angry. She'd seen him hurt or frustrated, but just like with the Secretary of State, he always remained calm. Dilya could just hang on him whenever she needed to feel that there was at least one person on the planet who'd accept her no matter what. He never complained when she did.

Kee was more complicated. Kee had killed for Dilya. She'd tracked her real parents' killers all the way back to Uzbekistan to get them. It was something Dilya could never repay.

Though Kee never said what she was feeling, there was no mistaking when she became angry. She roared like a scary lion despite her small size. But every now and then, Kee would hold Dilya close: so tightly that she couldn't breathe. Dilya cherished those rare moments even more than Archie's easy acceptance.

Those hugs had become less frequent lately because Kee was pregnant with her own child. She always spoke about Dilya having a brother or sister, but Dilya knew better. She was an only child and her real parents were dead. Nothing but a war orphan—as a boy at school had teased her until he'd accidentally fallen down a flight of stairs. She figured by the time the baby was born, or a little longer if she was lucky, she needed to have a backup plan in place. An escape route and somewhere to go.

She'd had one, once upon a time. Nanny to the First Family. But they hadn't taken her with them when they left the White House and all of her old fears were coming back.

The new First Family didn't have a baby and didn't need a nanny. Oh, they'd kept Dilya around to take care of their dog when they were too busy, but anyone could take care of a dog. Though that was a new angle she'd started working with Sergeant Linda—before

Linda became her friend. Maybe it would still work. If she could show how good a dog trainer she was, maybe they'd keep her around. Even if her new parents forgot about her because of their new baby.

For something to do, Dilya had taken to following Linda and Thor around the reception room. She'd stayed well behind—Linda and Thor were undercover after all and she and Zackie were double undercover—but never so far behind that she couldn't see how Linda was signaling Thor. To others it appeared as if she wasn't. But Dilya was watching closely and could spot the tiny signals.

But the one Dilya was learning tactics from wasn't so much her new friend. Though it was seriously cool to see how Linda moved through the crowd. She walked with all the confidence of a dangerous woman armed to the teeth—which she was, under her pretty jacket they'd chosen together. Dilya liked that image a lot and tried shifting her step and shoulders to match, but couldn't get it right.

But it was from Thor that she was learning tactics. The dog simply walked through the crowd, doing his happy-cute-dog thing. He had the act down so well that it was impossible to believe that he was thinking about anything else. He was even more undercover than her own "sullen teen" or "ditzy young girl" disguises. Don't *think* the part, *be* the part. She'd have to work on that.

"Hey, short stuff."

Dilya would have been irritated by the interruption, except that it was Former President Peter Matthews.

"Hey yourself, President Peter." It had been very important to him that she call him by his first name when they first met—before she understood how important he was. Not even his wife used his first name very often. "Where's the First Lady?" Geneviève Beauchamp Matthews was too tall and beautiful and perfect for Dilya to ever use *her* first name.

"Her flight was delayed. She and Adele will be in tomorrow if you're up for some babysitting."

"Always!" Dilya welcomed anything to make her important, even for a day. Too bad she couldn't think of a way to get him back here full time. Then they'd need her more often, maybe often enough to keep her if Archie and Kee forgot about her.

Linda and Thor had disappeared into the crowd down at the far end of the hall. Dilya wished she was taller so that she could see over people's heads. She should've worn heels instead of her red Converse, but they'd been part of her undercover-as-a-kid disguise. Maybe she could keep track of Linda by...

Rather than looking at President Peter, she kept staring into the obscuring crowd at President Thomas, his staff, and the visiting Prime Ministers and their staff.

"What are you watching so intently?"

"My new friend Linda. She and her dog are working tonight."

As planned, that snagged President Peter's attention—he'd understand what that meant. He gave her a hard look, then turned to follow Linda's progress. He was a foot taller than she was and could see much more. She could tell when he zeroed in on them. After that, she faded back into the crowd and watched him in order to keep track of Linda.

Archie was no longer talking to Secretary of State Mallinson, instead Kee stood close beside him. She did look really pretty and it was clear Archie thought so too as he didn't look away from her for a moment. Then he rested his hand on Kee's pregnant belly and got that dreamy look of his.

And Dilya's fears rose even higher. They were going to be a new family of three and she was going to be on her own again. But she wasn't eleven anymore. She was fifteen and could deal with this. For starters, she'd never spent a penny more of her allowance than she needed. For movies, she waited until they came to the White House. For music, she only listened to the free downloads. For clothes, the charity stores had plenty, especially for wild color combinations. People were always getting rid of old colors before the clothes wore out—they just didn't get how cool they looked together. Four years of savings should cover her food for a while if it came to that.

She couldn't access her college fund which was just filled with money from her work at the White House. Her new parents managed that. She was the first girl in her family to get schooling and she already knew more than her teachers. So why did she need college? She was going to need the money, but would have to figure out later how to get it.

Watching her new parents making their new dream of a family, she'd lost track of Linda and Peter. She waited and tried not to watch her new parents talking about a future that she probably had no part in. Maybe she would, but she couldn't count on it. What if—

Suddenly Thor emerged from the crowd.

He was different. The happy-dog act was gone. He was a soldier on a mission now.

Dilya watched closely.

Linda was intent and in soldier-mode, too. Dilya could see that Linda had palmed a small taser and held it hidden against her side in one hand while she held Thor's leash in the other.

She *knew* something. Now the criminal would be caught.

President Peter had seen it too and came back to stand beside her.

Chef Andrews joined them and she could only silence him by taking a chocolate treat from his tray. Didn't he see what was happening?

Moving quickly along the side of the room, Thor sniffed right and left and then honed straight in on—

"Oh shit!"

Chef Andrews wrapped an arm around her shoulders—whether for comfort or to keep her in place, Dilya couldn't tell. All she could do was watch as her world came apart even sooner than expected.

Thor had identified Archie. The dog had walked up, sniffed, and sat—clearly marking the criminal.

It took everything in her power to not be sick. It couldn't be. Not Archie. He was the one rock in her world. Yes, Dilya had expected him to become too distracted by the new baby to remember her. And why would Kee think much about an Uzbekistani war orphan that she'd plucked off a barren mountainside four years ago?

What almost took her to her knees though, wasn't the

unexpectedness of her plans coming apart too soon. It was that her new parents could be taken away from her that easily.

They might not need her, but she needed them. She'd never needed anybody, not really. Because she knew that, in less than a second, someone could pull out a gun and shoot them in the eye and they'd be dead.

But a world without Archie? Without Kee?

She'd always imagined it would happen, but now that the moment was here, she couldn't stand the thought.

No! She wanted to scream the words, but couldn't. All she could do was stand as she had stood as a child and watched her real parents be killed. Unable to help. Unable to do anything.

And her heart, which had died that day, was dying all over again.

Impossibly, Linda said something to each of them, and then she and Thor continued about the room.

Dilya broke out of Chef Andrews' tight grasp and raced across the hall, not caring what anyone thought as Zackie raced at her heels.

She slammed into both of them.

And Archie and Kee folded her against them. They held her. Hard. Like they used to when she was a little girl and had *needed* their comfort.

"Thought I was going to lose you for a second there, Dilya," Archie whispered it into her hair. She could hear the nerves in his voice because he could never truly hide anything from her. He'd been afraid for a moment even if he didn't show it to others.

"Never gonna happen," Kee growled as fiercely as ever.

And Dilya could only look up at them in surprise.

Dilya remembered picturing them together a long time ago, back when she first met them.

An inkling, the merest hint of a dream of Archie the String Man and "The Kee" and a Dilya-sized person. She'd forgotten that daydream.

But she understood now. They weren't going to be a family of three, casting Dilya out to make the vision come true. There would be a new baby, and they'd be a family of four.

As much as she wanted to watch Linda and Thor, she could see her new parents watching them for her. Maybe as long as they did, everything would be okay, so she just held them close and waited.

She could feel through their hugs when they both suddenly relaxed.

Linda and Thor had saved them. Now Dilya would have a family *and* a friend.

"Damn, Mallinson," Kee grumbled. "I hope they hang the bastard."

Secretary of State Mallinson? Dilya had never minded him much—he just saw her as the "little kid." But if he was the bad man, that meant there wasn't a Secretary of State anymore. And they'd need a someone to replace him.

She knew that her friend President Peter missed his old job by the way he went over to visit the new President every time he was here.

That gave her an idea.

Dilya would have to suggest the idea to Linda. Find a way to make it her friend's idea. Because if Former President Peter came back to work at the White House as the new Secretary of State, maybe the Former First Lady and little Adele would come back too. Then she could be a nanny and a dog sitter.

A nanny, a dog sitter, and part of a real family. That would be safe enough.

Wouldn't it?

ON YOUR MARK

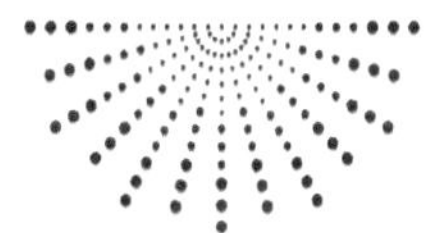

Jim Fischer and Malcolm the springer spaniel love their patrols safeguarding the White House. They walk the fence line, meet the tourists, and hunt the bad guys. Neither one ever searched for more, until now.

Reese Carver raced NASCAR. She abruptly left her front row starting position to join the U.S. Secret Service. The first woman to ever drive the Presidential limo—known as "The Beast" for a reason—holds the President's life in her hands alone. Or so she thought.

To save the President, the driver and the dog-handler must find common ground before their hearts get blown away.

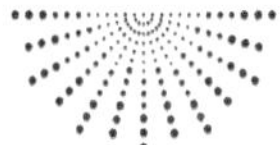

alcolm was happier than a horned toad at a mayfly festival.

And when his English springer spaniel was happy, Jim was happy.

It was one of those impossibly clear days that Washington, DC, dished out like dog treats in February. The chill winter days were probably behind them. In another month, even the occasional below-freezing nights would be nothing but a memory. Now it was an hour past sunrise, the temperature was already above forty, and the maples and beeches along the White House fence line looked as if the tips of their branches had been dusted with just the tiniest bit of bright green. The ornamental cherry trees were already glowing bright pink with the promise of the spring to come.

The air smelled fresh and vibrant with possibility. He loved the way that every city had its own smell. He'd now been in DC long enough that each season wrapped about him like fireflies on a summer evening with its own special particulars. Most of his life had been lived on the road in one way or another, but three years here just might be enough to anchor him in place for a lifetime.

He often wondered what Malcolm smelled on such days. The freshening grass? The latest civilian dog pee-o-gram on a tree trunk?

The track of the other US Secret Service PSCO explosives-sniffing dog currently on patrol?

Handling a USSS Personnel Screening Canine—Open Area, also known as a friendly or floppy-eared dog, around the White House perimeter was the best duty there ever was. He and Malcolm had been walking this beat for three years now, putting even the mailmen to shame. Just because a blizzard *and* a hurricane had ripped through last year, each shutting down the city, didn't mean the security at the White House put its feet up—at least not these six paws. The only things that had been moving in the whole area during either event were emergency services, the guards at the Tomb of the Unknown Soldier out at Arlington Cemetery, and White House security.

The snowstorm had been a doozy by DC standards, almost as deep as Malcolm's legs were long. The next morning had been a surprisingly busy day at the fence line as tourists had trudged through a foot of heavy, wet snow to get photos of the White House under a thick, white blanket. Most of the crazies had the good sense to stay warm in their beds that day.

Not even the worst of the crazies came out during the hurricane.

Today it was the sunshine *and* the madness that drew people to his patrol zone along the White House fence. Delineating the two before Malcolm picked out the madness-motivated ones had become one of his favorite games to occupy the time. He figured the visitors to the fence fell into five distinct categories, only two of which Malcolm was trained to give a hoot about.

The True Tourist. They would just stand and stare though the steel fence. It had been formed to look like the old wrought iron one, but was far stronger—a Humvee that hit this fence would just bounce off. These people were often the older set. They were easily marked at a distance by taking pictures of the White House rather than taking selfies of them *at* the White House.

The Clickbait Tourist. They'd barely glance at the magnificent building. But even if they never actually looked at it, everyone inundated by their social media feeds probably more than made up for the lack.

The Squared-away Vet. The ex-military who arrived to see the representation of everything they had given. Whether standing tall or rolling along in a wheelchair, they came to see, to try and understand. He liked talking to them when he could. Jim had done his dance. Nothing fancy—a "heavy" driver for three tours hauling everything from pallets of Coca-Cola to Abrams tanks.

The Mad Vets and the Crazies. These guys were damaged. The less toxic ones just wanted to tell their story to the President so that he "really" understood. But there was a sliding scale right up to the ones who wanted retribution. These were the fence jumpers. They might have a protest sign, an aluminum foil hat, a .45 tucked in their pocket, or a load of righteous wrath strapped to their bodies. No real plot or plan, they were solo actors and had to be stopped one at a time. He and Malcolm caught their fair share of those—maybe more because Malcolm was such an awesome explosives detection dog. These were the main target of the fence patrol.

The Terrorist. Bottom line, that's why his team and all of the others were here even with them all knowing they were, at best, no more than an early warning of any concerted attack. They'd all seen the movies *White House Down* and *Olympus Has Fallen*. It was amazing how much Hollywood could get wrong and still scare the crap out of you—definitely not entertainment to anyone who worked guarding the White House. They discussed worst-case scenarios all the time. And he sure prayed that it didn't happen until after he was dead and buried—though he'd wager that he could be pissed just fine from the grave if someone attacked his White House. Three years of walking around its perimeter, keeping it safe, made it at least partly his.

It was still early enough in the day that the fence line was almost exclusively the top three categories. The Mad Vets and the Crazies category typically didn't kick in hard until later in the day when their morning meds wore off.

He saw a Squared-away Vet standing at the fence. The officers were particularly easy to pick out. They liked everything in order and would instinctively find the exact centerline—at either Lafayette Square to the north or the curving line of the President's Park to the south like this one. As predictable as sunshine on a clear day, they would come to a halt at precisely the twelve or six o'clock positions and simply stare.

Normally they didn't notice him or react if they did. This one stared at him...no, at Malcolm, with eyes so wide it was a wonder that they remained in his head.

"*Gute Hund,*" he instructed Malcolm—training him in German avoided confusion with an alert word accidentally spoken in a sentence. He'd met a dog once trained with the numbers in Japanese: *Ichi*—sit. *Ni*—stay. *San*—down. *Shi*—heel... Pretty darn slick. He'd thought about retraining Malcolm to be bilingual for the fun of it, but it seemed a dirty trick to play on a perfectly nice dog.

Gute Hund—good dog—told Malcolm he was off duty and could relax and be a dog for a moment rather than a sniffing magician.

It also gave Jim an excuse to let Malcolm approach and really check out the veteran up close just in case he was a Crazy-in-disguise. Even "off duty" Malcolm would respond if he smelled something dangerous.

Nope, guy was clean.

Jim glanced back at his patrol partner and nodded to indicate he'd be stopping for a moment. PSCO dogs never worked the fence line alone. Sergeant Mickey Claremont followed five to ten meters behind him. He was a big guy, looking even more so because of the bulletproof vest over his warm coat clearly labeled USSS Police. The AR-15 automatic rifle that he carried across his chest was part of his primary duty of being backup in case Malcolm did alert to someone. His second job included making sure that nothing slowed Jim's and Malcolm's progress. But Claremont had learned that there were certain types of guys that Jim always stopped for.

"You handled dogs?" He asked the wide-eyed vet hovering uncertainly at the fence.

All he managed was a nod back.

"Been out long?"

Head shake...then a grimace.

"Don't worry about it, brother. The words will come back eventually."

"You sure?" Barely a whisper and now the guy was watching him.

"Three tours in the Dustbowl. Nothing fancy. A heavy driver on the Kandahar and Kabul run." A fellow soldier would know what that meant. Hauling heavy loads, desperately needed by the in-country teams, from the port at Karachi, Pakistan, across a thousand kilometers to Kandahar, Afghanistan, or another five hundred klicks to Kabul. And every millimeter past the southern Wesh-Chaman border crossing or the Torkham one to the north had been run in constant fear of being a giant target on a known road. They'd lost a lot of guys, but he'd made it out in one piece.

"Two tours in Baghdad. One in Mosul," the guy at the fence was back to staring at Malcolm. He reached out a tentative hand as if he was seeing a ghost, but pulled it back before he could test the theory.

"That's some hard shit, brother," Jim wouldn't have wanted that tour any day. "Just give yourself some time."

The guy nodded, almost desperately.

"Hit the support groups," Jim dug out a card from the stack he always carried and handed it over. "These guys saved my ass. Gotta get back to work now. Good luck, buddy. *Such!*" Like *soock* with a guttural German *ck—Seek!* And Malcolm went back to sniffing his way along the fence line. Even letting the guy know that there was such a thing as "getting back to work" would help.

Claremont folded in behind him and worked the second part of his job as they passed more tourists.

"Yes, he's a bomb-sniffing dog." "No, you can't pet him because he's working right now." "Yes, it's okay to take his picture but, no, he can't pose for a picture because he's working right now." And so on in an unending litany.

Jim was so used to it that the silence always seemed wrong after the crowds thinned out at night but the patrols continued.

They were nearing their one-hour limit. A dog's nose only went so long without a break. One hour on, half-hour off. Which was good, that gave him enough time to do the paperwork that was part of being a PSCO handler: patrol reports, daily security briefing, studying the faces of known risk agents and recent threats. A letter writer was usually just that, someone dumb enough to threaten the President's life. Some even put their return address on the envelope. A single visit from the Secret Service was usually enough to scare those dummies back under the wire. But it didn't hurt to have studied their faces in case they transitioned to The Crazies category.

That's when he spotted the sixth type of visitor to the White House fence—The Newbie.

REESE CARVER STOOD at the White House fence and tried to figure out what had changed.

Actually, she knew exactly what had changed, but she couldn't reconcile how different it *felt*. Two years driving for the Secret Service —mostly in San Francisco, LA, and New York. Six months ago she'd grabbed the brass ring and been accepted for the Presidential Motorcade.

When she first came aboard, she'd waited outside the gate in one of the escort vehicles.

Then they'd started bouncing her around: press corps van, support vehicles for carrying the staff who didn't rate a ride in the President's car or one of the spares, then Command and Control while the guys in the back handled route logistics on the fly, and even the front Sweep Car that checked the route out ahead of the Motorcade.

Hazmat had been hard on her nerves because she knew nothing about what those guys actually did.

Watchtower—the ECM or electronic countermeasures vehicle— was capable of suppressing remote explosive triggers. It could also detect incoming threats that used radar or ones that used laser-targeting and jam those as well. It had made her feel like she was constantly the precise target of the attack—even if there'd never been one. Roadrunner was also a mobile cell tower, satellite uplink, and everything else communications oriented, which convinced her she was being *constantly* irradiated. When she asked, the guys manning the vehicle hadn't said the feeling was completely wrong.

She'd even driven Halfback—the lethal Chevy Suburban that carried the Presidential Protection Detail immediately behind the President's limo. She'd liked that one. The agents were armed to the gills, including a pop-up-through-the-roof M134 Dillon Aero Minigun. Could have used that back on the NASCAR racetracks a few times on some of the assholes who thought ganging up to shut out a female driver was good sport.

With all these different assignments, it had gotten to the point where she'd driven every vehicle except for Stagecoach—the Presidential monster itself, also nicknamed The Beast for a reason—and the ambulance that always trailed along behind.

She'd liked driving the unimaginatively named Spares. The two identical copies of the Presidential limousine played a constant shuttle game with Stagecoach so that a terrorist would never be sure which of the three Beasts carried the President and which were the decoys. Any Spare driver worth their salt dreamed of Stagecoach breaking down and the President shifting into their vehicle—which had happened only five times in the last two decades, so the chances were low.

The Secret Service had hundreds of elite drivers, from the San Francisco SWAT team to the Capitol Police of the Uniformed Division. The competition to reach the Presidential Motorcade had been fierce.

Then she'd crossed the Motorcade drivers' "finish line."

Stagecoach.

Just this morning she'd gotten a wake-up call from the head of the Presidential Protection Detail, Senior Special Agent Harvey Lieber.

"Bumping you to driving Stagecoach, Reese. Get your ass in here." With Harvey, that wasn't some slur because she was a black woman with an ass that she'd been complimented on far too many times. All it meant was for her to get her ass in there. From him she'd take that, but not from any other asshole.

That call had changed the world.

A part of her was ready to do a victory dance.

Reese Carver—the first woman to drive Stagecoach. And a black woman at that. She wanted to do her dance on the heads of every male idiot who said a woman couldn't do it. Every jerk who'd tried to put her down—even after she'd smeared them off the NASCAR track…or maybe especially then. She'd learned the hard way to keep it all inside. Men were expected to brag, but one little smile out of place and it tagged a woman as a bitch. Fine. Whatever.

But the other part of her could only stand and stare at the White House. Next time she drove onto the grounds, it wouldn't be a matter of escorting the President. Next time he'd be riding in *her* car. She'd have his life in her hands.

"What am I supposed to feel about that?" She didn't have a clue.

"First days are always like that," a deep baritone said from close beside her.

"What?" She turned and looked up at the bright-eyed UD smiling at her. The Secret Service Uniformed Division guys always struck her as a little foolish. Didn't they get it? United States Secret Service meant Special Agent. Secrecy. Not parading around Washington, DC, dressed like a cop. They really should be called something else. Maybe —as they *were* standing on the edge of the National Mall—they should rename them mall cops. She liked that. She'd didn't come up with funny things on her own very often, but that wasn't half bad.

"Your first day?" He nodded toward the White House in a friendly fashion. His smile said that he was completely assured of his own charm. She'd never yet met a man like that who actually charmed her.

"Not even close," she warned him off.

"Oh," his smile didn't diminish. "You have the look."

"What look?" She didn't have a look. No one was supposed to be able to see what she was feeling. She'd learned that lesson the hard way a long time ago. "Like some lost fem in search of a big, strong, handsome man to protect her?"

He laughed. "Like you can see the White House, but it's spooking the crap out of you worse than a mouse at a cat convention. See that a lot on Newbies."

"Not." Keep it short. Make him go away. Nobody saw through her shields—ever. *So* not allowed. She looked away and down into the big brown eyes of a smiling springer spaniel. He was standing there looking up at her with his tongue lolling out. She reached out to pet him.

And he sat abruptly.

Reese froze.

It was the signal that explosive-detection dogs used to alert their handler that they'd found something. Out of the corner of her eye she saw the backup man shift his grip on his AR-15 semi-auto rifle as he moved for a better angle. Tourists continued streaming by as if nothing was amiss.

She straightened very slowly, keeping her hands in clear view.

The handler was still smiling, though his hand was now resting casually on the butt of his taser. "Been at the range recently? Malcolm will alert to the gunpowder residue on your sleeves and hands."

"Every day before work." She was a driver, not a shooter, but if it came down to it, she'd be ready. "An hour workout, then five magazines at the range."

"I do my workout after my shift."

He definitely had a very nice workout build—powerful without being overworked. But she wasn't real interested in yet another guy staring at her in her workout gear.

"Maybe I need to switch over to mornings. Though Malcolm here likes to start his mornings right off, then nap at the end of the day while I hit the weights."

So, he'd identified her as Secret Service and figured they'd be using the same gym under the nearby headquarters building. Not a giant leap. Despite what some people thought, protection agents' jobs weren't to be undercover in their suits; it was to be so obvious that no one would think of testing their resolve.

She gave him a little credit for not looking away from her face, despite his comment. So he wasn't a complete low-life. His accent said Oklahoma, his smile said self-proclaimed lady killer, but his light brown eyes, with hair to match, were definitely watching her slightest motion in a way that said professional.

"How about handing me your ID slow as a rattler on a winter day."

She unbuttoned her winter coat, then eased open the lapel of her suit jacket. She reached past her FN Five-seveN 5.7mm primary weapon and slipped out her leather Secret Service ID holder. Despite it having her badge and ID, he called it in. That was good—she liked that he was being doubly careful. When he also confirmed her signing time in and out at the range this morning, she was actually impressed. It was far more than she'd expected from a "mall cop" who flashed his charming smile as if it was all the ID he needed.

"Nice to meet you, Clarice Carver. Sorry for the trouble," he handed back her badge holder. The backup guy eased his AR-15, but not completely.

"Reese." She heard the soft click as the backup reset the safety on his weapon. She'd missed it coming off.

"To your friends?" and that smile was back. Asshole apparently thought it was beneath him to introduce himself.

"And my enemies."

"Good to know. You headed in or planning to stand and gawk a while longer?"

"Headed in," she hated that she'd been caught in a moment of weakness and just wanted to get away from him.

"Well, that's fine then. Me and Malcolm, we're at the end of our hour on the fence. we'll go in with you." And he nodded toward the gate another hundred meters down the sidewalk.

Reese tried to figure out how to shed the guy, but couldn't come up with anything.

He tossed a treat to his dog, then scrubbed his fingers into the dog's fur as it crunched happily. *"Gute Hund. Sehr gut!"* He said it in a squeaky high voice that the dog clearly enjoyed, but it made the man sound totally ridiculous—and actually a *little* charming.

Then he spoke to his dog softly. *"Such."*

And the dog changed; they both changed.

The dog rose to his feet and began sniffing his way forward through the crowd. The UD officer stepped out smoothly and the two of them were suddenly all business. His eyes scanned the crowd ahead of his animal, both of them on watch.

The change was almost shocking.

He was still the same guy. Even though she was looking at his back, she could tell by the way the crowd reacted to him and his dog that he was projecting the same easy-going demeanor ahead like a radar sweep. But by the way he moved—just enough on his toes to be ready for a quick reaction, scanning not where his dog was, but looking out and ahead—spoke of a highly trained professional. Even the positioning of his non-leash hand; it swung close beside the taser on his hip with every stride.

"I'm Claremont, by the way," the backup man was on the move as well and was now passing by her.

She fell in beside him.

"Reese Carver," she offered in return, but he just tapped his earpiece. *Right.* He would have been listening in on the same frequency that the dog handler had used. "Is he as good as he looks?" Reese nodded to the team ahead of them.

"Better. Three years on the fence line. Jim and Malcolm have the highest identify-and-capture ratio of any team by a factor of three times." Claremont smiled at her as if he was answering a very different question about just what kind of quarry the handler identified and captured.

Ladies' man. Didn't matter as it had nothing to do with her. It was his three years patrolling the fence that surprised her. If he and his dog were such hot shit, why were they still doing the beat cop routine out in the weather?

Jim wondered at just how stupid he'd been. He'd never even introduced himself—as if his mama hadn't raised him right. And now Claremont chatted up the hot Special Agent Reese like they were old pals. He couldn't quite hear what they were saying, but there was no mistaking Claremont's smooth Southern accent that slayed so many of the ladies.

That's when he identified Reese's accent. It was well masked, like she'd worked on it hard, but she was from the Carolinas just like Claremont.

Redneck trucker from Oklahoma didn't stand a chance.

Too bad. Special Agent meant she was good. But there'd also been a small code on her ID that said she was a member of the Presidential Protection Detail. He almost hadn't called in to confirm her identity because it was so unlikely for that to be forged. He finally had, just to see if he could learn anything else about her. No joy. The main desk had merely confirmed she was USSS and even pushing through to the range officer only confirmed that she had indeed logged five twenty-round magazines that morning. But that little code on her ID said that she was beyond exceptional in more than her looks.

Just two inches shy of his own six feet. Pitch black hair that fell straight to scatter over strong shoulders. Her deeply brown skin was smooth and creamy. It was her dark-dark eyes that had been so hard to look away from. There was something about them that both hid and revealed the woman at the same time.

And when she'd pulled back her jacket, he saw her trim waist with enough of a figure to not make the big Five-seveN handgun look ridiculous in her shoulder holster. The weapon said even more about her. What he could see of the handle had the shine that only came from being held for thousands of rounds.

As he'd returned her ID, he'd spotted the shooter's calluses thickening the web between her thumb and forefinger. She looked like everything a man could want and he'd messed it up something awful.

Sadly, it wasn't the first time. Maybe he was losing his touch. When Linda and her dog Thor had joined the White House team last month, he'd done nothing much about it. At least not right off. That had *seemed* like a good idea.

She'd been cute as hell, and he'd entertained a few thoughts. But while he'd been taking his time, she and her dog had gone on to save over sixty lives, including the President's. It was a Secret Service agent's wet dream—making that once-in-a-career save. Then, while he wasn't watching, she'd gone and fallen in love with the chocolate chef, which seemed a little unfair. It was like the Big Guy upstairs was smacking him in the face and shouting, "Wake up, dude."

The last girl to make him even think about wanting the long-haul had been Margarite of the sleek body, long red hair, and a laugh like Christmas sleigh bells. Though she'd hung with him for almost a year, she'd made no secret that her aim was always set higher. "You've walked that fence so long, there's a rut there with your name on it." Margarite had finally latched onto a Congressional aide who—with her street smarts at his side—was now in the running as a Virginia state senator.

He'd had a lot of time to think about it while walking the fence line. The sex had been good and the companionship great. But they'd been on such different tracks. He'd always been content to be who he was and she'd…never been. In the end he'd wished her well, though what he'd really wished was that she was still there beside him when he woke up in the mornings.

Oh well. He figured that, just like Malcolm, he'd keep patrolling ahead and someday he'd catch a scent and track the right lady.

Pity about Reese Carver though. She was quite something. He wondered what it might be like waking up next to her. It was a very nice image.

At the security booth, he and Reese stepped through the door while Claremont waited for the next dog team to come out.

They both showed their IDs and were waved through easily.

So Reese was known. *Of course* she was known. Her code said Presidential Protection Detail. That was a very small, very elite group. Strange that he hadn't seen her walking around. There was no way not to notice her.

IF JIM the dog handler was arrogant, Reese decided that his backup security was perhaps the least subtle guy on the planet. Pleasant, well-trained, and just about everything he'd said could be taken as sexual innuendo. He always said it as if it was a joke—no way to quite take offense despite her sensitivity being set on ultra-high. But it was getting old by the time they reached the entrance to the grounds. What the guy really needed, she decided, was new material.

Once through, Jim waved to a Uniformed Division woman headed out to take his place. She was preceded by a small, brindle-colored mutt. They looked as if they both belonged in suburbia somewhere, but he wore the harness of a USSS dog and his handler was vested and armed.

"Hey, Malcolm," the woman called out to the springer spaniel.

"Hey, Thor," Jim did the same to her dog. The two of them traded smiles as they passed.

Thor? Reese could only shake her head in wonder. That little mutt was the one who'd caught a potential bomber outside the fence and then saved the President's life just last month? Never judge a dog by its stature, she supposed. The female handler followed Thor as he trotted happily out the gate and joined up with Claremont before heading off on patrol along the other side of the fence.

She looked down at Malcolm and silently asked, *Anything you want to be telling me?*

He just wagged his tail at her.

Reese turned for the White House and almost ran over a teen standing there.

"Hi!"

How did some tourist and her Sheltie dog end up on this side of the fence?

Malcolm almost took Reese out as he and the Sheltie rushed to greet each other in the area usually reserved for her knees.

"Hey, Dilya," Jim said from so close over Reese's shoulder that it was all she could do to not jump.

"Hi, Sergeant Fischer."

"You don't call me Jim and I know you're up to something." He sounded just a little too relieved at having an excuse to say his name in front of her. At least he knew he had been a jerk.

"Doesn't replace a proper introduction, Sergeant," she muttered at him. Southern politeness said that you introduced yourself properly when meeting. And, in her experience, it was a bad sign when a guy couldn't be bothered to do that.

He might have blushed at being caught but he recovered fast, making it hard to tell. "Right. Sorry. Reese Carver, this is First Dog Zackie. Zackie, this is Reese," he addressed the Sheltie. Which explained what the dog was doing here.

"Hey," the girl protested.

Jim just grinned. "And this pint-size piece of trouble is Dilya Stevenson."

"Not the introduction I meant," but Reese could see that he knew that. She turned to the kid, "Hi." She never knew what to say to kids.

They would come up when she used to do publicity for her NASCAR sponsor. The boys were easy—they were either young enough to have a crush on her car or old enough to have a crush on a woman who won races in one. The young girls were tricky. They were either some weird mix of shy and tongue-tied that she'd never understood, or chatty-beyond-belief, which she'd both never understood or had time for. A lot of them idolized her as a symbol of all women or all African-American women or...

She was just a girl who'd grown up in a racing family outside Charlotte, North Carolina. They'd lived a five-block walk from the Charlotte Motor Speedway rather than out in the McMansions along Lake Norman with most of the other pro drivers. As a young girl, if she wasn't watching Pop or her brother racing, she was timing their competition or hanging out in the garage or the pits. The school bus never dropped her at home—it had always dropped her at the Speedway's back gate.

This Dilya was the first teen Reese had been near since she'd left racing and joined the Secret Service. Without even racing as a guide, she had no calibration for what the kid could want.

She was mid-teens, with that strung-out look of hitting her

growth, though she'd never be tall. Her skin was about half as dark as Reese's own but the tone was different, so not African heritage. Her hair fell in a thick ruffled wave almost to her elbows, but that wasn't her standout feature. It was her eyes. Impossibly green, they assessed Reese as thoroughly as Reese was assessing her. Except she had the feeling that those green eyes could see far deeper into her than the kid was letting on. Or than Reese was comfortable with.

Her parka was bright blue. Her jeans stonewashed. Her boots red cowboy. She also wore a beautiful, hand-knit scarf of brilliant colors.

The three of them—the five of them counting the dogs frolicking up and down the wide, secured street between the EEOB and the White House—headed toward the entrance to the West Wing. Left with no choice except to draft along, she fell in behind them.

Jim wasn't doing a lot to impress her so far.

"Are you on the New York shopping trip?" Dilya slowed down to ask her.

"What trip?" Reese hadn't heard anything about New York.

"Oh. Never mind." Her smile was pleasantly enigmatic.

Staffers were hurrying past. Dilya and Jim walked as if there was all the time in the world. Reese considered moving by them, but that seemed rude, even for her.

She scanned behind her to the fence line and saw nothing out of place. Thor and his female handler, with Claremont in tow, were just disappearing behind a large beech tree, still devoid of leaves. To her right she could catch glimpses of the grounds through the screen of trees: the children's garden, the basketball court, a hint of blue of the swimming pool, and the white facade of the south face of the White House.

When she turned back, Dilya was eying her closely. A Marine in full uniform had come up beside Jim. It sounded as if they were talking football scores. Didn't they get that it was February and the season was over?

"Maybe you both got off on the wrong paw," Dilya must have noticed the direction of her glare. "You know, I just read *Pride and*

Prejudice. They hated each other at first but it was just because they didn't know each other."

Reese swallowed hard. She barely knew the story, but it was a romance novel and they only ended one way. No way was this Presidential dog walker going there.

"You better not be saying what I think you're saying."

"What would that be?" The girl practically batted her eyelashes at her in all innocence. Inside the door, Dilya pulled out her security badge, swept it through the turnstile, then flipped the lanyard over her head.

Reese noted that it was an "All Access" badge: Residence, the Oval, Air Force One, even the Motorcade. She knew for a fact that neither the President nor the VP had kids yet, though both wives had just recently been reported pregnant—the security briefing beating CNN by less than an hour.

"Where did you come from?"

"Uzbekistan. At least I think so. I don't really know. I can still speak Uzbek, so I'm guessing I grew up mostly there."

"How did you end up here?" Reese was finding the conversation more than a little surreal. They stepped through the lobby and past the Situation Room entrance, where the Marine peeled off. There was a solid flow of people around them now, all moving fast and with purpose. Normally she'd be in perfect sync with them, but now she was with these slow-moving dog people and felt out of step with herself.

"I walked."

"You walked from Uzbekistan to the White House?" Reese only roughly knew where that was. North and west of Afghanistan?

"No, silly. I would have had to swim the ocean. I only walked to Pakistan."

Jim stopped so abruptly that Reese slammed square into his back. It was like walking into the SAFER barrier that encircled racetracks. The man was impossibly solid. She stepped back, but her nervous system felt as if she'd just been hit with a taser charge. No man should feel so real.

"You *walked* to Pakistan?" Jim was staring down at Dilya.

The teen shrugged.

"Is that hard?" Reese actually made the mistake of engaging him in conversation despite her plan to never waste her time on him again.

"You walked across the freaking *Hindu Kush?*" Jim ignored her and kept his attention on Dilya. "That's worse than surfing in a Texas hurricane."

Reese had heard of those mountains. Okay, that was hard. Beyond hard.

"With my parents, before they were killed. Then by myself until Kee found me." Dilya winced—perhaps at the memory, perhaps at talking about it at all. "Not fun."

"Not fun?" Jim's eyes were wide. "I drove that road nigh on a couple hundred times. It's the worst place I've ever seen to cross."

Reese looked at him again. More change. He'd driven the Hindu Kush a couple hundred times? That meant he'd been in the military, part of the war effort there. So, he wasn't just some dog handler, not if he'd done that.

"We didn't follow roads much," Dilya took a sudden interest in the First Dog, kneeling to comb his fluffy brown-and-white fur with her slender fingers.

"You really went all the way across those mountains?" Jim missed the teen's desire for a subject change.

"To Bati."

"The soccer stadium? The one converted into a US Special Operations fort?"

Dilya stopped fooling with Zackie and looked up at Jim abruptly.

"I delivered some loads there," he explained. "Fuel and food, mostly. Hauled out some pretty shot-up helicopters too."

"I lived there for over two years with my new parents," Dilya's voice was small.

"You were embedded with—" Jim glanced at Reese and snapped his jaw shut.

Dilya shrugged. "They rescued me from the middle of a firefight...

and then they kept me." She jolted to her feet and was gone so fast it was as if she'd never been there.

"Bati?" Reese asked as Jim gazed down the crowded hallway in the direction Dilya had disappeared.

"Forward operating base," he spoke as if he stood ten thousand miles away, looking at the scene. "Spec Ops. Very hush-hush. Home to the best team and best pilot of the entire Night Stalkers—that's Army airborne."

Hard to have grown up in Charlotte and not know about the Night Stalkers. They flew overhead all the time on their way between their base at Fort Campbell, Kentucky, and the Special Operations teams stationed at Fort Bragg, North Carolina. They'd done numerous demos at the Speedway before big races. Once even delivering the pace car from one of their big black helos.

"What was the pilot's name?" She wasn't sure why she asked. She'd only ever met one pilot years before, but the woman had left an indelible impression. A female Army helicopter pilot. Reese hadn't even known there were any. Reese *had* spent a really fun one-week stand with her gunner—a macho Latino named Tim Maloney—but it was the woman who stuck in her memory.

"Emily Beale. Most impressive woman I've ever met." Then Jim turned to face her and that Mr. Charm smile was back. "So far."

CHAPTER TWO

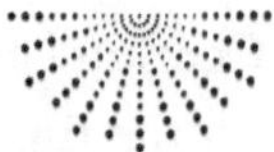

$\mathcal{R}$eese really didn't need this shit. She strode off along the short length of hallway remaining to reach the Secret Service Ready Room. It was the largest office in the entire West Wing, roughly twenty-five by ninety feet: about three times bigger than the Oval Office. If size implied power, the Secret Service were it.

She'd only been inside a few times. Normally the Motorcade assembled in the garage beneath the Secret Service headquarters five blocks east of the White House. She'd been on the grounds dozens of times, but almost always in her vehicle.

Jim and Malcolm veered off toward one of the jam-packed desks that filled a whole end of the room without even a glance in her direction. She watched out of the corner of her eye as he topped up a water bowl, played with Malcolm for a moment, then gave him some treats before directing him to a doggie bed. The guy sat at the desk and pulled out some paperwork.

Reese felt kind of irked. First no proper introduction, then—she'd thought—they'd been having a nice moment together with Dilya. Only to be followed by him turning all smarmy and now walking away from her as if she was nothing.

She hadn't been too weird, had she? She'd tried to be normal—but since she wasn't, it was hard to pretend. She'd managed a couple of friendly moments… And now the cold shoulder.

Fine!

Because she was female? Or black? Or… Didn't matter to her. No reason to care anyway what some dog handler thought.

She turned her back on him, walked through the briefing area that could seat thirty agents, and headed for the small side-by-side offices at the far end. They defined the dual nature of the Secret Service.

To the left, Captain Baxter, head of White House Detail for the Uniformed Division and Jim the dog boy's boss. To the right, Senior Special Agent Harvey Lieber, head of the PPD—the Presidential Protection Detail. He'd been her boss for over a year now, but with her promotion to driving Stagecoach this morning, their relationship had just changed. She was now his right-hand woman for all things Motorcade. Actually, his left-hand woman, as he always rode in the front passenger seat in any vehicle the President was aboard.

Reese knocked discreetly and waited at the threshold.

No response as he stared at his computer screen.

"Good morning, sir."

Harvey grunted but didn't look up. He was a good-looking guy. Tall, good shoulders, brown hair and eyes almost the same color as the springer spaniel's—easy bet he wouldn't appreciate that comparison. Rumor said he was single, but imagining a woman being up to his demanding standards was hard to do.

Though she *did* like a challenge, there wasn't any spark there for her. Besides, he was her boss and she *wanted* Stagecoach. He didn't push her hot button any more than mall-cop-turned-dog-walker Fischer.

He'd ridden with her several times, first out at the James J. Rowley Training Center and later in the Motorcade sitting with her in a Spare rather than with the President. At the time she'd thought it was merely odd, not getting that she was being tested to take over the helm of Stagecoach from Ralph McKenna when he retired.

He didn't look up from his screen as he reached out and pounded the flat of his palm against the wall. Not in anger, more as if… Oh, the shared wall with his Uniformed Division counterpart.

"What?" Captain Baxter stepped up close behind her. He was a crew-cut, gray-haired, one-man-army who was a White House institution. He was now on his fourth President as head of the White House UD.

Reese tried to move aside, but the office wasn't big enough to fit the three of them unless she sat down in the one open chair. And Harvey hadn't invited her to do that.

"We—" Harvey finally looked up and blinked at her in surprise. "Where the hell did you come from, Carver?"

"I've been standing here. Knocked and everything, sir."

"Sass." He looked past her at Baxter. "You've seen it?"

"I've seen it."

Reese hadn't, but figured that they'd know that and kept her mouth shut.

"Who the hell thinks these things up?" Harvey continued grousing.

"Not me."

"Doesn't make me feel any better."

After two years in the Secret Service, Reese was used to cryptic conversations, but this was getting awkward.

Then Harvey looked at her and narrowed his eyes. He squinted at her long enough that she couldn't help herself and spoke.

"What?"

"I'm gonna bounce you out of Stagecoach."

Reese didn't know whether to rage or cry. All she managed was a squeak as she'd just stopped breathing. She'd fought so hard, never really believing that she'd make the goal of being the President's driver—only two or three per decade made the grade—but that hadn't stopped her from gunning for it. And she'd made it only to have it ripped away on her first day?

It wasn't right. It wasn't fair! She'd—

"Just for the next three days, dammit. I've got three drivers out with that bug that's going around and I need a lead for a First Lady Motorcade. President isn't scheduled outside the Oval this week. So stop freaking out and take a goddamn breath, Carver."

She tried, but it wasn't working well. She tried again and managed a wheezing gasp that made Harvey smile and totally embarrassed her.

"Always good to know how bad you want it," Harvey enjoyed rubbing salt in the wound.

She restricted herself to a simple nod of acceptance. That was twice in one day she'd let her feelings show. *Get it together, girl.*

As to how bad she wanted it? There wasn't a single accolade higher than being the President's driver. It was the Daytona 500 and the Cup Series all rolled into one. It didn't have the high public profile, but that had never been what motivated her to drive.

So the First Lady needed a Motorcade? That meant…

Reese decided it was time to prove she wasn't a complete loser.

"Is it the shopping trip?" The girl Dilya had mentioned that. First and Second Lady both pregnant. Motorcade. It all made sense.

Harvey opened his mouth, squinted at her, then snapped it shut.

Chalk one up on the scoreboard.

Harvey turned to Captain Baxter. "Gonna need your best dog team, too."

Reese caught herself holding her breath again. Please *not* cold-shoulder Jim Fischer. He'd already deemed her too weird. That she knew he was right didn't help. Or maybe he was the one who was too weird with his non-introduction. Hinting she might be the best woman ever, and then just walking away from her cold.

Whatever he was, it was confusing the crap out of her and she wasn't interested in spending another second in his presence.

Captain Baxter didn't hesitate or turn, just calling out loud enough to be heard throughout the long room.

"Fischer! Get yourself over here, boy."

JIM WONDERED what he'd done wrong this time. Baxter was fussier than his own sister on prom night about getting everything downright perfect. An old warhorse like Captain Baxter fussing with his makeup—now there was an image.

Of course, Jim had witnessed far too many breakdowns, accidents, and just plain damn foolishness while driving the nation's highways—and the Paki-Afghani ones. He agreed with Baxter about getting it all right, but he'd thought he was running clean.

He flashed a *stay* sign to Malcolm as he shoved out of his chair and headed over to the Captain. Malcolm stayed on his doggie bed, but Jim could feel the spaniel's eyes tracking him across the room.

Reese Carver stood there beside the Captain.

Crap! Had she seen something and made a report? Griped about him double-checking her ID? He'd already received the "go away, boy" message loud and clear. He wasn't sure quite what he'd done to make her stalk off like that, but he knew when to steer clear. Apparently not soon enough. He shouldn't have even walked with her through security.

He thumped Thompson, one of the other dog handlers, lightly on the shoulder just to steady himself. Thompson's "Hey, Jim," sustained him most of the way over.

Reese had shed her heavy winter coat and now stood in a typical, dark gray Special Agent suit. Except *typical* had nothing to do with how it looked on her.

He barely managed to stop the whistle of surprise. He'd thought she was hot when all he'd seen was her face. That brief glimpse of her figure as she'd handed over her ID wallet hadn't prepared him for the woman standing here now. She looked dangerous, powerful, and sexy as a centerfold all at once. How did a woman do that?

She glared at him like he was a preacher man for the anti-Christ. He did his best to stop admiring her figure, but it was hard—real hard. She looked sweeter than a hot rod and more powerful than his old Kenworth T680 semi-tractor.

"Yeah, boss?" He focused on Captain Baxter's ugly mug. Far safer.

"Pulling you off the fence."

Jim shrugged his acceptance, but didn't like it. They'd offered him other jobs before, and he'd always found a way to turn them down. This one wouldn't be any different. He liked his walks with Malcolm. He'd seen what happened to other guys who aspired to more. They spent their days patrolling the insides of convention centers and meeting rooms, basement kitchens and garage entries.

Not for him.

Not for Malcolm. Dogs were supposed to be outside with room to roam.

"What is it with you people today?" Harvey growled.

Jim did his best to fix his expression. It was never a good idea to be upsetting the head of the Presidential Detail.

"You two bozos know that First Lady Anne Darlington-Thomas and Former First Lady Geneviève Matthews work for the UNESCO World Heritage Centre at a very *senior* level?"

He didn't pause long enough for either of them to respond, which was fine. He knew it, and if Reese was PPD, she'd certainly know it as well.

"Normally they travel from their offices here in the East Wing up to the UN building in New York about once a month for meetings. Well, this time they've added on a day of shopping, eating out, and going to a Broadway musical. Second Lady going along for the ride." Harvey rolled his eyes as if he was in pain. "The three ladies together will make a very attractive target," then Harvey stabbed a finger in his direction. "Not a single snide remark out of you."

He held up his hands palm out declaring his innocence, though the man was right. First Lady Darlington-Thomas was a short, pretty-as-could-be blonde from one of the best Southern families—with all the class and none of the expected attitude. Former First Lady Ms. Matthews was a tall, full-figured French-Viet beauty who could have had a career walking runways. Second Lady Alice Darlington was just cute as kittens—and a brilliant CIA analyst. The three together would be a total knockout.

And a very high-value target to some nutcase.

Jim glanced at Reese, offering a smile about just how funny the moment was, but all he got back was the chill professional in her Special Agent suit. Right, she was ready to scrape him off the bottom of her shoe like some of Malcolm's... Jim sighed. Yep, just like that.

Baxter at least offered him a sly grin of commiseration. Whether for Harvey's remark about the leading ladies or Reese's cold shoulder, he couldn't tell.

"They hit the Downtown Manhattan heliport in twenty-six hours. I'll get a logistics team on it, but NYPD is holding a big explosives detection exercise and are reluctant to pull any more dog teams than they have to. I promised to loan them a lead team. So, I want you two in the First Lady's Suburban and headed north now. You can drive there faster than I can get air transport in place. Route and area familiarization today. Pick them up at ten hundred hours tomorrow morning for a day in the city. UN meetings on Day Three, then home that night. I'll have a list of their planned stops before you get there. The rest of the team will be dispatched out of the New York office or fly in with her. You can buy a toothbrush and a change of underwear on the way. Now move."

Harvey Lieber had barely paused for a breath in the whole rundown.

"Well? Why are you two still cluttering up my office. Go!"

So much for even having a moment to blink.

"Let's hustle," Reese turned for the door, grabbing her coat on the way.

"Okay if I get my dog and jacket first?"

Reese made a show of checking her watch, then smiled at him—almost. "Only if you hurry."

It was a nice almost-smile, so maybe he hadn't been totally tagged as an asshole. That would be good as it looked as if they'd be rubbing shoulders for the next sixty-plus hours.

Jim grabbed Malcolm's emergency go-bag: dog food, water bowl, and doggie med kit. He snagged his full vest, which included his own med kit and extra rounds, then raced for the door with Malcolm at his side. He had to double back for his jacket.

JIM HAD SEEN the First Lady's Suburban before, a carefully unremarkable vehicle. Unlike the President's limo or one of the black-on-black escort vehicles, this was a pleasant bronze color. It was also armored and powerful, with tinted windows and a luxury interior. The back seats had been replaced by a pair of generous arm chairs at the rear and a pair of rear-facing narrow bucket seats forward for aides. It was a serious machine even without its lethal escort.

"Do it," Reese's soft-spoken command echoed in the low-ceilinged garage beneath the Secret Service Building. She nodded to Malcolm. So, her first words since leaving the White House were to his dog. He sighed.

"*Such!*" Jim told Malcolm.

Malcolm circled the Suburban in moments. Jim popped the doors and Malcolm managed to jump in without help despite the high step. In moments he'd sniffed over the interior as well. Other than the two weapons' caches built into the driver and passenger doors, he didn't find anything. He finally curled up on one of the seats and resumed his nap.

They were out of DC and on the B-W Parkway headed north toward Baltimore before he braved her silence.

"Sorry for not introducing myself."

Nothing.

"How long are you planning to hold that oversight against me?" Maybe the problem was that she was distracting as hell. Women had never made him tongue-tied before, but he'd sure messed up around Reese. He *knew* that he'd seen her having a Newbie moment at the fence as clear as bluebells on the Oklahoma prairie, though it still puzzled him. He was finding her harder to read with each passing moment.

Five or six miles rolled by before she responded.

"You're the kind of asshole who thinks that women aren't up to your standard. I can hear the Okie in your voice. You just a misogynist or are you a racist, too?"

"I'm—" He glanced at Reese's profile. It was one of those trick questions with no right answer. He'd never been accused of either one before and he didn't know what to do with it. Denying it wasn't the answer either, because of course that was expected.

"Yeah, that's what I thought."

That finally pissed him off. "You a lesbian bitch or do you just hate dog owners?"

"I'm not—" Then she stopped for a long moment before she snapped out a bark of bitter laughter acknowledging the trap. "Okay, you got me." She slipped through three lanes of traffic in one smooth move.

Another couple miles passed by in strained silence.

"Look—" "Listen—" they both spoke at once as they passed the Fort Meade exit. Rather than go through the whole you…no, you… then more silence scenario, he just plunged in.

"You're driving the First Lady's vehicle."

Reese still didn't glance away from the road.

"You aren't looking real happy about it."

That at least earned him a shrug.

"Why? It strikes me as pretty damned impressive."

Her hands had tightened enough on the Suburban's steering wheel that he could imagine the leather creaking under the strain.

"Okay. Fine. Don't tell me. Can we at least get some munchies? It doesn't feel like a road trip without Fritos and root beer."

"I don't want to delay getting to New York. There's a lot of ground to cover there before they arrive. Besides, you call *that* road trip food?" At least she was talking.

"Yep! The best." He put on his best hick accent. "I've done driven a couple hundert thousand miles or more jes' on that for fuel. Way-ell… that and a passel o' diesel go-juice. What about you, little lady?"

"Krispy Kremes and Cheerwine."

"Damn, woman. You travel on that sugar rush, you oughta be sweeter than you're being." Cheerwine was a sickly sweet, hyper-carbonated soda from North Carolina. Though he could have thought of a better way to say that, but that train had left the station so it seemed best to just let it go on by.

"And you oughta be more intelligent, but you aren't."

Again the silence dragged out right through Baltimore and onto I-95.

Reese Carver wasn't fitting neatly into any of the types that women always seemed to run into.

Roadhouse Girls were the ones who hung out at truck stops. Not the working girls, but rather the locals looking to be a little bad with a passing trucker. He'd certainly had his fair share of those back in his driving days, but had lost interest soon enough. Got to the point he'd rather just have a good night's sleep.

One step up were the Bar Chicks, looking to find some adventure between the sheets for a night or a week. Like the tackiness of bar floor on a boot heel, they always wore off even when he tried to hold onto one. Maybe faster when he did try.

The Show Girls were damn nice to look at and wholly untouchable. Convinced they were out of the league of everyone around them, and probably right about that.

The Nice Ones were hard to find. Girl next door. High school sweetheart. Stacie had been a nice one. She'd ridden as a shooter on his HETS—heavy equipment transport system, basically a damn big truck for hauling tanks around. They'd shared the route and a whole lot more for six months. But her tour had ended while his military career was just gearing up. She'd saved them both the pain and Dear Jim'd him on their last night together in Karachi.

The Pros. Again, not the working girls. These were the ones all bound up in their careers. They stuck, sometimes for a long while like the sultry Margarite. But they were always looking for what was next.

The Keepers…well, they were a myth of the highway. He saw them but, sure as Christmas falling in December, they were already taken.

Reese Carver was none of those. She had the career focus of the Pro, the iron wall and incredible looks of a Show Girl. But she had the feel of a Keeper without also being a Nice One, a combo he'd never thought of before.

One more try, then he was going to give up. Mama always said that taking problems head-on was better than tackling tapioca—not that he ever knew what she meant by that.

"I still don't know what I did to piss you off."

REESE'S HANDS were hurting from how hard she was gripping the steering wheel, which wasn't a good thing. A light grip was the secret to a good reaction time, but she couldn't seem to ease up.

"You want a list?"

In her peripheral vision she could see Jim shrug as if he didn't care.

Why had he really pissed her off? This wasn't like her.

She knew she was being nasty. It was a defense mechanism that she'd learned the hard way. Enough guys at the track had thought they could get away with grabbing her butt or breast because she was a black woman in a white man's sport. She'd never really noticed before, but it had made her tough. She learned young to be fast with a lug wrench—all that had saved her from a couple of really bad moments that she didn't want to remember.

But when had hard become nasty? She was never rude unless it was called for. Silent, yes. Obnoxious…

"You know Dilya?" Reese had found the best way to win was to slip up on someone sideways—though she didn't know why she'd started there.

"Thought I did. Walked across the Hindu Kush? She was probably at Bati when I was there. Guess I don't know her so much."

"She said something," and Reese couldn't believe she was about to repeat it, but it seemed she was. "About us being like the couple in *Pride and Prejudice*."

"So I'm the prejudiced jerk and something has wounded your pride?"

"You know the story?" She didn't, but that made sense with the title.

"Sure. Keira Knightley. I'll watch almost anything with her in it."

Which might explain his earlier brush-off. Reese couldn't help glancing down at her own chest. She was no stick-thin, flat-chested white chick. But if that was the way his tastes ran, then why had he been all Mr. Charm and smiles out at the fence?

"Can't say as it fits me," Jim continued. "Don't see myself as much prejudiced against anyone, excepting maybe the folks that tried to kill me overseas. What are you being prideful about?"

Reese sighed. Their stretches of silence had only gotten them through the first hour of the four-hour drive. They'd probably be tied at the hip for several days. Uncomfortable stony silence was still an option…just not a good one.

"Okay," Reese decided to face the real problem. "This morning, I get a wake-up call from Harvey Lieber that I'm taking over as driver for Stagecoach."

"Holy shit!" Jim twisted to face her. "You're the one they tapped to replace Ralph McKenna? The man is a freaking legend. That would scare the crap out of me too."

"I'm not scared." She *absolutely* wasn't scared, even if she'd been momentarily paralyzed at the fence line this morning. That *wasn't* fear, it was…something else. "I fought hard for that job. It's what happened next that is making me crazy."

"You're suddenly driving the First Lady's Suburban on a New York shopping trip," he said with an unexpected insightfulness for someone she'd accused of being an idiot.

Reese sighed. That was it.

"So, you're not only good enough for Stagecoach, but you're good enough to be bounced into the First Lady's vehicle on no notice. Strikes me as winning first *and* second prize at the county fair."

She hadn't thought of it that way. Now she was feeling foolish that she hadn't, yet this Okie dog handler did.

Reese actually glanced away from the road for the first time to look at him. Jim was back to watching the road, not her.

He was squinting ahead, but didn't seem to be looking at the traffic.

"Clarice Carver," he said her name slowly.

"Reese."

"Clarice Carver," he ignored her. "Used to be a NASCAR driver with that name. I seem to recall she was lighting up the track something fierce, then she just disappeared one day."

That was a past, a moment in time she didn't want to remember.

"Always figured you'd had kids or something."

Or something. No way was she going to be telling this guy about the worst day of her life.

"Used to follow NASCAR pretty close, before I went overseas. You did most of your racing while I was out and gone. Heard you were good though."

"I was the best."

IT WAS like the woman snapped back into focus in that instant. She didn't move, frozen hard at the steering wheel, staring out at the traffic, but Jim could suddenly see her clearly.

Maybe it was the pain in her voice.

Jim needed to call his sister. Sissy was always the red-hot NASCAR fan and could give him chapter and verse on every driver better than Pastor Daniels of Purcell, Oklahoma, First Baptist could quote from his Bible.

Didn't matter though.

"NASCAR to driving the President's limousine. I am sittin' here in the presence of greatness." What the hell kind of internal drive had it taken to do that? The kind that Margarite of the long red hair had always accused him of lacking.

No wonder Reese didn't have time for someone like him. She'd seen right through him and had practically been screaming to be left alone the whole morning. He hadn't done that real well either. He supposed now was as good a time to start as ever.

He glanced into the back of the Suburban.

Malcolm was snoozing and shedding in the First Lady's seat. He'd have to remember to wipe that down before they met the flight tomorrow morning.

Jim turned back to the road and flexed his hands. Even though he was a dog handler now, he'd spent so many years as a truck driver that sitting in the passenger seat felt completely useless.

He didn't even have road munchies to keep his hands busy at something.

CHAPTER THREE

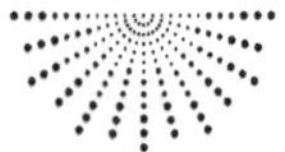

*R*eese was exhausted.

Wake-up call at six—with all of the emotional charge of being named to take over Stagecoach. Then the crash of thinking she was being bounced back out. On the road by eight, and hitting New York City by noon.

Harvey had sent a list of five stores, two restaurants, and a Broadway theater right on Times Square.

She'd dropped Jim at each place, where he and Malcolm had been met by an agent from the New York office familiar with the locale. While he'd been doing site familiarization, she'd scouted approach and getaway routes, driven in and out of garages until she knew the best access to each exit, including where to go to ground if they had to abandon the vehicle.

There was an odd congruency of knowing that Jim and Malcolm were doing exactly the same thing on the other side of the walls. Now that they were separated, they finally made sense together—working as a team to ensure their protectees' safety.

They certainly hadn't made any sense on the drive up. She supposed she'd gotten what she'd asked for. After unearthing her past, he'd been kind enough to finally leave her alone. Leave her alone to wallow in the pain of events she'd spent the last two years trying to forget.

At the end of the evening, they'd sat together in the car watching the patterns of movement as the Broadway show let out. How the crowd dispersed under normal conditions. Where the limos lined up. How many cabs sat in the queue.

Just on spec, they poked through the local bars and found one that seemed likely if the ladies wanted a drink afterward. The Rum House was a few blocks back from Times Square and didn't have the hard-packed, post-theater draw of Sardi's or Carmine's right on the Square.

"Can I buy you a round?" It was the first non-business thing Jim had said since Wilmington, Delaware.

"As long as the place has food," she'd had a knockwurst with sauerkraut from a street vendor about a thousand hours ago. The only one who'd eaten regularly had been Malcolm. It was nice watching how thoroughly Jim took care of his dog.

"Actually," he was studying the menu mounted by the door, "it does. Not much, but I'm past caring." It was the first hint he'd given that he wasn't utterly tireless in the pursuit of his duty.

He held the door for her, an unexpected politeness, then whispered as she passed close beside him.

"Watch this. It's always fun how these crowds react."

So Reese stepped in and waited. Jim indicated a small table by the window that would let them both sit with their backs to the wall: one facing into the bar, the other facing the window where they could keep an eye on the street.

He nodded for her to go grab the table. Only when she was seated and watching him did he start moving. But he didn't head straight for her. Instead, he guided Malcolm on a curving route that took him much more deeply into the crowded bar. It was quiet with the warm buzz of friendly conversations over soft, piped-in jazz.

While she watched, she decided that this place was a good choice. The Rum House felt upscale Old West. Worn hardwood flooring, heavy on the walnut and mahogany woods for décor, along with benches covered in dark leather and comfortable seats. The old-timey feel was achieved without being all phony about it. Hurricane-style lamps and circular styling of the woodwork simply evoked the era without getting cliché.

It took her a moment to see what was happening with Jim and Malcolm. Urban hipster couples would glance at the dog. Then look away. Then look back and up to see the tall, broad-chested handler. Some would go back to their meals. If it was a group of women however, their gaze intently followed Jim.

Had she really not noticed how handsome he was? And in this crowd, his good-old-boy attitude really stood out. Mr. Tall and Easy-going in his dark blue jacket with USSS emblazoned across its back in six-inch yellow letters. She'd never managed easy-going for a single second of her life, yet he looked as if he'd never been anything else. She could almost admire that.

Reese recalled their one actual contact, when she'd run into his back outside the West Wing Secret Service Ready Room. When he'd felt so impossibly solid and real. His long silences on the drive up had been uncomfortable at first, but by the end of it, she'd started to take on a little of his silence as her own. She wasn't used to that and couldn't decide if it was all bad or not.

Was the reaction of the women what Jim wanted her to see? Mr. *Guy* showing off how male he was?

Then he got a new reaction from a couple laughing over drinks.

Dog—turn away—Jim—turn away…

Then a double take so hard that the couple almost fell out of their chairs. The instant Jim was past them, they jolted to their feet without finishing their drinks. The man threw some bills on the table as if they burned him and then the couple raced for the door.

Jim didn't turn to follow their hurried exit; instead he shot her a big smile with a silent laugh behind it. At the far end of his wandering loop, he turned for her, continuing his wandering way through the crowded tables.

A group of three guys at a nearby table had the same massive double take-and-bolt reaction the moment they spotted Jim. No, the moment they spotted Malcolm.

This time they were close enough that she could see their faces go sheet white before they ran. One of them, while dumping bills on the table, accidentally tossed down a baggie of white powder. He looked at it in horror, then at Jim's back. He almost snatched it up, then, thinking again, he left the baggie on the table and ran out the door as if all the hounds of hell were after him rather than a sweet little springer spaniel who hadn't even looked at him twice.

Jim dropped into the chair beside her and Malcolm sat by his side. Jim wasn't laughing out loud, but he looked awfully pleased with himself.

Reese couldn't help herself and let the laugh out. After all the craziness and stress of the day, it was great watching people who didn't know that an explosives-sniffing dog wasn't trained to react to illegal drugs.

She laughed until it grew all out of proportion. It was like a release of so much she'd been keeping under hard control. She was going to be chauffeuring the three leading ladies of the current administration, and these people were freaking out about whether they'd be caught for having a couple hundred bucks of cocaine in their pockets.

Jim didn't look worried, he just waited her out until she could catch her breath.

Jim couldn't catch his own breath. He'd never imagined that the impossibly serious Reese Carver of the Presidential Protection Detail could laugh—and definitely not like that.

She was undone, and a shockingly beautiful woman emerged into clear view, no longer hidden by the serious, kick-ass heroine that would do just fine facing down Batman or Superman...or both at once. A stunning, black Wonder Woman in US Secret Service armor. All she needed was a sword and golden lasso of truth to complete the image.

Had *he*, with his little dance about the room, made her laugh like that? It did sound as if she was laughing with him and not at him, which struck him as encouraging—even if it was all out of proportion with the joke. He rubbed Malcolm's head to give her a moment.

Reese wiped at her eyes with a napkin and took quick sips from a glass of water that a waiter had rushed over.

Good service, another important aspect of choosing a locale to bring the First Lady's party tomorrow night. He'd also liked that the bartender working nearest the door was built like a bouncer and had traded a quiet nod of acknowledgement with Jim when he'd spotted the USSS on Jim's jacket. Subtle but watchful. Jim looked over at him while Reese finished her recovery. The bartender offered him a quick smile, clearly appreciating the joke as well.

A waitress cleared the abandoned tables, looking pleased at the generous payments dumped on each table. She delivered the baggie of powder to the bartender to deal with. The man grimaced, glanced one last time at Jim for saddling him with how to explain it to the police, then turned back to his other business.

"Thanks," Reese's voice was rough with the laughter, as if there had been pain behind it as well. "I guess I needed that."

"If you had told me before that you could laugh like that, I'd have no more believed you than a bright purple pinto horse."

"If I had told *me* I could laugh like that, I'd have called me a liar. Been a long time."

"Want to talk some about it?"

"Definitely not."

He ordered an Oklahoma Tropical Twister and she ordered a North Carolina Rum Cherry Bounce. The waitress was good; she didn't blink once at the two strange requests that had nothing to do with the big bad city. A pair of grilled Gruyère cheese sandwiches and a couple of sliders for Malcolm, without the buns or condiments, completed their order, and then they were alone again.

Still she wasn't talking, but he didn't want to let the moment go. It had been the first crack in the ice wall.

"Strange day," he started.

Reese offered a shrug of agreement.

He needed a new topic, without sounding like he was fishing. But he wasn't having much luck finding it.

"How did you get into dogs?" Jim could only blink in surprise at the sudden opening. All day, dark shades had hidden her eyes and her thoughts. Now the dim lighting of the bar seemed to do the same. Unable to read why she'd asked, he was still glad for the opening—surprisingly glad for it. It was clear that she was something special and, without him noticing, the brush-off had hurt. He knew he was good at what he did, but not being good enough for Reese Carver hurt.

"Mom gave me a German shepherd pup for my tenth birthday. I had to train him fast if I wanted to ride with Dad during the summers." He scratched Malcolm's head where it rested on Jim's knee.

"Ride with Dad?" Reese's tone could have been for a job interview. Very matter-of-fact and to the point. Maybe that was just the way she rode.

"He's an over-the-road owner-operator."

"You say those words as if they mean something," Reese said it deadpan with neither tease nor irritation. She was so neutral that she almost disappeared back behind her hard shell again.

"Long-haul trucker, which they call over-the-road. Owner-operator means that he's an independent who owns his own rig. Actually he owns nine of them. Now that us kids are all grown, Mom runs the business from the passenger seat—though she drives some too. My brother, sister, and two first cousins all drive for him."

"But not you?"

"Did local delivery during high school summers and long-haul a couple years after, once I was old enough to get my commercial ticket." Those had been good years. He wasn't sure why he hadn't gone back to them. Mom and Dad had found a lifestyle on the road that fit them, but he hadn't.

He told her how they stayed in touch despite the entire family's mobile lifestyle. He'd get a call every time someone in the family had a run that hit DC and they'd get together for a meal. Just last June, everyone had runs that hit Roanoke, Virginia. He and Malcolm had gone over for a couple days and they'd made a reunion out of mini-golf, BBQ, and some tall cold ones.

"Then the dogs," Reese interrupted his memories.

"Then the Army. Drove HETS—that's Heavy Equipment Transport System."

"Don't know those either."

"Big trucks. Seriously big," he liked sitting with her as if they did this all the time.

"You're a trucker kind of guy," Reese concluded and went silent as if the interview was now over.

"Was. Now I'm a dog kind of guy."

"Makes you the black sheep of the family," she nodded once to herself. She now had him well pigeonholed. He didn't know if that was comforting or irritating.

"Black dog—or brown-and-white in Malcolm's case—but yeah. How about you?"

How about her? Reese's past was a complete train wreck compared to Jim's ever-so-happy trucking family—*all for one and one for all.*

The waitress' delivery of their drinks bought Reese a few moments. The waitress guaranteed herself a nice tip by bringing out a water bowl for Malcolm.

Sipping the sweet rum cocktail that tasted a lot like home bought her a few more moments.

Like home.

That was all gone. Charlotte. The Motor Speedway. Her family.

"That was one dark thought," Jim was seeing past her armor once again.

She felt the automatic brush-off shrug ripple across her shoulders...and didn't like it. What was it about herself that she couldn't just talk to someone? She'd never known how to do that when she was a racer and she hadn't become any better at it in the Secret Service. Always a loner, just a highly skilled one.

For once, she was sitting next to someone who she *wasn't* in competition with. He was a nice guy, a dog handler, and *wasn't* after the same job she was.

"Okay, fine!"

"Fine?"

"I meant that for myself. I drove NASCAR."

"Already figured that." But he said it nicely.

"Made it to second row starting position. My dad had the fastest qualifying time for the race, so it was hard to feel bad about not getting the lead on the start. We started our last race at the head of the field; Number One and Two in a field of forty-three." She couldn't look up at Jim, instead seeing the heat shimmering off the Motor Speedway. A one-and-a-half-mile oval, it was going to be fast with the warm track giving the tires good traction. Turn 4 was in the shade of the grandstands. It would be slicker just at the moment that they transitioned from blinding afternoon sun coming out of Turn 3, plunging into the relative darkness of the shadowed Turn 4.

Every driver knew, and they were ready. That was where the accidents were going to be happening that day.

"I watched—"

Reese had never told anyone about this moment. Not the reporters, not the Secret Service interviewers.

"We were still running one and two after fifty laps. I was a car-length back when Pop lapped someone, or tried to. They banged fenders. A nothing contact. Such a little bump. But it was just enough to break his front end loose going into Turn 4."

She'd been drafting so close that she could see his face as the car spun a one-eighty. For just an instant he was traveling backward into the turn at a hundred and eighty miles an hour—nose to nose with her car. NASCAR racers rode the ragged edge of aerodynamically stable when they were nose into the wind.

"The wind caught the tail of his car. One moment he was right there in front of me," Reese looked out into the bar but all she could see was the track. "The next, he was tossed twenty or thirty feet into the air, slamming into the high fence. Flipping and spinning like a toy even worse than Richard Petty's historic crash."

A warm, strong arm across her shoulders was all that let her speak. All that let her breathe. She was caught up in the retelling and couldn't find any way out of it other than through.

"They have safety flaps in the roof that are supposed to break up the effect, but a weakened hinge broke and it didn't break up the unwanted lift. I got away clean, ducking under the wreck while it killed my father."

She sat up abruptly and faced Jim.

"I kept it cool. I ran safe and clean. Even when the pit boss came on the radio to tell me he hadn't survived, I held my line and raced. Some idea that I was going to win it for Pop."

"Did you?" His voice was a close whisper of sympathy.

She shook her head. "Blew an oil ring with ten laps to go. Engine tossed a rod and I was out. It happens."

Jim held her close. It felt so good to be able to turn into his shoulder and just be held.

Thankfully she'd buried the worst thing from that day so deep it didn't come out.

"My baby brother, always a little wild, died in the Argentine desert during the Dakar Rally. Pop died on the Charlotte Motor Speedway—his home track. I decided that I wasn't going to die there."

"What about your mom?"

When she tried to knock back her entire drink, Jim slipped it out of her hand and set it back on the table next to his own. Didn't matter. She drank so little that even half a drink had gone straight to her head, or why would she be telling a jerk of a stranger all that she was telling him?

"She was the smart one of the family. She left when I was three. Pop said she married a schoolteacher in Oregon. Didn't even call for the funeral."

Jim Fischer waited while alcohol, shame, and chagrin washed through her system like a bad fishtail. Waited while she stared at the tabletop as her heart threatened to throw a rod through her chest and end her. Finally she just stared at her fisted hands on the table.

Something bumped against her thigh a couple times on the side away from Jim, then a weight settled there. She looked down in surprise to see Malcolm looking up at her with sympathetic doggie eyes. Reese rubbed his head and felt a tiny bit better.

"He seems to like me."

"He has good taste in women."

Reese looked at him with surprise in her eyes.

"Not me," he held up his hands. "I have terrible taste in women. I always end up with the 'just friends' type." Now why had he paid her a compliment? She'd been hard-edged and pushing him away all day. And here he was handing her some cheap line. Except it didn't *feel* like a cheap line. She *was* an amazing woman, just not the type he ever landed.

"Just friends," she sounded thankful for the change of topic.

"Sure. Not a one of them has ever knit me a sweater."

Reese just blinked at him.

He took a bite of his sandwich, which had arrived at some point without his quite noticing. He looked down at the floor and saw that Malcolm had polished off his sliders *before* going to console Reese. He picked up the empty plate and slid it under his.

Reese Carver. She'd seen some seriously harsh times. Alone in the world, no wonder she'd brushed him off. He'd be scared to death of getting close to anyone again—the loss must have been horrific. Well, he might not understand how hard she'd brushed him off, but at least it explained things a bit.

He nudged her plate toward her. She nodded at it, but didn't take a bite.

"Ma always said that you could tell if a girl was serious if she knit you a sweater."

"I don't knit," Reese finally reached for her late dinner, keeping a hand on Malcolm's head.

"Ma either, but she swears it's true."

"So, I guess we're never going to be serious."

"Guess not." He knew he was out of the running, but he did wonder if Malcolm was going to get lucky tonight. He knew from experience that sad doggie eyes earned him a portion of almost any woman's dinner. Margarite had had no willpower where Malcolm was concerned. Jim had to admit that even being a long-time dog person, Malcolm could almost get by his own guard with that act.

Reese took a bite of her sandwich, then set it back on her plate without offering any to Malcolm.

He heaved out a doggie sigh and looked across her lap at him for aid in his nefarious plans. Jim simply shook his head, which earned him another doggie sigh.

He wasn't sure where to take the conversation from here.

He'd painted himself into a corner by bringing up relationships, which would be more likely with one of the people still streaming by on the sidewalk—despite the late hour—than with Reese Carver.

She was clearly done with the topic of her life after her cathartic upheaval. No tears. Not her. Never her.

"When did you learn to be so strong?"

That earned him a bark of laughter sharp enough to startle Malcolm.

"What?"

Reese opened her mouth, closed it again, and turned back to her sandwich. Malcolm did eventually get the tail end of a crust with a little cheese on it, but far less than his normal take. Reese was made of sterner stuff than most.

The crowd inside still wasn't thinning. The waitress swept up their empty plates and set down a dessert menu. Neither of them was more than half through their drink, so she slipped off to thirstier clients. Nearing midnight, it really was the city that never slept. Most of his New York trips had been to one loading dock or another. The tourist center of Manhattan wasn't a place he'd ever had to run an eighty-foot full-box rig, and riding shotgun with Reese all day had convinced him that he'd never want to try.

Tomorrow was going to be a long hard day. By unspoken mutual consent, they both clambered to their feet and shrugged on their jackets. He paid the bill and they drove across town to the hotel near the UN. A location team from the New York office was already on patrol there and nothing remained except to check in and ride up in the elevator.

At the door to her room, she stopped him before he could lead Malcolm to the next room down the hall.

"You know that you're pissing me off, Fischer?"

"Kind of hard to miss that."

She shook her head and her long hair was lustrous beneath the soft lighting of the long corridor.

He waited.

"You're making me think. I don't like thinking."

"What do you like?"

"Winning," she didn't hesitate a single moment. Then her voice went much softer. "That's what I've always been good at anyway."

"Doesn't sound like a bad thing."

"No... But it's a pretty damn lonely thing. Pop was dead—and I raced. You say it's strong, but you make me wonder if maybe I've turned hard. A stock car has to have a certain softness in the suspension or the tires break free of the track too easily. There has to be a give. You make me wonder if I have any give left in my suspension."

"So, what? You walked away from NASCAR three years ago and have focused solely on becoming the new Number One driver in the Secret Service?"

She shook her head. "Nothing else."

"Damn, woman. You need to get a life."

"I don't even know what that means."

Jim looked up and down the hall. Past midnight, it had the silence of a hotel—a well sound-insulated, luxury one. It was just the three of them, the burgundy carpet, and the sconce lighting of the flowered wallpaper. He'd always been more of a Holiday Inn Express kind of guy when he couldn't sleep in his rig.

"Jim?" Reese voice was a soft suggestion, barely audible in the long hall.

He looked at her, really looked at her. The sadness in her eyes would put Malcolm to shame—except with Reese he knew that it was neither a shame nor a genetic predisposition as it was with Malcolm. Today had taught him that it was completely against her nature to look that way.

He had no resistance. There wasn't even thought as he reached out and pulled her against him. He'd had the good fortune to have hugged plenty of women over the years, but holding Reese was the first time he'd ever hugged steel. Even as she leaned into him, her back was ramrod straight. When her arms came up around his shoulders, he could feel the impossible power of a woman who worked out for an hour every morning *before* starting her day—she wasn't Pilates fit, she was United States Secret Service fit.

Unable to help himself, he buried his face in her luxuriant fall of hair as they held each other.

She didn't ease into him, slowly relaxing until their bodies were melded together.

Reese Carver broke in a single slide of lost traction. One moment the woman of steel. The next pressed so tightly against him that he wondered if he'd ever been really held by a woman before.

It didn't last but a moment, but she showed him a window to a whole new world he'd never imagined.

REESE STEPPED into her room and turned on the light as the door snicked shut behind her. It was a small room, made to feel bigger with a large mirror above the dresser and mini fridge.

She looked at herself and studied the woman there.

Was that really her?

Suits had defined her since she'd been a kid. Her father had given her a full-body racing suit just like his when she was eight and she'd worn it with pride. The kids at school had teased her, but she hadn't cared, not really. Because it had her name above her left breast and Carver Family Racing across the back. By the time she'd donned her own Nomex racing suit and climbed into a car, it had fit like a second skin.

Three years in the Secret Service had done the same. Open-collar button-down shirt, dark blue or gray suit, polished black rubber-soled shoes, current issue lapel pin identifying her as part of the Presidential Detail at a glance. She slipped out of her suit coat and revealed the nylon webbing of her shoulder holster to the mirror's eye. That and the FN Five-seveN sidearm were a part of her as well.

But for just a moment in the hallway, she'd been a woman in a man's arms.

Even after an entire day of putting up with her bullshit attitudes and weird silences, he'd still held her as if she wasn't the disaster area that she knew herself to be. It was when he'd buried his face in her hair that it had undone her. She'd always thought of her hair as a shield—herself on one side and all of the bullies, assholes, and even the lovers carefully kept on the other.

Jim had taken no advantage of her. He'd somehow seen that for even a single moment, she'd just needed to be held.

The woman in the mirror looked back at her in confusion. If he'd grabbed her ass, or anywhere else, she'd have known what to do with him. A hot steamy kiss from an undeniably handsome guy pressed back against a hotel room door, that too was familiar.

But to simply be held. As he'd done at the bar when she'd told him the story of her father. The first time she'd ever told anyone that story in full.

And when they'd kissed, when she'd finally let him slip fully through the shield of her hair, it had been like pounding into Turn One.

Coming off the downshift.

Feeding the power toward Turn Two with the tires glued into the groove despite the g-force dragging her head sideways.

Not there yet, but feeling the anticipation of the upshift and hammer-down launch onto the backstretch.

Jim's kiss had been like a blast of nitromethane in a top-fuel dragster, firing off nerve endings she didn't even know she had. It was an adrenaline rush she hadn't felt since...

Her image scowled at her.

...since running one and two with her pop at the Charlotte Motor Speedway.

Yet when she'd tried to pull him into her room and find that high-octane finish, he'd refused.

"It's not that I don't want to, Reese," he'd looked right at her so there was no way to doubt his sincerity. "Don't know as I've ever wanted anything more. But as much as I'd enjoy tonight, I'm guessin' that you wouldn't be enjoying tomorrow morning much more than a cottontail rabbit on a highway—pissed off and feeling run over."

The fact that he was probably right didn't make her feel any better at the moment. Even as she tucked her sidearm under her pillow and undressed, she could still feel the suits that had defined her life.

How strange that some blind spot of Jim Fischer's didn't see her armor at all.

CHAPTER FOUR

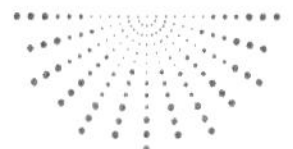

The day had been just as brutal as Jim had expected. That he'd spent half of the short night thinking about Reese asleep just next door hadn't helped matters.

Since when did he turn down a beautiful woman, no matter how much pain she was in? Since never. He'd learned that letting a woman have a good cry on his shoulder made him into a shining knight. And the sorry-for-doing-that make-up sex afterward was typically awesome.

But Reese was made of different, sterner stuff. She was like the difference between his old Kenworth semi-tractor with its cozy sleeping compartment versus a HETS tractor that hauled Abrams main battle tanks through the heart of a war zone.

He would've liked to start the day with something more friendly, but they'd barely had time for hello.

Morning route briefing over donuts and hotel coffee—really good hotel coffee, but of little help after a short night.

They'd had only a few minutes alone together on the drive to the Downtown Manhattan heliport but conversation had been about timing and logistics. Then he'd spotted Malcolm happily curled up in the First Lady's seat. Thankfully, among the weapons, gas masks, and other paraphernalia, the vehicle was also stocked with Windex and paper towels. He shuffled into the back and spent the last part of the drive cleaning up dog hair.

"Thanks, buddy."

Malcolm, who'd slept at the bar, in the hallway, and across his legs, offered him a lazy yawn that was hard to resist. He waved Malcolm out of the seat and onto the Suburban's carpeted floor.

"*Not* with the sad doggie eyes," Jim told him. "You know that doesn't work on me."

Malcolm sighed and moved to the floor. Jim began cleaning the back seat.

Reese's sad eyes of last night had certainly been gone this morning. She was back to pure Secret Service driver. It was a sunny day in February and her dark glasses were firmly in place, hiding all of her thoughts.

The moment he'd stepped out of the vehicle and onto the pier at the heliport was the very last he saw of Reese all day except at a distance.

He and Malcolm cleared the heliport terminal building, bathrooms, and finally the L-shaped pier that stuck out into the East River.

Reese rolled the bronze Suburban out onto the pier and turned it around, ready to depart.

He saw her watching him through the driver's window, but he and Malcolm were done scanning and there was no reason to delay. Back through the terminal, he was climbing into an idling black Suburban when he saw the white-top helo fly in over Brooklyn. An NYPD fast patrol boat circled beyond the pier while a helicopter gunship hovered above on Overwatch.

He shut the door and was whisked off to the first site on the First Lady's itinerary.

Other dog teams had secured the store, but he and Malcolm did a final walk-through of their precise route—information so compartmented that even most of the agents and NYPD didn't know it. Loading dock, freight elevator Number Three reserved for their exclusive usage, up to dresses, then over to shoes. He barely saw the ladies themselves as his work was done before they'd actually arrived.

He and Reese managed to exchange smiles as he headed out and was whisked off to the next site.

During the Broadway show, he'd constantly patrolled the lobby and backstage. The show had pyrotechnics and though there were two agents hovering over the technician and his supply of flammables and small explosives, the scent triggered poor Malcolm so often that they'd had to go for a long walk around the block just to calm his nerves.

Once they'd done the initial patrol at the Rum House—the place wasn't going to have nearly as many business-class cokeheads for a while—he'd mostly hung by the door, idly chatting with the bartender who doubled as a bouncer. It was a prime spot, anyone entering the bar would have to walk past Malcolm's sensitive nose.

Through the front window, he could just see Reese in the Suburban pulled close up to the curb with the rest of the Motorcade. She remained in the driver's seat, ready to evacuate the party at a moment's notice.

Harvey Lieber had been right, the three leading women of the White House were absolutely stunning together. He could see Ms. Matthews' calm sophistication, Ms. Taylor's class, and Ms. Darlington's whimsical sense of fun as the three of them laughed together over a late night snack.

Detra—the head of the First Lady's detail—flirted with him briefly each time she passed by on patrol. It seemed to just be a piece of who she was.

Beat Belfour—the head of Ms. Matthews' detail—gave him one withering look that said she be glad to neuter him slowly with a dull blade if he screwed up in the slightest. He actually wouldn't put it past her.

But it wasn't any of them he was thinking of.

The reserved agent who had sat at the front corner table with him last night occupied his thoughts so thoroughly that he was glad

Malcolm was the one watching the door because he was doing a lousy job of it.

REESE HAD ENJOYED WATCHING Malcolm and Jim doing their job throughout the day. Even at the end of it, the dog still had a bounce in his step and Jim still had a smile for her each time he passed by.

The First Lady's Motorcade was quite different from the President's. Thirty-five vehicles were reduced to five or six other than a police escort. They were seen as significantly less tempting targets for foreign attackers. Especially the current and former First Ladies, as both were immensely popular.

So she'd spent her day never more than three steps from her vehicle inside a highly secure area. Police and a Sweep Car led the way. Then her vehicle, with the head of the First Lady's Protection Detail sitting where Jim had been all yesterday.

The contrast was jarring. Special Agent Detra Willand was a voluble and cheery blonde. She maintained that attitude even as she scanned for bad guys before opening the door for the ladies to exit the vehicle. As they rolled along between sites, Detra had filled her in on news items and gossip as readily as route protection details.

Jim had been comfortable with the long silences as they'd ridden together around Manhattan. Detra was almost never silent, and by the end of the day, Reese was exhausted. She liked Detra. The agent would be a great person to spend a night out on the town with. But after a day together...the silence was welcome.

By the end of the day, sitting outside the Rum House and watching through the bar's front window as Jim was so perfectly vigilant, Reese could really appreciate him. She knew now that no matter how casually he sat at the end of the bar closest to the door and chatted with anyone who came up to him, he wouldn't miss a single thing.

He hadn't even missed that she *would* have hated herself this morning if she'd dragged him into her bed last night.

But that was last night.

She'd now had a whole day to watch him at a distance and think about it.

As usual, Jim departed minutes before her Motorcade did, rushing back to make sure the hotel was still secure as everyone reassembled in the vehicles. Once set, they rushed after him: police, Sweep Cars, her bronze Suburban with the three laughing women, and Detra once more chatting at her side. In the rearview mirror rolled Halfback—the heavily armed black Suburban that carried the rest of the First Lady's Protection Detail, a press van, the Roadrunner communications vehicle, and a police car tail.

When she finally reached her room, she was thrown by the Do Not Disturb sign hanging from Jim's door handle. Had she misread everything about the last thirty-six hours?

She considered knocking anyway and demanding answers. She considered pulling out her sidearm and shooting out the lock. Instead, she retreated to her room to fume in private.

Her foot crunched on a note on hotel stationary that had been slid under the door. In a heavy block print was a simple note: *Our rooms have a connecting door.*

Reese hadn't given the inner door any thought last night except as a possible avenue of attack. Jim clearly had.

Before she could second guess herself, she stepped over and unlocked it from her side. When she swung it open, she saw that Jim's was already opened a crack.

Moment of truth, Reese.

Jim Fischer wasn't some contest, some race she had to win. But he definitely made a hell of a door prize.

She nudged the door open a little wider. Malcolm looked up at her from where he sprawled across the foot of the king-sized bed and wagged his tail. In the background, she could hear Jim's shower running. Again, the door was cracked slightly open spilling the only light into the room. An invitation.

Reese had always been a morning-shower person. A fresh start to the day. Hot water, soap, green starting flag, go! Jim seemed to be more of a wash-off-the-day type, which always struck her as a little defeatist. Tonight perhaps she'd ignore that. But she'd only taken that single indecisive step into the room when the shower shut off.

She froze for a long moment while Malcolm watched to see what she'd do.

Never be here in the first place was most best option—hasty retreat and trust Malcolm to not give away her indecision. But now that she was here, retreating wasn't an option. The right solution? Pedal to the metal.

Reese stripped as she hurried to the far side of the bed. Jacket, blouse and slacks over a chair, shoes and underwear on the floor by the bed, sidearm under the pillow, she slipped between the covers. She wished she'd thought to swing the connecting door back into place.

She slipped down deeper in the covers and warmed her toes against Malcolm.

After another minute, Jim stepped from the bathroom. He was naked and backlit by the bathroom light. It made her catch her breath. He walked all day every day and his muscle definition, highlighted in the bright light, was incredible. Adding in workout shoulders and he was a vision sparkled by tiny drops of water.

Whether it was her sharp breath or his noticing the ajar connecting door, he spun to face the bed.

"Reese?"

She kept silent in the shadows, not sure if she could speak.

"Reese," her name turned thankful in his husky voice. It was enough to wash away her doubts. Though it wouldn't do to have him too assured of himself, not after the doubts he'd just put her through.

"Fischer," she kept it a simple acknowledgement she might use passing him in the hall of the West Wing.

She as much felt as heard his soft chuckle as he turned off the bathroom light. A dim nightlight in the bathroom spilled a soft glow into the room, just enough to track his movements. He crossed to the dresser first, where she heard a soft crinkle of foil.

"Pretty sure of yourself, buying condoms." And she didn't like that at all. Had he simply assumed that any woman would be glad to fall into his bed? It was almost enough to make her climb back out in the darkness.

"Part of Malcolm's med kit. If I have to bandage a bleeding paw fast, I won't have time to shave it before I tape it. Condom first, then tape over that so that I don't catch his fur."

"Oh," she pulled the half discarded sheet back into place. "Better not hurt a paw anytime soon," she warned the dog.

"Don't worry, I carry plenty."

"Were you a boy scout? Always prepared?"

"Eagle scout." He slipped in between the sheets and an exploring hand landed on the flat of her belly. "And not ready for you."

It was a corny line, except the way he said it, it didn't sound like a line at all.

Rather than sliding up to grope her breast, his hand continued around her waist, then hauled her against him as if she weighed nothing. He was even careful not to snag her long hair as he pulled them together.

No kiss, no grope. Instead, he pulled her into a hug as tight as last night's and held them together.

For a long moment, she could feel herself holding tension, like waiting for the starter's flag. In many ways it was the most adrenaline filled moment of the race—all anticipation and withheld action.

But Jim didn't start, instead he simply held her close.

As if he was waiting for something.

As if he was waiting for…her.

No man ever did that. Apparently Jim Fischer did.

She relaxed into him, sensations scorching along her skin as more and more of their bodies came into contact. Jim was warm from the shower and just a tantalizing bit cool from the sparkles of water that he'd missed toweling off. It made him feel more three dimensional. Like that moment she'd first run into his back in the West Wing— impossibly real.

He'd forgotten a razor when they'd stopped for essentials and she could feel his two-day beard as he buried his nose in the crook of her neck. Ignition sparks followed his hand as he brushed up to her shoulders, then slowly down her bare back and finally caressed her behind.

"*That,*" Jim whispered, "is an amazing ass."

Far too many men had said that in one form or another. She was black, not some ass-flat white chick. But she was so tired of men saying so.

Reese's arms were around Jim's back, so she couldn't punch him.

Instead she thumped a fist as hard as she could into his kidney.

PAIN ROCKETED up Jim's back. Not enough to make him scream as she had a lousy angle on him, but enough to engage a hundred percent of his attention. And to make him accidentally jam out his legs.

Malcolm responded with a yelp of surprise and a hard thump as he fell off the foot of the bed and onto the carpeted floor.

"Sorry, Malcolm," Reese whispered out into the darkened room.

"Sorry, Malcolm? He's not the one you just punched in the kidneys."

"He's also not the one who just told me I was hot because of the shape of my ass."

Jim groaned a bit as he tested his back with a careful twist. If that was a near miss, he couldn't imagine what a direct strike from Reese would feel like.

"Did I hurt you much?"

"Enough," he winced as he shifted.

"Good!"

Deciding that his fate was in his own hands, Jim reached under her arms and grabbed her behind again.

Because he kept his elbows out, her next swing bounced harmlessly off his ribs.

"This…" he squeezed her tightly so there was no question about what he was talking about.

She tried once more to thump him and growled at her inability to strike her target.

"…is a truly exceptional piece of anatomy on a beautiful woman. It also had nothing to do with why I'm in bed with you."

"Oh, but my breasts do?"

"Again, exceptional examples from what little experience I've had with them. Again, not particularly relevant."

"Okay, Fischer, why the hell are you in bed with me?"

"You mean other than it being my bed and you're the one who's in it, not the other way around?"

"Yes, other than that." He could hear her gritting her teeth and he liked doing that to her. A little payback for the kidney shot, a little bit keeping her off balance. He suspected that Reese was too used to a certain kind of man having a certain kind of expectation of this beautiful woman.

"Because from the first moment, you've been nothing like I expected."

She didn't even hesitate. "Because I didn't throw myself at you from the first moment?"

"Because you keep being so much more than I expect. Then I raise those expectations and you either blow right by them or go sideways around them."

"What did you expect?" She finally stopped any sign of struggling, but he wasn't going to let his guard down just yet.

"At first the wide-eyed newbie. But then Dilya liked you and that kid goes deep in ways I guess I'll never understand. You take the hit of losing your father. The way that happened, you could have hung it up and shriveled away worse than corn in a drought—most folks would. Instead, you come back as the driver of Stagecoach. Damn, woman! Then you've got an ass that feels as good as this," he stroked it more gently this time and just couldn't believe how soft her skin was over all that smooth muscle. "Is there anything you can't do?"

"Apparently, understand an Okie."

"Good, maybe that will keep you around a while trying to figure me out. Because you've sure got this good ol' boy mystified."

"Let's see if I can demystify a thing or two."

CHAPTER FIVE

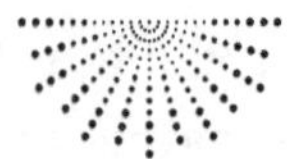

Not only did Reese know that she had a fine ass, when she woke up the next morning, she felt it too. Jim hadn't focused on it alone. In fact, he'd gone to some impressive effort so that not a single inch of her felt neglected.

Clothes in her hand, she headed to her own shower so as not to wake him—the man had earned his sleep. Gods, had he earned it.

Reese felt loose, like a cat on the prowl. Curiously comfortable with her nakedness in a man's room like she'd never been. She'd always been the one to race to the finish, won and done. Always first dressed.

Jim had refused to be hurried. And it hadn't been just his hands or his mouth. He'd rubbed her instep with the top of his foot like he was performing reflexology on the pressure points there rather than just a nice contact. When she'd looped a leg over his hips, he'd taken the time to massage the calf muscles and reshape her until she lay more tightly against him than she'd thought physically possible.

She stood at the connecting door and looked back at him. The predawn light leaking around the edges of the hotel curtains revealed him flat on his back and arms flung wide, like a man cut down in his prime. It made her smile. He somehow *knew* that she would want to be on top. No power games, no avoidance. He'd let her ride him and take control, the only way she'd ever found to reach that pinnacle of release. Yet Jim hadn't been merely compliant even then. Instead he'd teased, enhanced, driven her until she'd forgotten everything other than her own body and the man giving it all of his attention.

There really wasn't time this morning, but she wished she had a chance to see if he could take her to that same impossible place again.

That's when she spotted the butt of her handgun sticking out from under her pillow. She tiptoed back, circling wide around Malcolm, who lay on Jim's jeans and tracked her with only his eyes.

As she reached for her HK Five-seveN, a hand clamped around her wrist. It was startling. She hadn't slept with many white men, and the contrast of their skin was a surprise. Light and shadow. Whole and… Reese didn't know what she was, but definitely not whole.

Without a word, Jim slowly dragged her toward him. She should resist, she should protest. His grip was actually only tight enough to ease her toward him and would be nothing to break from. Instead she dropped her clothes. There was a muffled woof of surprise and then a quick rattle of his collar as Malcolm shook free of her clothes.

"Shh," Jim whispered to her. "Don't wake the kid."

"There isn't time."

"Hush. There's always time." And he pulled her in until she had no choice except to lie down against him, tucked inside the curl of his arms.

Resigned to the inevitable, not that she could really think of any reason to complain, she relaxed into him.

And he held her.

Nothing more.

Until she wondered if he had gone back to sleep.

She tried to raise up to look at him, but he rested his hand on her head and eased her back down onto his shoulder.

"Just lie still a moment. A man likes a moment to appreciate waking up beside a fine-assed woman."

In one night, he'd managed to turn a phrase that had made her livid as hell her whole life into a tease, almost an…endearment. He made it sound as if they had a deep and abiding relationship, not an absolutely incredible one-night stand. She was even less used to endearments than she was to lasting relationships.

As he continued to lie there, holding her close, she could almost believe in it though. She wasn't very skilled at relationships longer than one-night stands, because they required on-going civility. Or maybe because… Reese no longer knew. All she could think about was how nice it felt to lie here in a lover's arms and pretend nothing more existed.

"You know," Jim whispered softly.

"Yes?" Her voice was a smooth, liquid tone that she didn't recognize at all. It was the tone of a woman's voice in the movies before she made love to a man. Which sounded like a very good idea. She slid her hand down his stomach to see what his body's thoughts were on the subject.

"We're going to be incredibly late if you don't get that fine ass of yours moving right quick." Between one heartbeat and the next, Jim rolled out of her reach and she was watching *his* fine white ass as he strode for his bathroom.

She lay there for a long moment in disbelief, then rolled out herself and regathered her clothes and her sidearm.

"I'm sorry, Malcolm," she paused to rub the dog's belly with her toes. "But I'm going to have to kill your master. Just thought you should know."

Malcolm considered for a moment, then flopped onto his back so that she could keep rubbing his belly. She continued for a few more moments, then smirked at the half-open bathroom door as she headed for her own shower. If the man thought he was going to sway her choices and beat her that easily, he had another thought coming.

DAY THREE and Jim was done in. Even Malcolm was dragging and he never dragged.

It wasn't last night. He'd never woken up feeling so alive. He missed his first chance to keep Reese beside him because the woman went from asleep to full speed in about two seconds flat. He was a morning person too, but there were some limits.

But he'd had his chance when she came back for her sidearm. He found it there in the middle of the second round of the night's gymnastics. During the first he probably could have grabbed onto a hot exhaust manifold and not have noticed the burn—Reese felt that incredible.

When she slid back in beside him, he'd had his chance to imagine what it was like waking up next to Reese when she wasn't running off like a house afire. *Damned nice!* For all her hard edges and abrupt lane shifts, when she gave, she did it at full throttle as well—racing was definitely the right metaphor for Reese Carver. A breathtaking display of physical ability fueled by raw heat. Last night she'd seared his memories with her body until no one else's remained.

And this morning, when she strode across his hotel room wearing nothing but a smile… Well, nobody got that lucky and he wasn't sure why she'd decided it would be him. It really was a pity that they'd run out of time and he'd had to yank himself away from her. He had rather hoped that she'd join him in the shower, but he knew some women preferred to do such things in private and he hadn't wanted to pressure her.

"We gotta find a way to keep her around," he told Malcolm.

The dog barely looked up at him. It was their last stop of the day and they'd done their duty. The Downtown Manhattan Heliport was fully secure. They'd patrolled from the front steel gates along FDR drive, throughout the small parking lot, inside and out of the terminal building, the narrow driveway along one side of the pier, and around the various helicopters waiting to whisk the protectees back from where they'd come.

"Now just the ride home, boy."

Malcolm sighed and plopped his butt on the sidewalk by the front gate to await the Motorcade already en route from the UN.

The lead route vehicle came by, slowing down only long enough to exchange a wave with the head of the detail waiting at the gate. That meant the rest of the Motorcade was less than a minute out. Jim spotted the flashing lights far down FDR well before he could hear the sirens. He and Malcolm were done except for the ride home.

"Looking forward to putting more fur on the First Lady's seat?"

Malcolm looked up at him. Absolutely.

"Looking forward to a four-hour ride back to DC with Reese Carver?" Jim asked himself.

That sounded mighty good as well. Maybe on the way back she'd stop at a store for Fritos and root beer. Still odd not being the driver. Except for trading shifts on the long-hauls—they'd often do four hours on/four hours off for the entire duration of the Kandahar run— he wasn't used to the passenger seat.

Felt as if he was doing that in many ways with Reese Carver, hanging on for dear life in more ways than one.

He could hear the sirens now.

"Hang in there, buddy."

He wasn't sure which of them he was talking to. Neither was Malcolm.

REESE LIKED that Jim had *not* asked why she didn't join him in the shower. It meant that he was deliberately messing with her head and the game was still on. She was down with that.

The New York trip was in the home stretch—the final drive from the UN back to the Marine's white-top helos waiting on the pier. The three women in the back were talking softly and even Detra in the right-hand seat was quiet. It had been a long couple of days for everybody and they'd all be ready to be done with it and get back to DC.

They emerged from the last tunnel two hundred yards from the heliport.

Up ahead she spotted a man and his dog leaning against the heavy steel corner post of the front gate. She'd give a lot to know what he was thinking. Which was a surprise. Normally she didn't give a damn.

Actually, that wasn't right—normally she *knew.* Men were predictably interested in sex and power games. Yet even if Jim had been an enthusiastic lover, he'd been a very thoughtful and thorough one. He'd made sure it was about her as much as about him. Maybe he'd done that just to confuse her. If that was his intent, it had worked.

The six-motorcycle V was keeping the FDR's right lane clear. She followed the Lead Car closely, not liking the tightness of the space as they emerged from the tunnel, a tall concrete wall to her right slowly tapering down as the Motorcade climbed.

At a hundred yards out, they were just close enough to make out Malcolm's coloring, white-and-brown, but not yet close enough to separate out the small black police vest that also served as his harness.

That's when she spotted a flicker of movement off her left side.

Before she had even fully registered it, her NASCAR instincts had crashed her foot into the floor and had her heading right until she was nearly into the four-foot vertical wall that separated the highway from a parallel lane of merging traffic. The Suburban's big V-8 engine roared to life and they accelerated sharply.

Detra started some question from the passenger seat, which Reese ignored.

She barely had time to see the massive grillwork on the twenty-four-foot delivery truck arrowing in on her before it clipped her back end.

For half a second, terror slammed into her as her rear tires broke traction and went sideways. She bounced the right rear fender off the concrete wall. They'd have been pinned, perhaps crushed, but she reached the end of the barrier and was able to swing into the open merging lane. If she hadn't accelerated when she did, the truck would have rammed squarely into her door.

There were screams from the women in the back—high and panicked, like the screams of her father's tires as they broke free on the Charlotte Motor Speedway.

Then Reese recovered. They weren't going two hundred miles an hour, out at the performance limits of a racing stock car. This was a big, tough, four-wheel drive Suburban doing its best to climb from sixty to seventy miles an hour. She snapped the steering wheel right, then left to regain control.

The black BMW Lead Car that had been immediately in front of her veered into the left lane to clear a path for her, then the driver slammed on his brakes—smoking his tires.

In her side mirror, Reese could see the BMW take the blow. The big delivery truck plowed into the rear of the BMW—forty thousand pounds versus four thousand. That Secret Service driver had just bought himself a long stay in the hospital and her eternal thanks.

The rear of the BMW disappeared in a cloud of debris before the car was flipped up and over backward. It buried its nose through the truck's windshield.

Lurching to one side, the truck caught a wheel and tipped over, skidding along the road, throwing showers of sparks in every direction. The passenger compartment of the BMW was battered aside and spun into oncoming traffic causing a chain reaction of swerving cars, squealing brakes, and crunching metal.

Reese kept her foot in it as they crossed eighty miles an hour.

Congestion ahead—the police leading the Motorcade no longer clearing the path but rather blocking it as they slowed in surprise. She jumped the curb separating traffic from a two-way paved bicycle lane. She barely missed taking out two cyclists and a line of park benches along the sidewalk. With a sharp swerve, then a counter, she was able to avoid the cyclists, then the fire hydrant on the divider.

In a final glance back, Reese could see that Halfback—the heavily armed Suburban that had been on her tail—was also tangled up in the mess and now lay flipped onto its roof. Despite that, agents with MP5s and AR-15s were already out of their vehicle and surrounding the truck. At their lead was the fierce black woman who led former First Lady Matthews' detail. Her jacket was shredded and she was limping badly, but her weapon was out as she led the way.

Focus ahead.

The police motorcycles, unable to jump the curb, remained on the main lane of the FDR as Reese raced past them to the heliport's entry along the bike path. At the main gate, guards had their weapons up and one was waving her through.

Estimating the traction and the limits of the heavy Suburban, she waited as long as she dared.

Then she stood hard on the brakes to dump half her speed. At eighty, they'd just roll over for what she was planning.

Detra was shouting over the radio to have the helos ready. Not Reese's concern.

When the speedometer hit forty, Reese turned hard to the right, slapped the transmission down into second, and punched the gas.

The rear wheels broke free.

She counter-steered into the sliding drift, watching the big heavy stanchion on the far side of the main gate looming large and heading squarely at her own door. If she hit it too hard, there was nothing to stop her from plowing through it and dumping them all into the East River.

Holding the line, she suffered only a glancing blow that served to finish the drift.

Now headed down the pier at ninety degrees to where she'd been a moment before, she punched the gas, barely dodging around a hot dog vendor's cart. Down to thirty miles an hour but still in second gear gave her plenty of power when she goosed the engine.

A glimpse of Jim in the main parking lot, yelling toward the gate alongside the terminal that separated the parking lot from the narrow driveway onto the pier. They got it open just in time for her to barrel through without having to drive into it and risk hurting someone as she blew the inner gate off its hinges. The driveway between the terminal building and the edge of the pier was meant to be taken at five miles an hour—she didn't ease off the gas until she was nearing the helos.

One last time, she cranked the wheel and stomped down on the parking brake. The big Suburban went into a sideways slide along the pier toward the waiting Sikorsky White Hawk. She stopped under the edge of the spinning rotor disk—with a low dip of seven-foot-seven, her six-foot-two Suburban was clear. It might have given the pilot a heart attack, but Reese had trained on this. She'd managed to place herself so that the rear passenger doors of the Suburban were facing the helicopter's side door from less than ten feet away and any attack from the street would be shielded by the bulk of the Suburban.

Detra was gone out the passenger door and Reese could hear the women being unloaded from the rear and rushed unceremoniously into the waiting helo.

But all Reese could see was Jim and Malcolm racing down the pier toward her. He had his sidearm out—double-handed and aimed at the ground—and was swinging his head side-to-side watching for any renewed attack, but he was headed straight for her.

She didn't know if she'd ever seen such a welcome sight.

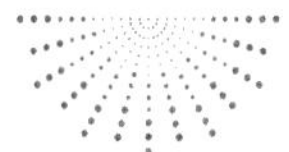

nknown.

By the end of the day, Jim wanted to beat anyone who said that word.

"Unknown" had been the conclusion of everything. Was the truck driver a solo actor? A terrorist? A psycho? Or had he merely fallen asleep at the wheel? The BMW Sweep Car's driver and his right-seat fellow agent had busted up ribs and arms but had survived. There wasn't enough of the truck driver left to identify. First, his head and torso had been shattered by the nose of the BMW ramming through the windshield, then a fire had broken out. The spilled gas from the broken BMW finally found an ignition spark as the First Lady's helo lifted well clear and headed to JFK to meet the waiting Air Force jet.

The man who owned the truck had reported it stolen thirty-six hours earlier and had been found in a bar next door to his shipping business, enjoying a pint and a roast beef sandwich. He, for sure, hadn't enjoyed the rest of his night. His original load of fifteen thousand pounds of exercise equipment for a new gym had still been aboard but was a complete write-off. Despite his apparent innocence, he and his company would be on a terror watchlist for a long time to come.

Another group of agents were scanning traffic cameras hoping for a clear shot of the driver's face, but with little luck.

Other than battered metal, the Suburban had come through unscathed. He, Reese, and every other agent who'd been on the scene spent the entire night in the New York Secret Service office in Brooklyn going through every step of the thirty-seven seconds from the moment the truck had veered across FDR drive until the Sikorsky White Hawk had lifted its wheels off the pier.

When finally released, he and Reese had collapsed into a bed together, with Malcolm—the only one who'd slept that night—sprawled happily at their feet. Jim had held her close as she once more recounted each action, each motion, every nuance of what she'd done and felt.

"For just an instant, when everything broke loose, I saw my father. Saw his car right there in front of me. Except this time there was no helmet hiding his face. It was as if he was trying to say something, but I couldn't hear it."

She doodled a finger on his chest.

He'd seen it all unfolding.

The big truck swinging wide ever so briefly, as if gathering momentum for its slash across the lanes of the FDR. Or perhaps to get away from the rushing phalanx of the Motorcade's sirens and lights. A moment of inattention, bouncing a tire off the low divider between directions of the FDR, then overcorrecting? There was no way to be sure.

Reese sliding free after banging off the wall and the Lead Car braking to take the hit.

Jim had known what Reese would do—had known what he'd have done in the circumstances—but didn't get to see it. He'd had to trust in her abilities as he turned to search for, and clear, anything that might slow her down.

The guards manning the inner gates were listening intently to their radios, unaware that five tons of armored SUV would be racing down on them in mere seconds. Unwilling to clutter the command frequency, he raced from the main gate toward the team manning the gate out to the pier. A quick hand signal had Malcolm following in a tight heel position, but on his right side, away from Reese's path.

He'd signaled and yelled for the agents to open the inner gate. They'd made it in time for Reese to race through.

He had ducked through himself moments before they slammed it shut and raised their weapons.

"Defend," he'd shouted, though they already were, and raced after Reese.

He'd almost choked as she slid the Suburban sideways beneath the spinning rotors of the helicopter. It was one of the slickest moves he'd ever seen…until last night when he'd watched the video of her passage through the main gate at speed.

"My dad," he told Reese as he held her in the dark until she finally wound down, "said that you're a crappy driver until you've driven your first hundred thousand miles. I didn't believe him, of course, until I had. Then I understood what he meant. I'd finally laid down enough miles to notice anything that *wasn't* normal. I've logged over a million now, and there's no way in hell I could do what you just did."

He could feel her shrug.

Everyone had been as impressed as hell when they'd seen the video, judging each slide so perfectly in an unfamiliar vehicle. She'd probably shaved five, maybe ten seconds off what any other driver could have done. But each time someone had commented on it, she'd shrugged it off.

"I wasn't the impressive one. It was the Lead Car driver who really did something, putting his life on the line without hesitation. All I did was drive."

"All you did was drive? You had one job, he had another. Even the very best drivers say they couldn't have done better; why aren't you letting that in?"

Again the shrug.

REESE LAY AWAKE a long time after Jim fell asleep.

He'd let her replay every instant of the incident until she was sure she wouldn't have done much different with a month's practice and planning.

Some way to prevent the necessity for the Lead Car driver's heroic act? None that she could think of.

Should she have worried about the truck in the other lane as they emerged from the tunnel? There was nothing to indicate that she should have.

Any race you finish alive is a good one. Any you complete with your car still running is a victory. How many times had Pop said that to her and her brother? But her brother had broken Pop's first rule shortly after Pop had.

He'd taken to racing motorcycles at a young age, and died attempting to jump a small ditch during the Dakar Rally in Argentina. A negligent moment—just five days after Pop died—not enough lift or maybe a crumbling edge…and he'd been flung headfirst into a tree. At least the death had been instantaneous. Pop had stayed conscious long enough for the ambulance to arrive, but hadn't even made it off the track.

By Pop's standard, she'd had a victory. By any standard.

Jim's final question rankled at her. So why *couldn't* she let it in?

CHAPTER SEVEN

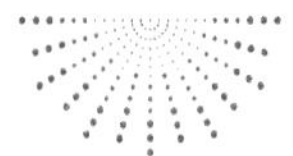

$\mathcal{B}$ack in DC, things fell quickly into routine—Jim's *old* routine.

With the intensity and intimacy of New York behind them, there was a distance in the present. Reese was the "golden one" from the moment they'd reentered Secret Service headquarters in DC. Lauded by everyone, he could see it eating at her. She disappeared in more ways than one.

She hadn't answered her cell phone when he tried it.

His text asking if she wanted to catch dinner—which he'd thought was fairly harmless—had received a two-word reply: *Need time.*

Now, a week later, Jim couldn't decide if he was as feeble as a glue horse for not pursuing her when she'd first tried to shut him out. What guy on the planet wanted to face the definitive "no" from a woman? "No" sucked. He had certainly received his share of "so long," "thanks," or that lamest of all "whatever" over the years. But not from the most incredible woman he'd ever been with.

He should have known something was wrong when he'd woken up that next morning. She'd already been up and dressed. No friendly teasing her back into bed. No quick snuggle to mark the start of a new day. It was still the old day—they'd gone to sleep about dawn after the long debriefing and it was just after lunchtime when they woke—so he figured that was fair, if regrettable.

"It's two o'clock and I'd like to get on the move before rush hour," Reese had told him as she finished fastening her shoulder harness.

Which he supposed was reasonable enough. The Suburban had only suffered cosmetic damage, so the two of them drove it back to DC for repairs.

No fresh news when they'd checked in, so the drive south had been mostly quiet, just watching the changes of the day as it rolled through evening and into night. He'd asked her a bit about racing, he'd told her some exotic stories of driving big rigs across the Afghan countryside, but for the most part they'd just fallen into the driver's rhythm of letting the road roll by.

Or so he'd thought. Until Reese Carver had evaporated.

He tried switching to a morning workout, but Malcolm didn't like the change-up in routine. After three days of not spotting her, he slid back into an after-shift workout.

Training Day came up on his duty roster.

It had been eight weeks and it was time for a refresher course for him and Malcolm out at RTC.

"Time to expose his nose to the stuff that explodes," as the course master Lieutenant Jurgen liked to say.

RTC was short for the James J. Rowley Training Center, the Secret Services' training grounds. Here they could attack helicopters and aircraft, drive militarized ATVs in the dirt, spin cars through twisted courses, and raid storefronts or skyscrapers. Almost every essential skill could be worked on here. The K-9 Training Center was a small corner of the complex. It contained an agility course and a mocked-up office building interior. For area work, there was a two-street town set up in a different section of RTC.

Tommy Jurgen was a tough sumbitch retired Marine and fellow Okie, so they got along just fine.

"So tell me," Jurgen didn't even let him get through the door of his office. No question what he wanted to know—Jim had been asked to tell the story all week.

So, he cracked a cold orange juice, tossed Malcolm a treat, and sat down to tell the tale of the most threatening attack on a Secret Service protectee in recent history. The newspapers had had a heyday of it, arguing both sides against the middle without the USSS saying a word: *US Secret Service saves the day,* and *First Lady nearly killed due to Secret Service negligence to detect the threat.*

The problem was that after a full week, there were still no leads on the truck's driver. Street cam footage had been pieced together over the entire thirty-six hours between the theft of the truck and the attack—and not one usable image of his face had been caught. They weren't even sure it was a he until the DNA analysis of the few teeth and bones that had been recovered. Beyond that, he was melting-pot American with no clear genetic history. Missing persons reports were being chased, but so far without any luck.

"Seems pretty unlikely for him to remain a John Doe for a full week," Jurgen scowled down at his boots. "Less'n he was tryin'."

"Yep," that had been everyone's conclusion. Jim told him the general consensus. "Deliberate attack by party or parties unknown. Assume significantly increased threat levels."

Jurgen scowled at the ceiling now as if searching for a different answer, but finally concluded, "Yep."

"Got another question for you." Jim knew he was fishing, but couldn't help himself.

"Fire away."

"You ever meet a Special Agent Reese Carver? Driver?"

Jurgen's smile grew quickly, in a way that had earned him the nickname Jerk Jurgen from all of the female officers. "Oh yeah. Majorly hot chick on the Presidential Detail. What about her?" Then he narrowed his eyes at Jim for a long moment. "No way! You?"

"I shouldn't have asked." Jim should have guessed at Jurgen's reaction. And it wasn't like Jim wanted that fact out in public, but he was absolutely desperate for any clues.

"Not a man in the Service hasn't looked at that piece of ass and wanted it," Jurgen was on a roll.

For the first time, Tommy Jurgen's attitude toward women

rankled.

Jurgen finally caught a clue and harrumphed himself back into being human. "Word is that no one, and I mean *no one*, gets much more than a hello out before she shoots them down outta the sky. Looked her up once. All set to be the top chick NASCAR driver, better than Danica Patrick, until her daddy and brother ate it in the same week. Had to be tough. Made her hard."

No, Jim decided. Not hard exactly. There'd been nothing hard about the woman in his bed. Cautious. Which meant...what? He didn't really know.

But Jurgen was expecting some reaction. Jim shouldn't have said anything in the first place, but he had. Now all he could do was try to make sure there was no reason for Jurgen to spread the story. So he offered his best nonchalant shrug and a "Huh," of defeat.

"So, she put another guy in the dust. Just another in a long list, buddy," Jurgen took the bait. "Time to stop thinking about women. You and Malcolm ready? I've got the course set."

"We were born ready. Right, Malcolm?"

The springer spaniel wagged his tail, clearly tired of all the talk.

An entire office complex had been built above the dog kennels within an innocuous-looking barn at the edge of the RTC campus. It would be spiked with dozens of different explosive compounds to be found by the team and keep them sharp.

As to not thinking about women, at least one woman, Jim didn't see that happening any more than him becoming a Nebraska Cornhuskers' fan after being bred-and-buttered on the Oklahoma Sooners. Nope, this trucker boy wasn't ready to give up on Reese one little bit.

"Let's do it." He slapped his knees as he rose and Malcolm jumped up ready to catch the bad guys, even if they were just pretend ones...today.

"SOMETHING EATING AT YOU?" Harvey Lieber had walked up to the desk Reese was using without her even noticing. When she'd glanced back during the attack, Reese had the best angle on the truck driver, but all she remembered was the truck's grill. She was flipping through the mug shot books on the chance that something would jog her memory, but so far no joy.

"No, sir. Just wishing I'd looked more carefully."

"Looked carefully enough to save your protectees. We're giving you the Director's Award of Valor for that."

"Don't want it, sir. I wasn't brave. Or *not* brave. I just drove. The two guys in the Lead Car—that was bravery."

"Yeah well, all three of you are getting one, so deal with it. Distinguished Service Award to your pal Fischer for fast thinking, too. Thinking of pulling him off Baxter's fence line detail and adding him to the Presidential team. What's your assessment?"

Reese wanted to say no, but knew that wasn't right. She remembered him racing to clear her way to the helos. On the camera footage, she'd seen him reacting several seconds ahead of any other agent—she'd still been bouncing off the wall and he'd already seen that she'd need a clear path. In NASCAR, races sometimes came down to thousandths of a second, making Jim's reaction time really stand out.

"He's a good man," was the very least he deserved.

Harvey Lieber narrowed his eyes at her for several long seconds, but she wasn't going to reveal anything else. He finally nodded to himself and turned away, making some inscrutable decision that she'd only find out about later.

"Are you two up to the Meryton Hall dance, or the Netherfield ball?"

Reese twisted around the other way to discover that Dilya and Zackie the First Dog had come up on her other side. She had the distinct impression that they'd somehow come to be there without Harvey even noticing. Dilya was dressed in form-fitting black—t-shirt, leggings, tennis shoes as dark as her hair—except for the bright rainbow-colored shoelaces woven between the eyelets in some strange and intricate pattern. Maybe this was her stealth mode.

"I don't know what you're talking about."

"You don't know *Pride and Prejudice,*" Dilya shook her head with sadness. "I'm reading her other books now. I like Fanny in *Mansfield Park*, but that's because she's sort of like me, not like you."

"Whereas I'm like…"

"Elizabeth Bennet."

Reese wondered if all conversations with Dilya were like this. "You'd have to ask Jim about the story, I don't know it."

"Oh, I can tell you, if you'd like, but it might spoil the fun."

"The fun." What part of any of this was being fun?

Dilya nodded happily, then thought for a moment. "I know what you need. You need to go for a walk. Too bad there aren't any rain-muddied meadows. C'mon." And she turned for the Ready Room's door without waiting to see if Reese followed.

At the moment, anything was better than staring at thousands of pictures in hopes of spotting someone she'd never actually seen.

Dilya had turned right out of the Secret Service Ready Room, but she didn't go up the stairs—which was a huge relief. Up those stairs was the First Floor of the West Wing, including the Oval Office. If Reese *never* went up those stairs, it would be fine with her.

Instead, Dilya lead her back through a warren of offices and through a small door that she needed her security badge to unlock.

"Where—"

"Shh!" Dilya held a finger to her lips, then whispered, "There's a press conference going on, I don't want them to hear us. But this way is shorter."

The low-ceilinged area was filled with racks of equipment. Stacks and stacks of computers, high-speed modems, and video processors stood in long rows. Despite the soft roar of fans, the area was warm with radiated heat. She saw labels on the racks: ABC, NBC, CNN… She looked up at the ceiling when a sudden roar of voices sounded above. They were directly under the Press Briefing Room and the gaggle was shouting out questions for the Press Secretary.

They were in FDR's old swimming pool—in the deep end. She looked at a small section of exposed wall and spotted the old tile that had originally walled in the pool. It was now covered with signatures of the press corps. FDR had swum here. JFK and Marilyn Monroe had probably frolicked together in this very spot. What were they…

Dilya had moved down to the far end of the pool. Zackie's nails clicked on the bare concrete floor that had replaced the old pool bottom.

Reese hurried along the cramped aisle to join her.

"This door leads into the Press Corps basement offices, but they should be empty right now." Dilya opened the door and led the way.

Down one side was a long line of tiny booths set up like the announcer's broadcast studios at NASCAR races. The door plaques showed that's exactly what they were: Voice of America, American Forces Network, Reuters, and more. On the left was a cubicle row, crowded aisles of small desks with cameras and notepads scattered about. There was a small rail with dozens and dozens of overlapping neckties dangling from it. Reese had no time for anything more than impressions as Dilya hurried along.

At one of the cubicle desks, a reporter hunched over a camera. Perhaps because the camera was broken there was no point in being upstairs at the briefing. All she could really see as they hurried by was the reporter's hands working on it. Close by lay a stack of several black boxes, each smaller than a pack of playing cards that must be some form of storage or battery she wasn't familiar with.

They passed a stairwell leading upward from which she could hear the clear voices of the press briefing breaking up. She raced ahead.

Past a tiny kitchen with two vending machines, a microwave, and an espresso machine with a picture of Tom Hanks above it, they came to another door. Again, Dilya slotted her ID and a flat panel at the end of the hall swung aside. Zackie pushed through first.

They rushed through after her as steps sounded on the stairs from the offices above. Dilya leaned on the panel and it snicked shut with seconds to spare. The sudden silence was echoing.

They were in a utilitarian hallway that Reese's sense of direction said was a basement beneath the White House Residence itself. There was the rattle of dishes and the hum of a dishwasher off to her left. To the right was a long wall with two doors, both labeled Storage.

Directly in front of them, in the middle of a long white hallway lit fluorescent white, stood a gray-haired woman. Her hair was back in a bun. She wore an unremarkable dress and a knit red cardigan. She looked like someone's grandmother, if not for her brilliant blue eyes that were watching the two of them closely.

"Miss Stevenson," the woman nodded to Dilya. "We meet at long last. And Miss Carver. This is indeed a treat. And where are the two of you headed in such a hurry?"

Reese opened her mouth, then closed it again. She didn't know. Now that she thought about it, she was simply glad that no one was about to shoot her for trespassing where mere Motorcade drivers were *not* meant to go. Yet she had the distinct impression that this woman had been standing here waiting just for them.

"Uh..." It was nice to see the supremely confident Dilya flummoxed by something. The young know-it-all had clearly been having fun messing with her. Turnabout was such sweet revenge.

"You may call me Miss Watson. Where were you off to, child?" The woman didn't offer to shake hands, instead keeping them clasped on the carved white handle of her stout wooden cane. It looked as ancient as she did.

"I was taking Ms. Carver to go and see Clive." Dilya's tone said that she was distinctly unhappy about the "child" comment, but wasn't comfortable arguing with an elder—at least not one as imposing as Miss Watson.

Their destination was news to Reese. Clive who?

"Of course you were, dear. And I know for exactly what reason. How convenient that he has just made me a small delivery this morning. Please, come to my office." Again without waiting for any acknowledgement, she turned toward the sound of the dishwashing.

A few steps along the hallway, Miss Watson opened a door onto a narrow spiral stairway. Firmly grasping the handrail, the woman navigated the spiral downward with surprising agility. When Dilya followed, Reese was left with no choice but to do the same. They emerged into an even more utilitarian hallway of the subbasement. Excess chairs, perhaps from the State Dining room, were stacked along one side of the hall. Fold-up tables could be seen further along. Doors were labeled Air Conditioning, Storage, Dentist—with no dentist at present—Elevator Machinery, and finally Mechanical Room 043.

Miss Watson unlocked the door to that last and slipped inside.

At first impression, it looked like a dark hole. The kind that people entered, then were never seen again. A dim desk lamp was turned on, revealing a battered steel desk and shelves of books.

"If you'd give an old lady a hand, my dear," Miss Watson waved at the joint of two bookcases—after the brightness of the hall it was too dim to read any of the titles.

In for a penny. Reese took in a breath and, hoping that she would still be alive to take in another, pushed. The two bookcases swung inward and apart, sliding easily out of the way.

A parlor, brightly lit with Tiffany lamps, was revealed. It had a white oriental rug, delicate armchairs, and walnut fixtures. Miss Watson shuffled past, and at the touch of a switch, a gas fireplace flickered to life beneath a large marble mantel that might have dated all the way back to George Washington. There were pictures of women's faces everywhere. The room was elegant. And easily the most unexpected place she'd ever been.

Dilya's wide-eyed expression said this was new to her as well.

Miss Watson crossed to a bright red ceramic Snoopy doghouse. Lifting the dog as a handle, she removed the roof and revealed a cookie jar filled with dog biscuits. She selected one and bent down far enough to hand it to Zackie, then pat her on the head.

"Please," she waved them to chairs while she busied herself with a white porcelain teapot covered in sweet peas.

Reese looked once more at the photos about the walls. They came from every era of the nation's history, some were hand-painted portraits, but most were photographs. She identified Spanish, Russian, German, and Vietnamese women as well as a wide variety of ones in American military attire.

"Yes," Miss Watson spoke without turning. "Many of the finest spies throughout history have been women." As if she already knew what question Reese was thinking.

She delivered teacups and small plates of delicate chocolates before sitting in a flowered chair across from them. Perhaps this Clive was the White House chocolatier. She knew he worked somewhere in the lower reaches of the Residence, though she hadn't been aware that the building went this far down.

"Tell me what you know but haven't spoken aloud, Miss Carver." She propped her antique cane beside her chair and picked up her teacup.

There was something odd about the cane. It had tarnished metal on the tip and rose in a long taper, wider at the top than the tip by at least an inch. The carved handle looked like old deer horn, handled so often that it had been burnished smooth. Rather than having a flat top to rest one's palm on, as an invalid's cane might, it curved slightly. More like a handle if one were to hold it horizontally.

"Yes, an elegant piece," Miss Watson didn't even glance toward it.

She had a disconcerting way of never looking at what she was discussing.

"Jim Bowie was nearly killed by this sword cane during a duel on a sandbar in the Mississippi. Instead, he killed the man who stabbed him in the chest with it. It was because of that fight that he purchased a large knife from a blacksmith—a knife that was popularized as the Bowie knife. The knife came after the fight, despite the popular story. He also was a spy for the Americans against the Mexicans before he was ultimately killed at the Alamo."

"Can I see?" Dilya set down her cup.

"*May* I see. And yes." At Miss Watson's nod, Dilya stepped forward and picked up the cane.

"Just tug sharply, dear."

Dilya yanked on the handle and a foot and a half of bright steel slid out of the scabbard. It caught the red light off the Tiffany lamps until it looked as if it dripped with blood.

Miss Watson offered her pointers on how to hold and wield a

sword. As Dilya practiced them, Reese noticed that Miss Watson's attention was on her, not Dilya.

Tell me what you know but haven't spoken aloud, Miss Carver.

Reese swallowed hard. Now it felt as if Miss Watson was a telepath placing her words directly into Reese's head.

She knew that she missed Jim Fischer and Malcolm. She shouldn't—not for how briefly they'd been together—yet she did. It was impossible that this unknown woman would be discussing that.

Therefore the topic, as it had tediously been all week, was the attack on the First Lady's Motorcade. Others were still debating between accident and attack, but she knew it was the latter. She also knew...but that was ridiculous.

Miss Watson smiled. "Yes, we *know* things even though there is no way for us to know them. That is the power of being a woman. You must learn to trust your instincts in life just as you did on the track. Tell me about the attack."

"I don't know your clearance."

"I should think that these walls speak for themselves," Miss Watson waved her teacup in a small circular motion that included far more than the unusual parlor in the deep subbasement that she occupied, perhaps even more than the White House itself. "But I don't care for such trivial items as what occurred. I already know all of that. I'm far more interested in what *you* know, but that others have not yet been willing to confront."

"It was a test." Reese hadn't known that for a fact until she said it aloud. But now that she'd given it a voice, she knew it was true.

"Oh my," Miss Watson stared down at her tea with pursed lips. "I had feared as much."

"A test of what?" Dilya paused halfway through a lunge with the blade.

"Of..." Reese didn't like the answer on the tip of her tongue. "Of Motorcade security. I have to tell Harvey. We have to lock it down harder." The realization slammed into her like a physical blow. She was halfway to her feet when Miss Watson held up a restraining hand. "What?"

"There is a question that you haven't asked yet, but which any of these women now hanging as memories on my wall would think of immediately."

Reese sat back and thought hard about what that might be. She even gave herself some time by eating the first chocolate. The deep flavors of strawberry and mint on a dark chocolate substrate almost served to distract her.

Almost.

"There is a hard-learned lesson by women of…" Miss Watson looked momentarily uncomfortable, "…my profession. Sometimes, an enemy's action is done to better understand our *reaction*."

Reese thought of racing, and it made perfect sense. There were times when you teased at a move, perhaps a couple times without executing it, to set up an opponent to be too slow to react when you finally did drop a gear to jump down to the inside of the track and take the lead from them. She'd done just that several times, but with a stock car. To do it with a Presidential Motorcade…

"But what did they learn?" Dilya slid the sword back into its cane scabbard and scooped up her third chocolate.

"That's the question, isn't it?" Miss Watson looked directly at Reese as if she knew the answer.

Dilya also looked at her for a long moment, then her eyes widened as if she too knew the answer.

Well *she* certainly didn't know it herself. The only thing they would have learned was…about Reese's driving. She was the latest unknown factor to be added to the Presidential Motorcade. Had they been trying to test her…or remove her?

She'd suddenly lost her taste for chocolate.

MALCOLM HAD DONE his typical stellar job on the training course. His sniffing score was at the top of the charts, and for a medium-sized dog, he'd done incredibly well on the agility course. For an hour he'd jumped over barriers, ducked and run through winding tunnels of plastic pipe, slalomed through stick gates like legs of fifty people in a crowd—all around proving that at four years old he was still a young dog in top form. Another half hour of attack training. Just because he was a "friendly" dog meant to be working among the public didn't mean he couldn't be dangerous when needed. Then a second run at an altered explosives course while they were both tired.

"I sometimes suspect your dog of cheating," Jurgen grumped as he signed off on the score sheet.

Jim looked down at his springer spaniel.

Malcolm gave back his best innocent look as if he knew exactly what they were talking about.

"Did you place all the explosives yourself?" Jim took a guess.

"Damn straight!"

"Wearing gloves?" Jim smiled.

Jurgen scowled down at Malcolm for a long couple seconds, then cursed when he figured out the drift of Jim's question.

"You little, four-legged sneak."

Jim burst out laughing. "Malcolm did a double find. He went after the explosives. And for the ones that were hardest to find, he went after the scent that the earlier ones had in common: you."

"That'll teach me." Jurgen offered a hard laugh, then thumped Malcolm on the ribs a few times to show that there were no hard feelings.

With his high scores, Malcolm had earned them an afternoon off.

Jim thought about hanging around until he saw what was next on Jurgen's agenda when a truck rolled up with a fresh load of ten dogs from Vonn Liche Kennels. Ten dogs tagged as candidates for the Secret Service's intense standards. He'd thought it could be fun, until he saw that they were all for the ERT.

The Emergency Response Team dogs were the toughest animals in the service: Dobermans, German shepherds, and Belgian Malinois. Driven, dangerous, and, after the long drive from Indiana, they would be a particular handful.

With thinly veiled excuses, which Jurgen saw right through but let him get away with, Jim and Malcolm made good their escape and climbed back into his pickup to head out.

The kennels and the bulk of the dog training area were in the farthest corner of RTC. Then there was the mock town, an area of tightly convoluted back roads for driver training, and then the main driving area for skid and turn training. The last was an open area of pavement a quarter mile long and a football field wide. If no one else was running, maybe they'd let him sign out a vehicle. Watching Reese on the videos, he'd learned more than a few tricks and wanted to give them a try. His job was no longer behind the wheel, but that didn't stop him from wanting to do it on occasion.

He pulled up beside the long line of battered Suburbans, Chevy Impalas, and Ford Tauruses that were used for agent's driver training. Once they were retired from the field, they were used and abused here. After they were truly worn out, they were repurposed once more for demolition derby training. *That* was a skill he was fine without learning—how to use another vehicle to bounce off for a change of direction or to shove into an assailant's path. Jim just wanted to try that high-speed drift.

Even as he opened his truck's door, he could hear the hard squeal of tires as someone worked the pavement on the other side of the garage. He rolled down the windows halfway and left Malcolm asleep on the front passenger seat. He'd earned his rest and the cool February day wouldn't bother him any. Jim tossed a light blanket over him anyway so that just his nose was sticking out.

After shrugging on his sheepskin jacket against the cool day, he walked around the end of the garage. Three guys were standing on the swatch of brown grass that separated the back of the main garage from the open stretch of pavement. They weren't doing anything, just watching.

Focusing downfield, he saw only one car on the big open area. It was one of the Beast limousines. The Presidential Motorcade only used three limos at a time: the President's and the two Spares. But the Secret Service actually owned twelve. Some were for backups when one or another was rotated into service. Others were for this.

The lone driver raced the car straight at them from the far end. With less than two hundred feet to go, the car slammed sideways into a four-wheel drift.

Before it even came to a stop, the rear tires smoked in reverse. With a hard cut, the driver was headed back the way they'd come, back end first. He could hear the engine clawing up against redline before the driver threw in the inevitable J-turn. A hard crank of the wheel. Rather than holding the sideways skid, they let the car drift around until it was headed nose-first down the field and the engine was gunning ahead in drive with almost no loss of speed despite the flip.

Jim strode up beside the guys watching. He'd expected to see Ralph McKenna out there taking one last set of spins before retirement, but instead he was standing here with the two head trainers. They all stood with their arms folded over their chests, just watching.

"Hey, guys."

"Hey, Jim," Ralph was the only one who glanced away from the driver long enough to identify him.

"Thought that'd be *you* out there."

"Technique's wrong," Arturo, the head trainer observed. "Ralph always hit the turn at five thousand RPM."

"That was fifty-five if it was a day," George, his assistant, added in.

"It was six flat. Hard against the redline," McKenna finished the conversation.

"Who…" But then he saw it. He'd watched the video a hundred times of Reese sliding the Suburban sideways at high speed to make it through the gate of the Downtown Manhattan Heliport. She'd judged it with such nicety that she'd barely scraped the driver's door, fitting the big vehicle through an opening only a few feet wider than the Suburban itself.

He got it now. She was slamming the monstrous limousine through the same maneuvers. There was a reason they called it "The Beast." With all of its armor and defense system, it was eighteen feet long, six feet high, and weighed in at eight tons—over twice his pickup with a full load. And she was making it spin and dance like it was a turbo-charged hotrod.

On the next run, she slammed it through a full three-hundred-and-sixty-degree spin, a full time around.

"Now why would she do that?" George mused aloud.

Jim glanced at Ralph and saw the small smile there, so he kept his mouth shut.

Reese did it three more times until she could nail the final direction every time.

On the next spin, when she was halfway through and facing away from them, he saw a pair of canisters shoot out of the front and blast out a cloud of smoke as she continued her turn.

"Is that tear gas?" The wind was drifting their way.

"Normally," Arturo growled. "Just smoke canisters for training here."

"She laid them down as a blind to anyone following rather than to clear a crowd blocking the way," McKenna said almost reverently. It was clear he'd never thought to do it himself.

Jim felt an itch. That was Reese Carver at the wheel. And it was clear that she was angry at something. She was slamming The Beast around like it was part NASCAR racer and part demolition derby.

"Anyone willing to bet a twenty she has another trick up her sleeve?"

They all turned to look at him for a long moment, then looked away.

"Aw, c'mon guys. Easy money." Even making clucking chicken noises didn't get him a taker.

As if Reese could overhear their conversation, she started her next —and he'd bet final—run from the far edge of the pavement.

What if instead of going into a drift to turn ninety degrees as she had at the heliport gate, she first wanted to blind those following her?

She gunned toward them from the far end of the field. For a quarter mile, she let the lumbering Beast gather as much speed as it could.

Then just as the guys were starting to get nervous, wondering which way they'd need to dodge and run, Reese slammed into a spin.

When her car was turned exactly one-eighty—with its rear end facing them—she launched another pair of smoke canisters out the front. Because they were standing on her side of the smoke screen, they could see the car continue to spin until it was headed off to the left at speed—a three-quarters turn nailed perfectly on dry pavement.

If it was a T-intersection, the attackers might barrel straight through the smoke screen and crash into the end of the road. If it was a through-intersection, they might race straight through and across the intersection in hot pursuit.

Either way, the Beast wouldn't be there. Masked by the smoke screen of the tear gas canisters, she'd be gone in an unexpected direction. Sideways.

There was an awed silence among the observers as Reese continued down the narrow side road she'd entered. Then with one more hard thrum of the engine, she came racing toward them backwards before flipping the car through a final J-turn and coming to a stop close beside them.

Reese sat there holding the wheel and staring at him as he started applauding.

Reese would rather Jim wasn't here. He wasn't supposed to be here. He was *supposed* to be at the White House, walking his precious fence line with his precious dog doing their precious sniffing. He—

She wanted to pound on something. Or someone. Jim was fast becoming a candidate as he led the applause.

How the hell had she gotten in this trap?

Miss Watson was right—it all somehow fit. *Reese* had been the target in New York. And for that to happen, it had to be an inside job. Which meant that she could trust no one! Once again she was out on the track all alone and no one to turn to.

She eased off the brake and, letting the idling of the big diesel engine put the car back into motion, drove along the small access road to the garage. She parked it by the other vehicles and turned off the engine.

A figure came up on the other side of the five-inch ballistic glass to open her door. She waited for Jim to fail. The Beast's doors didn't open by merely pulling on a handle—then any fool could run up and do it. One of the closely held secrets of The Beast was how to open its heavy doors from the outside.

But the door swung open anyway.

Ralph McKenna was standing there. He'd driven this car for a decade so of course he knew its tricks; he'd probably helped design them. The others were standing back a bit.

She popped her belt and clambered out, taking the hand that Ralph offered because she didn't trust her knees with how they were shaking. It wasn't fear. It wasn't stress. She didn't know what it was, but it was there and she didn't like it. She was such a mess that she should tell them here and now that she couldn't be the President's driver. Stagecoach—as the Beast was known whenever the President was aboard—was one rung of the ladder too high.

Ralph was no longer holding her hand, he was shaking it.

"When it comes time to put me in the ground, Carver, I want you driving the hearse. That way I *know* that I'll get to where I'm going."

"Not for a long time, McKenna." If the best driver in the Service told her that, it meant that she *couldn't* walk away. *Damn it!*

"Not a chance. I've got a cottage and a sailboat waiting for me in the San Juan Islands up in the other Washington. Time for me to go home. I know The Beast and his passengers are in the best of hands."

A double dare. Definitely no way out of it.

Arturo and George came up and shook her hand as well. "I can't see putting that in the standard training. I don't know if either of us could even do that move, never mind teach it to the poor *hombres* who come through here. Nice, Carver. Seriously nice."

Triple dare. Crap! All she'd done was drive. It was all she wanted to do. She didn't like whatever was messing with her knees.

Then they moved off and there was only Jim.

"Where's Malcolm?" She still wasn't ready to talk to him. She'd treated him like crap since New York and she wasn't ready to deal with that either.

"In the truck, sleeping off a hard morning of training," he hooked a thumb toward a big Dodge pickup with a crew cab and a short bed. Meant the thing was all for show because the bed wasn't big enough to haul anything. And it looked that way too, immaculately clean as if he spent the weekends polishing its glossy black surface.

On cue, Malcolm stuck his head up over the window sill and gave her a welcoming woof before disappearing out of sight once more.

"Can I buy you lunch? Know a good spot about ten minutes away. Great roast beef sandwiches. Beer if you're done for the day."

She was *so* done. Somehow he knew that she didn't want to talk about her driving. In the last five days she'd forgotten how easy it was to be around Jim Fischer. He never pushed her when she didn't want to talk.

"Fine." Her Pop would slap her butt a hard one for that kind of manners. "Thanks, that'd be great." A little better.

"Need a lift? Malcolm might insist that you sit in back…" he trailed off with a smile that appeared genuine.

She pointed at her ride, parked beneath a shade tree on the far side of the lot.

Jim glanced over his shoulder, then did a double take, which made her feel better.

"How did I miss that?" And he was on the move for a closer look.

At a loss for what else to do, she followed in his wake.

Pop had given her the rusting hulk for her fourteenth birthday, had it towed into the back corner of his racing team garage at the Motor Speedway. "You get it fixed up, honeychile, and you can drive it when you get to sixteen."

The 1969 Mustang Mach 1 had taught her not only how to fix a car, but why they worked the way they did. She'd torn the engine block of the Ramair Super Cobra Jet V8 down to bare metal and rebuilt it all the way up. The 4-barrel R-Code Holley carb had taken her a week to refurbish, and another three days before she figured out she'd put a float valve in upside down. Piece by painstaking piece, she'd put that car together with Pop's and his chief mechanic's training, but none of their help. It was all hers.

After a lot of soul searching, she'd decided to make everything as cherry original as she could until you lifted the hood. The engine, transmission, and suspension were all rebuilt with only one purpose in mind—speed. From the factory it would have run 0-to-60 in eight seconds. By the time she was done installing the nitro, it was well below five. Tuning the suspension had taken some work, but she could drag a quarter mile in the sub-ten-second range.

It had taken until she was eighteen to finish it, but by the time it was done, it was perfect. The jet black finish accented by a single, thin, red racing stripe down the side made it look fast standing still. The ram scoop in the middle of the hood, the rear louvers over the back window, and the rear spoiler made it look even more like a race car.

It was also the most fun ride she'd ever taken. A NASCAR stock car was a faster, tougher machine, but it was pure race car. Her Black Beauty looked classic, but flew like pure joy.

"Damn, woman. Is this thing street legal?"

"Depends on the street." It was nice that Jim could see past the pretty car down to the fact that it was a performance machine.

"Bet that's faster than Road Runner being chased by Wile E. Coyote. What do you call her, Jackrabbit?"

"Black Beauty."

At that he went suddenly quiet and looked right at her, "Of course you do."

She was glad that her complexion would hide the heat rocketing to her cheeks.

"Okay," he didn't push it. "Can you go slow enough to follow me in my truck? Or should I give you the coordinates of the nearest airport for you to fly into?"

"I'll keep it in first and we'll see how we do."

Jim nodded and headed for his truck.

She liked that he kept it simple. Though she'd definitely have to razz him about going exactly the speed limit as he led the way.

CHAPTER EIGHT

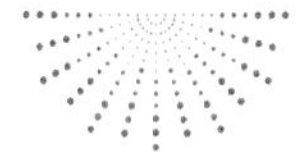

*J*im knew it was a gamble, but he took Reese home.

"What's this?" Reese asked as she climbed out of the Mustang. No, as she oozed out.

All the stress she'd been showing at RTC until he was afraid to touch her for fear she might shatter had fallen away during the short drive in her Mustang. If he didn't get her out of that suit and into his bed in short order, he was the one who was going to shatter. But he knew a frontal attack wasn't going to win the day, so he'd just follow her lead.

"Home. Not much, but I like it." The way she'd eased down from her drive was exactly how this place always affected him. He'd sunk the money from selling his rig and being a good boy with six years of banking his Army pay to buy five acres just a half hour outside of DC and ten minutes from the Rowley Training Center.

Malcolm hopped down and ran around to see if any deer or rabbits had passed through since this morning's run.

It had been all trees. He'd hacked an acre-sized hole right out of the middle and parked his fifth wheel along the north edge so that he looked out on the sunny yard. A small stream ran at the far edge of the wide lawn.

"Got a nice wood deck on the southern side," he led Reese around to it. "Should be warm this time of day."

Reese kicked one of the tires on his fifth wheel as she walked by. "This thing ever move or are you like most RV owners who should just build a damn home?"

"Every vacation and the occasional weekend. Malcolm and I like wandering the backroads. Done a whole lot of Maryland and Virginia. Thinking to start Pennsylvania next. Hoping to do the original thirteen colonies, but really see them, not just the highways I drove back in my trucking days."

"That explains the big-ass truck," Reese muttered to herself.

"Have yourself a sit and I'll go rustle up some sandwiches," he waved toward the two loungers he had out on the back deck. He'd glassed in the sides to stop any wind. He had an awning he could run out, but rarely did—he preferred looking at the sky and the stars even when it got cold.

He headed inside and Reese came in on his heels. She prowled through the place, which didn't take long. There was the big bed up in the nose of the fifth wheel. The dividing wall that made it a bedroom had dressers below and a built-in big-screen TV above that could be spun on a swivel to face either the bedroom or the living room. One side of the living room had a two-burner cooktop, small fridge, and oven. The rig's only pop-out was the living room, which allowed for a big sofa and a couple of lounger chairs. Toward the back was a bathroom and shower all-in-one, and a four-person dining booth that mostly served as his desk. There was a small outside swingout for a grill and a small storage bin that he kept stocked with wood for campfires.

"Not much, but all a man really needs." He began fishing out sandwich fixings.

Watching Reese prowl through the place was making it hard to concentrate. It had been a long time since a woman had been here. Maybe not since Margarite, and the contrast was startling.

Margarite had accepted that this RV and this property represented who he was—and that it wasn't her. She'd never really relaxed out here. Or around him, he supposed.

Reese filled the space with her presence as if she somehow belonged. She stood in the middle of the living room staring out at the lawn, backed by Loblolly pines and red oak trees, through the sliding glass door. She just seemed to soak it in. He knew that even if she never came back, it would take him a long time to get over looking at her standing there.

He concentrated on the sandwiches for all he was worth. He hoped that she liked the way he made them, because his mouth was too dry to even ask if she liked horseradish on her roast beef.

"Are you planning to look me in the eye anytime soon?"

He froze. He'd looked at her driving, at her hot car, at her in his rearview to make sure he didn't lose her on the way here.

"Seems kinda lousy of me not to, doesn't it?"

"It does."

"There's a problem though," he got his hands moving again. He finished the sandwiches, scrounged up a bag of chips that wasn't too decimated, and a pair of Cokes.

"What's that?"

"Look you in the eye, as likely as rain at a summer picnic, I'm gonna want to be kissing you."

That earned him silence.

Well, no guts, no glory. He turned slowly and looked at her. Those dark, mysterious eyes were watching him closely. Well, he'd been right. Even that brow-knitting expression she was wearing didn't change a thing. Three steps. That's all it would take, just three measly steps separated them.

"Even after the shit way I've been pushing you away all week?"

"Even after." He wasn't going to admit how much that pushing off had scared him—not even to himself was he going to be admitting that.

"Still feeling that way?"

"Seems I am." It was all he could do to not drop down on the carpet and drag her down with him.

"Dilya asked me if we were after the Meryton Hall dance or the Nettingfield Ball."

"Netherfield."

"She didn't explain herself."

"It means that either you've decided I'm a prideful jerk or that I'm actually dashingly handsome and alluring despite my vastly superior station in society."

"You walk a dog for a living," Reese rolled her eyes, but the frown had eased off to that cryptic partial smile of hers.

"You're nothing but a fancy chauffeur. Maybe we're in the wrong story."

"Not according to Dilya. So what's your role after the two dances?"

"Oh, I'm utterly fascinated by you either way, I'm just too shy to say so."

Reese finally laughed a little. "Shy isn't one of your problems. Being too nice might be one of them."

"Definitely the wrong story, then. So let's eat." Jim turned and picked up the sandwiches. He wasn't turning aside from the obvious path because he was too nice. Some instinct told him that going fast was going to make it "race over" way too soon.

Out of the corner of his eye, he saw her stumble a half step forward as he walked away. He hoped that was a good sign.

OUT ON THE BACK DECK, some part of Reese's sanity returned. She'd been within a moment of shoving Jim into that bedroom of his. It was right there, conveniently mere steps away. A man cave of dark woods and a big screen TV. Use his body, then leave him watching some ESPN.

She just wanted to lose herself in mind-blurring sex. Let a cathartic release help her forget, even for a moment, what Miss Watson had forced her to see.

Instead they were sitting on side-by-side loungers in the warm sunshine. The tall pines and oaks gave the property an other-worldly feel. It didn't seem possible that all the worries of DC lay so nearby.

Malcolm came back from his explorations, begged some roast beef from both of them, then curled up on a dog bed Jim had set close by his lounger.

The quiet of the place expanded, emphasized by the birdsong from the trees and even the quiet trickling of the distant brook, until it made her ears ring. Her apartment was in Friendship Heights and she'd forgotten what the country sounded like.

Jim knew that about her and simply ate. But it wasn't as if he wasn't there. Instead, her awareness of him grew and grew until it seemed as big or even bigger than the trap she'd fallen into.

"Get many visitors here?" Reese could hear cars, but they were so distant that she didn't hear them unless she was listening for them.

"Deer and rabbit. Got some moles over in the southeast corner that Malcolm catches on occasion. Had a coyote come through once. Raccoons come along to fish in the stream during the summer." His voice had a soft smoothness that made him easy to listen to but hard to keep track of the words. He was definitely talking about another world if those were his "visitors."

She considered as she took another bite of her sandwich. There *was* a very nice looking bed not ten feet away. But the sun-warmed deck and the canopy of blue sky were—

Jim reached across the gap between their loungers and took her hand. When she turned to meet his eyes, he was looking right at her. Not with a question, but with a need that she discovered she was sharing. At the slightest tug, she abandoned her seat and straddled over him.

Sensations jolted into her, even though they were both fully dressed.

"You doing something to me, Fischer?"

"Planning to, Carver."

It wasn't what she meant, but she leaned down to kiss him and decided to see how his plan went first—because all of hers were awful.

Reese Carver in a darkened hotel room had been fantastic.

Reese Carver straddling him and silhouetted against the blue sky was a revelation. He opened her jacket and blouse, then blessed a front-opening bra. Every curve of her chocolate skin looked as perfect as it had felt. He filled his hands with her and still wanted more.

When she leaned forward and lay her bare chest against him, it was liking hitting that home run ball—just ever so sweet, knowing it was right and clean even before it soared aloft.

He tried to never make comparisons between women, but Margarite had never wanted to do it outdoors. She'd been a DC woman with DC aspirations. They hadn't even done it on the couch very often. With Reese it seemed as if everything was irrelevant other than their two bodies coming together.

When she disengaged long enough to shuck her pants, he saw that the wonder of her didn't end at her waist. She still wore jacket, blouse, and disengaged bra as she helped him shed his jeans and sheathed him before she moved back over him. Her sidearm in its shoulder harness rubbed the back of his knuckles as he once more marveled at the feel of her breasts and the contrast of his light hands on her dark skin.

Sliding into Reese was better than backing a double-trailer rig in a dead straight line. She moved against him with a rhythm all her own as her fingers dug into his shoulders. Her long hair slid from its ponytail and fell around them like a private curtain against the world. Only at the very last did her eyes slide shut, but he was unable to look away from the wonder of her. The line of her arching neck the moment before the release slammed into her and had her hunching to absorb the force of it when it arrived. The taste of her moan as he dragged their lips together before his own wild release had him arching up against her as if he could somehow bring them closer together.

Together.

Jim had never felt so *together* with a woman in his entire life. *This* was a woman that he could never tire of. It wasn't that she brought a new and unfamiliar spice to sex—although she did. It was that… Jim didn't know what. What he did know was that he was permanently ruined for any other woman.

When Reese finally eased down against him, he could only marvel at the warmth and softness of this "hard" woman. Though the butt of her FN Five-seveN sidearm digging into his armpit argued the point the other way. He managed to slide it free and lower it to the deck.

She curled against him, burying her face in the crook of his neck.

He ran his hands up and down her back under her clothes. At first it felt as if she was merely snuggling. But he knew what a snuggling woman felt like and this wasn't it.

Somehow he was holding the "hard" woman again, even as she lay so completely against him. Reese was holding herself rigidly. As rigidly as he expected she'd been while putting The Beast through paces that no one else had ever seen before.

"Something you want to be talking about, Reese?"

She shook her head sharply enough to nearly bruise his jaw.

Maybe if he just held her a long while, she'd find what she needed —and he didn't mind that solution at all.

His bare legs were getting cold despite the warm sun. When he ran his hands down over her bare behind, it was covered in goosebumps. He tried chaffing her skin and it earned him a snort of laughter.

"If we don't move soon, you're gonna freeze the Secret Service's finest ass…et," he teased her.

It earned him a soft thump on the ribs, but then she unwound herself from him. She started reaching for her clothes, even holding her jacket closed, and he didn't like that at all. He scrambled to his feet, scooped up all of their clothes, and headed inside. Bare-assed, she followed, then doubled back for her sidearm.

He turned for the bedroom, dumped their clothes on the floor, shrugged off the few bits he was still wearing, and slid between the covers.

Reese stopped in the doorway and looked down at him—one hand holding her jacket closed and the other holding her sidearm. The hem of the jacket and blouse danced along her hips.

"You expecting something more, Okie?"

"Don't mind being comfortable while we're talking."

"Talking?" Reese eyed him skeptically.

"Talking. Oh, I got no more complaints than a tornado in a trailer park if you want to just have more sex, but I'm thinking that something's eating at you and this is as good a place as any to do the talkin'." He liked her smile when he really laid on the accent. Something about it worked on women and he wasn't the complaining type.

She hesitated for a long moment, then sighed. With a single shrug, she shed all the layers off her shoulders at once and stood like a black Madonna—an armed black Madonna.

Reese slid the sidearm under the other pillow and tucked into the bed beside him without a single point of contact.

"Now that ain't no way to be talkin'." He pulled her in until she lay against him with her head on his shoulder and her leg over his hips. He began toying with her hair. "By the way, you ever cut this and I'm throwin' you out with the dog."

"You don't lose that accent and I might do some cutting myself." She lifted her leg and slid her hand down around him to indicate precisely where she'd be trimming things.

"Whatever you say, ma'am."

She growled a little but left him intact, resting her palm once more against the center of his chest. Again she let the silence stretch a long time and he could feel her gathering her thoughts like the air gathering its strength. He just hoped that he survived the tornado when Reese unleashed it.

"Can I trust you? How can I trust you? And I'm not talking about sex."

"Didn't think you were," though he'd bet it would be easier if she was. "Always figured that had to be earned. Malcolm and I do our best to do that."

⸻

AND SOMEHOW THAT MADE A DIFFERENCE. Malcolm clearly trusted Jim for everything and Jim had won that trust through action and kindness.

"I'm in trouble."

She'd never understand how Jim's silence always helped her along. She'd always depended on men to pry out what they needed to know, because it was far safer to keep the rest to herself. But Jim simply waited for her own thoughts to form until she was ready to give them a voice.

"What if the attack in New York wasn't an accident?"

"Didn't think it was."

"What if it wasn't an attack either?"

"But—" then he stopped for a long moment. "A trial run?"

"That's what I thought at first. Then Miss Watson suggested—"

"Who?"

"Doesn't matter," Reese wondered just how few people knew about the spy in the White House basement. "What if it was a test?"

"A test," Jim rolled it over his tongue like he was tasting it. "A test of the Motorcade's defenses?"

This time she decided to keep her thoughts to herself and pray that Jim didn't reach the same scary conclusion she had.

"No. If it was a test, they were testing for something that they didn't know. You. They wanted to test what you could do, because you're what they don't know about."

She tried to stay perfectly still, to not give away her next thought. But she felt it along the entire length of their bodies lying together when the realization hit him.

"It's an inside job," he barely whispered it. "The truck wasn't stolen until after the New York team was mobilized. And to have it in that place, at that precise moment… But the Secret Service never had a traitor before…" The way he tapered off said that he agreed that they did now.

And that was the moment that Reese knew she could completely trust Jim Fischer. They were lying too close together for his shocked reaction to be faked. And his first, instinctive reaction was to crush her against him as if he could somehow protect her by simply holding her close. As if he could take the bullet to spare her.

The last man to protect her unconditionally had died in a shattered stock car.

Since then she'd forgotten what it felt like—had always relied on herself alone.

Then Jim sealed the bargain with a whispered question.

"What are we going to do?"

We. Not her. *We.* She could definitely get to like the sound of that.

CHAPTER NINE

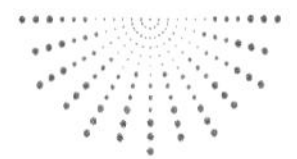

*J*im had asked for time to think about Harvey Lieber's offer to join the mobile team of the Presidential Protection Detail. This morning he and Malcolm marched straight in and took the job.

He and Reese had brainstormed through the long afternoon, then over a dinner of delivery pizza—his five acres in the woods wasn't *that* far from DC civilization. Malcolm had gotten his usual pizza crusts from Jim—Reese ate hers. After dinner, they were still nowhere on figuring out who else to trust.

It was an odd problem. The Secret Service trained them to trust no one except the other members of the team. But when it became impossible to trust the team…

He'd favored telling Captain Baxter—the man had run the White House branch of the Uniformed Division for four Presidents and been Jim's boss for three years.

Reese didn't know him from Adam and favored telling Harvey Lieber. He'd been with the President for nine years, ever since Zachary Thomas had been nominated for the Vice Presidency. But he'd always struck Jim as an unimaginative hard ass. He'd also been the one to personally promote Reese into her new position. Had that been a setup?

For the moment, they'd decided to keep everything to themselves.

They'd had sex again last night, but there was an overlay of tension now. Despite what the movies portrayed, being in fear for your life and suspicious of everybody did *not* enhance sex—not even in a them-against-the-world unity. They'd held each other close, but neither of them had slept well. Breakfast had been a fast and silent affair of leftover pizza. And the RV's shower wasn't built for two, even if they'd been in the mood.

"Welcome aboard," Harvey shook his hand and waved him into a chair. Malcolm plopped down at his feet as if the transition from Uniformed Division to the Presidential Detection Detail was the most normal thing in the world. He just hoped to god it was.

Baxter looked in, saw what was happening, and cursed. "Hate to lose you, Fischer. Make me proud." Then he was gone, back to his office with just that much ceremony.

"I'd like to give you a manual for your new duties, Fischer," Harvey was tapping his fingers together. "But we don't have one. We've never embedded a K-9 team inside the Motorcade before. They always travel ahead to prep the site. I've got reports of your work during the First Lady's trip, both prior to the event and during the event itself as well as your scores from yesterday's refresher training."

Jim didn't like that Harvey was still calling it "the event" rather than "the attack." Just because they couldn't confirm the latter didn't make it any less true.

"I'm assigning you to Agent Reese for now. You won't ride in Stagecoach, but she's already familiar with some of your methods. Tad Doogan is the head of the Motorcade, but he has enough headaches at the moment without adding another direct report agent to his list. I want you to work with the team and figure out how you fit into our processes."

"Yes, sir." Jim also didn't like that Harvey didn't refer to Malcolm, though he was sitting right there. Baxter would have said "you and your dog" or "you and Malcolm." Harvey acted as if Malcolm didn't even exist. With each passing second he was feeling better about advising Reese not to talk to him about their conclusions.

"Two more things. First, you do anything to screw up the efficiency of my Number One driver and you'll be walking patrol at a sewage plant." His tone made it clear that they were no longer discussing any on-duty actions.

Jim thought they'd been circumspect, but apparently not enough. Or did it somehow show on him? What would show? That he was completely gone on Reese Carver? He'd sure been wearing a goofy smile yesterday—Reese had commented on it a couple times. She didn't smile much, but she'd certainly come back to his bed for more, so it was hard to complain. But the tension today had wiped that smile off his face. At least he thought it had.

"Two, you've got forty-eight hours to get integrated into the team. "

When Jim looked at him in surprise, Harvey's grin was as plain evil as a rattler's.

"The President will be going to a new exhibit dedication at the flight museum at the Udvar-Hazy Center two days. From there, he's flying to Nashville to address the Cattle Industry Convention on his way to a triple header in his home state of Colorado. First, a speech at his alma mater of the Air Force Academy. Then on to the Olympic Training Center to have lunch with his mom, she's a swim coach there, and this year's athletes. Finally, a party fundraiser in Denver. Every stage has ground transport. Hope you like the hustle, boy." And Harvey turned back to whatever his next crisis was.

Jim scooted out quickly to let Harvey get back to it. Now he stood in the middle of the bustling Secret Service Ready Room wondering what the hell to do next.

He dialed Reese. Harvey had said he was assigned to her. It would be nice to hear—

"What?"

"That's how you answer the phone?"

"Yes. Now, what?"

Jim could feel her glower over the phone.

"Waiting here."

And he'd bet that wouldn't last long. "I'm assigned to you. So, um, where are you?"

"HQ Room 304," and she was gone.

He stared at the phone for a moment and wondered how to read her. Was she angry? They hadn't discussed him coming over to the Presidential Protection Detail. Maybe he should have. Or maybe she was just busy? No one focused on the lane they were in harder than a race car driver. So now he'd been demoted to a distraction?

"You got to wake up with her, dude." It might not have included wake-up sex, but she'd felt absolutely incredible in his arms. Not sure when he'd be back here in the West Wing, he gathered up all of his and Malcolm's most essential gear before heading out the door at a trot.

Dilya waved at him from where she walked the First Dog along the North Portico as he hustled out the gate into Lafayette Square and turned east for the six block walk back to the Secret Service Headquarters Building where he'd parked his truck to begin with. She looked as if she wanted to talk, but he wasn't ready for some question about the nature of his relationship with Reese if it was modeled on Regency England.

He wasn't ready to discuss it with himself!

Had he really thought that he was ruined for all other women by a couple-three nights with Reese?

He had. Moreover, it was true. Yet they hadn't spoken a word about what was happening between them; it had all been about work or in a silence that passed for understanding. If only he knew that it had indeed been understanding and not a path leading out the door and onto the open road.

Damn it! They *were* following the plot of Dilya's story. They were definitely in a relationship, as sure as the give-and-take of Elizabeth Bennet and Darcy, and they definitely weren't talking about it.

"Not a lot of Presidential Motorcades in your day, Mr. Darcy," he muttered as he crossed 14th Street against the light. A high-heeled blonde in a dark blue jacket and skirt so tight that it screamed look at me, eyed him strangely as he passed her by. That he didn't even give her a second look told him just how completely Reese had moved into his head and locked down his libido.

He slotted his ID at the security desk and headed up to Room 304. Inside was what he could only call ordered mayhem.

Cubicles were grouped in clusters down one side of the long room. Small signs indicated their functions: Route Security, Building Security, Police and Military Liaison, Air Transport, and more.

A dozen different agents were huddled around a central table. Built into its surface were eight large flat screens. Five displayed different maps: DC, Nashville, and three screens that must be Colorado. Each map had a red route and several blue routes.

He spotted an area that was labeled Motorcade Personnel and dropped his and Malcolm's gear there before joining Reese at the table. She was in the thick of it and looked as if she absolutely belonged. She didn't acknowledge his arrival with even a nod but, as she appeared to be at the center of three different conversations, he wouldn't take it personally.

<hr>

"SIDEKICK—" the President's Secret Service codename "—will be at the Udvar-Hazy Center for two hours," Tad Doogan's slightly nasal and very Harvard-haughty tone sliced into Reese's headache.

Even her tiny nod to Jim and Malcolm had been ill-advised.

"We're directly under the Dulles flight path. We'll move him by Marine One helicopter from the South Lawn direct to Udvar-Hazy. He is keynoting a brief ceremony to open the exhibit featuring the Combat Search and Rescue Sikorsky MH-60 that he flew during his service in Yemen, Somalia, and other classified locations. His old unit is having an on-site reunion afterward. We will then transport him again by Marine One helicopter to Andrews where he will board Air Force One."

"Why not bring Air Force One to Dulles?" Jim's question cut off every side conversation.

"And who are you?" Doogan did his best down-his-nose look at Jim. He had humbled entire teams with that look.

"I'm the Motorcade's new K-9 dog handler."

"And what do you know of the logistics of moving the President?"

Reese winced on Jim's behalf, but there'd been no chance to warn him about what he was walking into. Actually, she hadn't even thought to do so, which was yet another unkindness.

Jim had held her last night when she'd most needed it. All the prior day she'd been groaning under the load of new knowledge: safety, protection, and her inability to meet those needs. If she'd been even half a second slower to respond, the three leading women of the land would be a bloody smear on the concrete barrier wall of the FDR Drive in New York. But she hadn't been. And somehow Jim holding her had helped her come to terms with that.

"I know that flying him thirty miles in the wrong direction, from Dulles back to Andrews, wouldn't be my first choice for security. When I drove convoys for the Army, that was always a fear—they knew exactly where we had to go because there was only one road from Karachi to Kabul. But I see on each of your maps here that you have multiple routes in case of last minute changes. Bad guys *know* that the President always departs from Andrews Air Force Base. So, for once, I wouldn't." Jim shrugged easily as if he was impervious to Tad Doogan's ability to use his glare to burn a hole right through your ego.

"Actually," General Arnson, the commander of the Marine One helicopters, spoke up, "I'm going to agree with the young man. If we time the landing, we could taxi Air Force One into position here at the holding area from Runway 1R. It's one mile from Udvar to that point along a secure road inside the airport perimeter. Run a small Motorcade along that road, then get him in the air."

Apparently Arnson was also immune to Doogan's lethal abilities. But if she drove that short leg of the Motorcade, then she couldn't be in position in Nashville in time to be the driver there.

Doogan's glare was now boring holes in the table. There was a dead silence until he snapped out without looking up.

"Fine. Carver will drive Stagecoach from Udvar-Hazy to Air Force One. A relief driver will then move the car over to the service area at the east end of Runway 30 to load up on a C-17 and reposition it in Colorado. We will have a second Motorcade pre-positioned in Nashville. Essential Motorcade personnel will be provided with seats on Air Force One so that they don't fall behind. That includes Jamieson, Walker, Carver, and I suppose whoever you are," he waved a dismissive hand at Jim. "Now would everyone just start doing your jobs." He aimed a final eye-launched laser at Jim before stalking off. Everyone else dispersed rapidly into smaller groups or hurried to their desks.

"He's a real sweetheart," Jim whispered once they were the only two left at the central table.

"That was him in a good mood."

"How's *your* mood?"

"I missed Malcolm. Thanks for bringing him by," she kept her voice deadpan as she knelt down to pet the dog. And she did feel better. The impossible vice of pressure across her scalp had eased the moment the two of them had walked into the room.

Jim offered a sigh as heartfelt as his dog's for not getting his own slice of pizza last night.

Not wanting to give away how glad she'd been to hear Jim's voice on the phone, she'd kept her responses curt so that no one else could read anything into them. Her body had jolted at his arrival, evoking a hot flush of memories of how skilled a lover Jim Fischer was. He'd made any of her inadequacies seem irrelevant or even nonexistent, though she knew better. She could feel the heat brushing her cheeks, so she momentarily buried her face in Malcolm's fur. The heat Jim's mere presence was igniting throughout her body would have to wait for later.

How odd to be looking *forward* to a lover. She looked forward to a race or a challenging drive. Lovers were mostly for briefly soothing frayed nerves or finding a release for whatever was bound up inside her and couldn't find any other outlet.

"It's too bad humans don't have engine rattles and exhaust pipes."

If they did, she'd know exactly what they were thinking. What she *herself* was thinking. Instead it was all muddled up inside her, and Jim Fischer seemed to be the one causing more muddle than usual.

Jim was smiling in a way that promised a scatological thought was on his tiny, trucker mind. Not the kind of exhaust pipe she'd meant.

REESE CRACKED HIM UP. She saw everything as some version of a car, as if humans were so easy to diagnose. He wondered if her occasional humor was intentional. Of all the agents in the room, he didn't recognize a one he could ask. It was as if the Motorcade was a world that had somehow passed him by unnoticed for so long.

Phones rang, keyboards were pounded on, and a large calendar covered a whole section of one wall. An agent—with a habit of squeaking his marker in ways that were making both him and Malcolm twitch—was marking upcoming travel. Six-country, eight-day East Asian tour next month. Three days at the First Family's farm in Tennessee. A meeting on the Hill.

Each, he realized, required an immense mobilization of manpower and equipment. Layered on in separate colors were travels for other key protectees: Vice President, First and Second Ladies, Speaker of the House, a visit by the British Prime Minister. The more layers he saw, the more there were to see. It was a rare day where some element of the Motorcade wasn't on the move.

Before he hit complete overwhelm, he turned back to Reese and their next mission.

"So," he looked at the maps on the table, because if he looked one more time down her blouse as she knelt over Malcolm and admired the bra that he'd helped put there just a few hours before, he wasn't going to be thinking of anything except how soon he could take it off again.

"So?" She rose to her feet and looked at the projected maps with him.

"Primary Motorcade route," he traced the jogging blue line across Nashville.

"And alternates," she traced the red lines. "Some are designed to cross the main route so that we can bail out onto them if there is a traffic problem or a detected threat. Some don't and are true alternates in their own right."

"And you memorize them all?"

Her steady gaze said that was a given.

Right! Reese Carver didn't like repetitions of the obvious.

Had she pre-mapped a variety of routes through their relationship? He'd rather not ask.

"Where do I fit in?"

"I don't have a clue," Reese looked as if she was answering both questions, even though Jim had meant to be asking about the Motorcade.

"Okay, then, I'll start." He looked at her steadily and saw her eyes go a little wide.

"Maybe that would be good," she said it softly. Softly as in a bedroom voice. She was such a driven person that it had never occurred to him to take the lead in where their relationship might go —he'd been along for the ride and enjoying himself. Which might explain where Margarite and the other women of his past had gone, following their own lead with no guidance from him.

Well, he didn't like the idea of Reese Carver drifting away due to his negligence. He *hated* the idea of her with another man.

"When a dog team preps a site, we're done before the Motorcade arrives. By the time Sidekick or any other protectee shows up, we're typically done and gone. One or two will hang on to keep the site secure, but most of us move on to prep the next locale. We aren't embedded directly in the Motorcade by any prior standard of practice." He'd always preferred the fence line, but that hadn't freed him completely from site prep for the President's trips.

"The Motorcade," Reese tapped a few controls and the DC map was replaced with images of vehicles lined up across the screen. She swept her hands across the surface and split it into sections so that she could stack and enlarge them, now a long double line spanning two screens. "It's typically made up of twenty-five to thirty vehicles, if you don't count the motorcycle police."

"Seen it go by enough times," Jim studied the pictures. "Never knew you were one of the drivers." As if he was apologizing for not having noticed her sooner.

"We don't go looking for trouble," even though Jim was definitely giving her some. "But we're ready when it comes." She'd give it back twice as hard as he dished trouble out if it came to that.

He shrugged as if her threat was of no consequence. He tapped the image of the first vehicle to zoom in on it. A standard black sedan.

"Tell me about it," but he didn't seem to be talking about the vehicle. If he thought she was going to talk about anything else in this room full of testosterone-laden men, he had another think coming.

"That's the Route Car. It runs several minutes ahead of the Motorcade, typically with a small fleet of motorcycle cops who stop to block intersections as needed. They make sure the route is clear. Pilot car is another sedan usually. Their job is to make sure we follow the planned route. Don't want to get lost or turn into a cul-de-sac with a thirty-five vehicle caravan on your tail."

"Then a bunch of cop cars and more motorcycles."

"We call them Sweepers. Sweeping along at the front to make sure the road is clear."

"Then another sedan," he started to brush the picture off the side of the screen but she pulled it back.

"Don't dismiss it. This is a key car—called the Lead Car. It's directly in front of the main package: Stagecoach and the Spares. It's my buffer if anything goes wrong. Guide, early alert, and offensive driving. They're the best drivers outside of the limos. Remember the guy who stopped the delivery truck in New York by slamming on his brakes and taking the crash himself? That's the Lead Car."

Reese closed her eyes and hung on to the edge of the table as she continued. Wished they were in a place Jim could put his arm around her as the images came back.

"That driver died yesterday. Some blood vessel in his brain was too damaged. He was getting better, talking to his wife, and it just let go. Killed him almost instantly. The first the docs knew was from her screaming."

If it had come down to that moment and *she'd* been the driver of the Lead Car, would she have done that to protect the First Lady?

She supposed she would have or they wouldn't have chosen her to drive Stagecoach.

Unless she'd been chosen for some other reason. The first woman to drive Stagecoach. Or the first one they thought was weak enough to let an attack through? She glanced around the room. Was one of these guys, her fellow drivers, setting her up for the fall? What about Doogan? She could hear him being snooty over the phone to some poor Colorado police chief who probably deserved better. Or Harvey? Or…

It was the road to madness.

"That's my car," Jim stabbed a finger down on it and it zoomed in to fill the screen.

"*What?*" Her shout was loud enough to silence the room. Even Doogan paused in mid-phone-snoot to glance over at her.

"The Lead Car. That's my spot," he said it more quietly and the other guys turned back to what they'd been doing, though they did keep glancing over.

"*That—*" she swallowed hard and tried to temper her voice. All she could picture was Jim in the car as it was battered and broken on the FDR. "In reality, Lead Car is probably the most dangerous position in the entire Motorcade. It's the last line of defense."

"But," Jim tapped the image again and it zoomed in until all they could see was a tire. He pulled his hands away rather than touching the screen again. "I'm with the Motorcade. In fact, I'm guessing that it's unlikely that we'd ever be separated from the main Motorcade. But I'd still be first to arrive. That means Malcolm and I can deploy while Stagecoach is still coming to a stop. We'd be able to check the immediate area for as much as ten or twenty seconds before the President steps out."

"We don't release Stagecoach's door until we're positive the zone is safe," but she wasn't paying much attention to her own words as she considered the implications. She zoomed back until the entire Motorcade was in view. Reese had thought he'd travel in a support vehicle, maybe back by the inevitable press corps vans. But each of those were specialist vehicles: ambulance, hazmat, mobile communications center... Each was crammed with personnel. The Lead Car usually had just a driver and a spotter in the front passenger seat. There would always be room for Jim and Malcolm in the back seat.

"You sure?" She looked at him carefully.

Something about him had changed. He wasn't just some Okie trucker with an unexpected set of skills in bed. After what they'd both witnessed, it would take an immensely brave man to ride in the Lead Car. Doubly if they were right and the run at the First Lady's Motorcade had merely been a test. Suddenly her dog walker was the Army soldier who had driven through war zones for a living.

Jim nodded down toward Malcolm. "We're sure."

She knew how he felt about protecting his dog. If he was willing to risk both their lives, then he really was sure.

Then he looked at her, straight in the eye with no evasion, no blinking. Just that totally male smile of his that said they were now on a completely different topic.

"I'm sure."

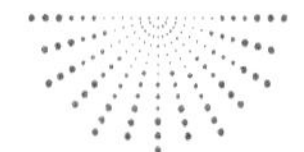

Jim followed Reese up the back stairs of Air Force One and tried not to feel like he was getting ready to leave the planet. He was certainly headed for a whole new world.

He'd been able to watch Air Force One just taxiing into position as their Motorcade had raced along the back road from the Air and Space Museum. Even for that short distance on a closed road, over a dozen vehicles had been involved: Route Car, Stagecoach, the five heavy-duty Suburbans carrying various aspects of the Secret Service, the cluster of press vans, and an inevitable ambulance. Overhead he'd been able to hear the pounding beat of Overwatch—a Marine Sikorsky Black armed to the teeth.

"I don't even hear it anymore. It's always there," Reese noticed where his attention had strayed. "Keep moving or you'll get run down."

Now the rush was for everyone joining the flight to race up the back stairs in the time it took the President and the senior staffers to ascend the front ones. The plane would leave when he was ready, not when everyone in the back was.

The members of the press clearly knew that as they crowded up the stairs behind him, most carrying small suitcases. For himself, he'd tucked a toothbrush and a change of underwear into Malcolm's pack and called it good.

He'd never walked under a 747 on the runway before and it was daunting how large it was. Planes never seemed that big when walking to them along an enclosed jetway. But this thing was massive. It blocked out the entire sunset sky. He could feel the weight of the responsibility of the Presidential load far more than from his first short ride in the Motorcade. All this, all these people, were to make sure that one man traveled safely.

At the head of the stairs, Reese headed out the left-side door into a seating area that looked like any other business class section he'd had to walk past on his way to the cheap seats. A glance behind revealed that the press exited the stairs via the right-side door.

"They get a boxed-in area on the other side of the fuselage from us. Fourteen seats, paid for by their agencies in the hopes of getting some tiny scoop from the President. They can't enter the rest of the plane without a personal escort by one of Harvey's boys."

"Harvey's girls don't count?"

She ignored him and led them to a pair of seats. The seats were generous enough for Malcolm to join them on the area between his feet and Reese's.

He was starting to recognize the faces who came into their side of the aircraft: four members of the PPD led by Harvey Lieber and two of the other drivers. The rest were unknown to him, but were easily identified as being attached to the plane rather than the Motorcade. They wore blue uniforms. Over their left breast, their name was stitched in white. Over their right was the Presidential Seal with "Air Force One" stitched above it.

"Is it me or is the air in here getting a little thin?"

"It's not you," Reese offered. "I've only been aboard a few times. Mostly I'm on the C-17 transport with the vehicles."

He wanted to take her hand, hold on to some concrete evidence that he wasn't so far in over his head. But he was...and he knew it. Two days assigned to work with Reese. He'd pictured at least meals and two nights together to explore a little of what was going on between them.

That idea had died in the first ten minutes.

"Joining the Motorcade is normally a three-month indoctrination. You have two days, so let's get to work."

Meals had been eaten while standing up or studying videos of simulated attack scenarios. Each had come with a twenty-page manual of what to watch for, position by position. The response scenarios had taken less than two minutes, but he'd had to watch some a dozen times to see how all of the pieces were moving at a deep level of coordination. Once he'd spent a day doing that, Reese ran him through a video he'd already seen dozens of times, the attack in New York.

A journalist had also taken a series of superb photos and videos that hadn't been available during his initial debriefing. The photographer had caught the feeling—and detail—of being right in the middle of every moment of the attack.

Step by step, Reese led him through the entire event second by second, displaying all of the different angles on the various screens of the central conference table. Much of the team had gathered around— it was the first-ever attack on the Motorcade in history that hadn't been repulsed while still several blocks away.

Each instant had a coordinated action.

"If a crisis occurs while you are traveling within our company," Tad Doogan had said in one of his tones, "I would highly recommend that you remain in your vehicle. Such an action will vastly increase the likelihood of survival for you and your animal."

Jim had wanted to brush off the warning, but Reese's deadpan expression stated that she'd heard worse advice.

As the frame-by-frame continued, Jim began to realize that perhaps she and Doogan weren't kidding. The agents who had poured out of the flipped SUV that had been caught in the truck's wreckage had moved quickly and aggressively to create a zone of protection despite how badly they'd just been rattled. And they'd done it in seconds.

On Day Two, they'd taken him out to James J. Rowley Training Center, but this time it was a full Motorcade, not just Reese. They moved into the winding streets of the simulated residential neighborhood.

They'd placed an agent in the back seat of the Lead Car with him. "Want to observe how you and your dog react."

Jim had served in the Army for six years and done dozens of training exercises here at RTC, so he hadn't expected anything surprising. He should have. The Motorcade was an attempt to reproduce the security offered by the White House and Air Force One, except in a mobile form. It was an incredible experience.

Malcolm's main complaint had been when the agent riding with them had asked him to roll up the window just because it was thirty-six degrees outside.

Jim's main complaint was that for two nights he hadn't slept with Reese Carver. Somehow, both nights he'd found himself driving home alone and he didn't like it one bit. He'd have been glad to plummet into sleep beside her and wake up together just getting dressed.

Instead, they hadn't so much as brushed fingers since that one morning in his fifth wheel. Reese was deep in the task, so deep that maybe she didn't even see that she was pushing him away.

He'd always been a family-oriented guy, he knew that much—he saw more of his parents and siblings, who were scattered all over the country, than most of his coworkers did who grew up in Baltimore or Charleston and had family nearby. Having Reese beside him when he woke up in New York and the one night at his place had him thinking about it for himself as well.

Reese had made it damn clear over the last two days that he'd been far too naive.

He glanced over at her as Air Force One roared down the runway, powering its way aloft with a surprising rate of climb. He almost felt as if he was an astronaut pushed back in his seat.

Reese sat with her hands folded in her lap and her eyes closed.

"What are you thinking about?"

"Feels like a stock car coming off the line," her voice was soft and whispery with nostalgia. "Pressed back in your seat. Two, three, four hundred miles of a challenging race just waiting for you to push the envelope. To find the edge and ride it through the heart of the pack. I miss it sometimes."

"Ever think of going back?"

She rocked her head side to side without opening her eyes. "Got a taste for doing something more important. Saving the First Ladies. That was something. We did that."

"You did." That had been clear from the videos. If she had been a single moment slower to respond, the entire rear of the Suburban would have been crushed. That had been clearly demonstrated by what the truck had done to the nose of the following Suburban instead.

"You'd have done the same," she opened her eyes and looked at him. It seemed it was the first time they'd had a moment to really look at each other in two days.

"I'm just a trucker, not—"

"Hate to break this up. You two are with me." Harvey Lieber was standing in the aisle by Jim's elbow. The climb had eased, though they weren't up to cruising altitude yet.

Jim hadn't realized how closely they'd leaned their heads together as they talked quietly over the four big engines' roar.

"Three of us," Jim popped his seatbelt and nudged Malcolm awake with his foot.

"Right," Harvey said dryly before heading up the aisle.

A glance at Reese. She didn't know what was going on either.

They passed through the luxurious guest area with eight seats for guests plus two more tucked in corners occupied by agents watching the guests. Lieber didn't stop as they moved past the staff area, a big conference room with eight executive armchairs and a line of couches along the wall encircling a sprawling table of walnut, or even the senior staff lounge where four people were huddled together debating something.

"Uh."

Harvey continued leading them forward past the galley and a

doctor's office presently configured as a small conference room.

They were fast running out of airplane.

A naval officer sat in the last chair in the long hallway they'd been following forward. At his feet sat the black leather briefcase of the nuclear football—the launch codes and communications gear that was never more than a hundred feet from the President in case he had to launch a strike.

Across from him sat a massive black man who Jim was fairly sure was the head of Secretary Matthews' protection. His hands were big enough that he could probably break Air Force One in two if he needed to.

Jim considered turning and sprinting for the back of the plane, but it wasn't nearly far enough away.

Harvey finally stepped through a double door bearing the Seal of the President painted in gold on the mahogany.

There was even less air here than there'd been at the rear of the plane.

REESE HAD BEEN within steps of the President any number of times, but she'd never actually met him. As a driver, her job was to stay behind the wheel of the car and be ready to move.

Now she was standing in his unoccupied office.

"He'll be with you in a minute. Sit. Don't touch *anything*." Then Harvey stepped out and closed the doors behind him.

She looked at Jim in desperation, but what right did she have to look there for comfort? For two days she'd tried to rediscover herself.

She depended on no one.

She needed *no one!*

Yet she'd spent almost every waking moment with Jim and enjoyed every second of it. She'd learned to anticipate his moods, partly by watching him, partly by watching Malcolm. Jim's sharp mind had been revealed behind his easy manner as they'd dissected video after video.

The only way to keep her head clear had been to get away—steer clear of him each night. Which had worked brilliantly. She'd lain alone in her bed both nights, thinking of him. Wishing him there beside her. Missing his silence in which to explore her thoughts.

Now she didn't dare speak. The President's flying office was a disorienting space—it felt twisted inside the square space. The President's chair was in the forward corner and a curved desk defined the power of the position by its sheer size within the small area. For visitors there was a single armchair near the hull and a curved sofa lined the other two walls. Anyone seated there would be a head shorter than the President.

Jim dropped onto the sofa as if it didn't matter and Malcolm climbed up beside him to rest his head on Jim's thigh.

Resigned, Reese was most of the way into the lone armchair when the door opened.

The President stepped in.

Jim jumped to his feet.

She tried to, but was past the tipping point and had to bounce off the cushion with all the guilt of a little girl caught playing in her parents' room.

"Stand up, Malcolm," Jim whispered and gave his dog a hand sign.

Malcolm rose to all fours on the couch and wagged his tail.

It earned Jim a smile from the President, which Reese felt was a good move coming off the start line.

Zachary Thomas was a tall man, with an open and friendly face—his Air Force background was clear in his bearing. He was closely followed by a man ten years his senior, former President Peter Matthews, now the Secretary of State.

"Hello, hello. Please sit."

Reese abandoned the chair and moved over to sit on Malcolm's other side on the sofa that wrapped around the wall. It was a long sofa, so perhaps she shouldn't have sat so close, but she liked being able to run a hand into Malcolm's fur. It reminded her of the few quiet moments the three of them had caught together over the last few days: a moment by the candy machine, a long silence as they studied a video while sitting hip to hip. Jim made it easy to treasure those brief moments.

She waited for the President to break the silence, which he did after only a few uncomfortable moments.

"I wanted to thank you both for the roles you played in saving our wives' lives. If you hadn't already been assigned to replace McKenna before that, I'd have requested you, Ms. Carver."

"Thank you, sir. It was a pleasure to serve."

"Except maybe during the accident?"

Reese felt the jolt and glanced at Jim, who grimaced.

"Told you," Secretary Matthews said casually.

"*Not* an accident. What leads you to that conclusion that it was an attack?" The President kept his tone casual, not showing the least bit of surprise.

She and Jim had agreed that they didn't know who to trust. But if they didn't trust the President and former President, what was the point?

"Too many coincidences. However, we," she glanced at Jim, who confirmed with a nod. It took her another breath before she could continue, "We have concluded that it was *not* an attack."

That got her both men's full attention. She wished it hadn't.

"Please believe that this isn't an egotistical statement, but we think the whole purpose was to test my reactions as a driver."

The President narrowed his eyes at her. But he didn't speak. Both men restrained what must have been a hundred doubts and questions. Instead, they sat on the edges of their seats and listened. Neither man was what she expected.

Damn Jim for his thinning atmosphere comment. She couldn't seem to get her breath.

"We believe, sir," Jim thankfully stepped in, "that they used the attack on the First Lady's Motorcade as an action-response test in preparation for an attack upon your own Motorcade."

"Why am I only hearing this now?"

"The timing, sir. To place a truck at that moment in that place indicates an inside job. We don't know who to trust, Mr. President."

"Reminds me of Emily," Secretary of State Matthews leaned back in his chair and smiled. "That's a very high compliment, by the way, Ms. Carver. She did something similar to Frank Adams, the head of my protection detail. That was shortly before my first wife's death."

The two men exchanged significant looks.

It had been before her time. All Reese recalled was that the immensely popular Katherine Matthews had died in a tragic helicopter accident. Their looks said there was little love lost there and that the truth was probably a very different story.

"Harvey," the President shouted.

Harvey Lieber opened the door and stuck his head into the room. "Find Cornelia and both of you get in here."

While the door was closed, the President continued. "If we don't count my wife and this guy here," he waved a negligent hand at Secretary Matthews. "There are no two people I trust more. Actually, I probably trust them more than you, Peter." It was a clear tease between two men who had been elected together and were now friends.

Secretary Matthews shrugged as if it was no skin off his back.

Reese felt Jim grab her hand for a moment deep in Malcolm's fur and squeeze it hard.

Trust.

It was a hard concept for her and he knew that. She wished that she understood him better. Or knew him better. Yet she trusted him, like no one else more than Pop. Even in front of the leader of the free world, he did nothing to try and bump her out of the lane. He made it clear that she was the force to be reckoned with, not him or his male ego.

Why she'd pushed him away the last two nights was now a mystery that she couldn't—

Harvey and White House Chief of Staff Cornelia Day entered and closed the door behind them. She was a slender, tall woman who had a lethal reputation. She ran the White House and the President's schedule like a metronome. There had never been a more on-schedule administration in history. Everything about her said DC elite: an immaculate dark blue skirt and blazer, perfectly tasteful makeup on a flawless complexion, haircut simple but perfect for her narrow face, and a Cordovan leather case for her tablet computer. Her nickname was "The Shark" and rumor said that even real sharks would never stand a chance against her.

Ms. Day perched on the far end of the sofa.

Harvey stood with his back to the door and his hands crossed in front of him.

"Tell them," the President ordered.

So they did. Harvey's scowl went dark, but he didn't say a word until they finished laying out all of their reasoning.

"Carver, you ever leave me out of the loop again, I'm parking your ass in a kiddie car amusement park. Both of you!"

Reese swallowed hard.

"Second," he turned to the President. "Reasoning is sound. I don't like it, but it makes sense. Not a hint from the—" Harvey spun to face her so quickly that she jerked back against the sofa.

He rubbed his forehead.

"What?" Until that moment Cornelia Day had restrained her input to a nod that had her collar-length, dead-straight hair pitching forward and back in a slicing motion as sharp as shark's teeth (Reese guessed that Jim would appreciate the metaphor). But Harvey's consternation had finally moved her to speech—a short, sharp command.

"NASCAR to my Motorcade. Draw me a roadmap, Carver."

"I left racing abruptly."

"Your father's death," Harvey nodded.

Reese had kept her mouth shut and let the press and everyone else believe that. But the President deserved the truth. She was having trouble facing Harvey, so she turned to the Commander-in-Chief.

"Putting my father's team sponsor in the hospital with a lug wrench after he tried to rape me as part of 'consoling' me over my father's loss. No witnesses. He didn't press charges, but he blacklisted me with the other team owners and I was left without a ride."

"Why didn't you press charges?" Ms. Day leaned forward. Despite her cold-blooded reputation, she appeared genuinely concerned and upset.

"I tried. The police dismissed it. He was an important man in NASCAR racing and the Charlotte business community. I'm a black woman who looks like this."

Reese wasn't conceited about her looks, but knew from experience that men were drawn to her for a reason. Even Jim had started that way. But he'd moved on. No mistaking that he liked her body, but he also liked *her*, which she knew she was being slow in processing.

"The police wouldn't even investigate. Besides it was a he-said / she-said and there was no evidence other than the beating I gave him. His punch to my gut and his throwing me around the room by my hair when I refused to cooperate didn't even show. I wear my hair this long as a clear fu… As a clear statement to myself of who is in control of my life."

"I'll fucking kill the bastard." Jim apparently cared less about language in front of the President.

In the telling, she'd forgotten Jim was sitting there beside her. She'd seen him quiet and sometimes frustrated, but mostly he was Mr. Pleasant with that big welcoming smile of his. His face was now dark with fury and his light eyes were as black as death.

She wrapped her hand around his in thanks.

"Don't," she told him. "He's not worth it. Besides, I did tell his wife, who has made it her life's mission to destroy his career and reputation. I suspect not because of what he did, but because I'm black. She's very 'traditional' Southern in all the worst ways."

"I could get to like you, Ms. Carver," the President said lightly to break the mood.

She tried to pull her hand back, but Jim had clenched it tightly, for all to see. Harvey didn't show any surprise, Ms. Day didn't show anything at all, and the President traded a smile with Secretary Matthews that was all too easy to read. It said, "Isn't that sweet?"

Well, maybe it was at that. But now was not the time to think about it.

"From there to my Motorcade," Harvey demanded through gritted teeth. Fury was clear on his face as well. It made her think better of Harvey as she understood his anger probably had very little to do with her holding hands with another agent in front of the President and a great deal to do with her past.

"I found a flyer stuck under the windshield wiper on my Mustang. I went to see a race…from the cheap seats. Only place I've ever called home was Charlotte Motor Speedway and I'd never seen a race from the stands. Now that all of the backfield was closed to me, it was the only way I had to get on track—buy a seat. The flyer was there when I came out. I figured it beat the dead-end future I'd seen myself skidding toward for that entire race."

"The Protection Force," Harvey groaned as if he was in pain.

"What's that?" The President asked while the Secretary chuckled. "What?"

"My doing, I'm afraid." Then Secretary Matthews must have spotted Reese's look. "Oh, not me personally. There's a little outfit called the White House Protection Force. One of my gifts to you, Zack. They're the ones who saved us all last month with Linda and Thor. In my book, there is no possible higher recommendation of Ms. Carver's skills than being picked by them."

Reese had certainly never heard of them.

"Who?" The President and Ms. Day asked in unison.

"Completely anonymous," Harvey complained. "I'd feel better if they weren't *always* right."

Reese wondered what else this Protection Force knew. She became very self-conscious of Jim's hand still holding hers. Did they know about how he cared for her? That was ridiculous, even she hadn't known that. Not until he promised to kill her three-years-past would-be rapist.

JIM WAS WATCHING Secretary Matthews throughout the exchange. This Protection Force might be anonymous to everyone else, but it was clear that former President Peter Matthews knew exactly who was behind the operation. Clear as mud on a hog, his father would say. Having hauled hogs in his early days, Jim knew that was pretty damn clear.

White House Protection Force. Somehow they'd reached out and plucked Reese Carver out of NASCAR, but she'd won her own way to the driver's seat of Stagecoach. There'd been no doubting her driving skills in the First Lady's Motorcade. And no doubting the look on McKenna's and the trainers' faces that morning out at RTC as she spun The Beast through paces it had never seen before.

It simply confirmed to him that she was special in so many ways.

"I just drive," he teased her softly while the others were debating what to do about this new threat.

"I do," she was paying attention to the other conversation.

"You're a goddamn miracle, Reese Carver."

She turned to face him at that. Her brow furrowed as she looked at him.

He could see a succession of emotions slipping over her beautiful features. Denial, the weight of the past, puzzlement, and finally a small flicker of hope as she whispered, "Really?"

"Really."

She swallowed hard and offered the tiniest nod that said she'd still need a lot of convincing.

"We should cancel this trip, Mr. President," Harvey was arguing.

"I refuse to huddle in fear, Harvey. That's the Protection Detail in you: lock me inside Cheyenne Mountain and let me out in four or eight years after I've turned into a babbling idiot. I'm not an Air Force captain because I hide from danger."

"But—"

"You're not an Air Force captain," Cornelia Day spoke up. "You're the Commander-in-Chief." She sounded as if she was offended at him acknowledging the lower rank.

"Drive straight ahead, sir," Jim spoke, though he hadn't meant to.

Everyone turned to look at him. In for ten tons, in for twenty— that was Mom's saying.

"I drove Karachi-Kandahar-Kabul for three tours, sir. And the answer is to be ready. The answer isn't to not show up in the first place."

"Could get to like you too, Mr. Fischer." The President turned to Harvey. "We're keeping the trip schedule. It's up to you and these two to keep me alive. Don't let me down or I'll be very disappointed."

Harvey nodded, but didn't move from the door.

The look he aimed at Jim made him wish that he still worked for Captain Baxter and was walking the fence line.

"You seriously think it's someone on my team?"

Reese didn't appear to want to talk, which left it up to Jim.

"When did you announce that Reese would be the driver for the First Lady's trip?"

"I told the team within minutes of when you left for site prep, but only our own people."

"Not the press or a public announcement?"

Harvey shook his head. "Not until the night before departure. And the route was never published, of course."

Jim nodded. "I had guessed that. We arrived in New York Tuesday noon to scout the locations. We met the First Lady's party at the heliport on Wednesday morning. We were an easy target anywhere in Manhattan, but it would have been hard to guess our route. The truck was stolen on Wednesday morning at four a.m. before the First Lady's party had even left DC."

"Thirty-six hours later," Harvey finished for him, "at 1600 hours on Thursday, the attack occurred. It was the one place they could be sure of our arrival route and time based on our public departure from the UN building."

Jim nodded. "Who knew about the trip in time for that truck to be stolen? Who knew our exact departure time from the UN and was poised to have that truck in the right place at the right time?"

"There's never been a traitor in the Secret Service. I'm going to find his ass and I'm going to grind him so far into the ground so hard that they'd need an oil drill to find his body." Harvey's snarl was one of the most dangerous sounds Jim had ever heard. No one faking it could make that sound.

Cornelia rose to her feet. "Thank you, Mr. President." Showing no fear, Cornelia eased Harvey Lieber aside as if he was an errant puppy and opened the door. She waved for them to leave, and Jim would have run except it took him a moment to understand that he couldn't disentangle himself from Reese's grip.

It had changed as they sat there. At first it had been comfort, no surprise to him at all that she'd successfully defended herself against some bastard rapist—he was just sick that's how she'd lost something she'd so loved. But now they were holding hands as if it was the most natural thing in the world.

And it was.

Jim had never been much of a hand holder. Margarite hadn't been either, which maybe should have told him something. So what did it say that he wanted to hold Reese's? Not to keep her close and safe— okay, not only that. But because he liked the connection there. Liked the way their fingers laced together as if they were the same hands despite the different colors of their skin.

As they rose to their feet, it was so hard to let go of her. And the President's knowing smile wasn't helping at all. He'd seen the President and his wife on TV—it seemed they were always holding hands. Holding on as if it was the most natural thing in the world.

When Reese finally noticed and went to extract her hand, he held on, earning him a puzzled look from her and a "good man" nod from the President. So he kept her hand in his as he led her out of the President's office.

Cornelia Day led them into the medical suite directly aft of the President's office. She shooed out the doctor and nurse. There were two chairs and a tiny couch. The operating table was folded up against the wall.

Ms. Day and Harvey took the two chairs; he and Reese were pressed hip-to-hip on the little couch, which he wasn't complaining about. Malcolm got the floor.

"Now. We're going to go through the entire trip step-by-step until it is second nature to all of us."

That's what they did for the entire hour-and-a-quarter-long flight to Nashville. And when nothing untoward occurred, Harvey and the two of them spent the next two hours to Colorado Springs doing the same thing.

They arrived at Peterson Air Force Base, Colorado Springs, at 2300 local time.

The President would sleep in his suite in the nose of Air Force One. Most of the Protection Detail would stay aboard as well, but the Motorcade personnel had no reason to remain aboard through the night.

Colorado Springs was at six thousand feet, almost a thousand feet higher than Denver, and was bitterly cold. A several-inch dusting of snow lay on the semi-arid desert.

All the vehicles of a second Motorcade were already pre-positioned inside the hangar, ready for tomorrow's events. Not being on duty until shortly before the Motorcade would have to roll, they grabbed a base car and headed for the nearest hotel.

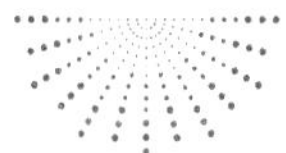

Reese had never been like this with any man.

They played grab-ass at the registration desk.

They would have had sex in the elevator if it had been more than two floors or in the hall if they'd been at the far end.

As it was, while he battled with the keycard, she stood behind him. Peeling back the coat she'd opened in the elevator, she yanked out his shirt hem and ran her hands over his flat stomach and up his chest, pulling herself hard against his back.

He had a workout chest, the legs of a man who walked for a living, and hips that her legs fit around like they'd been made-to-order.

Why in the world had she been avoiding that?

The *sha-shink* of the releasing lock was the only cue she needed to shove him against the door, pushing it open with his body. It was a good thing that Malcolm was fast on his feet or he might have been locked out in the hall and she'd have been helpless to pause long enough to let him in.

Jim let her pin him back against the wall. There was no questioning that he let her because even as strong as she was, he was in a whole other category.

"Reese?" Jim's voice was tentative. Cautionary.

"Don't you get," she spoke between attacking different portions of his and her clothing. "There are times when you don't talk. All you do. Is get naked." Both of their sidearms hit the floor with a heavy thump.

"This is one of those times?"

She finally had his pants off and grabbed him. The way he filled her hand was amazing.

He grunted hard into their kiss when she simultaneously rammed their mouths together to stop any more words.

Okay, perhaps she'd grabbed him a little too hard, but he felt so incredibly good. So powerful. So...male. For the first time in her life she actually wanted all she could get of his pure, unadulterated maleness.

It wasn't his anger at how she'd been treated in her past that wowed her—she'd already known he wasn't one of those guys.

It wasn't the way he stood up for her at every opportunity—though that was sexy as hell on several levels.

It was... She didn't know.

That almost stopped her.

She wasn't a wanton, not by any stretch of the imagination. But Jim Fischer made her feel so free at the moment that she wished she was one. Just for him. Even if it was just this once.

"I'm not stopping," she told them both, then gave him another squeeze to prove her point. "You going to do something about it, dog boy?"

"Well, if you insist." He kicked his shoes and pants free. With a shake of his arm, he managed to shuck the last of his shirt and jacket off his wrist. Then he squatted down just enough to shoot an arm between her legs. One hand grabbed her butt, the other wrapped around her shoulders; he scooped her aloft as if she weighed nothing.

Three steps later, he *threw* her down on the bed. Hard enough that if it had been a better mattress, she would have bounced.

"Ready?"

"Stop talking!" She was breathless from the magnificence of him. From that moment of flying before she'd struck the covers—floating loose in the instant before a gear shift once more threw power into her system.

And he did stop talking. He fell on her. His hands…his mouth… were everywhere.

Faster than had ever been possible, he drove her aloft until everything came apart.

But he didn't stop there.

Again and again he showed her just what was possible, then found a new way to break through the envelope and find even more performance from her fracturing nervous system.

He stuck to her like perfect racing slicks on a hot track until she couldn't know what was coming next and could only hang on for the ride. When he finally took her, when he finally pounded into her, there was little more left in her than a whimper.

But it was a whimper of joy from the body, not from her. Deep inside her, down at the heart of her body's engine, it was so much more.

Somewhere inside her, the past was burning away.

That bastard who had thought rape was his due.

Gone.

The drivers who had harassed her on the track…crowded her car into corners so that she ate a wall and was out of the race…who had done everything they could to prove that a woman didn't belong in a man's sport.

Blown away.

All of the times she'd somehow thought it was her fault. Her fault that she'd cracked up another car, even though they were always tapping her rear fender to break her loose. Her fault that she had come in second, not first, despite the on-track battles she'd surmounted. Her fault that…everything!

Gone!

Jim Fischer had just shown her that, in his book, there was no woman who deserved more. That she was special beyond her body— that it was only the stock equipment that he'd driven like a master tactician to prove to her who she might one day become, beyond her body's performance specs. There was a glimmer of light there that she'd never seen before.

Never imagined.

Yet Jim's passionate need for her had revealed it as surely as lights illuminating a nighttime racetrack.

She clung to him. A tangle of limbs in a cheap hotel, unable to let go, unable to ease up her double-armed throttle hold around his neck. All she could presently do was feel and know that she held one man— one fantastically special man.

CHAPTER TWELVE

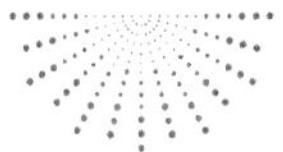

*J*im glared at the tires in frustration. The night had
brought a fresh dusting of snow that was slick to walk
on. Which meant it would be slick to drive on. Not what
he wanted on his first real mission with the Motorcade.

Colorado Springs road crews had already sanded the primary
Motorcade routes and were reportedly working on the alternates…
drawing massive "shoot me here" targets to his way of thinking.

"At least they've put on studded snow tires," he tried to find the
bright side of it all, but wasn't having much luck. Apparently chains
would be a major problem if someone shot out the tires and they had
to get away on the run-flat tires. Each one had an inner core of hard
rubber, but if the outer tire deflated, then chains would become loose
and could create a snarl. That had meant a change of tires. At the
moment he wasn't feeling very happy about *anything* changing.

"It will alter my spin rate, if I need to do one," Reese seemed to be
taking everything about the morning in that easy stride of hers.

He could only glare at the car as Reese headed off to consult with
the other drivers. No question that his mood was foul this morning.
And no question that he was doing a crappy job of hiding it from
Reese. Even Malcolm had picked up on it, moping about his feet.

"I should have stayed on the goddamn fence line." He understood *that*. He knew what to expect there.

Everything was confusing now. He'd spent two days trying to inhale Motorcade logistics but it was such a massive task that an entire vehicle was dedicated to just that. The ID car might run well back in the pack. Its sole task was route logistics and identifying any problems and changes on the fly.

So, he needed to let that go.

Even identifying his own role here was a challenge. He wasn't on the drop-in ahead team, patrolling a route, building, or crowd. He deployed twenty to thirty seconds ahead of the President as if that was enough time to find anything that all of the other dogs had missed. It made no sense.

Yet Harvey Lieber had asked him to join the Motorcade itself. Because a single time he'd been faster thinking on the ground in New York than most others? That had nothing to do with Malcolm. It had nothing to do with the last three years of his life as a White House dog handler.

"What's gonna become of us, buddy?" Malcolm looked up at him, clearly bored out of his skull. They were usually never bored. Not when they had the whole fence line to patrol. No tourists here inside the Peterson AFB hangar. No veterans in need of a little cheering up. No bad guys thinking they could directly breach the White House and live to tell the tale.

"C'mon, let's check out the cars. *Such!*"

And at the simple seek command, the life surged back into Malcolm. He jumped to his feet, glanced up at Jim until he pointed toward the front of the parked Motorcade, and headed off with the same joy he walked the fence. The vehicles were lined up in three parallel rows so that they all fit in the hangar.

"You've got it way too easy." Malcolm only had one thing in life to worry about. For himself, he couldn't seem to stop finding new things to add to the worry list. It was already longer than an elephant's leash and it just kept growing.

They circled both of the Spares and Stagecoach itself. Then they went over the Lead Car that they'd be riding in. The police escort was already in place, so he checked out their motorcycles and Sweep Cars. He even went over the Pilot and Route Cars, though they'd be well ahead of the Motorcade to provide early warning of any problems.

Reese joined him as he circled back down the far side of the line.

And the anger surged back in so hard that he almost choked.

"What?"

He could only shake his head. He didn't know! It wasn't at Reese, he knew that much, but he couldn't seem to put a good face on it—not even for her sake. It wasn't her past. The assholes in her past were obviously losers who'd never understood what she was. She'd survived them and come out shining.

There was no real way for Malcolm to inspect Halfback. It was in line directly behind Stagecoach and the Spares and was armed to the teeth. It was filled with weapons that were fired frequently and with the men who fired them. They even had explosives, just in case they needed to cut the President out of a wreck quickly. Still, he gave Malcolm a treat each time he triggered on the vehicle. It wasn't his fault that they lived in a crazy world that needed such things.

"Did I do something wrong last night?" Reese kept her voice low as they moved on to inspect Watchtower—the electronic countermeasures Suburban. It could block signals to IEDs, detect incoming aircraft or missiles, and a wide variety of other attacks. If anyone fired on the Motorcade, they'd discover to their dismay just how fast Watchtower could pinpoint their location and transmit it to Hawkeye Renegade—the counter-assault team vehicle farther back in the lineup.

"How could you possibly think that you did anything wrong last night, Reese?" He couldn't quite bring himself to look at her. That was okay. He had to pay attention to what Malcolm was doing, didn't he?

"Because you're being very weird this morning."

"Well it's not you. Okay? I couldn't imagine you being more incredible. You're a goddamn fantasy brought to life."

"I don't want to be someone's fantasy. I've had enough of that shit!" The anger shot to life in her voice.

"Doesn't keep you from being one." Reese Carver was certainly his fantasy. Gorgeous, amazing in the bedroom, skilled, intelligent, thoughtful... The best companion a man and his dog could ever ask for.

"Eat hot shit, Fischer!" And Reese spun on her heel and walked away.

"Well, that went well, didn't it?" he asked Malcolm. Two of the agents managing the senior staffer vehicles looked at him in surprise, then turned to watch Reese. Even pissed as hell, she had an amazing walk from behind. Only by gritting his teeth did he manage to avoid beating the crap out of them for staring at her so blatantly.

Thankfully Malcolm was busy working and didn't know enough to roll his eyes at Jim.

"Yeah. Total washout." He guided Malcolm down the line: Control, counter assault (which gave Malcolm just as much trouble as Halfback had), intel division, hazmat, Roadrunner (that could connect them to a satellite feed, into the Situation Room, or provide a local cell tower when there wasn't one), ambulance, and the rear guard vehicles.

About the time he reached the end of the last line, the two press vans rolled in, bringing the press corps back from their hotel. They tucked into the back of the middle row of vehicles so that they'd be in the right place for departure. The reporters moved clear, winding their way past the inner row of vehicles. They gathered around the base of the steps of Air Force One (there was a scheduled ten-minute press conference before they moved out, not as if anything had happened overnight). He and Malcolm moved in to check the vans.

Clean. Clean. Clean.

If he found one more thing that was clean and safe and secure he was gonna scream.

That was the problem.

They *knew* there was an attack coming. It was coming and there wasn't anything he and Malcolm could do about it. How was he supposed to protect the President? How was he supposed to protect Reese, when any threat was so far out of his league? How was he supposed to find explosives from *inside* the Lead Car?

He squatted down to give Malcolm a good rub. At least his dog would know that whatever happened, it wasn't his fault.

He squatted there, in front of the lead press van. There were two of the Chevy Express twelve-seaters. They were big enough, barely, to carry the press corps and their gear. It was the last of the all-American boxy vans. Even Ford had taken on the slick Euro-Japanese exterior profiling. He'd driven the delivery version of the Express plenty before he'd gotten old enough to pick up his commercial license and move into the big rigs.

There was a small box under the steel bumper that he didn't recognize. He leaned in to inspect it. A Brickhouse Security micro camera, smaller than a pack of cards. It could shoot eight hours of HD video without a recharge. As far as he knew, they only saved to an SD card, but could one be modified to transmit? That hadn't been included in his briefings about the Motorcade, but he'd come aboard so recently that it could be just one of a thousand things that there hadn't been time to learn.

He leaned out and saw that there was a matching one under the second van's bumper. On the next row of vehicles over he could see that neither the intel car nor the hazmat truck had them.

Turning the other way, he could see one under the bumper of Stagecoach. He was pretty sure that wasn't supposed to be there.

He pointed out the small camera to Malcolm, *"Verloren."* Lost. Maybe whoever had put them there had left the same scent on each of the cameras, just as Jurgen had left his scent on the explosives out at RTC. If they were all the same, that would be very suspicious. After Malcolm had a good sniff of it, Jim gave him the seek command and they began circling the vehicles once more.

Reese tried to think of the last time she'd felt this angry. All she could come up with was her pop's former team owner. Jim had made her feel so…violated!

Last night had been such an incredible experience. And this

morning she was just another hot fantasy calendar girl only fit to be a pin-up on some testosterone-laden grimy garage wall—her butt and breasts eventually coated in oily fingerprints from every mechanic who slapped it as they walked by.

One thing was certain, Jim Fischer was never going to touch her again.

Rather than feeling righteous, she felt impossibly sad.

"What the hell happened to you?" Harvey Lieber was suddenly at her elbow as she stood under Air Force One's wing with nowhere to go. She should be waiting by her car, but Jim was there, circling around them once more. Her interest in joining the press conference at the base of the plane's stairs was less than zero.

"I'm fine."

Harvey looked over her shoulder toward the Motorcade. "God damn it. I warned him."

"Warned him what?"

"That if he messed up my best driver, I was going to kill him."

"Don't!"

That earned her a Harvey Lieber scowl.

"I want the option to do that myself."

At that he smiled.

"Now I know you're okay. Get in your vehicle. We're almost ready to roll." Harvey walked over to join the President as he took last questions.

Okay? She was anything but okay. Though from Harvey's perspective, maybe she was. If she was head of the Presidential Protection Detail, she'd *want* her drivers to be in a foul, run-over-anything-in-my-way mood. And she was definitely that.

She stalked over to Stagecoach as Jim rose from looking under the front bumper.

He froze and looked at her. She could see there was some question written across his features.

To hell with him.

She opened the driver's door, slipped inside, and hauled it shut.

He came around to her window, the only one in the car that rolled down (though just three inches), so that she could talk to an agent or pay a toll if necessary.

Reese had no interest in talking to him and liked having the eight inches of armored steel and five inches of armored glass between them. Instead she placed both hands on the wheel and stared straight ahead. *Please, oh please. Let Jim Fischer get in her way.* She would run him down in a heartbeat!

Suddenly everyone was on the move.

Jim had never seen the full Motorcade load up all at once and it was a daunting sight. Thirty-five vehicles including the police escort. Except for the motorcycles, most vehicles had four or five people. The press vans and the assault team Suburbans had even more. Two hundred people on the move in a highly coordinated flow.

One side of the hangar doors slid open and the Route and the Pilot Car shot out into the morning brightness. Now that the door was open, even though they were still inside the hangar, a phalanx of four agents surrounded the President as they escorted him into Stagecoach.

Once Harvey Lieber had the Beast's door closed, he came sprinting around the nose of the vehicle. He shoved Jim hard enough to send him stumbling forward.

"You aren't in your seat in the next five seconds, we're leaving you behind."

Even as he turned, Jim saw the momentary flash of the Lead Car's backup lights as the driver shifted from Park to Drive. He sprinted over and opened the back door.

Malcolm leapt aboard and the car was moving while Jim still had one foot on the ground. He dove in, landing partly on top of Malcolm who thankfully had gone to the far side of the back seat. By the time he had the door closed and his seatbelt buckled, they were already well away from the hangar and racing for the airport's nearest exit gate.

Mack and Mark—the two agents in the front seat—were laughing at him.

But Jim wasn't in a laughing mood.

For twenty-seven minutes all he could do was stare out the window and worry as they roared across Colorado Springs, up I-25, and finally, at long last, onto the supposedly safe grounds of the Air Force Academy.

He'd sworn he wouldn't look back at the three Beasts following on the Lead Car's tail. They were busy doing their dance, playing a game of Three-card Monte at sixty miles an hour to hide which vehicle carried the President.

But Jim always knew when Stagecoach was in the lead of the two Spares—he could feel Reese glaring at the back of his head.

REESE KNEW that she should have stayed in her car, but the President was giving a thirty-minute speech to the student body of the Air Force Academy north of Colorado Springs and then having an hour-long meet-and-greet with top class members and the school's commanders. Dry. Scattered trees. Snow dusted thinly among the brown grass. Freaking freezing beneath a brilliant blue sky.

The instant she was out of the car, Jim Fischer came over from his patrol. He'd been fast and efficient, in exactly the priority order that they had worked out over two days of planning. It was impressive how much ground he and Malcolm were able to cover between the moment of their arrival and when Harvey approved the site as clean and opened the President's door.

Somehow sensing her desire to duck back into the driver's seat, he signaled Malcolm to slip into the narrow space between her and the door, then waved him to sit and stay.

Traitor! I thought you liked me.

Malcolm lolled out his tongue in a doggie grin.

Trapped in the open, Reese forced herself to face Jim.

"I've got a problem."

"More than one," she shot back.

Jim chewed on that for several moments before discarding whatever he was thinking. "I've got a problem because I don't know what is and isn't protocol on the Motorcade."

Reese bit back her unexpected disappointment. He wanted to be strictly business and she wanted… She wasn't sure, but running him over with Stagecoach was still an attractive option. She waited him out.

"Are spycams standard on the vehicles?"

"What are you talking about?"

He took her by the forearm and it was all she could do to not yank it away in front of the other drivers and agents who had remained with the vehicles.

Fischer—that's all she'd think of him as now, except maybe Asshole—tugged her forward until he was standing well to the side of her car. The Motorcade was lined up in the parking lot alongside Fieldhouse Drive that they'd blocked off in front of the six-thousand-seat Clune Arena. Then he squatted and pointed under Stagecoach's bumper.

She squinted, but didn't see anything. Then she pulled off her sunglasses.

There, in the shadows under her car, was a small black box.

"It's a miniature HD spycam. I know the model. Fully self-contained: camera, battery, and storage card. It's set to activate in motion-detection mode. I brought you over here to the side because it and the others are all aimed straight ahead."

"Others?" Reese could feel her skin go even colder than she could account for in the chilly morning air.

"Press vans, all three Beasts, back of the Lead Car, front of the Halfback and Watchtower, front and back of the ambulance."

"Of the ambulance?" She turned to look. That didn't make much sense, nor did the press vans. There were a lot of vehicles between the Protection Detail riding in Watchtower and the press vans. "How did you find them?"

"Pure chance on the first one. After that, I had Malcolm sniff them out. Same person touched every one. And they weren't wearing gloves, so they left behind a clear scent mark."

Reese actually looked Jim in the eyes for the first time since this morning. And all she saw was the professional. Fine with her, that's all she should be seeing at the moment. Besides, the professional was someone she completely respected. She looked back at the camera attached to her car.

"I can tell you one thing. They aren't ours."

THE ELECTRONIC COUNTERMEASURES from Watchtower said they couldn't pick up any signal from the spycams, concurring with Jim's own assessment that they were set to record only, not to transmit.

That calmed everyone's nerves down.

A thorough visual inspection of all vehicles showed that Malcolm had uncovered every one of them, which had earned him high praise from everyone except Harvey Lieber—who was still too pissed at someone having messed with his Motorcade—and Reese—who was still pissed at Jim himself, but he couldn't take the time now to figure out why.

They'd been on the verge of pulling them, but Jim intervened.

"Look. Whoever placed these is getting set to record some event. Maybe it's just more intel on Motorcade operations. Maybe not. I say that we leave them in place so that whoever it is doesn't get suspicious."

Reese was nodding, "I'd rather face an attack today than if we spook them and they do it at some unknown time in the future." She glared at Jim as if he was the one doing the attacking.

"We just make damn sure to take down anyone who tries to recover them," Harvey snarled with all the danger signals of an ERT— emergency response team—attack dog.

Jim hauled Harvey and Reese aside.

"We still don't know who to trust. Now the entire Motorcade knows about the cameras."

"Shit!" Harvey wasn't happy.

"Not all of them," Reese put in. "Only the drivers and assault teams. The press, senior staff, and the protection details still don't know we found them. They're all in with the President. Nothing's gone out over the radio except my request for you to leave the detail and come join us."

"Well, that's something."

Jim scanned the area, but the Academy had made a point of emptying out the broad parking lot prior to the Motorcade's arrival. Beyond its broad expanse, the Front Range of the Colorado Rockies kicked up the land into rough slopes with sparse trees. A glance at the gymnasium and Jim could see a line of Delta snipers along the roofline—each studying a different section of the surrounding hills through their scopes. Nothing moving out there except maybe some deer.

He, Reese, and Harvey went down the line, verbally spreading the order that the cameras' existence was strictly need-to-know, compartmentalized information. Also that they were to keep their eyes out for anyone who went near one.

They met up once more alongside Stagecoach.

"Record only. Video only. What use is that?" Harvey sounded even grumpier.

Jim let his gaze drift down the long line of vehicles. They were in a double line outside the south entrance to the Cadet Field House. The first half of the Motorcade was closer to the building, with Stagecoach exactly aligned with the entrance doorway. The second half of the Motorcade formed a layer of shield from the wide empty parking lot.

An attack here on the Air Force Academy grounds would be very unlikely. That meant that if it was going to happen, it was still in this mission's future. There were four more pending sorties: Academy to Olympic Training HQ, Olympic Training to Air Force One, then, after a short flight to Buckley Air Force Base at Denver, out and return to the political fundraiser.

It would be an external attack again, otherwise there'd been no point in testing Reese's driving in New York.

"Someone wants images of the attack."

Reese and Harvey looked at him, but he didn't want to be distracted.

The spycams had been placed so that they would be focused on Stagecoach and the Spares. Rear end of the Lead Car. Front of all three Beasts. Front of the two vehicles immediately behind the Beasts. Then a long gap all the way back to the press vans and then another skip to the ambulance.

"They want to record the attack *and* the aftermath." Which explained the ambulance. But it didn't explain the press corps' two Chevy vans.

He looked back at Reese.

"Those images of the New York attack. The ones that you had that I hadn't seen before, where did they come from?"

"Some news agency. I'd have to call Doogan to find out."

"Need to know?" Harvey cut in before Jim could.

Reese was already shaking her head because she figured it out just as fast as they had.

"But who put them there?" Harvey was starting to get back to focusing on the problem.

Jim shrugged. "A traitor inside the Service working with the Press would have plenty of access or…" He thought about the layout of the Motorcade in the hangar this morning and the Press Vans pulling up to the rear of the middle row. "That's it!"

"What's it?"

"This morning, when the Press Vans pulled into the Motorcade. The reports flowed out of the vans and wandered through the Motorcade to get to the steps of Air Force One for the President's interview. Each camera is a self-contained unit. It would take less than a second a piece to slap each one in place if it was prepped with a magnetic strip."

"The press." By the sound of it, Harvey just might kill the whole lot of them. Jim would bet that the President wouldn't complain. "At least we know where the cameraman is now."

Reese was nodding. "One of the press corps. Oh shit!"

"What?"

"I saw…" she squeezed her eyes shut. "Where was I? I saw a stack of small black boxes… Just this size. On a desk."

Her eyes shot open and she grabbed his jacket.

"The basement offices underneath the White House Briefing Room." Reese could half see the image.

"What the hell were you doing in there?" They both ignored Harvey.

"Someone working on his camera. I only had a glimpse. I don't know if I even turned in time to see the man's back. Can't even swear it was a man. But I remembered the boxes because I didn't know what they were." Once again she'd missed seeing a person of importance. It was like a gut punch.

"Fine. I'm losing the press vans from the Motorcade. They can scream all they want." Harvey raised his arm to swing his wrist microphone into position, but Jim clamped his hand over Harvey's arm before he could complete the gesture. They looked ready to come to blows.

"Never spook the enemy when you know where they are," Reese had learned that lesson a long time ago. The most misogynistic racers, she always kept them clear in her sights so she'd know the instant they moved in to attack.

"She's right." Again Jim Fischer supporting her, even after dismissing her as a mere fantasy. They *really* needed to talk.

"Besides," Reese agreed, "even if we remove the cameraman, they won't stop the attack."

Harvey glared. "Have you two been drinking the same Kool-Aid?"

Reese looked over at Jim. Their thoughts traveled the same paths so easily. Their bodies had too. How could he…

"Don't you dare get all gooey-eyed on me, Carver," Harvey snapped.

"I wasn't." *She definitely wasn't. She'd sworn to hate Jim Fischer forever, hadn't she? Then why was she still clutching onto his jacket?* She let go—so abruptly that both men noticed it of course.

"We need to just do what we do," Jim spoke fast enough to show that he too was uneasy. "We trust Reese's abilities to save the President."

"No pressure, huh?"

"Not a bit for a lady like you," and he offered one of his cheery smiles.

She punched him as hard as she could in the solar plexus.

He wasn't the least bit ready for it. Jim gave a long, gasping wheeze, then slowly folded down onto his knees making little *hee-hik* sounds. Malcolm licked his face as a reward.

She turned to Harvey. "I'm *not* getting gooey-eyed over some guy." And she was no man's goddamn fantasy.

Harvey held up both hands and backed up a step, but his smile said that he knew otherwise.

CHAPTER THIRTEEN

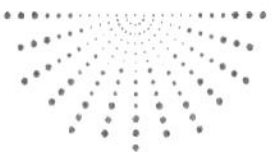

By the time Jim got his breath back and wiped the dog slobber off his face, the President's meeting was breaking up.

Again, he barely made it into the Lead Car before the Motorcade rolled out.

Mack and Mark had thought the whole thing was hilarious. Or was it Mark and Mack? They were both classic, six-foot, athletic agents with crew-cut dark hair. And it wasn't just that they looked and sounded alike—he was sure they were swapping names just to mess with him.

The trip to the US Olympic Training Center was almost an exact replay of the trip to the Academy in reverse. Three exits earlier they plunged off I-25 and down onto the city streets. The police had a rolling blockade set up blocks ahead, stopping all side traffic until the Motorcade whisked down East Platte Avenue going eighty miles an hour during what should have been the bumper-to-bumper lunchtime rush hour. The city was going to be a snarl for hours to come—a typical byproduct of a visit by the Presidential Motorcade.

He steered well clear of Reese, even volunteering to augment the local's dog teams. They continued their patrols around the perimeter of the secured site while the President lunched with this year's athletes and his mother—a former medalist and one of the senior swim coaches.

His gut still ached from where she'd caught him, but he wasn't going to rub it and give the guys any more reason to tease him. The entire ride down had been nothing but razzing from the front seat because, of course, every person waiting with the vehicles had witnessed it. He'd seen the blow coming and managed to partially tense for it—though not nearly enough with the power Reese could deliver.

Using Malcolm as an excuse, he left the patrol and grabbed a quick lunch at the Taco Bell on the corner. He had a beef burrito and Malcolm had a tray of diced chicken with cheese—he had a huge weak spot for cheese. One of the servers even gave him a service bowl of water.

Jim was halfway through his meal when Reese walked in with several of the other drivers. It was hard to hide in the crowd when Malcolm picked up her scent and trotted across the restaurant to greet her. Generally, Malcolm was so well behaved that there was no point keeping a leash on him, but he'd grown a definite weak spot where Reese Carver was concerned.

So had Jim.

Reese squatted down to greet Malcolm with a good rub, then looked up at him. After a moment, he could see her sigh deeply before waving Malcolm to return to him.

A minute later, with her plastic tray bearing triple beef tacos, she slid in across from him. He hadn't expected her to join hi—

"Hey, asshole, you okay?"

Or perhaps he did. "Needed to clear all this fresh country air out of my lungs anyway, I suppose." It earned him a flicker of a smile.

"Not apologizing."

"Figured," he bit into his burrito and ignored Malcolm's pleading eyes. He'd long since finished his chicken and cheese. "Mind telling me what I did?"

"You can't be that stupid." She still wore her sunglasses against the bright Colorado sunlight that poured in through the windows. It made it hard to read what she was thinking.

"Apparently I'm twenty-four cents short of a quarter. Mind explaining? Simple words so a dumb Okie like me can understand?" Not many people made him feel slow, but Reese always raced so far ahead that he was only now beginning to get up to match her speed.

She eyed him for at least half a taco from behind those dark lenses.

He was beginning to wonder if she'd ever speak again when she finally did.

"You called me 'any man's fantasy.'"

"No, I called you a goddamn fantasy."

"Well, I'm not."

"You sure are mine."

"Look," she aimed the bit-off end of her second taco at his face like a weapon. "I'm not some fantasy poster on a stupid-ass garage calendar."

"Shit! Is that what you thought I meant?" He could see how that might piss her off.

"Isn't it?" Reese was clearly aiming for scoff, but fouled that ball off into still-seething anger.

"Reese. I never even dreamed of being with a woman like you."

She opened her mouth to protest.

"And no, I'm not talking about your looks—which are incredible— or your body—which is awesome. I'm talking about *you*. I drove for a living from the moment I got my license to the day I got Malcolm. I know enough to *see* what you can do. What you did putting the Beast through its paces out at James J. Rowley Training Center. What you did to save the First Lady. No matter what you say, that isn't 'I just drive.' It was a goddamn miracle to watch. I *know* what that takes to do. I sure as hell couldn't have pulled it off. Ralph McKenna couldn't. You stunned him speechless out at RTC. Tell me what part of that doesn't fit fantasy woman."

"The part that makes *me* a fantasy girl," but this time she didn't make it an accusation. This time there was some humor and maybe a bit of surprise.

"Well, shit, woman," he leaned back and did his best to match her suddenly nonchalant tone. "Gonna have to get used to it if you're gonna hang around this ol' boy."

They ate in what he hoped was companionable silence until "Ten minutes!" squawked over their radios. They drained their sodas and hustled out the door as fast as the snarl of rushing agents allowed.

REESE HAD a lot to think about after they checked over the vehicles once more and she locked and strapped herself in.

Maybe the way Jim had actually meant it, being a fantasy woman didn't sound all bad.

Though she still wrestled with being more than a 'just a driver.' Granted, she wouldn't be sitting in this seat if that's all she was. But when she looked out the sideview mirrors and saw the rest of the vehicles arrayed around her, she felt very small.

When the President climbed aboard and called out his friendly greeting, she managed to respond. Secretary Matthews and Franks Adams followed him in, then Harvey closed the heavy door, which weighed as much as the door on a Boeing 757—over three hundred pounds—and hustled around to his own door.

Out the windshield, she saw Jim scramble into the back of the Lead Car. He turned around to smile at her and wave as Harvey buckled himself in.

"That boy is gone on you, Carver."

"Yes, sir." There was no denying it. And after his amazing speech, in a Taco Bell of all bizarre places, she was starting to feel a little gone on him.

A little gone on him?

Not even close. She finally understood that she'd crossed that line a long time ago. He saw her in ways that she certainly didn't see herself. As if she was somehow amazing. And he was forcing her, inch by grudging inch, to see those parts of herself.

The Lead Car moved out.

She could hear the President and Secretary of State Matthews in the back of the car. Every spare minute they'd been talking about some country or other. She'd only caught snippets: South China Sea security, Indo-Russian Zapad military exercise, Egyptian government. They sat at the far back and were hard to hear even though they left the glass partition down. Chief of Staff Cornelia Day, who sat in the rear-facing seat directly behind Reese's own, spoke rarely but the two men always listened when she did.

"We leaving anytime soon?" Harvey teased her.

Reese dropped into gear and quickly closed the four-car-length gap that she'd let open up between her and the Lead Car.

Out of the parking lot, down a quiet wooded block, and a left onto East Platte Avenue. The four-lane major thoroughfare was already closed eastbound for the short seven-mile run to Peterson Air Force Base and the waiting Air Force One. The President would make the short hop to Buckley Air Force Base outside of Denver, then hold onboard meetings while the Motorcade raced the ninety miles north to rejoin him. The next sortie for the Motorcade wouldn't be until the dinnertime fundraiser and they'd be there hours ahead of that.

Through the narrow congestion of the first few blocks, there was little to see except for the bare limbs of the tall maple trees. Dark clouds were building to the West and the bright sun in the blue eastern sky was getting squeezed out fast.

Then they fell off the edge. What little beauty existed in Colorado Springs—arid landscape just didn't sit right for a woman from the South—decayed into a depressingly familiar strip of light industrial and mini-mall sprawl.

On the plus side, the east and west lanes became broader and were separated by a low curb. The intersections were farther apart and the Motorcade began moving up to its normal speed. They were soon headed east at eighty miles an hour, little more than a long black blur to the people lining the roadside with their cell phone cameras.

She began counting down the miles like minutes: six to go, five, four.

A feeling of complacency that she recognized from her days of racing settled over her.

Stay in the slot and ride the groove home.

There was one key lesson she'd learned about that particular feeling—it was almost invariably wrong!

"Shit!" Reese raised her voice, "Everyone in back. Check your seatbelts." She heard two loud snaps. Complacency! Double shit!

Harvey looked at her in surprise.

"Hang on!" She couldn't see it coming—whatever *it* was.

But she could feel it.

JIM WATCHED the Pilot Car and the motorcycle sweepers flash through the closed intersection ahead, against the red light. Things like red lights had no bearing on the Motorcade.

They were passing the last big box stores. Over the rise he could see the first ramped exit as East Platt Avenue transitioned into the divided State Highway 24. That exit and one more would see them safely back onto Peterson Air Force Base.

Other than a Perkins pancake restaurant and a pawn shop, they were out of town.

"Looks like an armored car convention," Mack spoke up from the driver's seat. Jim had finally straightened out which of them was which. Mark rode shotgun, literally—with the weapon propped between his feet.

Jim looked between the front seats and out the windshield. On the far side of the intersection, eight armored cars—the heavy-duty ones that banks used to move cash—were parked four on each side of East Platte Avenue.

He didn't even need to think.

"Turn right!" Eight armored cars weren't a convention. They were the attack!

"Why?" But Mack slammed into a sideways skid before he even finished asking the question. The motorcycle cop who'd been stopping traffic at the intersection barely had time to dive away from his bike before they slammed into it sideways. The collision was enough to get them headed south on whatever road this was.

Jim pinned Malcolm to the floor under his legs and glanced back along East Platte. He saw the armored trucks already in motion off the sides of the road, plowing into the police escort.

Cop cars, motorcycles, and—he swallowed hard—bodies were scattered in every direction.

Twisting further, he saw that Reese had taken the turn better than they had, doing her job of sticking on the Lead Car's tail.

"Two more!" Mack called out.

At the end of the block, two of the big trucks were already rolling off the curb to block their escape. The attackers had anticipated this possible escape route. Did they have access to the alternate route plan, or was it simply good logistics? Either way, at the moment it was working.

Jim struggled to remember. The road to the left was called something Loop. Loop was a bad sign.

"Right again!" There weren't any other choices.

The Lead Car slewed onto the narrow two-lane road—lights and siren blaring.

Two leafless maples stood by the Pine Tree Square road sign. They blasted by a dry cleaners.

"What have you gotten us into, Fischer?"

"Damned if I know, Mack. Just don't slow down." They were on a very narrow two-lane lined with trees and a sidewalk.

"No shit, Sherlock."

Jim twisted to watch behind while Mack drove ahead.

Reese had managed the turn and was tight on their tail.

One of the Spares stopped sideways across the entry to the road, spanning all the way across the entrance.

An armored truck slammed into it at speed, plowing into it so hard that the truck's rear end lifted at least five feet off the ground. The Spare was blasted aside in a tumbling roll. The hit was hard enough to crumple the armored truck's front end. Goliath versus

Goliath, both had lost. But three more trucks raced into the breach their companion had made.

He keyed the mic. "They're pros, Reese. Serious pros."

There was no response, but their gazes met across the tiny gap that separated their vehicles. She gave him a sharp nod of acknowledgement.

Halfback came in behind. Revealing its true colors, the Suburban's split roof had been flipped open and an M134 Minigun had popped up. These trucks would be armored to B7 standards, able to survive a hit from a 7.62x51mm round. But the four thousand rounds a minute that the M134 could deliver was another matter. Despite the roaring engines, Jim could hear the distinct, chainsaw *Brap!* of the gun as it tore at the armored trucks.

He prayed for no stray rounds. The Beast could take it, far better than the armored trucks, but he was in a production Chevy Impala. Not so much!

"WE'VE STILL GOT HALFBACK," Harvey reported.

Reese had seen the Spare take the hit for her. Even inside the Beast's armor, the driver would be lucky to live through that blow.

"Where's the rest of the Motorcade?" President Thomas shouted from the back.

"Doesn't matter," she and Harvey yelled in unison. Harvey got the "sir" on the end—she didn't.

Whether the rest of the Motorcade was in the fight of their lives or quietly parked on East Platte Avenue didn't matter to her—they weren't here. That was all that counted.

The Lead Car twisted left, then right through a short-sharp S that was meant to be taken at ten miles an hour, not sixty. In another hundred meters it opened onto a large parking lot—if she could get that far. The lead armored truck managed to tap her rear bumper, but she didn't have any weapons back there big enough to stop them. She needed a missile.

As if in answer, a missile slammed down from above.

Overwatch—the Black Hawk helicopter that always flew above the Motorcade. Such a fixture that she never gave it any thought.

The third armored car disintegrated.

Halfback had been chasing so closely that they slammed into the wreckage. The Protection Detail poured out the doors of the destroyed vehicle even as it burned.

Now it was just her and Jim's Lead Car against the two remaining armoreds.

She had half a second to understand what she'd just done. It wasn't the *Lead Car* anymore. It was Jim himself who had seen and understood what was happening. *He* was the one protecting her and the President. Without him, they'd probably be dead on East Platte Avenue by now. He understood driving *and* battle.

Reese was willing to trust her life to his hands. And rather than being afraid, it gave her a renewed confidence.

In her rearview, she almost missed the streak of light slicing upward from the back of the second armored vehicle.

Jim could only watch in horror as the RPG shot upward from the rear of the second armored vehicle.

Overwatch, which had moved in for the kill, never stood a chance of evading.

They did manage to get the second missile off but it went astray and punched a smoking crater among the vehicles of the nearby parking lot.

The helo twisted and spun, tumbling out of the sky. Whether it was by chance or plan—it was hard to tell—the helo slammed into the second armored truck and both disappeared in a ball of fire.

"And then there was one," he whispered to himself.

"You wish," Mack didn't sound happy.

Jim spun around. They'd emerged into a vast parking lot. Some people were running, others were just gawking.

The long, low stretch of a super-sized Walmart store rose before them.

"Don't go around the side! It's one lane. Too easy to trap us there."

Mack slewed them into the frontage road along the front of the building. It was crammed with people. People, and two more armored trucks that must have come in from the original group on East Platte Avenue. He continued the turn and raced into the depths of the parking lot.

Someone lost their shopping cart and Mack slammed it aside. Jim half expected a squeaky toy moment on the windshield. Instead, big Number 10 cans of tomato sauce slammed into the Impala like mortars. One shattered the right side of the windshield as it shredded and they were all covered with tomato sauce. He'd have preferred the squeaky toy.

"Thanks, Mack," Mark must be okay to be complaining in that steady tone.

"Needed a shower anyway, Mark." Mack was fast running out of parking lot.

The other two armoreds were moving to block exits.

Jim had an idea. "Take us back, Mack. Straight at the main entrance."

"Wish someone here knew what they were doing, because it sure doesn't sound like you," but he did it anyway.

"Just gun it for all you're worth."

Jim spun around to face Reese, who was still right on their tail. They had outrun the armored truck by twenty yards and the gap was growing.

He spun his finger in the air and then jabbed a finger forward as if she was launching gas canisters from a spinning car. He could only hope she understood.

"You've got a radio, doofus," her voice sounded in his earpiece, "but I get it. How badly are you hurt?"

"Hurt?" Then some more sauce dripped out of his hair. "Tomato sauce. We're going to go left."

He saw her nod of understanding.

REESE RACED after the Lead Car, then braced herself. She'd only done this once and that had been on a quiet practice field. No narrow lines of parked cars. No people running away, screaming.

At least the people inside her car weren't screaming. Instead, a grim silence had settled over them while they waited for Reese to save them.

Some idiot started to back her Ford Fiesta out of a spot.

The Lead Car managed to swerve clear, but the Beast clipped the car hard. It spun away, bounced off a few others before Reese had raced by. The armored truck blew through it like it was week-old Kleenex.

Jim's car, as he promised, turned left, then left again, racing once more into the depths of the parking lot.

Reese started her spin as she exited the parking lane. In the broad pick-up/drop-off area in front of the store, she managed to get through her one-eighty. Harvey fired the tear gas canisters for her at exactly the right moment.

She let the spin continue but there wasn't enough room.

The side of the Beast slammed sideways into the four, six-inch concrete pillars that guarded the entrance. Three of them snapped off, but it stopped her sideways momentum. There was a hard thump and a sharp cry from the back. Perfect, she'd probably just concussed the President against the inside of a five-inch thick car window.

The Kevlar tires got traction and they shot aside mere moments before the armored truck came racing out of the cloud of tear gas. Braking too late, it flew past the pillars and disappeared through the front entrance of the Walmart in a cloud of glass shards and metal doorframes.

Gunning it for all she was worth, she headed deep into the parking lot once more.

She saw figures in black running in from East Platte Avenue.

The Counter Assault Team. There was blood on some faces. One ran with one arm hanging limp at his side and a rifle in his other hand.

In moments, one of the CAT unleashed an RPG. The rocket-propelled grenade raced across the Walmart parking lot toward one of the waiting armored cars. The grenade seemed to think about it for a moment after it hit beneath the lower edge of the driver's door. For a moment she thought it was miss. Then the explosion bloomed upward, lifting the truck and knocking it onto its side. The shot had been intentionally low for that purpose.

A second RPG, that must have been fired before the first one even hit, slammed straight into the now-exposed gas tank, and the truck disappeared in a ball of flame. Now that was *her* kind of teamwork.

The last armored truck was trying to make good its escape, racing along the front of the store.

Reese ran a long curve through gaps in the middle of the parking lot, then chose her lane.

"What are you doing?" Harvey shouted from the right hand seat where he'd been trying to coordinate all of the attacks and counterattacks.

Yes, it was her job to get the protectees to safety. It was supposed to be her only job. But she had another idea.

"Get him!" President Thomas shouted from the back.

Precisely! She was sick to death of people ramming her, battering her, trying to beat her down when she was just trying to run the race.

Well, not this time.

In her lane, she raced the Beast back toward the building.

Maybe the armored truck didn't see her coming.

Jim had the Lead Car racing along in front of it. He'd punched out the back window and was firing round after round into the armored truck's windshield with a shotgun. The armored's windshield was tougher than that, but it was likely badly star-cracked.

She slammed into the side of the armored car at over thirty miles an hour.

It flew sideways into the massive block-concrete wall of the Walmart and disappeared inside the store.

Reese backed up, ready to ram it again.

Harvey rested a hand on her arm, "Enough. They're out of the contest."

Reese glanced out her side window.

The Lead Car sat there, not ten feet away. Jim and Malcolm were grinning at her as Jim held his shotgun aimed at the sky. She could see the red sauce still matted in his hair.

It was easy to grin back.

Then the Lead Car pulled away and she turned to follow. She could feel that her Beast was limping. The hood was twisted up, the status indicator showed that three of the four tires had been blown and she was running on the inner tread. But she was running.

They covered the last two miles to the airport slowly, with no Motorcade, but they delivered a healthy President and Chief of Staff to Air Force One. Secretary Matthews would be wearing an arm cast for a while. Frank Adams nearly carried him aboard they were moving up the stairs so fast.

The blue-and-white plane already had its engines running and was in the air before she had a chance to park the Beast out of the way.

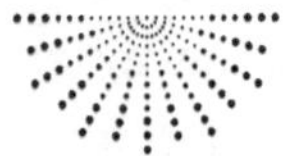

*R*eese sat wide awake in the silent darkness trying to understand what was happening to her and how she'd come to be here.

Jim lay asleep with his head on her lap; he had a hand wrapped lazily over her bare thigh. Her hand was tangled in his hair, which was almost as soft as Malcolm's, who lay upon her feet. She was warmed by two males...*her* two males.

It was an uncomfortable thought for such a comfortable position.

A comfortable position in...

She sighed, softly, so as not to wake her boys.

She'd often been asked about the possibilities of sex in a stock car —invariably in the crudest of ways. And the answer was that it was wholly impossible. A stock car had a single bucket seat wrapped in a steel roll cage. Steering wheel, stick shift, and protective padding turned it from seat into cocoon for one. It was not a place for claustrophobes.

Not that she'd disliked the image, just the jerks who tried to use it as an opening line. Sex in a hot racing car. Two very good things in the same space.

She'd never thought to have sex in their current location however.

She, Jim, and Malcolm were on the homebound leg back to Andrews Air Force Base in the guts of a C-17 Globemaster III jet transport. The Beast limousine had been loaded aboard with the three other surviving vehicles from the Motorcade—there'd been eight aboard on the way out. Air Force One and the President were already safely back in DC; the Marine One helicopter seeing to the final stage of returning the President safely to the White House.

They'd been over Kansas when Malcolm had come up to her sitting in one of the forward crew area seats. The other drivers with her were either fast asleep in their seats or involved in an intense game of poker. The C-17's crew were sitting up forward with the pilots.

She and Jim were the only other ones awake…except that she didn't see Jim anywhere.

Malcolm appeared anxious to return to his master, so she waved him away and, after only a moment's consideration, followed the dog. He'd led her past the first three vehicles in the massive cargo bay only barely lit with red nightlights. Just enough light so that she didn't trip over the front-and-rear chains anchoring each vehicle to the deck so that they couldn't shift in flight.

At the rear of the aircraft had sat the battered Beast. Her car.

And the massive rear door had been propped open, ever so slightly.

She'd hesitated again, longer that time. It hadn't been difficult to guess what awaited her—a truly amazing man—but the implications were huge!

To make love with Jim Fischer in the back of *her* car was part teenage fantasy. But that car was also all that she was.

No. She'd only *thought* it was all she was. Jim had proved to her that she was more than just the car she drove. She was also a woman that he wanted to survive—the one he believed in so deeply.

That had been enough to have her pulling open the door, allowing Malcolm to climb in where he curled up on the President's seat.

Then she'd stepped in herself to join the man waiting for her.

She hadn't been convinced that it was the right choice, but she'd stepped in anyway and pulled the door shut.

And now, despite what they'd just done, she still wasn't.

The question was, did she want to be convinced?

Inside the Beast, the outer world had gone away. The tinted windows dark enough to allow only the softest glow from the plane's red nightlights to filter into the car. The heavy armor cut off the massive roar of the four big Pratt & Whitney engines, and her ears had popped when she removed her earplugs.

Initially they'd simply sat on the forward bench talking about the car, the Motorcade, and their narrow escape from the attack.

The reporter, a long brunette, had put on a real show of horror at the whole situation, even as she was caught recovering a camera from the bottom of the flipped and destroyed Spare—though the driver had gotten off with only a broken wrist.

She'd been promised Pulitzer material and a million-dollar bonus to keep her mouth shut about how she got the images. She'd signaled her accomplice the moment the First Lady's Motorcade had left the UN, and the instant that the President's Motorcade had left the Olympic Training Center.

The other side of the chain had been less obvious until she finally revealed that she was sleeping with a Saudi prince from a renegade branch of the royal family. Or at least that's what they were calling it now. Who knew the actual truth. The prince in question had regrettably died during "an accident" shortly after his arrest. The king had promised more answers soon.

The Beast's armor made the car so well insulated that their own body heat soon had them opening, then peeling off their jackets.

She remembered how Jim's smile had made peeling off her blouse seem so natural just moments later. Any residual hints of chill had been scorched away by the attention he'd lavished upon her willing body.

It was only as they were deep in the throes of their encounter that she began to *appreciate* the location.

They were in the Beast.

They were in *her* car!

A charge had run through her as that insight fought its way through the blinding heat that Jim had generated to replace the last of the cold. It didn't take long before they'd fogged the windows.

"It's like the mile-high club, only better," Jim had whispered close by her ear.

"We were over a mile high in the Colorado Springs parking lot," she'd teased.

Being made love to in the Beast, inside an airplane, while flying six miles up in the sky should have been the upper limit. But Jim had found a way to pack the power of turbo-charged adrenaline rush into a moment of such gentle perfection that the explosion of their bodies should have launched them into orbit.

Thankfully sound traveled no better out of the Beast than it did inward, because the cry that burst from her was unstoppable. She'd never felt anything like the joy that Jim had pumped into her body as she'd knelt over him in the deep leather seat, her hands braced on the ceiling, his hands firmly clamped about her waist and his face buried between her breasts.

Would it last?

When she'd finally come down, when she had at long last managed to flop bonelessly into the seat beside him and he'd laid his head in her lap, she could finally ask the question.

But the question, she now knew, was pointless.

She *knew* it would last. The pleasure they gave each other might someday become familiar, but she suspected that too would always be exceptional. The least experience with Jim far overshadowed the best moment of anything prior.

But even that truly didn't matter.

Jim didn't just want sex with her. Neither did he want to change her into someone she wasn't. He would always be the patient, even-tempered person in their relationship. And she would always be the quiet one who had to be coaxed into facing anything inside her.

Inside her.

She could feel Jim inside her. And from far more than the delicious sex.

She could feel him inside her like a light. Like the green flag fluttering high above the track the moment before it flashed downward to launch the cars on their way.

He believed in her. Not merely her ability to drive, but also her ability to make the right decision in crisis. He stood inside her with a purity of faith as clear as her father's had been. Perhaps more so.

Her father had never seen past the next race, the next season. All he'd focused on was the edge of the envelope...and it had killed him. There was more than the next race. There was more than the points-ranking for the season.

Reese hadn't understood that before.

Yet Jim always saw all of the futures ahead of them.

She brushed her hand through his hair and listened to his sleeping breath. Yes, he'd showed her how to see more than the next time at the wheel. He'd taught her how to believe in a future she'd never even given thought to—never mind dreamed about or believed in.

And still her beautiful man slept in her lap in the back seat of *her* car.

She wiggled her toes under Malcolm.

He at least woke up enough to sigh happily.

Jim slept on, unaware of the change he'd made inside Reese's heart.

It was okay. He'd have years and years to learn about those changes.

So would she.

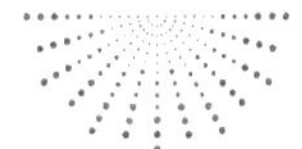

J im stood on the broad white marble step at the west end of the White House Rose Garden amid the June roses.

Malcolm stood by his side; his coat brushed until he shone in the bright sun.

Captain Baxter stood by his shoulder as best man. "Got you through the Uniformed Division. Least I can do is get you through a damned wedding without you screwing it up."

Ralph McKenna had flown in from retirement in Washington State for the wedding and to walk Reese up the aisle, then had to fight Harvey Lieber for the privilege. Last Jim had heard they were both going to walk her down the aisle.

Seated across the Rose Garden lawn were K-9 members and Motorcade drivers as well as the President, senior advisors, and all of his own family—their big rigs were parked out at his place.

Out at his *and* Reese's place.

Their home.

She'd gotten shaky when he gave her a key to the place, which had given him an idea. For his wedding present, he had signed half of the property's deed over to her because he wanted her to have a real home again.

Reese had cried so hard that he'd considered calling 9-1-1 before she finally recovered. *Together,* she'd promised. Together they would build a house there someday. A house with an extra bedroom for a child. She hadn't argued when he'd insisted that it would also have a shower big enough for two.

Instead, they'd had wedding eve sex that was so gentle and so perfect that *he'd* almost cried.

Secretary Matthews stood there beside him as he'd be performing the ceremony.

"You've got your flag?" Jim whispered to him.

"I do. That was an excellent idea." He pointed behind the potted rose tree that defined one side of the altar. The furled black-and-white checkered flag—the exact same brand and size waved for winning a NASCAR race—was ready for Secretary Matthews to flourish over their heads when Jim kissed the bride. President Thomas had given him special permission to replace the standard Sunoco gas emblem in the middle with the Presidential Seal.

He heard the soft rumble of the big diesel engine only moments before her car pulled into sight. Eighteen feet of shining black, armored Beast rolled along the driveway that encircled the south lawn and stopped by the garden entrance near the South Portico.

Dilya climbed out of the front passenger seat—Reese's bridesmaid. Dilya had been horribly frustrated, trying to fit them into her whole *Pride and Prejudice* storyline. He'd never been prejudiced and being prideful was not a problem for Reese. Getting her to acknowledge her own worth and value was the challenge—though why such an amazing woman had so much trouble seeing it was beyond him. While she'd gotten better about it over the last several months, she would never understand how truly incredible she was. But that was okay—he did.

Jim was watching the back passenger door and completely missed the moment when the driver's door on the far side swung open and Reese stepped out of the car.

His laugh was first, but only by moments—the rest of the wedding party caught on quickly.

Harvey Lieber and Ralph McKenna exited from the rear doors.

Because, of course, Reese Carver drove the limousine to her own wedding.

The laughter died like an eighteen-wheel blowout as she stepped around the car into clear view.

Reese Carver was a vision.

Her long black hair fell behind her shoulders in a single shining wave. She wore a dress of white lace. It was off the shoulder, with a low collar that revealed her lovely neck and collarbone. The long-sleeved, open-patterned, white lace down her arms was backed by the warm, dark luster of her skin. The dress clung to her curves, the lace spilling past where the lining ended at mid-thigh to once again tease with more hints of her skin until her athlete's legs were ultimately revealed by the scalloped hem.

"You lucky shit!" Dad whispered from where he stood at the first row of seats.

Mom elbowed him, but since she was busy dabbing at her eyes with a tissue, there wasn't much force behind it.

Some White House lady photographer with long silver hair moved in to take photos.

Dilya led the way in a dress that made her look far more like a graceful young adult than a precocious kid almost grown. Someday, she was going to make some guy seriously happy…and keep him seriously challenged.

But it was only Reese that he could see walking toward him.

Malcolm trotted down the aisle to join Reese, then turned to walk back with her—nearly causing Harvey Lieber to go down.

Jim could see his mouth move as he swore silently.

But none of that mattered.

All that mattered was that the distance between Reese and himself was closing with each passing second. Soon they would cross the finish line together and *that* win would last them a lifetime.

IN THE WEEDS

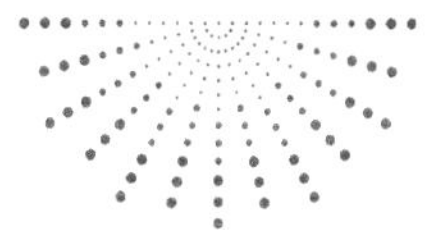

Colby Thompson likes nothing better than his Secret Service patrol of the White House South Lawn with his trusty German Shepherd, Rex. The role fits them both down to the ground.

But when his childhood nemesis **Marine Corps Major Ivy Hanson** steps off the Marine One helicopter, his comfortable existence flies apart.

Assigned together, they end up in the battle of their lives to protect the President. But can they step forward to find love, and leave their childhood feud back In the Weeds.

CHAPTER ONE

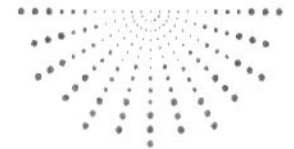

It was still confusing. *Major* Ivy Hanson—recently promoted to White House Liaison to Marine Corps HMX-1 squadron—didn't match the woman inside her head. She brushed the cool metal of her golden oak leaves and they were definitely on *her* shoulders: not captain, major. For the tenth time she double-checked that the Eagle, Globe, and Anchor insignias on the collar points of her Marine Corps dress blues were fully upright.

They were.

She really had to calm down about this. She was a Marine—though at the moment it felt as if that was the only thing she knew for certain.

The VH-3D White Top helicopter eased out of Joint Base Anacostia-Bolling, gaining altitude slowly. The President's helicopter—which would be designated Marine One if he was aboard—was a strange, anachronistic beast of a machine.

For years Ivy had flown one of the newest helicopter types there was: the massive and highly innovative MV-22B Osprey tilt-rotor. And now she was aboard the President's vintage helicopter: a fifty-year-old machine that was somehow maintained into a far more perfect condition than her prior ride. The ancient White Top also carried more armor than her MV-22B and was far more luxurious.

Instead of the sharp bite of hydraulic oil and unrelenting reek of jarhead sweat, the cabin smelled of lemon furniture polish and fine leather. Which, to a former combat pilot, was wrong on so many levels that it was better not to think about it.

Despite the soothing, air-conditioned, and well sound-insulated environment keeping the heavy load of rotor noise at a comfortable distance, her nerves continued flying sky high just as they'd been ever since she'd gotten dressed this morning.

There was a feel to dress blues that no amount of wear or dry cleaning could remove. From the steam-ironed pants' crease to its brass buttons to the gold of her major's oak leaves on her shoulder boards, blues were something special—somehow *other*. The stiff collar reminiscent of the high leather collar that had earned them the nickname "leathernecks" over two centuries ago was a badge of honor every Marine wore proudly. She always felt stronger, more powerful in her dress uniform. And far taller than she was—which was especially neat as at five-four she didn't come up to most Marines' shoulders.

Her full flight gear from her eight years piloting the MV-22B Ospreys came a close second as her favorite clothing, but there was a small and very egotistical part of her that loved the dress blues: all of her service ribbons on display, her aviator wings flying high above them—the Corps in all its righteous glory. No ceremonial sword today, but hers was so short to match her frame that she always felt a little foolish when she brandished it. She was fine without her sword.

But she was sitting in the observer's seat rather than the pilot's. That too was intensely disorienting.

A glance aft didn't reveal thirty Marines loaded for bear or a 155 mm howitzer ready to unleash havoc thirty kilometers past wherever she dropped it. Instead it revealed the President's armchair, another facing his, and a long bench seat for six aides. Directly behind the President was a seat for his personal aide. And at the back corner, just aft of the rear door, was one last seat for the head of the Presidential Protection Detail. At the moment, Ivy was the only person in the cabin other than the Marine Corps crew chief who sat in the seat closest behind the pilots.

She was seated sideways, instead of facing ahead. Coming at her new assignment sideways was okay, as long as she got there.

Because it was *exactly* where she wanted to be.

REX ALWAYS WANTED to be somewhere else and constantly hauled at his leash to prove it.

Colby guided him down the South Lawn of the White House, leaning back against the leash's pull. His German shepherd was on the hunt for any hint of explosives and he was one hard-charging canine Secret Service agent.

Rex cracked him up.

He treated sniffing for explosives as if they were the most important thing in the world, which was exactly what he'd been trained to do. The joke was that he was a dog. EDT—Explosive Detection Team—dogs didn't really care crap about explosives. They just knew that they got a treat if they found some or checked a whole area and found none. Rex was super smart about everything except his treats—which had almost flunked him out of the Secret Service's dog school. It had taken Colby a lot of work to teach him that giving false positives didn't earn him more goodies.

Colby scanned the grounds. Two floppy-eared dogs working the outside of the fence line, checking on tourists. From here he could make out two of the three vans that housed ERTs—Emergency Response Teams of dog and handler. The handlers would be watching everything using binoculars through the tinted windows, ready to release their dogs if needed. Those dogs made Rex look mild by comparison. An ERT dog would go after explosives, but that wasn't their primary job. They trained to take down fence jumpers—hard. He traded waves with another ERT team strolling the close perimeter around the White House itself.

He and Rex had risen to the top of the puppy pile, earning them the informal title of Lead Dog. Colby had come to enjoy wrangling the various handlers and types of dogs. But his favorite were times like this, when it was just him and Rex checking it all out.

The one thing he'd never let go of as he moved up the ladder was the South Lawn patrol. They'd been doing it together for the last four years of the six they'd been working together. He'd gotten Rex when he was two years old and they trained together, then started over at the Capitol. For a while they'd been loaned out to different teams: the Speaker, the home of the Vice President, and visiting dignitaries.

Four years ago they'd made the grade and been advanced to the White House. Now they both had the routine down. Zigzagging back and forth, they crisscrossed any possible path the President could take from Marine One to the White House. Every line from the South Portico of the Residence over to the outside door of the Oval Office.

Even though Colby knew it was just a training flight coming in this morning—he didn't bother telling Rex or taking it any less seriously. Though this flight would be a pain. Some new honcho was coming in on a free ride and their undue pride was always hard to swallow, but Colby timed it just like normal anyway. He and Rex worked their way down the lawn until they arrived in the landing zone itself at the same time as the groundskeepers. They were rolling out the trio of two-meter aluminum disks to protect the lawn by making temporary landing pads for the helicopter's three landing gear.

A quick sniff by Rex to make sure that someone hadn't jumped the fence in the night—undetected by patrols, rooftop snipers, or the array of motion sensors—to plant a bomb under Marine One's landing pads. It was all clear and the big red disks with their white crosses at the center were flopped into place. Fast work with a tape measure assured the guys that they'd dropped them spot-on to match the helicopter's undercarriage. A quick glance at the spacing told him they were expecting one of the VH-3D Sea Kings rather than a VH-60N White Hawk, the only two types of aircraft authorized to land on the White House lawn.

"Hey, one of these days, you should set them up for something huge like a Chinook or maybe a tiny Little Bird and see what those flyboys do."

"You want to piss off a Marine Corps pilot, I'll leave that to you." Jonesy, the head of the groundskeepers, grinned at him. He also kept a watchful eye as his crew pinned down two six-inch-by-twenty-foot strips of canvas in an L-shape that would give the pilots their centerline and final nose position.

"Hell hath no fury like a pissed-off jarhead," Colby agreed.

"Ain't that the truth, bro. You up for poker on Friday?"

"Sure. I need some easy cash." He guided Rex in an expanding spiral around the helicopter's landing zone until they reached the trees.

"Too bad you still owe me twenty from last week," Jonesy called.

Colby pretended he hadn't heard as he guided Rex through the last lap of the spiral.

Nothing to report, boss, Rex's expression said as he looked up at the end of it.

Colby lobbed a couple of treats and Rex snatched them out of the air with sharp snaps of his big jaws.

He gave Rex the hand sign to relax. He couldn't see the inbound helo yet, but if they were on time, they'd be here in two more minutes. And one thing could be said for Marines, they were always on time—no matter *what* was in their way.

TODAY'S FLIGHT was only three miles. But those three miles were along the *most* highly-engineered, regulated, and secure flight route in the country. Which might be exactly why Ivy liked it so much.

For every pilot who made the grade to fly to the White House, hundreds applied. The posting was considered the highest honor for a Marine Corps flyer. These were the very best pilots in the entire Corps, meaning the best in the world—no matter what any other unit thought.

She'd always dreamed of being a Marine One pilot—a member of the most elite flying team anywhere. But she'd found something even better. Only one flight officer at a time made it to being the HMX-1 liaison to the White House Military Office.

And that was her.

Newly promoted Major Ivy Hanson. A field grade officer. Her parents had nearly died with pride, especially Mom. One more rank and she'd be the same grade as Lt. Colonel Marina Hanson (retired).

The pilots were hers—not to command, that was still General Arnson's billet—but she would be assigning all of their missions.

Starting today.

From the *White House!*

In charge of all operational planning for the unit. She'd tell them where and when she needed heliborne assets and General Arnson would make sure that they delivered every single time.

She kept her breath under strict control, because she was a Marine and never showed nerves or doubts. The overwhelming excitement was harder to keep hidden. She was a professional and that's all her team would ever see. But she could hear her heart pounding louder than the muffled rotors. And the adrenaline was almost as sharp at the back of her throat as the lingering hints of the half-burned kerosene from the cold engine start.

Once off the tarmac at Anacostia-Bolling Air Base, they turned due west. A quarter of a mile across Hains Point—the southern tip of East Potomac Park—to the middle of the Potomac River.

"Any problem, Captain?" She called forward to the pilot. It was weird that the sound insulation was so good she didn't even need an intercom headset. There was something intrinsically wrong with that; it hardly felt like a helicopter at all.

"Why do you ask, Major?" She knew Walters well enough to hear the amusement in his voice.

"Your rate of climb is below simulator profile. Just wondering if there's a reason."

"No reason that I can think of, Major." But neither did he begin to climb more rapidly.

The crew chief pointed out the side window. She turned and

looked down at the island below just as one of the two decoy helicopters—Presidential helos typically flew in packs of three, constantly shuffling places to keep the President's actual position hidden—flew by them even a little lower.

The thirty-six holes of Hains Point Golf Course covered this entire end of the island. They were low enough that she could see the main rotor's downwash blow away one golfer's hat and another's umbrella. They passed so close that she could see players shaking their little putters at them as their balls were rolled about the green. At least that explained why the pilots chose to fly so low. In addition to the rough and sand traps, this particular golf course had the occasional air hazard.

It reminded her of the day she'd found out that Drill Sergeant McKinnon, much to her surprise, wasn't a sadistic asshole. Or perhaps that he wasn't *just* a sadistic asshole. On graduation night from Officer Candidate School, she'd spotted him drinking quietly in the back of a Marine bar while her class was whooping it up in the front. He'd waved her over. She could still feel the nerves that had shaken her as she crossed the room, but it was one of what she'd come to think of as McKinnon's Laws.

Being a Marine doesn't mean that you're not afraid. It means that you don't give a damn if you are.

Once she sat, he'd looked at her a long time in silence, but she'd waited him out until he'd finally acknowledged her with a nod of what actually looked like satisfaction.

"You're gonna be one hell of an officer, Second Lieutenant Ivy Hanson. So let me tell you all the things you're going to want to do wrong." And they'd talked right through last call; she'd still been on her first beer after many of her classmates were facedown on the floor and being shoveled out the door.

Another of his laws was: *You're going to want your people to behave perfectly. They're Marines, so they will when it matters. Don't sweat the small stuff. They'll respect you for letting them be human. But* you *draw the line and don't let anyone cross it. Ever! Or they'll run right over you.*

Batting down golf balls with a twenty-million-dollar helicopter struck her as small stuff. But they already knew that General Arnson expected them to land inside a ten-second window every time—even on a training flight like this one—and that she'd expect no less. The Army's Night Stalkers said plus or minus thirty seconds in any battlefield, and they delivered. But these were the fliers of Marine One and nobody kicked ass like the Corps.

Across the golf course and over the Potomac, they finally reached the mission profile's altitude. There was nothing like the DC skyline from five hundred feet.

COLBY GLANCED up at the snipers on the West Wing roof.

Two of them had their rifles aimed high and due south. With their spotter scopes, they were always the first to see the approaching helos. By their very steadiness, he knew the guys had picked them out. That placed the helos out over the Potomac and just turning north.

He wondered how the Marine Corps pilots felt, knowing they were in the sights of the snipers. Wouldn't be his first choice, but they were Marines, so what did he care?

Four years—more importantly four DC springtimes—and he still wasn't used to working here. The Presidential Park was stunning this time of year. The new-mown grass smelled rich with May sunshine. The trees were all leafed out, but still brilliantly green—the darker shades of summer were a month away yet. The morning breeze was out of the west, from over the vegetable garden. Nothing much to smell from that quarter yet, just lots of green shoots; though there was a hint of chlorine from the freshly refilled swimming pool. The Rose and Kennedy Gardens lay to the north of his current position so he couldn't smell them even though they were already rich with lush flowers.

Perfect season to take a girl for a walk through them, except he didn't have a girl since Elsie had given him the heave-ho. And escorting a congressional secretary around the White House grounds like it was good place to bring a date wasn't exactly the best idea…no matter what Elsie had thought.

Just as well. Rex had never liked her much, which should have told him something a lot sooner than 20-20 hindsight. Rex was happy now because he'd gotten back his spot on the couch. And Colby was done with clubbing, never a big hit with him anyway, and was back to his ESPN and action flicks. He knew it was a stereotype, but anything was better than pounding sound systems among bodies so tightly packed together that they were indistinguishable—when the whole point of going in the first place was to "be seen."

"Need to find us some girls, boy." Not that Rex had the anatomy to care about those anymore.

Colby wasn't sure how much he himself cared either.

Elsie had been fun, and watching her dance never failed to fire up his libido. Too bad that was all she'd fired up. They'd been good together in bed, but not much heat otherwise—either good or bad. They hadn't fought often, but they hadn't done the whole close-couple thing either.

He looked aloft and spotted the trio of helos as tiny black dots. That placed them even with the Pentagon.

Colby still felt the thrill every time. It didn't matter if it was the President himself or an empty training run, there was something majestic about watching them approach that he'd never tire of.

This time they'd told him to there was a sole passenger for him to escort to security. Captain Baxter—the head of the Secret Service Uniformed Division for the White House—wasn't big on extra words, like who the hell Colby was meeting. Just some officious official who'd finally earned enough rank to con a ride on the helo. He would be so totally full of himself after the HMX-1 ride that Colby suspected he'd want to unleash Rex on the pompous jerk by the time they had crossed half the lawn.

Colby backed off from the three landing disks and watched the helos come in.

———

Ivy couldn't decide where to look. The crew chief was grinning at her, but it was impossible to be blasé about the ride or the amazing view.

There were a few days that particularly stood out in memory: her first ever solo in a Bell UH-1 Huey, four combat missions that she wished she didn't remember quite so accurately in her nightmares, and a few others. She knew today would join those.

Once they were at altitude past the golf course, the flight had smoothed out as a serious focus took over. She checked the time mark on the dash when they crossed above the Arland D. Williams Jr. Memorial Bridge. Just five seconds early for this particular profile— her kind of flight.

The Pentagon dominated the view to the west. To the east, the Tidal Basin cherry trees bloomed like a bridal bouquet gone madly pink—past their peak but still radiant in early-May glory. Then the majestic turn that placed the Jefferson Memorial due east and the Washington Monument dead ahead.

Pilots flew it a hundred times in the simulator before they were allowed to even fly as copilot. She had "ridden" along on twenty of those simulations herself so that she could witness all of the primary emergency scenarios.

But to be able to fly the route itself, even as an observer, was like a miracle. Never expecting to command them, she'd been gunning for the post of Presidential pilot since boot camp, a fact she hadn't even told Drill Sergeant McKinnon. Though proving that nothing ever got by him, just this morning she'd received a text from him, his first contact in years. He'd spared two whole words for her: *Go Marine!*

She'd been shocked that her heart hadn't blown right out the chest of her dress blues. In an excess of pride, she'd sent back *four* words that, of course, he hadn't replied to: *For the Corps, Sergeant.* In hindsight, she should have sent *Semper Fi!* Short for *Semper Fidelis,* always faithful. Two words for two words.

She'd broken McKinnon's Law of: *Never use extra words. They only serve to cloud the communication.*

Tough! She was damn proud of what she'd done and she was a

major so she'd use four whole words if she felt like it. If McKinnon had ever laughed, she could imagine him laughing at her. But it was impossible to imagine he ever had, so she was safe on that account.

They crossed the middle of the National Mall between the very top of the Washington Monument and the World War II Memorial at the foot of the Reflecting Pool three seconds behind schedule. No one but a Marine would notice.

McKinnon had been right. Let the boys have a little fun when it didn't matter and they'd perform all the better when it did. The pilots wanted this flight to be perfect as badly as she did.

Nothing had prepared her for the real view of the White House from the air—something so few ever saw. In the simulator it had looked amazing: interactive video simulated from high-resolution 3D imaging. But that was nothing compared to the real thing. Now she was looking down on the South Lawn from above as the pilots eased between the trees, doing the trademark quarter turn down between the treetops to turn the President's helo door so that it faced the White House. There it was, the center of government—the home of the Commander-in-Chief himself.

And her new office.

She'd probably never get to take this ride again, so she'd promised herself to pay attention to every detail, every moment. Yet between one eyeblink and the next, they were settling down on the lawn, landing on the trio of six-foot aluminum disks rolled out to protect the lawn.

Of course, during the last few meters of the landing itself, the pilots were unable to see the disks themselves. But no Marine pilot would take that as an excuse to miss landing precisely on those hidden disks. No signalman stood by waving batons, just those two strips of canvas. Marine Corps pilots didn't need anyone else's help to nail a landing.

Contact two seconds early—dead zero as the shock absorbers fully took the weight of the seven tons of helicopter, fuel, and extra armor. She thumped a fist on Captain Walters' shoulder and she heard his pleased chuckle.

They went through the full routine: cycling down the engines before the Marine crew chief opened the forward door and lowered the stairway. He then did a military march, three steps out, six steps to the rear, and three steps in to lower the rear door and stair. The front door of the helo was reserved for the use of the First Family and the crew chief. All others used the rear stairs.

So she placed her white, field officer cover squarely on her head and walked down the length of the cabin. At the rear stairs she made her own neat right angle turn and descended down onto the grass of the immaculately manicured White House lawn. Per protocol, the crew chief had returned to stand beside the forward stairs. There he stood at parade rest with his hands clasped behind his back, ready to aid or honor the President. As she stopped two steps in front of him, he saluted sharply.

She couldn't resist looking down at the wheels first. The center of all three white crosses were hidden by the black rubber of the tires—hitting the marks within six inches in the blind on a six-foot disk. She returned the sergeant's sharp salute, then shot a thumb's up to Walters, who grinned in relief. *Go Marines!*

McKinnon's Law: *Let them know when they done good and you never have to tell them when they done bad. They'll know.* His corollary, which she'd also proven many times: *Tell them about the second screwup. Third time ask yourself if they're really Corps material.*

"Thank you, Sergeant Mathieson." She automatically checked the crew chief's uniform. He was one squared-away Marine. Too bad about the officer-enlisted gap, because he was also damn fine looking in his dress blues. He had three bronze hashes on his sleeve, marking twelve years of service. He'd earned his right to stand there and look magnificent.

"A pleasure, Major." His smile said that he might be thinking the same thing about her. Nothing would ever happen there, but it didn't hurt her ego in the slightest.

She almost wished the Press Corps was around so that someone would get a photograph of her striding this one time across the South Lawn in her uniform.

When she turned to walk up the lawn, Ivy nearly tripped over one of the biggest German shepherds she'd ever seen. He was wearing a US Secret Service vest and a giant-sized doggie smile that revealed equally large teeth.

"Hey there, Saint Ives!"

Ivy sighed. Only one person had ever called her that.

Colby had taken his normal station on the back side of the helo's landing area, between there and the distant fence. This was his station, keeping an eye out for any last-minute fence jumpers. Once the helo was down and stopped, he'd circled around the tail, arriving just in time to see the back of the officious official.

Except the officious official was a pint-sized Marine in full dress blues, a female one. As trim and perfect as a wind-up doll, complete with her hair wound into that donut-shaped bun that female Marines wore. They never had a single strand astray because that would be against regulations and even a Marine's hair follicles followed regulations. She looked a hundred percent delectable and he no longer minded having to escort her to the White House. Maybe she'd like a personal tour of the White House.

He hadn't been ready for when she turned to salute the sergeant by the front stair. It was a profile he'd know anywhere. Moving closer didn't change who it was. Their families were neighbors and her older brother was still his best friend. But when did Ivy Hanson start to look like this? She'd been overseas so much these last several years that he'd only seen her in passing.

Rex moved in to sniff her just as she did a military about-face and almost trompled him.

"Yipes!" Her cry of surprise as she stared down at the dog and fought for balance was pretty funny.

"Hey there, Saint Ives."

She closed her eyes in a deeply pained expression.

When she'd turned to face him, it was like being hit by a taser blast. Little Saint Ives transformed into a Marine Corps officer in her dress blues was messing with his head. She carried a dark blue leather-encased tablet computer that managed to make her look even more official and impressive.

That's when he noticed her shoulder insignia.

"Major? Whoo-hoo! When did you get them pretty little leaves on your collar?" He had to say something to distract himself from the conflicting thoughts she was firing into his brain. Little Ivy and sexy Marine Corps major was a very weird juxtaposition.

"Last week," she heaved a sigh. Even the dress blues couldn't conceal the very pleasant movement of her chest. Then she opened her eyes again, which were bluer than the DC springtime sky.

"Would you mind getting your dog out of my way?" Rex had sat after giving her a good sniff.

Colby looked down at her. He'd always remembered her as a little bit of a thing, three years younger besides. She'd always been cute as hell, but she was completely under the best-friend's-little-sister rule: no touch, no look, no think. Hell, he'd practically helped raise her. It was a rule he'd always been fine with, mostly. He'd certainly never told Reggie about any stray thoughts to the contrary. Or Ivy. She'd have flattened him even if he could have picked her up one-handed.

But she didn't look like anybody's kid sister in her Marine Corps uniform. She was breathtaking.

"Colby," she let a Marine growl into her voice, sounding almost as gruff as Rex, who cocked his head to listen to her. That was funny enough to give him back the power of speech.

"Afraid not, Ives. Rex is sitting for a reason. Want to explain it to me or should I frisk you?"

"You. Wouldn't. Dare!" She shifted her weight to her back foot. The Secret Service had given him enough hand-to-hand combat training to recognize a fighter's stance when he saw one. That's when he remembered that one teased Saint Ives at their own risk. She'd been a taekwondo black belt by junior high and judo black belt in high school. Or was it jiu-jitsu? Dangerous as hell either way. More than once she'd taken him down despite the age and size difference.

Even before she'd become a Marine, she'd always fought like a girl —to win.

"It was range work and you damn well know it. He's looking right at my sidearm." And Rex *was* staring at her holster. Detection dogs triggered to spent powder. Then she pulled out her White House ID, looped the band over her head, and held it out for Colby to see. She had full Proximity Clearance—which meant that not only could she stand beside the President unescorted, but she was also one of the select few outside the Secret Service who were authorized to be armed in his presence.

He should read her badge, but he couldn't look away from her photo. Not even for a White House badge had Ivy been able to lock down that brilliant smile of hers. It was like she was looking right at him, as if he was a ray of sunshine on a winter's day.

Then he managed to look up from her photo and into her face. Not so much with the smile—sunshiny or otherwise.

His leaning down had placed their faces entirely too close together. She didn't get this close to anyone.

Typical jerk, leaning in so close. Colby knew he was a handsome SOB, but the emphasis was on being a son of a bitch—and not in the good, Marine Corps sense of the word. He looked really good and... she'd clearly lost her mind.

The last year that she'd spent with HMX-1 had been brutally hard, trying to live up to the impossible standards that challenged every single jarhead in the squadron. General Arnson drove his Marines just as hard as he drove himself. She'd never served with such an exceptional team before. But it had also meant she'd had no time for more personal liaisons.

And now Colby stood so close that she could smell—

McKinnon's Law: *Marine first, second, and third. Everything else comes fourth.*

"Back off, Thompson." He jolted away as if she'd slapped him, his eyes a little wild.

So much for her dignified arrival at the White House.

She glanced back and caught Sergeant Mathieson's smile as he marched the six steps from closing the rear door of the White Top and returned to the forward stairs. He turned to climb the stairs himself and his smile was hidden from view. Then she spotted Captain Walters' grin through the pilot's side window. She really didn't need this.

Ego don't mean shit in the Corps. And McKinnon's wisdom wasn't helping her ego at all.

"What are you doing here?" Colby said it as a whisper.

"I'm the new HMX-1 liaison to the White House Military Office."

"The WHMO?" That earned her a whistle of surprise. "You know that those guys are a little freaky, right?"

Hard challenges are what Marines live for!

"Damn straight!" Ivy wasn't sure if she was answering Colby or an imaginary McKinnon. Though Colby was right. The WHMO was one of those quiet agencies that almost no one had ever heard of. Yet Marine One, Air Force One, the ceremonial Marine sentries, the Nuclear Football with the President's launch codes—all that was only part of what they did.

"What are *you* doing here?" She tried to step around Rex, but he shifted to keep giving his warning signal. Colby put on his best innocent look, which never fooled anybody.

"Any landing of the Marine helos on the South Lawn is part of Rex's and my patrol. We secure the passage, the landing area, then act as backup on standby. If I'm right there," he pointed off to the side as if she cared what he did, "then I'm not in any Press Corps photos either."

Overhead, the helo's engines began whining to life. The rotors swung through their first lazy turn. Then another. Burning kerosene replaced the smell of fresh-mown grass.

When Ivy again tried to step around Rex, the low growl that emanated from his chest was loud enough to be easily heard despite the escalating noise of the twin turbine engines. She froze in place. In fact, she was fairly certain that she stopped breathing entirely. He really was huge; his shoulders practically reached her waist.

Colby flickered a hand sign to Rex to ease off. But the dog was too busy pointing his nose at her sidearm. He tried again. Still nothing.

Ivy offered him a smirk. Still the same old Colby, never having his act together.

Ivy's smile wasn't all happy and friendly like the one on her ID—it was more, *What a goon!*

He signaled Rex one more time, but he was too busy looking at Ivy. Who could blame him? Somewhere over the last few years while he hadn't been paying attention, she had tipped over from being a cute, feisty, pain-in-the-ass to being a gorgeous Marine warrior. He finally had to call out, *"Gute Hund."* Rex looked up at him but didn't move until Colby remembered to fumble out a dog treat.

Once he had happily chomped it down, Rex sprang to his feet and let Ivy step past. She didn't scowl at the dog, but she did scowl at him. Not his best day's work.

Behind them, the helicopter's rotors wound up to full speed. But he didn't look. He was too busy trying to catch up to the striding Marine a head shorter than he was.

"Such," he told Rex with the hard German ch. *Seek.* And they were alongside Ivy in a moment.

"Because of course a German shepherd speaks German," Ivy didn't ease up from her military perfect posture as she strode across the lawn. Her voice carried easily over the roar of the departing helo. She'd never been soft-spoken, but the Marine Major carried an authority that he wasn't sure what to do with.

"Of course," he agreed amiably. Actually, it was a very common practice among military and Secret Service dogs to train them in German. It avoided confusion in a crowd. The number of German words spoken by the Secret Service in general conversation were few and far between, so it also decreased the chances of a false signal to the dog.

But what Colby was wondering about was if Ivy's perfect posture was a leftover from all the ballet she'd done as a kid or martial arts as a teen? Or was it pure Marine? Whichever it was, she was making it damn hard to remember the best-friend's-little-sister rule at the moment. Major Ivy Hanson was a serious woman who looked amazing in her dress uniform.

"Don't you have something else to do?"

"Nope, can't think of a thing." Rex was tugging ahead, sniffing the air that he'd just checked coming the other way before the helicopter had landed. Unlike the friendly, floppy-eared dogs who patrolled among the tourists on the outside of the White House fence line, Rex was eighty-seven pounds of hard-driven canine who had never learned to be easy on the leash when he was on the job. He'd dump someone as small as Ivy right on her face as he charged ahead.

Then Colby looked over at her again.

Marine tough. Not a button or hair out of place. Enough ribbons on her chest to tell him that she wasn't good at what she did—she was exceptional. Of course he wouldn't expect anything less from Saint Ives.

Maybe she'd be just fine handling Rex.

"Colby, I know how to walk to the damn White House alone."

"You can try, but it's not gonna happen."

"And why not?"

"Because for roughly the next ten minutes, I've been assigned to be *your* liaison to the White House."

"For reasons beyond understanding."

"For reasons of security. You've entered the White House grounds without passing through Security. Just because they let you onto the Anacostia airbase and aboard a White Top helo doesn't cut it with the United States Secret Service. That means that you have an escort until you're registered as being on the grounds. Think you can put up with me for that long, Saint Ives?"

"I don't know. It will be hard. But we Marines are used to

shouldering heavy burdens." She delivered it in a flat tone, but that smile of hers slipped out and lit up her face.

It was a good thing the White House kitchen was in the basement of the Residence. That's where her brother, Reggie worked—so he wouldn't be able to see what was going on.

What was going on?

Colby didn't know. But he knew he wanted to see Saint Ives smile at him like that again—really soon.

Then Rex swung left as Colby stumbled off to the right. He was thinking of Saint Ives *how?* Reggie would kill him.

Off balance and looking the wrong way, Colby went down on the South Lawn—face first. Leftover grass clippings were plastered to his face and he brushed at them frantically.

Rex spun to look at him in surprise. He heard a sharp laugh from one of the Delta snipers on the roof of the West Wing.

Saint Ives didn't even break her stride, but it was easy to imagine her eye roll. Easy money said she'd make a point of rubbing in his clumsiness as well.

———

The White House loomed. Ivy had been here dozens of times working with the White House Military Office as part of her training, but she'd never stood on the South Lawn before. She'd also never arrived by helicopter, but it was still the same White House. It was still the same WHMO.

Except it completely wasn't.

It was as if she'd teleported down onto another planet and was caught in one of those *Star Trek* back-in-time episodes.

Here she was, walking across the South Lawn. The long arms of the East and West Wings wholly overshadowed by the towering white facade of the Residence. Fifty meters wide and twenty high, it looked as if the mass of sandstone was going to tumble down the gentle slope and crush her.

Overseas, she'd seen far too much of Libya and plenty of Iraq and

Yemen from the air. Her Marine Expeditionary Unit—MEU—had gone on to Syria at the same time her requested transfer to HMX-1 had come through. She still felt bad about that. However, after the recent attack on the Presidential Motorcade, she was feeling less guilty. The President needed the best protection there was. That's why the Marines were on the job.

But now she was a sole Marine—without the two thousand other Marines of her MEU—walking toward the most imposing facade in the nation's capital. Perhaps in the world.

Walk like you own it!

Yeah right, Sergeant. It was an act of sheer will to remain upright despite her knees gone to liquid.

She held the line set by Colby. The South Portico with its twin sweep of stairs was off to her right. And to her left, the Oval Office dominated the South Lawn from its corner. It actually didn't look like much, a curved wall with a lot of windows and several tactically placed trees that would mask the Oval Office from a distant shooter. But even though the President was at Camp David with the Australian Prime Minister, the Oval Office was there and she could feel the windowed eyes watching her every step.

Colby had been guiding her toward the Rose Garden. The entrance there led into the hall that ran between the Press Briefing and Cabinet Rooms. Past those lay the main floor of the West Wing, but there was a stairway around the first corner that would allow her to descend into the far less scary ground floor of the West Wing.

"Does it still spook you every time you walk here?" Ivy whispered her question to Colby as she crossed the paved circular driveway for the South Portico.

When he didn't respond, she looked over at him, except he wasn't there. He was behind her, trotting to catch up. Rex had a happy smile and lolling tongue as he had a chance to move with a springy lope rather than dragging at his leash.

"What happened to your knees?" His dark slacks were brightly grass-stained along with one of the elbows of his white shirt.

Colby just glared at her like he was some kind of pissed. About what, who knew? Or cared? Not her.

Ten minutes. That's what he'd said. *Fine!* She was a Marine. She could cover a kilometer wearing a forty-pound rucksack in under ten minutes—she could certainly deal with Colby Thompson for that long. Thank goodness they didn't have to work together.

She turned back just in time to plow into a small Shetland Sheepdog that yipped in surprise as a young voice called out, "Zackie!"

***

COLBY MANAGED to grab Ivy's arm before she plummeted to the ground. As a result of his grasp, they performed a small whirling dance. He almost had their balance right—except Rex, as he'd been trained to do during the unexpected, firmly braced himself to act as a support if needed.

Instead of support, the sudden tightening of the leash in his hand tipped Colby's own balance past recovery. If he'd let go of the leash or Ivy at that moment, she might have been fine. But some part of him hadn't cooperated and he was dragging her down with him.

With a sharp twist, he managed to get his back to the lawn and take the brunt of the fall—squarely on his spare: the Glock handgun that he kept at the small of his back. Pain sliced up his back.

The rigid black brim of Ivy's hat cracked him sharply enough across the bridge of his nose to bring tears to his eyes. And the impact of her fist, tightly clutched around her tablet computer, nailed him in the solar plexus.

"What the hell?" Ivy shouted at him from an inch away.

All he could answer with were small *whoop* noises as he desperately struggled to take a breath. That Ivy continued to lie full upon him made it even harder to recover.

He'd only ever let himself think about how goddamn cute Ivy was —and even that little bit only on rare occasions before he caught himself. He'd never thought of what it would be like to actually touch her or...

Lying full upon him, she didn't feel like a best friend's little sister under a no-touch-no-think interdiction. She was no longer the little girl he'd practically helped raise.

Colby inhaled through his nose to force his breathing to slow down. It was the fastest way to recover from a solar plexus hit. But it also filled his senses with her scent. She smelled of glory and gunmetal, of spring grass and not even a little bit of the teenage girl running down the beach in a hormone-busting sleek one-piece. As she struggled to free herself, she nearly cut off his nose with one of her collar-point insignias. She felt so light, except against his diaphragm, which was registering a weight somewhere between elephant and lying under one of the wheels of Air Force One. *Whoop. Whoop.*

"Let. Go. Of. Me." Ivy ground out the syllables like a military command.

It took him a moment to identify that his hands were still firmly clenched about her upper arms. Serious biceps and triceps there for a woman. Rex was sitting off to the side holding his own leash, which Colby had finally dropped, between his teeth.

It took Colby several moments more to unclench his grasp without setting off more spasms in his chest.

In seconds, Ivy's weight was gone. She now stood, brushing at her immaculate uniform. No grass stain would dare impinge on her perfection.

Perfection. That was Ivy Hanson's specialty. That's why he'd tagged her as Saint Ives when she was all of five. The nickname had worked on several other levels as well—particularly in that it had always irritated her.

Saint Ives *lived* to be in hot pursuit of the absolute perfect. Nothing less, in herself or others, was ever tolerated. As a kid he'd first thought it was ridiculous. Then later, a little terrifying.

By the time she'd hit high school and was entering state-wide martial arts competitions, he'd wondered what he'd been missing by not trying harder to achieve something—anything. He was smart enough that he'd been able to loaf through high school without much effort. With Ivy jarring his attitude, he managed to kick a little ass in college with solid grades and a state swimming championship.

He'd always been a good swimmer. The Thompsons and the Hansons had side-by-side cabins near Ocean City on the Maryland barrier islands. They'd all been swimming through the breakers since the time they could walk. College had simply honed that natural ability until it felt as if he owned that skill.

By the time he made the Secret Service, it felt as if he was in control of his life. Dog handler at the White House totally rocked.

Then Saint Ives shows up. She'd driven him to become who he was, even if she didn't know anything about that. But instead of living up to that standard, suddenly he was in high school not-living-up-to-his-potential mode again. It wasn't fair.

He sat up once his gut muscles could tolerate a sit-up. A sit-up square into a giant face lick by Zackie.

"Dilya! Get your dog off me!" But he smiled and scrubbed the Sheltie on the head, making her wag her tail happily, to show there were no hard feelings. It wasn't the First Dog's fault that it was so excessively cheerful; just part of the breed.

"She's not my dog."

"As good as."

He looked up at Dilya. The teen was the First Dog's handler as well as the on-site babysitter for the former-President-turned-Secretary-of-State's child. And now with the First and Second ladies both pregnant, she was soon going to have her hands full. It was a good thing she was finishing high school a year ahead next month.

"You hear from the schools yet?"

"Georgetown. Political science and international affairs double major. So, I still get to play part-time nanny and dog sitter here."

"Wow! You go, girl. Too bad you weren't born in the US. I'd vote for you for President." Dilya was seventeen, brilliant, and—he had to blink a few times—fast becoming a gorgeous young woman. Her Uzbekistani medium-dark skin and long black ruffled hair were offset by brilliant green eyes. She was taller than Ivy, but gawky-teen slender rather than Ivy's ever-so-nice, hyper-fit, Marine Corps trim. The guys were definitely going to be hounding her heels.

Though Dilya also mysteriously seemed to be at the center of everything that happened around the White House.

"President is too visible. Maybe I'll run the CIA instead. Or maybe the Secret Service, then you could work for me." Then she bit her lower lip, clearly something she hadn't meant to say.

Dilya had that same driven enthusiasm that had always made Ivy such a standout.

She hurried on, "I was just walking Zackie when I spotted the helo. She wanted to say hi to Rex."

Colby rose to his feet and gave Dilya the same treatment he'd just given the First Dog: a big head rub to mess up her hair. Though he wouldn't be trying that on Major Ivy Hanson.

"Hey!"

"You heard the helo, knew the First Family wasn't due back yet, and were in too much of a hurry to grab Zackie's leash as you used her as an excuse to rush and see what was going on."

Dilya just grinned at him and held out her empty palms.

"I shouldn't even introduce you."

"Oh, she's Major Ivy Hanson, the new HMX-1 liaison to the WHMO," Dilya *did* know everything. "Hi, I'm Dilya. Sorry about Zackie."

Ivy scowled at him rather than the dog.

"Are you okay, Ives?"

"Little slow with that question, Colby. This is your idea of a welcoming committee?"

"No, Rex and I typically reserve this particular type of greeting for visiting heads of state. The Pope and I had a nice roll around the fountain one particularly sunny afternoon." He pointed to where the big fountain splashed cheerfully farther down the South Lawn. With the helo gone, it was the loudest sound there was. The traffic on Constitution Ave beyond the Ellipse was muted by comparison.

"I'm thinking that my brother wouldn't hold it against me if I killed you right now."

"He still owes me fifty bucks from poker the other night, so he might offer to hold me down. Just saying, in case you need to take up a posthumous collection for my funeral expenses. Of course, then you'd have to put up with Rex. He'd whine pitifully if something happened to me."

Ivy looked down at his German shepherd. "You sure about that?"

Rex sent him a questioning look, like: *What are we standing around for?* Or perhaps it was a doubtful look, like: *Miss you? Maybe yes, maybe no.*

***

COULD she have found any less dignified approach to her first day? Thank God there *hadn't* been a Press Corps photographer around. Ivy brushed at her uniform again, but couldn't find any grass stains.

Rex didn't look like a whiner. More like a furry, four-footed Zulu Cobra attack helo—lean and lethal.

She really needed to have a long talk with Reggie about his choice in best friends. Colby Thompson was definitely a lower life form, the kind a woman scraped off her boot after stepping in it accidentally. He'd always been a lazy, arrogant jerk wholly convinced of his own self-worth with little to no justification.

Then he leaned down to pet his dog and take the leash from the dog's mouth.

But he didn't look useless. Nor had he moved like some bumbler. Her martial arts training let her understand the move he'd done to take the hit of the fall himself. It wasn't something he'd thought about, then done; there wasn't time. It had been an instinctively trained act, trained to the point of reflex, to protect those around him. The fact that it was also a decent and selfless act must be strictly a coincidence.

And lying on him, he hadn't felt useless. Instead he'd...

As he turned to chat with the teen, she could see the grass stains on his white Uniformed Division shirt: both elbows, one shoulder that must have dug in hard to get so green, and a clear imprint of the backup piece at the small of his back that had to really hurt to land on. But no complaints. Instead he'd asked if she was okay. This wasn't any version of Colby Thompson that she recognized. This wasn't the boy who'd taught her to read one moment and started a food fight that she'd been the one to get in all the trouble for the next moment.

Watching his back, she could appreciate other changes in him. He was no longer the whip thin Colby she'd grown up next door to. Somewhere along the way he'd earned himself seriously broad swimmer's shoulders. The rest of his body showed that he made his living on his feet: powerful legs, trim waist, tight—

She was *not* looking at Colby Thompson's glutes.

But she could still feel the strength of his arms as he wrapped them around her to protect her from the fall.

She was a Marine Corps major. She didn't need anyone to protect her. Her aircraft had often been the tip of the spear—first on the ground delivering forward teams beneath the watchful eye of the leading gunships. The only protection she needed was provided by the Corps.

Colby and Dilya appeared ready to chat all through the sunny morning. Zackie and Rex had sat close beside their handlers and were holding a tongue-lolling contest.

Ivy punched Colby on the shoulder, the unstained one to avoid staining her knuckles. Not hard enough to knock him off balance, but hard enough that she double-checked to see if she'd just punched a brick wall. Again, solid muscle and Colby Thompson, hard to equate the two.

"Right. Sorry. Later Dilya." He reached out and messed up the girl's hair again.

He tried that on her and she *would* kill him. Why did guys always think that was so cute? She shared a glance of commiseration with Dilya as the teen struggled to get her hair to lie properly again.

Ivy punched Colby's shoulder again—hard—on Dilya's behalf.

"Hey, what was that for? We're going already." He began leading her once more toward the West Wing.

Ivy glanced back to see Dilya shove enough hair aside to uncover a wide grin. Ivy found it very easy to smile back before she followed Colby.

Today was supposed to be about stepping into her new job and confirming relationship roles. She checked her *Star Trek* wrist watch —its silver face etched with the lines of the top of the NCC-1701 Enterprise's saucer section was sufficiently elegant and understated to be permissible with her uniform—stated that she still had fifteen minutes before her meeting with Major General Markham, the director of the White House Military Office.

Yet against all common sense, she had the sudden notion that perhaps she'd just had the most important introduction she'd have today. The President's dog walker had known who she was, had the run of the grounds even during an HMX-1 landing, and her innocent teenager act didn't fool Ivy for a second—though Colby appeared to have swallowed it whole.

Or...Ivy was imagining everything and there was a force field around Colby Thompson that projected mental aberrations on unsuspecting Marine Corps majors. That hypothesis at least had a higher degree of plausibility.

As they crossed through the Rose Garden, she glanced back once more.

Dilya had produced a tennis ball from somewhere and was heaving it far out onto the South Lawn. The Sheltie went bounding after it. It could have been any girl playing with her dog. But it wasn't. This was the White House and everything here had more meaning than it would anywhere else. Just as Ivy was turning away, Dilya's bright eyes swung to inspect her again. Focused. Thoughtful.

Yes, the girl was not what she seemed.

The Rose Garden itself was something of a disappointment. In none of her prior visits had she actually been out to see the gardens. The Jackie Kennedy Garden on the far side of the South Portico was a riot of brilliant blooms. The Rose Garden itself was a broad, rectangular expanse of perfectly trimmed lawn. Only the border had trees and flowers. The bright pink of the magnolia tree blossoms were brilliant, but the narrow border of roses and immaculate box hedges didn't impress her much. It was so formal. A rose garden should be a lush affair that abounded with masses of blooms, not some carefully constrained study in rectangles.

Hopefully she wouldn't be disillusioned by trading her chance at being an HMX pilot for the WHMO position.

Colby led her up the broad steps at the far end of the Rose Garden. Atop the steps they crossed the West Colonnade and Colby held the door open for her into the West Wing.

Did that have more meaning too? Colby Thompson had never held a door for her once in all the years growing up together. She'd have remembered if he had, just because it would have been so unusual. He'd been far more likely to "accidentally" let one close in her face. And she'd been just as likely to "accidentally" kick him in the shins shortly afterward.

He had also managed to keep her from disgracing herself and her uniform on her first day. What meaning did that have?

Facts are all that count. Marine officers love conjecture, but never lose sight of the facts! McKinnon had been mostly right about that one. She'd learned that there *were* times to ponder an enemy's intentions, but never to lose sight of the facts.

Fact: She knew Colby Thompson's failures as a human being far too well.

Fact: None of those appeared evident in the man holding the door for her.

Hypothesis: Maybe he was a pod-person, a secret alien substitute in Colby clothing.

Conclusion? She was flying deep in a total brownout.

CHAPTER TWO

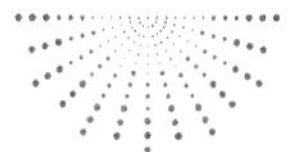

"You're a sad case, Thompson." Captain Baxter's bullhorn voice echoed through the big Secret Service Ready Room in the West Wing's ground floor. It made every agent look up, first at Baxter, then invariably following his glare (as clear as a laser on a foggy night) to the green grass stains all over his clothing.

Colby groaned. He just wasn't going to get a break today. He'd handed off Ivy to security and was gunning for the clean shirt he kept in a desk drawer. The Ready Room was the largest contiguous room in the West Wing. Only the Situation Room was bigger, but it was chopped into eight or ten spaces, or so he'd heard. Even though he walked by it every time he came in the west entrance, he'd never walked through those guarded doors—which was fine with him. He'd seen the looks on the faces of the people headed in and out of there. Merely grim meant it was a good day.

"My office. *After* you've changed." Baxter bullhorned again, then withdrew into his tiny cube of an office at the far end of the room.

The head of the White House Uniformed Division—which included all of the dog handlers—was a fixture. Rumor was that, when FDR had the West Wing basement dug and built out beneath his fifth cousin Teddy's original structure, they'd unearthed the Captain already at his desk—and built the Ready Room around him. Of course there were also rumors that he'd served in every conflict since the days of Genghis Kahn, so it was hard to tell if the basement rumor was true. Either way, he was as formidable as the bedrock he'd been carved from.

Rex stretched out on his dog bed after Colby stuffed a couple of treats inside a Kong toy and then dropped it for the dog to wrestle with.

Colby dug out a fresh shirt and stripped off the soiled one. He didn't keep extra slacks here, so his knees were just going to be grass-stained all day. He got a round of applause and some catcalls from the eight other agents currently in the room as he stood bare chested by his desk. *Whoops!*

He took a bow.

And stood up to look directly into Ivy's eyes as she passed by the Ready Room door on the way to the White House Military Office that lay another fifty feet down the hall.

Her gaze on him lasted only for the two strides it took her to pass by. Not even a hesitation in her step despite her head turned sideways.

As he was pulling the fresh shirt over his head, he heard a male exclamation of surprise. When Colby dragged the shirt down enough to see, he spotted a staffer now standing framed in the doorway, still stumbling to regain his balance. He looked as if he'd just been rammed by a pint-sized Marine juggernaut who hadn't been looking where she was going. Colby found that strangely encouraging, though he had no idea why, as he hurried to Captain Baxter's office while still tucking in his shirt.

Two offices defined this end of the Ready Room: Baxter's, the lair of the all-seeing eye; and the office of the head of the Presidential Protection Detail, which seemed to be rarely occupied. Harvey Lieber traveled with the President but also wasn't an office sort of guy; he was always stepping out for meetings or to check on his detail. Colby saw far more of Harvey while he was on grounds patrol than he ever saw of Baxter—which was fine with him. Colby had worked for Baxter for four years at the White House and, still, he was scary.

Colby knocked on the door and Baxter looked up from some report to eye him. "Yes?"

"*You* wanted to see *me*, sir." *Correcting Baxter? Smooth move. Real smooth.*

The captain's office was a study in military precision. His steel desk had precisely one file on it, closed automatically at Colby's knock and exactly centered in front of the Captain. There was an inbox that was empty and an outbox in the same condition. Six secure file cabinets and a single folding metal chair for guests. One wall had portraits of the Captain with the last six presidents—all shaking hands, all signed—and the other had a small shelf bearing an American flag folded into one of those triangular wood-and-glass display cases. There'd been a lot of speculation among the agents about whose coffin that flag had originally covered, but no one knew. And sure as hell, no one asked.

"And why would I want that, Thompson?"

Colby had long since learned that Baxter hated people who spent too much time thinking before replying; he wanted his agents to move fast and decisively at all times. But Colby could think up no quick answer so kept his silence. Apparently it was the right choice as Baxter continued one breath later.

"Now that you're done rolling around on the grass and making a disgrace of the uniform..." His baleful gaze didn't make it clear whether he was merely interpreting the stains on Colby's uniform or had somehow used his all-seeing eye to glare when Colby had taken down Ivy Hanson.

Baxter often displayed an odd sense of humor in unlikely situations. Not the least hint of a smile this time. So he probably hadn't been witness to the situation where he had totally embarrassed himself, otherwise Baxter would have made something more of it.

"Sorry, sir. I snagged Rex's leash and—"

Baxter made a pinching motion to indicate Colby should close his mouth. As it seemed likely that Captain Baxter would consider it beneath contempt to have picked up the gesture from a Bruce Willis movie, Colby was left to wonder how Bruce Willis might have picked up his trademark hand sign from Captain Baxter.

"You've been on site at the White House for four years with Rex, and one year as the head of the White House grounds dog teams."

"Lead Dog, yes sir. Four years here as of tomorrow. And four fine and fun years they've been, sir." And when was Colby going to learn to keep his trap shut? Apparently on the twelfth of never. But he hadn't thought that anyone would notice the anniversary except him. He'd been thinking about taking Rex out for a beer and two burgers to celebrate. He should remember that nothing got by the captain.

"Sit down and shut up."

Colby double-checked that Rex was still on his dog bed. He wasn't yet done wrestling the Kong toy into submission. The big boy really was a laugh riot—a dog as smart as Rex mesmerized by a toy that resembled a six-inch-high black-rubber snowman.

He sat and Baxter kicked the door shut.

"You've been a real asset, Colby."

The captain's tone sent a chill up his spine. He'd been fired once in his life, from a teenage summer job doing pool maintenance. It didn't get much lower than that. But now Baxter's tone—

"As much as I hate to do this..."

Colby could feel his breath going arrhythmic, as if something far worse than Ivy Hanson was punching him in the solar plexus.

"I'm taking you off Lead Dog."

Colby froze—afraid to move because he might shatter. Like really might. Making the Secret Service was the one thing he'd ever done really right. To leave, to lose Rex—who belonged to the Secret Service, not to him—meant that...

"I need you in foreign travel."

"You need...what?" He felt whiplash as the conversation veered in a wholly unexpected direction. Baxter's grimace said that he just might be enjoying himself.

"Agent McPhee's Rusty is retiring. He's eleven and should have been retired two years ago, but he's the kind of dog who hates to quit. Rex has proven that he doesn't spook. The helos don't throw him.

You've had him around jet transports several times and the reports say there were no issues."

"There weren't." Colby was still as befuddled as his dog was by food hidden inside a toy.

A lot of dogs, even the ones who had been trained to keep working through gunfire and explosions, hated helos and flying on jets. Colby often wondered if it was the high whine of the turbine engines—which hurt his own ears badly enough, never mind giant doggie ears—or perhaps they thought that an aircraft was like a car that was too big and fast to chase so they must be, plain and simple, wrong. Whatever it was, Rex seemed to look at any aircraft and just shrug.

"Also, you're single. Heading up the dog teams for the Presidential travel detail is brutal enough without maintaining a relationship in the middle of them. You're not paired up with anyone I don't know about?" Baxter, of course, knew everything about everybody.

Colby could only shake his head. Elsie had given him the boot several months back because he "just wasn't a long-term kind of guy." *Hell!* He could have told her that…if she'd ever cared to ask.

"McPhee broke his ankle stepping in a gopher hole out at Camp David about an hour ago. I was going to overlap you for a week, starting with the President's return this afternoon, but that's out. Effective immediately, you're transferred. I've got Malcolm sniffing for the Motorcade, but I need someone on the helos. And I need someone to keep all the travel dogs out of my hair. That's you and Rex. Here's your primary contact." He handed over the file he'd been reading. "Read that before you head over."

"Who will take over my former role?"

"I figure Linda Hamlin and Thor can't do any worse job than you two do."

Ouch! Thor was a scrawny mutt. Though Thor and Linda had saved the President's life in his first month at the White House—which proved they had the chops. There were also a lot of other things to like about Linda, but she'd married the White House chocolate chef, so he'd been careful to only admire her from afar.

"You'll show her the ropes. Any questions?"

"Yes, sir. No, sir."

"Out, Thompson. And try not to disgrace the Secret Service any more than usual."

"I wouldn't ev—"

"Out."

Colby got out and headed to his desk to study the file. Rex had finally freed his snack from the toy's interior and made quick work of it. He now watched Colby intently as he crossed the room.

"It's gonna be good, boy. It's gonna be good." He knelt down to give Rex a big scritch. And it *was* going to be good. Presidential travel. That meant he and Rex would be off to see a bit of the world, domestic and foreign. "Sounds like an adventure."

Rex didn't seem upset by the change. Of course, he had always been the steady one of their team—the elder statesman. He'd left puppyhood behind while he was still under a year old and now took everything right in stride.

Colby was less certain. He'd been born and lived his whole life in Maryland. College had been in Baltimore and his Secret Service training had been at the James J. Rowley Training Center just outside DC in Laurel. Other than the two three-month trips to FLETC—the Federal Law Enforcement Training Center in Georgia—he'd never been out of the state.

"About time we did a little adventuring, huh, boy? Stretch our legs? Maybe ride the big plane with the main man? Could be fun."

Rex appeared ready for it.

Colby glanced at the file Baxter had handed him.

No *way* was he ready for it. He didn't need to open the file; the label alone already told him too much about who he was reporting to.

Colby didn't turn to look at Baxter. He didn't need to see or hear him. Colby could *feel* the captain laughing his ass off.

CHAPTER THREE

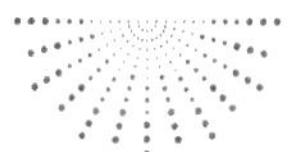

Major General Markham of the United States Air Force offered a "Welcome Aboard" greeting that Ivy quickly discovered was indistinguishable from a Drill Sergeant's first day briefing of new recruits, except with less yelling. He was concise, to the point, and he required one hundred and twenty seconds to impart his sage wisdom. Even appropriate "yes, sir" and "no, sir" comments were superfluous and she abandoned them inside the first fifteen seconds of the one-twenty.

Three minutes after entering the near silent White House Military Office, she was sitting at her desk—one cubical in a pod of four—and feeling a case of vertigo. Her head spun like she was the first-ever person through a starship's experimental transporter. One moment she'd been flying aboard an HMX-1 Sea King. The next wondering if this...*this* was what she'd been looking forward to?

Markham had made it clear that HMX-1 should do its job and not bother him because he was busy with "important" matters. The fact that she was female was a crime. The fact that the Marines had allowed her in was a travesty. The fact that she had served four tours flying forward combat with the most decorated and most blooded Marine Expeditionary Unit of the seven MEUs was irrelevant. She was in the White House now and was not to disturb him with such minor shit as Marine One—a job that should belong to the Air Force anyway as they were the ones who were supposed to do all the flying for the US military.

She'd barely managed to *not* point out that the Army, Navy, Marines, and Coast Guard had all fought hard with Congress to keep flying elements because the Air Force was such a pain in the ass to work with. The USAF was territorial, officious, and...

Ivy sighed.

And Markham was a prototypical two-star general in any service. Too old and passed over too many times to ever make three-star except as a retirement bump, which should have been done a decade ago no matter what the man's age was. He was old-school military, with no respect for anyone who'd come on board since the elder Bush's war to free Kuwait from Saddam.

There was a line of demarcation in the military. Oddly, it wasn't at the end of the Vietnam War—they'd all hit mandatory retirement by now and even fossils like Markham didn't go back that far. Rather it was at the start of Afghanistan and Iraq Wars in 2001. The earlier Desert Shield and Desert Storm conflicts had been traditionally fought battles for the most part. Fought with equipment not all that different from Vietnam—heavy bombers and massive troops with Special Ops mostly under the radar.

But in Afghanistan and Iraq, tanks and Humvees fell to cheap-ass, homemade IEDs, and it was up to the MRAP to change ground warfare. Marines and Special Ops stalked in where Army grunts used to stroll. The Air Force found no major military installations to bomb in those pitifully downtrodden nations. Helicopters had taken larger roles than jets, and air-to-air dogfights were a thing of the past because it was only a matter of a few minutes' work before neither country had any air force at all. The allies quickly achieved supreme command of the air—if you didn't count surface-to-air missiles— leaving the Air Force with too little to do. Few of the old-schoolers understood the fundamental changes, and officers like Markham denied the shift with every breath and action.

Ivy had never known anything else. She'd joined the Corps years after the jets flew into the Twin Towers and the Pentagon to light the fuse in Afghanistan. There, the Marines led the way with the unstoppable kind of force only they could bring. They also led the way on innovative technology like her MV-22B Osprey tilt-rotor aircraft. At long last, a full decade behind the Marines, the Air Force was finally getting serious about the best helicraft in the sky.

And HMX-1 was the best helicopter squadron flying anywhere. *That* was the reason they were entrusted with the President's life. The USAF's 1st Helicopter Squadron—who'd once shared the Presidential transport role with their even more ancient Hueys—had been given the boot decades ago. So long ago that only the Air Force even remembered it or kept mentioning it. She'd damn well make sure that HMX-1's reputation continued no matter what the director of the WHMO said or thought. She was going to ram the Marine Corps right down the throat of every stuck-in-the-mud, narrow-minded, misogynistic—

"Don't let the old man get to you."

Ivy flinched. Despite being a Marine, she actually flinched.

"Hi," a handsome blond man held out a hand as he sat in the chair across from hers.

She gave it a Pavlovian shake, still too jarred from her unexpected dismissal to respond normally.

"Major Steve Curnow. Air Force One liaison. Don't let the old man get to you. He doesn't micromanage unless you screw up."

"I'm a Marine."

"Which means when you screw up, you do it at full speed. Good. That's the way we like it here. Special Agent Tish Tolman, there to your right, is Motorcade and Secret Service liaison. McPhee is our traveling dog man, but he's out at Camp David with the First Family so we usually just ignore him. As long as the four of us keep our noses clean and get the President where he needs to go, Markham leaves us alone."

Ivy allowed her shoulders to sag with relief as she shook Tish's hand and it earned her a laugh from the other two. She didn't like ignoring a superior officer unless he was a superior asshole. Actually, they were the most dangerous to ignore as they typically took offence so easily.

Tish could be short for Morticia from *The Addams Family.* Her hair was straight and dark and her complexion fair enough that she'd burn instantly if ever exposed to the Maryland sunshine. The fact that she *wasn't* burnt told Ivy just how many hours this team spent at these desks. After nine years of working and flying more outdoors than in, she wasn't sure that she liked the sound of that.

Was it too late to approach General Arnson about dropping into the pilot's seat the next time one opened?

No challenge is too tough for a Marine. Not one of McKinnon's Laws, it was a Marine law, ground into her soul by the bootheel of nine years of service and a twenty-five-year Marine Corps mother.

Their four cubicles were all open toward a small table that would automatically be the center of any conversation. It was just a chair spin from her own desk to the team desk. There were a dozen pods like it crammed into the room. What she'd first taken for Markham-cowed silence, she could now hear was the soft buzz of professionals doing their jobs. That made her feel much better.

"So, what's on the boards?"

"Are you always all business?" Tish asked in a surprisingly high and sweet voice, making her seem gentle and soft. But she was Secret Service, so the soft part was probably only skin deep.

"I'm a Marine," Ivy repeated her earlier answer. It was a Marine Corps trademark: absolute focus and commitment to each and every task.

"Yep! She's a laugh a minute," a deep voice sounded behind her.

Ivy closed her eyes. She really didn't need this.

"Go away, Colby." She opened her eyes and looked straight into the deep brown gaze of Colby's German shepherd. His breath smelled like doggie treats. "I don't need you either."

The dog rested his muzzle on her knee, probably shedding a million hairs that would never come out of her dress uniform slacks.

"Apparently you do. Have they told you about McPhee yet?" Colby stepped into the small circle but did nothing to call off his dog.

"What about him?"

"His dog's retiring. So, he's going to get reassigned. I'm his replacement. Except he broke his ankle in a gopher hole—McPhee, not his dog—about an hour ago, so I'm your man ahead of schedule."

Exactly what she didn't need. "Can't he just get another dog?"

Colby sauntered over to the only open chair and dropped into it as if he was at a backyard picnic. He stretched his legs out far enough under the table that they were nearly touching hers. She was grateful for the thick-soled Oxford shoes that were part of a Marine's dress uniform as she kicked him in the shins. Only after she did so did it remind her of old times. He jolted but pulled in his feet only a few inches. Then he grinned just as goofily as his dog—who she'd started scratching between the ears without thinking, creating yet more dog hair.

"Minimum six months to train up a new animal. Besides, it doesn't work that way. One agent, one dog. In the entire history of the Secret Service dog teams, there've only been one or two times an agent got assigned a second dog. That's probably half the reason McPhee and Rusty hung on as long as they did."

He sounded so casual. He even looked casual, slouched in his chair with his fingers laced together and resting on his stomach. But she knew Colby Thompson, and while he might be fooling everyone else, maybe even himself, he wasn't fooling her for a second. Colby was only truly still when something was freaking him out.

She remembered Colby as a kid, when their families went to a restaurant together. He'd start by balancing a knife on his fork like a teeter-totter to find the center of balance. Then he'd stack on a spoon and have to reconfigure the balance points so that everything rocked on the back of the fork. Then he'd slowly spin test his assemblage. She used to wait until he almost had it, then subtly jar a table leg with her foot while innocently looking the other way. He never complained amidst the clattering collapse of his silverware arrangement, instead merely started over. He didn't fidget so much as tinker, but he was never truly still.

Except now.

Was it his presence here? Or hers?

"You know," he turned to Steve and lowered his voice confidentially, "when Major Hanson was younger she'd—"

This time she kicked him hard enough under the small table that he yelped. It was also enough of a jolt for Rex to lift his nose off her other knee and heave a sigh before moving to curl up at her feet. She brushed at her trousers, but the attempt was wholly ineffective. At least he didn't drool. So far. Tish reached back to her desk and tossed over a lint roller, which helped a little.

"As I was saying earlier... What's on the boards that I need to know about?"

Steve and Tish were smiling at each other. Neither of them had missed what had happened either. Maybe she'd lost some of her subtlety the day she became a Marine. Steve gave her the login to the scheduler for her tablet.

"Meeting at Camp David ends in two hours," Tish began rattling off from memory even as the information populated Ivy's screen. "Marine One scheduled back here in time for a lunch meeting with senior staff. Next travel is tomorrow morning, all fairly routine. A one-dayer. Landing at Cape Canaveral, Florida. An HMX out-and-back to the Gulf Coast Conference at a hotel in Orlando with Mexico, Cuba, and the five surrounding states' governors attending. Motorcade on the ground just in case. Then HMX back to Canaveral for a nighttime satellite launch. It's one that the President sponsored while he was still VP. Back in DC by two a.m. if all goes to plan. In our beds by three. Cut and dried, as much as these things ever are."

"Ouch!" Colby still hadn't eased up despite his whole casual act. "Not exactly a tourist timetable."

Thankfully, Steve laughed in his face, sparing her the need to.

Ivy couldn't believe this was happening. Cape Canaveral? Had she just died and gone to heaven? A shot at seeing an actual launch? She'd always promised herself that one day she'd make it down there for one…except she'd be stuck here at the White House.

"Looks like Rex and me are gonna be doing some runnin' about in some purty interestin' places."

Ivy considered kicking him again, just for vengeance. He'd always been the brains of the Reggie-and-Colby show and spoke perfect English when he cared to.

Rex had shifted without her noticing and was now asleep with his chin resting on his crossed paws—which were crossed on her shoe. Her right foot was tingling its way to falling asleep. She wiggled her toes, which earned her a happy sigh before Rex rolled his big head against her shin. Oh, fine! Now she'd have dog hair there as well.

It was unfair that Colby was going to get to see all of those things, and she wasn't. It was *her* dream, not his.

Except…

"What's after that?"

"Three days after we get back, there's a day trip up to Ottawa for trade talks with their prime minister. Then, the week following, we've got a France, Germany, UK round robin. It's fully scheduled, advance teams are already in place. Then quiet until Memorial Day, when we're scheduled for a trip to the First Lady's family farm in Tennessee —that one we have down. So, planning is good on at least that one for the moment."

"Perfect," Ivy wasn't above a tiny bit of subterfuge. "I'm going to take Marine One logistics local."

"Huh?" Steve and Tish looked at her in surprise.

"I've reviewed the last two years of operations reports and I want to try taking the liaison team on site for maximum efficiency. Our problem isn't data coordination back to this office. Once the trip has begun, our problems are out there in the field: communications delays, rapidly evolving scenarios that we don't have eyes on, and the like." She liked the way that sounded. Ivy almost believed it herself.

She checked in with her inner McKinnon while the others at the table exchanged puzzled expressions. Not a single McKinnon Law came up that she was violating. She might be stretching the *Trust your own impressions over everyone else's facts* law to her own purposes, but not by much. Besides, it *sounded* right—something she'd learned to trust.

"We'll set up a standard speed-dial conference number. Anyone hits it and our other three phones ring. Steve travels with Air Force One. Tish gets out there with her motorcade advance teams."

"Oh boy," Tish rubbed her hands together. "There's got to be better pickings out there in the world than here."

"Pickings?"

"Men," Tish looked at her as if she was a dunce. "Cute ones, like Colby. But there's no way he's going to look at me with you in the room."

Colby shrugged a "Maybe so."

"I'm with the helos," Ivy blocked anymore comments on such a stupid topic. There was no way that there was anything between them —ever! "And Colby is…" She wasn't sure where.

"I go in with the helos' transport. Jim Fischer and his dog Malcolm travel as part of the Motorcade, but McPhee was always on the helo advance team."

Ivy hadn't intended to force herself closer to Colby; farther away would be definitely preferable.

Treat your planning screwups like they're genius master strokes. Your instincts may be smarter than you are—lord knows I've done what little I can to train them. Besides, it saves you sounding like a damn fool when you try to unravel one. Great! Thanks, Sarge.

"Let's do it."

"You *are* a Marine!" Tish grinned at her. "I'll get us a speed-dial conference number," she headed over to the desk for the White House Communications Agency, another arm of the WHMO.

Ivy checked her master schedule.

"The advance helos for tomorrow's flight are shipping out this afternoon. Colby and I will hop a ride back on Marine One after it delivers the President." If a chance to take that flight again meant she had to travel with Colby, she'd even do that.

STEVE TURNED BACK to his desk and got on the phone setting up his own travel arrangements. It left just the two of them, and Ivy was bent over her tablet computer, clearly trying to ignore him.

"You just want to see a space launch," Colby guessed.

"Not so. It will offer me an eyes-on analysis of HMX-1 operational processes in the field." But a bit of a blush colored her cheeks and she was careful not to look up at him. She'd always been a crappy liar. Even her fibs as a kid had never flown. Well, they worked well enough on Reggie, but Colby had always been able to spot them.

"You were hyped on Star Trek reruns since you were two."

"I don't remember that far back," she kept her face down but Colby had the impression that she wasn't making much progress on reading her screen.

"I do. One of the best ways Reggie and I had of dumping you. You'd always be following us around—like that's what a pair of five-year-old secret agents wanted, a two-year-old brat chasing after them—unless we found you some television show or movie set in space. Didn't matter. *Star Trek, Star Wars,* one of those awful 1950s things. You loved them all."

"Colby!" Her voice was practically a hiss. "It's a good thing that your dog is sleeping on my feet or you'd get a busted kneecap and spend the next month in physical therapy."

"He's *what?*" Colby ducked down to look under the table. Sure enough, he wasn't just asleep on her feet. He looked like he was moving in to stay. "Well, that's weird."

"Why? Dogs like me. I'm likeable."

He wasn't going to comment on the second part of that. He was still having problems with the best-friend's-younger-sister-who's-really-a-pill memories that seemed to be bounding to the fore. It was far easier to recall her thrashing him in miniature golf or taking flash pictures at precisely the wrong moment of what was supposed to be his and Reggie's double date-first kiss with the Ivanov sisters. It was harder to remember from moment to moment that she was a Marine sitting in the White House West Wing. With his dog asleep on her foot.

He looked again, but Rex absolutely was.

"He's not generally a big fan of women."

"Maybe it has to do with the *kind* of women you bring home."

He just raised an eyebrow at her.

"That wasn't an offer, Thompson."

"Yes, ma'am." He wanted to snicker, but it seemed to get caught in his throat. So he saluted her instead.

"Will you just go get ready? We're out of here on Marine One at 1230 hours sharp. Go away! I have work to do."

He clambered to his feet, but had to nudge Rex awake with his boot to get him moving. Not even a pat from Ivy, though Rex was looking for it. One thing he had to say for Ivy, she didn't offer either of them any encouragement.

"YOUR SISTER'S HERE." Colby leaned against the doorway into the White House Kitchen.

"Uh-huh." Reggie was sprinkling herbs he'd just minced into a giant soup pot as if one shred more or less was going to make or break the soup.

Colby had parked Rex in the small Secret Service office in the basement of the Residence and then ducked around the corner to harass Reggie while he mooched a meal. He'd done it so often that even Chef Klaus, the executive chef, did little more than offer his customary Teutonic scowl at Colby's arrival. Colby was careful to always throw a five or ten into the jar to cover food costs—Reggie had lectured him the first time about taxpayer costs, even on leftovers, and Colby had never forgotten.

The White House kitchen was in full swing, but just for a luncheon so there were only four chefs working at the moment. A knife hammered against a cutting board, mincing garlic faster than his FN P90 submachine gun on full auto. There was a sharp sizzle of bacon on the griddle that made Colby's stomach growl—he'd have to snitch a piece for Rex or he'd never be forgiven. A rattle of plates being stacked on the warming shelf as someone else hustled by on their way into the produce fridge. Overall pretty quiet. If it was a state dinner, he wouldn't go near the place.

"Ivy looks hot in her dress blues." Colby wasn't quite sure how he'd ended up here on such a crazy morning, but he had a free half hour and no longer had a patrol duty to fill it with.

He'd gone to his truck in the Secret Service HQ garage and snagged his emergency go-bag. Then he'd tracked down Linda and Thor, her scraggle-haired mutt with one of the best noses in the business, to discuss her taking over the Lead Dog role at the White House. Linda had been a little startled—apparently Baxter hadn't warned her. Typical.

Linda was still new enough that he had to explain that was Baxter's idea of a rip-roaring, hilarious joke. Thor had been fine with it though. Colby had given her access to all his files on the dog teams and then felt lost and at loose ends. Until it was time to go, there was nothing more for him to do.

So he and Linda had walked and talked their way to the White House Chocolate Shop, which was run by her husband. The Chocolate Shop was about twenty feet from the kitchen so Colby had dropped in on Reggie.

"Ivy's really grown up. She's changed a lot." More than he'd ever imagined possible. Yet in other ways, she was still that same driven girl he'd always known.

"Uh-huh." Reggie's attention had moved from his soup to cutting up a loaf of sourdough bread, totally missing that Colby had just said his little sister was hot. Which she was, but he wasn't going to actually think about.

"I've decided to marry her."

"Uh-huh." Reggie stacked the slices neatly in a lavender-colored glass serving bowl so that it looked more like a flower arrangement than food.

"We're going to name all of our kids after you."

"Sure."

"Even the girls."

"Fine. Wait… What?" Reggie blinked at him in surprise.

Colby did his best to keep a straight face.

"Ivy's here?" Reggie looked around the kitchen as if he expected his little sister to pop out of a cabinet the way she used to when she was trying to scare them. It had never bothered Reggie, but Colby had jumped every time. She'd loved that. The time she'd jumped out of the refrigerator when he'd been after a soda had almost given him a heart attack. Only belatedly had he noticed all of the shelving and contents neatly stacked off to the side. She wasn't above elaborate preparations for her traps—she'd been wearing long johns and a parka while she waited. He'd also spotted a book because Ivy never just stopped. He'd never again opened a refrigerator without first checking for the slightly open door providing an airgap.

Colby put on his best smirk for Reggie.

"Oh right. She starts today." And just that fast, Reggie was gone back to his lunch prep.

Colby should know better than to bait his best friend when he was cooking. They'd cooked together a lot growing up, but for Reggie it had always been a thing. For Colby it had been an excuse to hang out with his friend and eat amazing food.

"You're getting married, huh?" Reggie was often tuned in, even when he was tuned out. "How did she take the news?"

"Like the trooper she is."

"She's not a trooper, she's a Marine. And you'd be all black-and-blue if you'd tried suggesting anything as stupid as marriage because she'd have kicked your ass."

"I've got grass stains on my knees," he went for pity points. Except, he'd kept a fresh pair of pants in his go-bag, so there was nothing to show.

No deal. Reggie didn't spare him a glance anyway. "Let me guess, you tripped over Rex and did a face plant."

Even best friends weren't supposed to know things like that.

"So, what are you really doing here midday?"

"Grade bump. At least I think it is. Presidential travel detail."

That actually got Reggie's full attention. "Hey, Colby, that's great."

"Hope so." A pinch between his shoulder blades made him shrug.

"Seriously! Don't you get it? Lead Dog at the White House is great and you earned that. But you just got bumped to the Presidential Protection Detail. That's huge."

Colby hadn't thought of it that way. Did that mean he now reported to Harvey Lieber, the head of the PPD, rather than Baxter? Was he supposed to trade in his slacks and jacket for a black suit? The captain hadn't said anything about that.

"You always were the slow one of the team."

"As if you're such a genius. Your little sister's sharper than you."

"Ivy's sharper than both of us put together."

Right next to the no-touch rule for little sisters was the always-agree-that-they're-exceptional rule. Of course, in Ivy's case, that was easy because she absolutely was.

Reggie had cut some more bread and was throwing together a massive BLT sandwich.

"Better make a pair of those. Ivy and I fly out together in about fifteen minutes."

Reggie's hands froze halfway through slicing a tomato. Then he very slowly looked up at Colby. "You *and* Ivy?"

"Uh-huh," he did his best to echo Reggie's earlier distracted tone.

"You and Ivy." Somehow the paired sandwiches had tipped Reggie's internal alarms where a tease about marriage hadn't. He'd always been a food guy. Colby remembered having to explain how girls flirted—in foodie terms—for Reggie to get it.

She's not going to offer you the main course of steak unless you go through the minestrone soup first. And you're not going to get the minestrone kiss without some major antipasti. Before that, you've got to have hors d'oeuvres to convince her she even sits at the table with you.

Explained that way, Reggie's success rate had risen, as had Colby's. Though the Ivanov sisters had ultimately slipped away unkissed.

"As part of the bump, I got assigned to the White House Military Office. We're headed out for a couple days. Together." He did his best to drop the last word suggestively, but he could feel his voice shift strangely. He and Ivy together for a mission. Two days was more than he'd seen her in the last five years.

In silence, Reggie finished the two sandwiches and wrapped a napkin around a few extra bacon slices for Rex. Colby would have been happier if Reggie was groaning or slinging some shit back at him. Instead he handed over the wrapped sandwiches with a look that said one thing very clearly: *You go there and I'll kill your ass.*

Colby shrugged like: *as if that could ever happen.* Besides, Secret Service training versus chef training, he wasn't worried. Though Reggie did have access to some seriously sharp knives.

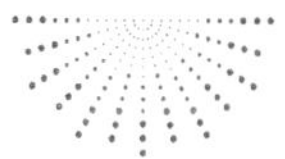

"What's in the bag?"

"What's it worth to you?"

"Rude," Ivy commented with no heat. She stood in the West Wing Colonnade and had been watching the sky even though it was still too early for the Marine One flight returning the President from Camp David. This time the Press Corps had piled out of the West Wing and were ganged up along the rope line.

But now she was looking up into Colby's dark eyes…and would rather she wasn't. He was very hard to look away from. He was so unexpected that she—

"Hold it, would you?" Colby handed her the bag, dropped his satchel at her feet, then stepped away to join a female dog handler who had just walked past.

Ivy watched as they walked together along the rope line that kept the press gaggle at bay. Several of the reporters greeted Colby and Rex, though none reached out to pet the dog as he sniffed them. She could hear the greetings for the other agent and dog as well: Linda and Thor.

Ivy watched as Colby instructed Linda on the proper search pattern, starting at the West Wing doors and working their way down to the landing area. There was a kindness that surprised her. Not that Colby was an unkind man. But it was easy to see the calming effect his instruction had on his teammate. They finished their patrol just as the groundskeepers rolled out the aluminum disks for this afternoon's flight. Introductions all around: friends with the groundskeepers.

That had always been Colby's trademark: Mr. Easygoing. In high school, the girls had flocked to him. Not because he'd been anything special in those years, but because he'd been friendly and kind. He'd always been attractive, really attractive, and he'd always known it, which was a major turnoff to her. Except, where it had once been the only card he had to play—and why not? It had worked on flocks of high school girls—he didn't seem to be using it anymore.

He escorted Linda to a position that would be between the helo and the fence, gave a final instruction, then shook hands with her before striding back across the lawn toward her. The tall man and his huge shepherd walking across the White House lawn as if they belonged. It was a walk worthy of a Marine.

Walk any turf as if you own it. That places fear in the enemy's heart, especially if you do it on their home soil.

Colby followed McKinnon's Laws instinctively, without any training by the Corps.

She remembered the bag she was holding and looked inside so that she wasn't watching Colby as he returned to her side. Two sandwiches. She hadn't even thought about food. A Marine Corps major having a major blood sugar crash on her first day would not be a good thing. Her flight suit had a small pocket that she always kept stocked with energy bars. She hadn't even thought about needing to do that in her dress blues even if there was a place. Her metabolism didn't have a lot of leeway and Colby had remembered that about her. She hadn't even been aware that he knew that.

Colby arrived and reached into the bag without ceremony. He snagged one of the sandwiches and a folded paper towel. He unwrapped several slices of bacon for Rex, then bit down on his own sandwich. "Damn, your brother even makes a sandwich something special."

"You saw Reggie."

He glanced up at the roof of the West Wing and nodded—more to himself than to her. "Better eat fast."

She pulled out her own and bit into it. BLT with avocado and the special mayo spread that he'd invented just for her. "A little chili for zing because it's so you, slivers of tarragon for your sweet heart—" a *so* big-brother-got-it-wrong detail (more than one boyfriend had labeled her heart as pure steel...with wire barbs) "—and a touch of lemon juice for the sunshine you bring." It was sufficiently the taste of home that it almost brought tears to her eyes.

"Sure I saw him. Told him we were getting married."

"How did he take it?" Colby wasn't the only one who could deliver a straight line.

"He thought it was a little odd that I wanted to name all our kids Reggie, but other than that he was cool with it." Colby's voice always gave him away. He'd tried to make a joke and Reggie hadn't been amused. Her brother was always so serious. It had definitely made Reggie and Colby an odd pair growing up.

"Works for me."

Colby choked on his sandwich.

Whereas having an older brother and Colby to practice on, she'd learned to never give away anything she was feeling.

They finished the sandwiches just as the White Tops flew into view beyond the Washington Monument. Three Sea Kings in a shifting group—even *she* couldn't pick out which was Marine One at the moment—and a pair of heavily armed Black Hawks flying overwatch patrol. Those were the pitch black helos of the 160th SOAR Night Stalkers who were best known for being lethal, even by Marine standards.

"Though maybe we should name the dog Reggie instead of our kids," she continued as much to distract herself as anything else. Her nerves were attempting to rematerialize. "Wouldn't want my brother getting a swelled head, thinking he was important or something."

She could feel Colby's shock take another hit.

This was even better than jumping out of cabinets to get a reaction out of him.

His joke had died twice now and Colby didn't know what to do with it.

Reggie had taken it seriously, when he was supposed to laugh.

And Ivy, its real target, hadn't reacted at all. Instead she'd talked about what they should name their dog as if she already had pictured their whole life together.

Did he even know her?

He considered asking her what she was actually thinking or feeling…but he decided that he didn't need that kind of joke backfiring on him a third time. And what if suddenly it wasn't a joke? He definitely couldn't deal with that.

He stuffed the empty sandwich bag into his gear while the President, his entourage, and the press did their dance and cleared off. Then they left the shade of the big magnolia and headed down to the helo. Once aboard, he dropped into the first seat and suddenly the Marine crew chief was glaring at him.

"What?"

The Marine's scowl grew darker.

Ivy sat in the armchair opposite him, but her smile was wicked.

Now what?

"You might want to look at the seat back you're sitting against so casually."

He leaned forward enough to turn and look. There, like a target at the middle of his back, was the Presidential Seal woven right into the fabric.

"Holy shit!" He jolted out of the seat, stumbled over Rex, who had laid down in the aisle, and plummeted onto the bench seat on the other side of the aircraft as the helo lifted.

Ivy burst out laughing.

The lethal-looking Marine Corps crew chief did not. Colby had clearly desecrated a holy sanctuary.

"Give him a break, Sergeant McShea. He's merely Secret Service; he can't help screwing up."

And Baxter had told him not to embarrass the service. Not much luck so far.

Rex looked at him as if to say to get his act together, then settled into his standard helicopter mode—naptime.

"Fine. Do that. I won't tell you that it's only a three-minute flight."

Ivy patted Rex's head and he sighed happily. "I think that renaming him Reggie isn't very fair to such a nice dog."

Between Rex's size and typical unrelenting drive, most of Colby's past girlfriends had been afraid of the German shepherd. Not Ivy, of course. She'd never been afraid of anything.

Ivy Hanson. A dog. Kids. It was a crazy image, but that didn't mean he hated it either. Maybe that was the problem. It was surprisingly easy to imagine waking up next to her—which was not where his thoughts about women typically started. His imagination was far more about the lying down together part. He'd found his share of attractive women over the years, but—

Hold on a sec!

Now he was thinking of Ivy as an attractive woman?

Not just pretty or good-looking, but actually attractive? Literally? Like he was attracted to her? That was so strange that—

The helicopter began descending rapidly. He glanced out the window. They were flying low enough over a golf course that he could easily read the flag numbers on the greens as they flapped in the wind off the rotor. *Crap!* He'd just missed his one-time-ever chance to see the White House takeoff from the other perspective.

But it wasn't the image of the South Lawn that stuck in his mind. It was the image of Ivy lying down next to him that was occupying his thoughts. Of course, he'd never be stupid enough to suggest such a thing seriously. Because Reggie had been right, Ivy would kill him if she found out.

As he watched out the window, he saw a blur flash close by the window. Like a giant bird. Or a tiny F-14 Tomcat fighter jet.

It seemed impossibly close, yet looked as if it was far away to be so small. Before he could make sense of it, there was a loud crunch like a pure steel gull hitting the side of the helicopter.

He was about to ask Ivy if everything was okay when the helo lurched sideways.

An ear-shattering scream pierced even the presidential sound insulation!

That definitely wasn't normal.

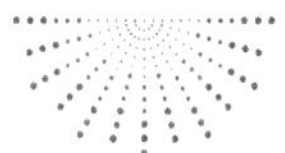

*I*vy knew the motion the instant they entered the sideslip. An engine's cry was bad news, but an auto-rotation landing could always be achieved.

This wasn't an engine failure sound.

The sideslip was the loss of the tail rotor followed by the rending steel of the transfer shaft blowing through its bearings. They weren't going to be landing under any sort of control.

"Buckle up! We're going down."

They tightened their seatbelts in unison yanks.

She tried to figure out what she could do for Rex when Colby scooped the big dog into his lap and clamped his arms around the German shepherd. Despite his size, he'd picked Rex up as if he weighed nothing.

It was crazy at this moment, but it was a visceral reaction—a body memory of how solidly he had held her as they fell on the South Lawn. Of his strength and power in ways that she'd never experienced in a man before. The fact that it came from Colby Thompson wasn't something she had time to consider at the moment.

Colby looked right at her, but didn't say a thing. Good man, the

Marine in her thought. No scream. No questions she couldn't answer. No panic.

She glanced out the window and was impressed at his lack of panic, because she could feel her own adrenaline kicking into high gear as the breath choked in her throat.

Without the rear tail rotor to counteract the spin, the helicopter had begun a death spiral. The rotors turning one way and the helicopter itself forced to rotate in the other. Normally the tail rotor pushed the tail sideways against the engine-induced spin to hold the helo in straight-line flight. Not anymore.

Flashes of the golf course.

Anacostia Air Base so close, but completely out of reach.

The blue slash of the Potomac.

The trees between the golf course and the park at the south tip of the island.

A radio call by the pilot, "Marine 173 going down, south end Haines Point." His voice calm and clear, but he didn't waste time repeating the call. Other than that, he and the copilot fought the controls in silence. The crew chief braced himself and kept his silence as well, knowing their fate was out of his hands.

The Air Base.

Blue water.

Because the pilot had been flying so low over the golf course, they were below fifty feet when the failure had occurred. It had sounded like a bird strike. Out of the death zone. The death zone for a helicopter started at fifty feet and ended at four hundred. Below fifty, you mostly fell out of the sky. Above four hundred, you could set up an autorotation (unless you lost your tail rotor), and have some choice in where you came down. Even without the tail rotor there were some things that could be done with enough altitude.

In the death zone…

Well, it was aptly named and she was glad to not be in it.

Didn't mean this wasn't going to hurt.

Ivy's body instinctively strained against the controls—controls that she didn't have. Her left foot jammed into the plush carpet, just in case some bit of the tail rotor still existed. She rocked her non-existent cyclic to the right in hopes of using the airframe's body angle to some advantage against the increasing spin.

She looked up and saw Colby clutching Rex to his chest.

But he was watching her.

As if he wanted to say something.

As if he didn't know what to say.

Maybe he—

They slammed in.

Momentum heaved her against her seatbelt.

Her hands, clutched to the seat arms, were torn loose as the helo flopped about like a dying fish.

Colby twisted, taking the brunt of the hit for his dog, just as he had for her forever ago on the South Lawn.

Rex knocked the air out of Colby's chest just as effectively as Ivy had earlier. Only this time it was much less fun. He couldn't even make a small *whoop* noise as the helo tumbled through a full roll.

He held Rex tightly so that he didn't drop his dog down onto Ivy as she was momentarily directly below him. Then struggling not to drop him on the ceiling as they both dangled from his seatbelt. Finally he crashed onto his back with eighty-plus pounds of dog flopping into his chest.

Struggling dog.

Wet dog!

Water poured into the cabin and in moments he was not only breathless, he was also underwater.

Rex kicked free, landing a few final injustices on Colby's body that might have made him scream if he'd had any air and not been underwater.

Finding his seatbelt, he struggled free and popped to the surface, banging his head on the helicopter's entry door as the helo now lay on its side.

He managed a small *whoop* for air just as Ivy surfaced inches from him.

Some joke about how good the wet look was on her, darkening her sun-bright hair to a rich gold, didn't have the air to be voiced. It had always been a good look on her when their families went to the beach —something he'd definitely looked forward to each summer.

Then a large wet muzzle surfaced between them, driving them apart.

Colby grabbed Rex again to protect them both from the dog's swimming feet. His paws were big enough that it was surprising he wasn't walking on the water, not that there was much room as the cabin kept filling with water.

Ivy popped the latch on the door and pushed it up.

No more water poured in—though small waves slopped in over the edges filling in the last of their air gap. The door was up in the air or she wouldn't have been able to swing it open against the water pressure. He managed to get his feet on the edge of the bench seat below, but by the way Ivy kept kicking his shins, she was treading water.

They stuck their heads out.

The helo lay on its side in the Potomac shallows off the south point of the island. Water lapped around them.

He gave Rex a heave up and out. After a brief scrabbling of claws on metal, he was gone with a splash that sloshed water back over his and Ivy's heads in a wave.

"Thanks," Ivy sputtered out a mouthful of Rex-flavored river water and glared at him.

"Aim. To. Please," he managed to gasp out on three micro-breaths. Then he reached out underwater, wrapped his hands around her waist, and heaved her upward as well. His hands could practically wrap all of the way around her waist. So trim, yet so brilliantly fierce. He'd always enjoyed that contrast in her.

He managed to place her high enough that she was able to sit on the edge of the doorframe. Unable to resist, he grabbed her by the ankles and flipped her off the helicopter and into the river.

She flopped back-first into the water and sloshed her own wave into his face just as the crew chief surfaced beside him.

"Pilots are clear, out the front windshield," Sergeant McShea announced with a sputter.

They shared a nod, then boosted themselves up and out of the helicopter together.

Their door was about all that showed above the choppy water. Just that and a single rotor blade sticking straight up—giving the world a twisted, twenty-foot middle finger for dumping it into the Potomac.

The beach lay fifty feet away and a crowd was already gathering.

Rex had reached the shore and was keeping the crowd back by shaking off great clouds of cold water. Ivy hung on to one of the wheels that dangled just below the surface and offered a smile at seeing the two of them emerge safely.

This time, Ivy *was* unleashing that big smile of hers in his direction and it felt damn good. As if he'd never done anything so right as being alive at this moment.

"Apparently they all think," he nodded toward the shore, "that a crashing helicopter is somehow unusual in these parts."

"A crashing HMX-1 helo is unusual. It has *never* happened before in our entire history." And that big smile of hers switched off. He was gonna miss that unless it came back for a spell. Colby decided that he was good with working on that.

He and McShea slid down into the water together, just as the pilots swam around from the other side of the aircraft. One had a bloody nose, the other was grimacing and appeared to be swimming one handed, but they'd all survived.

"Nothing like a minor miracle on a Monday morning," the crew chief revealed a sense of humor that Colby somewhat suspected was unbefitting a Marine. Colby chuckled to promote his bad behavior.

"Miracles? I always blame those on Saint Ives," Colby called out as they swam ashore together.

"Saint Ives?" The bloody-nosed pilot burst out laughing—which was cut short when he swallowed a mouthful of the Potomac. No question, that nickname would be traveling around.

"Colby!" He could hear Ivy's teeth grinding.

Very near the shore, they plowed into a raft of duckweed. In moments, their every surface was covered in the tiny tri-petal plants until they looked like they'd caught alien-green measles or something. Getting their feet down in the shallows, they waded the rest of the way to shore, raking handfuls of plants off their faces, hands, and clothes. At least they weren't slimy, merely infinite in number.

He reached over and hauled handfuls of the water weeds out of Ivy's hair, then wished he hadn't. A man only got to handle a woman's wet hair if they showered together. It was a shockingly intimate feeling—until she slapped his hands away hard enough to sting.

The one-armed pilot had a broken wrist, but they were all alive. As one, they clambered across the steel railing that the helo had flattened in its death roll and sat on the grassy bank facing the one-bladed protest of the otherwise submerged aircraft. A weekday morning crowd of thirty or so people kept a respectful distance.

The other two helicopters in the flight had been in the lead when theirs went down. One continued to base, but the other circled back and was descending to land on the lawn above the beach. The crowd was brushed back even farther as the five of them huddled to keep their backs to the blast of rotor-driven wind and grit. Rex ducked low in their wind shadow and closed his eyes.

As soon as the helo was down and the blast abated, Rex rose to his feet in front of them. He gave another shake, finding yet more water in his thick coat to spray in all of their faces. It was mixed with gritty sand and a jillion more tiny duckweed leaves.

A chorus of complaints sounded.

"Hey, you can't get any wetter."

As if to prove him wrong, Rex walked into his arms, licked him in the face, then gave himself a final shake.

At least, because this time Colby was hugging Rex's head, most of the spray went sideways—into Ivy's face.

"Good boy," he whispered in Rex's ear.

CHAPTER SIX

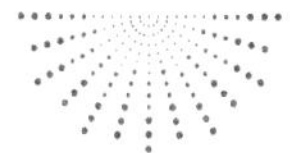

"Turnabout is fair play," she warned Colby as they stepped off the Sea King helicopter that had fetched them across the narrow Washington Channel to Anacostia.

She was wet, dirty, had lost her cover, and could only hope that the dry cleaner could deal with the damage done to her uniform—dress blues were hideously expensive. Her return to Joint Base Anacostia-Bolling was far more ignominious than she'd imagined possible. For over seventy years, HMX-1 had never had a flight failure or other accident. They had the best service record in the world—and she'd been on the flight that had just ruined it with their plunge into the Potomac. Forever after, from this moment on, the Marines Corps would always have to say, "Zero mission failures…except this one time when the new White House Military Office liaison was aboard and—"

"What do you mean: turnabout is fair play?" She'd forgotten about Colby and Rex as they stood close beside her.

"Meaning, if you leave my side, someone actually *may* shoot you."

"After being knocked out of the sky, I'm not in much of a mood to be shot. Guess I'm glued to your hip." He offered her one of his teasing smiles. Two could play that game.

"Good thing we aren't getting married or I might read something into that." As she turned away, she caught an odd expression on Colby's face. But by the time she turned back it was gone and the cocky dog handler was once more in place. Now it was *her* mind that was playing tricks on her.

"What's your clearance?"

"I'm Lead Dog, or I was," his face fell at that.

Surprise. Surprise. Colby Thompson had actual feelings. She almost ribbed him about it, but couldn't get past the sad face.

"Which means what?"

"It's not an official title, but it still has a lot of meaning inside the team. I was head dog handler on the White House grounds. They didn't work for me, but if they had a problem, they came to me first and it was my job to solve it before it hit the Captain's desk."

"Which tells me nothing about your clearance."

He flicked his badge at her, which had somehow survived the crash and their swim on its lanyard. "I've got armed proximity to the President status, just like you. Anything that isn't code-word classified or eyes-only I have full access to, if I was dumb enough to want to read any of that crap."

She had to respect that. It took over a year to get that clearance as she well knew; *if* you could get that clearance. Now that she thought of it, she remembered the FBI interviewing her about Colby some years ago in her role as friend (yeah, right) and neighbor (not by choice). It had taken all the kindness she could muster at the time to not shout "Hell no! Not him!", figuring someone else they interviewed would take care of that. Apparently no one had and he'd made it in.

Ivy didn't like being wrong, but looking up at the man beside her made it difficult to argue. If it was anyone other than Colby, she'd be respecting the hell out of him at the moment.

Had he been interviewed when she'd earned her clearance? Probably. She decided not to ask what he'd said. And definitely not what he thought about saying but hadn't.

They weren't authorized to move away from the Sea King, so she kept them standing out under the midday sun as they dripped.

Even soaking wet, one didn't just unbutton a dress jacket. You wore it or you went and changed. *Spit and polish all the way down to your soul.*

"HMX-1 has a split personality." Ivy spoke up to fill the weird silence between them. Besides, split personality was the best way to describe what newbies were walking into here.

"Like you and your big brother?"

"Hey, he's your best friend. I'm only related to him because we accidentally have the same parents."

"Yeah. That and he'd kill someone with one of his chef's knives if they even looked at you funny."

She glanced at Colby but he didn't seem to be joking. "Really?"

Colby just scoffed at her. "I made that joke about naming our kids after him and almost got a ten-inch Wüsthof up my nose."

"Huh." Reggie had never seemed like the protective type. More like the quiet, overly-serious chef, leave-me-alone type. Yet he'd always hung with Colby, which had never made sense to her in either direction, even if it had to them.

Colby and Rex were looking around the airfield. Rex shook himself again, but was thankfully out of water to shed.

"This used to be a big airport back in the day," she explained. "The runways and hangars have all been filled in with office buildings now, except for this one hanger and the helo landing area." Six helicopter-sized squares bordered in yellow-and-brown lines were painted on the bare concrete. All of them empty except for the bird that had just ferried them onto the base. Even now, a team was prepping it to tuck away into the hangar.

"You have your own dog team," Colby was watching the team that first went through their rescue helicopter. "Guess they want to make sure I didn't smuggle any explosives or bacon aboard on the thirty-second ride over from Hains Point beach."

"Don't even joke about explosives around here."

Then they came over to inspect him. Rex took one sniff of the new dog and turned his head away.

"What was that?"

"Dogs have always confused Rex. He thinks he's human and is never sure what to do about lower life forms except to ignore them."

The Marine's dog sniffed Colby with no interest at all before moving off.

Now that they'd been cleared, she led him toward the hangar.

"Split personality," he reminded her.

"Right. Three bases, two classes of birds, two birds in each class. We keep White Tops based here for fast access to the White House, a few more over at Andrews, but our main installation is forty miles downriver at Quantico."

"Three airfields. Check. And you guys own the landing pad on the South Lawn since you chased away the Army and Air Force back in the '70s. That makes four."

"Okay, four."

"Except that we at the Secret Service only set it up for you temporarily. Then we take it away and roll it into storage. So we're the ones who control whether you have four or three."

"Shut up, Colby."

"Yes, ma'am."

She'd never really noticed what a great smile he had. Had he always? She tried to remember, but that all seemed so long ago.

They stepped through the open hangar door into the cool shade. Eight helicopters were stowed there. The tech team was fussing over the engine of one. Two others were being waxed. When she needed to check her uniform, she could see her reflection in the shine of any HMX-1 helicopter—except the one now crashed into the river. Despite that, at the moment she strongly suspected that she'd be smiling and didn't want to be caught doing that by Colby Thompson. Bantering with Colby had always been fun.

"White Side and Green Side," she focused once more on her introduction as she headed to a supplies shelf to find Colby some spare clothes. Size Marine large to span his chest and height.

"Couldn't you just call that top and bottom of the helo? Why do you paint the helos two colors anyway?"

Ivy considered picking up a handy crescent wrench and going after him with that instead.

COLBY LOVED MESSING with Ivy's brain. He'd done it a thousand times growing up. She was just as focused and almost as serious as her older brother, which had made her an easy target. Reggie just shrugged off Colby's best digs like a duck and rainwater, but Ivy's revenge was always charmingly devious.

When Ivy had been trying to learn her single-digit addition and subtraction, he'd asked her what was "two minus three." That had shut her up for a good long time. Later he'd asked her, "Why does swimming have a double m, but dancing only has one c?" And a myriad of other traps that he'd learned first by being three years older. Though in later years, she'd pulled ahead of him and he'd had to get more creative—like picking her up over his head and throwing her into the ocean right after she'd stretched out to sunbathe on the beach. Which he'd had to leave off doing as her martial arts skills had improved.

Of course he knew that the two colors of the helo wasn't what she'd meant about White Side and Green Side, but he wasn't going to tell her that.

Ivy skipped the teeth grind and went straight to malevolent glare just as he'd hoped.

And his would be a reasonable assumption to anyone who didn't know better. Each of the helos was painted a glossy forest green except for the very tops, which were painted a white that reflected the errant sunlight beam coming in one of the high windows so strongly he was surprised that the crews didn't wear sunglasses to work on that aircraft.

"White Side," her voice sounded as narrow as her glare, "are the White Tops for transporting the President and other heads of state. Top secret clearance, with presidential special access or better, is required to even enter this hangar. We have a desperate time getting pilots and service personal because of how long it takes to obtain that level of clearance. Green Side are the civilian transport aircraft—which are painted all green. Here we're White Side only. At Quantico, there's a patrolled security gate between the two. They can't even hand a part or a tool across the line because it might have been tampered with."

Colby felt a bit of a chill and it wasn't just because his soaking wet clothes were now cooling rapidly in the hangar's shadowed interior. He wished he was standing back in the sunlight. It was a given that these guys were serious, but now maybe he understood the reaction of the crew chief at him even sitting for a moment in the President's seat.

"White Side flies the Sea King and a modified Black Hawk called a White Hawk. We're replacing the Sea Kings with VH-92 Superhawks, but those are still in testing for another few years. Green Side flies MV-22B Ospreys for missions like transporting the Press Corps and senior staff. They just retired the other aircraft."

"Which makes it two sides, but one of them has three aircraft and the other only has one. Doesn't seem very fair to me."

"Shut up, Colby. This new anal side of you isn't charming."

"I'm completely charming. Just ask me."

Ivy didn't take the bait. Instead, she punched a finger at the floor close by a bathroom. "You. Sit. Stay."

Rex's look said, *She's talking to you, buddy. I've already got my butt on the floor.* He'd sat down as soon as they'd come to a stop. Colby didn't sit, but he did stay.

Two minutes later a woman walked out of the bathroom and Colby almost didn't recognize her.

The wind-up-doll perfect Marine Corps major in her dress blues was gone. The white cover—as Marines insisted on calling their hats (which was probably now at the bottom of the Potomac or flowing out to sea)—was now a Marine-green garrison cap with its little ridgeline running front to back. Shoes to boots, trousers to camo pants, and the dress jacket with all of its ornamentation was now a USMC drab green t-shirt that clung tightly enough to show a perfect outline of her sports bra. In addition to her earlier sidearm, she now wore a KA-BAR knife almost as long as the thigh it was strapped to. A camo jacket hung loose off her shoulders, which also bore a small pack. If not for the wet dress blues in a plastic bag, he might have thought she'd done one of her parallel-world alternate-self things.

Protocol perfection had switched over to down and didn't-mind-getting-dirty Marine.

"Well, that's a relief," he told her.

"What?"

"*This* Ivy Hanson I recognize."

"Is this gonna be some crap about the past?" She waved him toward the bathroom to change.

"Absolutely!" Then, instead of explaining, he handed her Rex's leash and went to change. It was easy to see the parallels between Ivy and the squadron she flew with—lovely but hard.

"So what are you on about this time, Colby? What's this old crap you want to dredge up now?" She shouted through the door.

"Well," he considered and decided what the hell, she could only kill him once. And if she busted in on him now, he'd be naked and who knew what interesting places that might lead. "Now that you're dressed to get some work or ass-kicking done, just seems more like you."

"I can kick your ass just fine in my dress uniform."

"Don't doubt it. But your dress uniform is so goddamn impressive that it distracts from the amazingly beautiful woman wearing it. Your working gear lets me see you clear as day."

For once, she had no snappy comeback to that. Maybe he should try telling her the truth more often. Though he wished the door wasn't separating them so that he could see her stone silent reaction.

THE FOUR OF them stood in a line on the tarmac of the HMX landing field at Anacostia: her, Colby, Rex, and General Edward Arnson—commander of HMX-1.

"Well, that's not something you see every day," the general's tone was certainly drier than she was, despite a change of clothes and two hours listening in on the debrief of the pilots.

One of the VH-60N White Hawks hovered above Anacostia. At the lower end of the cargo line, it dangled the battered Sea King helicopter it had just fished out of the Potomac.

"There goes our perfect no-accident record," Ivy couldn't believe that she'd been on the flight that had destroyed a seventy-year Marine Corps tradition.

"Don't blame it on the Marines. Blame it on whoever was flying the F-14."

She turned to Colby, as did the general. He clearly didn't know what Colby was talking about either.

"It was odd." He cocked his head much the way his dog would as he studied the descending helo—the helo they could have so easily died in.

They all kept a respectful silence as it came to rest on it wheels not twenty meters away. Within seconds, the lines to the hovering White Hawk were released and a phalanx of mechanics moved in to see what had happened.

"Just before the impact—" Colby resumed.

"What impact?" She didn't remember any impact, just something broke with a bang followed by an awful rending sound as the rear rotor ate itself.

"The F-14."

"Colby! What are you talking about?"

"Well, that's what I'm trying to tell you."

"Could you do it in a less of your typically laconic manner?"

"Could, if you'd hush up some."

She could see General Arnson on the other side, grinning down at her. He wasn't much given to grinning in her experience. She bit down on her tongue—hard—to make sure she kept her silence. It wasn't an easy thing to do around Colby. Something in him just made her want to keep poking at it to see what hid underneath.

"Just before we went down, I spotted an F-14 coming in fast from," he hesitated and looked across the Washington Channel and the Anacostia River to where the helo had plunged into the river not a quarter mile away. "It came from our back quarter, out of the northwest."

"I couldn't have missed an F-14," Ivy's tongue ached from her hard-clamped teeth as she released it and blood flow resumed, reminding her why she'd been clamping down on it in the first place.

"You must be mistaken, son. I'd have noticed an F-14 in the corridor. It would have shaken us hard flying that low. I was standing in the hangar when you went down." He nodded over to the big building behind them, which would have a clear view of the accident. "First I heard of it was a shout from Jake that something was wrong with the approach. Saw you spin in. There's no way to miss an F-14. Besides, the military retired the last of those over a decade ago."

"Maybe it was a bird, Colby."

He looked down at her. "Unless seagulls have developed twin vertical stabilizers, glass cockpits, a four-missile array under the wings, and a steel-gray paint job, I'd say it was a might more likely it was a Grumman F-14 Tomcat. Remember, we built an awful lot of fighter jet and helicopter models together after we ran out of spacecraft. You still have those?"

Ivy bit down on her tongue again. That was something else she'd forgotten about Colby, his infinite patience in teaching her how to make models actually look as good as the image on the box. He might tease, but he was smart as hell—even when he'd been lazy about everything else, his mind missed nothing. The details of that nine-inch model built across a couple of stormy afternoons had been cataloged neatly away until he needed it twenty years later.

"I couldn't figure out what was up. It looked incredibly close, but looked small at the same time like it was..." He tentatively stretched his arms out until his hands spanned four or five feet. "It still doesn't make sense."

"An RC." It was the only way that an F-14 could be that small but still have the level of detail Colby was describing.

The general was now scowling at her.

"Radio-controlled model—RC. Models come in all sizes. They sell kits that you can fly with a remote. Fly fast. Like a hundred miles an hour."

"Some pissed-off golfer with a toy took down one of my helicopters?" General Arnson's scowl was gone—and had been replaced by a dark fury. "I almost lost five personnel and a helicopter, and scrapped a seventy-year safety record, because of a goddamn toy?"

"Six personnel," Colby corrected him, cool as could be.

Ivy had been eyeing potential escape routes and wondering if there was a bomb shelter big enough to save her from one of the general's rare but legendary explosions. But Colby was facing straight into the storm.

"Six?" Arnson ground out.

Colby pointed down at Rex, who looked up eagerly, knowing he was the sudden center of attention. Probably hoping for a treat.

Instead of killing Colby on the spot with his bare hands, the general laughed (though it was a grim sound) and leaned down to pet Rex. "Six it is. Glad you made it too, boy."

The general raised a hand and a lieutenant appeared at his elbow.

"Warn the dive teams. They're looking for the remains of an F-14 model, one to two meters across. Get a team to shut down Hains Point Park and check every damn person for a radio controller or whatever the hell it is they use to fly those things. Tell them not to kill the bastard before I do."

"Yes, sir!" The lieutenant saluted.

The general snarled at him, and the lieutenant broke into a run toward the hangar.

In unison, the four of them moved forward to inspect the damage to the helicopter that had almost killed three of them.

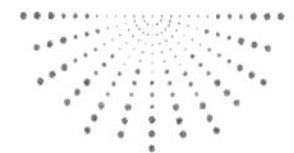

Three hours later, they were little wiser.

Approximately a third of a model F-14 lay spread across three tables in a hundred pieces. The transmitter had been destroyed, so there was no information to be gotten there. The kit manufacturer had confirmed that it sold a model with that serial number five years before. The Secret Service had a field agent at the purchaser's doorstep within twenty minutes of obtaining his address. He had registered his kit to get the warranty, but sold it for cash at a RC fly-in last October because he'd upgraded to an F-22 Raptor.

"I don't know who he was. Just your average white kid with more money than sense. Said he'd never flown an RC, but wanted the F-14. Knew he'd crash it on its first flight, but he had the cash. Figured mine was the good side of a four-hundred-dollar lesson for the kid. Wish I'd kept it, though. F-14 was the last of the truly great pilots' birds." That had been in Ohio.

The opinion of the Washington, DC, RC club president, that to fly the F-14 at full speed to impact a helicopter's rear rotor was "a fine piece of flying," almost got him beaten to a pulp by the Marine Corps forensic team. But the only F-14 model he knew about in the whole club was quickly accounted for.

Ivy definitely considered tracking him down herself and offering him a lesson or two on tact.

No radio controller had been located in the park. The plane could have been easily operated from a boat and the search was expanded to see if the controller had been dumped in the Potomac, but nothing had been found in the muddy depths.

Now they were out of time and the Marines of HMX-1 were never late. A VH-60N White Hawk was prepped and waiting for them.

As she'd grabbed the contents of their recovered go-bags from the big clothes dryer they kept in the hangar, General Arnson stalked up to Colby. She managed to blend into the background by sorting her dry clothes from Colby's into their respective packs. It was a surprisingly intimate process, unwinding one of her bras from his briefs—he was a briefs man and she'd bet that he looked good in them. In *just* them. *Whoa! Divert all power to the shields!*

It also helped that General Arnson's whispers were at a level that most officers issued commands. "I got one word for you, Thompson: *careful.* Be careful that you don't mess up my best officer and I won't be forced to make sure you get demoted from dog handler to dogshit cleaner for the rest of your natural born life. We clear?"

Colby had the good sense to reply, "Clear, sir."

Ivy had to puzzle at what the general was talking about as she handed over Colby's packed bag and they moved toward the waiting White Hawk together. There was no doubt that the general was referring to her—though as his "best officer," which was far more than he'd ever said to her face. If he'd meant it, the fact that he'd even said it made her feel as if she was in her dress blues again—with the sword this time.

But how would Colby mess her up? Irritate her to death perhaps, but she was missing something. It bothered her that Colby appeared to have immediately understood what the general had meant.

Colby settled into a seat—not the one with the President's seal on it; actually he chose the one at the very rear of the aircraft—and told Rex he was a good boy. Ivy sat next to him in the much smaller helo for the flight from Anacostia over to Andrews Air Force Base. She'd forgotten that the White Hawk seats were narrower and they were practically rubbing shoulders. That, in turn, reminded her of something Colby had said just before they were separated by the debriefing teams.

"You called me beautiful."

Colby burst out laughing loudly enough to attract the pilot's attention from the duties of preparing for flight. "You always were a tenacious girl, Saint Ives."

"You paid me a compliment?"

"Might have. Took you long enough to notice."

If Ivy was any less of a Marine, her jaw would be down.

Colby Thompson had paid her a compliment? Several? At least two.

He'd acknowledged that despite his Secret Service training, she was still probably the more capable fighter. Which was true, she was a Marine, but it was unexpected of him to admit it.

And he'd called her beautiful.

Not cute. Because of her size, she'd heard that enough to spit fire at any guy who said such a thing.

But Colby had called her beautiful. Colby. Her.

This was a time to speculate about the enemy's intentions and to hell with McKinnon's Laws.

If Colby was just messing with her, she'd get him back but good. And why hadn't she done just that? *Well, of course I'm beautiful. But if you and your dog were in a pageant together, guess who'd win?* Though Colby had grown up to become some serious eye candy and—

She needed to make an appointment for a new brain—soon.

Ivy jolted when the crew chief came aboard and slammed the double door shut. The rotors wound up and in moments they were headed aloft to Andrews Air Force Base.

On the other hand:

Query: What if Mr. Oh-I'm-so-cute-while-I-play-with-my-dog-on-the-helicopter had meant it? What if he'd actually *meant* his compliment?

Query: What if his teasing joke about marrying her and naming all their kids Reggie hadn't been completely a joke?

Conclusion: Then she *would* have to kill him. Now would be the opportune moment. While she'd been thinking, they'd climbed up to a thousand feet over Maryland. Nobody would think anything of it if his body suddenly plummeted out of the sky. Crew Chief McShea was a Marine—he'd cover for her. Though maybe not. Colby had done one of his everybody's-friend things after their plunge in the Potomac.

Secondary conclusion: It was the coward's solution anyway, unbecoming of a Marine. No, if he actually had meant what he said, she'd kill him one-on-one with her bare hands, somewhere that she could hide the body. That would be far more fitting for someone like Colby Thompson.

So, the Marine in her understood the situation.

But the woman was just a little bit charmed by Colby Thompson calling her beautiful.

CHAPTER EIGHT

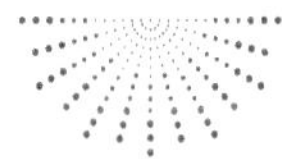

The C-5 Galaxy cargo jet boomed and echoed its way south along the East coast. He and Ivy weren't the only ones aboard the massive plane. Three VH-60N White Hawks, including theirs, had been loaded aboard the Galaxy after having their rotor blades folded back along the tail. The vertical rear rotor also had to be folded down, but otherwise the massive jet swallowed the three helicopters whole. That hadn't even *begun* to fill the cavernous interior. Their crews, plus a ground team with their service truck, plus seven vehicles for the Presidential Motorcade and all of their personnel were aboard as well.

The upstairs seating, which spanned the rear third of the plane above the cargo deck, wasn't even full. He could tell the old hands: most of them were asleep before takeoff. He'd heard that about the top soldiers—they could sleep anywhere. It was only the third flight of his life—one of his Georgia training trips, he'd gone by train—so there wasn't a chance he was going to be sleeping anytime soon. He wished there were windows so that he could see, but there weren't so he couldn't.

Pure willpower had fought off the intense wave of claustrophobia. That, and he didn't want to embarrass himself in front of Ivy.

Because of Rex, Colby and Ivy had claimed front row seats to get some extra foot space where Rex could lie down. Of course Rex was a dog, which meant he automatically filled every available inch. As a result he and Ivy had no room at all for their own feet. Their front row was actually at the very tail of the plane because all the seating was installed facing backward.

"They put it this way so that our backs are padded for nose-first crash landings," Ivy was smiling. Smiling!

He had to assume it was a joke—hoped to hell it was.

Then on takeoff someone whooped out, "Hey! A C-5 that's actually working." That earned laughter and catcalls from others.

"Actually working?"

Ivy leaned in close enough that her scent filled his brain and he could hardly understand her words as she spoke barely louder than the roar of the four massive engines. "The aircrews have nicknamed the Galaxy as FRED—short for Fucking Ridiculous Economic Disaster. C-5s aren't exactly known for their maintenance and reliability record."

Just what he didn't want to hear.

Unable to stand it, as soon as they were at cruising altitude Colby unbuckled and descended the steep stairway into the cargo hold. An air pocket almost flipped him off the side of the ladder even though he was clutching both handrails. The South Lawn never did that to him, except when Ivy Hanson was walking across and sending her own shock waves into his world.

No windows here either, but at least he could pace around the perimeter.

The helos and other vehicles were chained down to the deck in a double file in the plane's belly—as tightly packed as a Dupont Circle traffic jam. Down past the three Beasts—as the President's limos were known. Up the other side past the Halfback, Watchtower, and Roadrunner SUVs—protection detail, electronic countermeasures, and the mobile communications platform that could be used to run a war if necessary. Last in the row was the elite counter-assault-team

SUV codenamed Hawkeye Renegade. The CAT guys were sitting in the flip-down seats built into the plane's side.

No friendly waves and trades of dog sniffs. Just a terse nod, so expressionless that he didn't know how to interpret it. They were close beside their vehicle and methodically stripping and cleaning their weapons. They looked more lethal than even the Delta Force snipers who manned the White House roof.

Finally, he lapped around the three helicopters with their folded-up rotors and then once more past the Beasts.

The earplugs made all but the simplest conversations impossible. He traded grunts and a wave with the CAT guys on his second lap. By the third lap they were ignoring him as a fixture of the flight. Maybe he'd just walk across the country, one plane length at a time.

Near the end of his third lap, someone grabbed his arm.

With little ceremony, he was shoved into one of the parked White Hawks. Unable to focus his eyes on the two facing armchairs to determine which was the President's, he collapsed across the aisle onto the bench seat that ran the length of one side. Rex hopped up into the open space for the President's legs. Ivy dropped into one of the armchairs, yanking the doors shut behind her.

His dog was following *her* around—just goddamn perfect.

She pulled her earplugs.

He did the same. Because of its presidential sound insulation, the inside of the helo was blessedly, almost painfully quiet. His ears rang from the sudden silence after wading through the C-5's roar.

"What the hell is wrong with you, Colby?"

"Wrong with me? There's nothing wrong with me. I've been on a plane twice in my life: for the flight down to the Federal Law Enforcement Training Center in Georgia and back. Twice. My entire life. It would have fit in this cargo hold. It was just a Boeing 737 so it probably would have fit with its wings still on. But *that's* not the problem. That makes this all old hat to me. Did you know that the C-5's hold is longer than the Wright Brothers entire first flight at Kitty Hawk? There's something really unnatural about that, too—just saying. Though that isn't my point either."

He wasn't sure what his point was, but he couldn't seem to stop ranting at Ivy.

"This morning my life made sense. White House perimeter security. Lead Dog. Keeping it all safe. Now I'm bouncing around the country to protect a President I've never actually met. Rex trusts me, but who the hell am I supposed to trust?" He might have been shouting a little by the end of it. It was hard to tell.

"This is only your third-ever flight? How did you get between states and countries in the past?" Like *that* was the important question.

"I fucking walked, Hanson!" Now he was definitely shouting, but was helpless to do anything about it. "I'm not some ultra-decorated super-duper Marine Corps pilot genius who has flown all over the world, okay? I'm not used to sitting backward for when we come crashing down out of the sky." That just *had* to be a joke. More likely no one survived if one of these monsters crashed. "I'm just a guy who's been to Georgia a couple of times. What the hell are we flying toward?" He waved a hand toward the nose of the helicopter. "I don't know! I've never been there! And what the hell am I supposed to be doing when I get there? I don't know. I've never done this. You're the big hot-shot liaison. Care to explain my job to me in some brilliantly anal retentive administrative detail? Huh? Huh? I'm just a high-paid dog handler. And you are so..." *Shit!* There was no safe way to finish that sentence as she watched him intently with those lovely blue eyes of hers. Watched him like a bomb with the timer fast running down to zero.

"That's the back of the plane. That's the front," she pointed toward the tail of the helicopter.

Right. This helo had been loaded backward to save space, overlapping tails with the White Hawk parked in front of it. *Crap!* He didn't even know which way he was going. He had to clench his jaw or he was going to be sick.

"Who are you, Colby Thompson?" Like he was some sort of total loser.

"Eat shit, Hanson!"

***

Never in a hundred years would the Colby Thompson she knew have admitted a weakness. And whoever this man was sitting across from her, he had just told her he was terrified!

Actually, Ivy had met so few men who would admit to feeling vulnerable—no matter how out of their depth they actually were—that she couldn't come up with a single name.

"Colby?"

"What?" He snapped out more sharply than his German shepherd.

"You're spooking your dog." Rex was indeed looking at Colby with alarm written clear across his furry face.

"Aw shit," he knelt down on the carpet and grabbed Rex's head, then rested his own forehead against the dog's. "I'm sorry, boy. This isn't about you. You're doing great." And he kept his forehead there until both he and the dog seemed calmer.

Which was about the sweetest thing she'd ever seen. It felt as if she should look away because the moment was so private. But she couldn't.

After Colby returned to his seat, he rested his foot on Rex's side. She was about to protest at how crass that was, using his dog as a footstool after the beautiful moment they'd just had, when Rex flopped on his back in the narrow aisle. Colby began rubbing his dog's belly with his foot.

Neither of their families had been dog people. By all rights they should have been, growing up in a kid-friendly neighborhood and having side-by-side cabins at the beach. But they hadn't. Yet Colby had finally found something to care about. And he appeared to be a natural at it.

Ivy wanted to slap herself. She needed to stop seeing Colby through the lens of the past. She didn't know what Lead Dog really was, but if what he'd said was true and not just bragging, it meant that he'd become one of the very best at what he did. He was the guy the *other* Secret Service dog handlers came to with their problems.

The past didn't fit the present man at all.

So, discard the past. Think of the man. Competent, but out past the stretch zone and into a hot-landing-zone type panic.

"Colby—"

"I'm not some goddamn idiot, Ivy. I know I'm in over my head. I've onboarded enough new dog teams to know irrational panic when I see it. I just don't know what to do with it."

"You act as though everything is fine."

He squinted at her.

"You think I've never been scared? Freaking out is part of being a pilot. When tracer fire is punching holes in your fuselage and your Marines are stuck inside, taking the hits with no way to fire back, and you're just praying to the gods the enemy fire doesn't punch out a critical system and bring your whole aircraft down out of the sky in a ball of flaming fire. Right then? Trust me, you're freaking. Training kicks in. You do the next task that's right in front of you. Chaff release, restore failing hydraulics, evasive maneuvers—whatever you can."

"Whatever's right in front of me?" Suddenly Colby had that half smile he always wore just as he was about to zing her. She'd learned to let him have his teasing moments. Partly because it was usually fun, partly because it made the revenge so much sweeter. But the shift this time was so fast.

"Exactly!"

"No matter what the consequences?"

"Well, hopefully it will fix things, but sometimes not."

"And you're sure about this?" That half smile was still growing. That was one of the things about Colby's teases—she could see them coming, but even with all the years of practice she could never predict what they'd be. Something about aircraft. Or flying.

"Worked every time so far." Maybe about travel.

"Fine, let's see how your luck is holding."

"*My* luck? You mean *your* lu—"

And Colby leaned across the narrow aisle and kissed her.

She'd guessed wrong again.

COLBY HAD EXPECTED any number of possible results: top of the list being a head-twisting slap. In anticipation, he'd casually rested a hand on her shoulder, placing his arm as an effective block. Because she was sitting sideways in the armchair, her other hand would be blocked by the back of the chair.

Instead, her burst of laughter broke the kiss. In seconds, he joined in. There was no way to stop it.

He and Ivy. There wasn't a more unlikely couple on the planet.

It was like they were sixteen and nineteen again, but it felt more as if he was eight and she was five. Except they'd never "stolen" a first kiss from each other. They both would have screamed "Cooties!" and run in opposite directions. She'd grown up sleek and beautiful and he'd really enjoyed watching her once she had.

Actually kissing her had never been part of any program.

Ivy managed to catch her breath first. She held out a hand as if to shake his.

Unsure what else to do, he took it and shook it firmly once.

"Hi, I'm Major Ivy Hanson." *Not a kid anymore.* He heard the unspoken part clear as day.

"Lieutenant Colby Thompson at your service, ma'am." And suddenly he wasn't holding her hand prior to some martial arts throw or grabbing her to heave her overboard. Instead he was holding the hand of a beautiful woman.

Using their clasp, he slowly drew her back in. She watched him carefully with those wide, blue eyes, but neither did she resist when he kissed her again.

This time it wasn't at all about who they'd been.

Somehow, at least for today, Ivy had become the only sensible thing in his world. A day that had begun so normally had spun out of control. And when she'd explained her theory of panic was the moment he'd understood what was really throwing him off his usual even keel.

His problem wasn't all of that other noise—that was merely making him a little nuts. His problem, since the moment she'd stepped off that helicopter onto the close-trimmed grass of the South Lawn, was Ivy Hanson.

He'd sworn at her, cursed her right to her face, and her response had been to sincerely try to help him. Cool under pressure he didn't doubt. But there had to be a woman in there somewhere.

And here she was, clear as day physically—an exciting combination of lovely and lethal. And so straight-ahead. No wonder she was a Marine Corps major. It was as if they'd invented the Corps for people like her—focused, straight-ahead thinkers. That trait was what had always made her so fun to tease: her absolute willingness to walk right into any trap he set for her.

The combination was amazing, but it was the woman who was dazzling him. He'd never have pegged Ivy Hanson as having kindness.

Or such a taste. Each moment she let his kiss continue added another layer of richness, of depth, of wonder. He'd been "lucky in love" and knew it. He'd had some fine women share his bed. None had tasted so vibrantly alive as Ivy.

Her hand pressed against his shoulder as a slow, steady pressure, driving him away even as she leaned into the kiss. Finally, she pushed enough farther with her arm than she leaned in that the kiss slipped apart with just the slightest tug of her teeth on his lower lip.

Anime girls didn't have eyes as big as hers were at the moment. Their brilliant blue shone brighter than a DC summer sky.

Continuing to use her arm as a lever against his shoulder, she slowly pushed herself back into her seat.

"I could ask why…" But she didn't.

He was glad she didn't, because he had no good answer to that. Any glib response had been erased by the surprising depth of that kiss. Her brow furrowed as she puzzled at it. Ivy really *was* the cutest thing on the planet. Not physically cute, which was how she would take it if he said anything, even though it was true. But linear, hyperrational cute. That kiss had just dropped his prior experiences of women right in the deep end of the pool where they'd all sunk with no idea how to swim. And she was busy thinking it through.

"I think instead I could ask, 'Since when?' "

"Well, since you're asking questions instead of running your pigsticker into my gut, I s'pose I should try to answer that."

"Please."

It took everything he had not to laugh in her face. Her eyes were still unnaturally wide, her breath was running in short hard gasps, yet her voice was perfectly calm. Marine training he supposed.

"At first I thought it might be the moment you stepped off that helo this morning without even a hair out of place."

"So, it's just lust." As if she could deal with that.

"Then I recalled that red-white-and-blue one-piece you wore at the beach for July 4th the year you turned sixteen. Please tell me you still have that swimsuit. You looked beyond amazing in that."

"So you're just interested in my body."

"But now I'm thinkin'," he stretched out the moment by leaning down to rub Rex, who sighed in his sleep, "I'm thinkin' that it goes back to maybe when I was five and you were two, following us everywhere. You made Reggie nuts, but..."

"You're so warped that teasing me to death was your way of saying you liked me?" Ivy concluded in a tone of judge, jury, and executioner.

"I was five. Sue me."

"And you aren't just messing with me now?"

"I'm not a big thinker, Ivy. I'm a Be Here Now sort of guy. And after that kiss, being here now sounds pretty damned good to me."

"But—"

"You're already thinking six steps ahead."

She nodded with a grimace that said it probably caused her at least as much trouble as it saved her. She'd always been the one with a plan.

"Remember what our favorite books were?"

"What are you talking about, Colby?"

"Reggie's favorite book as a child was written by Julia Child. Yours was..."

"The Little Engine That Could." And it had been. He'd helped teach her to read from that book. There'd been most of six months where he couldn't turn around without finding Ivy clutching her favorite book and looking up at him with her little girl eyes begging him to read it to her. She did that long after she could read it herself.

"You were always way past the train making it up and over the mountain with a trainload of toys. I bet you have never once thought 'I think I can.' You were always 'What can I do next?' Pretty damn humbling, Ives. Remember what mine was at that age?"

"Winnie-the-Pooh," her voice was little more than a puzzled whisper. It would have been impossible to hear outside the helicopter's sound insulation.

"Winnie-the-Pooh," he confirmed. "Know why?"

She shook her head.

"Because I'm like Pooh. He's the ultimate Be Here Now kind of guy, just dropping in on his other pals in the Hundred Acre Wood. So, no, I wasn't thinking ahead about messing with you, or setting you up for something. I was thinking about how much I wanted to kiss you. Enough that I didn't even care much what your revenge might be."

"At least I think before I act."

Which was true. It had taken him a long time to realize that because Ivy always thought so damn fast, it looked like simple reaction; but it never was.

"Unlike me. I just wanted to kiss you, so I did. What are you thinking, Saint Ives?"

"I'm still thinking that you're messing with me intentionally."

He raised three fingers in a Boy Scout salute. "As God and the Scouts are my witness—"

"Save the shit for someone who cares, Thompson." But she said it with a smile.

"Yes, ma'am."

He tried to wait her out, but she wasn't having anything to do with it. He looked around the helo, even out the windows, but all he could see was a black SUV to one side and the steel side of the C-5's hull to the other. That left him to think about what had just happened.

"Hell of a kiss though, wasn't it?" He'd never actually imagined kissing her, but now that he had, it was hard to think of anything else.

Ivy just nodded.

"Want to try it again?"

She shook her head.

No! She *absolutely* didn't want to try it again.

Her job, her *life* did not have any possible interpretation that allowed a kiss from Colby Thompson. The first peck, maybe. It had been almost cartoon funny—even less likely than some of the Captain Kirk kissing the alien seductress scenes.

The second one, though? Clearly, she'd slid off into some alternate reality. Who knew that hormones could shift her world track—temporarily only, she prayed—to include such a thing? It was a Jean Luc Piccard and Beverly Crusher kind of kiss, full of meaning and history and—

So not! *Where are my damn shields!*

Ivy Hanson and Colby Thompson—*that* belonged on the far side of the galaxy through a very twisted quantum space that...

She didn't know *what* it did!

But it certainly didn't leave her heart racing faster than the time she'd been shot down and saved her crew as much by luck as by skill.

That was it!

She must be injured and lying in some hospital bed again, suffering from a painkiller-fueled delusion, like the one time she'd let a handsome Austrian *oberstleutnant* convince her to try skiing. Southern women should not be made to downhill ski. It had caused her to swear off dating all Austrian military men ever since—and German and Swiss military while she was at it.

So why in the world did her fantasy include a scorching kiss from Colby Thompson?

She looked down at Rex. He was lying across Colby's boots but had his front paws and nose resting on hers. He was looking at her as if telling her to get her act together.

Ivy didn't have dreams where she could see each expression as it moved over a dog's face in real time. Her dreams were crazy, swooping swirls of adventure ever since that Saturday when she was eleven and she'd watched too many sci-fi movies in a row—only to relive them all mashed together in her sleep. Gort and Robby the Robot dancing to the *Star Wars* theme, while Princess Leia and Spock debated the nature of effective rebellion over a game of holographic chess played between *Jurassic Park* dinosaurs and *Blade Runner* replicants all singing the five tones of *Close Encounters of the Third Kind* in thirty-two-part harmony that slowly fractured as more and more of them were killed off by phaser blast and light saber-wielding Klingons.

She'd learned never to try and explain her dreams to anyone. Not since the one time she'd tried to explain one to Colby.

"You laughed in my face." He had. Years ago. But her present dream had included an undeniably real kiss.

"No, I didn't. I kissed you. Well, the first time, yeah. Besides, you laughed first. But that second kiss was no laughing matter."

"Then what was it?"

"Stupendous!"

"That's not what I'm talking about." Kisses with the Colby Thompsons of the world were *not* supposed to be stupendous, even if it had been. "It wasn't. It was just an aberration, that's all. An aberration that's never *ever* going to recur."

"Ivy, sweetie."

"Sweetie? You were doing so well, Colby, right until that moment." *Patronizing bastard.*

"You know it was an amazing kiss." He offered one of his smarmy Colby grins. "Bet you just can't wait for another."

"I... *What?*" As if she didn't *know* what she wanted. As if she hadn't had to fight every step of the way to beat her way into the Marines. She didn't deserve this kind of shit from anybody. Not her brother, not Colby, not anyone.

Ivy popped the door on the VH-60N, climbed out, and closed it quickly—almost catching Rex's nose and cutting off Colby's attempt to backpedal. She didn't look back to see either of their faces in the window.

There was no free weight set on this plane. No punching bag to work out on. She needed to beat on something badly.

There was also nowhere to hide.

Unless…

She strode forward as if she had a purpose. As if.

"Well, I screwed that up pretty royally, didn't I, boy?"

Rex sighed and returned to lying on his feet, sprawling out over the President's carpet.

"She smell as good to you as she did to me?"

A second sigh.

"She tastes even better."

Rex ignored him.

"And she is some kind of pissed right now. I just—" He didn't know what had come over him at the last second. He'd suddenly found himself pushing Ivy's buttons—hard—and he knew right where they were. Like he'd backslid into some past version of himself and couldn't stop it.

Ivy didn't mind being laughed with, but she hating being laughed *at.* Hate was too mild a word. He'd seen her shut out friends for life for doing that to her. In hindsight, he was perhaps the only person he knew of in her entire life who'd ever gotten away with it.

"And I just told her she didn't know her own mind. Shit! I guess I deserved her storming out on me."

Rex fell asleep.

"And now I'm sitting in the President's helicopter talking to myself because even my dog isn't listening."

Nothing was happening.

"Sitting where the crew chief will shoot us for just sitting, even if you weren't shedding all over the place." While probably not true, it was enough to motivate him to get moving. He swung open the door, then roused Rex so that they stepped down from the helo together. When neither of them was shot, he took it as a good sign. The fact that Ivy was nowhere to be seen was, perhaps, less of a good sign.

He circled around to the other side. The boys of the counter assault team were apparently done checking their weapons but hadn't gone back upstairs.

For lack of anything better to do, he flipped down the next seat that ranged along the side of the cargo jet's fuselage and sat with them. Once he introduced Rex around and had given him a treat for each "positive" he found on all the guys as they petted him, they relaxed enough to start asking him questions. A few were about the White House, most were about Rex and how he could respond to various attack scenarios. Not a single question about Ivy, which was good.

"YOU GUYS ARE ALMOST HUMAN. When did that happen?" Ivy teased the Air Force crew and it earned her a laugh and some flak about being a toy soldier. They had an entire habitat on the upper deck. It stretched from the wings forward with no access to the aft passenger cabin except through the big cargo bay down below.

It began just forward of the wings where there was a seven-seat area for military couriers who couldn't risk mixing with the general population of mere soldiers. A small living and bunk area for the relief crew. Typically they were aboard only for long missions—since with midair refueling the C-5s could span the globe. But carrying the President's motorcade and helicopters, they wanted to be prepared for everything, and an entire second crew was along even for the short flight down the East Coast. In addition to the standard four on the flight deck—pilot, copilot, and two engineers—they also had a navigator who only flew for special missions.

She'd managed to talk her way into the flight deck's observer chair by waving around her White House Military Office appointment. It was nice that it had some use other than saddling her with Colby Thompson. She'd also wager that being Lead Dog wasn't going to get him permission to climb the forward stairway. She could use the distance.

Out the front windshield, she could see that they were hugging the coast, slipping between brilliant white lumps of cumulus clouds scattered across the blue sky. She could see just a little of the eastern seaboard of the Carolinas below, dotted with giant spots of cloud shadow.

She'd somehow fallen into one of those shadows down in the cargo deck with Colby, closed inside a helicopter. Now she was once again up in the sunlight, talking about foreign missions, the lousy conditions at different overseas bases, and the food at Ramstein in Germany versus Lemonnier in Djibouti. Familiar. Competent.

How could Colby never have left the East Coast? Not even to Florida?

As she chatted with the crew, making a point about how luxurious the Air Force had it with beds and baths and room to walk around, she thought about that.

Colby had started out the conversation very differently than he'd ended it.

He'd been overwhelmed. Afraid even. Of travel. Of his new role. Of leaving the familiar grounds of the White House.

Had he let his fears show because she was the only person around? As close and he and Reggie were, her memories of eavesdropping on their heart-to-heart chats had been much more in guy speak.

"Thinking of France for a couple years." Her brother spent two years at the Sorbonne's culinary school. But she'd overheard him checking out the idea with Colby long before he mentioned it to their parents. He'd never thought to ask if she'd miss him.

"Leaving DC?"

"Yeah, need to get away from your stink. Maryland ain't half far enough."

Then they'd gotten really deep.

"You cool with it?"

Colby's manly, worldless shrug of "Why wouldn't I be?"

And yet he'd *spoken* to her. Told her he was afraid and recognized that in himself.

The Air Force guys teased her back about having an entire eight-hundred-foot Landing Helicopter Dock ship to wander around with her MEU. "Yeah, real luxurious, guys. Two thousand Marines crammed aboard and we aren't even allowed on go up on deck to see the sky most days because of constant flight operations."

It earned her the "smallest violin in the world" pity gesture.

She responded with an equally friendly flying middle finger and they moved on to reminiscing about other operations.

How had she responded to Colby's cry for help?

She'd told him to never show it. Stuff it down deep and never let anyone know.

And that's just what he'd done.

And when he'd started to say something about her, she'd told him that he was pointing at the wrong end of the plane. Real smooth.

So, instead, he'd kissed her and called her sweetie as if either of those was okay.

If he was smart, he'd never risk speaking to her again because who knew what new ways she'd find to slam him down. She was showing about as much emotional depth as her big brother. The New Colby had peeked out into view and her answer? She'd squashed him like a bug. He probably did the kiss and "Sweetie" thing just to chase her away. It was certainly something Old Colby would do. Or a Colby with the least sense of self-preservation.

Except for that kiss.

Better than she'd ever imagined possible.

Had she ever imagined kissing him?

Wait! She had the timeline wrong. Colby had kissed her, really kissed her. Then, when she'd slammed into him about laughing at her crazy dreams half a lifetime ago, he'd pushed her away hard: "Sweetie, I bet you can't wait for another."

"Assholes!" He'd been a complete and total asshole. But then…so had she. They both were.

The Air Force crew was looking at her strangely.

"What?"

She'd lost track where she was. They'd been waiting for a laugh or mock indignation or some response to something. By the look of it, it was their third or fourth attempt—then she'd called them all assholes. And not in the kindest of tones.

How could she explain…without explaining. The smiles died and the moment withered just as she imagined Colby's smile had when she'd slammed the door in his face.

"We're starting our descent," the captain finally spoke and the rest of the crew got busy. The Air Force captain had barely tolerated her up here in the first place and joined in none of the banter. Now his message was very clear.

She might pilot a helicopter rather than an airplane that weighed four hundred thousand pounds empty, but she could tell they weren't actually doing anything yet—other than *looking* busy. She took the hint and thanked them for the view.

"Anytime," and they made it sound sincere. Even might have been. Except the captain, who said nothing.

As she descended the ladder, she spotted Colby huddled up with the shooters of the Counter Assault Team. They appeared to be having a grand old time. And she'd been worried that she'd hurt him. Or not listened to him well enough or something. Nope, nothing actually upset him. Maybe the whole vulnerable thing had been the act. The kiss hadn't been part of that. It had been part of "Sweetie, I'm sure you deserved it when I laughed in your face." That was the real him.

Fine, Colby Thompson. You're on your own.

Of course, with friends like her, maybe he didn't need enemies.

She descended the steep stairs quickly and circled around the far side of the parked vehicles where he wouldn't be able to see her. When she ascended the rear ladder to the seating area, no one looked up at her except for Rex, who must have caught her scent as she went by. Colby missed the cue from his own dog.

Ivy couldn't stop wondering if that was a good thing or bad as she met with the HMX crews upstairs. Or after she strapped in alone in the front row of seats once the descent finally began.

Colby stayed downstairs with the guys.

Fine.

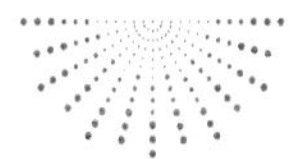

Everything got much more lively when they landed at Cape Canaveral. There were two runways, one in the heart of Kennedy Space Center. The other, an overlong strip built specifically for landing shuttles. Flights using the latter runway were so restricted that there was no taxiway, just the main strip—meaning traffic must not be a problem. Their C-5 Galaxy apparently rated.

The CAT guys had warned him, so he'd been waiting close by the rear ramp when it was finally lowered. He'd been told that the unloading would be a good opportunity to get run over and it would be best to just get out of the way.

When the back of the plane cracked open and the stern of the cargo bay began lowering, the heat and humidity had rolled over the top of the angled ramp and crashed into him like an unexpected tidal wave. It felt wrong and it smelled wrong. As if somehow the humidity made it achingly dry. And it was thick with sea salt against his tongue, like an ocean that someone had forgotten about and left cooking too long on the burner.

Ivy grabbed his arm and dragged him down the ramp, jumping off the side just as one of the SUVs rolled backward down the slope and onto the sizzling pavement. Even with the CAT guys' warning, he'd been stunned into place. He checked the tires of the descending vehicle, but they didn't appear to be melting when they hit the pavement. According to his watch, six in the evening was not late enough to be visiting Florida. He could feel the heat driving through the soles of his boots.

"This is insane."

"It's a heat wave. Never gets much above this. Still, it's cooler than Camp Lemonnier," Ivy didn't looked wilted at all.

"Which is…"

"Horn of Africa, Colby. You really should get out more. This is mild. And you get used to it."

"I like DC just fine." But that wasn't what Captain Baxter had set him up for. He'd set him up for travel, probably worldwide travel. "Next you're going to say that I need one of those t-shirt that says 'Whining' with a big red circle and slash over it."

"Marines never whine. I don't know what's up with you Secret Service types."

Neither did he. He never complained about anything. Of course, compared to the last twelve hours, most of his life had given him very little to complain about. Even when it had, he'd always made a point of acting as the positive force in the group. Ivy apparently brought out his dark side or something.

"You and Darth are close I guess."

"What was that?" She'd been watching the unloading.

He decided to keep his thoughts about Ivy's power and the dark side of the force to himself.

One of the Beasts eased down the ramp, the long limo carefully tended by two loadmasters and a small phalanx of Secret Service techs. It was closely followed by two more SUVs.

"Come on." Ivy led him into the relatively cool shade beneath the aircraft. They walked past the eight tires of the left landing gear, each taller than he was. Much more tolerable.

Of course she hadn't felt like the dark side of the force. Not until *after* he'd kissed her and the fury had lashed out of nowhere.

"I didn't kiss you to make you angry, Saint Ives."

"I wish you wouldn't call me that." Again, she answered the wrong part of the question.

"Goddamn it, Ivy!" Colby grabbed her arm and dragged her to a halt beneath one of the jet's massive engines, so monstrous that it felt like it was going to fall off the wing and crush them at the least excuse.

Maybe he no longer cared if it did.

"Now you're going to make me angry."

Ivy just squinted at him like he was a bug.

"Fine," he turned to continue forward when he heard her voice softly behind him.

"Then why did you?"

"I…don't know. But it wasn't to piss you off. And it wasn't a tease. I did it because…I wanted to."

"Well, don't. It's confusing."

Yeah, like that was news. He kept going, but stumbled to a halt when he and Rex reached the nose of the plane. Or rather where the nose was supposed to be.

Instead of sticking out the front of the plane, the nose section had swung up and out on massive hinges until it was three stories above them pointing upward at the hazy blue sky. In its place, a forward ramp had been extended and the White Hawk helicopters were being rolled off out the front of the plane.

"Go to work," Ivy prompted him from close by his elbow.

Of course that's all she cared about. He didn't look at her. If he did, it would just make the hurt worse.

Don't. It's confusing.

It wasn't like he knew why he kissed her in the first place. She was always too smart for him, living in some stratosphere to which he didn't belong. Too smart, too motivated, too good to do anything other than succeed.

Rex.

He understood Rex. Sniff, eat, nap, get treats. Dog actions broke down into such simple categories.

"*Such,*" he ordered.

And Rex sought.

Simple. *That* Colby could take comfort in.

They circled and crawled through each helo. They checked every technician working on the birds: the ones unfolding the rotors, others from the base who arrived to fuel the helos, two more techs doing systems checks. They sniffed at the flight crews as they assembled to pre-flight the helicopters in preparation for a test flight.

Ivy moved forward to talk to the flight leader. Thankfully Rex had already checked him and they didn't need to go near Ivy, but he could feel her attention tracking him. Like there was some sort of dog leash between them now.

Since the moment of the kiss, he'd had an incredible awareness of her.

On the flight, he hadn't been watching for her, yet had somehow glanced up and recognized her boot from all others as it hit the first rung of the ladder down from the Galaxy's flight deck. Forcing his attention back to a friendly argument with the CAT shooter's ridiculous preference for the old Colt 1911 with .45 rounds over Glock 19 pistols with 9mm was the only thing that kept him from watching how she moved.

He *had* tapped Rex's shoulder to draw his attention to her so that Colby could track her by the motion of Rex's head—up the rear ladder to the passenger deck without coming anywhere near him.

Shit!

For something to do once his inspection of the helicopters was complete, he guided Rex over to the wing shade on the far side of the C-5. The monster plane had "knelt," squatting down on its wheels until its belly almost rubbed the tarmac to make the unloading easier. It also had the advantage of blocking his sightlines beneath the aircraft to see Ivy. He scanned the scrub grass and low brush while Rex lay down on the pavement and rolled over as if it was a comfy heating pad.

"How do you do that with all that fur?"

Rex sighed happily, laid his head back, and fell asleep with four paws in the air.

The interesting parts of Cape Canaveral lay south of the airfield, warped by the heat haze. Impossibly tall gantries were scattered about like individual skyscrapers, each missing their city. In the far distance, there was a small group of truly massive buildings. Ivy could probably tell him about each and every one: purpose, history, and God alone knew what else. Only the fifty-story tower of the Vehicle Assembly Building, where the rockets were assembled for launch, stood out clearly. At less than two miles away, it alone commanded the southern vista.

This section of the Cape was a lonely place. Due east was nothing but a line of low trees—mangrove and Brazilian pepper, one of the C-5's loadmasters had told him—cutting off any view of the nearby ocean. To the north, only a few tall condos peeked above the trees. To the west, again nothing.

Maybe he'd just act like those lone skyscrapers. Ivy hadn't been in his life or much in his thoughts for several years prior to this morning. No loss. He'd just go back to ignoring her, standing alone on the baking runway beneath a strangely hazy sky—blue, but definitely not DC blue.

Did sleeping dogs get homesick?

"It feels desolate, doesn't it?" Ivy spoke from close behind him.

Between one heartbeat and the next, Rex flopped over from upside down, dead asleep to sitting up and looking for a pet from Ivy.

She looked impossibly sad as she complied.

Colby could ignore many things, but he couldn't ignore that.

She hadn't expected this feeling.

Shuttles had landed here. Right here!

Cape Canaveral.

Kennedy Space Center.

After a lifetime of dreaming, she'd finally made it to the heart of America's space program. And all that struck her was the vast emptiness.

The isolated runway.

The lone C-5 jet.

Except for the quickly assembling HMX-1 fleet and the Motorcade, the silence was echoing. Air Force One would be arriving early tomorrow and everything would be ready. Where was the drama? The excitement?

"Why didn't you ever go for being an astronaut, Ivy?"

Colby's question surprised her. "I..." She didn't have a good answer to that. Because almost no one ever made that grade? Well, she'd guaranteed that she wouldn't by never trying.

"I guess that I never really thought to try. It was all too far away, too magical."

"Reality looks a lot like hard work."

"Well, that's a downer, Thompson."

"No! No!" Colby turned to face her. "I'm fine with hard work—"

"Didn't used to be."

"Maybe you could grant that I grew up somewhere along the way."

"Sure...sweetie!" But that was wrong. Ivy shrugged an acknowledgement that felt as if she was saying he was right. Earlier today it would have been a sarcastic *Yeah, right!* But it didn't feel like that anymore. This Colby Thompson was too impressive to deny.

"I like a challenge. Gives me purpose. You taught me that."

She looked at him in surprise, but he continued too quickly for her to ask what he meant. If she didn't know better, she'd say he was sorry he'd spoken that thought aloud.

"I love working with Rex and the other dogs. Just... It seems as if there should be more, somehow. I don't know. Just whistling in the wind here." He turned back to face the low green wall that bordered the long runway. "There are hundreds of agents and dozens of dogs working to keep the President safe. That doesn't count all of the other forces we recruit from police and military. I've caught my fair share of fence jumpers, and Rex has tagged a couple of wannabe bombers, but nothing big. Which I suppose is good, but it still feels...small."

"I feel like that all the time. I think that's what makes me keep pushing."

"Sounds right. But it doesn't sound like me. Maybe it's just this place."

Colby knew her that well, to know what sounded like her even when she didn't. He knew her better than anyone other than…maybe not even herself.

The salt wind seemed to be taking the daylight with it. The sun, now a bloody orange orb, set beyond the helos as the first one lifted aloft for its test flight. Soon the other two followed.

"Shouldn't you be there?"

Where she should be was back in the White House Military Office, acknowledging the report that the HMX-1 team was ready. Here, she'd already seen that the operations team was fully prepared to carry out their tasks without her poking her nose in. She would complete the mission, but perhaps her idea of being in the field hadn't been the best. All she'd managed to do was get shot down.

"I…" the words seemed to be trapped in her chest. "I don't know where I'm supposed to be."

Colby wrapped a friendly arm around her shoulder for just a moment and Rex nuzzled at her hand, both of which made her feel better for no reason she could identify.

"We'll figure it out, Saint Ives."

"Why do you always call me that? I'm not from Cornwall. And he's the patron saint of lawyers. So that can't be it. Tell me it isn't the dumb nursery rhyme."

"*As I was going to St. Ives, I met a man with seven wives. Each wife had seven sacks. Each sack had seven cats. Each cat had seven kits. Kits, cats, sacks, wives. How many were going to St. Ives?*"

"One. The narrator who meets the man, etc. who are going the other way."

Colby looked down at her carefully. "You've always gone your own way, Ivy. Full bore, crashing over anyone who tries to become an obstacle."

"Doesn't sound very nice, does it?" However, it did sound more than a little true. Just like her, in fact. The little engine who could…no matter what was in her way.

"It's one of the things I admire most about you. You're beautiful, funny, and you have a kiss so good that I still can't get my head around it. But your stand-out feature is your determination. It's as clear and direct as…as a rocket flight—always going your own way without any doubts or questions. I'm sure that it makes you an awesome Marine, but that's why I was wondering that you never went into space."

"I was only ever a pilot. No advanced degrees in science or robotics."

"And NASA doesn't use pilots?"

"I was only ever a *helicopter* pilot. To pilot for NASA, you have to be a *jet* pilot first. Jets never interested me."

"You're a funny woman, Saint Ives."

"Ha-ha funny?" She wasn't feeling like laughing at the moment.

The three VH-60Ns came racing in from over the horizon, high enough to glow brightly in the sun that had already left the runway in shadow. Low enough to suppress conversation for the few moments of their passage.

"Not to me, Ivy. Funny as in each time I think I understand you, I discover that I don't at all."

"Welcome to the club. I don't understand me either most of the time. I'm a Marine who doesn't fight. I'm a Marine pilot who no longer flies. How did I think that was a good thing?"

"I did learn a few somethings about you over the years." Colby's look seemed kind, which must be a trick of the fading light. She didn't deserve it after the way she'd shut him down.

"Which is?"

"Anything you do is a good thing. Anything."

His tone said that he firmly believed that. And knowing of his belief helped ease her own doubts. Made her once again remember how proud she'd been as she approached the White House.

"Colby?"

"Um-hm?"

He saw her as more capable than she saw herself. When she wore her Marine Corps cloak, Major Ivy Hanson knew who she was. The woman-Ivy was more of a total-frame-loss accident that had happened long ago. But maybe, just maybe, there was hope for a woman named Saint Ives.

And she felt that way because of how Colby was looking at her. Because of how he spoke of her. Because of how *he* made her feel.

The three VH-60Ns hammered down out of the dark, landing on the pavement to finish their test run. Maybe it was time for her to test a thing or two herself and see how they progressed.

She stepped forward into Colby's arms and pulled him down far enough to kiss him.

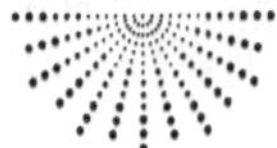

Colby woke in the darkness with a start. The soft sound of the air conditioner said motel room. The soft snore close by the side of the bed told him Rex's location. He must be on his back again; he only snored when he was upside down.

The woman, a mere outline in the white nightgown standing close by the bed—no more substantial than a ghost—her he couldn't place at all. The red LED clock informed him it was still short of midnight.

Rex's snore cut off.

Not a ghost.

The woman…

"Ivy?" They had kissed at sunset. If he'd needed proof that the first kiss wasn't a fluke, the second one had proved that it was because it was even more incredible. Her body had tucked against his like a custom fit. Her soft moan of pleasure had nearly taken him to his knees as he wrapped his arms more tightly about her. Ivy Hanson kissed as she did everything else: with her whole being.

Then the flight leader had appeared out of the dark to report on the successful test flight. Which had led to a review of the next day's mission and the multiple sorties that would be necessary to provide for the President's itinerary. Which had looked simple on paper, but

Colby had rapidly learned was anything but. Even the two-point-seven miles between the shuttle runway and the launch viewing area had to be carefully considered.

Because of the events that had landed them in the Potomac that morning, she then became involved in discussions about changed security measures in case another drone approached any of the HMX-1 flight paths. Firing a hundred-thousand-dollar Hellfire missile capable of punching a hole in a Russian tank at a small object weighing ten pounds wasn't a solution. He'd made sure she ate at one point, but she'd been so deep in it that he'd finally taken a ride to the hotel with Sergeant McShea.

"Ivy?" His room ghost hadn't replied.

There was a slight movement of the gown that might reflect a nod.

Unsure of what else to do, he slid to the far side of the bed as he folded open the covers.

The ghost took a step forward, stumbled on Rex, and flopped down onto the bed completely unlike an ethereal ghost. There was a brief scramble as Rex moved to a new location on the floor and Ivy attempted to untangle herself from her second crash landing of the day.

"So much for my dignity," she mumbled.

"Or any indecision about climbing into my bed. As you're now sprawled in it."

"I told the clerk my mag card key had died, then gave him your room number to reprogram it to. Not exactly a high security place."

"Not complaining. Surprised as hell, but not complaining." As they spoke, he tried to lean in to assist her. Instead of finding her elbow, he found something else wonderfully soft beneath smooth flannel. "Whoops!"

When he went to pull away, she grabbed his hand and kept it against her breast. "As good a place to start as any."

"Ivy? Maybe we should talk first?"

"Why?"

Of course Ivy Hanson would be as straight-ahead about sex as she was about everything else.

"Because…"

But Ivy had gotten herself straightened out, slipping under the covers and moving against him. There was something about a woman in flannel that begged to be touched. And on Ivy's body, every touch was a wonder. That lean strength of hers was unlike any woman he'd ever been with. She had the strength of a bodybuilder and the lithe slenderness of a dancer.

This was, uniquely, Ivy.

Little Ivy—who didn't feel little at all.

Reggie's little sister—but Reggie was a thousand miles away.

She was—

Her kiss removed his last attempts at rationalization.

He scooped her against him and groaned at the feel of her so close, so real. There would be no shedding of her nightgown, they were already too tangled together. He wanted to feel her flesh to flesh, but through the ever so slight barrier of flannel, she also felt enticing and fantastically exotic as he stroked up and down her body.

Each slide of Colby's hands seemed to peel a layer off her skin. This HMX-1 liaison to the WHMO had just spent five exhausting hours in an intense review of procedures. So immersed that she hadn't even noticed when Colby had left. One moment he'd been there, with Rex asleep at her feet, the next they'd both been gone. There hadn't been a moment to miss them, but she did.

His hand stroked down over her behind and tugged her thigh up to drape over his legs and the Marine Corps major washed away faster than her thirty-second combat shower had rinsed off the Potomac.

She liked that he slept without pajamas or even underwear. Someone as male as Colby Thompson would of course sleep in the nude. Studying his body, as he was clearly doing to hers, revealed so many things she already knew but hadn't known.

Colby's strength had been breathtaking when he'd caught her on the South Lawn this morning. Again when he'd lofted her out of the sunken helicopter as if she was weightless. But it was also reminiscent of the visceral thrill when he would sweep up a young girl and heave her into the ocean. He'd always been the strong one of the three of them.

Lazy and directionless, sure. Though he wasn't directionless at the moment as he shifted to take her breast with his mouth through the thin cloth, forcing her to arch into the powerful sensation.

She could get past his guard with subterfuge, but never with strength. Now he was using all that glorious muscle to keep her tight against him. The hand at the small of her back that said she wasn't going anywhere, not that she wanted to. Even the leg, which had slid between hers until she'd clamped it between her thighs to hold tight to the sensation, was solid with the muscle of a man who walked for a living.

When he finally peeled the layer of flannel, one slow, agonizing, spectacular inch at a time, she finally lost all track of Ivy Hanson. In Colby's arms she was simply a woman. Not just some girl. Not a mere crazy-hot kiss—emphasis on the crazy if she was in bed with Colby Thompson.

In Colby's embrace she felt more female than with any other lover she'd ever had.

Most lovers made her painfully self-aware. Each move, each touch considered and measured. There was no flight plan with Colby. Every touch was natural, normal, unplanned, and a nerve-tingling escalation over the one immediately before, which had been an escalation of…

The first waves slammed through her and she felt no embarrassment that she climbed the peak alone. How could she, with Colby's hands upon her in the most personal ways. Without her noticing, he had spooned her back against his chest. The arm her head pressed against continued around her so that she was completely pinned. His other hand had drifted down between her legs and driven her aloft without her even noticing what he was doing.

She had no metaphors for the sensations. She should. Flight, combat, something. But she couldn't recall anything except for the intense blasts from her nervous system as she gave herself completely over to him.

Control. She *always* had control. Was always the one *in* control. Could always—

But not this time.

Everywhere Colby led her, she was helpless to do more than follow.

When he slid on some protection, she tried to ready herself. Ready for power. Ready for rough handling and hard driving.

He eased into her so gently that she almost wanted to cry. As if he worshipped her, rather than just finally taking what he really wanted. The climb this time was so much slower and so much more certain that when she crested it was like a long, smooth ride home after a dangerous mission.

When they were both done, he didn't roll away. He didn't just collapse on her either, though she'd have welcomed the weight of him. Instead, he simply held her, kissed her neck, and whispered her name in her ear as she drifted away into the silence of space.

* * *

COLBY'S first sight was a puzzled frown on Ivy's face. Morning had happened outside the curtains and enough light entered to see her clearly. She sat cross-legged on the bed, once again shrouded in her snow-white nightgown. It wasn't her anger frown—which brought a chilly winter snap to her light blue eyes.

"Sadly, that doesn't look like a frown of considering how soon we can jump each other's bones again."

"What?" She'd been concentrating on something so deeply that she actually startled when he spoke.

"Good morning, Ives. Where did you go?" He brushed a hand over her cheek and enjoyed the impossible softness of her fair skin.

"Good morning." She neither leaned in nor flinched away. Back to being unreadable.

And, typically, she didn't answer the more important part of what he said. He wasn't going to let her dodge it this time. "Ivy?"

"What?"

"What are you thinking about so hard?"

"The President's flight schedule."

"Bullshit."

She shrugged, but this time there was a hint of a smile.

"Well?"

"I'm not a very sexual person."

Colby couldn't even manage a *bullshit* remark. His jaw wouldn't retract enough for him to form any words.

"I just assumed I was broken somehow. Inside."

"So not," he managed. "By the way, it feels awesome to be inside you. Just in case I didn't make that clear last night. Need another demonstration?"

"Not just yet," she shook her head. Her fine blonde hair, out of its Marine Corps bun, danced around her shoulders. It was so light that it seemed to glow, even without the sun shining on it.

"Well, that gives me a little hope."

"What are you expecting out of this, Colby?"

"Expecting? Out of what?"

"Out of you and me being together."

"We're together?"

Her eyes found the icy blue so fast it made his head spin.

"It was a joke, Ivy." He sat up to face her, though he kept a sheet and blanket over his lap.

Her scowl didn't agree. She never was good at recognizing jokes. Reggie could get into it when it was just them and a couple beers, but not Saint Ives. A tease, sometimes, but a joke didn't work for her.

Wait. They did. At least they used to. The only times they didn't work on her was when they mattered—when it was something important. Then she had no sense of humor at all.

She began to back away.

Grabbing her hand to stop her retreat earned him a hard right cross to the gut, or would have if he hadn't blocked it.

At a loss for what else to do, he dragged her into his arms and held her for a moment until she stopped struggling. No head butt to break his nose. No knee to the balls or whatever other lethal mayhem she'd been trained how to deliver. So, just a pissed off woman rather than one who really wanted to get away.

Once she stopped fighting, he eased her back, keeping both hands on her upper arms to at least buy him a moment to speak before she escaped out of his bed and maybe back out of his life.

"Look, Ivy. This is all new to me, too. I wanted you since the moment you stepped off that helicopter. Hell, probably since you were still jailbait sixteen and I was too-old nineteen—even if I didn't know it at the time. It does not mean that I have a clue how to handle whatever this shit is that's going on between us. You are so incredible to make love to, it's like nothing else that's ever happened to me."

She looked down at her clasped hands, shaking her head. It caused a blonde cascade that hid her face.

He risked unleashing one arm to brush her hair aside. The blue eyes that finally looked up at him were softly gray now. Gone was the fury, but the perplexity of the morning's frown had returned.

"It's the best night I've ever had too," her voice was a bare whisper.

He guessed that she was no more in the mood for delving into it at the moment than he was. "How do you feel about mornings?"

With a narrow squint, her eyes seemed to shift back to true blue. Blue backed by a hint of a smile. "Mornings, huh?"

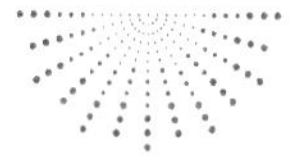

"Hell of a smile you've got there, Major."

Ivy tried to turn it down, but Captain Juarez, the flight leader, just grinned at her efforts.

"You should see the other guy," she riposted and did her best to be dignified as she accompanied him to Marine One. She'd fly as passenger on one of the decoy helos, but wanted to make sure everything was squared away on the designated primary bird.

The image of Colby, sprawled beneath her, with his palms cupping her breasts and his eyes practically rolled back into his head with the intensity of his pleasure just wouldn't go away. It was a good image. Rex had popped his head up over the edge of the bed at Colby's groan, then snorted and lay back down on the floor.

Mornings indeed.

But she hadn't felt like laughing. Morning sex with Colby wasn't some quick passage at arms. It was a drawn-out, ecstatic adventure that had left them breathless as they'd finally bolted for showers and rushed to change. Breakfast was a couple power bars and hotel-room coffee as they drove back to the airport.

They hadn't said a word, but there had been a thousand little touches: energetic towel rubdowns that were almost as erotic as the sex they'd just washed away, Colby tweaking the alignment of her oak leaf insignia on the collar points of her camo blouse, both reaching for the elevator button at the same moment.

Though he had teased her as she'd struggled to put her hair up into the accepted donut bun as the car jounced along.

She felt sixteen again. Not the incredibly painful moment of losing her virginity to Gregor on his parents' couch, but the fun, flirting (she could now admit) moments with Colby. These were the teen hormones that had noticed Colby the collegiate athlete and driven her to find new ways to tease him.

It was time to get her head in the game.

"Colby, you're with me." She ignored Juarez's smirk. "I think your best position—" was lying sprawled beneath her "—will be in one of the decoy helos. We'll land ahead of Marine One. That will give you perhaps thirty seconds to test the immediate landing area prior to the President's arrival."

He nodded, "Should be enough."

"Then you can expand into the crowd ahead of the President, which will already have been checked by other dogs, but I'd rather trust you and Rex's nose as a doublecheck."

Again, the simple nod.

No power games with Colby. Which was interesting; there hadn't been any in bed either. It was something she'd come to expect from any lover. They had some need to control or manipulate the petite— gods but she hated that word—Marine Corps officer.

Not Colby.

Not even when he'd grabbed her this morning. She hadn't known what she'd been reacting to, still didn't. But the longer he'd held her, instead of getting angrier, the quieter she'd become. Leaning into him was a place of forgetful peace. Maybe that's why he so confused her. She was Major Ivy Hanson 24/7…except in Colby's arms when she simply became Ivy the woman. She had no clue who that might be.

He and Rex headed off to recheck all of the helos and the flight crews.

She'd never had much success being a woman. "A Marine with

female body parts" had always fit her image of herself. Colby didn't even see the Marine in her. Maybe it was some sort of sick echo of jailbait teen lust on his part that had made him—

That wasn't right either. If it had been that, then he *would* have been that manipulative, controlling jerk she'd met in so many others. Colby was… She wasn't any more sure of what he was than what she herself might be. As much as she hated to admit it, they were going to have to talk at some point. But not too soon, as she had no idea what she wanted to say.

"There," someone called out.

Ivy realized that she'd been studying her reflection in the side of the Marine One aircraft for this first sortie. Trying to see herself in the soft image—wax bright over dark green paint. A dim version of herself. Was that what she was? It wasn't the Marine who looked back at her, but rather a dim reflection of a woman. That was new.

She turned to see where everyone else was looking.

At the far end of the long runway—0900 hours and already shimmering in heat haze—a black dot headed straight in. It rapidly expanded to the massive 747 of Air Force One. A brief puff of smoke as it touched down and the tires jumped from hanging still in the air to spinning at a hundred and fifty knots…and the President was down.

While the plane taxied, her phone rang, it was the WHMO group call.

"Everything fine here on Air Force One," Steve reported.

"Motorcade is good," Tish waved from where she was hanging out with Colby's Counter Assault Team guys—eight tough-as-hell dudes and a slender Goth in equally black clothing.

"Looks like you found some guys."

"Oh, they're *so* sweet!" From what Ivy could see at a distance, it looked as if the most lethal assault team on any security detail anywhere didn't mind at all being called sweet. At least not by a woman as cute as Tish.

"HMX-1 helos are clean," Colby's voice was heavy, like a hammer spiking the last nail into a coffin and ending all further conversation.

They all signed off as the 747 rolled to stop and things began happening very fast.

Before, she'd always been in her place: pilot, crew, something.

This time she could simply stand and watch the logistics with no defined purpose herself.

Almost identical in size, there couldn't have been two more different aircraft.

The Air Force gray C-5 Galaxy's bulk squatted low on its wheels. The high wing reached out from atop the fuselage and angled down, giving the plane a slightly sad and droopy aspect. The tail ramp and nose still gaped open, making the aircraft appear to be no more than a hollow tube. It looked every moment of its thirty years of hard service.

Air Force One might be the same age, but it was in sparkling condition, sporting the brilliant blue-and-white of the presidential livery. Its wings, attached to the bottom of the fuselage, angled up with perky energy still raring to go. It even bore the Seal of the President close by the President's door as a stamp of hard-won pride. The luxury aircraft rolled to a stop near the gathered HMX-1 helicopters and the stairs were lowered as an honor guard formed up around the aircraft.

The press and Secret Service agents poured down the rear stairs like an untidy river that splashed against the pavement. The press hurried to the bottom of the President's forward stairs as if they hadn't just been on a two-hour flight with him. Of course they were only rarely let out of their rearmost compartment in flight and perhaps the President hadn't visited them this time. How much could have happened in a two-hour flight that they demanded a comment since the boarding press conference? This was the leader of the world's most powerful nation, so perhaps a lot.

The Secret Service dispersed in a much more orderly fashion: some to surround the base of the President's stairs, a few to the HMX-1 aircraft, and others to the motorcade vehicles that had been delivered yesterday.

Colby met up with another dog handler near the lead Beast limo.

She recognized Clarice Carver, the President's driver. That must make the man and dog beside her Jim Fisher and Malcolm. The English springer spaniel and Rex had a slightly longer conversation than Rex had with the Marine Corps dog at Anacostia, but Rex broke it off first.

Two Secret Service agents and a dog. They made a sweet family…a sweet family that had saved the President's life during an attack on his motorcade.

What had she done so far? Been aboard for the first-ever downing of an HMX-1 helicopter was her high-water mark. So to speak.

"Hi!"

If Ivy hadn't been a Marine, she'd have jumped out of her skin.

"He is awfully handsome, isn't he?" Dilya continued blithely as she looked over at Colby. She'd popped up as if teleported in.

Zackie was circling Dilya's knees, pausing to sniff Ivy's, then circling back the other way once she reached the end of her leash. She vibrated with nervous energy.

"You have slept with him by now, haven't you?" Now those mysterious green eyes were inspecting her.

Ivy nodded before she could stop herself.

"Was it wonderful?" The girl sighed like a hopeless romantic.

"Worth waiting for." An answer which surprised her. She'd barely seen Colby since joining the Marines. But if last night and this morning were any measure, he was absolutely worth waiting for. At least the sex. The man she still knew almost nothing about. Well, she did, but—

"Waiting," Dilya sighed. "I get so tired of waiting. I'm like the only senior girl in the whole high school who hasn't made it with a boy yet. You have no idea how completely scared they are when I tell them I work at the White House with the President. I've barely even been kissed."

Ivy could only raise an eyebrow at Dilya in surprise. First, she was a beautiful and exotic young woman. Second, this was way more information than—

"Not even that, really. A peck on the lips doesn't count, does it?

Especially not when it was only an excuse to grab my breasts. Maybe some nicer boy would come near me if I had only sprained Kevin Gerber's wrist," she offered a heartfelt sigh. "But I broke it. Actually, both of them."

Ivy couldn't help remembering Gregor's fumbling efforts during her own first time. If the event itself hadn't been so painful, she might be remembering the fingerprint bruises that had taken days to stop showing on her own breasts, hurting long after any other pain had been forgotten.

Then Dilya's smile turned wicked. "Wearing dual casts, I bet he couldn't masturbate for months."

Ivy could only laugh.

"Did you know it only takes seven pounds of pressure to break a wrist, but nine pounds to break a nose? I looked it up. Maybe if he tries it again, I'll see if fifteen pounds is really enough to break his neck," she continued in a happily conversational tone.

"I'd stick with breaking wrists." Maybe this slender and pretty girl *did* know how to break necks. Actually, by Dilya's age, she was well on her way to a second black belt and had been trained to *not* break someone's neck in sparring practice. How far she'd come from seventeen to arching against Colby's glorious body like a wild thing.

"Right. Less jail time." Dilya nodded as if filing away the information. "Oh! Here we go."

Dilya hopped aboard the helicopter just as the President strode up followed by a pair of top advisors. They were deep in conversation.

Ivy had meant to be gone before the President's arrival, but now she was standing close beside the door of his White Hawk, opposite the Marine Corps crew chief who *was* supposed to be there. Too late to do anything else, she saluted as the President strode up.

"Two Marines," President Zachary Thomas stopped and returned their salutes. "You guys have to stop doing this or I'll get a swelled head."

"Sir, yes, sir," she and Sergeant McShea responded in unison.

Crap! She was in battledress uniform. Not her dress blues. Not even her service uniform. She wanted to melt right into the pavement and disappear. She wasn't supposed to be meeting the President on this trip. She was supposed to be an observer tucked out of sight on a decoy helo. Except she wasn't. She was here.

The President almost stepped past—maybe he hadn't really noticed her and this would pass unremarked.

Then he glanced down at her shoulder boards. "A major guarding my door. To what do I owe the honor?"

"Inattention, sir." *Dumb. Dumb. Dumb.* "I'm supposed to be over there," she nodded toward the second alternate aircraft. "I was distracted for a moment."

"By Dilya, I noticed. She's good at that. The little sprite wanted to see the launch so badly, I couldn't turn her away."

"Something we have in common, sir." And if the President thought Dilya was still some cute little girl, he wasn't paying attention.

He smiled down at her, "Major…?"

"Ivy Hanson, sir. White House Military Office Liaison for HMX-1. At your service." She remained at rigid attention.

"Carry on, Major Hanson. Glad to have you aboard. Wait…" he narrowed his eyes for a moment. They were mid-brown, going with his dark-brown hair. Gray was already starting around his temples. "Hanson? You were on that flight that went down yesterday. Why don't you take the seat opposite me? I'd like to hear about yesterday's events first hand."

"There was only one true eyewitness, sir," she waved toward Colby, who was standing by the helicopter she was supposed to be on.

"Bring him along," the President climbed aboard.

Unsure what else to do, she waved Colby over to join them.

He looked down at Rex uncertainly. She gestured again and Colby finally joined them with his dog leading the way. Rex sniffed the President, accepted a pat on the head, and looked about for something else to find that might earn him a treat. She'd already learned to recognize how he thought. She wished Colby was even half as transparent.

"Special Agent…?" President Thomas greeted him.

Colby, apparently comfortable in any environment, corrected the

President. "Lieutenant, sir. Special Agent is for the protection service. I'm just a dog handler for the Uniformed Division of the Secret Service. Colby Thompson, and this is Rex."

"I've seen you on my lawn a number of times."

"Four years, sir. Since it was President Matthews' lawn. Rex and I love that patrol. We're typically out by the fence when you arrive or depart."

"Better than crashing into the Potomac?"

"That had its moments as well, sir."

Wasn't Colby ever nervous? This was the President of the United States he was talking to and he sounded as if he was at a baseball game. Whereas she'd crashed and burned like an early Redstone rocket—which didn't fit the metaphor at all no matter how true.

***

THE PRESIDENT WAVED them all aboard.

Unlike the Sea King helicopters, where the President had his own entry, everyone except the pilots used the main door. A two-panel swing-aside, like an armored, glossy-green French door, opened in the side of the helo.

Colby waited as if his feet were riveted to the runway. He couldn't seem to lift them as the two advisors and Ivy climbed nimbly aboard and all settled on the bench seat running along the far side of the aircraft. For them it was an everyday occurrence. He'd just met the President for the first time about ten seconds ago.

He checked in with Rex, who seemed to be breathing just fine. *Show off!*

President Zachary Thomas looked at him and smiled. "Nerves?"

"I had them once upon a time, but they don't seem to be working at the moment. I suppose that nervous systems are like that."

"Try stepping on one of these birds as the President. That'll jangle your brain worse than a cattle stampede."

"Suppose it would, Mr. President." Up close and personal he was no less daunting than he was on television or chatting with the press gaggle on the South Lawn. His casual-Coloradan attitude was even more obvious in person. Colby climbed aboard, careful to sit in the armchair facing backward rather than the one with the Presidential Seal. Rex settled on Ivy's feet, as well as those of the other two advisors seated beside her. The aisle was narrow between the sides of the two armchairs and the bench seat; Rex filled it completely and none of them would be moving their feet anytime soon.

The President settled into the armchair opposite Colby's.

Only then did Harvey Lieber, the head of the Presidential Protection Detail, climb aboard. His scathing look at Colby as he attempted to step over Rex without banging his head on the ceiling, which was only about four-six high, was worthy of a carnival contortionist attempting to turn himself into a pretzel. Then he had to step over Zackie, who had curled up between Dilya's feet directly behind the President.

When he finally made it into his seat at the very rear of the aircraft, the look he gave Colby was unreadable. Did he now work for Harvey and was he now Number One on Harvey's dogshit list? Or was Harvey upset with dogs aboard Marine One in general? Or… Harvey was much easier going than Captain Baxter, but he hadn't risen to the head of the PPD by being a candy-ass either. Yeah, they needed to straighten all this out, but this probably wasn't the moment. No more likely than straightening things out with Ivy…ever.

Last aboard was McShea.

That's what finally broke Colby's petrification.

The crew chief stepped aboard, knelt very formally to close the doors behind him, then attempted to move to his seat at the very front of the aircraft. Rex had only partially blocked the rearward aisle, but he completely filled the forward aisle. The crew chief, so immaculate in his dress blues, had clearly never dealt with eighty-seven pounds of German shepherd cluttering up his aircraft.

Rex huffed grumpily when Colby signaled him to sit up. Then he simply laid his big head in Ivy's lap, huffed out a breath, and waited for the crew chief to get by—the equivalent of an exasperated doggie eyeroll.

McShea balanced himself with one white-gloved hand on Colby's shoulder—that he dug in hard enough to claim payback, but not hard enough to show any real anger.

Everyone finally settled, and the rotors began spinning to life.

"So I hear that you didn't enjoy your first flight on my helicopters," the President began.

"Oh, Rex enjoyed the swim well enough. And we finally found Ivy's cover when they fished the helo out of the Potomac, so it could have been worse, sir." It was a little tricky to recall that the man sitting so casually across from him was the Commander-in-Chief and that Colby would probably be better off if he kept his mouth shut.

Over one of the President's shoulders he could see Harvey watching him intently. Over the other, he could just make out Dilya's grin. That gave him a little courage.

"You saw the F-14 model that took out the helo?"

"Yes, sir. And two people on the jogging path did as well so I'm fairly sure I wasn't hallucinating. It was a quiet morning in the park until we crashed in, so they are the only other witnesses. They saw it moving fast and low, barely five feet above the river. I saw it just for the instant before it smashed into us. Climbing hard from our rear quarter. It was a good line of attack. A real pro job from what I would know. General Arnson agrees with me, especially as we weren't exactly standing still."

"Defense suggestions?"

Colby could only blink in surprise. "Sir, I'm sure that people far more qualified than myself have been studying that closely for the last twenty-one hours."

"They have. Defense suggestions?" And the steel tone of an ex-Air Force CSAR captain turned Commander-in-Chief brooked no evasion. Combat Search and Rescue meant that he'd been as exceptional as the HMX pilots in his way.

Colby watched out the window for a moment as they climbed aloft while he considered it.

The helo tilted its nose down to gather more speed and the President—seated toward the rear from Colby's position—now seemed to loom above him, even larger than life. They turned west and for just a moment he had a clear view of Kennedy Space Center. Scattered around its base were samples of their work. Instead of a car lot, they had massive rockets, as big around as a house and twice as long. His view of the launch pads were fast dwindling in the distance.

He glanced at Ivy, who was twisted around to stare raptly out the window behind her. She really should have gone to space…but then they never would have run into each other again.

Colby did his best to look thoughtful until the space port was dwindling behind them.

"What do you think—Ives?" He barely remembered in time that she hadn't been real happy about his calling her Saint Ives. She'd be even less happy if he did it in front of the President, as her instant scowl proved.

"She's much better at this kind of thing that I am, Mr. President."

IVY WAS GOING to kill him. She hadn't paid any attention to the conversation. How many times in her life would she get to see Kennedy Space Center from the air? One. And now Colby had hung her out to dry in front of the President—and she was about to make a second impression even worse than her first.

Colby was a dead man. But he spoke again before she could decide whether to go straight to murder or implement some torture first.

"How do you stop radio-controlled models and drone attacks?" At least he gave her the damn question again.

"FCC," she responded without thinking.

"You mean the FAA. The Federal Aviation Administration," Colby tried to correct her.

"No," *Doofus!* Her, not him. FAA was exactly what she'd meant, but that's not what had come out.

Assume your mistakes aren't mistakes until proven otherwise. Admit your mistakes, but a Marine Corps officer's brain is often right for reasons you may not understand at first. McKinnon's Law.

"No, I meant the Federal Communications Commission." Now, why had she thought that? "Restriction and jamming of radio frequencies. The FAA was caught flat-footed when the hobby drone market blew wide open. The old radio-control law—if it's below this size, that speed, so many feet altitude, we're just going to ignore it—was allowed to hold control for too long. Now they're trying to regulate something that has already slipped out of the box. Shut down their frequencies. Jam them just like we do with cell phones in combat areas to keep the enemy from remotely triggering explosives. Same idea, different frequencies."

"Told you she was smart. All I could think to do was sic Rex on them." Colby actually had the temerity to wink at the President.

She'd felt like she was babbling. There was something else there, but for the life of her she couldn't figure out what it was.

The President glanced over his shoulder at Harvey Lieber.

"We already do this on the motorcades," Harvey responded. "The Watchtower SUV that travels second behind the limos serves precisely that function."

"*Shit!*" Ivy remembered what she was missing. She scrabbled at her belt and shoved Rex aside so that she could rise enough to scramble forward to kneel between the pilot's seats.

The crew chief had yanked his sidearm. Before she could reassure him, Colby's sidearm was against the chief's temple.

Rex was now on full alert. His snarl filled the cabin loudly enough to have both pilots looking back at them wide-eyed. Rex was moments from leaping to take out the crew chief's throat.

"Really should learn to trust your own, buddy. Now ease the weapon." Colby's voice was low and sounded incredibly dangerous.

He didn't understand that Marines guarding the President were trained in scenarios where anyone on the team could be a traitor. And that McShea wasn't going to ease off until he'd been reassured this wasn't the start of an attack—not even at risk of his own death.

Time to move slowly. She placed one hand on McShea's sidearm and eased it downward with a light pressure. Laying her other hand on Rex's head quieted the dog. Colby looked at that in surprise, then reholstered his own sidearm with a shrug. Easing forward, she leaned into the cockpit far enough that she could speak to the pilots. The copilot had his own sidearm drawn, held mostly out of sight close by his belly in case he needed it. Out the front windshield, she could see that they were fast approaching their destination.

"Captain Juarez. Can you confirm for me that Marine One aircraft never travel without ECM jamming on? Not even when returning to base?"

"I can confirm that. Full ECM on all official maneuvers."

"Thank you, Captain."

Ivy eased back into the cabin, still moving slowly, making sure to reassure Rex as she did so. She buckled herself back into her seat as everyone watched her closely. She noted that neither the crew chief nor the copilot had reholstered their weapons. She'd have to remember to commend them later on their vigilance. That's how she wanted her Marines around the President, act first and apologize for killing any potential aggressors later.

"So, Major, what is the reason you swore in my face?" The President asked it in a perfectly normal tone.

"I swore in your face, sir?"

"Rather vehemently," Colby was grinning.

Dilya giggled. As she'd proven earlier that she wasn't some bubble-headed teen, Ivy suspected that Dilya had calculated that to be a tension breaker. It seemed to work. McShea, at least, put away his firearm. Ivy deciding against turning around to check on the copilot's actions.

"My apologies, Mr. President. I'd realized something that I should have recalled yesterday. I can't imagine how we missed it. We need to review our debrief procedures, but the F-14 model was a scenario we had never previously anticipated."

"Which is?" Colby prompted.

Right. Get to the point, Saint Ives.

"It was neither an accident nor a random attack. It was a strike by an expert."

"How do you conclude that?" Harvey Lieber's voice was suddenly pure ice. As head of the Presidential Protection Detail, there was nothing that he would find more upsetting.

A random attack was unlikely to succeed because of the security bubble around the President. But a planned assault would take the Secret Service's capabilities into account. An *expert* assault implied that its planning included actual knowledge of those capabilities. It was the nightmare scenario. Even the attack on the Presidential Motorcade in Colorado had been mostly an application of brute force. This was far more dangerous.

"That F-14 model should have fallen out of the sky when it flew so close to us. Our ECM—electronic countermeasures—block almost every frequency, except for a very few that we're using ourselves. Frequencies that we're constantly changing. Pull out your cell phone. You won't be able to place a call. All of those frequencies are blocked within a hundred meters or more of this aircraft. That F-14 should have fallen out of the sky rather than performing a pinpoint maneuver."

"So the drone's transmitter wasn't randomly damaged by the crash with our tail rotor. It was *designed* to self-destruct, to hide how they did that," Colby was nodding. "Slick."

Harvey began to swing up his radio, which *was* on an authorized frequency, but Ivy held out a hand to stop him.

"You were about to call in an abort on the visit?"

"Yes, ma'am!" Harvey snapped out.

"Don't. It almost had to be an inside job. If you perform an abort, they may just go underground. You can't keep the President locked away forever."

"Now," said the President, "I believe it's my turn to curse. My apologies, ma'am, but *damn straight* you aren't doing that, Harvey. I expressly forbid it. We need a solution, not a retreat."

"Sir!" Harvey protested, but the President shook his head.

"I flew Combat Search and Rescue for multiple tours. I'm not getting chased out of the sky by some nutcase, no matter how smart they think they are. Figure something out."

The helicopter flared for its landing before settling gently on its three wheels.

"Please hold your seat for a moment, sir."

When the President turned to Colby, he continued.

"I'm supposed to have landed at least thirty seconds ahead of you, sir. Until Rex and I have secured the area, we're going to ask you to stay aboard. I don't like that Marine One landed without Rex first checking the landing zone. You're not going to die on my watch, Mr. President."

President Zachary Thomas clenched his jaw tightly at the restriction, but finally nodded when Lieber rested a hand on his shoulder to keep him in his chair.

Colby opened only one side of the double door built into the side of the aircraft, keeping the President shielded by the armor built into the other door. Ivy tried to follow Rex out onto the Orlando hotel front lawn, but Zackie raced out first, dragging Dilya in her wake. At least Dilya made it look that way, but the dog weighed so little that the girl could easily have picked up the dog.

"Trust me. I have similar problems with her," the President explained. "She and that dog are always underfoot at the oddest of times."

At times that Dilya finds most interesting. But Ivy kept that thought to herself and instead followed with what dignity she could muster as the President laughed.

To one side stood the Disney Dolphin Hotel, a nine-story, stuccored edifice that rose another eighteen stories to a triangular pinnacle in the center. Atop either end of the main roof were massive smiling dolphins—each six or seven stories high themselves. To the other three sides of the narrow green lawn sprawled a man-made lake. Wide, low passenger boats carried hotel guests to and from Epcot. And today, each was manned by a team of Secret Service agents. She looked but didn't see any agents in the little swan paddle boats, which would be worth the price of admission.

Colby and Rex had circled Marine One and the second decoy helo that they were supposed to have arrived in. The other decoy remained aloft—better able to react in case of an emergency. A pair of gunships hovered in the distance providing cover.

As Colby and Rex proceeded up to the hotel's entrance, Dilya and Zackie tagged closely behind. Apparently Zackie had a new hero and was mimicking Rex move for move, even if the First Dog didn't know what it was searching for.

Ivy did her best to only show her Marine Corps discipline as she marched up the slight slope from the water's edge to the glass-and-steel main entrance. Past the hovering staff and Secret Service agents, Colby radioed just as Ivy caught up with him.

"Lieber, this is Thompson. Clear."

Ivy didn't have an earpiece, as she was just along as an observer. Colby was her way to stay connected with what was going on. She hated being dependent on him. She still wasn't sure if she was even talking to him.

Then the President, his advisors, and a team of agents brushed by her into the hotel. Into the hotel and out of the bounds of HMX-1 for the next seven hours—which they would spend in intense negotiations with Mexico, Cuba, and the governors of the five Gulf Coast states. All she could do now was wait.

MAY IN FLORIDA was enough to melt a man. And to dissolve a dog.

So he chose one of the deep leather armchairs in the vaulted lobby and listened to the water fountain that splashed merrily into the big sandstone-edged pool.

Dilya had been a distraction for a while. She'd wanted to know everything he could tell her about how to control a dog off-leash. Rex was very mellow when he wasn't under the *seek* command—his elder statesman mode—so they worked with hand signals and voice commands until Rex paid attention to her as well. He wished he could ask Rex what was going on. First, he seemed to have fallen head over all four heels for Ivy. Now, he was accepting commands from a teenager.

Zackie proved to be far less of a bubblehead than the Sheltie had first appeared. Once she understood a command, she followed it every time. Soon, Zackie was trotting about the lobby with a bright click of her nails on the terracotta flooring in patterns that, at least roughly, matched each of Dilya's gestures.

Now they were off practicing their new skills elsewhere in the hotel.

"You know what she's probably doing?" Ivy slipped into the next chair over.

He'd noticed her in the shadowed bar at one edge of the lobby, sipping a Coke. He idly wondered if she still crunched the ice cubes in her teeth—a sound that had always sent nearly-painful shivers up his spine.

He shrugged, unsure of how he was supposed to be reacting to her. Childhood friend? Except they hadn't really *been* friends. They'd been almost enemies—more like adversaries in ways only the closest family members might be. And now that he'd slept with her, the whole "childhood" thing was a moot point. She was more of a woman than…maybe anyone else he'd ever bedded. She took and gave and groaned. She melted and attacked, was vibrant and alarming. Ivy was—

"Dilya is probably sending Zackie running into the President's meetings so that she has an excuse to chase after her and eavesdrop."

He wouldn't put it past her. But it wasn't some teenager and her dog that he was thinking about.

"What's going on, Colby?"

"Me and Rex, we just be hanging." After an hour's exposure to Zackie's high-strung energy, Rex was taking a hard-earned nap.

"Hanging at the Disney's Dolphin Resort doesn't sound like hot babe territory. More like moms with families."

"You're here."

"You calling me a babe, Colby?"

That sounded like dangerous territory. "I don't know what the hell you are, Ivy. Do know that I've never wanted a woman the way I want you at the moment." He kept his voice calm so that he didn't attract the attention of any of the other agents or aides who flowed through the lobby in a near constant stream.

Ivy didn't reply for a long time—long enough for him to look over at her.

"I'm not used to men thinking about me that way," her voice was a whisper.

"Get used to it, lady, because I definitely do. Especially after last night. Hey, this is a hotel. I bet they have rooms. Rooms with beds in them."

"Colby," her tone landed deep in shut-the-hell-up territory. Which sounded like an excuse to keep teasing.

"Hot showers. Hell, I'd settle for a broom closet at the moment if it meant I could get my hands on you."

AND THAT'S what she was to Colby: some babe to "get his hands on."

Yes, last night *had* been amazing. Colby Thompson was a spectacular lover...yet about as deep as the man-made pond in front of the resort—as in not very.

"There's a whole past family-brother-relationship thing going on that you're not paying any attention to, Thompson."

"I didn't know Marines did that."

"Did what?" She wanted to slouch lower in the soft armchair, Colby made it look so comfortable. She never slouched, especially not in her dress uniform. She should be working. While Colby had been working with Dilya, she'd checked her queue. There were three options for the upcoming trip to the Ottawa trade meeting. Preliminary field work for the Pacific Northwest fisheries tour, including a haul over to Japan to once again try to cut down their whaling activities. And a prospectus for the Quito, Ecuador, Climate Conference.

"I didn't know Marines invited their whole family into relationship discussions."

"What are you talking about?"

"What I'm talking about is you, me, and a comfortable bed. What you're talking about is beyond me. What's your family doing in the middle of this conversation?"

"And your family, Thompson."

"Hey, I didn't invite them into this conversation. I was just thinking about sex with you and—"

"And that's all you're thinking about. A man with a dick where he's supposed to have a brain."

Colby snorted out a laugh hard enough to attract the attention of a Mexican and a Cuban government aide conferring hotly in the next set of armchairs over.

"Been called a dickhead before, but never quite like that."

"Tell me it isn't true."

"It isn't true."

As if she believed that.

"Ivy, all I'm talking about at the moment is great sex. It's not as if we're getting married."

"That's not what you told my brother Reggie." Why was she arguing with him on this? Yes, the sex was great. No, not a chance did she want to be in a relationship with Colby Thompson. So *why* was she arguing that he wasn't being committed enough?

"Okay, fine. Let's invite our moms into this. Mine has asked me enough times about getting together with you that I should have her on a loop recording."

"She did? I didn't know that." How could she not know that? She'd followed Reggie over to the Thompsons' nearly as often as Colby had come to their house.

"I always figured it was just a sign of how disappointed she was in her only child's lack of motivation." Colby seemed to slip even lower. If he wasn't careful, he'd end up on the floor with Rex. "She probably figured you'd set a good example or whip me into shape or something."

"That doesn't sound like her." Mrs. Thompson was a Beltway lawyer, specializing in high profile divorces—known for representing the wives of philandering congressmen, senators, and other officials. Yet, despite that, she always seemed to have such a positive attitude.

"If not that, then maybe it's because our moms are already best friends and just wish they were related. We'd be their only chance unless they switch sides and run off together."

"Doesn't sound like either of our moms, the latter part. You could both switch sides and marry my brother."

"So not. First part is true though. Our moms might as well be sisters anyway." Colby glanced over at her. "Anything your mom says?"

"Not directly."

"She's a Marine. I thought everything Marines did was forthright and direct. What does she say instead?"

"We can be subtle when it's called for. Every now and then she points out how handsome you are."

"How handsome I am?" Colby shoved himself upright and raised his voice. "How *handsome* I am? Your *mom* says that? Shit! It looks like I've been chasing the wrong family member."

She was on the verge of taking him down, hard, even if half the lobby was staring at them. And then she caught on that Colby was teasing her. Somewhere along the way, she'd taken him seriously on the topic of relationships. He was right—she was the one who'd hauled their families into a conversation about casual sex. She hated that she'd fallen for it.

Ivy considered throwing him into the deep end of the dolphin fountain, but her mom was right: Colby was incredibly handsome. And, no, he wasn't chasing the wrong family member.

Besides, the fountain wasn't more than a foot deep.

HARVEY LIEBER MIGHT NOT HAVE BEEN able to send the President home, but he made it clear that he wasn't going to trust him in the air unless he had to. Instead of a twenty-minute helicopter flight, the President took a forty-five-minute, sixty-mile ride in the Beast. The

Secret Service punched down a sealed-off corridor at the peak of Orlando rush hour, closed Highway 528, and roared down the empty two-laner and into the twilight at well above the speed limit.

With Jim and Malcolm the springer spaniel covering the Motorcade, he, Ivy, Dilya, and the two dogs were the sole occupants of the three helicopters returning to Cape Canaveral.

"Kept him running, did you?" Colby asked the girl. Zackie was passed out during the flight—a state he'd rarely witnessed the Sheltie in.

"Might have."

"Learn anything interesting?"

Dilya looked at him with a puzzled expression. So disingenuous that he might have bought it if not for Ivy's snort of laughter.

The teen shifted to a bright smile and shrugged off her defeat easily. "Not all that much really. Mexico is still trying to hold on to old styles of energy production; drilling the Gulf is how they've always propped up their economy. Now that we can generate the oil more cheaply and more safely with fracking—that's such an ugly word, isn't it? It's like the word itself causes even more people who don't understand it to hate it. Words are so fascinating that—"

"No one can sidetrack us," Colby warned her and she actually frowned for a moment before giving in.

"Cuba is far too desperate to be concerned with any ecologic considerations. They were more worried about being nice to the governors of the two particular states that border the Gulf. They're nearest to Florida, but their economics minister hovered around the Alabama and Mississippi governors. He wanted to know all about their casino operations and how he could rebuild the old Cuban casinos as if it was still the 1950s and they could get Hollywood and tourism money pouring in. 'Green oil' he kept calling it. 'Green oil for our economy.' I liked that analogy. I think the governors liked it too. As if it made sense to them."

"Are you the one who gave it to him?"

She stumbled to a halt as if she'd just accidentally showed her poker hand. Then she shrugged like she didn't know what he was talking about and became interested in whatever was out the window. He checked, a twilit expanse of Florida's never-ending lakes.

Note to self: never underestimate Dilya.

Ivy unleashed one of those million-watt smiles on him.

Note to self: never underestimate Ivy either.

He wanted to continue their conversation from the hotel lobby, but not with Dilya there.

"Aren't you going to at least talk to her?" Dilya was now eyeing him curiously.

"Yeah," Ivy said, sounding far more casual than her usual Marine Corps self. "Aren't you gonna talk to me?"

"About what? The startling way your eye color seems to shift with your mood? The way your hair catches the sunlight, even when there isn't any? Or, there are other things I could point out."

Ivy actually blushed, so maybe it was a good track to pursue later… in private.

"Duh! Tell her what you like best about her. That's what girls want to hear."

"What I like best about her?"

Dilya nodded.

Ivy set her jaw and glared at him, but the color was still bright on her fair cheeks.

"What I like best about you." There were a surprising number of things to like about Ivy Hanson. But best? "Your absolute and complete determination that you can make the world a better place through sheer force of will. I know it changed my life for the better."

Dilya must have been keeping an eye on Ivy, because she punched him in the arm with a job-well-done gesture.

"Your life?"

"I told you. Would never have amounted to much if it wasn't for you. You made being determined look like it was fun. I've never been a particularly driven guy, I know that about myself. But you've made me want to be a better one and I've tried. You kind of lent credence to the old nickname: Saint Ives, the patron saint of Colby Thompson, the sad sack."

That's the moment that Ivy finally shed the last of her "Old Colby" bias. She could feel it sloughing off and falling out of the helicopter just as she'd considered disposing of Colby's body yesterday over the Maryland countryside.

Colby *embodied* the better man. He still wasn't driven, displaying none of that edge that she knew cut other people away from her side. But he was steady as a rock. Was he also as loyal as his dog? It actually wouldn't surprise her if he was.

And he'd done it because of her? No. Erase the question mark. He *had* changed himself because of her.

"I'm not anything special. I'm…"

But Colby was shaking his head and offering her a smile that she remembered from the bedroom this morning. No, from that very first moment on the South Lawn when she'd turned around and almost fallen over Rex. She hadn't recognized it at the time, but it had reflected a genuine pleasure at seeing her. Despite the teasing, the banter, the fumbling, and even the stupid comments each time he became uncomfortable—he looked at her as if she was a joy to be with.

She definitely wasn't a joy. There had been plenty of grunts under her command who had made that clear. Their opinions were solidly backed up by the abort-style exit strategies of her past lovers. She earned respect. She earned obedience. She rarely earned pleasure at her presence.

Ivy the Marine didn't go away around Colby, but it also wasn't the part of her that he saw. And that scared the crap out of her.

Yes, a Marine never showed fear, never ran from a fight. But this handsome, patient man from her past who had somehow metamorphosed into her present made her want to launch her heart right at him.

JUST BECAUSE THE President hadn't ridden in the HMX-1 helicopters didn't mean that they were put away on their return to Cape

Canaveral. They would remain parked by the C-5 Galaxy, available on a moment's notice until the President was safely back aboard Air Force One. That had meant that he and Ivy were free to go and watch the launch.

Well, moderately free. Harvey Lieber didn't believe in letting assets sit idle any more than Captain Baxter had.

The public would also be at this launch, so Rex and Colby moved into the crowds ahead of the President along with Malcolm and Jim from the Motorcade.

Ivy trailed along in the wide wake that Rex cut through the crowd. But she was enjoying herself hugely. It felt an awful lot like the way she used to tag after him and Reggie so long ago. She gawked like that little kid as they walked through the dramatically lit Rocket Garden.

"Look! Look! Look!" She tried to point in every direction at once. "Both of the Mercury rockets—the Redstone *and* the Atlas—Gemini, Juno, Titan." She named each like it was her favorite pet ever. "Look at them all standing on their tail fins as if they were still ready to leap into space right now." She slapped her hands together sharply enough to startle Rex, then slashed one skyward as if she could take off like Superman. Or Superwoman.

When they reached the Apollo/Saturn V Center, she practically swooned, sighing like a movie heroine in love. That rocket was so big they had laid it down in a cradle rather than erecting it vertically like the others. And still it dwarfed them. She was right, it was incredible.

"This is when they knew how to dream," Ivy told him. "The shuttle was a delivery van compared to these racing cars. Nixon made us give up space."

"No, he authorized the shuttle. That's what got us to orbit."

"Trust me, Colby. The day we began work on the space shuttle was the day we gave up on reaching the planets. Nixon invested an extra hundred billion—a one-third increase—in 1968 alone into the defense budget to destroy Southeast Asia. At the same time, in just six years, he cut NASA's budget from six billion (which was already the lowest in four years) to three. We were supposed to be on Mars in 1986. I could have gone there if—"

She bit it off hard, looking sour and angry. Like everything else, she took this completely to heart as a personal affront.

He took his attention off Rex long enough to wrap an arm around her shoulder. She leaned into him for a moment as if seeking comfort. He liked that. He liked learning that Saint Ives did have a vulnerability and was even willing to share it with him, however briefly.

He couldn't think of what to say as they made their way to the NASA control room, called a Firing Room.

"Well, they're dreaming again, Saint Ives."

She nodded as fiercely as Dilya sometimes did. Then she gazed longingly with puppy-dog eyes out toward where the rocket would launch later tonight. Why couldn't she see that in herself? *This* was obviously where she belonged. All the echoing silence of the distant runway was vibrantly alive here at Kennedy Space Center, especially in this pre-launch moment.

"How often do they launch here, Ivy?"

"Every twelve days globally. They're expecting growth to one every two days this year or next. A third of that is US, probably growing to half. Most of that from right here," she sounded dreamy. Then blinked at him in surprise.

"That sounds like a lot of launches."

"It does, doesn't it?" And for the first time since they'd rushed out of bed this morning, that smile was back. That smile of hope and what was possible.

They'd arrived in the glass-walled room where the President was the guest of the NASA management team. The floodlights out at the launch pad three miles away shone like a star in the Florida night. He led Ivy over to a corner where they'd still have a view.

"Secret Service trick to being invisible," he whispered to her, "be exactly where everyone expects you to be."

"But not anywhere that they'd normally look," Dilya said as she and Zackie slipped up by Ivy's elbow.

Ivy looped an arm through Dilya's as they both leaned back against the wall, well out of the common sightlines.

They were raptly watching the goings-on.

To their left through an interior wall of glass window, long rows of computer stations were manned by serious, focused personnel. On their level, raised enough to look down over the entire floor, was the primary row of control stations. There were only six seats at the station and the launch director striding back and forth, hovering over their shoulders.

At either end of the upper platform were a pair of glassed-in rooms. On the far side, the Operations Support Team were the top-tier of decision makers. Ivy whispered that they were the senior flight and manufacturing personnel who would give the Launch Director the final go/no go. They themselves were in a similar glass box with all of the officials.

"Nobody in this area has any say-so, but they're too important to shut out." And indeed, the NASA Administrator and his deputy sat to either side of the President while others hovered as nearby as they dared.

Harvey Lieber, far from being inconspicuous, stood in the center of the only doorway into the room. Nobody was getting near the President without going through Harvey first.

It was a real problem here. NASA security was like an itch he couldn't scratch. They were an independent agency, but they needed a serious lesson. Colby figured that even without his badge, he could have entered this room given only minimal planning and a minor dose of razzle-dazzle. Security was still based in old-fashioned metal detector thinking. The White House had a multi-layered defense system far beyond most buildings, but—despite being the center of the American space program—this site was little more secure than a post office. Those guys at least had a healthy paranoia about how unpredictable civilians could be. NASA seemed to think that if you were dressed like an engineer, then you must belong.

If not for Rex and Malcolm, who was also on patrol, he could have walked in with an entire knapsack of Semtex and taken out whole sections of the complex. They'd blocked all of the obvious routes and methods, but the Secret Service had plugged those decades ago. The kind of attacks the Service planned against could breeze in here on a tourist pass.

So Colby kept a careful eye in the one direction that Harvey couldn't see without fully turning around. Harvey spotted that and gave him an infinitesimal nod of acknowledgement. Which, in the grand scheme, wasn't bad. It was more than Captain Baxter had typically offered.

The closer the launch came, the lower the numbers rolled on the countdown, the harder it was to not watch Ivy and Dilya rather than Harvey's back.

The brilliantly blonde Marine Corps major was the same height as the dark teen, but they could almost be mother and daughter with how greedily they both watched the monitors and the small star of light that was the distant launchpad.

Mother and daughter.

Imagining Ivy with her own mother only evoked images of how alike the two women were. Ivy's coloring had come from her father the chef, but her small build and attitude had come straight from her Marine Corps mother.

Watching Ivy with Dilya made it easy to imagine Ivy with a precocious daughter of her own. Of *their* own? Was *that* the image in his head? Despite her mother's decades of service and his own mother's constant tales of high-profile divorce, both of their parents' marriages had been very stable through the years.

Relationships that grew too deep were his excuse to find fresh pastures. But Ivy, who felt like the freshest ground of all, also dated back to his first memory. What was up with that?

The clock was finally released from the final planned hold at nine minutes. The other glass cubicle, filled with its specialists, must have given approval for the launch. The excitement grew palpably as single-digit minutes became double-digit seconds and ultimately they turned single-digit as well.

Three.

Two.

One.

At zero, the star of nighttime floodlights was suddenly overwhelmed by the brilliant glare of the rocket. The clock reversed.

One.

Two.

Three.

On four, the tiny rocket balanced atop the huge ball of light climbed impossibly slowly out of its own steam cloud. But climb clear it did, clawing aloft until it seemed to find its gait, then it roared aloft.

But it wasn't the rocket's glare that captured his imagination. It was the fire's glow on Ivy's shining face as she tracked it upward with her whole being.

Somewhere in the background, the announcer declared they were five-by-five and continuing on profile. All good to go. Cheers broke out around the room. The NASA administrator and the President were trading solid handshakes of congratulations.

And Ivy stared aloft with tears streaming unwiped down her cheeks and a smile bigger than all of space lighting her features.

He liked his life just fine, but he'd never felt the way she looked. No woman, anywhere, had ever looked that happy.

He'd thought Ivy was done with changing his world, but he'd been wrong. He wanted to be a part of that joy so badly it almost hurt.

CHAPTER TWELVE

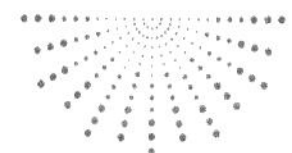

*I*vy wasn't used to waking in a man's arms, but she could get used to it quickly if it kept feeling like this. And despite its newness, she felt instant awareness about the identity of the man holding her. Perhaps it was because of the massive dog lying by her feet like the world's best foot warmer, but she didn't think so. She leaned into Colby's smell, so unchanged from when they were younger yet completely different.

In their youth, he'd sometimes carry her piggyback, at least until she'd started tickling him whenever he did—she hadn't been able to resist. He'd reluctantly agreed to be her sparring partner when she needed to practice a judo move, at least until she'd misjudged a grapple and throw, bloodying his nose so badly that it had taken hours to fully stop.

Breathing him in now, he smelled like home. As familiar and safe as her childhood room.

Safety.

Colby Thompson?

That part of him wasn't completely new, but most of it was. It was like the transition from a Bell TH-57 trainer (the 206 to civilians) to the majesty and power of the MV-22B Osprey. It was bigger than the transition from a solo Mercury rocket barely reaching low Earth orbit to an Atlas V moon rocket. Younger Colby and the man presently sleeping with his arms still wrapped around her couldn't be more different. He was the Falcon Heavy rocket, the biggest rocket since the Saturn back in the 1960s.

She'd been emotionally exhausted after the long day and the launch. Riding back to the C-5 Galaxy within the President's Motorcade, the President and Dilya were quickly airborne and headed back to DC on Air Force One. It was midnight when they began breaking down and loading the helos. Three a.m. before they unloaded at Andrews Air Force Base back in DC. At four a.m., they'd crawled into Colby's bed. She had no real memory of her arrival here. Up the stairs, through a darkened room, shed clothes, and pass out curled up in his arms.

Now, she was awake, realizing how spontaneously she had gotten where she lay and feeling a bit wanton. She hadn't even asked, but then again, neither had he. She'd simply climbed into the taxi with him and ridden back to his place.

This wasn't confusing enough, let's go back to bed together because the sex was better than having a warp drive in her own personal starship.

Real deep, Ivy.

Who needed deep when it felt and smelled this good?

She snuggled back in and let the exhaustion take her back under.

HE'D FELT her wake up, but hadn't said anything at first. And then when she didn't, it finally became so awkward that he wasn't sure what to say so had kept his mouth shut.

Colby had spent the entire night in uncharted territory. Rex hadn't tested it for safety with his nose, wasn't even trained to help him detect potential hazards and traps. Colby was out here on his own, stumbling into pitfalls and triggering explosions all on his own.

In the middle of the night, Rex had snuck up onto the bed, and Colby couldn't figure out how to stop him without waking Ivy. Now, his feet were numb and tingling below where Rex lay across them. They had so little blood flow that they could probably be amputated without him even noticing, until Rex moved and the nerves all came roaring back to life.

That's what Ivy had done to him. She made it feel as if he was roaring back to life—a life he'd never known he was missing in the first place. And it hurt!

He'd named the uncharted territory somewhere around dawn. It was the land of the *What If* in the future possible lives of one Colby Thompson. Definitely not a place he'd ever been before. Thinking ahead wasn't a major pastime for him or Rex. He liked that about his dog: they were both very present-tense sort of guys.

Ivy was anything but that.

What if Ivy wanted more than a fast fling for old times' sake? But there was no "old times' sake" between them for that to happen. She wasn't some sexy, ex-girlfriend looking for a one-night revisit to old triumphs. She was… He didn't know. So he'd continued the game as its sole and unwilling player.

What if she *didn't* want more than a fast fling? That didn't sound like as much fun as it usually did.

What if it became *more?* What if they both let that happen, then she left the Marine Corps to pursue a job in space? She'd end up in Cape Kennedy or Houston, or, God help him, maybe she *would* walk on the surface of Mars someday. Meanwhile, what would Colby be doing?

Walking the South Lawn.

Rex still had a couple good years in him if everything went well. But eventually Rex would be retired. And then one day his pal would go to sleep and never wake up…not a prospect Colby could even face.

When had he become emotionally dependent on a dog? Attached? Sure. He loved the furry beast. But to have Rex as the deepest emotional relationship of his life sounded pretty lame.

And he was flung back into the land of *what if.* What if this fling-that-didn't-feel-like-a-fling turned into more than a fling? What then? He and Ivy?

Reggie would kill him, that was a given.

Their moms would probably be thrilled. Their dads...well, they'd be dads. They'd raise a beer and call it a job well done.

What would Ivy do? What would he do?

It was better not to tell anyone...especially himself. The less he knew about this, the happier he'd be. But he couldn't seem to get there. Not with Ivy curled in his arms as if she'd never belonged anywhere else. Her hair, so light he could barely feel where it lay upon his chest and cheek, smelled of springtime and that joy that she wore like an inner skin—letting it shine through her fair outer skin whenever the mood struck her.

He wanted to hold on *and* run away both.

He felt her go back to sleep. He considered waking her, because maybe it *was* time they had a talk. Tried to figure out what was—

The phone by his bed rang so loudly that he felt as if he'd been plugged into an electric socket. He was—normally—a very deep sleeper, so he kept it loud.

By the second ring, several things had happened.

Rex leapt to his feet on the bed.

Only by quickly scooting sideways was Colby able to avoid being castrated by one of Rex's massive paws.

Ivy jolted awake.

Having learned a thing or two, he managed to get a hand between her and his solar plexus to block any random incoming elbows. He even managed to get his face out of her hair and turned to the side so that he didn't get headbutted as she too jolted to life.

His balance tipped precariously at the edge of the mattress, but he held on.

Until Ivy dove for the phone on the nightstand, placing a breast squarely in his face.

That did it.

All balance and control gone, he tumbled down onto the carpet, where Rex and Ivy both looked down at him in surprise.

"Hello?" Ivy answered his phone. At least she said something like that, her voice was still thoroughly sleep-fuzzed.

"It's for you," she handed it down to him.

"It *is* my phone."

She blinked her eyes hard a couple of times, looking around the room as if uncertain quite where she was. It was Saturday morning. The only person who called him on Saturday morning was his mother. They usually checked in with each other about whether they could fit in a family meal over the weekend.

And *Ivy* had answered the phone. This was bad in so many ways.

"Hi, Mom." There had to be some way to avoid explaining the woman in his bed. No, that wasn't the problem—Mom was used to that. There had to be some way to avoid explaining quite *which* woman was in his bed.

"Not your mom, Thompson," General Arnson snarled into the phone. "Was that my best officer who answered?"

"Um, yes, sir." This was even worse than Mom.

"And what did I say about you messing up my best officer?"

"You didn't say anything about *mussing* her up though." Not his best comeback, but he was lying naked on the floor with an equally naked Ivy looking down at him quizzically and that was a very distracting vision. Her hair was loose and tangled, making a charming golden halo about her face. It was a vision he wouldn't soon forget.

There was a stony silence on the phone.

For lack of anything else to offer to keep him out of the future job of dogshit cleaner, he kept his own silence.

"Why aren't you at the White House?"

"Because we—" should have said *I* "—got in at four a.m. And perhaps I should mention that it's Saturday."

"You don't understand the trouble you're in, Thompson. Neither does Major Hanson."

"Trouble, sir?" *We're both in trouble?* Colby mouthed the question to Ivy.

She furrowed her brow for a moment, then shrugged. Which set off some very nice secondary effects down her body that he did his best to ignore. At least until he got off the phone.

"Harvey Lieber is unwilling to place the President's life in *my* helicopters until we have a solution. HMX-1's next mission is supposed to be Ottawa. That's Monday morning. You and Major Hanson have forty-eight hours to solve this. I expect you to arrive in the White House Military Office in twenty minutes and not move your asses a single inch until you get this done."

"I live thirty minutes door-to-door from the White House."

"Make it in twenty-five," he snarled, leaving no doubt that it was the limits of his patience.

"We aren't even dressed," some idiot part of himself just couldn't resist. But the instant he said it, he knew he was a dead man.

"Twenty-*four!*" And the line went dead—thankfully before he could think to point out that Rex needed a morning walk as well.

IVY'S ATTEMPT TO detour to the Navy Mess to get coffee and something breakfasty was blocked when General Arnson spotted her coming through the West Wing lobby.

"Where are your dress blues?"

"Still water-logged from my swim in the Potomac." All she'd had in her go-bag were battledress uniforms. And her spare blues were in her apartment on the other side of town from Colby's apartment. It was embarrassing to come to the White House dressed so casually, but she hadn't had any other option. The general was immaculate in his uniform.

"Where's Thompson?" The general looked ready to commit murder.

"Taking Rex for a quick walk," she nodded toward the West Wing's entrance. "He thought it might be better if his dog didn't pee on the lobby security desk." They'd split tasks to save time—he'd walk Rex and she'd get breakfast—but her part of the job wasn't working very well. She tried leading the general over to the mess, but he didn't appear to be in the mood to move so she was stuck.

"Thompson." He said it completely deadpan. "You have a history?"

"Not the way you mean. We grew up next door to each other."

"Assessment? And don't give me any happy smile crap. I can see that part of it all over you already."

Ivy had been sure that her best deadpan was firmly in place. "I—" she tried to start, but Arnson's scowl stopped her and she had to try again. *Happy smile crap all over her?* He was right, that couldn't be what was happening. Except she could feel that it was.

"Colby Thompson. If ever there was an unambitious man, he's it. Always was. However, he has risen to his current position through skill and hard work. It would never enter his mind to maneuver or be a political animal."

"A top soldier, but no officer."

"A natural leader, but no cutthroat attitude to match."

"How many throats did you cut before you came to my attention at HMX-1, Hanson?"

"As few as possible," she risked a smile.

The general returned it readily enough before continuing in a softer voice. "Being a Marine officer means that you toed the line— and you toed it hard. You know and I know that anyone who waivered from the standard of the Corps was *meant* to be left in the dust."

"Yes, sir."

"Do you think you and your unambitious lover can get my helos back on the job?"

She wasn't comfortable with the word lover, but that wasn't something to point out to a pissed-off general.

"If we fail, it won't be for lack of killing ourselves, sir."

His grim nod said she'd better come back dead if she failed.

"Any assets you need, *any*, get them. Call my cell at any hour if some dead man tries to stonewall you. And Hanson…"

"Yes, sir."

"You cut any throats you have to. Even dog boy's. I want my birds back in the air."

"GOT ANY THROATS I CAN SLIT?" Ivy lay her head down on the desk, not even bothering to shove aside any of the paperwork.

"How about mine?" Colby was too exhausted to slouch and barely managed a slump in his own chair. Three shifts had cycled through the WHMO without making them much wiser.

The organization chart of who was informed of flight operational frequencies hung on one wall. They'd managed to reduce the list by a third—General Arnson's approval for that had arrived less than six minutes after they'd sent him the proposal.

Three different radio experts had reviewed the operations frequency selection methodology—the White House Communications Agency was a part of the WHMO, so they didn't have to go far to find the top people in the field. Between them, they generated an entirely new set of protocols that required half as many frequencies and actually improved operations and crisis communication efficiency. Because that one was more convoluted and had broader ramifications to HMX procedures, it required Arnson *nine* minutes to approve it. Harvey Lieber's approval—as the Presidential Protection Detail was also involved—arrived six minutes later with the note: *Good work. But it's not enough yet.* That had sapped what little energy had sustained them through the round-the-clock shift.

"Twenty-four hours down," Colby rubbed at the back of his neck, but that didn't help either. "Twenty-four more to go before the President is on the move again. You know, if you'd gone to space, neither of us would be in this pickle."

"Next time he goes into the Oval Office, let's sneak upstairs and padlock all the doors shut from the outside."

"Nah," Colby forced himself not to lay his head down on the table right next to Ivy's. "Then Harvey Lieber, as head of the protection detail, would have to shoot us. And that would lead to all sorts of awkward problems."

"Like the general not being able to kill us himself for not fixing this problem."

"Right. Besides, being killed twice doesn't sound like much fun from our end of it either."

"I'm hungry," Ivy told the diagram of the F-14 model's flight path and attack line that her head lay on.

"I'm too tired to be hungry," Colby agreed. The only one who'd eaten regularly had been Rex. Colby looked at his watch. "It's 0600. Sunday, I think. The Navy Mess won't open for a while."

"The White House has a kitchen. I know because my brother works there."

And the chances of running into Reggie at this hour on a Sunday were thankfully very low. "We'll circle out across the South Lawn for Rex to do his thing."

It still took them a couple of minutes to generate enough enthusiasm to stand and another to get moving. Once he was outside, Colby felt as if he could breathe again. This is what he and Rex were used to. Walking the lawn, out in whatever the weather was. This inside desk work just wasn't right for a man and his dog. But that was a problem for another time.

"I love this time of day." The dawn had painted the entire sky in roses and pinks. Blues were still several minutes away and for the moment there was a hush on DC. Too early for the traffic or the protestors, even the birds seemed to be holding their breath.

Rex piddled on a couple of rose bushes on their way to enter below the South Portico. The ground level entrance passed through the Diplomatic Reception Room.

"Are we even supposed to be in here?"

"Sure. I'm Lead Dog. Clearance to go anywhere, even the Residence if I could justify the need." Though he'd only been through this entrance a few times over the years.

"I thought you weren't Lead Dog anymore."

Colby felt the gut punch. Ivy rested her hand on his arm in immediate sympathy.

"I'm sorry. I wasn't thinking."

"It's okay. I've got to get used to it."

"I feel like I'm making the room dirty just by breathing in here."

She tucked her hand around his elbow as they stepped further into the room. After that, he didn't care if they were supposed to be here or not.

It was one of the four oval rooms in the White House, all roughly the same size. Predating the one in the West Wing were the three in the Residence. Stacked up, one per floor, the Green, Blue, and Yellow Ovals formed the grand curve of the South Portico giving the White House its distinctive shape.

The Green was a pristine space. Its elegance so extreme that Colby had always felt it was stark. The rug was a vast terrain of pale blue and gold with the emblems of the fifty states worked into its perimeter. White doors, white walls, white ceiling, crystal chandelier.

"It feels chilly," Ivy's voice was barely a whisper.

"Elsie, uh, this woman I knew, would have liked this room." Several of his former girlfriends would have. The high-end furnishings, the obvious history of it all. He liked that Ivy would be more comfortable in a room with a battered but comfortable couch and a coffee table you could prop your feet on rather than one you'd be afraid to brush against.

"Did you dump her or she you?" Ivy missed nothing, of course.

Colby ignored the question and instead looked at the wallpaper mural. Zuber wallpaper, he'd been told, worth over sixty grand and put in place by Jackie Kennedy who had salvaged it from some mansion about to be demolished. He'd never really had time to look at it. Stylized scenes of nineteenth century America, back when there'd been much less of it. Boston Harbor, Niagara Falls, New York Bay— with a skyline that looked nothing like in the movies by about a hundred stories. It wrapped all the way around the room from waist height to eight or nine feet.

He looked at Ivy and she was as wide-eyed as he felt.

"Yeah, out."

She nodded quickly and they exited the far side of the room. The Central Hall had none of the pomp. Red carpeting, massive white arches supporting the upper three stories of the Residence that felt a little too low just because of the arches' heft. It was immaculate, but far less scary.

"Maybe I'll avoid that entrance in the future."

"Good idea."

He dropped Rex off on the dog bed that was kept in the corner of the small Secret Service Ready Room before ducking down the hall to the kitchen. At this hour, there should only be one of the staff chefs manning the place. They could grab whatever was at hand and get right back to work. Stepping in the door, he was almost run over by Chef Klaus, the executive chef—who didn't even bother to slow down, assuming the world would get out of his way.

The kitchen was in full swing.

Klaus strode up to a chef surrounded by massive crates of vegetables. He might be a Teutonic hardass, but he was also an amazing chef. He stopped beside the chef surrounded by crates of peas still in the pod, tiny brilliant green zucchini, and bright yellow, star-shaped pattypan squash.

"It is not some hammer you are beating them with. It is a chef's knife. It is a tool of art, not war. One extra ounce of pressure and we see it mar the flesh," he watched the poor chef make another cut. "No! No! No! Do not slow down. Slow is as bad as too hard. Gentle and fast. Then you get smooth slice. *Jawohl?*"

The chef nodded as Klaus continued to watch his every motion.

Colby was glad that he hadn't followed Reggie into being a chef. Reggie had tried to nudge him that way, but Colby had never had the deep passion about food that his best friend did. He was a better-than-average cook from all the meals they'd made together, but that was a long way from being a chef.

Reggie was studying one of the massive soup kettles as if it was a set of nuclear launch codes.

"Maybe if we step away quietly," Colby whispered. "He won't notice us. Then we can run for our lives."

Ivy looked at Colby in surprise.

"You're afraid of Reggie?" But they were best friends.

"We're in a kitchen filled with knives and cleavers. Consider it the better part of discretion."

"We're armed too," she patted her sidearm and dragged him the last step into the kitchen. "What's that, Reg?"

There was no reason for Colby to be worried, her brother didn't even look up from his soup. There was no heat coming from it. In fact, the air felt cooler near it. Chilled pureed soup of some sort. Colby would probably know what it was just by looking at it, but she didn't have a clue other than it looked creamy, smooth, and green. Maybe a space ooze that would leap out of the pot and turn them all into pod people.

"Watch." Reggie picked up a squeeze bulb attached to long rod. He squeezed the air out, dipped it in a bowl of an orange liquid, and sucked some of it up. Then he turned to his soup and, pressing the bulb once again, slowly formed a small orange globe that bobbed on the surface. He then stabbed it with a syringe of something dark green. Setting his implements aside, he picked up a soup spoon, scooped up the orange globe with some soup, and held it out for her to taste.

She took it off the spoon. Bright mint was the first flavor to hit. She might not know how to cook oatmeal, but living with Dad and Reggie, she'd learned how to eat and taste. Waiting past the initial surprise of mint, the smooth depth of fresh peas rolled over her tongue. But there was a citrus tease from the globe that had her biting down on it. In a minor explosion of flavor, bright orange sunshine flooded her mouth, finishing with just a hint of original mint and lemon that he'd injected into the center of the globe.

"Oh. That's wonderful. Spring in a spoonful. Make one for Colby."

"For Colby?" Reggie almost jumped out of his shoes when he looked around to realize that Colby was standing close beside her. Shocked out of his chef mode, his eyes immediately tracked down to where her hand was still looped around Colby's elbow. It felt so natural there, she hadn't thought anything about it. Well, to let go wasn't going to happen. She wasn't doing anything wrong.

Reggie slowly made another and held a spoon for Colby.

She watched him as he tasted. It was as if she could see so much more of the dish just watching his face than tasting it herself. The balance of the salt and pepper. The choice of chicken rather than vegetable broth behind the primary pea flavor. And when he bit into it, the smile that touched his lips made her want to kiss him so that they could share that taste. They had been together for just two nights and again she was imagining intimate, sharing moments with him. And where might *those* moments lead? To equally connected and intimate sex. It wasn't a question; it was a given with how it felt to lie against his body. How it felt to simply hold his arm.

"A little more lemon in the mint center," Colby suggested.

"Then a little more pepper in the soup—no, just on the surface," Reggie concluded. "The pepper will accent the lemon, bringing the final taste to life but I don't want to unbalance the soup for today's Rose Garden luncheon." Which explained why the kitchen was so busy at such an early hour.

They watched him in silence as he made another pair of globes. Scooping them onto fresh spoons, he ground the tiniest bit of pepper on each before handing them over.

The globe now burst to life in her mouth, "Oh my God!"

Colby just offered a thumbs up.

Chef Klaus joined them. This time Reggie selected a small sundae glass from the shelf above his station. He poured in a ladleful of the soup so carefully that it didn't splash the sides. He then floated another of his orange-mint-lemon balls in the middle, topping it with the tiniest amounts of pepper, sour cream, and chives.

The chef inspected it carefully, perhaps for visual effect, then tasted it, showing absolutely no reaction.

Ivy wanted to beat up on him for not loving her brother's beautiful soup.

He took another spoonful, of just soup this time, and waited for a full thirty seconds after tasting it again. Then he set the glass down, nodded, and walked away.

"Wait! What about—" but Chef Klaus had moved on.

"That's high praise from Klaus, Ivy." Reggie actually smiled. "High praise indeed."

"Because he didn't say anything awful?" Ivy was still outraged.

"Yep."

"Well, ignore him. That was really something special, buddy," Colby slapped Reggie on the shoulder.

Which once again drew Reggie's attention back to them. Somewhere in the tasting, she'd let go of Colby's arm, but that didn't change what her brother had seen. He looked back and forth between them. Maybe Colby was right and they should have run when they'd had the chance. Did the energy between them sizzle so brightly that it glowed like some force field? If so, she should feel much more impervious than she did. Instead she wanted to stare at her feet like a bad little girl.

"How did this happen?"

"How did what happen?" And there was the Colby she knew. His subtle tease, forcing Reggie to actually state what he meant.

"You two. I should beat the shit out of you, Colby. That's my little sister."

"Hello, standing right here. I'm not in the third person."

Reggie ignored her and glared at Colby and looked as if he actually might try to tackle him right here in the kitchen. "Together. How?"

Ivy and Colby glanced at each other. And again there was that hint of a smile that told her Colby was about to zing his best friend.

Even better to zing in stereo.

They turned to Reggie in unison, then, as if they'd planned it and practiced it, they both shrugged and said, "No idea."

<hr>

"He didn't look very happy." Even by the end of the breakfast he'd served the three of them, Reggie had still been grumpy. Maybe because Ivy had kept poking at him throughout the hurried meal of cheese and mushroom omelets with a blueberry marmalade scone and hot chocolate.

Colby had focused instead on enjoying a White House breakfast as fast as he could. He knew that, with Reggie, it was best to just let him stew on things a while. Despite being his sister, Ivy had never learned that lesson.

"I can't see why it matters to him," Ivy grumbled as they retrieved Rex. He scarfed his egg-and-cheese doggie omelet off the paper plate in two gulps. "It's *my* personal life, not his."

"When it comes to protective older brothers and their little sisters, it's very personal."

"Well, it shouldn't be."

"It would help if I wasn't his best friend."

"Why? He already likes you. Better than me sleeping with some stranger."

"It doesn't work that way between guys. Besides, I'd rather you didn't do that."

"Sleep with strangers? Why?"

"Becoming rather partial to sleeping with you myself, Saint Ives."

She rolled her eyes at him.

"Missed sleeping with you last night."

"We were working side-by-side all night. Straight through. And we —" she unleashed a tonsil-deep yawn "—have to get back to it."

"Sure, but I liked the sleeping together part." And he had—even if it was now most of two nights he hadn't slept. Holding Ivy was a real treat. If he'd ever dated a snuggler before, he didn't recall it. Sleeping with Ivy made a man feel as if he was somehow more than a man. Ivy gave a hundred percent of her attention to sleeping beside him just like she did everything else.

"I'm done in. We've got to get *some* shuteye. I'm unsafe to fly at this point."

"I'll keep you out of any cockpits."

Rex had stopped without Colby noticing. Colby hit the end of the leash and still Rex didn't move, forcing Colby to a halt. His dog was staring down the long Central Hall. They'd progressed most of the way from the midpoint where the Secret Service Ready Room was, back to the Palm Room to return to the West Wing.

Behind them, trotting along by herself as if she hadn't a care, Zackie came silently toward them over the red carpet.

Ivy laid her head on his shoulder, not even bothering to turn, simply falling asleep because they'd stopped moving.

Zackie traded nose sniffs with Rex, turned around, and trotted back the way she'd come.

Normally Colby would shrug it off. The dog was Dilya's problem, or the First Family's. But the little Sheltie was moving with purpose just as she had at the conference center in Florida, after the training Colby had given to Zackie and Dilya. Then the Sheltie sidetracked to sniff a potted plant before cutting over to the other side of the hall.

Colby caught the barest glimpse of dark hair peeking around the corner, then a whispered command echoed down the odd acoustics of the long hallway. Zackie snapped to and continued on her way back to Dilya.

It was too early to play games, but she probably hadn't sent Zackie to them just as a game—nothing was ever that simple with Dilya. Besides, he liked the kid. The kid who might never have been a kid according to the stories he'd heard about her war orphan past. Despite his exhaustion, he was intrigued.

He unclipped Rex's leash and gave him the hand sign to move ahead fast.

"Geh Herum! Links!" Go around! Left! He added the whispered command as a last minute thought.

Rex swung left into the first corridor at a fast trot.

Colby began his countdown. *Seven.*

Zackie disappeared around the far corner where Dilya waited.

Six. Five.

Colby made a point of turning the near somnambulant Ivy toward the exit, but kept his head turned just enough to see down the Central Hall in his peripheral vision. "Wake up, Ives. You don't want to miss this."

Four. Three.

The top of Dilya's head peeped around the corner once more, with Zackie's nose down by her knees.

He had to pinch Ivy to get her attention.

Two. One.

Ivy startled and turned just as Rex caught up with his target.

With a loud *"EEP!"* Dilya stumbled out into the middle of the hall. Zackie launched forward as well. Then Rex, emerging from where he'd circled around and run down the back corridor, stepped on Dilya's foot and leaned into her. She tumbled to the carpet and Rex proceeded to sit on her before looking happily down the hall toward him. He completely ignored Dilya's protesting laughter and Zackie running excited circles around the pair offering bright yips that echoed painfully down the hall.

He and Ivy strolled back, but he didn't give Rex the heel command. It was another new behavior, pinning Dilya in place. Apparently you *could* teach an old dog new tricks.

"Good morning, Dilya."

She managed a gasped, "Morning," as she shoved ineffectively at the dog who probably weighed as much as she did.

Rex apparently decided it was a back scratch and began wagging his big tail, beating her about the head and shoulders with it.

"What trouble are you up to?"

"Brea-thing." Her gasp had devolved to a wheeze as she gave up and crossed her arms over her face protectively.

Colby slapped his thigh and Rex trotted over, eliciting a final "Oof!" as he pushed off. He gave Rex a couple of well-earned treats.

Dilya sat up rubbing her belly. "That was...so cool. I never saw him...coming. If Zackie hadn't turned...at the last...second, Rex might have...run me...over." She spoke quickly despite her breathlessness.

"No. I didn't give him an attack command. So he just tries to corner the prey, not disable it."

"That's good I guess."

"Why were you stalking us?"

That finally woke Ivy up the rest of the way.

Apparently this wasn't some amusing dog test. Dilya had wanted their attention for a reason—even if she'd earned more of it than she'd counted on.

"I was told to find you. Quietly."

"How's that working for you?" Colby offered her a hand up.

Dilya shrugged uncomfortably as Ivy glanced up and down the long central hall. No one around, even though they could still hear the controlled mayhem coming from the kitchen at the far end of the corridor. Rex's run and Dilya's half-choked giggles hadn't attracted anyone else's attention.

"Now that you found us," Ivy turned back to the girl, "care to tell us who told you to do so?"

Dilya shook her head as she attempted to get control of her hair that Rex's tail had completely tangled. "It's better if I show you. She's not the sort of person who is easy to describe. She keeps...changing."

Colby waved for Dilya to lead the way.

Ivy couldn't think of who she meant. First Lady Anne Darlington-Thomas was a very steady person—at least on television or when aboard HMX-1. She seemed the unchanging type, actually, very consistently herself. But Dilya didn't lead them up the main stairs. Instead she cut through the Curator's Office. Ivy barely had time to take in the space—four desks and floor-to-ceiling bookcases. Ever since the Kennedys' declaration of the White House as a museum, the office of the curator had become the repository of all historical items and in charge of all displays—from the portraits of the Presidents on the wall of the Oval Office to the furniture in the Lincoln Bedroom.

In moments, they were out the other side of the empty office and into the back corridor. From there, the staircase narrowed and led downward. She had no time to see anything of that level, as Dilya led them down once more.

Ivy noticed that Colby had signaled Rex ahead of them and he suddenly veered into a doorway. All she could smell was cleaning products. The steady thrum of massive air conditioning units seemed to echo along the white walls and bounce off the concrete floor like it had been slapped away. But Rex had picked some thread out of the Residence's lowest reaches.

Dilya stopped at the door Rex had entered.

The German shepherd was sitting in front of an old woman. She sat behind a battered steel desk in a tiny room surrounded by dusty bookshelves. Lit only by a down-focused desk lamp, she should look like an evil spider lurking in the shadows. Instead she looked to be a dotty librarian who had absentmindedly wandered in off the street and never been heard from again.

The walls of books were much more tightly packed than the pleasantly jumbled shelves of the curator's office. Here they crammed into any available space in apparent disarray. The few titles she could make out in the dim light reflected off the desktop were even more of a misfit than the woman in the basement: *The Military Cipher of Commandant Bazeries, Caesar Cypher Quick Reference, and Polygraphiae.* Other titles often included: *Code, Crypto, Analysis, Enigma...* She was in a spy library in the White House basement.

Strange objects hung on the walls above the cases, some even dangling from the overhead pipes that gurgled with rushing water every now and then. Wrong sound for flushing toilets. Maybe they were below the dishwashing room—she didn't know anything about this part of the White House.

A number of the wall "decorations" were strange, clandestine-looking weapons that she was amazed had made it in through security. Actually, it was a surprise that the *woman* had been let in through security. Mother Hubbard and her knitting belonged in fairy tales, not a clandestine library on...being clandestine. Except for her eyes—which seemed to miss nothing.

The room shifted Ivy over into Marine Corps officer defensive mode. Something about it sent a chill up her spine. She stepped away from Colby so that they'd have two angles of fire if necessary.

"Oh, no need for that, my dear," the woman said in a surprisingly pleasant voice for an alien impossibility lurking in the dark of the

Residence's lowest basement. The small desk lamp illuminated almost nothing other than a multicolored sock she was knitting and her bright-blue eyes.

Colby's arms were crossed casually over his chest, his hand nowhere near his sidearm.

"I expect you'd like a dog biscuit," the old woman addressed Rex. Then she looked up at Colby. "If you would be so kind as to call him off, Mr. Thompson. I'm not likely to explode, but there are many smells in this room he won't like."

Colby glanced down at Dilya, who held up her hands in denial.

"I didn't say a thing. Miss Watson knows everything."

Colby tapped his thigh and gave Rex a treat when he returned to his master's thigh.

Too trusting! Ivy kept her position in one corner and did her best to ignore the prosthetic arm that dangled just over her head.

Miss Watson rose, proving that she was actually quite tall for a dotard granny. Then she and Dilya approached one of the bookcases and pushed on the middle. The cases swung back to either side, revealing a long and cheerfully lit parlor, complete with armchairs, little side tables, and a snug fireplace crackling away beneath a solid marble mantel. The walls were covered with photographs of women, mostly in military uniforms—though not all US military.

Ivy glanced up the moment before she stepped forward to inspect the room more closely. The brighter lamplight from the cozy sitting room illuminated the prosthetic arm above her head. A glint of steel and she was focusing on it differently—not stainless like an armature, rather gunmetal gray. There was a rifle embedded in the structure of the arm, with a barrel that ended flush with the palm. A deadly handshake.

Someone had written across the arm, in neat strokes of violet nail polish, *Mission accomplished! All my love, Binky.*

Ivy checked quickly, but the strange Miss Watson appeared to have both hands as she lifted a pair of dog biscuits out of a Snoopy cookie jar and offered a big one to Rex and a smaller to Zackie. Apparently she wasn't Binky herself.

"It's a pity you've already eaten as I just made a lovely quinoa and salmon breakfast torte, but I'll fix you some tea. I'm sure your nerves are far too jangled from the last few days' experiences for coffee."

They were soon settled in chairs clothed in delicate sepia-toned fabric of world maps. With a set of colored pushpins, they'd make fine diagrams for mission planning or mapping out global geopolitical dynamics.

The tea was served in delicate porcelain cups adorned with sweet peas. Dilya, perhaps as part of some innocent-teen-girl disguise that she'd long since blown, was sitting cross-legged on the floor between the two dogs, a hand resting on each as they settled in for a nap. All three of them appeared to trust Miss Watson, which was interesting in itself.

"I expect that you are tired enough that we should postpone any pleasant chit-chat until some later opportunity. You must both come back when you have leisure time and perhaps some more recent shuteye."

"So, why are we here?" Ivy didn't like this. She appeared even more grandmother-kindly in the parlor than she had at her desk, but knew far too much. After a long hesitation and a tiny confirming nod from Colby, they settled into the luxurious wingback chairs close by the gas fireplace. Ivy did her best not to imagine that colored pushpins weren't poking into her own back as her life changed more every minute.

"Terribly difficult to have logs delivered here, so I've had to accept a gas artifice," Miss Watson seemed to be pursuing pointless chit chat despite her prior comment.

Ivy resisted the mild hypnosis the jumping flames offered. It was easy to forget first impressions in this cozy space. Perhaps she'd have a space like this in her and Colby's house...though without the rifle prosthesis. And— Without Colby! She really must be tired to think such things.

"On December 4th, 2011," Miss Watson continued her very pleasant tone, "control was lost of a Lockheed RQ-170 stealth drone named the Sentinel—a flying wing model—while it was patrolling over Iranian airspace. Our government has, naturally, insisted that it was over Afghanistan when it malfunctioned and crashed. The Iranians have insisted that they interrupted its control-and-guidance system deep within their own borders and landed the drone themselves. It took them three years to reverse engineer and copy the aircraft."

Not so much with the chit chat apparently—unless this was Miss Watson's idea of charming conversation. Besides, Ivy knew about that drone. There were some who argued that they had simply done a nice job of plastic work for the published photographs but didn't yet have a working model.

Though it seemed an odd tale for Mother Hubbard to be telling. Or was she Mother Goose? Ivy wasn't sure. She had grown up on science fiction and dreams of space—which hadn't helped her fit in with little girls at all. They played with dolls and she built intricate scale models of the LEM lunar lander and the *Serenity* spaceship from the *Firefly* TV show.

No. Models that Colby had helped her build. Did he remember that? She hadn't. Not really. She looked over to see if Colby remembered, but he showed no signs of it. Not that she'd said anything aloud. The flickering fire, hot tea, and lack of sleep were ganging up on her.

"The Iranian's copy is fully functional, in case you are interested. Not as refined perhaps, but still, very effective."

So much for the plastic theory.

"Seven days after its initial loss, the President of the United States requested its return. He was very polite, though he was careful to admit no wrongdoing or to apologize. Iran offered to return it free of charge. Actually an Iranian *toy manufacturer* offered to return twelve of them—in 1/80th scale rubber toys." She waved a negligent hand toward one corner of her dingy inner office visible through the swung-aside bookcases. Dangling from one of the pipes was a hot pink model of a flying wing drone about a foot across. "You have an interest in drone control systems, Ms. Hanson."

Ivy startled upright and almost slopped her tea in her lap. The few people who knew that should not include some odd woman in the deep basement.

"More specifically, how to block them."

Ivy's hand drifted to her sidearm. Colby casually dropped Rex's leash. His dog popped up his head from his pending nap and looked at him. So, Colby wasn't as excessively trusting as he appeared—apparently ready to unleash the lethal weapon that was his dog.

"My, but you two are so cute together. They make such a charming couple, don't you think, Dilya?"

Dilya squinted up at them from her spot on the floor. "Seem like an odd couple to me."

"Oh, now there was a charming code breaker if ever there was one." She freshened everyone's tea and set out shortbread cookies in the shape of cherry blossoms. Did their shapes change with the seasons?

"Who?" Ivy bit her tongue too late to keep the question from slipping out. She didn't like this Miss Watson commenting on a relationship she didn't understand herself. Maybe if she *had* gone to space the way Colby had suggested, she'd not be here and then this wouldn't be half as confusing because she wouldn't know about it.

"Tony Randall. He starred in the television serial entitled *The Odd Couple* for years as an intelligent, but rather fussy gentleman who is burdened with the slovenly Jack Klugman as a roommate. Tony was also an exceptional code breaker for the United States during the Second World War. Although that role is one of his least known."

"Anything you want to be telling us?" Colby actually teased her in a somewhat suggestive tone.

"Oh dear, no. I wasn't even born yet, Mr. Thompson. Besides, Mr. Randall was happily married well before he was recruited to the Army Signal Corps. But most of the codebreakers were women and my mother said that Tony was particularly charming, always doing his best to make everyone he came in contact with laugh as it was an arduous and stressful occupation. Apparently he was also a wonderful dancer. He was a semi-professional ballerino for a time."

Ivy was wondering if it was the exhaustion or if she'd fallen down some White House rabbit hole into an alternate reality.

Miss Watson leaned forward so abruptly that Ivy slammed into the back of her chair. The woman's voice shifted to surprisingly sharp and businesslike—not befitting an old grandmother at all.

"You are missing the most simple fact that apparently eluded the mechanics of the RQ-170 as well. Minimizing frequency selection mitigates the problem, but doesn't solve it. The problem is that the moment you broadcast on a frequency, any electronics store scanner can overhear that. Yes, the Sentinel drone had an inertial guidance system in addition to its GPS guidance. But it also had a command-and-control frequency. Once used and identified, it was simply a matter of beaming a stronger signal at the drone and overwhelming more remote, less powerful instruction sets."

"Encryption?" Colby asked.

Miss Watson waved her hand at the open bookcases. "Codes, ciphers, cryptograms: they all have their place. But a sufficiently powerful computer—or rather a sufficiently powerful network of computers—can overcome that. Electronics have made codes both more secure and more predictable."

"Then what's the solution?"

Miss Watson sipped her tea and eyed Ivy as if willing her brain to solve it for herself. But struggle as she might, there was still a need to communicate between pilots, ground teams, overwatch patrol, and so on. They even had to keep the channel for the President's personal panic button open at all times.

"Don't transmit?" Dilya guessed.

"Close," Miss Watson acknowledged with a smile.

"Don't transmit in any way that can be detected," Ivy knew the answer, but wasn't sure—

"Give the girl a gold star."

"But how can we…" But Ivy could see it. Transmit, but never from the Presidential aircraft. Use a laser-encoded communication system for point-to-point communication with another helo—one outside the ECM-suppressed area. And let them relay transmissions. This setup would provide an undetectable point of communication without impeding its efficiency by more than any other electronic relay. All possible with standard equipment already aboard the HMX-1 one aircraft.

Colby and Dilya were watching her closely. Why? She looked down at her own hands and realized that she had frozen in place with the teacup half raised to her lips. She made a point of completing the gesture and sipping the sweet peppermint tea before replying.

"Thank you, Miss Watson."

CHAPTER THIRTEEN

"We still don't know who she is," Colby fumbled for his apartment keys with little luck. It had taken only minutes to get Arnson's and Lieber's approval. But then they had to rush out to Anacostia and work with the pilots to perform test flights and work out a dozen unanticipated bugs with the plan.

The three HMX-1 helicopters of any Marine One mission were always shifting in position. If they shifted so that one helo was above the rotors of another one, the blades chopped up the laser-based transmission.

And the interface between the radio and the laser system wasn't direct. It required a human relay because the data bus interfaces on the voice-to-laser transmission systems were not CAAS compatible. And that had only been the beginning.

The problems dragged on through most of the day, and his hands were no longer working well enough to unlock his own door. With two hands, he finally managed it and they stumbled into his apartment in the middle of Sunday afternoon.

"Dilya's trust is a good sign though, don't you think?" Ivy was still riding high on finding the solution. She was bubbling with energy. If a person could effervesce, then Ivy was the woman on the planet closest to doing it.

The signs of their hurried departure thirty-six hours ago were everywhere. Grabbing his vest from the closet had dislodged several jackets, which spilled onto the floor and caught under the door. Rex tried to jam through the narrow gap right after Colby stepped into it. The door didn't budge, which stuck the two of them fast.

Ivy shoved against the middle of his back and he tripped over coats and dog to land squarely on the middle of the living room carpet.

She yanked her jacket and blouse off with a single hard, overhead yank at her back collar.

"Get naked, Colby. I'm in the mood to celebrate."

He was in the mood to pass out cold as he'd now missed two nights sleep. Then she dropped her weapon's belt—her sidearm thumping down with a heavy weight—then shed the rest of her clothes. The woman was an amazing sight. This wasn't some darkened hotel room. Or some half-awake glimpse of her while he stumbled through a phone call with General Arnson. This was Ivy Hanson, far more glorious than he'd ever imagined her, wearing nothing but her dog tags.

"If I must," he conceded. But he wasn't fast enough for Ivy, who had his boots and socks off and was working on his pants before he managed to undo his vest. He had it off, but still wore his t-shirt by the time she got the rest of him naked.

Then...she dove on him. Landing no more gently than she had on the South Lawn, at least this time she didn't inadvertently punch him in the solar plexus.

But the impact was no less.

She was everywhere. Nuzzling his neck one moment. Digging her hands hard into his butt the next while making a happy humming sound.

Thankfully, she'd kept some protection handy from last night, stashed in a back pocket for something. She straddled him then, in a total shift from wild to still, she eased down on him so slowly that it seemed there was time for the afternoon sunlight to shift across the carpet before they fully came together.

Her eyes were closed long before she completed the move, but he couldn't look away.

He and Saint Ives. Sex on the living room floor. It was beyond awesome.

Her back arched, then her head bowed down until he was surrounded by the long fall of her blonde hair as she ever so slowly reversed the process.

Cupping her face, he pulled her down enough to kiss her as he almost slid out of her and she began the impossibly slow return. He swallowed her deepest groan of pleasure and did his best to hold on, because—while her slow movements were absolute torture—they were *exquisite* torture.

And with each movement, with each moment, he knew that he'd never find another woman like her. No with her dedication, her passion for her job, and definitely not the way she felt and smelled.

She added a side-to-side gyration to the beat of a very slow drummer that blanked his mind until all he could do was give up what little control he had and take the ride with her.

When she finally let the release take her, take them both, he wondered if he'd ever seen anything as amazing as the smile of ecstasy painted across Saint Ives' features.

* * *

IVY DIDN'T REMEMBER MOVING to the bed. Maybe Colby had carried her. Never in her life had there been such a release. It was as if she'd been filled with pure light. Turned into a being of nothing but light.

It was too bad, really.

Could a being of pure light still have sex with Colby's incredible body? It would be very sad if she couldn't. Could a being of pure light ever move again? Her limbs felt disconnected, her body floating.

It was just dark and Colby's steady breathing told her he was close beside her and out cold. She dug her toes through the covers into Rex's side for a moment and received a happy sigh.

Good.

That meant beings of pure light *could* still interact with those of mere mortal stuff. Based on that encouragement, she rolled over until she lay fully on Colby's back.

His breathing grew a little more labored, but didn't change particularly. For a while, she was content to ride up and down with each cycle of breath—a languid but deliciously comfortable carousel horse.

"Colby Thompson," she whispered in his ear. "Wake up, Colby Thompson."

"Why?" The softest grunt of a reply.

"Because…I'm hungry." For more Colby Thompson.

He reached out a hand for—his phone. He punched in a number.

"Hey Jake, this is Colby. Yeah, Unit 42. The usual, but make it a large. Yep, a side of bacon, too. Thanks, you're a champ." And he hung up the phone, burying his face back in his pillow.

She lay there, and it seemed he was falling back asleep. "Wake up, Colby Thompson."

"No," his reply was muffled.

"Sex. Colby Thompson."

He made a thoughtful hmm sound that rippled down his back and into her chest.

"Must be quick, Colby Thompson," she shifted to whisper in his other ear. "If you just ordered pizza."

"Might have."

"Sex. Colby—" was all she had time for before he rolled over, pinning her beneath his back.

With the smooth grace of an athlete, he twisted about and pinned her in place with his hands and lips. He never gave her a chance to even sigh in happiness: not during a hand brush over her breast or a kiss planted firmly between her legs. Unable to find protection in the bedside table, he slung her over his shoulder with all the ease of a beach towel and headed into the bathroom. When she struggled, it earned her a sharp slap on the buttocks—not hard enough to do more than sting.

Before she could retaliate, he found protection, sheathed himself, and shifted her until they were chest-to-chest. He never let her feet touch the floor, instead slamming her back against the cool tile between a towel rack and the door. As perfectly gentle as this afternoon's lovemaking had been, tonight's was anything but. With her legs locked around his waist and his palm supporting her behind, he took her.

There was no other way to describe it, he simply took her.

And she was powerless except to give. She'd always made sure that she was in perfect control during sex. Had even convinced herself that she could only find release if she was.

Colby proved she was completely wrong and he took her body, her kiss, her very breath, until she really was just a vessel of light absorbing his unquestionable corporeality.

Sex doesn't equal love. Reminding herself of that wasn't having any particular effect. She was swooning. In moments she'd be completely gone.

Then her first release slammed away all thoughts.

Still Colby didn't relent.

Even as the shudders rolled through her, he took her higher and higher, even better than the rocket launch. His final liftoff tipped her into a second-stage burn that she hadn't known she possessed. She had to pound her fists against his shoulders because the power slamming through her body couldn't be contained, not even within a body made of pure light.

And when the mad pulsing waves finally eased, his kiss was gentler and deeper than the deep rumble that had reached them from the rocket's launchpad a full twenty seconds after they'd witnessed liftoff. It didn't matter that it was an unmanned satellite launch, her heart had gone aloft with it into the fiery heavens. She had wanted to be there like an ache in her body.

At the moment, she couldn't imagine wanting to be anywhere else. Ever.

Colby held her gently as he carried her back to bed and deposited her there with a kiss. Moments later, he yanked on a pair of sweatpants and headed for his door. Doorbell. Pizza. How mundane after a lover had just launched her right through the stratosphere.

When the phone rang, Ivy answered it without thinking.

"Hello?"

"Is…ah, Colby Thompson there?" A woman's voice this time. She'd recognized General Arnson last time and handed off the phone as fast as she could hoping that he hadn't recognized hers. This time she'd be a Marine and take the challenge head on.

"Mrs. Thompson?"

"Ivy? Well, I certainly didn't expect to hear your voice on my son's phone. Oh! *Especially* not sounding so languid. I'm so pleased for both of you. That's simply wonderful. Oh, your mother and I always hoped the two of you would get together. How long has this been going on? I'll just strangle him for not telling me sooner." Her voice rose higher and accelerated with each statement acting like a fresh booster rocket.

"We didn't—"

But they totally had.

"We aren't—"

But what if they were? "Together" implied things that they hadn't discussed even a little.

Colby stepped back into the room carrying a large pizza box and two beers, with a roll of paper towels tucked under his arm. His sweatpants rode low and his bare chest looked awesome. He hesitated in the doorway and offered her a puzzled frown.

"The sex is amazing, Mrs. Thompson." She offered Colby her best radiant smile as he gawked at her and lost the paper towels, which bounced onto the floor. Hopefully he'd be more careful with the pizza. "Don't know why we didn't think of doing this sooner."

"It's just the way of it. I did the same dance with his father for months. Then *pow!* And I never knew why I made him wait so long. An engineer. I *never* expected to be swept off my feet by an engineer."

"Literally, I hope."

That earned her a knowing laugh followed by a happy sigh. "He still does. Tell Colby I was just worried when he didn't come over for Sunday dinner. He usually calls if he's not going to make it. Even at his age, mothers worry."

"I may have been busy distracting him. But he's standing here half naked and carrying a pizza."

"Ooo. Why didn't I think of doing that? Tomorrow night. Definitely tomorrow night. Wearing nothing except one of Steve's shirts."

"Or maybe just one of his ties and nothing else."

Colby's face went white and perhaps even a little green. Apparently guys didn't talk about sex with their moms.

"Even better. I like the way you think, Ivy. I'll leave work early to make sure I'm home first. Have fun, dear." And she was gone.

Ivy hung up the phone, well aware that she was still completely naked and lying back on Colby's pillows, still in sex-magazine-model-in-training mode apparently.

"Your mom says hi."

When he still didn't move, she clambered out of the bed, bent down to fetch the paper towels, and couldn't resist running her hand up the inside of his sweatpants and cupping him.

"Yummy. Maybe later. Pizza first, I think." She secured the box with a slight tug and carried it back to the bed with a happy swing to her hips.

Colby didn't make her feel like a Marine with inconvenient woman parts. He made her feel like the luckiest woman on this planet. And since the rest of the planets appeared to be unpopulated—except maybe whatever hid under the ice on Europa, besides it didn't really count even if there were females of some weirdo sub-ice species—she decided to stake claim to the entire solar system while she was at it. And that was mightily lucky.

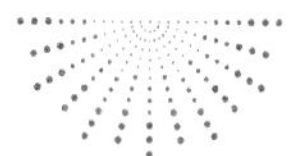

olby had never been comfortable in a suit. Wearing one of the President's suits and walking across the White House lawn only worsened the sensation.

Harvey Lieber was trusting of their communications solution, but not *very* trusting. So Colby was playing body double, having donned one of the President's cowboy hats (he didn't wear them often, but today "he" did). With a pair of sunglasses and Ivy in her dry-cleaned dress blues talking to him intently so that he had an excuse to keep the brim of his hat down low because of their difference in heights…

"You make a good decoy for the President, Colby."

"That's Mr. President to you."

The Motorcade had left the basement of the Treasury Building very quietly fifteen minutes earlier, without sirens and only a minimal police escort. They'd be most of the way to Andrews Air Force Base by now. If everything went right and no one tried to kill him, they and the President would be arriving to board Air Force One at roughly the same moment.

Rex hadn't liked the idea of traveling with the President. It had looked like the whole plan was going to go awry on that point alone until Dilya trotted out of the tunnel that connected the White House

East Wing basement to the Treasury Building garage. She'd had Zackie and a day pack, and without even hinting that she hadn't been invited on the trip to Ottawa, she strode up to Rex. She'd given him a good head rub, taken the leash from the President's hand, and done exactly as Colby had taught her—leave no doubt about who was in control.

"C'mon, Rex. Time to go." She'd climbed into the Beast limousine and, after one bewildered glance back at Colby, Rex had followed her in and lain down on the floor. Zackie was ecstatic—even by Sheltie standards—to have her big buddy Rex along for the ride.

The President had merely shrugged at Dilya's abrupt appearance, shaken Colby's hand, and said, "Good luck, Mr. President." That was fifteen minutes ago.

Now, it was just him and Ivy coming down the front lawn. The press had been told that there'd be no statement or time for questions on the South Lawn. The fourteen reporters lucky enough to get a seat on Air Force One were following the fake Motorcade. Everyone else had left an hour ago—taking vans out to Anacostia to board a greenside MV-22. Air Force One would reach Ottawa in under an hour, the slower Osprey needed almost two.

So there were only a few stringers left at the White House. None had bothered to come out for a photo of the Marine and the imposter walking down the lawn. Even if they didn't know that's what was going on.

He saluted the Marine standing at attention by the helo's door. Not McShea—he'd gone ahead with the other helos shifted up to Ottawa for transportation to the meeting. The Marine saluted back, then did a sharp doubletake.

"Carry on, Sergeant. It's all with good reason."

The Marine glanced at Ivy. No, he looked at Ivy like she was a side of meat he wanted to take home. The man was too damn handsome for his own good and knew it.

"Stow it, Sergeant Mathieson," Ivy said in a tone that implied things Colby didn't want to be thinking about Ivy and other men.

"If you say so, ma'am." He actually gave her a leer. If he really was

President, Colby knew who his next appointment to Nome, Alaska, would be.

Colby clambered aboard, forgetting about the hat. He almost knocked it off, revealing his hair, which he wore much shorter than the President. He made a point of avoiding the President's chair until Ivy grabbed his arm and shoved him into it. She sat in the armchair directly across from his.

When the Marine sergeant boarded after folding away the stairs, he offered a glare that could scorch Colby's image irreparably into the fabric of the seat. Apparently all Marine crew chiefs were very protective of the President's seat. With this asshole, he was fine ignoring the man.

"It's for security, Sergeant. The President is traveling by another route." Ivy's reassurances did little to assuage the man.

"At least I have you here to protect me," Colby told her once the crew chief turned to other duties.

"Tell me why I should bother," Ivy made a point of yawning as if bored, but it carried longer than fit the joke. They'd slept through the afternoon and evening, but somewhat less during the night after they eaten most of a large pizza.

"Because you already can't live without me," he teased.

"I thought it was the other way around."

"Well, could be," he had to admit as they finally lifted off the South Lawn.

Ivy twitched and collapsed deeper in the seat opposite him.

"Ivy," he signaled for her to lean in close, as close as the seatbelts allowed.

She watched him the way cats watched Rex—with a great sense of caution and some alarm. Rex hadn't even sniffed at one since a long ago feline had tried to quarter and section his nose with a swipe of claws.

And that was when Colby knew. Dad had always said that Mom had simply taken his heart and run away with it after their first date. He didn't know if a swim in the Potomac, a space launch in Florida, and tackling a major security problem was the kind of thing Dad had meant. But Colby understood *what* he'd meant.

After his parents, the number of people on the planet he cared about as much as he cared about Ivy Hanson totaled precisely zero. Her first homecoming was his first memory. He remembered her dogging his and Reggie's footsteps, but he also remembered an awful lot of good moments.

She was a voracious reader. With her Marine Corps mom often overseas and her father running a restaurant and a household, Colby was the one she came to when she didn't understand a story. He'd been the one stuck trying to explain the cruelty of twelve-year-old boys to her.

If she'd been a remarkable kid, she was an astonishing woman. A woman he hadn't known he was waiting for.

It was as if the focus shifted as they lifted up and over the National Mall. Maybe it was sitting in the President's chair, but he could see more clearly now. He'd climbed up out of the weeds and, looking back, could see that he and Ivy had a common path that went back a long way. And it was so easy to imagine what that path looked like going forward as well—without the duckweed.

Ivy finally leaned closer as the helicopter's rotors, finally up to speed, lifted them off the South Lawn. The seat belts let them lean just close enough to whisper despite the pounding rotors.

"What?" Her caution ran even deeper than his.

"Could be that I can't live without you. Maybe. Maybe not. But I do know one thing." Did she remember all of the good times as well as all the teasing?

"What's that, Thompson?"

"I have no idea how I lived without you this long." Not what he'd been intending to say. He'd started out to say something about how he couldn't live without the awesome sex. But it had shifted, morphed by the President's chair, into some strange, impossible truth.

"Get a grip, Thompson." Ivy's expression definitely agreed about the strange and impossible.

For the first time in his life, it felt as if he actually had one. "I've got a grip. Trying to live up to your standards, you've already made me a better man than I ever set out to be, Ivy. And while I do love your body, it's nothing compared to how I feel about you."

"Whoa!" Her eyes went as saucer wide as the day she'd asked him where babies came from and hadn't let him escape answering. He could still feel the heat in his cheeks from that long-ago conversation. Or maybe it was the heat from what he'd just said.

"Whoa!" Colby said himself and flopped back in the President's chair. "I didn't just say what I think I just said. Did I?"

"Not unless I heard what I didn't just hear. Or didn't hear what I just heard. Or…" She took a slow, deep breath before asking softly. "Did you just say you…loved me?" She mouthed the last two words silently as if even the sound of them had been scared away.

"Uh," Colby looked around the helo, but he couldn't even pet Rex as a distraction because Rex was in the Beast with the real President.

Love was a word for moms and dads. It was a word for a man's best friend—at least of the four-footed kind, not for Reggie. But was it a word for someone he'd known his *whole life?* And for *her* whole life?

He didn't think so. Yet maybe it was.

"Colby?" He could hear the strain in her voice.

He tried to look away. He really wanted to watch the approach to Andrews Air Force Base. He wanted to look down on Air Force One from the sky.

But he couldn't look away from *her,* from Ivy.

There was the right question. Was love a word for describing Ivy Hanson?

"Yes."

"Colby, what did you just say?"

"Yes." He'd just said yes.

"What are you saying yes to, that I just said your name?"

"Yes," he teased her, which wasn't at all what he'd meant.

She scowled at him as the wheels settled on the pavement close beside the shining bulk of Air Force One. They taxied forward, entering the massive hangar that could hold all four of the big executive jets: the identical pair of 747s used for Air Force One, and the pair of 757s used for Air Force Two duties for the Vice President or when the First Lady traveled alone. The shadows seemed to bring them even closer.

Sergeant Mathieson lowered the forward door and descended to stand at his station as the engines wound down to silence. The helo pilots were busy with their logbooks. He and Ivy were alone for just a moment.

"And yes, I said what I said."

"Which was?" How typical of Ivy to not let him off the hook.

"Yes, I can't think of a better word to describe how I feel about you." He tugged on the President's cowboy hat and clambered out of the Chair of Truth before something else slipped out, like how easy it was to imagine spending the rest of his life with her.

"Typical, Colby," she muttered to herself as she descended the stairs behind him. "Can't even say the word."

He decided against pointing out that she hadn't said "the word" either.

Ivy was in a bad reentry burn. Her heat shield—the shield that kept men away from meaning too much to her—was badly cracked and burning away. Would it last long enough for her to survive whatever this newest game of Colby's was?

The Motorcade raced into the hangar and stopped on the back side of the helicopter, out of everyone's view. When the President emerged, Colby handed over hat and sunglasses, then shrugged off his jacket and flipped it over his shoulder. Taking up Rex's leash, Colby now looked much more like himself.

He had looked important, even daunting in the President's seat on Marine One. And so sure of himself. So...impressive. As impressive as the President in his own way. When had that happened?

Never avoid the question! One of Drill Sergeant McKinnon's Laws. *If you're asking it, there's a reason. Be damn sure you figure out the answer...*

preferably before it kills you. And this one definitely possessed lethal qualities—like death and destruction to her sanity.

"Okay," she muttered to herself as she followed Colby and the President out of the hangar. "Do I love Colby Thompson?"

"Duh!" Dilya said from close beside her. "Dumb question."

"Why is it dumb?" Even with Zackie in tow, the girl had a serious stealth mode.

"He isn't just amazing. He's amazingly amazing."

Ivy couldn't believe that the kid was quoting *Hitchhiker's Guide to the Galaxy* at her about being in love.

"It isn't *possible* that I love him."

"Why not?"

"Because he's like a big brother to me. Maybe even more than my own brother."

"But you had sex with him. You told me that."

The President headed for Air Force One's forward stairs—the entry for the President, special guests, and senior staff—to greet the press and then climb aboard. Colby led them toward the rear stairs that had lowered from the center of the tail section for everyone else to use.

"I did." Not that she was comfortable discussing her sex life with a teenager—though she didn't seem to have much choice at the moment.

"Was it good sex?"

Ivy eyed Dilya, but the teen didn't blink. Not hiding behind any facade at the moment, Dilya was daunting as well.

"It was *amazing* sex," Ivy did her Marine Corps best to answer honestly.

Dilya sighed happily. "I knew it. I just knew it. That doesn't sound like you're thinking of him as a brother very much."

She wasn't at all, was she. Meaning that had been a lame excuse.

Never use an excuse. They just hide the answers.

She wished McKinnon could have been a *little* less helpful. Then maybe she could have avoided all of this.

But she hadn't.

Maybe if she'd gone to space as Colby suggested. Or left for space right now…

But she didn't want to avoid Colby. Didn't want to miss out on all they could have shared.

Did she love the boy who had let her weep out her first-ever fifteen-year-old heartbreak on his shoulder? Did she love the man who kept trying to convince her that it was never too late to pursue her real dream of space? Did she love the man who saw past the uniform? Colby saw *her*. He was incapable of seeing her any other way because he knew her too well.

"You know what true love is?" Dilya asked without a hint of teenage innocence.

"Uh… Why don't you tell me? Then I'll see if I agree."

"First Lady Anne Darlington-Thomas told me it was two things. First, you can't imagine *not* living your life beside someone. She said that test worked for both men and women. But she said women were lucky, because they had an even better measure."

"What's that?" Ivy climbed the stairs into the back of Air Force One. Thankfully Rex had pulled Colby up well ahead.

"Can you imagine giving birth to any man's child other than his?"

Ivy didn't need to think about it for a second. Not an instant. She'd give anything to be able to hold Colby's child in her arms. Dilya was right; it was the gut punch question when the answer couldn't be denied. But could she stand to live with him for all the years to come? That was a much harder question.

Ivy sat beside Colby in the Secret Service section at the tail of the airplane. Dilya used her First Dog privileges to head forward as if she hadn't just dropped a ticking time bomb in Ivy's psyche.

Colby didn't even seem to notice as he slid his fingers through hers and took hold of her hand. It was so natural.

She was so screwed.

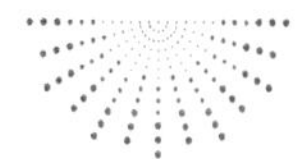

One hour to Ottawa. One hour in which not a single word had passed between them. Colby was cool with that.

Ivy had asked for no more impossible confessions—thank God. Nor had she offered any of her own. But it was clear what she was thinking by the way she fell so quietly asleep on his shoulder, never breaking their handhold.

He could do this all day, every day.

And apparently he was comfortable with it—as the impact of landing startled him awake with his cheek resting on her hair.

Their fingers were still slipped together.

And Harvey Lieber was glaring down at them.

"You two think this is going to work." He made it a demand rather than a question.

Colby looked at Ivy. Was it going to work? He didn't know. But he knew he'd be an idiot if he didn't try.

Except why was Lieber asking about his relationship with…

Oh. He wasn't. He was asking about the HMX-1 helicopters.

"Nothing is ever a hundred percent certain," Ivy stated as if she was quoting someone.

Harvey harrumphed.

Colby could feel his pain. From Ottawa's Macdonald-Cartier International Airport to Harrington Lake—the Canadian PM's retreat —was forty kilometers through the very heart of Ottawa city past a million people along unfamiliar roads and bridges. Or an eight-minute flight on an HMX-1 aircraft out over sparse suburbs. Less exposure in time. Far more hazardous if attacked.

"Okay, here's how we're going to play it." And he began to explain. Colby could only groan.

AIR FORCE ONE parked at the south end of Runway 32, well away from any of the passenger or cargo handling areas.

Two large hangars faced the area where Air Force One, several helicopters, and the backup Presidential Motorcade had all been parked. Between the hangars, a barracks building that would have housed the pilots and mechanics had been appropriated as an operations center. A lone, bright orange helicopter was parked off to the side by a building with a medical transport sign.

"It's an old QRA," a Canadian security agent informed her before continuing his patrol.

"A what?" Colby—again clothed as the President—whispered his question in her ear as they crossed to one of the HMX White Hawks that had been moved up the previous night. The President, wearing a Secret Service vest and leading Rex, along with Dilya and Zackie, headed toward one of the backup helos.

"Quick Reaction Area. It was where they staged emergency alert fighters at the peak of the Cold War in case of a Russian attack. They could be airborne over the capital in less than three minutes. Those square blocks we spotted out behind the hangars, those were probably missile silos, which I'd guess were nuclear armed back in the day."

The airport itself was strangely quiet, as there would be no takeoffs or landings while the American President was on-site.

"Let's get a move on, 'Mr. President.'"

"Lead the way, Major Hanson," Colby said with all the

graciousness of the President himself. Banter with Colby had always been fun—he was just as quick to hand it out as she was. Something she'd found far too rarely.

The two of them climbed aboard one of the White Hawks. This time it was again Sergeant McShea waiting for them—the crew chief they'd gone swimming with in the Potomac four days ago.

Four days? *Four days!* Ivy was clearly losing her mind and it was all Colby's fault.

"Um, Colby?" McShea asked.

"Salute when addressing the President, Marine!" Colby snapped it out but backed it up with a big smile. Because of the last-minute change, she hadn't thought to warn the Marine crew. Her area of responsibility.

Tish was loading up in the Motorcade and had probably kept her Motorcade people in the loop just fine.

McShea saluted automatically, probably Colby's intent. Then he'd offered a slight, but very amused smile. "Welcome aboard HMX-1, sir!"

"Carry on, Sergeant!" Then Colby banged his hat and head hard against the White Hawk's low entry. It took everything she had not to laugh in his face as he collapsed into the President's chair.

"Ow!" Colby reached up to remove his hat.

"Don't! The press corps are watching. Look at me." Ivy clambered over to the bench seat that would force Colby to look away from the open door. His face wasn't *that* good a match for the President's.

"Sure, just as soon as my eyes stop swimming."

McShea had them locked in moments later and they were quickly aloft.

"Now we hold our breath."

The eight-minute flight was uneventful, but she couldn't relax until they were on final approach to Harrington Lake—which was the name of the mansion, not the lake it commanded. The helicopter circled once over the big house, the luxurious lawn, and the lake shore. What she saw were the security checkpoints, the patrols, the Emergency Response Team van parked near the entry to the grounds.

The Prime Minister's country getaway lay northwest of Ottawa. The mansion sat by itself in the only cleared area along a quiet narrow road. Over three thousand acres of forest surrounded the lone residence. A few cottages and outbuildings, and a large vegetable garden dotted the clearing. The house faced a grassy beach and a stunning view of Lake Mousseau complete with a pair of boat docks. The lake itself was long and narrow, stretching out of sight between darkly green, towering conifers on steep shores.

The three helos of the HMX flight settled onto the broad lawn in back of the house. The two overwatch Black Hawks circled above.

Ivy watched carefully, but during the unloading, none of the Canadians appeared to notice that she and a Secret Service agent—without his cowboy hat—stepped out of one helicopter while a teenage girl led his dog out of the one the President had flown in.

Under the auspices of trade negotiations, they had eight hours to wander the grounds.

Ivy was at a loss of what to do with herself. It was late morning. A lone heron flapped lazily by overhead. A small contingent of Canadian geese had stopped off on their northbound journey and were fishing quietly along the shores of the lake. Otherwise, the wildlife had been scared off by the sudden invasion of two countries' security forces.

The President, Prime Minister, and their advisors had settled in comfortable chairs in the front garden. The house itself was a two-story colonial revival with steep roofs, generous windows, and a large sunroom topped by a balcony. It was very pretty, for a twenty-room "cottage." For her and Colby, she'd prefer a cozy house where they were always in each other's way. That's how they'd both grown up: bedrooms for sleeping or teenaged pouting and a merry great room that always had puzzles, cats, cooking, and maybe a game on TV.

She wanted that closeness again (though it had often irritated her as a teen—hence the pouting part of bedroom usage). And she *did* want it with a man like Colby.

A man *like* Colby? Was there such a thing other than the original?

Ivy watched him as she chatted with the flight crews. They'd staked out one of the docks closest to their helos to enjoy the sunshine. Their easy laughter had sent the geese farther up the lake for peace, so the only sound was the soft lap of tiny waves against the rocky verge.

Colby circulated with the other dog teams, patrolling the perimeter.

She could see him gathering up respect as he progressed, along with the occasional baggie of dog poo.

The respect came naturally to the man. The sense of play from his boyhood was still there, but the rest of it was a hundred percent self-made. But it was a self-made that she completely recognized because it was so based in who he was.

Now, if only he hadn't instilled those doubts in her.

She was a Marine. Five tours, ten years. It had earned her a role at the White House Military Office. Someday, it might even earn her the lead. Would she become as bitter and stodgy as Major General Markham and his two-minute-and-no-seconds welcome lecture?

"What have you done to me, Colby?"

He looked up at Ivy in surprise. "Nothing. You've been avoiding me all morning."

"No, I haven't." To prove her point—because she always had to— she sat down next to him on the grassy beach. She held a piled-high picnic plate from the spread the Canadians had set out for lunch that was at least as generously mounded as his own.

"Sure you have. You've kept your pilots wrapped around you like a security blanket. So, what could I have done to you? Nothing. They would have sunk my body in the lake if they knew that I'd touched so much as a hair on your head. See," he nodded at the nearby dock before forking up a maple-flavored meatball. "Even now they're planning my demise should I even look at you inappropriately."

"I mean, you have me questioning my whole career." She sounded grumpy, but bit into her chicken-avocado sandwich so she couldn't be too upset.

"Just trying to keep you on your toes, Ives. How did I do that?"

She glanced up at the sky without looking at it. Glanced up as if… looking at space.

"Oh. So go for it."

"Just like that?"

"Just like that."

"Don't be an idiot, Colby."

"Can't help it. Comes with the territory."

She shook her head and set down her sandwich. He knew the look. It had to be something bad to kill off Saint Ives' appetite—she'd always been a hearty eater. Which was a good thing, because with her metabolism she needed to be or her blood sugar plummeted through the floor.

With two fingers, he gave a meatball to Rex. Rex approved and licked his fingers completely clean. Then he picked up his own sandwich, trying to set an example for Ivy, but she wasn't buying it.

"It's already passed me by," her voice was the barest whisper.

"You said that before, but you're wrong."

"No. You are." Of course nothing with Ivy was simple. She had a persevere-against-all-odds streak so wide that it was sometimes hard to tell it apart from stubbornness.

"I'm not wrong, Ivy. You can do anything you set your mind to. You are five-foot-four and barely crack a hundred pounds. Yet you're a highly decorated Marine Corps pilot. You qualified for HMX-1— which I have on the best of authority is almost impossible to get into. I know this because you told me yourself. And you're so exceptional that a man of General Arnson's caliber selected you to represent his outfit at the WHMO. Go ahead, tell me there's something you can't do."

She didn't respond, but she started eating again, which he took as a good sign.

The silence stretched out between them. Birds fluttered down to see if they were offering any treats. He tossed a twist of pasta salad out toward a red-winged blackbird, but Rex's lunge for it spooked the bird away. A flock of black-capped chickadees settled for a moment but were gone before he could break off any breadcrumbs for them. Even after they finished and Rex had licked their plates clean, they sat quietly and watched the wind ruffle across the lake's surface.

"There's one other problem," Ivy said at length.

"What's that?"

"Say I did go for the astronaut program or even volunteered for a Mars mission and was accepted. I'd be in Florida."

"I wasn't a big fan of that heat wave, though the evening was nice enough. I'll bet the winters are great. Seems all right to me."

"You'd be Washington."

Colby hadn't thought about that. There was no way he could leave Rex to some other agent. Not even for Ivy Hanson.

But that wasn't the right answer either.

Now he knew where her appetite had gone.

———

A CHILL WIND was making up along with the thick clouds to the south by the time the meeting wrapped up. The meeting had moved inside after lunch and the agents on the grounds were soon scrounging up jackets. The pleasant day had decided that May wasn't quite done with winter yet. Weather services reported that the cloud ceiling was still acceptable for the flight back to the airport but that bad weather was moving in fast.

Everything kicked into high gear.

Crews were pre-flighting their helicopters.

Tish stopped by to check in, wearing a massively oversized USSS jacket that one of the assault team must have loaned her. She confirmed that the Motorcade, which had traveled empty across Ottawa just in case they were needed, was ready to roll.

Security agents from both countries gathered up their gear.

Ivy had taken advantage of the quiet afternoon to log some flight time with Captain Juarez so that she could stay current. Circling above the Canadian lakes and forests had served as both a wide-area patrol and a bit of welcome distance from Colby.

Once she was back at Harrington Lake, she'd sat alone out at the end of the farthest pier and no one had disturbed her except the waves starting to kick up in the contrary wind.

She'd only ever wanted one thing: to be the best Marine Corps officer.

And she'd achieved that in so many ways. She'd met her goals.

So set a new one.

It sounded like a McKinnon Law, but it felt as if it came from her.

The problem was that she now wanted multiple things.

She loved the Corps. There was a reason that there was no such thing as an ex-Marine—it was going to be a part of her forever.

Colby had reawakened her dream of space. And he was right. She just might have a chance. Even her few days so far at WHMO would put an indelible stamp in her file that said she had the organizational skills to be of use as a mission planner, perhaps even a mission commander. And while an MV-22 Osprey might not be a jet, it wasn't a helicopter either. It was an immensely technical hybrid that brought far more skills to the cockpit than the simple little White Hawk she'd just logged a couple hours in. That should look good as well.

And she wanted one other thing. One that made the second dream impossible. She wanted Colby Thompson. Not for a night's tumble. Not just for that. His mere presence brought a piece of her to life that she'd forgotten, or perhaps never understood. Ivy wasn't used to being a woman as well as everything else. But also…

She'd been happy as a Marine. It had fit her well.

But Colby had brought her back to the feeling of pure joy. To a thrill that had made her want to tease him, to interact with him.

But he was—

But *she* was—

She'd gotten nowhere but flying in circular orbits all afternoon that had insisted on looping back over themselves faster and faster.

And now she was standing in the middle of the Prime Minister's backyard all alone. If she didn't hustle, she was going to miss her flight back and be *stuck* in the middle of nowhere during a chill downpour. The Motorcade had already rolled out, headed back across Ottawa. If you weren't ready when the President was, you got left behind.

Colby, Dilya, and both dogs were aboard one of the decoy birds.

She wasn't ready to face either of them.

The President's staff were already aloft in the second decoy.

That only left her one option—Marine One. Thankfully, the President waved for her to hurry, so she clambered aboard just moments before McShea closed the doors.

The only other person aboard was Harvey Lieber, seated behind the President.

"Glad you decided to join us," the President's voice sounded hoarse.

"Did the meetings go well?"

He nodded as he leaned back tiredly in his seat. It made his cowboy hat, which Colby had once again returned when they landed, slide down over his eyes. The man wanted his privacy, that was his option, so she focused her attention out the window.

Racing from the countryside back toward the airport under the edge of the darkening storm, the trees gave way to housing. Soon they were over thick suburbs with the city lights ahead. They were approaching the Ottawa River. Curiously, they passed over a sprawling golf course—though at a thousand feet up there was little chance of disturbing the few remaining golfers trying to finish a round before the storm hammered in. Darkly massive thunderheads marched in from the east—garishly lit by the last of the sunlight cutting in below the cloud cover to the west.

Looking down at the golf course gave her both a shiver and a smile. Remembering the helo pilots messing with the golfers. And Colby and Rex taking a helicopter crash so professionally—dealing with a situation that threw untrained people into panic.

Colby was *highly* trained. The Secret Service were at least as selective as the Marine officer corps—the Presidential Protection Details equivalent to Whiteside operations of HMX-1. Yet, Colby had made the grade. If ever there was a man to match her, impossibly it was her childhood nemesis. If ever there was a man to push her ahead, it was oddly enough the man who never pushed himself.

She *was* a Marine.

She *wanted* space.

But she *needed* Colby. The woman that she'd almost lost, Colby had found and brought back from the brink. She could have ended up like General Markham—entrenched at the WHMO, bitter and old before her time. Colby would never let her get away with that. Just by being himself.

Her escape from a similar fate had been so close. Now if only she could figure out—

She didn't see the attack coming any more this time than she had last time.

CHAPTER SIXTEEN

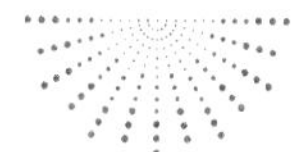

There was no crunch and cry of rending metal.

A shattering crash sounded from the cockpit. Then a scream that could only be human as the helo lurched badly.

Some body memory had Ivy diving into the cockpit even faster than Crew Chief McShea.

The windshield was gone. Juarez was dead. He had to be with half of a model jet smashed into his chest.

His copilot had his hands still on the controls, but he was screaming from a face half torn off by one of the model's wings.

She slapped the seatbelt release on Juarez and tried to yank him clear. He outweighed her by at least double. McShea reached over her shoulder and grabbed Juarez's collar. With a single yank, he hauled the pilot across her lap and into the back.

Diving into the seat, Ivy grabbed the controls. No time to move the seat forward or put on a seatbelt, she perched at the forward edge of the seat and stretched her toes out to reach the rudder pedals. The Captain's headset was gone, so she took a moment to reach out and grab the one off the copilot's head. The muffs thankfully cut off most of his on-going cries.

543

The controls fought her as she struggled to gain control of the spinning helicopter.

The copilot—why couldn't she remember his name?—clutched his duplicate of her controls with a death grip.

"McShea. Get him off the controls."

Rain and snow drove into her face, forcing her to squint. Combined with the cloud cover, it was so dark it might as well be night for all she could see.

McShea made a grab at the copilot, but the man—Merton—didn't let go. Instead, the controls jerked hard and almost flipped them onto their backs, driving the nose aloft. She slid back into the seat. Without her feet on the pedals, they spun in a hard circle counter to the spinning rotors.

There was a sharp crack as McShea broke Merton's arms with a powerful blow, then hauled him out of the way.

Ivy struggled to right the aircraft. The centrifugal force of the spin was strong enough to slide her forward once she leveled out the nose. It was almost enough to fling her out the missing windshield, but she managed to regain control before that happened.

The ground was—where?

There. On the right. They were falling sideways out of the sky.

She keyed the mic switch on the back of the cyclic control.

"Mayday! Mayday! Mayday! This is—" she shouldn't identify that the President was in trouble "—HMX-1 going down."

"Roger that," someone replied calmly. They'd know that she was past their help until she was down, so there was only silence on the airwaves. They could be calling in rescue and aid units on another frequency, but as long as she was in the sky, this frequency was now hers.

She got them upright, but something else had been damaged and they rolled hard onto their left side. Each attempt to correct their position with the cyclic joystick between her knees was met with odd jerks and jumps. Linkages were broken or damaged.

A glance at the altimeter. Three hundred feet. In the heart of the Death Zone.

Except on the radio there wasn't only silence.

There should have been. The laser transmitter should be dead silent without input.

A high-pitched tone warbled at the upper edge of her hearing, like a supersonic dentist's drill.

"Carrier wave. Someone tell Colby. Carrier wave!"

CHAPTER SEVENTEEN

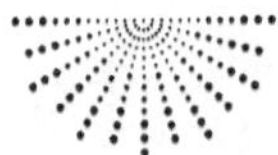

$\mathcal{C}$olby could only watch in horror as Ivy's helicopter pitched and rolled its way out of the sky.

"Colby!" The pilot was shouting at him. "Colby!"

"What?" He'd sat close beside the crew chief. That placed him near the cockpit.

"Major Hanson said to tell you 'carrier wave.' That mean anything to you?"

Carrier wave? For a moment it didn't, then he remembered a discussion they'd had with one of the WHMO's radio communication specialists. In an instant, he knew she'd used the radio.

No, they—the bad guys—had *been using* the radio.

And a carrier wave meant that the attacker wasn't using some empty frequency, as their new protocols had peeled most of those away. Nor were they using a high blast of power to override the jamming on any one frequency. Instead, the attackers were using the *primary* communication frequency, but only using the very highest part of the signal as a carrier for their control commands.

Communication hadn't been the problem.

Their problem had been identifying which of the three shifting helos was the actual Marine One with the President aboard.

By launching that initial attack over the Potomac, they must have known that the Marines would eventually stumble on the idea of not letting Marine One ever transmit by radio. Instantly, its simple silence on the radio would identify which helo carried the President.

But that meant—

"Set your electronic countermeasures to broadband. Block all frequencies," he shouted to the pilot.

"Are you crazy? If I do, no one can communicate."

"Exactly! Including the attacker with his aircraft. Do it. *Now!*"

The pilot snarled and made some adjustment to the radio console between the two pilot seats.

Moments later, a large model aircraft impacted their helo's steel nose directly below the windshield. Colby had seen it falter with the loss of a radio signal and lose the crucial meter or so of altitude that was all that kept it from coming in through the windshield.

That's what must have happened to Ivy.

He looked out the window for her helicopter. It took him a moment to find it, and when he did, his heart stopped.

Ivy fought the controls, but it wasn't doing her much good. Each moment she managed level flight, she added all the lift she could manage to slow their plummeting descent.

But those were stolen moments.

They spent far more time tipped onto their side, once even flailing through a full roll.

Setting up an auto-rotation was out of the question. She still had some power to work with—in engine Number Two. She'd been forced to pull the fire T-handle on Number One as the turbine must have ingested something nasty. She had enough power to maintain level flight, but not sufficient control.

Where to land? Assuming she could find any control to make a choice even possible.

The snow now blasted through the missing windshield. It stung worse than a Libyan sandstorm.

The golf course was out of reach.

In fact, either shore was out of reach. They were going down in the Ottawa River. But it wasn't some gentle flow like the Potomac. There would be no giddy banter as they raked handfuls of duckweed out of each other's hair.

Here, the Ottawa River was over two hundred meters wide and narrowing rapidly for the hard pinch at the heart of Ottawa. She'd seen the Remic Rapids south of the Champlain Bridge before. They weren't a waterfall, but she had no desire to be beaten against those rocks.

"FOLLOW THEM DOWN!" Colby shouted.

The pilot half-turned to face him, then nodded and turned back. The upward slam of Colby's gut into his chest told him they were dropping altitude fast.

He began stripping off his jacket and vest. He dumped his sidearm as well.

"What are you doing?"

Damn it! He'd forgotten about Dilya. He turned to console the frightened teen, but that's not who was looking at him. No. The girl who now faced him was the war orphan he'd heard about—the one who had seen a *lot* of war before being picked up and adopted by one of the military's top snipers.

With the facade ripped away, he now saw that she'd never been young.

"I have to go in to save them." Because he had to save the President. No matter what. And if he didn't save Ivy, there wouldn't be any point in any of it. Next time he had a chance, he wasn't going to fool around with any word games—that was for damn sure.

"I…" Dilya hesitated, then suddenly looked ready to cry. "I'm a lousy swimmer. Oh God. I should have learned better. You don't swim in Afghanistan's rivers. Especially not girls. I have to help. If you think I can, I'll go in. But I don't—" Her voice remained calm and steady even as tears started rolling down her cheeks—tears of anger at her own shortcomings.

He bent down to quickly unlace his boots. A good trick against the bucking descent of the helo.

"You can do two things, Dilya. First, once I'm in the water, I won't be able to see very far. I'll look to you to point me toward anyone who is washed away. Don't lose track of anyone. Can you do that?"

She nodded fiercely and he didn't doubt her for a second.

"Second, make sure Zackie doesn't try to follow Rex and me into the water."

That got the choking half laugh he'd been hoping for.

He swung open the two doors until they latched off to either side, then leaned out and looked down.

Ivy's helo was so close that it felt as if he could reach out and touch it. But she was even closer to the river.

IVY FOUGHT FOR A LEVEL SPLASHDOWN. They'd be jarred harder, but it might give them a moment of float time to escape the helo before it sank. It might not. White Hawks weren't big on floating.

Twenty feet up, whatever damage she'd been fighting in the control system finally gave way.

She'd been dragging the cyclic back and to the right when it simply let go and she slammed her elbow into the edge of her seat back.

No time to curse or compensate, she was flung up and forward as the nose dropped out from under her.

Weightless, with no seatbelt to hold her, she was flung out through the missing windshield. How close she came to the spinning rotor blades she'd never know. She slammed into freezing water and was driven under.

Good idea.

She dove as deep as she dared to get away from the churning

blades that should be shattering themselves against the surface of the water.

Unable to hold her breath against the freezing cold any longer, she fought to the surface. The rain-shrouded darkness was lit by brilliant punches of two spotlights. Both were aimed behind her at the floating wreckage.

Even as she watched, one of the helos slowed to hover above the scene and a swimmer jumped off the side. A massive dog followed close behind, removing any doubt as to the swimmer's identity.

The water was moving—she could see the Champlain Bridge coming up at warp speed. The rocks of Remic Rapids lay not far beyond the bridge.

Ivy knew she should be doing something, but the water was so cold that it was hard to concentrate. Dunk training had taught her what fifty-degree water felt like—this was definitely colder.

Swim. That was it. That's what she was supposed to be doing.

She tried to stroke out with her right arm—

Pain screamed up from her elbow.

Not so much with the swimming.

COLBY SWAM through the bits of floating wreckage.

No one. No one.

Then his next stroke slammed onto someone's back.

The President.

"Mr. President?"

"Uh-huh!"

Dazed, but conscious. He kept staring up at the spotlight centered on him, blinking hard but not thinking to look down.

Colby pulled his head down. A big hard bump on the back side. Maybe a concussion.

"Look at me, sir."

He managed that.

"Don't look at the light. Look at me. Got it?"

"Okay."

Rex swam up at that moment.

Colby took the President's hands and wrapped them firmly around Rex's harness.

"Hold onto Rex, sir. Hold on hard."

"Okay," the President squinted his eyes as if it took all of his concentration to do so, but he seemed to have a handle on it.

When Colby swam away, Rex dutifully followed in his wake, dragging along the President.

The next body he rolled over had a massive hole in his chest. One of the pilots by his gear. The next body he rolled over coughed and sputtered as soon as he rolled into the air.

"McShea. Buddy! Good job getting the President out. Where's Ivy?"

"Uh-huh," he was no better off than the President.

Then he grabbed Colby's shoulders and shoved him underwater.

Colby knew that drowning men would climb atop one another to save themselves. Colby prepared to hit McShea in the gut to force him to let go when the man released him back to the surface.

"Sorry. I had to push off. To get…this." His voice was still wavery, but he held a lifting collar in one hand, dangling on a line from the hovering helo. In moments they had the President's head through it and the helo crew was winching him aloft.

Together they found Lieber in rough shape and got him winched aloft after the President.

McShea was flagging badly. It took little argument to convince him to go aloft as well.

"Ivy!" He shouted at McShea as his feet cleared the river.

McShea shook his head, then raised his arms in an I-don't-know gesture that almost slipped him free of the collar tucked under his arms.

Then Colby remembered. Dilya was his eyes tonight.

He had to backstroke out of the spotlight. The snow shifted to rain and pummeled down on him hard.

There! Dilya squatting in the doorway of the helo hovering above him.

Her arm was out, pointing firmly downriver.

IVY LEARNED many things about herself as she flowed between the pylons of the Champlain Bridge, which shuttered the bridge's roadway lights into a surreal strobe light.

One, she was going to dress far more warmly in the future.

Two, she'd never again complain about how cold the ocean was by the family's Maryland beach cabin.

Three, there was only going to be one real tragedy if she died tonight. If she did, she was going to lose a lifetime with Colby.

No way was she going to let that happen. She tucked her injured arm into the half-zipped front of her light jacket. The shivers were continuous now as she heard a growing roar.

She could almost see her brain shutting down, the life signs on the med bay monitor drooping lower and lower with each pulse.

The helicopters weren't the roar. They were still on the upstream side of the bridge, illuminating whatever was in the water.

An eddy flung her around and she saw the cause of the roar. Even in the darkness, the whitecaps of the Remic Rapids caught the glow of the bridge's streetlights.

This was going to really hurt.

She braced herself just as something slammed into her from behind and forced her face underwater as if she wasn't wet enough already.

Wet enough already?

She surfaced to a mouthful of wet dog fur just as a strong arm wrapped around her waist.

Colby. She wanted to burrow up against him. Hide, just for a moment.

But there was something important.

And it was happening soon. Really, really soon.

If only she could remem—
"The rapids!"
"Hang on!" Colby shouted back.

COLBY DUCKED down under the water, grabbed Ivy's thighs, and with all his strength, heaved her upward.

Someone on the White Hawk helicopter hovering right at water level must have grabbed her, because she kept going upward after he'd lost all momentum.

Kicking hard, he surfaced again with a shoulder under Rex and heaved him up and through the door as well.

But he himself had run out of time.

Heaving Rex aloft had driven him back under.

Just as he surfaced once more, the helicopter lifted abruptly out of reach. He could see Rex's rear legs still dangling out the door as water poured out of the helicopter's cargo bay.

Then Colby felt the blow to his chest as he was flipped head over heels by the rapids.

CHAPTER EIGHTEEN

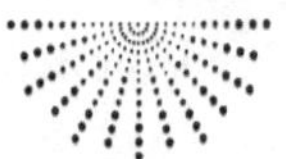

*I*vy had never in her life screamed in fear.

And she didn't this time either.

It was stark terror that erupted from her throat as Colby slammed into the rapids. She didn't even care when Rex made it to all fours and sprayed everyone with a massive shake of his coat.

The searchlight swept back and forth over the white caps. Colby's passage through the rapids should only have taken seconds, but she couldn't see him anywhere. Had he survived it?

It was the sharp-eyed Dilya who spotted him. Some swirl of the current had dragged him sideways in the river. Her limbs were shaking too hard with the cold to throw herself in to save him. The helo swooped in close and everyone leaned out to pluck him from the racing water.

In moments, he too was aboard. Blood was streaming down his face from a scalp wound. But it was easily staunched by her palm, so it couldn't be too deep.

Dilya had her fists in both dogs' collars. The President lay along the bench seat with McShea and the rescue helo's crew chief checking him over.

Colby lay back against her knees as she sat in the President's seat. "Let's not do this again, Saint Ives. Deal?"

"Deal!" And she wanted to laugh. Is that how his marriage proposal would sound? Casual, a little teasing and whimsical, both backed up by a smile for humor? She'd be disappointed if it didn't.

She watched out the still open door as they gained altitude over the river.

Piercing the sheeting raindrops, she spotted a series of red dots. A line aimed right at...

She twisted around and saw the dot—on the President's chest.

A rifle's aiming laser.

She instinctively dove forward enough so that the light was on her own chest instead. Then braced for impact...

No bullet slammed into her. No wound erupted in the middle of her chest, geysering blood.

If it wasn't a guiding laser for a bullet, maybe it was guiding—

A fast-moving shadow in the rain.

No time to act, a shout erupted from her.

COLBY TRIED to sit up as Ivy shouted, "Rex! Fetch!"

Rex pushed off the far bench, breaking free from Dilya's grasp and slamming Colby aside.

He launched out the door and into the air.

What Colby saw should have been impossible.

Fifteen feet out from the side of the helo and thirty feet above the rushing darkness of the river, Rex's jaws clamped down on the wing of a model plane that was rushing straight at the helicopter's side door.

It was moving fast enough that it would have wounded or killed anyone in the flightpath.

Rex was snapped around cruelly, but he hung on to the model's wing and together they plunged down into the river.

Even as Colby scrambled to look down, there was a roar like a buzz saw. One of the overwatch helicopters must have traced the origin point of that laser. Whoever the attackers were, they were done for as the minigun unleashed on them.

Their gripe with the President, whatever it was, had just been definitively settled. And if there was anyone behind them, he'd trust the Secret Service to ferret it out.

CHAPTER NINETEEN

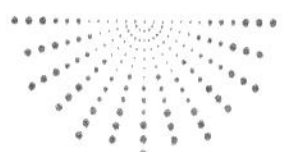

Ivy was touched that the President had sent a jet at his own expense down to fetch them from the Cape for the ceremony.

"Not Air Force One," Colby noted, "But a Gulfstream is still a class act."

General Arnson personally flew their helo from Andrews to the South Lawn.

Ivy noted that even he wasn't above messing with the golfers as he climbed out particularly low over The Courses at Andrews that lay behind the Air Force One hangar.

But once again she didn't get to see the approach to the South Lawn. She was far too busy staring at the incredibly handsome man beside her. They both sat on the side bench—they certainly weren't going to sit in the President's chair, not even with her bridal gown as an excuse.

She had debated about wearing her Marine Dress uniform, including the Congressional Medal of Honor she'd been awarded for managing to only somewhat crash the Marine One helicopter with the President aboard. But that wasn't how Colby made her feel. He made her feel like a hundred percent woman.

"I didn't go overboard-girlie, did I?" She brushed a hand over the dress that was the first she'd worn in at least a decade.

"No one would ever make that mistake about you, Saint Ives." Colby leaned in and kissed her very convincingly. The dress wasn't bouffant—though it wasn't a bad word for the kiss that sent happy sighs rippling all through her. It had no great gobs of taffeta all over its surface. Instead, she'd chosen a sleek dress, but with a lace over-collar that made her seem more curvy than she was. The skirt had a lovely flair and swoop to it that somehow made her look taller. She'd tried heels once, for almost ten feet in the wedding store, and almost insisted on Army boots after the experience.

Colby had opted for a tailored suit. His own Director's Medal of Valor had been left in a drawer at home. At home. Not quite her cozy cabin on the Maryland beach dream—that would come later. For now they had a small house close by Cape Canaveral. It *was* right on the beach so that they could go swimming together every morning before work. After her swim in the Ottawa River, she never complained about the overly warm Gulf Stream current that flowed by their beach. The chill of thinking she'd lost Colby to that cruel water had never truly left her.

She still couldn't believe she'd made the astronaut corps. Maybe it was NASA's access to the tape of her plunging flight. Or maybe when dredging up the helo had revealed the extent of the damage she'd fought against—it shouldn't have been able to fly at all, but she'd fought it down out of the Death Zone all on her own. Piloting wasn't just about jets, and NASA had finally seen that.

Life had seemed so short in that moment and it made every moment since twice as precious.

"You shouldn't have let him see the dress," Dilya greeted her the moment Master Sergeant McShea opened the helicopter's door. Then her maid of honor squealed like the teenage girl she sometimes was and threw herself into Ivy's arms. "You look beyond amazingly amazing. He's so lucky! You get that, don't you?" she asked Colby over Ivy's shoulder.

"Maybe," Colby shrugged noncommittedly. Dilya barely had time to frown before he simply bent down and scooped her into a hug that left her feet dangling well above the ground.

Dilya hugged him back hard and seemed reluctant to let go.

"Hey, he's mine," Ivy reminded her. "You don't get to keep him."

Dilya nodded, but sniffled a little once her feet were back on the ground. And did her best to glare at Ivy. "You get how lucky you are too, right?"

"I'm going to say 'I Do' when it matters. Does that count?"

The girl nodded fiercely and again teared up. To hide it, she knelt down to greet Rex.

"Hey, boy." She gave him a big hug. "Zackie will be so glad to see you, c'mon."

Rex limped alongside her as she led the way up to the White House Rose Garden. Rex's limp didn't pain him but it would never fully heal, disqualifying him from the Secret Service. His fall with the model plane had cut a tendon that the surgeons had to shorten to put back together. But he was certainly plenty healthy to fulfill his role beside Colby as the new Lead Dog of NASA's security.

Colby held Ivy's hand, keeping her back for a moment.

Together they looked at what awaited them. A full Marine Corps Honor Guard, so beautiful in their dress blues, with swords. She would get to walk through an arch of swords after the ceremony because even though she was an astronaut now, there was no such thing as an ex-Marine.

Their families and much of the administration, including the First Family, were chatting together on the front lawn. No sign of Reggie, probably off making some last minute adjustments in the kitchen before serving his Best Man duties.

A tall, elegant woman, with lovely long gray hair and wielding a camera, came down the lawn. Miss Watson—who, as Dilya had said, kept changing—snapped a photo of them, winked, and moved on.

Ivy realized that it was the photo she'd always wanted but never imagined. Her, on the South Lawn, in front of an HMX-1 White Top helicopter, but in a way she'd never imagined. Wearing a wedding dress with the man she'd always be able to say she'd spent her whole life with.

Colby squeezed their joined hands. "Luckiest man alive, Saint Ives."

"You are," she smiled up at him.

At his laugh, she leaned her face into the center of his chest.

They had the whole universe ahead of them.

IF YOU LIKED THIS, YOU'LL LOVE THIS COLLECTION!

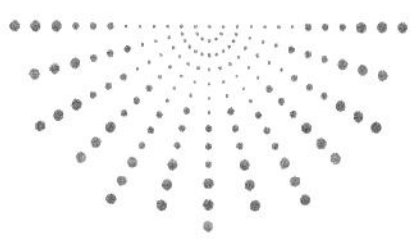

Available exclusively at: www.buchmanbookworks.com

DANIEL'S CHRISTMAS (EXCERPT)

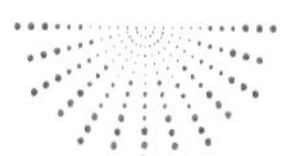

THE NIGHT STALKERS WHITE HOUSE #1

Daniel Drake Darlington III pushed back further into the armchair and hung on for dear life. Without warning the seat did its best to eject him forcibly onto the floor. Only the heavy seatbelt, that was threatening to cut him in half he'd pulled it so tight, kept him in place.

"You never were the best flier."

Daniel glared at President Peter Matthews as Marine One jolted sharply left. They occupied the two facing armchairs in the narrow cargo bay of the VH-1N White Hawk helicopter. The small, three-person couch along the side was empty. The two Marine Corps crew chiefs and the two pilots sat in their seats at the front of the craft.

"I'm fine," Daniel managed through gritted teeth. "I just don't like helicopters."

President Peter Matthews sat back casually. Apparently all the turbulence that the early winter storm could hand out had not interfered with his boss' enjoyment of Daniel's discomfiture.

"And why would that be?"

The President knew damn well why his Chief of Staff hated these god-forsaken machines. Even if Marine One was probably the single safest and best maintained helicopter on the planet, he hated it from the depths of his soul along with all of its brethren of the rotorcraft category.

"My very first flight. I suffered—" a jaw rattling shake, "a bad concussion. Then we crashed."

"Yes," the President stared contemplatively at the ceiling less than foot over their heads.

Daniel kept his head ducked down so that he didn't bang it there as they flew through the next pocket of winter turbulence.

"That was one of Emily's finer flights."

And it had been. If the helicopter had been flown by anyone of lesser skill than Major Emily Beale of the Special Operations Aviation Regiment, Daniel knew he'd have been dead rather than merely bruised and battered. Thankfully the Army trained the pilots of the 160th SOAR exceptionally well, even better than the four Marines flying the President's personal craft. And Major Beale was the best among them, except for perhaps her husband.

The tape of that flight and the much more fateful flight a bare two weeks later had become mandatory training in the Army's Special Operations Forces helicopter regiment. To this day he knew his life would have ended if he'd been aboard for that second fiery crash. The crash that had taken the First Lady's life a year ago.

But that didn't make him like this machine one whit better.

"There's home." President Matthews nodded out the window just like any tourist. Any tourist who was allowed to fly over the intensely restricted airspace surrounding the White House.

Daniel managed to look toward the window as the helicopter banked sharply to the left. Please, just let them land safely and get out of this storm. The White House did look terribly cheery. November 30th, she wasn't sporting her Christmas décor yet, but she was a majestic building, brilliantly lit, perched in the middle of the most heavily guarded park on the planet. Another jolt and he squeezed his eyes shut.

He did manage to force his eyes open as they settled flawlessly onto the lawn with barely the slightest rocking on the shock absorbers.

In moments the door slid open and a pair of Marines stood at sharp attention in their dress uniforms as if the last day of November were a sunny summer day, and not blowing freezing rain at eleven o'clock at night.

Daniel stumbled out and managed to resist the urge to kneel and kiss the ground. For one thing, it would stain the knees of his suit. For another, the President would laugh at him. Okay, he'd laugh even more than he already was.

Both feet on the ground, Daniel found himself. Managed to pull on his Chief-of-Staff cloak so to speak. He grabbed his briefcase and kept his place beside the President as they headed toward the South Entrance. They each carried umbrellas of only marginal usefulness that the Marines had thoughtfully provided. Now that they were on the ground, Daniel didn't mind the cold rain in his face. It meant he was alive.

"I'd suggest turning in right away, sir. We have an early start tomorrow."

The President clapped him on the shoulder, "Yes, Mom."

"Your mother is over in Georgetown."

"Well, I'm not going to call you 'dear' so don't get your hopes up there."

Daniel had come to really like the President. Even at the end of a brutally long day, including a flight to Kansas City, then Chicago, and back, he remained upbeat with that indefatigable energy of his. He was easy to like. There'd now be no oil workers' strike in Kansas City and his Chicago dinner speech had benefited the new governor immensely.

"You go to bed too, Daniel."

"Just going to drop off this paperwork," he held up his briefcase.

The President headed for the Grand Staircase and Daniel turned down the white marble hall and headed over to the West Wing.

Somewhere behind them in the dark, the helicopter roared back to life and lifted into the night.

Buy now to keep reading. Available exclusively at:
www.buchmanbookworks.com

ABOUT THE AUTHOR

USA Today and Amazon #1 Bestseller M. L. "Matt" Buchman started writing on a flight south from Japan to ride his bicycle across the Australian Outback. Just part of a solo around-the-world trip that ultimately launched his writing career.

From the very beginning, his powerful female heroines insisted on putting character first, *then* a great adventure. He's since written over 60 action-adventure thrillers and military romantic suspense novels. And just for the fun of it: 100 short stories, and a fast-growing pile of read-by-author audiobooks.

Booklist says: "3X Top 10 of the Year." PW says: "Tom Clancy fans open to a strong female lead will clamor for more." His fans say: "I want more now…of everything." That his characters are even more insistent than his fans is a hoot.

As a 30-year project manager with a geophysics degree who has designed and built houses, flown and jumped out of planes, and solo-sailed a 50' ketch, he is awed by what is possible. More at: www.mlbuchman.com.

Other works by M. L. Buchman: *(· - also in audio)*

Thrillers

Dead Chef
One Chef!
Two Chef!

Miranda Chase
Drone·
Thunderbolt·
Condor·
Ghostrider·

Romantic Suspense

Delta Force
Target Engaged·
Heart Strike·
Wild Justice·
Midnight Trust·

Firehawks
MAIN FLIGHT
Pure Heat
Full Blaze
Hot Point·
Flash of Fire·
Wild Fire

SMOKEJUMPERS
Wildfire at Dawn·
Wildfire at Larch Creek·
Wildfire on the Skagit·

The Night Stalkers
MAIN FLIGHT
The Night Is Mine
I Own the Dawn
Wait Until Dark
Take Over at Midnight
Light Up the Night
Bring On the Dusk
By Break of Day

AND THE NAVY
Christmas at Steel Beach
Christmas at Peleliu Cove

WHITE HOUSE HOLIDAY
Daniel's Christmas·
Frank's Independence Day·
Peter's Christmas·
Zachary's Christmas·
Roy's Independence Day·
Damien's Christmas·

5E
Target of the Heart
Target Lock on Love
Target of Mine
Target of One's Own

Shadow Force: Psi
At the Slightest Sound·
At the Quietest Word·

White House Protection Force
Off the Leash·
On Your Mark·
In the Weeds·

Contemporary Romance

Eagle Cove
Return to Eagle Cove
Recipe for Eagle Cove
Longing for Eagle Cove
Keepsake for Eagle Cove

Henderson's Ranch
Nathan's Big Sky·
Big Sky, Loyal Heart·
Big Sky Dog Whisperer·

Love Abroad
Heart of the Cotswolds: England
Path of Love: Cinque Terre, Italy

Other works by M. L. Buchman:

Contemporary Romance (cont)

Where Dreams
Where Dreams are Born
Where Dreams Reside
Where Dreams Are of Christmas
Where Dreams Unfold
Where Dreams Are Written

Science Fiction / Fantasy

Deities Anonymous
Cookbook from Hell: Reheated
Saviors 101

Single Titles
The Nara Reaction
Monk's Maze
the Me and Elsie Chronicles

Non-Fiction

Strategies for Success
Managing Your Inner Artist/Writer
Estate Planning for Authors
Character Voice

Short Story Series by M. L. Buchman:

Romantic Suspense

Delta Force
Delta Force

Firehawks
The Firehawks Lookouts
The Firehawks Hotshots
The Firebirds

The Night Stalkers
The Night Stalkers
The Night Stalkers 5E
The Night Stalkers CSAR
The Night Stalkers Wedding Stories

US Coast Guard
US Coast Guard

White House Protection Force
White House Protection Force

Contemporary Romance

Eagle Cove
Eagle Cove

Henderson's Ranch
Henderson's Ranch

Where Dreams
Where Dreams

Thrillers

Dead Chef
Dead Chef

Science Fiction / Fantasy

Deities Anonymous
Deities Anonymous

Other
The Future Night Stalkers
Single Titles

www.ingramcontent.com/pod-product-compliance
Lightning Source LLC
Chambersburg PA
CBHW032152180726
48284CB00001B/19